XKARNATION

REBORN AS A DEMONIC TREE
BOOK 2

aethonbooks.com

REBORN AS A DEMONIC TREE 2
©2024 XKARNATION

This book is protected under the copyright laws of the United States of America. No part of this publication may be reproduced, stored in a retrieval system, or transmitted, in any form or by any means, without the prior permission in writing of the publisher, nor be otherwise circulated in any form of binding or cover other than that in which it is published and without a similar condition including this condition being imposed on the subsequent purchaser. Any reproduction or unauthorized use of the material or artwork contained herein is prohibited without the express written permission of the authors.

Aethon Books supports the right to free expression and the value of copyright. The purpose of copyright is to encourage writers and artists to produce the creative works that enrich our culture.

The scanning, uploading, and distribution of this book without permission is a theft of the author's intellectual property. If you would like to use material from the book (other than for review purposes), please contact editor@aethonbooks.com. Thank you for your support of the author's rights.

Aethon Books
www.aethonbooks.com

Print and eBook formatting and design by Josh Hayes.

Published by Aethon Books LLC.

Aethon Books is not responsible for websites (or their content) that are not owned by the publisher.

This book is a work of fiction. Names, characters, places, and incidents are the product of the author's imagination or are used fictitiously. Any resemblance to actual events, locales, or persons, living or dead is coincidental.

All rights reserved.

ALSO IN SERIES

Reborn as a Demonic Tree
Reborn as a Demonic Tree 2
Reborn as a Demonic Tree 3

Check out the series here! (tap or scan)

1
ASHFALLEN SECT'S NEW MEMBER

The rebirth gave Ashlock an opportunity to retake control of his life as throughout his life in this new world, he had constantly felt forced into situations and compelled to react to threats as they arose.

Naturally, such a lack of independence was expected from a human mind abruptly torn from the modern world and thrust into a tree with no warning or guidance and expected to flourish in an ancient world of cultivators where impulsive youths could imbue their weapons with the fire of their souls and attack him for the slightest grievance.

It had been overwhelming and challenging, with each day feeling like a battle for survival. But experiencing the chill of death and having Senior Lee appear to explain his situation made him appreciate life more deeply.

Although his system being temporarily offline for the next week and his cultivation rapidly recovering to its previous strength should have made him uneasy, Ashlock only felt relief as he finally felt in control.

It might have been merely an illusion of choice provided by the system, but his mindset had significantly improved since fully becoming a tree. It was immensely satisfying to be asked if he wished to be free and to resolutely say no.

This was now a life he had chosen and was ecstatic to have.

As the late afternoon sun shone on his leaves and filled him with warmth and life, Ashlock tried to push aside the many threats and goals Senior Lee had laid out in his mind. The Patriarch, beast tide, and

Monarch Realm World Tree in the Celestial Empire that wanted to eat him could wait as right now he was just a half-grown tree on a desolate mountaintop.

The Dao Storm may have given him a rebirth of both body and mind, but it had also stripped away the pavilion he had called home for the last decade, and he felt naked and exposed without those white walls and red vines surrounding him on all sides.

This vulnerability was somewhat alleviated by the thousands of demonic trees encircling him, offering a fraction of their Qi through the mycelium network. Each tree contributed a tiny amount, but combined, he could sense his Qi intake was at least five times faster than when he had done it alone, and he knew that as the demonic trees evolved into spirit trees and grew, his Qi intake would only increase.

"Thanks for the help," Ashlock muttered. "I'll pay you guys back once I have some Qi to spare, but for now, keep helping Dad grow big and strong to protect you all, okay?"

A faint wave of happiness emanated through the network from the few demonic trees scattered throughout the vast forest that had been nurtured from his Demonic Seeds directly and were old enough to have developed a spirit.

With the new demonic forest addressed, it was time to refocus on the humans.

Since his system was offline, Ashlock had no way to check how much time had passed for him to complete his soul merge, so he didn't know the situation with the alchemy tournament as it was supposed to start a week or so from when the Dao Storm struck, but that wasn't important for now.

First, he needed to get his Ashfallen Sect in order. As Senior Lee had mentioned, the human ego that allowed him to form connections with the humans and raise them into dependable allies placed him above the other world trees that had been taken advantage of and ultimately perished. He planned to use this advantage to its fullest.

The Ashfallen Sect was his sanctuary for nurturing and raising dependable allies, and in a world of egotistical cultivators fond of displaying wealth, first impressions were crucial.

The rogue cultivator Diana had led up the mountain said some harsh words that hurt to hear but were true. There really was nothing up here except a tree on a desolate mountain. Not much for a supposed sect that had made some big claims and was running the entire region from the shadows.

Despite the truth in rogue cultivator Douglas's words, Ashlock still had to assert his authority, so upon Diana's request, he demonstrated his presence by staring down the sect's newest member through his {Demonic Eye}.

The muscular man with golden brown hair and some of the most chiseled muscles Ashlock had ever seen instantly knelt under his gaze and trembled like a leaf.

Strangely, this scene reminded Ashlock of Senior Lee's comment that bodies were merely vessels for a person's soul.

Back on Earth, Douglas could have been a world-class fighter that no one would dare confront—due to his tall stature and formidable presence—unless they were heavily armed. Yet, here in a cultivation world, he knelt from a mere glance from a superior being.

Since Ashlock was already using his Demonic Eye to showcase his presence, he decided to examine Douglas's Soul Core, as that was one of the primary advantages of observing someone through his Demonic Eye.

Douglas clenched his teeth as Ashlock's gaze intensified.

Ashlock could see the man's quivering Soul Core desperately attempting to keep the turbulent earth Qi within his body under control. "Third stage of the Soul Fire Realm with an impure spirit root," Ashlock mused as he slowly closed his bark to conceal his eye, feeling pity for Douglas.

"A bit too weak for combat but should be suitable for construction with his earth affinity," Ashlock mused while closing his demonic eye.

Of course, if Douglas impressed him with his efforts, Ashlock would be generous and send the man to the Mystic Realm for training, and if he truly amazed him, some truffles might find their way to him.

However, that was for the future when Douglas had proven himself to be a reliable ally worth investing in, as, for now, he was far from being fully integrated into the Ashfallen Sect.

Ashlock had been lucky with Stella, as they had been together from the beginning, and Diana had spent over a year getting accustomed to how Ashlock did things before Stella showed up and formally introduced her to him.

Though Douglas was about to get a crash course on the life and his position within the Ashfallen Sect, Ashlock almost felt bad for the man.

Douglas's ranting and cursing about being glared at by a tree had angered the awakened Stella, and she was looking at the man with a gaze that could kill.

"*I asked to see your leader, not be glared at by some cursed tree!*" Douglas yelled into the mountain as his hands continued to tremble on the stone. Sweat dripped from his hair, and his breathing was erratic. "*I was told my cousin would introduce me to a rebel sect. I expected it to be somewhat shabby, but this is absurd! Stop messing around, and let me see your leader. Intimidating me like this will get us nowhere!*"

That was unexpected. Ashlock was curious about the sales pitch the girls had used to persuade people to come work here. He had anticipated mortals or maybe late Qi stage cultivators to arrive, but a third-stage earth affinity cultivator exceeded his expectations.

Diana stood calmly beside Douglas. Her hand was slightly shaking, but she seemed to have mostly resisted his demonic glare. Nonetheless, her dull gray eyes observed the man, and a faint frown appeared on her face.

"*Patriarch,*" Diana spoke flatly, "*please forgive the man for his crude words. Douglas is a cousin of Mister Choi, an old friend, and was the only rogue cultivator willing to join our sect on such short notice.*"

This was the second time Ashlock had heard the phrase "rogue cultivator." What made a cultivator rogue? Was the man a criminal or something? Regardless, Ashlock was sure he would find out soon. His cultivation was still recovering, so he didn't want to waste Qi on telekinesis to communicate, so he flashed a single leaf once to say yes.

"*I thank the Patriarch for your kindness,*" Diana said, and then she turned to Douglas, who was slowly rising on his wobbly legs. "*Introduce yourself and then take the oath to join the Ashfallen Sect.*"

The man was a mess, but he finally found his balance. He took a deep breath and said, "My name is Douglas Terraforge, and no, I won't take the oath."

A brief silence passed, and Diana scowled. "Either recite the oath or die."

"*Now, just rein in your fucking temper for a moment, Miss. I think we got off on the wrong foot here.*" Douglas took another shaky breath and continued. "*Please understand that signing an oath is close to a bloody slave contract. I only followed you up this damnable mountain with expectations that haven't been met!*"

"What did you expect?" Stella said coldly from the bench while leaning on its armrest.

"Where is this fucking hostility coming from?" Douglas replied. "I apologize if I offended your Patriarch. But cut me some slack, okay? It's just the first time I have seen people taking orders from a fucking tree before!"

Stella frowned and glanced back at Ashlock—he could feel the brief warmth in her eyes, which then transitioned back to cold when she looked back at Douglas. "This tree, as you call it, is our Patriarch. He is currently recovering after defending against the Dao Storm that nearly destroyed Darklight City, but at his peak strength, he is in the Star Core Realm."

She then gestured around. "I'm sure you saw the ferocity of the Dao Storm from the streets of Darklight City? Such a storm naturally wiped out the beautiful pavilion left behind by my family. That is why there is nothing here except us and a rapidly regrowing tree."

Douglas nodded. "I see, so the Ashfallen Sect consists of you two rude women and a tree?"

Diana reached over, gripped his shoulder, and said in a low, threatening tone, "We are fine with sharing our secrets only after you recite the oath and stop insulting us."

Douglas shrugged. "The way I see it, I'm dead either way. You two are clearly far stronger than me since I can't guess your cultivation stage, and that spirit tree made me quiver with just a glance. I'm simply asking for some clarification on what I'm even swearing a fucking oath for!"

Honestly, the man was more confrontational than Ashlock assumed most were used to in this world, as most just bowed to the strong without question, but he liked the guy's attitude. So he flashed his leaf and groaned when he saw the timer in the corner of his interface add another half an hour to his recovery time.

Diana saw his flashing leaf and removed her grasp from the man's shoulder. "Fine. Stella can explain things to you."

"Perfect," Douglas said. "I just need to know some surface-level details. I understand the pavilion was taken away in the storm, so it's just you three... I can't believe I'm including a tree as a person."

"Well, you better get used to it." Stella crossed her arms under her chest. "The Ashfallen Sect is the true ruler of this land—"

Douglas seemed confused. *"Isn't that the Redclaws?"*

"The Redclaws answer to us and have already recited oaths of loyalty," Stella snapped back, silencing Douglas. *"With just us three, we fended off and eradicated the Winterwrath and Evergreen families and ruled the entire region from the shadows. As some random schmuck, you have been brought here to construct a place befitting of us—"*

"With what?" Douglas replied.

"What?" Stella stopped her ramblings and glared at Douglas, clearly infuriated at how he didn't care about everything she had just claimed.

"You want some majestic palace to show off your big egos, right? So what do you plan to build it from? Hopes and dreams?" Douglas continued as Stella furrowed her brows. *"Do you have an architect? What about a budget for the materials? Or mortals to furnish the place?"*

Ashlock felt a little foolish. Although he had left the girls to handle the job, he had seen how the White Stone Palace had been constructed. Hundreds of mortals had streamed up and down the mountainside like worker ants. To expect a single cultivator to do the entire thing himself was unreasonable.

Douglas continued to rant. *"As some random schmuck, did you expect me to build an entire palace at a wave of my hands? Should I also keep the place clean for you once it's built? Should I dress up in a maid outfit and sing a song for you fine ladies?"*

"Shut up," Stella shouted, and some of her immaturity leaked through her confident facade. Before Douglas could retort, Diana stepped in and lectured the man with as much enthusiasm as a dead fish.

"Douglas, we have many people to rely on. Even if you can't see them, they're here. We have connections in the city, including Mister Choi. We can mobilize the Redclaws to secure as many mortal servants as needed, and there's an abundance of building materials all around. If that's not enough, we have thousands of dragon crowns on hand to purchase anything."

Diana's rant reminded Ashlock that he needed to get the Redclaws back to work. Sadly, they were buried deep in the mine, under thousands of meters of rock, waiting out the Dao Storm, and he didn't want to add another day to his recovery time to portal them out.

"Fine." Douglas crossed his arms. *"If what you say about the resources at your oh-so-powerful sect's disposal is true, I don't mind*

reciting the oath. But let's be clear: constructing a palace with a wave of my hand is beyond my abilities. However, I could carve some rooms into the mountain right now."

For some reason, Ashlock had been far too focused on getting that sense of safety that being surrounded by pavilion walls gave him when the actual logical solution all along had been to build the Ashfallen Sect inside the mountain.

Now that Douglas brought up the idea, it seemed almost too perfect for many reasons. First, building a giant shiny palace atop a mountain was an ideal way to blow their cover and attract the attention of others when the Redclaw's white palace was supposed to draw everyone's attention.

Second, it wasn't certain if the beast tide included monsters capable of burrowing through rock, but the Dao Storm had taught him that above-ground structures were futile against cataclysmic events unless they were runically enchanted.

Finally, his hollowed-out roots could serve as tunnels to connect the rooms. He should have Douglas start in the mine and work his way up from there.

Ashlock decided to use a little bit of Qi to manipulate a rock and write out his plan on the ground, which earned a rather funny yelp from Douglas as a rock floated past his head.

His plan? Have Douglas take a ride down his root with the help of Diana and then dig a tunnel to get everyone out of the mine.

His only hope was Larry wouldn't try and eat the new guy.

2
A BIZARRE SECT

Douglas tried to ignore the awkward tension in the air as he finally felt the shivers that ran through his body subside. It was difficult, but he pushed the terrifying truths he had seen in the spirit tree's ageless gaze to the back of his mind.

He had come here at the request of his cousin, Mr. Choi, to whom he owed a lot after fleeing the Terraforge family in his youth. However, although he greatly respected his cousin, he never expected to be deceived like this.

His cousin had made this elusive Ashfallen Sect sound like the place of his dreams, where he would finally be recognized as a valuable member and be surrounded by people capable of fighting against the Blood Lotus Sect and the cruel noble families he had come to despise so much over the years.

Yet there was far less here than he had been promised. Even taking a step back and overlooking the lack of a pavilion due to recent events, there were only two members of the sect, and neither was in the Star Core Realm.

Of course, they claimed they were taking orders from this enigmatic tree, which was shedding its bark as it grew upward at an alarming rate. But even if the tree was as powerful as they claimed, everyone knowledgeable about spirit trees understood that they weren't much different from ordinary trees, except for producing slightly better fruit or having bark imbued with Qi, making it more valuable.

But a spirit tree smart enough to even talk? Order around humans? It was inconceivable, and he wasn't seeing it—a rock flew too close to his head with enough speed to make a whooshing sound past his ear that woke him from his inner stupor.

Douglas immediately looked toward Stella as the culprit, as he had felt a hint of spatial Qi leaking from her when she had thrown that brief tantrum earlier. *Foolish child trying to take my head off when I wasn't looking,* Douglas cursed to himself but was surprised when Stella followed the rock and watched it scrape against the ground.

Had it not been her?

"The Patriarch is conversing with us," Diana said confidently, as if that made any sense.

Douglas knew trees couldn't control rocks, nor were they literate. Curious, he walked over and was surprised that Diana made no move to stop him. Even Stella didn't pay any attention, her full focus on the squiggles on the ground.

Douglas squinted hard at the etchings but couldn't make sense of their meaning. *Are they pulling my leg? This is just a load of random squiggles. Although they do look a little similar to the runic language I know...*

He honestly half believed this entire situation was one massive joke set up by his cousin. His suspension of disbelief could only be stretched so far before he threw his hands up and demanded to be let in on the joke.

Stella was busy murmuring to herself, and Douglas could see the seriousness on her face through the gaps in her blond hair. She wasn't really his type, but he could appreciate a beauty when he saw one, and seeing her reading some squiggles for an elaborate joke was rather endearing, he had to admit.

"Okay, I got it." Stella straightened her back and turned to him. "Once you say the oath and pledge your loyalty to the Patriarch of the Ashfallen Sect, we can continue."

"Did your tree tell you that?" Douglas carefully held back his smirk when he saw the coldness in Stella's eyes. "Whoa, all right, fine."

Truthfully, he had planned to say the oath from the beginning.

He had been unable to find any employment back in Darklight City due to his less-than-stellar track record and lackluster skills. So when his cousin contacted him for this job, he was thrilled.

Even if these girls wanted to pretend and live in their delusions, it was fine by him as long as he got paid.

Being a cultivator wasn't cheap, and he had a mountain of debt to clear off sooner rather than later. Life as a rogue cultivator was hit or miss with job offers, and he had an addiction to beast cores that needed to be satisfied.

Not only would he go insane if he let the heart demons win, but if his cultivation remained stagnant at the third stage of the Soul Fire Realm, his enemies would soon surpass him and come knocking.

Douglas looked at Stella's serious face before shaking his head and heading to the tree. "You want me to pledge loyalty to the tree, right?"

"Loyalty to the Ashfallen Sect, which the tree is the Patriarch of, so yes," Stella confirmed with a nod.

Douglas looked at the tree's cracking and warping trunk as it rapidly grew upward. It was a marvel to witness, and his hand still shivered slightly from the memories of that gaze. Undoubtedly, this tree was special, and he was curious to learn more about it.

The things I do for a paycheck, Douglas cursed as he wet his lips, closed his eyes, and made his link with heaven through meditation.

He brought his hand up to his chest and rested it near his Soul Core as a sign of respect, even if he thought they didn't deserve it. I bet this oath won't even work. There's no way heaven acknowledges this Ashfallen Sect as a real thing, Douglas thought as the world's energies swirled around him.

"I, Douglas Terraforge, pledge my loyalty to the Ashfallen Sect." Douglas tensed up as he felt tremendous pressure descend upon him. It was as if an eye of heaven was glaring down at him and recording his every word with intense scrutiny. Holy shit, the Ashfallen Sect is recognized? Douglas couldn't believe it. Fools did fake oaths all the time. Heck, he had done a few throughout his life, but he had never felt heaven's interest in an oath this intensely before.

Gulping and keeping his eyes closed, Douglas continued with the standard pledge of loyalty. "If my loyalty is to falter, may my cultivation be forever crippled and my heart demons unleashed upon my unfaithful soul."

And he truly meant it. To heck with the Ashfallen Sect being two girls playing the most well-crafted joke—this was serious business.

As those final words left his mouth, he felt a chain of heaven's intent wrapping around his Soul Core. It was cold, and he almost wanted to clench his chest from the chill, but he kept his hand steady.

He could tell the phantom chain led out his body toward the spirit tree before him. He instinctively knew that any betrayal to the Ashfallen Sect would result in the chains fading away and allowing the heart demons to devour his Soul Core.

Most curious was how he had sworn loyalty to the Ashfallen Sect, yet the chain linked to the tree rather than to an abstract concept of community that dictated most sects. It was as if the tree was the Ashfallen Sect, and he could tell that his oath would be voided if the tree perished.

"A sect entirely run under the canopy of a spirit tree," Douglas murmured as he opened his eyes and saw the tree in a new light. For a tree to earn the direct interest of heaven was a feat that he could only marvel at. Perhaps the tree was responsible for far more than it was letting on.

A clap from Stella across the empty mountain peak drew his attention.

"All right, Douglas." Stella smiled, but it was cold and almost scary as if she knew something he didn't. "You will be going with Diana down into the mines—"

Douglas felt his mind freeze. Dark memories of him taking on work in the mines for meager pay during his darkest hours made him break out in a cold sweat. That one memory of him running out of Qi in the middle of a mine collapse and being buried for two days because there was no air to waste on circulating his breathing technique to recover his Qi made him shiver.

"Mines?" he blurted out. "I thought you hired me for fucking construction, not to crawl around on my hands and knees in the dark for some darn spirit stones. Hire some mortals for that shit."

Stella glared at him with a look that could kill. "Douglas, you shmuck, stop interrupting me and let me finish. Maybe then we can actually get something done today?"

That was fair. Douglas had been a little confrontational since arriving here, but it wasn't his fault! Everything had been so far from expectations, and everyone here was so unreasonable.

Stella huffed, and then, after seeing Douglas remaining quiet, she continued, "As I was saying before being so rudely interrupted. You will join Diana down in the mines. Your first task will be building a tunnel from the mine to the outside so the people trapped there can escape."

"What people?" Douglas asked. "Why are they trapped down there?"

Stella waved him off. "Don't worry about that. Just take this." She held her arm out, and a black cloak materialized in her hand out of thin air. There was no flash of gold from the many spatial rings decorating her fingers, nor any whiff of spatial Qi.

How had she done that?

Douglas had to admit he was impressed and eyed the cloak with a hint of awe as Stella approached and shoved it into his hand. "Wear this cloak. As the newest member of the Ashfallen Sect, we need to keep your identity well hidden. This is a cloak of concealment. It comes with a big hood to hide your face."

"That's it?" Douglas had to admit the cloak was made of decently soft and durable material, and it was equipped with a massive hood he would expect cultists to wear, but did such a cloak with that name really do nothing impressive?

"Yeah, that's it." Stella shrugged. "Diana will also give you a mask. Just keep your mouth shut down there and follow Diana's orders. Don't interact with anyone if possible."

"What—" Douglas tried to ask more questions but was interrupted as something was shoved into his other hand. "A mask?" he mumbled, inspecting the black wooden mask.

"Put it on," a slightly distorted voice he recognized as Diana said. Looking up, he saw the black-haired girl wearing an almost identical mask to his, but it was bone white.

"All right, all right," Douglas grumbled as he fastened the mask to his face, put his arms through the cloak, and tightened it around himself. He couldn't see himself, but he guessed he looked rather menacing.

"Looking good," Diana said flatly as she gestured for him to follow her. "We'll take the fast route down."

"Fast route?"

Diana nodded. "Yeah, it's right down here."

Walking over and following her gaze, he saw a dark hole in the ground that seemed to lead to a tunnel of some kind. Upon closer inspection, he noticed it looked like the inside of a tree root.

"You want me to go down here? How far is it?" Douglas felt at ease when surrounded by rock, but a thick tree root wall between him and the mountain rock would isolate him from his environmental strength.

Diana was already climbing into the hole with water from the air liquifying around her hands. "Don't worry, just follow me and keep your head facing upward if you don't want to drown."

It was impossible to tell if she was joking or serious, with the creepy white mask obscuring her facial features and her flat tone. However, the strange woman had already vanished into the hole, and he could barely see the tip of her head at this point, so he reluctantly began to climb down into the tunnel.

"Not coming?" he asked Stella, who had returned to the bench and was lying lazily under the tree's canopy with a smile on her face, and her eyes looked suspiciously full of endearment at the rapidly growing tree.

She tilted her head toward him at his words and scowled. "Just leave Tree and me alone."

"O-okay…" He felt like scratching the back of his head in confusion but couldn't take the girl's wrathful glare that hinted at her peak-stage cultivation realm. Why was nobody in this sect normal? What had his foolish cousin roped him into?

With a sigh, he allowed the dampness of the tree root to engulf him, and he began to fall…and fall. Faster and faster. Concern rose quickly in his chest as the wind howled past his ears, and he plummeted through the mountain.

Was this an elaborate way to assassinate him?

He was confident that he would survive the fall with his sturdy body, but he would need a few moments to heal with a pill. Was Diana waiting at the base with a dagger, ready to slit his throat?

His heart pounded in his chest, and his Soul Core hummed as the earth Qi he had stored up in his body rushed to reinforce his legs to brace for the incoming impact. He felt his entire body tense up, and just as he sensed the ground drawing near, he hit a wall of freezing water.

"Ugh—" Douglas choked as water smacked him in the face and rushed into his mouth and nose. Diana's advice of keeping his head up echoed in his mind as he plunged through the water and landed on a floor with far less speed than before.

Coughing up a lungful of water while crumpled on the ground, Douglas rolled over to see Diana standing there, looking down at him with her hands on her hips.

"You didn't listen to my instruction about keeping your head up, did you?"

Douglas groaned in response as he tried to push himself up and walk on his shaky legs. "I did listen…"

"No, you didn't," Diana snapped back. "Now you're wasting my time, being pathetic because your brain is too full of useless thoughts."

Douglas then felt all the freezing water weighing down his clothes, being pulled away by a mystical force and gathering in a ball above Diana's open palm.

Today has been the worst, Douglas thought as he finally got to his feet and towered over Diana. However, she had already turned her back on him and begun making her way down the mushroom-lit tunnel.

It was at this moment he truly felt like a lackey. Sighing, he trudged behind the woman and marveled at the luminescent mushrooms. Then when there was a fork in the tunnel, a black root he hadn't even noticed on the floor suddenly lit up with lilac flames.

"The Patriarch is guiding us to his people," Diana said flatly as she followed the flames down the widest tunnel. "These mushrooms are also his creation."

Douglas remained quiet, but he had to admit the tree continued to impress him. He had spent his fair share of time in the mines, and lighting was always an issue, yet he had never seen such a simple solution. The mushrooms that emitted a blue glow were a great idea.

After a while, Douglas could hear the echoes of chatter emanating from deeper within the tunnels. Before they rounded a corner, Diana stopped and looked him up and down. "Douglas, don't speak a single word unless I give you permission. Understand?" Her voice was a whisper imbued with Qi, but it reached his ears with unsettling wetness. "We have a facade to maintain that ensures loyalty around here, and I don't need your loud mouth ruining things."

Douglas could feel the threat of instant death dripping from every word, so he resolutely nodded without saying anything—luckily, that seemed to appease the woman.

"Good—follow me." Diana turned and rounded the corner. Douglas obediently followed and marveled at the expansive cavern he was greeted with. However, the cavern didn't impress him so much as the number of people.

Hundreds, if not thousands, of people were gathered around a seemingly artificial stream running through the cavern's center. There was a strong smell of food wafting from the far embankment of the river, where he saw many mortals gathered around small mountains of belongings and quietly chatting among themselves over bowls of food.

Meanwhile, on the closer side, Douglas noticed many cultivators sitting in stone-cold silence. An awkward tension existed between the two groups, but their arrival quickly drew the cultivators' attention first, likely due to their use of spiritual sense.

A sudden burst of flames appeared a step before them, vanishing a second later and leaving behind an aged man with sharp eyes and crimson hair.

To Douglas's surprise, the man, whose heavy presence indicated he was in the Star Core Realm, gave a deep bow to Diana despite her being an entire realm below him.

"Grand Elder of House Redclaw humbly greets the Ashfallen Sect." The Grand Elder spoke calmly, and within moments, many other elders from the Redclaw Sect rushed over to bow alongside him.

"Raise your heads." Diana barely paid the Redclaws attention and walked between them, surveying the cavern for something.

"Mistress, if you will forgive the question…" The Grand Elder wore a worried expression.

Diana tilted her head over her shoulder. "What?"

"Our Peak…Darklight City…the Blood Lotus Sect." The Grand Elder chose his words carefully, his shaky voice betraying his true thoughts. "Does anything remain after the fearsome Dao Storm has ravaged the lands?"

Diana chuckled and waved the Grand Elder off as she ventured deeper into the cavern. "The immortal handled it—there's no problem."

"That is truly unfortunate— Wait…what?" The Grand Elder caught himself mid-sentence, his jaw hanging open.

"Your lack of faith in the Ashfallen Sect displeases me." Diana was now near the stream, and Douglas felt the urge to hurry over and join her as she casually strolled about like she owned the place.

"I…I…" The Grand Elder was at a loss for words. "I will repent! Forgive me."

"Don't bother," Diana replied coldly. "Just gather everyone near the river's source. This oaf over here will dig a tunnel to get you guys out, and you can see the situation yourself. Although I will mention it's a different world out there. Quite a few more...trees."

Douglas wanted to respond to the insult since it made him feel foolish in front of many powerful cultivators and one of the noble families' Grand Elders. But he let it slide and quietly followed Diana alongside a large group of cultivators and curious mortals, making sure to keep his hood down.

Once they approached the wall at the far end of the cavern, Douglas could see the hollowed-out tip of a black tree root poking through rock, with crystal-clear water gushing out.

"All right." Diana pointed to the wall beside the pipe on the cultivator's side, "Underlord, if you follow this pipe, you will create a tunnel to the outside...eventually."

Underlord? Was that his secret name? Not wanting to get scolded for asking questions, he went along with the context clues and placed his hands on the stone wall to begin his technique, but Diana interrupted him.

"You need to make it very wide."

Douglas just grunted in response. What did she mean by wide? He spread his arms out as if indicating how wide she wanted it, and the masked woman shook her head. "Make it wide enough for ten people across and five people tall."

Huh? Did she understand how much Qi such a feat would require him to use?

Seeing his confusion, Diana helpfully added, "It needs to be wide enough for Larry to get out. Anything smaller simply won't do."

Deepening his voice as much as possible to mask his identity, Douglas replied, "Who's Larry?" His curiosity got the better of him, and he also wanted to know because he believed Diana was mistaken. Who could be ten people wide?

Diana's hand twitched as a blade to slice his throat appeared in a flash of gold between her fingers, but she relaxed at his simple question. "Take a look for yourself."

There was a commotion behind him.

Turning with apprehension, Douglas saw the crowd of mortals and cultivators part as a shadow loomed over them.

He stumbled back a step and felt the cold stone against his back as a monstrous creature loomed into view. The most enormous spider he had ever laid witness to stared him down with scarlet eyes that seemed to glow in the dull blue light of the mushrooms filling the cavern.

Diana walked over without fear and patted the monster's leg, which looked like a tree beside her. "This is Larry, the Patriarch's pet."

Douglas paled. *That thing's a pet?*

"Wait, who is this little guy?" Diana said as a small black snake smoothly made its way down her arm and carefully coiled around her neck like an exotic necklace.

The little snake's pink tongue poked out and licked Diana's neck with curious affection.

Douglas just stood there frozen. What in all the nine realms was going on?

3
THE INFAMOUS OAF

Ashlock observed the entire scene through his spiritual sight, facilitated by his roots that covered nearly every inch of the cavern. He hadn't actually told Diana where to instruct Douglas to dig the tunnel; he had simply assumed the earth affinity cultivator could peer through the rock or something and determine the optimal route.

Her words, however, rang true. If Douglas created a tunnel beside the black root, they would find themselves a thousand meters up a mountain —close enough to the ground, in his opinion.

He had to admit that there was a certain satisfaction in watching an egotistical cultivator shiver against a wall while confronting something he considered nothing more than a pet.

Once again, he hadn't instructed Diana to tell Douglas to make the tunnel wide enough for Larry, but she had taken his pet into account and even sought out the spirit beast when she entered the mine.

"Now little Kai has taken a liking to her," Ashlock mused as he observed the tiny F-rank grass snake coil around her neck. He felt happy when all his sect members, including his pets, got along. Regrettably, he knew this harmony was only temporary.

Eventually, he would need to expand the Ashfallen Sect, as he couldn't tackle every issue alone. Having Stella and Diana around had already saved him from death on numerous occasions, and both his pets were also contributing to his continued survival.

"Hopefully, little Kai can advance to S grade soon. That way, I can have Larry protect me, Maple watch over Stella, and finally, little Kai take care of Diana." Ashlock was aware that it would require a significant amount of time and many hunting trips to elevate little Kai to such a level, but with his Mystic Realm and the ability to teleport people within his sphere of influence, once he extended his roots far enough into the wilderness, he could send Diana and Kai on missions.

Reining in his wandering thoughts, Ashlock shifted his focus back to the cavern and saw that Douglas had begun working. The solid rock appeared to morph around him and then crumble to dust as he advanced.

Due to Diana's request to widen the tunnel, he had to move sideways more often than forward to enlarge it. This continued until he paused and approached Diana, who was conversing with the Redclaws.

"What do you want?" Diana inquired over her shoulder. When Douglas didn't reply with gestures, she summoned a dagger to her hand again and tilted her masked head. "Speak, oaf. What is it?"

"Can I make the tunnel through the mountain and then expand it afterward for that thing—err, I mean Larry?" Douglas spoke gruffly through the mask. *"My Qi reserves are running low, so I need to take a break soon to recover."*

Ashlock was almost taken aback by how polite he sounded, although his accent remained rather rough.

Diana slowly nodded. *"That does make sense. Sure, go ahead."*

"Thank you." Douglas wandered back to the tunnel and resumed his work.

Ashlock had given the man the E-grade cloak of minor concealment he had received from the sign-in spree he had conducted before the Dao Storm. With Douglas's large size, a cloak darker than night that didn't reflect light, and the black wooden mask, the man looked like some kind of undertaker who would patrol a misty cemetery with a metal shovel.

After a few minutes, Ashlock grew bored of watching Douglas effortlessly tunnel through the rock and planned to return to the surface, but he caught a conversation between a Redclaw Elder and a youth at the last moment.

"Is that big oaf really part of the Ashfallen Sect? He seems so weak compared to the others—" the youth began to ask the Elder, and Ashlock was baffled by how swiftly the color in the Elder's face drained away, as if he had seen a ghost.

Hundreds of conversations occurred in the cavern, and just like when he was a human in a busy train station, it was all white noise until his brain latched onto certain keywords that interested him, such as his name—or in this case the Ashfallen Sect.

Even as a mountain range–spanning tree, his focus could only be on one thing in a single place at a time. However, he naturally honed in on this particular conversation because, unlike the one Diana was having with the Redclaw Grand Elder, which consisted of mere pleasantries and trivial talk, this one smelled of drama.

And what else was a sick tree recovering from a near-death experience supposed to occupy his time with other than eavesdropping? Even his system had abandoned him for the next week!

When those words left the youth's lips, the Elder had already spun around and clamped a hand over the boy's mouth. "Don't ever say such a thing."

"Why—" the boy started through the Elder's hand but was silenced by a glare.

The Elder glanced around the cavern quickly and then spoke in a hushed whisper. *"If an immortal from the heavens above descended and called the Blood Lotus Patriarch a dog—do you dare refer to the Patriarch in the same manner? Words are relative. An oaf to the Ashfallen Sect is an existence that rivals our Grand Elder's authority to us."*

The boy's eyes widened at his Elder's words.

"You see that cloak he's wearing?" the Elder said, and the boy slowly nodded. *"It's of perfect quality. I saw it up close. Every stitch seemed as if the gods themselves crafted it. If something appears mundane in this world, look closely at the fine details, and the truth will be revealed. Do you believe an oaf of our level could wear such a thing?"*

The Elder took his hand from the boy's mouth, and the obedient youth kept his yapper clamped shut.

"Those who flaunt their wealth or cultivation are fools—true masters lurk in the shadows and conceal their true power until the final moment since those who flaunt are the first to perish." The Elder offered a genuine smile and ruffled the boy's hair. *"So if you don't want to die, don't go around calling a grunt worker from the sect above us an oaf, all right?"*

The boy nodded vigorously and then ran off to the other youths, likely to spread the news.

Ashlock felt that the Elder had taught a valuable lesson, even if he did find it amusing that they thought he cared that much about Douglas. Perhaps in the future, he might care, but for now, he had only known the rude man for a few hours, and his first impressions had been subpar at best.

In truth, he had sent the man down into the mines to get him away from Stella, as she wasn't in a good mood right now, and he was being confrontational. Douglas was already learning his place within the sect after only a few hours, but it would take a bit longer for him to mature and for Stella to mentally recover from seeing Ashlock's charred stump.

He could have wasted a day's worth of Qi to form a portal to get everyone out or widen the hollowed-out root that provided the cavern with water and let people escape that way

Both options would slow his recovery, but getting them out as soon as possible was necessary—the surface needed the Redclaws.

Just from a quick glance after he returned to the surface with his {Eye of the Tree God}, he could see that Darklight City was now overrun with demonic trees, and people were out in the streets trying to chop them down.

"I hope none of the homeless kids try to fill their bellies with poisonous berries." Ashlock cursed at the thought. He needed to get back to his full power to regain control over his surroundings, but for now, he would have to rely on his subordinates to fill in for him, and for that, they needed to escape the cavern.

Naturally, looking at the trees also led Ashlock to question the origin of these demonic trees. His best guess was the cursed blood he had unlocked just before the storm.

The question now on his mind was whether he would have survived even without turning the storm into trees His roots delved deep into the mountain, and even with such a small part of his trunk remaining, he had managed to survive. Maybe he would never know until another cataclysmic event came along to try and end his life.

"Hey, Tree."

Ashlock felt a small hand tapping on his trunk, so he returned to the courtyard and saw Stella still lying there, looking up at his canopy with a vacant expression.

Ashlock flashed a leaf with Qi to show Stella he was listening and was happy to see it hardly added a few minutes to his recovery time. As his cultivation rapidly recovered, things got easier. If he had to guess, he would surpass the Qi Realm within the next hour and then spend the next week shooting through the Soul Fire Realm, and by the week's end, he would resume his previous state of cultivation.

"I really don't like that guy at all," Stella grumbled. One hand rested on his trunk, and her face was buried into her elbow. Although her expression was obscured, he could tell she was upset.

"Why did he expect me to know everything about his capabilities? I have never even met an earth affinity cultivator before." She then sniffled. Was she holding back tears? *"That jerk then ranted at me about how to build things as if I'm an uneducated idiot."*

She then laughed sadly. *"I mean, I am uneducated, but that's not my fault. There was nobody there to teach me! Tree...what should I do? If every new person in the sect is smarter than me, they will think the Ashfallen Sect is run by idiots like me, and then you might look bad."*

Ashlock found it unfortunate that her insecurities were flaring up again. She was such a bright and capable person, but she failed to see it, as there was never anyone around her while she grew up to offer words of encouragement or advice.

It pained him to see her so distraught. Without a mentor for cultivation, she was already touching the Star Core Realm at sixteen years old, and from what he had seen, that was unbelievably impressive. She'd also learned to translate an ancient runic language in a single year, and considering her somewhat lack of social experience, she had handled meetings with Grand Elders hundreds of years her senior with style.

She was an exceptional person all around, and he was incredibly proud of her. So to see her lying on the bench and feeling like a failure somewhat enraged him. But at the same time, he could understand her plight.

He hated to admit it, but she wasn't exactly the best person to be the face of the Ashfallen Sect due to her lacking education, especially in politics. It had worked out so far, but her immaturity sometimes snuck through, and she had yet to be confronted by someone she couldn't bully with her superior cultivation or with Larry backing her up.

She needed time to grow up and learn the skills the other scions had. It was important to remember that she was years younger than both Diana and Douglas, so some inexperience was expected. The situation reminded Ashlock of those university graduate jobs that demanded years of work experience from someone who hadn't worked a day in their life.

"I should just let Diana handle everything," Stella grumbled as her arm fell to the side, and she looked up with red eyes at his canopy. *"Then I can stay here and protect you from harm while she handles all the annoying people."*

As endearing as that sounded, he didn't want a moody Stella hanging around him for the next week. He had a lot to plan and needed to focus on recovering.

Looking within himself, he saw his dim Star Core slowly refilling with Qi that funneled in from his leaves and the many demonic trees around him. Luckily, since he still had a Star Core, he could manipulate Qi outside his body despite being limited to the peak stage of the Qi Realm.

Because of this, he looked around the desolate mountain peak. The storm had destroyed almost everything. Even the badly damaged runic formation surrounding him had been ripped apart, and only shards remained here and there.

Using telekinesis, he grabbed one of these shards with a pointed end to write on the stone nearby.

Stella turned her head toward the sound and slowly read aloud what he had written. "Just keep doing your best. That's all I will ever ask for."

Stella held back a sniffle. "That's so kind, Tree—"

The scratching sound continued as Ashlock wrote out one last line.

"Now stop crying so I can sleep." Stella read and then laughed while she wiped her tears away. *"Okay, okay. Sorry, Tree. I'll let you sleep and go cultivate..."*

Stella wiped away the tears on her sleeve and got up from the bench. Then, after a long stretch and slapping her cheeks to wake herself up, she looked around the empty mountain with a frown. "Wait, where can I cultivate? There's no runic formation anymore?"

She wandered over to the approximate area where the last runic formation courtyard had been. She had to step over some piles of rubble, and there was still the general outline of where the pavilion had been as the foundations had survived the storm.

Surprisingly, the runic formation was still there. Although it was just a husk of its former glory, as the silvery spirit stone lines hadn't survived the storm.

Stella crossed her arms and hummed to herself as she wandered around, seemingly trying to think of a solution. Only then did Ashlock realize Stella had only ever cultivated within a runic formation.

When she built that massive runic formation that had surrounded him while he was asleep all those years ago, he had felt the drastic change when he woke up. The formation had attracted and condensed all the Qi in the nearby area around him, making cultivation easier.

Stella began to grumble to herself as she kicked some random rocks, which ironically distracted him way more than she had while being moody. After a while, she gave up on her rock-kicking and summoned some spirit stones to her hand from one of her spatial rings.

The weird silvery metal reminded Ashlock of mercury, and he watched as Stella inspected the rock, then looked at the runic formation, and then back at the rock. This continued for a while, and the frown on her face grew with every look. Eventually, she sat down on the runic formation and tried to jam the silvery rock into the grooves of the formation to little effect.

It was obvious she had absolutely no idea what she was doing. Hadn't she claimed a few years ago that she had been the one to install the runic formation that surrounded him?

"No way she told me that just to sound more useful," Ashlock wondered. It was common for children to lie to their parents about their achievements. But the more he thought about it, he realized how silly he had been to assume a child could have constructed such a massive runic formation around him. She must have gotten some help from somebody.

"Agh, how can I fix this stupid thing?" Stella cursed and stood up and began to walk toward Ashlock. *"Maybe I should ask that shmuck Douglas how to do it—"*

She paused mid-step from her own words and scowled. *"No, he will call me an idiot. I can figure this out!"*

Ashlock sighed as he watched Stella march back to the runic formation with a newfound determination. She stood there with her eyes closed, and moments later, her golden spatial rings flashed with power, and a stack of books materialized.

She sat down, picked a random one from the pile, and skimmed the first page. "Nope," she said as she chucked it to the side and reached for the next one. "Nope, again."

Leaving Stella to distract herself, Ashlock looked over the mountain with his {Eye of the Tree God}. From up above, he marveled at the beautiful sight. He didn't know how sustainable this mountain forest of demonic trees was, considering the lack of soil for nutrients, but he was sure he could work out a system of some kind to keep the forest alive.

"I could bring nutrients through my roots in the wilderness and exchange them with these demonic trees for Qi," Ashlock mused as he debated the idea. Ascending a single stage in the Star Core Realm had already been a tall order, but now that he was entirely a tree and his Star Core was the size of his trunk, he had a lot more Qi to collect to ascend and he needed all the help he could get.

He still couldn't believe a spirit tree was out there at the peak of the Monarch Realm. How long had it been cultivating to achieve such a level of power, or did it also have a system like him?

Maybe he could ask the world tree if they ever met. He was sure he could grow his roots to meet theirs if given enough time, no matter how far apart they were.

While Ashlock was observing the mountain range of demonic trees, he saw a streak of flame arching through the sky, and when he focused on it, he saw the Redclaw Grand Elder standing upon a sword of crimson as he zoomed toward the White Stone Palace that still stood after the Dao Storm.

"Oh, Douglas must have finished with the tunnel," Ashlock concluded, glad his subordinates could finally return to work. But then he was distracted by a surge of Qi through one of his roots.

Switching views back to the mountain peak, Ashlock saw Douglas fly out of the hole in the ground that led to his hollowed-out root, followed by a water spout, and unceremoniously land on his face a few meters away.

Diana, with little Kai wrapped around her neck, effortlessly followed and gracefully landed on her feet. She then looked around and spotted Stella surrounded by a mountain of books and furiously muttering to herself.

"Hey, Stella," Diana said flatly. *"What are you up to?"*

Stella whipped her head around and scowled. "Learning about runic formations."

Diana took off her mask and furrowed her brows. *"Why? Just ask Douglas; it's one of the most common jobs of earth affinity cultivators, as only they can really turn the spirit stones into a liquid form unless you have an artifact... Why are you glaring at me like that?"*

There was a tense moment, and then Stella hurled the book she was holding across the courtyard while huffing, clearly annoyed at being told her efforts over the last hour had been futile and her only option was to ask Douglas to fix it.

Ashlock seriously debated activating {Hibernate} and ignoring everyone for the next week.

4
RUNIC FORMATIONS

"Did someone mention runic formation?" Douglas shouted, pushing himself out of the rubble he had fallen face-first into. He was drenched, with a thick layer of dust from the wreckage covering him from head to toe. Even his brown hair had turned white from the grime.

Diana casually walked over and effortlessly extracted the water and dust from Douglas's clothes, forming a ball above her palm that turned into a dusky snow globe. With a flick of her wrist, the water ball transformed into mist and was carried away by the wind.

She then crossed her arms and lectured in a monotone voice, *"Stella, why are you in such a bad mood today? The Patriarch is recovering, and we have Douglas here to rebuild what was lost in the Dao Storm."*

Stella scowled over her shoulder, but then her eyes widened. "Diana, why is there a snake around your neck?"

"Mhm?" Diana hummed until she remembered the tiny black snake. *"Oh, this little guy? Not entirely sure. He was sleeping on Larry's back and then took a liking to me."*

"He's so cute!" Stella ran over and extended her finger. The snake cautiously approached but reeled back and tried to hide behind Diana's neck. "Hey, why is it scared of me?"

"Maybe because you have a fat squirrel on your head." Diana rolled her eyes as Stella reached up and felt the soft white fur of Maple.

Ashlock witnessed how Maple appeared out of nowhere and perched himself on top of Stella's head. Somehow, the squirrel seemed weightless, so Stella rarely noticed when he decided to sleep on her head.

"Maple, when did you get here?" Stella grumbled. *"And why do you keep running off? Where were you when the Dao Storm hit?"*

Ashlock was glad the squirrel didn't seem to mind people doubting him, as Maple didn't react to Stella's words and continued to sleep. Likely recovering from the monstrous ability he had unleashed on the Dao Storm.

He was still unsure of Maple's full capabilities as that attack on the Dao Storm had been the closest to him actually getting a glimpse of what he could do.

"Aww, what a majestic squirrel—"

Stella grabbed Douglas's outstretched hand by the wrist, keeping it firmly in place. The giant man still wore his black wooden mask, so his expression was indiscernible, but the gasp of surprise told Ashlock that Douglas hadn't expected such a strong reaction to his innocent gesture.

"If you touch a single hair of Maple's," Stella warned, *"don't blame your death on me."*

Maple watched Douglas lower his hand to his side, and then seemingly satisfied, the squirrel closed his eye.

Would Maple have really killed Douglas? "Hey, Maple. I know you can hear me. I know Douglas and Diana aren't in the mutual pact, but please don't kill any of my sect members for small transgressions against you, okay? Their survival and growth directly benefit me."

Maple sprawled out on Stella's head with his limbs far apart but gave Ashlock a thumbs-up. With the murderous squirrel under control, Ashlock realized that Larry was still missing.

Expanding his spiritual sight, which now covered most of the mountain peak, he saw the massive spider crawling up the mountainside at a sluggish pace.

"The brute must be hungry," Ashlock mused. Larry had been confined to the cavern for some time and couldn't go hunting. "Well, I need him to help translate for me up here, as I don't want to waste Qi while I'm recovering. He can go hunting after."

Communicating with Larry required only a tiny bit of Qi compared to controlling a slab of stone with telekinesis and accurately writing out a message.

Douglas rubbed his wrist. *"Stella, I apologize for trying to touch your pet."*

"No apology necessary. I should have warned you earlier since you two haven't been formally introduced." Stella pointed up at the dozing squirrel. *"This is Maple. He emerged from a rift leading to a hellish dimension, where a monster with an eye many times the size of our Patriarch lurked. He may appear cute, but he might be the strongest one here. Also, he is not my pet."*

Maple, indifferent to both insults and praise, continued sleeping. Sometimes, Ashlock wondered if he had a pact with a mythical squirrel or if Maple was actually a sloth in disguise.

Douglas removed the black mask from his face and, taking Stella's warning seriously, examined Maple as though he was a ticking time bomb.

Stella shifted her focus from Douglas to little Kai, the snake wrapped around Diana's neck. "Have you named the snake yet?"

Diana hummed in thought. *"I don't think I should. It acts strangely friendly, like the Patriarch's other pet, so it might already have a name—"*

Just then, Larry crested the side of the mountain peak, and Ashlock informed him through the tether about the grass snake.

"Kaida," Larry declared gruffly, drawing the attention of the girls and Douglas. "He is the newest guardian under Master's eternal guidance!"

Stella took a moment to translate the words in her head before gasping in understanding. "So the snake is called Kaida and is Tree's pet like you?"

Larry slowly crawled closer and huffed a plume of ash from his mouth. *"Mistress, I'm far from a simple pet like that small snake that can do nothing but look cute. I am Master's faithful servant and part-time executioner!"*

"Sure you are." Stella rolled her eyes.

"Forgive my question, but you can understand the spider...ahem, I mean Larry?" Douglas asked. The man tried to maintain his composure, but Ashlock could tell he was bewildered from watching the two speak in a language he couldn't understand.

With pride, Stella practically stuck her nose in the air and switched back to the common tongue. *"Of course I can! The Patriarch can only communicate via the ancient runic language, so I learned it."*

There was a brief pause as Douglas processed the information. He looked between the squirrel, Stella, and then Larry and eventually just shook his head. "The Ashfallen Sect continues to surprise me." Douglas nervously chuckled as he rubbed the back of his neck. "Is there anything I can do to help? You mentioned something about a runic formation."

"Ah." Stella's joy instantly vanished. "Yes, our runic formations were destroyed in the Dao Storm, and I tried to fix it myself."

"Formations?" Douglas seemed surprised. "You had two up here?"

Stella reluctantly nodded. "There was a smaller personal one that my father used when he was still alive. It was constructed of high-quality stone and strengthened by runes to withstand stage ascensions up to the Nascent Soul Realm."

Douglas whistled in appreciation. "That must have cost your family a small fortune to have built."

Stella shrugged. "No idea. It was here when I was born."

"Right." Douglas glanced around. "And where was this other runic formation?"

Stella gestured with her chin toward Ashlock. "I replaced the entire courtyard surrounding the Patriarch with premade portable Qi-gathering arrays."

"Huh? Why did you do that?" Douglas rubbed his chin.

"Well, long story short, there was an incident with lightning…the first of many." Stella smiled at the memory. "Tree got knocked out, but I saw he was recovering slowly, so in desperation, I sold everything left in the pavilion of any worth and went to Darklight City to buy those portable formations."

Ashlock felt a mix of warmth and shock, knowing what Stella had done while he was asleep. The thought of such a young girl venturing into the city alone to sell items belonging to her family to create the Qi-gathering formation that had surrounded him broke his heart. Although it had been beneficial, he still cursed the lightning for causing such a situation.

Douglas furrowed his brows. "Why didn't you just hire an earth cultivator to create one for you?"

"I was about ten years old at the time and terrified everyone was out to kill me." Stella sighed. "Also, it wasn't like I bought them all at once. I went down there and bought a few, brought them up here, laid them around Tree, and quickly realized I needed more. I only stopped once the *old man at the shop started giving me an odd look and I ran out of money."*

Douglas walked over and began inspecting the remnants of the central courtyard. *"Bloody hell, you filled this entire area with them? That must have cost a fortune."* He then bent down and picked up a stone shard. *"And low-quality materials as well. No wonder it didn't survive the storm."*

Stella shrugged. *"Actually, that formation has been in disrepair for years. People kept coming here to fight, and they destroyed a bit of it each time. Honestly, I had been debating replacing it with something more proper, but I lacked the funds to do so"*—Stella raised her fingers weighed down with golden rings—*"but now I have the wealth of hundreds of people stored in these rings."*

If there was one thing the Ashfallen Sect had, it was now a vast wealth. Of course, it wasn't sustainable income, but it was a sizable bounty they acquired after slaughtering hundreds of Evergreen and Winterwrath cultivators.

But if they wanted to hire many mortals and buy materials to create things, they would need a more reliable source of income, and Ashlock was still betting on alchemy to be the Ashfallen Sect's main export.

That was why he wanted to keep pushing ahead for the alchemy tournament despite all the risk. Obtaining a top-tier alchemist he could keep within the sect and have teach Stella or maybe Diana would be very beneficial.

And who knows? Perhaps the alchemist tournament of Darklight City can become a yearly event that brings in more wealth and talent to the city.

Douglas's eyes lingered on the many golden spatial rings on Stella's finger and then grinned. "Well, it just so happens I am for hire!"

"We already hired you," Diana said flatly, petting little Kai's head. *"You belong to the Ashfallen Sect now."*

"Ah…" Douglas paused. *"Wait, we never discussed pay!"*

Then, when Diana frowned, he quickly added, *"I won't demand any pay for spending a few hours building that tunnel, but if you want me to repair or build a runic formation, I will need at least a few dragon crowns for my efforts…"*

Ashlock realized that Douglas's words were true. They had somewhat bullied the man into signing an oath without ever discussing the benefits or pay.

"*Pay?*" Diana raised a brow, interrupting Ashlock's musing. "*Why would a member of the Ashfallen Sect need payment?*"

Douglas's expression darkened. "*I need payment. I have mountains of debt and beast cores to buy! Why else would I come and join your sect?*"

Stella pulled one of the spatial rings free and tossed it to Douglas, who fumbled and almost dropped it.

"*That should pay off your debts, and we will need to work on your beast core addiction,*" Stella said seriously, glancing briefly at Diana.

Douglas put the ring on his pinky finger and closed his eyes. A small glow of power emanated from the ring, and Ashlock could tell the man was searching its contents. Finally, his eyes snapped open, and he gasped. "Is all this for me?"

"*Sure.*" Stella shrugged. "*I think it's rather pathetic you care so much about some wealth anyway when you are now a member of the Ashfallen Sect. Diana and I have grown tremendously in cultivating without needing dragon crowns or spirit stones, although that might change soon now that our pavilion has been blown away...*"

Ashlock suddenly got a terrible feeling that he had been spoiling Stella a little too much over the years with free cultivation resources and gifts. Had he acted like a rich parent and spoiled his child rotten?

"*I don't know what to say,*" Douglas spoke slowly. "*This is more money than I have ever seen in my miserable life. How can I repay you? You want to repair the runic formation, right? I can do that right now!*"

Seeing Douglas so appreciative of her gesture, Stella seemed to cheer up. "*That would be much appreciated, as trying to reach the Star Core Realm without a runic-gathering formation is a futile endeavor.*"

Stella then crossed her arms. "*However, I want you to teach me about runic formations.*"

"*Teach you?*" Douglas rubbed his chin. "*I can do that.*"

What followed was Diana relaxing on a bench under his shade while Stella and Douglas stood over the runic formation that Stella used to use for cultivation before the silver lines were destroyed.

Douglas got down on one knee, placed a palm on the formation, and closed his eyes. *"I will return the runic formation to its original form first and then explain its function."*

Ashlock saw the hard stone covered in deeply engraved lines that were chipped and damaged seemingly morph into a watery, clay-like substance and then ripple as the engraved lines were wiped and redrawn.

Once the runic formation looked new, Douglas opened his eyes. *"All right, the best place to start an explanation about runic formations is naturally the runes, also known as words of power. They are basic instructions that heaven understands. Depending on your goal for the formation, you will merge various arrays that are small collections of runes."*

Douglas then pointed toward the outer edge of the formation. *"Since this is a super basic Qi-gathering formation, it's simply one massive Qi-gathering array using the runic word for 'gather.' However, most of the Qi gathered by the array replaces the Qi inside the spirit stone lines."*

"Why would the Qi be used by the array?" Stella asked while Douglas brought out some spirit stones from the golden ring Stella had just given him.

"Well, you can't write words of power in the dirt with a stick—heaven only recognizes instructions provided through intent, also known as Qi, which the spirit stones contain."

Douglas injected some of his own Qi into the spirit stone, and it melted from a solid into a liquid, now resembling mercury. *"Although the formation could gather twice as much Qi for you to use for cultivation, the spirit stones within the formation would need replacing regularly. So it's a cost-versus-performance thing."*

Slowly, Douglas brought out more spirit stones and filled all the grooves with the silver liquid. The grooves didn't look that deep, but Ashlock was surprised by how many spirit stones were needed to complete the formation. Such a small formation had gobbled up handfuls of spirit stones already, and it still wasn't complete.

While Douglas was hard at work using his earth affinity Qi to transform the solid spirit stones into a viscous liquid, Stella was busy studying the runic words.

"Hey, Douglas, what's the difference between this and the ancient runic language?"

"Oh, that old language?" Douglas mused. *"I am using a more*

streamlined version of that old language here. Fewer lines are needed to convey the same message to heaven, so it's cheaper, and runic formations using the new version can also be more compact."

"Does that mean I could make my own runic formations with the ancient language, then?"

"Absolutely, those old runic masters are obsessed with it," Douglas replied. "Runic formations that use the ancient language are ideal if you have a lot of wealth and room to work with, as they connect with heaven better and are therefore more efficient. But the language is mostly dead, and few bother to learn it, including me."

Douglas then returned his focus to the Qi-gathering formation full of spirit stones. "Stella, come place your hands on the formation and activate it. All you have to do is direct heaven's will toward it to get the cycle going."

Stella nodded and got down on her knees beside Douglas. She then placed her hands on the formation and closed her eyes. A moment later, the entire thing lit up with a silver glow, and through his spirit sight, Ashlock could feel the Qi in the area gravitating toward the formation.

And as he focused more, he could see that the silver lines absorbed around half the Qi that gravitated toward the formation while the other half hung around within the formation's circumference as if there was an invisible bubble.

"Perfect, you can take your hands away now," Douglas directed Stella, and she complied by standing back up and looking at the active formation.

Douglas then summoned an artifact from his spatial ring. It looked like a soldering gun with a hole in the top. *"Stella, this artifact lets you carve out lines in the stone, and then you put a spirit stone in the top, and the artifact converts it to liquid."* The man then pushed the artifact into Stella's hand. *"Why don't you try it? You could rebuild whatever formation you want around the Patriarch. I can direct you."*

Stella gripped the artifact in her hand and gave Douglas a weak smile. "Thank you for this, Douglas—"

"No, no." Douglas shook his head. *"Thank you for taking me in and helping me start a new life."*

The man tapped the golden ring on his pinky. *"The funds in here are more than enough to pay off all the debts that have been weighing on my mind for over a decade."*

Stella's smile grew a bit. *"That's nice. Then I hope you don't mind helping me cover every inch of this mountain in a Qi-gathering formation for Tree?"*

"Err, that might be a bit much—" Douglas started.

But he was swiftly silenced by Stella's excitement. *"Of course, that would just be the start. Can we create defense formations? Ideally, ones that can deflect lightning and pesky Dao Storms. Ooo! How about one that increases the growth of trees? Is that possible?"*

Douglas just let out a long sigh and pinched the bridge of his nose. Ashlock could feel the man's pain, but Stella raised some good ideas that he hoped they would implement over the next few days while he was out of action.

It was going to be a hectic week—Ashlock could already tell.

5
TREE HATES THE COLD NIGHT

As the mountain was enveloped in the darkness of dusk, Ashlock observed Stella drawing lines on the ground with a paintbrush in one hand and a pot of black ink in her other.

Ancient runic symbols painted by Stella surrounded him, which his {Language of the World} skill seemed to automatically translate in his mind.

As Stella went about her work of writing the ancient runic language onto the ground with the paintbrush, Douglas was watching from the sidelines and offering advice when Stella asked for it.

However, his guidance proved disappointing. His initial lecture on runic formations had been helpful to Stella, but his knowledge beyond the basics was limited. It became clear that Douglas's expertise in runic formations was superficial at best, as though he had acquired the skill merely to pad his resume and secure higher-paying jobs without actually being proficient.

"So you really know nothing about the ancient runic language?" Stella inquired as she continued painting. Considering the size of the formation she wanted to create, Douglas had advised using his techniques to create the grooves rather than the handheld artifact he had given her.

Douglas shook his head. *"As I said, those old fogies obsessed with runic formations learn it, but I've never been one to hole up in the library and study dusty books. All my runic knowledge was picked up here and there while working the trade."*

Stella grumbled to herself, and Ashlock could tell the little bit of respect she had built up for Douglas this afternoon had vanished. Although Stella was uneducated due to her circumstances, she was a curious and bright girl who picked up things quickly. Because of her intellect, she did have the natural snobbish attitude studious people had toward muscle heads, which he could relate to.

Back on Earth, he was the type of guy to spend most of his time glued to a chair playing games or studying. Perhaps that was why he reincarnated as a tree? It suited him, to be honest.

Setting down the ink pot and brush, Stella stepped back and scrutinized her work. "Are you sure there isn't a way to specialize this Qi-gathering formation for a tree?" she asked her unhelpful assistant, and as expected, Douglas shrugged. Ashlock had concluded Douglas wasn't the sharpest tool in the shed.

Diana, who had remained on the bench the entire time, gave her two cents. "Spirit trees cultivate with both their leaves and roots, right?"

Ashlock decided to confirm that with a flash of Qi.

Stella hummed to herself in thought, and then her eyes widened. *"I think I got it! So this runic formation just gathers Qi and traps it within the area above the formation, right?"*

"Right…" Douglas replied, clearly unsure of where Stella was going with this.

"So is there any way to send the gathered Qi into the stone below so Ash can absorb the Qi with his roots, too?" Stella asked excitedly.

Douglas rubbed his chin. *"It could work—defensive formations make use of transfer arrays to channel the gathered Qi to a storage array. In this case, you could just treat the tree's roots as the storage array and make use of several transfer arrays…"*

Stella beamed. *"So how should I do it?"*

"I will make the engravings super deep to reach the tree's roots and ensure the engraving is wide enough so there's room to add more engravings on the inside wall, which can be the transfer runes. You could also inlay it on top of the surface Qi-gathering runes, but it can muddle the meaning of the runic words and make them less efficient."

Douglas then added gravely, *"But this formation will be extremely* expensive. At least a hundred if not a thousand times more spirit stones will be needed than what you used for your personal Qi-gathering formation. The sheer size of this endeavor is hard to fathom."

Stella waved him off as she walked back to pick up the paintbrush. *"The Patriarch's cultivation is priceless. He is the pillar of the Ashfallen Sect. If he had abundant Qi to work with, the entire sect would prosper, and a few mere spirit stones are laughable in comparison."*

Amusingly, the first person to agree with Stella's assertion of Ashlock's importance was Larry, who had been quietly waiting off to the side of the mountain peak. The giant spider would have been crawling around his branches, but since he was ten times his original size, Ashlock doubted his branches could even support the colossal creature's weight.

"Master's recovery comes before anything else!" Larry stated gruffly, and Stella nodded to the giant spider.

"See? Larry gets it."

Diana and Douglas, both clueless about the ancient runic language, exchanged a puzzled glance.

Douglas shrugged and walked closer to Stella. *"Are you done with the first layer of Qi-gathering runes? It's getting late, and I want to head to Darklight City to pay off my debts tonight."*

"Oh?" Stella turned her head, paintbrush still in hand. *"Are they even open this late? I thought most stores closed at dusk."*

Douglas blinked in confusion, then laughed. It began as a chuckle, but soon he was wiping tears from his eyes. Stella just stood there, pouting.

"What's so funny?" she kept asking as Douglas tried to recover.

"Your innocence..." Douglas started but burst out laughing again. *"Sorry, sorry. Forgive me,"* he said between gasps, wiping his tears. Eventually, he caught his breath after much effort and tried to calmly explain. *"These debt collectors are people of the night. They don't run a store where I can just walk in. So it's more of a back-alley situation. That's why I found it so funny. Imagining those thugs running a store was hilarious."*

"Back alley?" Stella frowned. *"Doesn't sound like a great place to conduct business."*

"You haven't run into debt before, have you?" Douglas said bluntly, and Stella shook her head.

Weirdly, Douglas suddenly had a warm smile on his face. He didn't say anything else, which seemed to irritate Stella even more, but they eventually returned to the matter at hand.

"Yes, I'm done with the outline." Stella placed the brush and inkpot into her spatial ring. *"You can do your part now."*

"Sure thing." Douglas got on his knees, and within seconds of the man's hands touching the stone, Ashlock began to panic. It was as if he had been standing on solid concrete, and it suddenly transformed into mud underfoot. The solid stone ground he had felt so comfortable in liquified and turned into viscous sludge.

If not for his roots delving so deep into the mountain, Ashlock feared he would sink. In fact, his body did begin to sink slightly, and he felt his trunk being engulfed by the stone.

Thankfully, the quicksand-like technique was finished within a minute, and Ashlock found himself surrounded by meter-wide and five-meter-deep engravings in the courtyard that followed Stella's paint. Through his spiritual sight via his roots, he could look up and see the sky through the gaps.

Ashlock had never felt so exposed, as if he was naked, as ridiculous as that sounded.

He then yelped as he felt Stella drop down into one of the gaps, which were barely wide enough for her to fit in. She then brought out the artifact that Douglas had given her, and after inserting a spirit stone into the top, she began carving the ancient runic word for transfer into every available inch of rock.

"Make sure to use high-quality spirit stones for the transfer runes," Douglas shouted down into the hole. *"The spirit stone quality doesn't matter so much for the gathering runes, but for the transfer, quality is of utmost importance; otherwise, you will lose a lot of Qi to the surrounding stone."*

"Okay," Stella nonchalantly replied as she carefully carved out the runes. Before, she had just been painting with a paintbrush, so mistakes were more tolerable. However, it was clear from her determined face that carving into the rock was a more permanent affair requiring much more concentration.

While Ashlock tried to get over the squirming feeling of someone walking on top of his roots, he watched Douglas walk off the mountain peak and begin to descend the mountainside. Although he had sworn loyalty to the Ashfallen Sect, Ashlock decided to keep tabs on the man to see what he would do.

"Larry," Ashlock said through the tether, *"tell Diana to tail Douglas. I want her to keep him safe."*

The spider huffed in acknowledgment and crawled over to where Stella was working.

Ashlock wasn't only worried about betrayal; he also feared that Douglas would be taken advantage of. Stella was clueless about money, and Diana didn't seem to realize the implications of a man going to pay back a mountain of debt suddenly with a spatial ring full of wealth.

The ignorance of rich kids.

Debt collectors did want their money back eventually, but they preferred to keep their victims in eternal debt to keep the interest rate mounting up. Suddenly turning up one day and paying off all his debts would raise suspicion about where he got the money, and they might even rob him on the spot.

Diana was in the eighth stage of the Soul Fire Realm, making her far stronger than almost everyone else in the area, and Ashlock had witnessed her superior fighting abilities firsthand many times. Especially with her corruption-filled attacks, he was confident she could triumph even when outnumbered.

Ashlock still didn't like the guy that much, but Douglas had shown some promise and seemed to be fitting in, so it would be annoying to lose him to some thugs already.

Larry looked down into the hole and conveyed his message in the ancient tongue to Stella, who half listened to what the spider had to say as she concentrated on her craft.

"Diana, the Patriarch wants you to tail Douglas," Stella spoke quietly over the sound of the artifact in her hand—using her spatial Qi to cut a deep groove into the rock—as Douglas hadn't made it that far down the mountain yet. "Keep a distance and only help if he gets into trouble."

Diana stood up from the bench, her black, modern-style clothes blending into the darkness of dusk. A thin smile appeared on her face. "A stealth mission from the Patriarch? My favorite."

She then scratched Kai's head. *"You should stay here, little guy. Where should I put you?"*

The black snake curiously looked around, and its little pink tongue flickered out toward Larry.

Kai's actions confirmed that all of Ashlock's pets inherited his language capabilities, and there was a strong chance that Kai would be able to hiss in the ancient tongue soon.

Obeying the snake's choice of resting place, Diana deposited the tiny snake onto Larry's back, giving Kai a smile. "I'll be back before dawn. See you soon."

Diana then slowly walked toward the mountain edge, and before Ashlock knew it, she had vanished into the darkness.

Ashlock would have tailed Douglas himself from the sky with the {Eye of the Tree God}, but he had discovered a problem he had outgrown in the past: fatigue when the sun set. A terrible sleepiness gnawed at his mind, and he struggled to stay conscious as the sun dipped beyond the horizon. Only moonlight kept him somewhat awake, but it wasn't enough to keep him awake much longer.

He had awoken in the late afternoon, so it had only been a few hours since he experienced rebirth and became fully a tree. His roots now felt like his toes, and he could manipulate them freely without much thought or direction. His branches felt like fingers, and while they were still too sturdy to wave around like a hand, he believed he could direct their growth.

And finally, his leaves, which he hadn't been able to chop off in the past—with nothing but a thought, the stem released its hold, and a leaf fell to the stone below.

He now had total control over his body, which came with the downsides of being a tree. He felt a natural urge to grow fruit to spread his seed and expand in all directions in search of nutrients and Qi. He also felt terribly tired without sunlight and already dreaded the upcoming winter months.

"Maybe Stella can build me a greenhouse formation?" Ashlock wondered. It was a good idea, as it would allow him to stay active during the winter months and maybe even stave off exhaustion during the cold, dark nights.

"Hey, Larry, ask Stella if she can make a heat-trapping formation."

The spider relayed his words, and Stella paused her engraving, looking up at the spider, clearly annoyed. *"Tree, stop being so demanding. Can't you see how much is already needed? And you want me to add even more features? And a heat-trapping formation? Do I look like a runic master to you? I have no idea what I am doing here, and that Douglas bastard is useless at teaching!"*

That was fair, but Ashlock had half expected Stella to blindly agree. Since when did she say no to him? Was she in her rebellious teenage stage? She was sixteen years old, so it was maybe a bit overdue.

Whatever the reason, it was fine; winter wasn't for a few months anyway, so there was plenty of time to turn the entire mountain range into a greenhouse. Obviously, he didn't forget about his children; they needed to be warm during winter, too!

"Mhm, it might be good for the Redclaws as well." Ashlock wasn't sure how a heating array would work, but he assumed it would have something to do with fire Qi.

"Ugh, I'll think about this tomorrow." If Ashlock could let off a minute-long yawn right now, he would. Was there anything else that needed his immediate attention before he slept?

"Oh, yeah. Larry, do you need to eat?" Ashlock spoke through the black Qi tether, and the spider perked up.

"Yes, Master," Larry spoke gruffly as he rotated to face him. *"I can sleep without food for centuries, but I used up a lot of energy during the Dao Storm, so my hunger festers."*

That made sense. Much like human cultivators who could put off eating for a long time due to their cultivation, eventually, they too needed sustenance. "While I sleep tonight, go out hunting. Take little Kai with you and feed him some scraps. I need him to get stronger and evolve like you."

Larry gave an awkward bow and then crawled off with his usual eerie silence that didn't match his colossal size.

With only Stella left, working diligently to build the most monstrous runic formation he had ever seen, Ashlock couldn't help but wonder how they planned to fill these massive grooves with spirit stones. Even all the spirit stone deposits he had encountered in this mountain wouldn't be enough.

Alas, that was a question for tomorrow when the sun shone on his leaves and warmed him.

With nothing else of note for him to worry about, Ashlock allowed exhaustion to consume him. Being a tree could be quite challenging at times.

All he could hope was that Douglas would be fine and Diana wouldn't cause too much carnage in Darklight City while he slept.

6
(INTERLUDE) HUNTER BECOMES THE PREY

Diana felt the wind rush past her ears and ruffle her hair as she dashed between the branches of the dense demonic forest that sprawled between Red Vine Peak and Darklight City. The place reeked of death and decay, emanating an eerie atmosphere that was difficult to describe.

Once a haven of greenery, the area had transformed after the Dao Storm. Diana refrained from questioning the Patriarch's abilities, but she couldn't help but wonder how Ashlock had survived the ferocious tempest, even managing to turn the storm into trees.

Legends spoke of the Monarch Realm's capabilities, where individuals were believed capable of creating a miniature world within themselves, allowing them to contemplate and expand their understanding of the natural laws governing the world.

After all, if a cultivator could create a world through sheer will, who was to say they couldn't comprehend the greater world around them at a fundamental level and bend reality's laws to their whim?

Diana believed that was what Ashlock had accomplished. Despite being in the Star Core Realm, he had seemingly bent reality's laws and converted the violent water and wind Qi of the Dao Storm into nature Qi in the form of trees. She couldn't quite fathom if that even made sense, but then again, what about the Patriarch did make sense? The tree could materialize objects from thin air and tear rifts into other dimensions.

Brushing aside her thoughts, Diana focused on her mission, nearly losing her footing while leaping between two demonic trees. In mere minutes, she had caught up to Douglas, who strolled leisurely down the forest path, whistling a pleasant tune.

Although it was a relatively safe area devoid of beasts, a very thin sheen of brown earth Qi surrounded the man's body, which was a common practice for cultivators traveling alone. It was better to slowly drain one's Qi while maintaining a thin shield than to be caught off guard and lose one's life.

Diana might not have been the most proficient assassin, but fortunately, her target was an earth-affinity cultivator known for dull senses and poor awareness. So she didn't need to worry about creaking branches or rustling leaves as she trailed close behind. This was why Diana and Stella could converse when Douglas wasn't far away without fear of being overheard.

As long as Diana kept her distance and never touched the ground, she was confident the man wouldn't detect her presence. However, if she was to land on the ground, he would instantly sense her, as earth cultivators naturally detected vibrations through the earth, akin to a spider.

Every affinity has its strengths and weaknesses. For earth cultivators, superior close-combat skills set them apart from almost all other affinities. In the event of a war between the Blood Lotus Sect and another demonic sect in the wilderness, the Terraforge family would lead the charge with reckless vigor.

Even outside of combat, their ability to alter terrain made them incredibly valuable for constructing buildings and runic formations, so the Terraforge family and other earth cultivators were some of the richest and especially made a lot of money whenever the sect had to relocate due to a beast tide.

Compared to the Terraforge family, Diana knew the Patriarch didn't care much for the Winterwrath and Evergreen families as they were highly environment dependent, and they would only ever move the sect to a frozen area if there were no other options as keeping mortals alive in icy conditions was difficult.

Cultivators always needed to consider the environment and surrounding Qi. For instance, Diana's heightened senses and agility were enhanced by a thin veil of mist emanating from flowers growing on a few demonic trees throughout this eerie forest.

The mist allowed Diana to tap into her powers and techniques without expending time and Qi on creating water herself. For example, she could manipulate the mist into a violent cloud or powerful water jets capable of slicing through rock.

This environmental advantage made natural affinities highly sought-after.

Many families within the Blood Lotus Sect possessed exotic affinities, such as the Starweavers with their cosmic affinity or the Skyrend family, known for conjuring multicolored lightning bolts, but they were considered specialists.

Diana paused on a branch, feeling the rough wood beneath her palm as she rested. In the distance, Douglas reached the gate of Darklight City. With no trees between her and the city, Diana had no choice but to wait, lest she risk Douglas discovering her pursuit.

Darklight City had changed a lot since Diana's last visit mere days ago.

The entire city was enshrouded in darkness under a forest canopy as towering demonic trees engulfed most of the sky. The sound of axes chipping away at the wood reverberated throughout the city like a cacophonous chorus.

Despite the city's infusion with nature creating a certain beauty, illuminated only by moonlight, Diana empathized with the people and understood why they were cutting the trees down. An almost sulfuric stench, characteristic of the soil surrounding demonic trees in the wild, permeated the air, and their bundles of poisonous berries threatened life here.

In the short time since demonic trees had overrun Darklight City, Diana was surprised to already notice numerous bird carcasses littering the streets, victims of the toxic berries, left unabsorbed by the trees due to the lack of soil. She even saw one of these carcasses rotting in a well that was supposed to supply the locals with fresh water.

Yet despite the random trees in the road or growing out of the side of buildings, the entertainment district's streets buzzed with activity, which made tailing Douglas easy. The large man stood out in the crowd, and the ambient noise diminished any chance of him detecting her footsteps among the others.

Whenever possible, she leaped between the city's demonic trees. However, she often had to walk through treeless patches where residents had chopped them down. In the forest abundant with water Qi, she could have moved silently through the mist, but the city's scarcity of water Qi put her at a disadvantage compared to Douglas, who could manipulate the earth beneath his feet.

Luckily, Diana didn't expect to fight Douglas tonight; instead, she worried about the debt collectors he had mentioned. Her privileged upbringing as the daughter of one of the sect's most powerful cultivators had left her uninformed about the underworld dealings of rogue cultivators.

As Diana continued to follow Douglas, the area grew livelier, and the women on the street shed more clothing the deeper she got until they were nearly naked, beckoning passersby outside shady establishments that reeked of musk.

Diana may have been naive, but she recognized this as the pleasure district, where sin tempted many to indulge in nights of forbidden delight. Cultivators publicly frowned upon such activities, though some secretly partook behind closed doors.

Uninterested in such matters, Diana focused on her mission. Eventually, Douglas stopped before a brothel and hesitated to enter. He fiddled with the spatial ring on his finger and steadied his breathing.

While Douglas was preoccupied, Diana examined the building for entry and exit points. Once she confirmed Douglas had mustered the courage to confront his past and entered, she slipped through a hole caused by a demonic tree root growing through the brothel's roof.

She filled the attic with mist to obscure herself from other cultivators' spiritual sight, sitting cross-legged as she scoured the entire brothel for any sign of Douglas.

Aside from the moans of mortals engaged in their nightly activities, which made her feel rather uncomfortable, she soon located a room emanating several Qi auras. A weak runic array, riddled with gaps, surrounded the room.

"If you're going to pay for a runic array, at least do it properly," Diana grumbled. Her eighth Soul Fire spiritual sight had no trouble penetrating the feeble array. "Now let's see how Douglas is doing…"

Inside the room, Douglas flaunted his third-stage Soul Fire cultivation, facing a clearly drunk and irate man barely at the first stage. A few mid-stage Qi Realm goons stood behind the drunk man, evidently terrified of Douglas.

A wooden table piled high with Gold Crowns and a few Dragon Crowns stood between them. The sheer amount of money on display made Diana gasp, realizing why such a debt caused Douglas considerable mental stress.

"Ten thousand Gold Crowns and twenty-five Dragon Crowns." Douglas grinned. "Including the thirty-five percent yearly interest we agreed upon. Feel free to count."

The man, his face flushed from alcohol, interrupted pleasure, or sheer rage, glanced at the mountain of money and then back at Douglas. "This isn't the amount we agreed upon."

Douglas raised a brow. "Oh? What would be the correct amount, Venik? I wouldn't want to scam such a good friend, after all."

"Are you mocking me?" Venik shouted, spittle spraying the floor. "Who else would give someone kicked out of their own family money to cultivate? As a friend, I helped you—"

"Thirty-five percent," Douglas roared back, his booming, Qi-empowered voice making the drunk man shrink. "What kind of friend charges thirty-five percent interest, Venik?" Douglas's massive hand shot over the table and gripped the drunk's throat, turning his face a shade of purple.

"T-thirty s-seven p-percent," Venik gasped.

"What?" Douglas tightened his grip, and Diana noticed light gray flames coating Venik's neck, and a sudden gust filled the room. It seemed Venik was an air-affinity cultivator, giving him no chance against Douglas inside an enclosed space.

"You owe me thirty-seven percent!" Venik screamed, attempting to pry Douglas's fingers from his neck. "That's the number we agreed on after you missed last month's payment."

"Fine." Douglas tossed him to the ground like a wingless bird. His ring flashed with golden light, and a few more Gold Crowns joined the pile.

As Venik lay gasping for air, Douglas crouched down and forced the man to meet his gaze. "Our business is over. I never want to see your damn face again. Do you understand, you fucking bastard?"

Venik opened his mouth, but instead of words, an intense burst of wind shot forth, knocking Douglas back into the table stacked with coins. They tumbled onto him and the floor like a mini waterfall of gold.

Unsurprisingly, Douglas was unscathed, his robust body immune to most attacks below his cultivation stage—especially those from wind cultivators, known for their weak assaults at lower realms.

Venik wasted no time stumbling past his line of goons, hoarsely shouting at them to hold Douglas off while he regained his footing. Douglas surveyed the mid-stage Qi Realm cultivators and shook his head. "Debt slaves, right? Just stay back…"

Unfortunately, they didn't listen to his words.

As they charged, Diana felt the floorboards tremble. Douglas grabbed one assailant and hurled him through a wall, filling the room with wood splinters and dust.

Chaos erupted as the mortals discovered their beds weren't wobbling due to their passionate activities but because the unstable building—burdened by a tree growing on its roof—couldn't withstand people being thrown through its walls.

Diana almost felt bad for those goons that died from being hurled through the walls until she saw Douglas grab a cultivator mid–roundhouse kick and rip the person in half, showering himself in blood.

That final death seemed to instill enough fear in the remaining goons, who turned tail and fled, leaving a blood- and dust-covered Douglas alone in the room.

"Damn bastards," Douglas cursed. His spatial ring flashed with power, making the mountain of coins vanish.

"Why should I even pay those lowlifes back?" Douglas grumbled to himself. Opting not to use the door, he punched a hole in the room's far wall and leaped into the alleyway below.

Had he looked skyward, he might have caught a glimpse of Diana atop the crumbling building, observing his every move.

"This is troublesome," Diana muttered. The commotion would attract attention, and Douglas wasn't doing a good job of concealing his involvement. As a member of the Ashfallen Sect, Diana could pull some strings to avoid punishment for Douglas, but that wasn't the main issue.

Douglas was supposed to stay low-key, and if such a rogue cultivator managed to dodge persecution, people would start asking questions and investigating his background, which would be problematic.

Should she help him slip out of the city stealthily or focus on silencing Venik, who had already made it several streets away using his air affinity?

Diana hopped to the neighboring building while contemplating her options as the brothel completely collapsed, and the demonic tree slammed into the building across the street.

Fortunately, her dilemma was resolved when Douglas, already donning his cloak of concealment, smartly fastened a black wooden mask to his face. The cobblestone alleyway split open, and Douglas sank into the ground—a common method for earth-affinity cultivators to move around by essentially swimming through the earth.

"Venik it is, then." Diana grinned, summoning two black daggers and dashing after the man through the darkness of the night.

The streets blurred beneath her as she rapidly closed the gap, never losing sight of the man who appeared like a firefly in her spiritual sight. As she approached, she abandoned her stealth at the last moment, her eighth-stage soul fire coating her dagger as she aimed for Venik's neck.

The man turned around with wide eyes and gasped, "Selena—"

Diana experienced a brief moment of confusion over the man's dying words, wondering if he had mistaken her for someone else. However, she found her answer when a tendril of shadow lashed out and smacked her dagger from her hand, saving Venik at the last moment.

Diana quickly glanced toward the source of the shadow tendril, then back at where Venik had been, only to find that the drunkard had vanished.

"Tsk, a Nocturne," Diana cursed as she retreated while keeping her spiritual sight active. It was hard not to notice the darkness all around her shifting as if alive. Then, before she knew it, she found herself in a world of eternal darkness, with only the blue flames of her soul providing light.

7
A NOCTURNE'S DEMISE

The darkness enveloping Diana shifted from an empty void to a dreamscape—a world that seemed real but fell apart under scrutiny. The verdant meadow of lush grass lay still as if painted, and the horizon blurred, making the sky appear to be melting.

Diana tried to steady her mind and recall her father's advice on handling Nocturnes, rare but dangerous threats that sometimes appeared when dealing with demonic sect scions.

Nocturnes, also known as dream eaters, were abominations that shadowed their hosts like haunting spirits, doing anything to keep them alive and preserve their food source.

"Selena, was it?" Diana called into the dreamworld, catching a glimpse of movement in this motionless landscape. She spun around to find the shadowy figure of a young girl.

Diana knew the real body lay on the ground, where an eerie specter of a girl with similar features to Venik floated where a normal shadow should be.

"You were his sister, weren't you?" she said solemnly. She had never met a Nocturne, but knowing their origin made the scene before her horrifying.

To create a Nocturne, a sacrificial ritual was needed to bind a relative's soul to one's own, allowing them to consume the relative, often a sibling, for a surge in cultivation.

This dark, secretive demonic practice also granted the added benefit of transforming the relative into a Nocturne, like Selena for Venik, that would protect the host from the shadows.

But there were severe consequences. Apart from brutally murdering a sibling, Nocturnes had to be fed, consuming their host's dreams and sanity for sustenance. And if the host ever reached the Nascent Soul Realm, the Nocturne could take over the infant soul and be reborn.

This fierce urge to keep their host alive for sustenance and the chance at a new life made Nocturnes exceptionally loyal protectors.

Diana now understood why Venik acted tough in front of Douglas, despite being a wind-affinity user two Soul Fire stages below him. A guardian always lurked in the shadows, watching.

A moment of silence passed as the shadow figure refused to answer, but the ghostly form trembling with grief betrayed understanding.

"I need to kill Venik," Diana declared, and the Nocturne howled. A chilling wail filled with anguish echoed as though pierced by countless needles. The dreamscape quivered, and hundreds of shadow tendrils shot forth, but Diana swatted them away with ease. It was weak.

The Nocturne faced a hopeless situation. If Diana killed Venik, the creature would perish without its food source. On the other hand, if they fought until sunrise, the dreamscape would shatter, and the Nocturne would burn under the sun's glare.

As Diana deflected more tendrils, she pondered Venik's motivation for subjecting his sister to such a fate. Had his parents arranged it, or had he performed the ritual himself? When Diana was involved with other noble scions, she hadn't heard of a wind-affinity Azurecrest child named Venik.

If Venik had done it himself, the ritual would have been done out of desperation for the benefits, as his rate of cultivation would decrease drastically since the Nocturne siphoned Qi. And he would also be unable to sleep or meditate without feeling haunted, which would deeply affect his state of mind.

Also, if Venik ever reached the Nascent Soul Realm, the Nocturne would devour his new infant soul, denying him the semi-immortality of being a Nascent Soul Realm cultivator.

All of that for a reliable bodyguard no stronger than the host suggested Venik couldn't leave his back to anyone other than his own sister's ghost.

Venik must have been insane or desperate for protection, either from family members vying for power or from numerous enemies he had made.

Neither option sounded good. Venik was a tumor that needed to be culled, especially since, with the death of his Nocturne, he would soon become consumed by heart demons, just like how Diana had been before Ashlock saved her with those truffles.

Diana continued slashing at the tendrils with her Qi-covered blade while gradually filling the dreamscape with her haunted mist technique. She could shatter the dreamscape with her cultivation, but the Nocturne would escape. She aimed to kill it first and then pursue Venik.

Although the dreamscape looked like it stretched for many miles, it was only around the size of a large courtyard. Soon enough, she could lock down the location of the Nocturne that was running around while its wails filled the entire space with her mist.

"There you are," Diana muttered as she dashed through the mist.

She tore through the shadowy figure a moment later as if it was smoke and seized the Nocturne's throat. She was about to tighten her Qi-coated grip and kill the spectral abomination when she hesitated. The wailing ceased, and the young girl, no older than ten, gazed at Diana with eyes full of innocence.

Was this some kind of trick to make her hesitate? Her father had only briefly mentioned this threat and simply said to kill the Nocturne to escape. Was there really no other way?

"Don't hurt Venik," the girl said in a distorted, eerie voice. "He was my brother, and I still love him."

Diana hadn't known Nocturnes could speak.

"Why?" Diana frowned. "He killed you and turned you into an abomination. How can you still love him?"

Was it some kind of mind magic that made the abomination loyal?

The Nocturne's eyes grew dull as if recalling a painful memory. "Venik had no choice. Our father forced this upon us."

"Father? Who's your father?"

"Grand Elder of the Azurecrest family. He received an order from the Patriarch..." The girl hesitated.

"Which was?" Diana pressed, knowing that the Patriarch rarely gave direct orders. But as a true demonic cultivator with little regard for human life, anything he meddled in was bound to be twisted.

"He wanted more airships and, therefore, more pilots. Our family is the main provider of these pilots. But he wanted them within a year."

That was enough for Diana to piece together the rest. Noble families were often vast, sometimes consisting of dozens of branch families and thousands of members in total. But not all family members were created equal. Out of those thousands, only a few hundred would reach the Soul Fire Realm, and only a tiny handful of those had the potential to reach the Star Core Realm.

As the largest producer of wind-affinity cultivators, the Azurecrest family was invaluable to the sect's continued existence, operating airships that enabled trade between cities and mass evacuations during inevitable beast tides.

With every Azurecrest family member in the Soul Fire Realm already employed in the airship industry, if the Patriarch demanded a new batch of pilots to appear overnight, the Azurecrest Grand Elder likely resorted to something truly horrific to meet the quota.

"Your father forced everyone in the family to kill their siblings to turn them into Nocturnes in order to increase their cultivation, didn't he?" Diana asked, and the little girl's eyes widened before she nodded.

"So please don't kill Venik. I was the weaker of the two, and he promised to make me a new body in the future."

Diana could barely stand the innocent belief in her eyes. Venik, a middle-aged man, had only reached the first stage of the Soul Fire Realm with the ritual's boost. His chances of reaching the Nascent Soul Realm before his lifespan ended were nonexistent. The girl was being deceived.

Diana suspected that Venik was aware of his slim chances and had resigned himself to his fate, abandoning the path of cultivation. His negligence was the reason he remained stagnant at the first stage in the realm for such a long time.

"Why did Venik charge Douglas such high interest? Do you know?" Diana questioned the Nocturne, and the ghostly girl shuddered.

"He couldn't stand me," the girl replied. "He spent all the money on alcohol, drugs, and women to drown me out. I kept urging him to cultivate, but he claimed he couldn't."

Diana suspected that he was simply lazy and unwilling to cultivate, but there was a genuine possibility that he couldn't. Possessing a Nocturne made cultivation significantly more challenging, as it was nearly impossible to enter a state of deep cultivation.

Diana tightened her grip around the ghost, and the girl cried out, "Why?! Why kill me? Let me go back to my brother…"

"Then let me out of the dreamscape," Diana retorted. "Maybe I can save you both." But the girl adamantly shook her head.

"I can see it in your eyes." The girl sobbed. "The eyes of a killer. You will kill my brother if I let you go. I just know it."

Diana had killed many people, including her own cousin, in front of Ashlock before her family was wiped out. Reflecting on it, that had been the last time she felt anything for taking a life. Since then, she had slain cultivators en masse without any qualms.

Had something broken inside her? Her father had used her as nothing but a tool, even threatening her life if she didn't go and kill Stella Crestfallen. But the situation was different this time. Ashlock had requested she follow Douglas; everything after that was her own decision.

Now, with her hand around the neck of a technically innocent person she wasn't compelled or ordered to kill, a disquieting sensation welled up in her chest. This was unlike the other lives she had extinguished over the years; this was a mercy killing. The girl believed she had a chance at life, but Diana knew that she would forever remain a Nocturne, feeding off her brother's dreams and sanity while watching him squander his cultivation.

Diana was fast, but Venik was still an air cultivator. She knew he would soon escape the maximum range of her spiritual sight and vanish forever into the darkness of Darklight City, never to be seen again.

"I'm sorry," Diana murmured, and her eyes turned dull as she twisted her Qi-coated hand and felt the Nocturne's neck snap. Her Qi flooded its spectral form, and the ghost wailed like a boiling kettle. The girl's body solidified and then crumbled to dust between Diana's fingers.

The dreamscape shattered, and the bustling noise of the street overloaded her senses. A few passersby gave Diana an odd look as she had likely appeared out of nowhere, but they soon walked on.

Diana observed the dust scattered in the breeze. Mercy killings evoked a distinct sensation that she loathed, but she tried to convince herself it was for the best to end the Nocturne's suffering.

Empowering her legs, Diana leaped onto the roof of a nearby building and expanded her spiritual sight. At its edge, she could sense Venik's presence. She had almost been too late.

Regrettably, the little girl had been right. Diana fully intended to kill

Venik tonight. He knew too much about Douglas and, with the death of his Nocturne, which had been holding off the heart demons like a dam, was now gone.

He would lose all sanity by sunrise.

Ashlock awoke to the crack of dawn the very moment the golden sun rays hit his leaves. He felt his entire biology slowly speed up under the sunlight's tender care.

The sound of stone cracking accompanied the morning birds, and Ashlock soon located Stella, still laboring to create the enormous runic formation. However, he was delighted to notice a section of the runic formation had already been completed and seemingly activated, as he felt Qi being drawn to the spot, then transferred down through the rock and directly to his roots.

Checking the countdown timer in the corner of his eye until his system was restored, he saw it had decreased significantly to only three days. Seeing that an increase in Qi intake drastically affected his recovery time made Ashlock very thankful for Stella's hard work and gave him an idea.

What if he used {Hibernate} since it increased his cultivation intake? He assumed now that he was fully tree that the experience wouldn't be quite so harrowing. But, even if it was, he could endure a few days if it helped him recover even a few hours faster.

With his mind still awakening, he surveyed the rest of the mountain peak. He wanted to ensure everything was fine before hibernating for a few days to complete his recovery.

As the sunlight bathed the mountaintop, Ashlock saw Douglas emerge from the rock as if stepping up a staircase, shaking off the dust and rubble that clung to his shoulders. He was alone—Diana was nowhere to be seen.

Ashlock was relieved that Douglas appeared to have handled his debts without issue. It made sense if Diana was lagging a bit behind, but even when he used {Eye of the Tree God} and searched the surroundings, he couldn't find her anywhere.

"Oh, you're back?" Stella said as she leaped out of the hole she had been carving ancient runes in and looked around. She was clearly concerned about Diana's absence but didn't want to ask Douglas.

Douglas grumbled as he removed the mask. *"Yeah, I'm back. There was a fight, and I ended up taking back the money."*

Stella raised a brow. *"What happened? Did they try to rob you or something?"*

"Kind of." Douglas scratched the back of his neck. *"To be fair, it was mostly my fault. In hindsight, I might have insulted that Venik bastard a little too much, but he deserved it."*

"Venik?" Stella asked. *"Who's that?"*

"He pretended to be my friend, loaned me money at my lowest point, and said I didn't have to pay him back until I got back on my feet." Douglas chuckled sadly. *"That was a lie. Once I got some work, he said there had been interest the whole time, and if I didn't pay it back, he'd have people smear my reputation, and then nobody would hire me."*

Stella nodded. *"Just to be clear, I gave you that ring filled with coins without expecting any interest."* She then smiled sweetly. *"But if you betray Tree, then I will demand your soul as payment."*

Douglas chuckled to brush it off, but Ashlock could see the slight fear in his eyes, as he knew Stella was serious. "I will take your words to heart," he mumbled, depositing the mask into his spatial ring.

"So what happened to this Venik fellow? You killed him, right?" Stella then froze when Douglas shook his head.

"He surprised me and got away. As an earth-affinity cultivator, there's no way I could catch up to someone from the Azurecrest family. But even then…why would I kill him? He was a bastard, sure, but he did help me in the past…"

Stella's glare made Douglas shrink back. *"Anything, and I mean anything, that could threaten to expose Tree's existence must be eradicated. That lack of bloodlust will come to bite you one day. We are in a demonic sect. Act like it. Do I make myself clear?"*

"Yes," Douglas answered quickly. *"But what should we do, then?"*

Stella looked at Darklight City in the distance. "I wouldn't worry."

By the afternoon, Diana walked up the mountainside with a vacant expression.

"Did you get him?" Stella asked. Diana nodded absentmindedly—her golden ring flashed with power, and a man's severed head appeared in her grasp.

Douglas cheered. *"You really killed that bastard."*

"You did a good job," Stella said, smiling and patting Diana's shoulder before pausing after seeing her face. "What's wrong?"

Ashlock was also worried. Diana looked like someone who had just done something they deeply regretted.

"I...I don't know. Some circumstances around it don't sit right with me." Diana let out a long sigh. *"Ugh, I just can't tell if I did the right thing."*

"Trust in yourself some more," Stella reassured her with a smile. *"Doubt only leads to festering heart demons. Right?"*

"You don't want to know the circumstances?" Diana seemed bewildered.

"Only if you want to tell me." Stella withdrew her hand and turned to jump back down into the hole to continue her work. "I trust in your judgment completely."

Diana stood there for a while, her mouth never quite able to form words. Eventually, she just muttered, "Thanks," under her breath, and a thin smile appeared.

"Hey, she may trust you," Douglas spoke from the side, *"but I would love to know these circumstances if possible. Venik had been a good friend of mine at one point."*

Diana nodded and then explained about the Azurecrest family and the Nocturne that had been feasting off Venik's soul.

Ashlock knew he lived in a demonic sect and had seen their ruthless culture and disregard for life. Still, he hadn't heard of many real demonic techniques or rituals outside the pill furnace that the Patriarch wanted Stella to become.

He could see why Diana had been distraught about the murder, as the siblings had been forced into a rather unfortunate position by their father. Still, Venik did sound like a terrible person, and Ashlock found his care for human life outside the group he cared for to be fleeting.

Did humans care when a forest was chopped down? When trees were burned to death for heat? Those pavilions were made out of the corpses of his fellow trees, and even right now, he could feel the waves of pain and despair through the mycelium network as the demonic trees in Darklight City were chopped down.

But with the mass murder of his fellow demonic trees aside, as he could do little to help them right now, the news of these Nocturnes and the activities of the Azurecrest family were concerning.

Douglas stood silently for a long while, staring at the decapitated head in Diana's hand.

"It all makes sense now," he eventually said. *"The sudden change in his personality, his insane desire to hide away from his family, and even his surprising jump in cultivation, which gave him the strength to run his brothel and order around those goons."*

A single tear rolled down Douglas's cheek. *"I had even met Selena a couple of times in the past. She had been such an adorable little sister to Venik. I can't imagine him doing something so horrible."*

Diana shook her head. *"Don't put all the blame on Venik. The Patriarch's greed to...save more people from the beast tide..."* She paused, clearly conflicted.

Ashlock concluded that this was a very messy situation where nobody was fully in the right. The Patriarch wanted more pilots for airships, which would mean more people could escape certain death. Venik had become a terrible person due to what his father had forced upon him, and Diana had essentially mercy-killed them because they could threaten the Ashfallen Sect.

"I'm going to go cultivate and clear my mind," Diana said, shaking her head. *"I need to contemplate a few things. Can I use the personal formation, Stella?"*

Stella popped her head over the hole's edge. *"Of course, all of us can use it. We are a sect now. This isn't just my home."*

Diana smiled and nodded in thanks.

Stella then glared at Douglas. *"Don't just stand around being useless. Come help me with this formation, and I'll teach you some ancient runes."*

With everyone busy and the loose end of Venik seemingly dealt with, Ashlock activated {Hibernate} and set the timer for two days. He hoped the extra Qi intake while he slept and the completion of the runic formation would shave an entire day off his recovery time.

When he woke up, he expected to see his sign-in system back online, and then it would be time to get down to business. Unfortunately, the alchemy tournament would require a lot more work than he had initially anticipated, especially in light of recent events.

Also, he would need to devise a plan to make the people of Darklight City coexist with his new children and maybe even silently eat those that had hurt them.

8
TREE TALK

[Hibernation Mode Deactivated]

"Tree! Hey Tree, wake up!"

Ashlock was roused by a system chime and the sensation of a hand patting his trunk, accompanied by Stella's persistent voice.

His mind felt even more sluggish than when waking from an ordinary slumber. He felt so slow and just wanted to go back to sleep.

"Treeeee!" Stella cheered. *"You woke up! I can sense it."*

"Huh?" Ashlock mumbled as his thoughts accelerated. "Woke up? When did I fall asleep…"

It was then that Ashlock realized something truly astonishing. Unlike the previous occasion when he had utilized {Hibernation} and endured every passing second, this time, he had simply activated the skill, set a timer, and drifted off. Two days had elapsed without his awareness…

Why couldn't he have had this skill back when he was a human?!

"System?" Ashlock inquired aloud. "Are you operational?"

Idletree Daily Sign-In System
Day: 3508
Daily Credit: 7
Sacrifice Credit: 0
[Sign in?]

It was present... It was genuinely there! A tiny part of him had worried that by becoming a full-fledged tree, he would lose his system. However, there it was in all its glory.

He had managed to employ system skills like {Hibernate} and {Eye of the Tree God}, so the likelihood of it having completely abandoned him was slim. Still, Ashlock needed to witness its return to feel reassured.

Letting out a sigh of relief, Ashlock felt much more awake now. But, to ensure his system was fully working, he summoned his status screen to check if his skills had changed.

>[Demonic Demi-Divine Tree (Age: 9)]
>[Star Core: 2nd Stage]
>[Soul Type: Amethyst (Spatial)]
>[Mutations...]
>{Demonic Eye [B]}
>{Blood Sap [C]}
>[Summons...]
>{Ashen King: Larry [A]}
>{Infant Grass Snake: Kaida [F]}
>[Skills...]
>{Mystic Realm [S]} [Locked until day: 3515]
>{Eye of the Tree God [A]}
>{Deep Roots [A]}
>{Magic Mushroom Production [A]}
>{Lightning Qi Barrier[A]}
>{Qi Fruit Production [A]}
>{Blooming Root Flower Production[B]}
>{Language of the World [B]}
>{Root Puppet [B]}
>{Fire Qi Protection[B]}
>{Transpiration of Heaven and Chaos [B]}
>{Devour [C]}
>{Hibernate [C]}
>{Basic Poison Resistance [F]}

Everything appeared precisely the same as before his rebirth. His race hadn't changed, nor had any of his skills. "Does this mean the system was linked to my tree body rather than my human soul all along? Or did merging my human ego with the demonic tree body carry over the system?"

The more Ashlock tried to unravel the mysteries surrounding the system and its origin, the more he felt a headache coming on. It was easy to just turn a blind eye to it and accept its presence, but why did he have a system if one really thought about it? Why didn't anyone else in this world have systems? Were they unique to spirit trees? Or just him? What made him so special?

"Ugh…" Ashlock groaned. These weren't questions to be contemplated immediately after waking from a pleasant two-day slumber. If his system was accurate, a week had passed since the Dao Storm, meaning Darklight City had been dealing with his new offspring for some time, and there might be news about the alchemy tournament scheduled to begin soon.

"Treeee, stop ignoring meeee." Stella stood beneath his canopy with her hands on her hips.

Ashlock went to flash his leaf with spatial Qi to show he was listening when he realized something. His level of control over the Qi on his trunk was perfect now, as the entire trunk was his Star Core. "There's no way, right…"

Filled with immense anticipation, Ashlock effortlessly wrote the words 'Good Morning' in lilac flame across his trunk like a whiteboard. Stella stumbled back in surprise, gawking at the words.

Ashlock was equally astonished. Although his previous method of communication—writing on the ground with telekinesis—wasn't vastly different from this, it felt significantly more convenient.

'Is everything all right, Stella?' Ashlock inscribed on his bark with the flames of his soul, and Stella nodded vigorously.

"Sorry for waking you. Did you sleep well?" Stella asked with a radiant smile. *"I finally completed the Qi-gathering formation a few hours ago and wanted to check on you."*

Ashlock looked around him, and sure enough, the sheer volume of Qi amassing around him was extraordinary. A single breath during his meditation technique brought in an incredible amount of Qi, but compared to the size of his new Star Core—thousands of times larger than his old one—it was still a mere drop in the ocean.

Nonetheless, a drop was better than an atom. The runic formation, combined with the Qi he received through his roots from all the other demonic trees, made his cultivation rate faster despite his new colossal Star Core.

Essentially, he was cultivating more rapidly than ever before and should reach the third stage in the Star Core Realm soon.

'I had an amazing sleep,' Ashlock wrote, and after Stella finished reading it aloud, he added, 'This runic formation is incredible, thank you.'

Ashlock tried his best to ignore Douglas, who stood off to the side, making amusing facial expressions that alternated between disbelief and amazement as he glanced between Stella and Ashlock's trunk. It seemed he still found the idea of a talking tree absurd.

"I need to learn to read that," Douglas finally spoke up from the side. "How long did it take you to learn the language to this level, Stella?"

"Mhm?" Stella shrugged. "Only about a year of studying day and night with endless love and devotion."

"Oh." Douglas seemed taken aback.

Stella giggled. "Diana gave up after just a week. It's really not easy to learn such a complex language. I can see why they created a far more streamlined version that you learned for runic formations."

"Yeah...the streamlined version is so different it might as well be another language," Douglas replied with a chuckle.

While they chatted, Ashlock inspected the runic formation more closely and noticed that the large holes Stella had used to engrave the transfer runes had been filled with a mixture of rock and spirit stones.

'Do we have any spirit stones left?' Ashlock wrote, and Stella shook her head.

"We used every last one. I either underestimated the spirit stone requirements for creating runic formations or overestimated our spirit stone reserves," Stella said, tapping her chin. "We may need to start cracking down on the mine and demand more from it... I can see why it was so sought after now. These runic formations are essential for cultivation, and I haven't even started on runic formations with other uses, like defensive ones that can create Qi barriers."

Douglas nodded from the side. "Why do you think runic formation masters are paid on par with beginner alchemists? It's a seriously lucrative business."

Douglas's statement made Ashlock realize he didn't know much about alchemists. He knew they existed since someone had to be making the pills they were consuming, and when his {Qi Fruit Production} skill upgraded to A grade, he was able to produce a cauldron fruit that facilitated alchemy, which suggested the practice's existence.

'How rare are alchemists?' Ashlock wrote, and Douglas answered his question after Stella read the words aloud.

"Very rare; there are just so many hurdles to overcome," Douglas said, counting off his fingers. *"First, you need a near-perfect spirit root, as the ingredients have to be combined within your Soul Fire, and you don't want any impurities; otherwise, you'll always be fated to create mediocre pills. Next, you need to reach the Soul Fire Realm with an intense focus on Soul Fire manipulation and control. If those two hurdles weren't enough, you must spend countless years studying—time that could have been spent pursuing cultivation and vast resources to practice with."*

Diana walked over, stretching her back with her arms behind her head, and added, *"Don't forget the brutal exams. They are questioned about thousands of herbs and need to memorize every combination. My cousin tried to become an alchemist, but the examiner chewed out the poor boy."*

Ashlock was glad to see Diana seemed in a better mood, but he found that hard to believe. Why make the exam so hard? Couldn't the alchemists just memorize a few basic recipes and then work from there? Ashlock spelled out his question in flames, and Diana soon answered with Stella translating.

"Simple answer: those alchemists are way too prideful. But it's a bit more complicated than that," Diana said, lowering her arms and putting them in the pockets of her modern-style hoodie. *"Alchemists only get paid so much because they are rare. If everyone could become a low-tier alchemist, then the prestige those bastards enjoy would soon vanish."*

Ashlock now understood the situation perfectly. Those old alchemists wanted to gatekeep the industry to keep it exclusive and maintain their high wages due to the lack of supply. It was smart, but Diana's words also gave Ashlock hope for his tournament's success.

Many aspiring alchemists were likely to be in attendance that couldn't get approved as official alchemists. He only needed one semicompetent person to show him and his three sect members how to perform alchemy.

Also, hearing how valuable they were made Ashlock want to pursue the idea of turning the Ashfallen Sect into a well-known alchemy sect. That way, they could get enough money to buy spirit stones and build more formations by trading with the merchants.

Ashlock's wandering thoughts were interrupted when a sudden wave of pain and fear shot through his roots. It was coming through the mycelium network near Darklight City.

His vision blurred as he switched views to the location of the pain, where he found someone trying to chop down a demonic tree that had his roots wrapped around it. This tree was located on the city wall, somewhere his roots could reach. It seemed that while he slept, his roots had naturally linked up and wrapped around this and many other demonic trees.

"The system mentioned something about automatically connecting with nearby demonic trees before my rebirth," Ashlock mused as another wave of pain washed over him, reminding him of the situation at hand.

The mortal's iron axe cleaved into his root that wrapped around the helpless tree, barely making progress. Cutting through the root of a Star Core demonic tree as a mortal was a futile endeavor.

Ashlock debated opening a portal and devouring the fool but realized that wouldn't solve the issue. He needed to come up with a realistic solution.

Taking a figurative step back, he tried to identify why they were trying to chop down this particular tree. It was growing sideways out of the city wall, causing the wall to crumble around its roots. Upon closer inspection, he noticed damp cracks caused by water damage.

"Ah, the digestive fluids," Ashlock realized. "That is indeed a problem."

The wall appeared sturdy enough to survive an attack from demonic beasts, so a tree growing from it shouldn't be such a significant issue. However, even the strongest walls weren't immune to water or corrosive fluids designed to dissolve the hardest demonic beast corpses.

Ashlock confirmed his roots were intertwined with the demonic tree and surrounding its trunk. With his full focus, he tried to project a message to the tree: "Calm down and relax. Stop trying to hunt—let me take care of you."

He accompanied the intent-filled message with a wave of Qi and all the nutrients the tree could ever need via the mycelium network. To his surprise, the tree responded with a wave of happiness.

"Stop producing berries and corrosive fluid. I will provide for you…"

As far as he could tell, his connection to the tree wasn't much different from before he became a fully fledged tree, but it seemed to understand him—could he speak tree now?

Through his roots, he felt the tree's roots gradually dry up over an hour. He could do things quickly for a tree, and if one thought about it, the fact this tree could stop producing corrosive fluid in just an hour was impressive.

"Good kid." Ashlock sent over more Qi and nutrients, attempting to train the tree like a puppy, always rewarding it for a job well done.

Ashlock confirmed he could communicate and train his children. If he repeated this process for all the trees in Darklight City, they should all be spared.

He could always have Douglas work to relocate those blocking roads or crushing buildings via his portals. All his children deserved to live, and the more that survived, the more trees he had to siphon Qi from.

Since his roots grew around the trunks of the trees, he could also grow mushrooms or flowers to decorate them and make them more appealing to the locals.

Ashlock set to work, making his roots tunnel under Darklight City and creep up through pavement cracks to meet all the demonic trees in the city. He was baffled at how fast his roots grew. His new Star Core was like its own nuclear power station, surging an obscene amount of Qi down his roots.

With a plan in place, Ashlock had to leave the helpless demonic tree on the wall for now. He shifted his view back to Red Vine Peak and wrote a message on his trunk for Stella.

'It hurts.'

Stella practically tripped over her feet as she dashed up to him. "What hurts, Tree? Are you okay?"

'They are slaughtering my children. It hurts,' he wrote in lilac flames, and he had never seen Stella look so furious. The air around her crackled with golden lightning, and reality was distorted by the spatial Qi leaking from her core.

"Tell me where to go. Who should I kill?"

Ashlock quickly outlined his plan, explaining that the demonic trees would stop producing corrosive fluid and emphasizing that the trees provided him with more Qi, helping him grow faster.

He had never seen Stella so motivated in his life.

"Portal me over to the Redclaws, Tree!" Stella said as she fastened the white mask to her face.

Ashlock sighed in relief as Stella calmed down and no longer looked like she was about to commit genocide on the mortals of Darklight City.

Creating the most stable and impressive portal to date, Ashlock connected Stella to the White Stone Palace. As she stepped through, everyone in the palace courtyard wearing crimson robes instantly bowed to the arrival of the Ashfallen Sect's mistress.

The Grand Elder rushed out of the palace within moments and gave a deep bow. "Mistress, how may we serve?"

He raised his head and added, *"Preparations for the tournament have hit a few hurdles, so I sent out news of the tournament's delay to all the attending families. But the elusive Silverspire family refused and said they were coming today—"*

"Silence," Stella said, raising her hand. *"I care not for some pathetic noble family. Why are you all standing around here when the immortal's children are suffering?"*

The Grand Elder blinked in confusion. "Pardon?"

9
ASHLOCK RELOCATING HIS CHILDREN

Ashlock watched the scene unfold in horror.

His relationship with the Redclaws had gone far beyond the point where Stella could mess up and he could simply eliminate them without a second thought.

They were too valuable to be disposed of now.

So why had she mentioned something like that?

Stella sighed at the Grand Elder's question and replied, *"The immortal expended great effort to transform the Dao Storm into new life. Wouldn't you consider those beautiful red trees his children?"*

The Grand Elder appeared bewildered, which was entirely understandable. Even Ashlock was somewhat confused by Stella's words, but fortunately, the Grand Elder dismissed her weird comments with a respectful bow.

"Mistress, please enlighten this old man with your request, as I am not sure I understand your profound words."

Ashlock let out a long sigh of relief. Stella had salvaged it somehow.

"It's rather simple. My immortal ancestor came out of seclusion to deal with the Dao Storm." Stella then pointed off into the distance at the huge demonic tree that occupied Red Vine Peak and was easily visible without the surrounding pavilion. *"He was enraged when the storm dared to uproot the beloved demonic tree that he had nurtured for so long, so he bent the natural laws to turn the Dao Storm into a forest of*

trees, so his favorite demonic tree wouldn't feel alone anymore while he was in seclusion."

"I see..." The Grand Elder slowly nodded. *"So the demonic tree holds great significance for the immortal?"*

"More than just significant," Stella replied, crossing her arms. *"That demonic tree is a spirit tree capable of basic thought, and it is connected to all these newly born demonic trees."*

"A spirit tree, you say?" The Redclaw Grand Elder stroked his chin as he observed the tree in the distance.

Ashlock really didn't appreciate being gawked at as it made him feel naked, nor did he condone Stella saying he was only capable of basic thought! Was that a roundabout way to call him stupid or something?

Stella nodded. *"Not just any old spirit tree. It has a fragment of the immortal's soul inside, so it could care for me and the Ashfallen Sect like a guardian in my ancestor's stead while he cultivates. You know...just like Larry."*

The Grand Elder's eyes widened as panic seemed to set in. Meanwhile, Ashlock found it astonishing that they would believe Stella's words, but in fairness, her explanation was more plausible than claiming he could communicate and had a sign-in system.

Stella gestured to Ashlock in the distance. *"Every time a demonic tree is cut down, the guardian feels pain, as does the immortal whose soul is linked to it."*

"I understand now." The Grand Elder bowed deeply again. *"I should have foreseen such a consequence with all these trees appearing. I hope you can forgive this foolish old man; I can only beg for your mercy."*

Stella approached and placed a reassuring hand on the Grand Elder's shoulder. *"You have performed admirably so far, and the immortal is pleased with you. Don't dwell on this too much, but we must find a solution swiftly."*

The Grand Elder straightened and adopted a serious demeanor. *"We could impose the death penalty on anyone caught even touching the trees. My family is small, but we could work tirelessly to enforce this if the immortal wills it."*

No. Absolutely not. Ashlock wanted the trees to live for his own selfish reason of generating more Qi. That was not a justification for taking people's lives so brutally. What if someone genuinely ignorant, like a playful child, touched a tree? Would the child be killed on the spot, no questions asked?

Ashlock had been concerned that Stella might be somewhat psychopathic when she seriously asked if he needed her to wipe out Darklight City, but now he wondered if they all shared this trait.

Fortunately, Stella shook her head. Ashlock had never been more relieved that he had provided Stella with a pre-outlined plan before she left. Otherwise, he wouldn't be surprised if they went to commit mass murder.

"Although measures need to be taken, we still have to consider the lives of Darklight City's people." Stella sighed. *"Those are words straight from the immortal. I personally would have agreed with you otherwise."*

"I fucking knew it," Ashlock groaned. He really needed to rein in her misguided loyalty—it was getting out of hand.

"So what should we do?" the Grand Elder questioned.

"The immortal understands that some trees must be removed, such as those obstructing roads or crushing buildings. So an earth-affinity cultivator from our sect, as well as any other earth-affinity cultivators seeking employment, can be hired to free the trees, which the immortal can then transport away via portals."

The Grand Elder nodded. *"That can be arranged, although it will be costly. I hope you have enough Golden Crowns on hand."*

Stella smiled, removed two of her golden spatial rings, and placed them in the Grand Elder's hand. "This should be enough for now. I broke the seals for you."

Ashlock watched the transfer of money with a pained heart. Why was everything to do with cultivators so expensive?

After inspecting the contents of the ring, the Grand Elder nodded. *"This is a generous amount. Should I proceed with fulfilling your orders?"*

With a simple nod from Stella, the Grand Elder took to the skies, leaving a blazing trail of crimson flame as he rode his sword toward Darklight City.

With Stella now calmed, she approached the Elders standing off to the side. "How goes the tournament preparations?"

They exchanged glances, and eventually, a stern woman replied, *"To be honest, not great. We are a smaller family and don't have much influ-*

ence within the Blood Lotus Sect. As you may know, alchemists are rare and considered strategic resources hidden from prying eyes. So unless the rewards are truly extravagant, they'll likely show up with no one better than complete novices."

"I see..." Stella drummed her fingers on her crossed arm. Ashlock could tell she was carefully crafting her words to avoid sounding foolish in front of the Redclaws.

Elder Mo was next to speak up. *"That issue aside, we have secured the training grounds of the Academy as a venue to conduct the tests, but there's a slight problem... Actually, would you like to take a look?"*

"Sure," Stella agreed. Ashlock then opened a portal to transport them directly to the entrance of Darklight City. This was another reason he wanted the trees to remain in the city: he could wrap his roots around them and use the trees inside the city as anchor points for portals.

"I hope you can see the other issue," Elder Mo said with a chuckle as the group stood in the stands of a building resembling a colosseum from ancient Rome. The primary issue Elder Mo referred to was that the place looked more like a zoo enclosure filled with demonic trees rather than a suitable location for a tournament.

"Indeed, Elder Mo, this won't do at all," Stella agreed. *"We should be able to remove these trees within the next few days. When is the event scheduled to start?"*

Elder Brent, the Elder Ashlock had seen on the wall that first spotted the approaching Dao Storm, spoke up. *"I can answer that. We sent out a notice of delay a few days ago to everyone who had shown interest in participating. Some met the news with sneers, others with annoyance. For them, the event will start in a month. Only one family completely ignored our notice, though."*

"The Silverspire family that the Grand Elder mentioned earlier?" Stella guessed. Elder Brent nodded in confirmation. *"I never really dabbled in Blood Lotus politics. So what are they known for?"*

"Wealth derived from creating spatial rings and being self-entitled, arrogant bastards," Elder Mo grumbled.

"They created these?" Stella looked at her golden spatial rings.

Elder Mo glared at them with annoyance. *"Unfortunately, their spatial rings are one of the largest exports of the Blood Lotus Sect, so they naturally receive special treatment from the Patriarch."*

A brief pause in the conversation led Ashlock to realize how certain affinities seemed more valuable than others. For example, what could the Redclaws really provide the sect other than firepower?

"Which families agreed to participate in the tournament?" Stella wondered aloud while looking at the horizon.

The stern woman known as Elder Margret replied, *"Participate is a strong word. They're essentially just sending inexperienced alchemists as a ploy to check out our presence here in Darklight City and see if they can seize a piece or the entire city from our hands."*

"But to answer your question," Elder Margret continued, counting on her fingers, *"of the seven remaining families, excluding us and the ones that have been wiped out, five showed interest."*

"Oh?" Stella raised a brow. *"Who isn't coming?"*

"The Nightrose and Silverspire families."

Ashlock was confused as he had never heard of this Nightrose family, and hadn't the Grand Elder said the Silverspire family was on their way?

Stella mirrored his concern to the Elder, who helpfully replied, *"The Silverspire family doesn't have Soul Fire—they have liquid metal cores that aren't suitable for alchemy. I assume they're coming to find a way to profit from this event rather than participate, as they hate being left out. As for the Nightrose family, I'm surprised you haven't heard of them, considering they're the Patriarch's family. They're very mysterious and prefer to hide their powers, so their refusal was expected."*

That was a lot of information to take in. Ashlock finally learned the name of the Patriarch's family. "I wonder what type of affinity the Nightrose family has? I should ask Stella when she returns to the mountain," Ashlock mused.

It was also interesting to learn that some affinities didn't have a Soul Fire. Did they follow a different cultivation system than everyone else? He was now even more intrigued to see these Silverspire people who were apparently on their way despite being told to wait.

Elder Margret added, *"Those sending someone of importance are the Voidmind, Starweaver, Terraforge, Skyrend, and Azurecrest families."*

Ashlock hadn't encountered most of those yet, but the Terraforge family rang a bell as they were mentioned in regard to Douglas and, finally, the Azurecrest family. After hearing from Diana what happened to Venik and his sister, he had a bone to pick with them.

Stella nodded sagely, but Ashlock suspected she didn't know about those families, either.

"*Are they only sending their own family alchemists?*" Stella inquired. "*Make sure the tournament is open to everyone who wants to participate.*"

"*You sure?*" Elder Margret questioned. "*The quality of alchemists that haven't passed the exam could be detrimental—*"

"*Then they won't win,*" Stella snapped back. "*This is a tournament that only lets the best win, right? Why should we care what those snobbish alchemists think? There could be talent out there being wrongfully ignored!*"

Stella then lowered her voice and added, "*Also, we will only have a few people show up if we keep the entry requirements so high...*"

"*Ah...*" Elder Margret blinked in realization and then scribbled something down on a piece of parchment. "*That is a good idea. I will allow rogues to participate. It's good that we delayed the tournament by a month to give them time to head over here and prepare.*"

The group continued to converse for a while, and after an hour or so, the skies became filled with noise. Airships floated over the demonic forest–covered city, and a few low-rank cultivators empowered their voices with Qi and shouted to the streets below from the platforms.

"***By orders of the Noble Redclaws and the Mortal Council, those found harming the demonic trees will be fined a Silver Crown as they are now deemed a protected species by the city. If you wish to remove a demonic tree from your home or street, you can pay ten Copper Crowns and enquire at the nearest guild building for an earth-affinity cultivator to remove it.***"

Ashlock was surprised at how quickly the Grand Elder had put his plan into motion, which made things a little awkward as the city was enormous, and his roots didn't even cover a fifth of it. Fortunately, only the nearest half of the city was affected by the demonic trees, as the further one got from Red Vine Peak, the fewer demonic trees were present.

After a while, the city buzzed with people rushing toward guilds and requesting demonic tree removal. Ashlock was sure many of them would regret their decision once he decorated the demonic trees with beautiful flowers and magical mushrooms—something he planned to do overnight.

Darklight City would wake up in the morning to a city they could hardly recognize. But while the sun was still up, he wanted to test out moving these demonic trees in the colosseum via his portals.

Back on Red Vine Peak, Ashlock opened a portal next to Douglas, who had been meticulously checking that the runic formation surrounding him was working properly. The man made eye contact with Stella through the portal, who gestured him through.

Once he stepped through and saw the colosseum filled with demonic trees and a portal opened next to one of the trees that led to a random spot in the wilderness, Douglas seemed to understand his task.

Jumping down, Douglas landed in a cloud of dust and got to work. The ground turned into the same weird, viscous state Ashlock had experienced two days ago, and he slowly pushed the tree up from the ground, roots and all.

Almost effortlessly, Ashlock used telekinesis through the root coiled around the demonic tree, guided it through the portal, and set it down on the lush grass of the wilderness. "Kid, dig your roots deep into the ground to stabilize yourself."

His root was naturally cut off when the portal snapped closed, but he had roots just below the surface of the wilderness, so he used them to help the demonic tree stay upright while it found its footing...rooting?

"This is going to be a tiring process, isn't it?" Ashlock sighed as he returned and worked alongside Douglas to move another one. Honestly, the fact he could lift trees with his mind was baffling, and it seemed to entertain the Redclaw Elders as well, as they stood watching with immense interest as trees many meters tall were uprooted and then floated through portals.

"The immortal is doing all this while cultivating two mountains away?" Elder Mo whistled in awe, and Stella grinned proudly from the side.

"He sure is."

Things were going smoothly until late evening when Ashlock noticed something on the horizon approaching. Due to its size, he thought it was a giant cloud, but he was soon proven wrong when an airship that looked vast enough to be a floating city cast a looming shadow on Darklight City.

"*Tsk.*" Elder Mo put his hands behind his back and grumbled, "*The Silverspires are here. We should prepare to meet them—they hate tardiness and will raise a fuss that we can't afford right now.*"

Stella nodded and gestured for the Elders to lead the way.

Just looking at how large and majestic the Silverspires' airship was made Ashlock realize how small the Redclaw family was compared to the true powerhouses of the Blood Lotus Sect.

All he could hope was they didn't eradicate the Redclaws and seize Darklight City for themselves, because if they did, he would be shooting his roots through portals and popping that pompously big balloon.

10
(INTERLUDE) RYKER VON SILVERSPIRE

Stella stood beside the Redclaw Grand Elder, her stomach churning with nerves. Despite her efforts to steady her breathing, the flashy display of wealth and power from the Silverspires, along with her limited knowledge about them, eroded the confidence she had been carefully building over the past few weeks, particularly through her frequent interactions with Douglas, who often challenged her on various subjects.

Looking up, she saw the Silverspire airship, a weirdly ring-shaped contraption comprised of a metal tube suspended by hundreds of white balloons hovering above the White Stone Palace. The airship dwarfed the mountain, prompting Stella to wonder how many Azurecrest cultivators were employed to keep it airborne.

"They refused to elaborate on the reason for their visit," whispered the Redclaw Grand Elder, his voice laced with fiery Qi. "Nor did they disclose who is coming. We can only hope it isn't one of the Silverspire Grand Elder's children. They are absolute nightmares to deal with."

Stella nodded, her gaze fixed on the gradually descending airship. It seemed destined to encircle the White Stone Palace like a ring. As time passed, Stella could only see the metal tube—presumably the living quarters for the airship's inhabitants—and the white balloons as they encapsulated her entire vision.

A bridge made of metal slabs, connected by chains, shot out and anchored itself into the rock near the White Stone Palace's gate, its two large hooks digging deep into the mountain.

Once this spectacle concluded, a hiss echoed as two sliding doors at the top of the bridge parted. A short child dressed in a white suit appeared, followed by a man who announced, "Please welcome the seventh son of the Silverspire Grand Elder, Ryker von Silverspire!"

The Redclaw Grand Elder emitted a quiet groan, which Stella detected only because she stood beside him. His fears had materialized— a son of the Silverspire Grand Elder had arrived. However, as Stella observed the child in the pristine white suit struggle to walk down the bridge, she couldn't help but think he was rather small. Was he merely five years old? What could he possibly be doing here?

Everyone except Stella and the Redclaw Grand Elder offered the young Silverspire a modest bow as he passed. Eventually, the child and a weary-looking butler stood before them.

Up close, Stella could appreciate their distinctive appearances. For instance, Ryker's hair resembled iron threads, while the butler's hair looked like pure silver, accompanied by a stream of liquid silver orbiting around him.

"Please forgive my rudeness and unexpected arrival," Ryker enunciated as clearly as a young child could, his voice betraying his youth with a lisp and high pitch.

The Grand Elder gave the child a nod and turned to the butler, clearly demanding an explanation with his gaze. Although the Silverspire family was evidently far superior, Stella appreciated that they still showed some respect for the Redclaws on their own turf.

"There were certain circumstances that we hope you will understand after further discussion away from prying ears," the butler said, his expression grave. "Would you please show us inside so we may discuss this further? Or would you prefer to board our airship and converse there?"

"Inside is fine. Please, follow me," the Grand Elder replied before leading the way into the White Stone Palace. Everyone bowed deeply as he passed.

The butler gave Stella an odd look, which she felt was warranted, considering she was wearing a mask and had blond hair that didn't match the rest of the Redclaws, but she still took issue with his attitude nonetheless.

"She is a trusted outsider," the Grand Elder explained as they traversed the empty hallways devoid of anything lavish.

"Big Sister, what's your name?" Ryker asked, stumbling forward as he tried to keep up with the adults' brisk pace. "Mine is Ryker von—"

"Yes, I heard the first time," Stella replied. "My name is Stella."

"Stella...Stella..." Ryker repeated her name a few times, seemingly committing it to memory. "I like that name. Reminds me of the twinkling stars."

Unsure of how to respond to such a compliment from a child, Stella remained silent.

"So?" the Grand Elder inquired with his arms crossed. They all sat in a grand yet rather empty reception room. The Grand Elder's cultivation surrounded them, ensuring that no wandering spiritual sights below the Star Core Realm could eavesdrop on their conversation.

"As previously mentioned, this is Ryker von Silverspire, the seventh and youngest son of the Silverspire Grand Elder," the butler began. "And my name is Sebastian Silverspire. I am from a branch family and have been entrusted with the young lord's safety."

Stella glanced at Ryker, who sat quietly on an ornate wooden chair beside Sebastian, swinging his short legs as he stared at the floor.

Sebastian paused before leaning forward and continuing. "As you may know, our family follows a similar but different cultivation path from many other families here in the Blood Lotus Sect. We have to absorb the Qi from metals matching our current realm. Do I need to explain more?"

Stella absentmindedly nodded without thinking, as she really did want to know, so the man continued.

"Quick explanation, then. Our Soul Cores are metal, and to upgrade to the next realm, we must condense our metal cores and transition them into a higher element. Copper represents the Qi Realm, iron the Soul Fire Realm, silver the Star Core Realm, gold the Nascent Soul Realm, and finally, platinum the Monarch Realm. However, that is just a speculative guess, as we haven't had someone manage to cultivate that far. Anyway, I digress."

Sebastian gestured toward Ryker. "As you can see, the young lord resides in the lower stages of the Iron Core Realm, or in your terms, the

Soul Fire Realm. As for myself, I am in the first stage of the Star Core Realm, or in our terms, the Silver Core Realm."

Stella managed to conceal her surprise. She had been used to encountering families with one or perhaps two Star Core Realm experts at most. But for the Silverspire family to employ Star Core Realm experts as bodyguards...they must have far more Star Core experts than the Redclaws, Evergreens, Winterwraths, and Ravenbornes combined.

"To be in the Soul Fire Realm at such a young age, the Grand Elder must be very pleased with Ryker's performance thus far," the Redclaw Grand Elder mused, frowning. "But I still don't see why you two invited yourselves here to Darklight City, despite our informing you that the tournament has been postponed."

"Father is going golden!" Ryker announced, clenching his chubby fists. "I must fight my scary brothers and sisters for the leftover silver."

The Redclaw Grand Elder's eyes widened, but Stella had to admit she wasn't following the conversation at all.

"It's as you suspect, Grand Elder," Sebastian confirmed. "Our beloved Grand Elder has entered seclusion in hopes of emerging triumphant and entering the Nascent Soul Realm or, as we call it, the Golden Core Realm."

"So this fight between siblings?" the Grand Elder asked hurriedly. "What does that refer to?"

"If the Grand Elder is to succeed in his ascension to the Golden Core, instead of creating an infant soul, he will create a Silver Core that can be passed down to the next generation," Sebastian said, his expression darkening. "Before going into seclusion, the Grand Elder declared he would pledge his newly created core to whichever of his children could generate the most profit for the Silverspire family while he was in seclusion. If one of his children were to absorb this core, their cultivation would soar."

The Redclaw Grand Elder leaned back in his seat next to Stella, letting out a long, drawn-out sigh that seemed to drain all his energy. "So let me guess, Ryker von Silverspire has come here in search of great profits?"

Sebastian nodded. "All the children fought over which city they would conduct business in, and Ryker drew the short straw—ahem, I mean, he was fortunate to draw Darklight City, so here we are."

"I thought you said there was nothing here, Sebastian?" Ryker asked with childlike innocence. "And you said on the airship that it was being run by a useless group of fire cultivators—"

"Silence, Ryker, before I take you back home." Sebastian glared at his young lord, causing the little boy to shrink back in his seat.

"Excuse him." Sebastian offered a weary smile. "Some things are best left behind closed doors, don't you agree?"

The Redclaw Grand Elder's eye twitched from the words, but he quickly composed himself and asked seriously, "So now that you're here, what do you plan to do? You know you can't just come and set up a business here on our land without our permission and without paying taxes to us."

"I don't even know what any of that means," Ryker grumbled as he crossed his arms. "Mother thinks I'm a genius, but I only like to cultivate. What do I know about selling stuff?"

Sebastian reached over and patted the boy on his back. "You may not win, but your mother believed this was an excellent opportunity to see the wider world and broaden your horizons. What kind of five-year-old should spend all day sitting on a mountain of Qi-rich iron and cultivating?"

Stella decided to interject into the conversation with some questions of her own. "Ryker, besides the airship and Sebastian here, did you come with anything else? Maybe some starting capital or an idea of what business you want to do?"

"Err..." Ryker twiddled his thumbs. "Mother gave me some starting funds, which I'm pretty sure is against the rules, but all my siblings already had some money, and I had nothing, so it should be fine...right, Sebastian?"

"Ryker's mother gave him a thousand high-grade spirit stones and fifty thousand Dragon Crowns." Sebastian frowned. "I do feel his mother was a little too enthusiastic about this contest, but it should be fine."

So he's a rich fool—that's more money than the Ashfallen had with all the stolen wealth combined, Stella thought as she analyzed the boy. She was no business guru herself, but even she had some ideas for businesses. However, this kid seemed clueless. Could she somehow extract those spirit stones from his hands to create more runic formations for Tree?

"So you came here with nothing but funds and the hopes of beating your well-established and richer older siblings?" the Redclaw Grand

Elder asked and groaned in despair a little when Ryker nodded enthusiastically.

The little boy then raised his hand. "I did have one idea actually that my sister gave me when I drew this city."

"Oh?" Sebastian asked, clearly intrigued. "What is it?"

"Alchemy!" Ryker exclaimed. "I hate spending my allowance on expensive pills, so wouldn't it be awesome if I had my own alchemist? Also, my sister said those with the fire affinity make excellent alchemists."

Sebastian's face darkened. "Young lord, I'm not supposed to offer too much advice, but please remember your sister may love you very much, but she will still try to feed you bad information to win. Alchemy is…resource intensive, to say the least."

Ryker naively tilted his head. "Does that mean it's expensive? I have a lot of money, though… And aren't you people having a tournament to find one? Can I…err…hire the winner from the tournament?"

"No, you can't," Stella snapped. "The best alchemist is for us. You could hire the others that compete in the tournament, though."

"But I want the best one." Ryker crossed his arms angrily as if someone had stolen his favorite toy.

Stella took a breath to calm her thoughts before she accidentally revealed too much. "What do you know about alchemy?"

"Nothing," Ryker grumbled.

"So how do you plan to train these alchemists or source the materials they need to perform alchemy?" Stella inquired.

"As I said, I just like to cultivate all day. I have no idea about this stuff." The brat then looked at her with sparkling eyes. "Big Sister wearing the cool mask, what do you do?"

"Well, I…" Stella hesitated, unsure how to answer his childlike wonder. She wanted to head back to Red Vine Peak and ask Tree about his opinions on this. She saw an opportunity, but there were also massive risks. If the Silverspire family came to know about Ash and his capabilities, it could be disastrous.

Sebastian added, "I'll be honest here. If you two can take Ryker under your watchful eye and help him set up a profitable business, you will have gained great favor with a future Elder of our family. If not—its next leader."

Stella found that hard to believe, looking at the little brat. And those were empty words to her, as she planned to remain here through the beast tide with Tree, so having a connection with a family planning to abandon this place was nearly useless.

"And if we refuse?" the Redclaw Grand Elder asked, and Sebastian frowned. "Then we will leave. We understand he is young and inexperienced, and to force him upon you would be impolite. Although we still plan to set up a business here and pay the required tax…"

"That sounds perfect—"

"Hold on," Stella interrupted the Grand Elder. "Let me go check with someone about this. I will be right back."

As if on cue, a rift materialized in the middle of the Redclaw Grand Elder's protection field, as if it wasn't even there. Through the portal was the view of the setting sun from atop a mountain and a weird mist.

Under the confused gaze of both Sebastian and Ryker, Stella stood up and gracefully walked through the portal, which collapsed behind her with a pop.

"Who is she?" Sebastian asked, his gaze lingering on where the portal had been.

"Someone with an even more frightening background than your young lord." The Redclaw Grand Elder chuckled. "Don't worry. She will be back with an answer that I'm sure will satisfy you both."

11
RUTHLESS NEGOTIATIONS

The portal collapsed with a soft pop, and Stella said nothing as she trudged over to the bench beneath Ashlock's canopy. She collapsed onto it with a long sigh, closed her eyes briefly, and murmured, "That was exhausting. I can't tell if the child or his guard was more annoying to deal with."

Stella was clearly not cut out for politics after spending a childhood alone, but unfortunately, she was the only one other than Larry who currently knew the ancient language.

Ashlock wished he could combine Diana and Stella's talents somehow.

He would request that Diana learn the ancient language, as she was far better at handling politics, but it was clear she had no desire to learn it. According to Stella, Diana had given up after just a week of studying and proceeded to spend the next year in the library cultivating and reading random books.

"You could hear all of that nonsense, right?" Stella said, her voice laced with exhaustion. *"How did I do?"*

'You did great,' Ashlock wrote on his trunk. Stella translated it in record time, and Ashlock started thinking she was fluent in the ancient language. She really was a genius.

"Thanks." Stella smiled. *"I came back here to inquire about your opinion, Tree, as you are the Patriarch of our sect. Personally, I think we should work with Ryker somehow."*

It was a great question, as Ryker von Silverspire could bring significant fortune to the Ashfallen Sect through wealth, connections, and family. It also helped that he was a clueless child, making it easy to draw him to their side or convince him of certain business ventures without him asking too many questions.

However, it was a double-edged sword, particularly due to Sebastian. While Ryker might be easy to manipulate, the presence of his Star Core–level guard would make extracting money from the young lord a challenging affair.

If they could somehow get rid of the guard, everything would be perfect. But how? There was no way the guard would leave if asked and entrust Ryker to a rival family.

As Ashlock's mind raced with solutions, Diana appeared, walking through the haunted mist she had coated the entire mountain peak in to obscure it from the Silverspire family.

"*Stella, you look exhausted,*" Diana said dryly. "*What happened over there? Mind catching me up?*"

Stella groaned at Diana's comment and explained lethargically, "*Ryker von Silverspire, the seventh son of the Silverspire family, is here. Their Grand Elder is ascending to the Nascent Soul Realm, and all of his children are fighting over an inheritance.*"

"*Right...what does that have to do with us, though?*" Diana asked.

"*Whichever child generates the most profit for the Silverspire family will receive the inheritance. So Ryker has come here to set up a profitable business.*"

"*Oh? That's great,*" Diana said, grinning, a rarity for her. "*Anyone from Silverspire is loaded with wealth, and you say it's the seventh son? Must be quite young.*"

Stella nodded. "*Yeah, he's a little brat. His guard said he's only five.*"

"*He has a guard?*" Diana inquired, and Stella nodded. "*That's unfortunate. I was hoping he came alone, but I guess that's an unreasonable assumption. Do you know if this guard reports everything back to the Silverspire family? If so, we need to be careful around him.*"

Stella shrugged. "*I didn't ask, but that's a good point. I think the guard makes working with Ryker a significant risk for us.*"

"*What's the time frame?*"

"*For what?*"

"The fight for the inheritance," Diana said as she sat beside Stella on the bench. "Depending on the time frame, we might be able to pressure them a bit. I assume the guard wants the best for the child? If so, maybe we can get him to stay away while we extract the money from the child."

"They said it would take the Grand Elder a year or so to ascend, but from the sounds of it, that's just a guess."

Ashlock understood Diana's implication and had to agree. They were dealing with an impressionable young child who had been given far too much money for anyone his age to manage, and he had a strict timeframe to make a significant return. So they were the ones with the upper hand here.

For Ashlock, the spirit stones and dragon crowns would provide ample resources to rapidly develop the Ashfallen Sect and perhaps even Darklight City. The gamble was worth taking, but only if they could remove Sebastian as an obstacle.

"Did you suggest any business ideas to Ryker?" Diana inquired.

Stella shook her head. "No, but the kid is dead set on starting an alchemy business."

Diana glanced at Ashlock's canopy. "Just to clarify, our plan is to develop into the alchemy business using those cauldron plants and all the ingredients we can grow, right?"

Ashlock flashed his leaf to signal agreement. Diana couldn't read his words, but she understood his gestures.

"I see. It makes sense." Diana rubbed her chin in thought. "We're a small sect with a unique advantage that we need to capitalize on as much as possible. Alchemy is undoubtedly the best way to quickly gain fame, connections, and money."

"Why do we even need the brat's money? Can't Ashlock handle everything?" Stella asked, apparently nursing a headache. "It would be so much easier to just tell them to leave."

Diana reassured Stella with a warm smile. "Let me handle it, okay? This is a big opportunity for us. You may think Ashlock can do everything on his own, but can he manufacture porcelain pill bottles and grow every single ingredient?"

She looked up at Ashlock's canopy. "Can you grow spirit grass?"

Ashlock looked through his options, and he actually could grow spirit grass with his {Blooming Root Flower Production} since the grass was counted as a type of flower.

Flashing his leaf once, Diana appeared surprised. *"Wait, you can? Huh, good to know. Well, I'm sure there's something you can't produce that we may need to purchase, and think of all the formations we can build with those spirit stones!"*

"I know, I know." Stella waved her off. *"You go deal with it."*

"Sure, leave it all to me," Diana said, standing to depart. *"Patriarch, I'm thinking of telling them we plan to establish an alchemy guild, hence the tournament. I'll offer Ryker the opportunity to invest his wealth into it for a share of the profits. Something small, like ten percent. That way, we can pursue our own interests, take all of his money, and keep everyone happy."*

It was an excellent plan, but Ashlock added, 'We'll construct our alchemy workshop in the mine. Inform them that Ryker can visit anytime, but Sebastian can only come if he swears an oath of secrecy.'

Stella relayed his words to Diana, who nodded in agreement. "Sure, I can tell them that. Anything else?"

Ashlock felt confident in letting Diana manage the remaining negotiations. He wanted to focus on transforming Darklight City into a floral paradise overnight. There was also another issue he had been delaying and intended to address that night. 'Stella, accompany Diana and retrieve a Fire Qi–producing flower from the Redclaw Grand Elder.'

Stella groaned after reading the message, but as the loyal girl she was, the sloth-like human stood up from the comfortable bench and joined Diana. "I'll get the flower and leave right away."

Stella reattached her black wooden mask, and Diana mimicked her action by summoning a different white wooden mask than Ashlock had seen before.

"How many of those things do you have?" Stella asked, and Diana shrugged.

"Quite a few."

The Qi in the air shuddered as space tore itself apart. It was astonishing how easy Ashlock found conducting spatial techniques across his body after the merge. Just like before, he made sure to keep the portal aimed away so he wouldn't expose himself.

Sebastian maintained his composure as he watched the smug Grand Elder sitting across the table from him. It had been several minutes since the mysterious girl left, and the Redclaw Grand Elder refused to elaborate on her origins or her supposed powerful backing.

Who in the sect could have a more powerful backing than his young master? Especially in a remote city like this? In fact, how had the Redclaws even gained power here?

Things didn't add up, and Sebastian felt uneasy about trusting Stella. Was she from a rival demonic sect? Or a hidden child of the Patriarch?

Had he made a mistake by not bringing more Star Core experts with him to this backwater city? He had researched Darklight City before coming, and although it was impressively large, it was ultimately a mining city with no other noteworthy exports.

The fact that such a small family with a single Star Core cultivator could rule over such a vast city indicated the low level of development here. It was so primitive that he had even mistaken the city for a forest when he had gazed idly out the airship window.

Sebastian nearly jolted in his seat, barely reining in his orbiting liquid silver in time to prevent it from obliterating the rift in space that reappeared. Through the portal, he saw two women backed by a dense, swirling mist with eerie shadows of ghoulish creatures lurking in the dark.

Stella was the first to step through, her blond hair in a ponytail and the same black mask hiding her features. Due to the thin sheen of spatial Qi at the peak of the Soul Fire realm coating her skin, Sebastian had no way to use spiritual sight to bypass the simple wooden mask and see her true appearance.

"Sebastian and Ryker, this is Diana." Stella gestured toward the slightly shorter woman at her side. Diana wore a white wooden mask, and her short black hair covered the top half. Sebastian also noted that she wore artifact clothing more suitable for combat and stealth operations than Stella's traditional garments.

Stella then addressed the Grand Elder after briefly introducing her companion. "Grand Elder, I require a Fire Qi–producing flower from you."

The elderly man appeared perplexed by the request, but his golden ring flashed, and a beautiful crimson flower materialized in his hand. "I hope this Blaze Serpent Rose satisfies him. It's a common flower from our home region near an active volcano."

Stella carefully took the exquisite flower, twirling it in her hand before depositing it into her spatial ring. "This should suffice. I will take my leave now."

Sebastian silently observed their interactions, and his lifetime of political experience allowed him to discern who held the upper hand in the relationship. Stella's ability to demand something without reason from a Grand Elder suggested her backing was above the status of the Redclaws. The mysterious male figure they referred to as "him" might even be at the peak of the Star Core Realm.

This was dangerous. Ignorance was the best way to find a knife in one's back.

"Big Sister!" Ryker called out, and Stella looked over her shoulder.

"Mhm?"

"Can I come with you—"

"No." Stella ruthlessly cut off the young lord with a resounding no and vanished through the rift that instantly closed behind her.

Sebastian was baffled. He had never seen someone so averse to making a deal with the Silverspire family, and he was fully prepared for Stella to agree to his young lord's request so he could follow him through that portal and learn what lay beyond.

But to think they weren't even interested, do they not want to exploit us? Sebastian mused as he eyed the new masked woman who gracefully sat beside the Grand Elder. "Let's get to business, shall we?" she said without pause.

"What type of business?" Sebastian asked.

"The type where I make an offer, and you either take it or leave and do your own thing without any assistance."

The stream of liquid silver orbiting Sebastian briefly sped up as he failed to conceal his rage at being so disrespected. Did they think they had the upper hand here? These country bumpkins were far too arrogant.

Diana tilted her head, her featureless wooden mask mocking him. "A guard of the elusive Silverspire family can't even control his emotions during civil negotiations? How sad. Even your young lord has better manners."

Sebastian's eye twitched, but he managed to maintain a cool expression. It was always important to control one's facial expressions during a negotiation, and he couldn't help but notice that the women from this mysterious group were way ahead of him in that regard, thanks to their masks.

"Excuse me, it was a long journey here." Sebastian offered a fake smile. "So what is this business proposition?"

"We plan to run an alchemy guild here. We have a nature-affinity cultivator that specializes in producing plants for alchemy, so we will have no need to go out and buy or harvest the materials ourselves."

Sebastian narrowed his eyes. A nature-affinity cultivator capable of growing such a wide range of spiritual plants could land a job fit for an emperor with the big alchemy guilds. Why would they be out here in this remote city, working with these people?

Diana continued, "With production sorted, we are now sourcing alchemists. Once this is done, we can begin producing groundbreaking products that will shake the market." She then raised her finger. "With this limited knowledge, if you agree to pledge all the wealth previously stated to Stella, we will give you ten percent of the profits."

"Only ten percent?" Sebastian frowned. Most alchemist startups failed spectacularly, as they could never compete with the bigger and more established guilds that already offered rock-bottom rates achievable through mass production and special deals with suppliers.

Diana then lowered a finger. "If you choose to learn more, I can give you a tour of our facilities and plans after the tournament, but the highest percentage I am willing to offer then is five percent."

Sebastian raised a brow; he had never heard of a negotiation tactic like this before. But to be fair, he was just a guard from a branch family. He had never been one to run the Silverspire businesses.

"And finally," Diana balled her hand into a fist, "if you still don't take the deal and approach us as we begin production and after seeing our groundbreaking products, the highest deal I can offer then is one percent."

"I want to work with Big Sister!" Ryker exclaimed from the side with childlike excitement. "It sounds so cool!"

Diana didn't even glance at Ryker; her faceless mask remained fixed on him. He could feel her piercing gaze through the mask and didn't like it one bit.

"I will give you a few days to decide," Diana said as she stood up and walked toward the doorway of the room, past Sebastian. "But don't keep me waiting too long, okay? Time is money."

Sebastian didn't even turn to see her leave, but he could feel a sudden surge of Qi and then a pop of air as the rift collapsed, swallowing the woman.

The Redclaw Grand Elder chuckled from his chair, seemingly enjoying the entire show. "Ruthless, aren't they? It helps when they have such a backer." He then leaned forward and whispered, "If I were you, I would invest my soul for just one percent so my family could live peacefully for the next few eons. If you had seen the miraculous things that I have over the past few months, you would agree…"

Sebastian ignored the man's words. It was clear they were working together, so the conman would obviously spout such nonsense to draw him into a deal. Ten percent wasn't bad per se, but jumping at the first offer of business for all their money could backfire terribly and squander his young lord's chance at the silver core inheritance.

He glanced to the side and saw Ryker, who seemed to be enjoying the whole experience. His childlike innocence on the matter made it harder to shoot down his dreams due to Sebastian's own world views.

Getting up, he gave a friendly smile to the Grand Elder. "I will discuss things with Ryker and give Diana a satisfying answer in a few days. Until then, we will retreat to our airship."

"You can stay here," the Grand Elder said resolutely. "I want that ugly ship gone. It's blocking the beautiful view of the scarlet forest."

Sebastian just let out a tired sigh. It wasn't worth arguing with these bumpkins anymore. "I thank the Grand Elder for his hospitality, then." He then turned to leave with Ryker, and a servant took them to their rooms.

The airship soon left without them on it and would return in a year's time. Ryker was busy running around the spacious room while a team of maids unpacked their possessions.

Meanwhile, Sebastian looked out the window at the vast scarlet forest and the distant peak surrounded by a haunted mist.

He needed to learn more about this place and that mysterious group that seemed to be ruling from the shadows.

"I guess a little look around wouldn't hurt," he mused, preparing to explore his new home. He refused to let Ryker be robbed due to his naivety and lose all the money his mother had provided him.

12
CHERRY BLOSSOM

The spatial rift snapped closed, and Ashlock watched Diana return from her meeting with a joyous smile as she removed the white wooden mask from her face and stored it away in her spatial ring.

He had naturally been listening in on the conversation between Diana and the Silverspires through his roots, so he left her and Stella to chat on the bench under his shade as he knew how the meeting had turned out. While awaiting the Silverspires' reply, he would keep pressing forward with his plans throughout the coming days.

As dusk descended upon the mountain peak, Ashlock felt his tree body slow down as the sun's warm embrace vanished. If anything, this reminded him even more of why he wanted that brat's spirit stones so he could request Stella or Douglas to create a heating array.

Concerning heating arrays, Ashlock had a few things to set into motion before falling asleep, as he wanted them done before the Silverspires started snooping around.

Stella had placed the Blaze Serpent Rose in a patch of dirt that had once been his mushroom garden that had been decimated by the Dao Storm. The solitary crimson rose, twisting upward like a serpent and cloaked in spikes, stood proudly in isolation.

Through his spiritual sight, Ashlock observed a slow transition of the Qi around the rose's petals to fire Qi. It seemed to be the perfect flower to rejuvenate the Redclaws' cultivation.

Casting {Eye of the Tree God}, his gaze ascended to the skies, surveying the forest of scarlet-leaved trees blanketing the mountain range. It was, without doubt, the most awe-inspiring sight he had encountered in his two lives. The feeling was amplified by the fact that he shared a connection with every tree via their roots and received a faint echo of their emotions.

Interestingly, those trees birthed from the recent Dao Storm seemed to possess infant egos, enabling communication with him. Yet they appeared to lack any affinity, just like the other demonic trees. Ashlock had presumed that the older trees he had nurtured would have developed spatial affinity cores or at least exhibited signs of doing so by now, but that had not occurred so far.

Could he possibly guide them toward a specific affinity by altering their environment?

Casting his vision to the forest at the base of the mountain range between him and Darklight City, he noted that there were still many typical green trees. The air was heavy with water Qi due to a mist originating from the Serene Mist Camellia, which were tiny pink flowers he had grown on his roots that coiled up their trunks and along their branches. It was adorable seeing his blood red–leaved children have small pink flowers growing on them.

"That area is already saturated with water Qi, so I doubt it's suitable for planting these Blaze Serpent Roses," Ashlock mused, continuing his survey. Though not a botanist, he understood plants thrived best in suitable environments. Unfortunately, there were no volcanoes nearby, but there were mountains that were kinda like volcanos—just without the magma and extreme heat.

The mountain had no green trees, only his demonic trees sustained by nutrients and Qi delivered by his roots. Otherwise, they had no business flourishing on the mountain. The thought of his offspring dying if he perished as they would be cut off from nutrients was grim, so he dismissed it and continued examining the scarlet tree-covered mountain beneath the White Stone Palace.

"Since this area is very Qi neutral with nothing but nature and air Qi, this should make a great place for the Blaze Serpent Roses," Ashlock concluded, so he brought up his B-grade {Blooming Root Flower Production} skill.

So far, he had only used the skill to grow the abundant Serene Mist Camellia, as the Blaze Serpent Rose had been unavailable in the menu, having never seen it before. Now, he could select the fire Qi–generating flower, and the system menu asked him where to plant them.

Ashlock had the ability to bloom a single flower at a root's tip or select a large area for automatic growth. A feature he deeply appreciated, given the vast ground to cover in a limited time. He could already feel his body preparing for slumber.

"This is going to cost a shit-ton of Qi." Ashlock cursed as he thought about how large of an area he wanted to select. The thought of draining the Qi he had amassed during his recovery for some flowers was far from thrilling, but this was something he had been putting off, and it needed to be done. The Redclaws deserved better than this.

With a single thought, he selected the vast, sprawling forest on the Redclaws' mountain. He could almost swear the system lagged for a second, struggling to process his request.

His Star Core, now thousands of times larger, blazed like a furnace as Qi gushed out of it in streams down his roots and through the mountain.

In his spiritual sight, he could see a literal tidal wave of Qi rush down the mountainside through the roots as all the trees along the way rustled and glowed with Qi.

Then something magical occurred. Since the sun had dipped below the horizon, the scarlet forest was bathed in darkness. This made the wave of crimson light cascading down the mountain all the more noticeable as Blaze Serpent Roses bloomed on the demonic tree trunks, each glowing like a firefly and producing a soft light that caused the scarlet leaves to shimmer.

Ashlock paused for a moment, captivated by the breathtaking spectacle, momentarily forgetting the massive Qi drain from his body that made it possible. His mind struggled to comprehend the scale of what he just did, as only gods should wield this type of power.

Stella and Diana had also risen from the bench, drawn by the sudden change in the ambient Qi. Diana parted the haunted mist that had obscured them from the outside world, and together like immortals lording over creation, they watched the spectacle unfold in silent awe.

A flurry of activity erupted from the White Stone Palace. The doors swung open, and the Grand Elder, along with the other Elders, rushed out. They watched, awestruck, as fire Qi swirled around and illuminated the mountain.

Once they regained their composure, they turned toward Red Vine

Peak, clasped their hands, and bowed deeply in gratitude. Ashlock couldn't deny the satisfaction he felt from their appreciation.

They needed each other. Ashlock could cultivate an ideal environment for his followers by manipulating local flora, using his Mystic Realm to train them and producing mushrooms with life-altering effects for cultivation pills.

In return, they could gather resources like spirit stones to construct formations that could enhance his cultivation speed, help him stay awake during winter and dark nights, and perhaps even create defensive formations to shield him from another Dao Storm.

Setting aside his sentimentality, Ashlock knew his time tonight was limited. With the sun set, his body was slowing down, preparing for sleep. He needed to act fast if he wanted to bless Darklight City with mushrooms and flowers overnight. He would also have provided fruit, but the system only permitted him to grow fruit from his branches.

Ashlock first summoned his {Magic Mushroom Production} skill and selected the entirety of Darklight City. "All right, I need to be careful here." He mentally frowned as he scrolled through the options. His mushroom-production ability was A-grade for a reason, as it let him add some seriously overpowered psychedelic effects.

He could, if feeling generous and suicidal, gift the city with spirit root–improving truffles, but he couldn't fathom a worse idea. His goal was a low-cost, aesthetically pleasing, and potentially edible mushroom.

He also had to be careful regarding the mushroom's smell because giving the mushrooms a sweet scent might sound nice in theory, but if the entire city smelled like an American candy store, then people would start feeling sick pretty quickly.

Finally, as exhaustion threatened to pull him into slumber, he chose the Oyster mushroom that resembled a stack of gray pancakes that grew on the side of trees and were known for being edible.

As for added effects? He made it so they glowed in the dark with a soft green glow. He also made them absorb the city stench, as even without a nose, he could tell Darklight City was a shithole. It didn't take a genius to understand that since all cities out here in the wilderness were ultimately temporary due to the beast tides, investing a lot of money and time into building a proper sewage system wasn't at the top of anyone's list.

In addition, he made the mushrooms fast growing but terribly bland tasting. He considered enhancing their flavor, but it would have added to the Qi cost for the production and maintenance of the mushrooms. He also didn't want the mushrooms to be over-harvested.

They also contained a minuscule amount of his Qi, which meant that anyone who consumed them could utilize them as a weak cultivation resource.

Satisfied with his creation, Ashlock allowed the mushrooms to proliferate in clusters on all the demonic trees in the city.

[Warning: Nearing Star Core Output Limit]

If the Qi demand for the Blaze Serpent Roses spread across the entire mountain range wasn't enough, transforming Darklight City into a mushroom haven seemed to push the limit.

Fortunately, his production skills required a high initial Qi investment, but subsequent maintenance was minimal, assuming the mushrooms weren't all consumed or the flowers all plucked.

"Just one more addition…" Ashlock thought lethargically, summoning the {Blooming Flower Production} menu. With his remaining Qi dwindling and sleep's call intensifying, he quickly selected a flower that held a special place in his previous life's heart: the cherry blossom, one of the most beautiful flowers in the world.

He deliberately chose a flower that didn't emit any ambient Qi or possess any special effects. It was a simple cherry blossom, but that was all he needed to transform Darklight City from a dreary, mining-focused metropolis into a lively and beautiful city.

With his vision darkening, he confirmed his selection, feeling another drain of Qi from his body toward the demonic trees in Darklight City.

"At last, I can sleep," Ashlock murmured, succumbing to slumber.

Sebastian's eyes shot open as he felt the morning sun's rays streaming through the window. He calmed his meditation technique, causing the swirling metal Qi around him to dissipate. A glance to the side revealed Ryker peacefully cultivating atop a small mound of iron ingots.

Using his spiritual sense, he could tell that the mound was almost depleted of Qi, rendering the Qi-dense ingots into mere mortal metal, which was of little use to them.

"Young lord," Sebastian called out softly, careful not to startle the boy from his deep meditation, which could have negative consequences.

Ryker's eyes sleepily opened, and he yawned. Then, after rubbing his eyes, he looked at Sebastian and smiled. "Morning, Sebastian!"

Sebastian's eyes narrowed. "Were you cultivating or sleeping?"

Ryker whistled nonchalantly, looking away.

"You fell asleep while cultivating, didn't you?" Sebastian chuckled and shook his head as he walked past the boy toward the grand room's door. "We should head to the city for breakfast. Would you like to join me, young lord?"

Still half asleep, Ryker rose and stumbled after Sebastian, which was adorable.

Sebastian reached to pat the boy on the head, but his hand was swatted away. "Sebastian, I'm a grown boy now! Stop treating me like a child."

Sebastian just blinked as he watched Ryker, who barely reached his waist, march down the hallway and past a legion of maids that bowed as he passed.

"They grow up so fast, huh?" Sebastian muttered. "Replace the metal piles in the room and prepare for a city visit," he instructed the maids as he quickly followed his young lord, a smile gracing his face at Ryker's nonsense. However, his smile faded into confusion as they moved further from their living quarters down winding hallways.

The White Stone Palace seemed nearly deserted, with only a few Redclaw family maids loitering around. He extended his spiritual sense to survey the entire palace, detecting a large gathering outside in the courtyard.

"I wonder what everyone's doing outside," Sebastian wondered, his voice echoing down the empty corridors.

"Maybe to meet Big Sister?" Ryker suggested with a smile, quickening his pace.

Sebastian doubted it, unable to sense any spatial rifts or the presence of those women. As they neared the reception area leading to the courtyard, the silence was eerie, yet he could sense an immense amount of Qi just beyond the door.

Before he could utter a warning, Ryker had already dashed ahead, pushing open the door that should have been too heavy for a five-year-old. His iron core realm cultivation, however, enabled him to perform feats beyond his years.

Sebastian caught up quickly, baffled to see all the Redclaws seated silently in the courtyard in lotus positions, absorbing the abnormal amount of fire Qi in the air. Was there a gathering formation nearby? He wanted to ask one of them, but there was nothing more discourteous than interrupting another cultivator's meditation, so he decided to keep Ryker close by and walk past them all to the palace gate.

"Wow..." Ryker whispered as he gawked at the spectacular sight. The demonic trees around them on the mountains radiated an orange glow, with fire Qi swirling around that hadn't been there last night.

Sebastian shared Ryker's astonishment. Having traveled the world during his three hundred years of life—one of the few benefits of the sect's constant relocation due to the beast tides—he had never witnessed such a magical sight.

As they descended the mountain and strolled through the forest, they reveled in the cooling mist swirling through the foliage. If only the acidic smell of the demonic trees could be eradicated, it would make for a relaxing place to contemplate life.

"What an odd place," Sebastian remarked as he saw mist-emitting flowers growing from thick black roots that coiled up the demonic trees. Most curious was how the regular green trees had nothing unusual about them.

Exiting the forest, they were welcomed by the vast wall of Darklight City adorned with scarlet trees. Most striking, however, were the thousands of pink petals carried by the breeze, dancing in the air before settling at their feet.

Getting past the gate by flashing his cultivation, he marveled at how the demonic trees within the city walls didn't seem to have any acidic smell or grow any poisonous berries. Instead, mushrooms were growing on their trunks.

He even spotted some children in rags, happily plucking the mushrooms from the trees and munching on them.

While few things brought a genuine smile to his face, Sebastian found himself in an unusually good mood in this city. However, Ryker's stomach rumbling quickly reminded him of their original purpose.

Despite Ryker's high cultivation, his young body still required sustenance for growth.

Walking a bit further down the street, he saw a man in a black robe crouching before a demonic tree obstructing the road. Dark-brown earth Qi swirled around his hands as he pressed them into the ground, forcing the tree upward.

Suddenly, Sebastian felt an overwhelming amount of spatial Qi flood the area. He watched in awe as the tree broke free from the ground, floating in the air above the street.

Many bystanders had halted their activities to watch this spectacle, and they all gasped in shock as the air shuddered, tearing open to form a rift. The uprooted tree then slowly drifted through the rift, and after the tree had vanished with a massive gust of air that rustled his robes, the rift snapped shut.

"Excuse me," Sebastian addressed the back of the black-cloaked earth cultivator. The large man turned around, and Sebastian was surprised to see that the man wore a black mask very similar to the one he had seen Stella wear.

Could this man also belong to that mysterious group?

"Yes?" The man's voice was gruff, distorted by the mask.

Sebastian smiled. "Fellow Daoist, I have a question for you…"

13
APEX OF THE VOID

Ashlock grumbled to himself, guiding yet another tree through a rift and situating it a thousand miles north. Here, he was constructing a colossal wall of demonic trees. This wall was to serve as an early warning system against incoming threats, such as another Dao Storm, beast tide, or perhaps wandering cultivators like the merchants.

Ever since the crack of dawn, Ashlock had tirelessly relocated trees across Darklight City. His quick thinking the previous night had eased the residents' anger toward the demonic trees. Their newfound beauty and the edible mushrooms they bore were a welcome surprise. Most of Darklight City's inhabitants were poor, so a sudden source of free food sprouting in their backyards or atop their houses was appreciated.

He had also commanded all the demonic trees through his roots to stop producing digestive fluids and poisonous berries.

Despite the residents' newfound acceptance of the trees, those obstructing the roads had to be removed. Transporting ore, food, and people from the mountains and farms through the city to the city's airship station was paramount to the citizens' livelihoods.

Over twenty hired earth Qi affinity cultivators, including Douglas, were hard at work uprooting trees, and he needed to attend to each one.

Every tree was precious to him, and he didn't want any of them to perish by being transported via mortal means, so he was happy to handle their transport himself.

The only unhappy aspect of the arrangement was his Star Core. In the morning, it had been as dim as when he'd nearly died, but by mid-morning, it had recovered just enough for him to utilize telekinesis and open rifts. He couldn't keep up this level of usage forever.

Ashlock was beginning to comprehend why cultivators chose to avoid conflict, seeking solitude in caves or quiet places for meditation. Not only was it to avoid interruptions like Stella once experienced, but also to accelerate their cultivation by not wasting Qi on pointless conflict.

To progress to the third stage of the Star Core Realm, Ashlock had to accumulate so much Qi that his Star Core literally couldn't contain anymore, forcing it to expand. He would never attain that level of Star Core capacity if he continued to deplete his Qi on flowers, mushrooms, and levitating trees through rifts.

"Maybe I should consider hibernating for a few years," Ashlock muttered to himself, meticulously situating the tree he'd moved through the portal a dozen meters from the last one in the tree wall. He was careful to space them adequately to avoid impeding their growth.

Despite the current tranquility, Senior Lee's words still resonated in his mind. He possessed something a Monarch-level threat desired. His only solace was that his formidable adversary, another tree thousands of miles south, remained unaware of him.

Yet cultivation was a process that couldn't be rushed. He didn't want to face a day when an irate world tree sent an army of mighty celestial cultivators after him, forcing him to hasten his cultivation to the Monarch Realm before he met his end.

After carefully positioning the demonic tree amongst its siblings, Ashlock's vision blurred as he covered a thousand miles in a second, reappearing on the street above Douglas.

"Do you work with someone called Stella or maybe Diana?"

Ashlock paused at the sound of a familiar voice from the previous night. Glancing down, he spotted Douglas being approached by Sebastian, who had Ryker in his company.

"And if I do?" Douglas retorted, prompting Ashlock to prepare for opening a rift next to Douglas, ready to pull him through with {Devour}. Revealing information to a potential enemy would undoubtedly breach his oath of loyalty.

"Well, hypothetically speaking, if you did know them, I was hoping to ask for your opinion about them. We're considering partnering with them for a business venture, but I have some reservations I'd like to address." Sebastian responded courteously, with Ryker nodding in agreement.

Douglas snorted behind his black mask. "Ask such questions, and you may find an eight-legged demon visiting you at night."

Sebastian frowned, clearly confused. Ashlock was also a bit baffled by Douglas's answer as he had half expected the oaf to spill the beans, but he had stayed surprisingly tight-lipped.

Douglas turned to leave and perform his duties, but Sebastian chuckled and asked an unusual question. "Fellow Daoist, forgive my earlier misguided question. I was hoping you could recommend us a good restaurant around here?"

"This is the industrial sector," Douglas replied. "Not much gourmet fare around here for someone like you. I suggest heading deeper into the city center where the wealthy mortals reside."

Sebastian shook his head. "We're exactly where we want to be. If we plan to conduct business here, we should familiarize ourselves with the locals, wouldn't you agree?"

Douglas shrugged and sauntered off, leaving behind a final, dismissive remark. "I'd rather eat dirt than anything around here."

Ashlock would have liked to observe the two Silverspires' actions further, but he needed to guide Douglas to the next tree for removal by floating a pebble in front of him.

From his vantage point high in the sky, through the {Eye of the Tree God}, Ashlock felt like he was playing a game of *Pac Man*, guiding Douglas through the winding streets toward each tree obstructing a road. This elevated perspective allowed him to manipulate multiple trees simultaneously with telekinesis and open rifts for them across the city.

If one ignored the ancient Chinese–style architecture and replaced the trees with starships, he would be convinced this was a scene out of a sci-fi movie as the floating trees cast looming shadows on the land below before blinking out of existence through rifts.

The whole operation was a bit too out in the open for his liking, but if he attempted to move each tree individually, it would take months. The number of trees to be relocated was simply too great, and he didn't want the townsfolk to take up their axes once more and harm his precious children, so he had to do them all at once.

Wielding this magnitude of power, something his previous body and smaller Star Core couldn't manage, Ashlock began to grasp the god aspect in his {Eye of the Tree God} skill. It felt as though he was a deity managing some city-builder game, yet each decision he made had very tangible consequences on his continued existence.

One such repercussion was already making itself known as his gaze drifted over Darklight City Academy. Ashlock tuned in to a troubling conversation.

An elderly man with pitch-black eyes and hair as if woven from the void itself stood outside the Academy's library, scrutinizing a demonic tree.

"We must alert the Nightrose family," the man murmured to his nearby assistant, who bore similar void-like characteristics.

Startled, the assistant nearly dropped the equipment in her hand being used to measure some aspect of the tree that Ashlock couldn't discern. "Elder Voidmind, is that truly necessary? It's merely a tree infestation. We shouldn't trouble them with such minor issues—"

She was cut off and shrunk back as the man shouted at her, *"What about this is trivial? Thousands of spirit trees appeared a week ago, bringing the city industry to a halt. That alone I could ignore, but their biology has altered overnight! That's unnatural. There has to be a force controlling these trees, causing them to mutate identically and simultaneously!"*

He plucked a mushroom from the tree, waving it in front of his assistant. *"When have you ever seen a demonic tree sprout mushrooms? And just last night, there was an acidic scent from the tree, now completely absent!"*

"That is...odd," the woman conceded with a weary sigh.

"It's not just odd," the man retorted. *"What if these mushrooms release toxic spores? Or if all the trees detonate simultaneously? I turned a blind eye before because demonic trees are well-documented; although bothersome in the short term, they can be felled and removed. But if their biology can adapt overnight, they pose a significant threat."*

"They are being dealt with, aren't they?" the woman countered, pointing to the sky as Ashlock moved a demonic tree through a portal a few streets away.

The Elder tracked the tree's movement through the portal, furrowing his brow before rubbing his eyes. "How is it floating like that?"

"Artifacts, I assumed," the woman responded, returning her attention to her apparatus.

"I don't see any artifacts on the tree, just an abundance of spatial Qi." The man's eyes widened. *"There shouldn't be a spatial-affinity cultivator with enough Qi to lift trees and transport them through rifts in the entire Blood Lotus Sect! What is happening?"*

Ignoring his assistant's response, the Elder sprinted across the manicured garden. Ashlock watched, surprised, as the old man effortlessly vaulted three stories high to land on a nearby rooftop.

"So he's a powerful cultivator and apparently an Elder of the Voidmind family; he's undoubtedly a threat," Ashlock muttered, tracing the Elder's path as he hopped across the rooftops, clearly making a beeline for the floating tree and the recently opened rift leading to the wilderness.

"Damn, I see his aim now." Ashlock attempted to hasten the tree through the rift, but the Elder was relentless. His skin became enveloped in black flames that resembled a liquid void, and with a single stride, the air rippled, and he re-emerged from a dark opening atop the trunk.

"He's definitely reached the Star Core Realm." Ashlock cursed. The Elder was evidently formidable, his aura causing Ashlock's rift to quiver as he passed through.

Ashlock was surprised it took this long for a powerful cultivator in the city to get suspicious, with three entire families being killed, his ascension to the Star Core Realm practically broadcasting his existence, and the heavens opening up multiple times. Had this man been so engrossed in his library books that he had overlooked the turmoil outside?

Whatever the reason, Ashlock was now in trouble. The man was standing upon the tree that had successfully made it through the rift and was now a thousand miles away in the wilderness.

"This is certainly not natural," the Voidmind Elder murmured, surveying the extensive line of demonic trees forming a wall. *"The deeper I look, the more alarming the anomalies appear. Why didn't anyone bring this to my attention sooner?"*

The Elder stroked his sorry excuse for a beard while contemplating for a moment. Ashlock wasn't sure what to do. If the man truly tried to contact the Nightrose family, he would have no choice but to intervene with lethal force.

"Please, don't…" Ashlock whispered, but to his dismay, the Elder's spatial ring pulsed with energy, and a communication jade materialized in his open palm.

"Fool, you should have just stayed inside with your books," Ashlock yelled, his trunk splintering open, exposing his {Demonic Eye} to the outside world for the first time since his rebirth. A rift materialized, and Ashlock glared at the Voidmind Elder through the flickering portal.

Ashlock recognized the Voidmind Elder was likely stronger than him, so he opened with his most powerful attack. However, to his surprise, the Voidmind Elder met his gaze with indifference.

And through the demonic eyes gaze, Ashlock confirmed a distressing fact by staring into the man's blackened soul. The Voidmind Grand Elder was at the apex of the Star Core Realm.

The rift trembled, and Ashlock panicked as the Voidmind Elder, enshrouded in wrathful void flames, materialized just a meter away from him. His vacant eyes instilled a deep terror in Ashlock.

"So you're the perpetrator?" The Voidmind Elder scrutinized him, dismissively ignoring his {Demonic Eye} as if it was nonexistent.

Reacting instinctively, Ashlock cast {Devour}. Black vines erupted from the ground, coiling around the Voidmind Elder, but his liquid void flames effortlessly annihilated them on contact. Ashlock's Star Core flared, channeling spatial Qi down the black vines in a futile effort to shield them from the Elder's flames.

Watching his lilac flame–coated vines dismissed with such ease made Ashlock panic as he lacked many other offensive options.

"Stay back!" Ashlock cried, expending every ounce of spatial Qi he possessed in an assault on the Voidmind Elder. Portals blinked open and closed, Qi-infused leaves were ripped off and hurtled toward the man, and the black vines radiated with lilac fire. Yet everything was reduced to ashes by the void flames.

"Interesting," the Voidmind Elder murmured as he extended a void-crafted claw shrouding his hand. *"It's been over a millennium since I've encountered something from beyond this realm."*

His hand effortlessly bypassed Ashlock's spatial Qi defenses, shattering them as it penetrated deeper into the open fissure in his trunk. In that moment, as the Elder's void-coated fingers reached to touch his eldritch eye, Ashlock realized he had fucked up.

He knew portals were a two-way street, but his recent arrogance had clouded his judgment. Playing god for the past few days had allowed his pride to grow, blinding him to his vulnerabilities.

He was a nurturer and provider, as all trees were. Not a conqueror or destroyer. That was why his role was to raise his subordinates and pets to accomplish this.

Yet where were his guardians in his time of need?

His eldritch eye swiveled slightly to glance past the Voidmind Elder reaching into his trunk, and he caught sight of Stella and Diana, who had been silently cultivating. Everything had transpired so swiftly, but his exploding portals seemed to have roused them from their meditation.

The expression on Stella's face was devastating. A mixture of disbelief and sheer terror washed over her as she darted glances between him and the intruder, frozen like a deer in headlights and also by the Elder's wrathful gravity.

"H-head librarian?" Stella muttered under her breath.

The Voidmind Elder either didn't notice the girls or deemed them too insignificant to even harm a single wispy hair on his balding head as he gave a mysterious smile. "This eye will make a fine addition to my collection."

Why had he sent Larry away? Why had he asked for a Qi-gathering formation rather than a defensive one? Where the hell was Maple, and why had he been such a fool?

The void-coated fingers grasped his eye and attempted to pull it out but couldn't. Ashlock then realized that the void flames didn't seem to harm him. Shouldn't he be burning alive right now?

[As a Demi Divine tree destined to grow throughout the nine realms, you are completely immune to the void.]

That was a relief, but the sensation of an ancient man stroking his eye made him want to recoil and scream, so instinctively, he snapped his eyelid shut.

"Why won't it come out—" The Voidmind Elder blinked as the slit in the tree slammed closed, taking his arm with it.

A brief silence ensued as the Elder gazed at the spot where his arm should have been, then back at the now-closed trunk. He then smiled eerily and began to laugh maniacally.

From his shoulder, void Qi began to spew forth, taking the form of a depthless, shadowy arm. It writhed and convulsed as though struggling against the man's control.

Ashlock just stared at it in horror through his spiritual sight. What was he supposed to do now?

14
ABYSSAL GAZE

Realizing his immunity to void-based attacks, Ashlock found some comfort in knowing he wouldn't be reduced to splinters by the Voidmind Elder's newly formed arm of pure void. But his mind was troubled by concerns for the girl's safety.

He wasn't certain if Larry could even stand against a peak Star Core cultivator, yet he had to try. "Larry, return immediately!" he called through the tether. A confirmation pulsed through their connection, but dread still choked him. Would Larry make it back in time?

The Voidmind Elder stopped cackling with manic laughter as he seemed to notice Stella and Diana, who were frozen off to the side, their legs trembling under this Star Core Realm gravity. Even Ashlock felt his branches creaking from the pressure, but he was naturally more resistant as a tree also in the Star Core Realm compared to the girls who were fleshy beings in a lower realm.

The Voidmind Elder's hollow gaze lingered on the girls, a spark of recognition flickering across his weathered visage. "Ah! Stella Crestfallen, is that truly you?"

"Head Librarian," Stella wheezed as the gravity tightened around her. "Please...spare the tree."

A sinister smile spread across the Elder's face. *"Ever since you sought my aid in deciphering those ancient runes, I've wondered who this Ashlock might be. I delved into the archives, spent countless hours in fruitless research, and eventually resigned myself to not knowing."*

His gaze turned back to Ashlock, scrutinizing. "So this spirit tree is Ashlock, yes? It hardly seems ancient or powerful enough to be from the old era." His voice, eerily detached and calm, heightened Ashlock's unease. What was this man plotting?

Under the crushing gravity, Diana was the first to succumb, her knees buckling beneath her. Stella quickly followed suit. "Please, Head Librarian!" Stella cried, tears welling in her eyes as she pleaded with the ground beneath her. "Spare the tree! There must be a way to restore your arm…"

The Voidmind Elder slowly walked over. Every step he took had the weight of a deity behind it as the formation Stella had carefully created just days ago shattered below his feet. *"You dared to hoard such a treasure? Do you have any idea how long I've been stuck at the threshold of the Nascent Soul Realm? Centuries! I even lost my position as the Grand Elder of the Voidmind family when my brother surpassed my cultivation by achieving a half step."*

He knelt down, gripped Stella's chin with his gnarled hand, and forced her to meet his abyssal gaze. *"Look at me, child. Do I strike you as someone with the patience to wait for another opportunity? It doesn't matter who discovered or nurtured this spirit tree all this time."* His grin was predatory, his words chilling. *"Even if it takes another century, I will extract that divine eye from the tree and savor its essence. There's nothing you can do about it—"*

In response, Stella sent a golden bolt of lightning through her chin into the Elder's hand, causing him to stumble back, his arm spasming. "Only I may touch Tree!" she yelled.

Diana gave Stella a peculiar look, to which Stella retorted, "Obviously not like that."

"What did you mean then…" Diana began, but her words were cut off by the Elder's furious outcry.

"Despicable girl! You dare to ambush this old man after I've assisted you!"

Ashlock had no idea what Stella had insinuated and was even more confused about the man's words. Were all high-rank cultivators so arrogant and delusional? The man did say he was ancient, and his elderly appearance, despite being in such a high realm, suggested he was telling the truth.

"So his aim is to consume my eye to attain the Nascent Soul Realm?" Ashlock's bark shuddered at the thought, and he frantically considered ways to assist Stella. Alas, the Elder's strength far outmatched either of the girls', rendering them virtually helpless. His own Qi reserves were critically depleted, and he had already failed to make a dent in the Elder's defenses.

His system was equally worthless in this situation. With only a meager amount of credits saved and an inventory devoid of high-grade items, Ashlock was at a loss. "If I could somehow trick him into drinking my cursed sap and transform him into a tree...or if I could just delay him long enough for Larry to arrive, we might have a chance."

Creating a portal to whisk the girls to safety had also crossed his mind, but the Elder had already demonstrated his uncanny ability to traverse portals near-instantaneously. Furthermore, Ashlock's strength was at its peak when the Elder was within proximity of his trunk.

"Head Librarian, don't be rash," Stella said carefully. "I have truffles that can improve your spirit root or help you comprehend heaven and overcome your bottleneck!"

The Elder scoffed, dismissing her offer as if it was the most absurd thing he'd ever heard. "At least propose something plausible. For centuries, every waking moment of my existence has been dedicated to surmounting my bottleneck." His voice escalated. "I've aligned myself with merchant groups, delved into rifts in search of opportunities, mastered alchemy in attempts to concoct medicinal pills, and meditated for decades uninterrupted!"

His eyes narrowed. "And now, obstructing my path to the solution I've been seeking, stands a girl destined to become nothing more than a pill furnace. If you truly possessed such an exceptional cultivation treasure, you would have already consumed it to save yourself from such a miserable fate."

"What if I've already eaten one of these truffles?"

"Do you take me for an imbecile?" the Elder roared. "Do you believe that rare cultivation resources simply sprout from trees?"

Stella, still pinned to the ground by the Elder's formidable gravitational force, grunted as she struggled to raise her head. "Please! I'm not attempting to deceive you. What do you stand to lose by allowing us to prove the existence of these truffles? The tree isn't going anywhere, and we pose no threat to you."

The Elder glanced at his void arm, seemingly struggling to maintain control. "Delaying tactics are futile. My only interest lies in the divine *eye nestled within the tree. Compared to its potential, your hypothetical truffles are a trifling waste of my time."*

"But—" Stella shouted at the ground. The Voidmind Elder just kept walking closer.

"Even if they existed, you attacked me." The Elder grinned. *"Such an act warrants a punishment far graver than death."*

A wave of intense, murderous intent engulfed the entire mountaintop, prompting Stella and Diana to try summoning swords from their spatial rings as the Elder got too close, but the tips of their blades were forced against the floor by the pressure.

This was the insurmountable difference between realms that was almost impossible to overcome. What level of power would the man wield if he got through his bottleneck and made it into the Nascent Soul Realm? Ashlock didn't even want to imagine.

"Don't kill her!" Diana shouted. *"What about the wrath from the Patriarch? Her body is…reserved for him."* She winced at her words as if in disbelief they even came out of her mouth.

"That old buffoon?" The Elder sneered, spitting to the side. *"Once I attain the Nascent Soul Realm, what is there to fear? Moreover…"* His gaze refocused on Stella. *"You would make an excellent vessel for my nascent soul."*

Events unfolded in a swift blur. The Elder's pure void arm morphed into a sword of utter darkness. Poised over Stella's head, he readied to execute her.

Ashlock's near-depleted Star Core roared to life with its dying breath—over ten portals materialized between the Elder and Stella, but the sword cleaved through them easily. Ashlock also sent more black vines coated in spikes with {Devour} at the man, but the void flames enshrouding the man deleted them out of existence before they could even leave a tear in his cloak.

A cataclysmic eruption of spatial Qi ensued as all ten portals were annihilated, followed by a piercing scream. Then a dreadful stillness enveloped Ashlock. He knew his defensive efforts had been futile in shielding Stella, who had been unable to lift her head to see the blade destined to end her life.

"Oh?" The Elder's confused voice gave Ashlock a hint of hope, and as the flash of spatial Qi faded away, it revealed a defiant paw holding the void blade a few centimeters from Stella's blond hair.

Maple, perched on Stella's head, stood tall with his white fur shimmering radiantly under the noon sun. His mythical golden eyes met the gaze of the Grand Elder. He then twisted his paw and ripped the void blade in two, compelling the Voidmind Elder to retreat and regain control over the leaking void from his arm.

Stella reached up as the immense pressure lessened. "Maple!" she happily shouted as the squirrel accepted head pats.

A wave of relief washed over Ashlock as one of his most powerful allies finally appeared, but he knew he wasn't out of the woods just yet. The Elder had suffered some damage from Maple's attack, but through his pact link with Maple, he could tell that blocking the attack had taken a lot out of the squirrel despite his defiant stance.

"A void creature?" the Elder asked through clenched teeth. *"Are you the guardian of this tree? Is that how it has remained unclaimed for so long?"*

The man reached up and stroked his wispy beard while scrutinizing the squirrel. *"Ah, that explains the fate of the previous families. I assumed internal strife, but they must have discovered the tree and quarreled over it, right?"*

The Elder wasn't far from the truth. Ashlock wondered how he would react when he saw Larry—but the spider was still outside his portal range, and Ashlock doubted whether Maple could hold off the Elder on his own for much longer.

Unexpectedly, a pure silver blade materialized in the Elder's hand. It seemed to sear his flesh, causing him to wince as the void flames coated his hand receded. "A blade wrought from divine metal," the Elder elucidated, wearing a smug smile. Through his pact with Maple, Ashlock felt a wave of fear. Clearly, this sword posed a significant threat.

With a void step, the Elder virtually teleported across the peak via fractured space and slashed with the divine sword at Stella and Maple, the air shuddered as a shield of void from Maple's paws appeared, but the blade cleaved through it easily. Maple redirected the sword's trajectory with his claws, spraying silver sparks and leaving deep gashes in the side of the blade.

With the swing completed, the Elder retreated, a deep frown etching his features. "Stronger than anticipated," he muttered before launching another assault. This time, Maple's timing was off—though the blade was still deflected, it took a thin layer of Maple's fur and flesh in the process.

Maple nursed his injured paw as black blood trickled down and dripped onto Stella's forehead. She tried to raise her head to look up at Maple, but the pressure from the Elder's gravity had increased once more.

"Maple! Are you okay?" Panic crept into Stella's voice as she noticed the blood pooling on the stone beneath her.

Meanwhile, despite being pinned to the stone by the pressure, Diana had managed to cast her mist technique, slightly dulling the Elder's senses and providing Maple with some assistance.

Ashlock also kept casting {Devour}, but the vines were getting thinner and coated in less spatial Qi as he tried to save up enough Qi to cast a long-range portal to bring Larry here.

The spider was far out in the wilderness and would soon reach the wall of trees he had started building, which served as the current limit to his range out into the wilderness.

Maple and the Elder clashed repeatedly, but it was clear that the Elder had a slight upper hand as Maple sustained more and more injuries. Ashlock surmised that if Maple didn't have to shield Stella, he could unleash a full-power attack as he had against the Dao Storm. But the risk of injuring Stella or leaving her vulnerable to the Elder's attack rendered him to a defensive stance, doing his best to repel the onslaught.

After a while, Ashlock felt a pull on his tether with Larry. His vision shifted from the mountain peak to a distressed Larry stationed near a wall of demonic trees, with Kaida clinging to his back. "Master, I am here!" Larry's gruff voice echoed.

Using the last drops of spatial Qi in his Star Core, a portal that wobbled at the edges as if unstable manifested, and Larry crawled through without hesitation.

The Elder's eyes bulged as he saw the looming shadow of Larry through Diana's haunted mist behind Stella. Eight glowing red eyes glared at him as Larry leaped through the mist and landed between the Elder and Stella.

Larry shot forth an ash-coated limb with lightning speed, nothing more than a blur. The Elder hastily raised his heavily damaged divine sword to parry the strike, only to have the blade shatter under the sheer force of the blow, sending him sprawling to the side.

Staring at the broken silver hilt in his hand, the Elder cast it aside with a frustrated huff. "Another guardian beast." His voice trembled with rage as he inhaled deeply. "What rotten luck to have salvation so close yet remain just out of my grasp."

His entire body flared up with Qi, and he muttered, "Reality Rend." Reality ripped apart as if the man had peeled back the wallpaper of the world and stepped through the tear. Beyond lay nothing but darkness. Time seemed to distort, his figure elongating infinitely as if teetering on the edge of a black hole. The spectacle was baffling, but one thing was clear: this wasn't an offensive maneuver; it was an escape attempt.

If he succeeded, he could inform the Patriarch, gather his allies, and perhaps even the Grand Elder of his family that was supposedly stronger than him.

"As you so rightly stated, Stella Crestfallen," the Elder's distorted voice echoed across the mountain peak, "the tree cannot run!"

"Neither can you." A voice Ashlock had never heard before made his soul shudder. The day turned to a starless night as if the heavens had turned the lights off. In the distance, he could see the Voidmind Elder swimming through the liquid darkness surrounding them.

Ashlock found the strange voice's source, expecting to see Stella and Maple. However, only Stella was visible—Maple had vanished.

An enormous, pupil-less eye that Ashlock recognized from his unsuccessful S-rank summon from years past loomed over the mountain peak like a small sun. It tracked the fleeing Elder, who glanced over his shoulder, his vacant eyes widening in terror. "A Worldwalker?"

The eye offered no response to the Elder's question. The world quaked and fractured as if subjected to an immense external force compressing the void. The Elder attempted to resist, but he was overpowered. Moments later, the eye vanished, replaced by the warm sunlight as Ashlock found himself back in the real world.

Hovering in the midst of the mountain peak was the Elder, trapped in a bubble of nothingness, struggling against the crushing force yet managing to resist complete obliteration.

Maple had returned to his perch atop Stella's head, his golden eyes full of curiosity as they met Ashlock's. The voice from earlier resounded within Ashlock's mind. "I can't hold him for much longer. Open your eye. Your trunk will serve as his prison."

"You can speak?" Ashlock was taken aback. Maple had never

communicated with him before. And the eerie eye in the sky... Had that S-rank summoning attempt from years ago not failed after all? Could Maple be the Worldwalker?

Maple bared his teeth. "Do it now."

With no other choice as he saw the bubble begin to crack, Ashlock reluctantly opened his {Demonic Eye}, and the bubble containing the Elder floated through the gap and settled next to his eye.

Then after he closed his trunk, the bubble burst, and a very enraged Elder was unleashed within his body.

What the fuck kind of solution was this?

15
A MORAL DILEMMA

Elder Voidmind felt his peak stage Star Core burning in his chest as he desperately resisted the compressive force enveloping him. It was as though he was imprisoned within a collapsing pocket dimension, and the only thing preventing it from imploding into a singularity and obliterating him was the outward pressure exerted by his own Star Core.

His sight and senses were completely eclipsed; his Qi was powerless against the crushing force, leaving him isolated in a void that felt so unfamiliar.

But then, all of a sudden, the collapsing realm shattered, and the Elder let out a gasp as he was enshrouded by spatial Qi. Although it wasn't as dense as his own Qi, enabling him to push back in spite of his drained Star Core, it was still almost suffocating.

After shouting some obscenities at his situation before quickly entering a meditative state honed over centuries, reaching out to the ever-present whispers of the void. To his relief, he detected faint traces of void Qi emanating from below and rapidly absorbed them.

Ashlock gazed down with his {Demonic Eye} at the Voidmind Elder inside him. The sensation was deeply unsettling, given that his entire body had transformed into his soul. Consequently, the Elder was essentially cultivating within his soul.

"Thank the heavens this bastard isn't a spatial-affinity cultivator. Otherwise, he would cultivate me to death." Ashlock shuddered at the thought. But what was he supposed to do now?

Fortunately, the Elder seemed engrossed in cultivation, allowing Ashlock to switch his focus to the chaotic scene outside his trunk. Stella was frantically circling him while anxiously questioning Maple, the mystical squirrel of dubious origins resting atop her head. "What did you do, Maple? What if the Elder has an axe and carves his way out?"

Maple, wounded and exhausted, merely snorted in response. This seemed to be his usual state after performing a major technique, leading Ashlock to speculate suspiciously about the squirrel's true power level. It was as if he was a super-powerful being trapped in a weak body that couldn't handle much of his true power... Ashlock felt like squinting suspiciously at the squirrel.

Now that he thought about it, there had been too many occasions where Maple's true strength had come into question, the last big one being the attack he had unleashed on the Dao Storm.

Even after what he had seen mere moments ago, Ashlock still found it hard to believe Maple could be that Worldwalker he had tried to summon years ago, as the system had claimed the summon failed. But the giant eldritch monster had shifted out of view at the last second, and then Maple appeared asking for a pact... There was no way they were the same monster, right?

"Maple, are you a Worldwalker?" Ashlock queried through their mental link. The squirrel merely glanced at him before closing his eye, falling back into slumber. "I know you can speak now. Stop pretending!"

Alas, the squirrel remained as elusive as ever.

Meanwhile, Diana cast a worried glance at Ashlock's trunk. Eventually, she voiced her concern. *"Even if Ashlock is capable of confining the Voidmind Elder, how do we justify the head librarian's sudden disappearance from the Academy to the city?"*

Stella halted, furrowing her brow. *"Why would we need to explain anything? How could they possibly suspect us?"*

Diana gestured toward Ashlock. *"Even I can detect the void Qi radiating from within the tree. The spatial Qi does partially obscure it, but those attuned to the void can sense it from a great distance."*

"Hmm..." Stella mused, her gaze drifting to the damaged runic formation beneath her. "Could we construct a Qi containment array?"

Diana glanced around. *"I suspect you would have to completely redesign and replace the Qi-gathering formation we are currently using, and even if we had the spirit stones on hand to do such a thing, would Ashlock appreciate it? His cultivation will completely stall, and he will be unable to replace the Qi he has been using over the last few days."*

That was terrible news, as who knew how long the Voidmind family would continue to snoop around looking for their Elder?

Furthermore, Ashlock's Soul Core was nearly completely depleted. Just a thin layer of spatial Qi left on the inside of his trunk maintained his normal operations. If that was the volume of Qi he was stuck with until the Voidmind family gave up their search, he would be in big trouble.

"Also, there is a lot of void Qi floating around here after the fight." Diana added, *"If we were to build a containment array, then that void Qi would never leave, and if the Voidmind family ever came here, they would catch on straight away."*

Prompted by this, Ashlock felt compelled to inquire, 'How formidable is the Voidmind family?'

Stella relayed the query, and Diana responded, considering Stella's lack of insight into Blood Lotus Sect politics. *"They rank among the top three in the sect in terms of high cultivation individuals, albeit they remain a minor family overall."* Diana then gazed at the horizon beyond Darklight City. *"They govern the City of Slymere and maintain strong ties with the merchants."*

So incredibly dangerous, then. The Voidmind Elder inside his trunk was already in the ninth stage of the Star Core Realm, and his brother was supposedly a half step into the Nascent Soul Realm.

Ashlock's gaze fell upon Maple, the slumbering squirrel perched atop Stella's head. Without question, the squirrel was the most powerful among them. However, could he withstand two individuals of the Elder's caliber if they arrived? Unfortunately, Maple's lack of transparency about his true power made it hard to plan a defense around him.

Stella added, *"The Voidmind family also intends to attend the alchemy tournament."*

This reminded Ashlock of another Voidmind individual he had encountered in Darklight City: the assistant who had been studying the demonic tree and had witnessed the Elder's hasty departure through the portal. "Shit," Ashlock cursed. "Shit, shit, shit. What should I do? She's the only loose end that could connect the Elder's disappearance to the demonic trees."

The fact Darklight City was so overrun with demonic trees and how they floated through portals was suspicious enough and already drew far too much attention. However, someone knowing with certainty that these trees were linked to Elder Voidmind's disappearance was a problem.

Ashlock hastily wrote, 'A woman from the Voidmind family witnessed the Elder enter one of my rifts at the Academy. What should we do?'

As usual, Stella read it out loud. And while Diana mulled over his question, Stella answered, "We should kill her, obviously."

"Huh?" Diana seemed taken aback. "*Why is that the obvious solution?*"

Stella tilted her head as if looking at a fool. "Because...anything that threatens Tree should be eliminated?"

"*So you would exterminate an entire sect to ensure Tree's safety? You must realize that virtually everyone would attempt to control him if given the chance.*"

Stella nodded with a smile. "*I don't care. I would kill anyone that may harm him.*"

Although Ashlock appreciated the kindness behind Stella's intentions, he wasn't certain that was a good way to go about things. He had no problems with killing anyone standing in front of him, waving a sword around, and threatening him, but preemptively dispatching assassins based on mere speculation seemed extreme and likely to complicate matters.

But then there was the flip side of how brutal this world was and how important it was for him to protect those around him. Unable to decide, he left Stella and Diana to argue it out.

"Well, I disagree." Diana crossed her arms. "*I was born into a lineage of assassins. So if Ashlock ordered me to go and kill someone, I would without question. But since he asked for our opinion here, I think killing this woman is a mistake.*"

"But...you killed that Venik person just because they knew of Douglas and his sudden increase in wealth?" Stella retorted. "*Aren't you being a hypocrite right now?*"

Diana exhaled a weary sigh. "*That's part of why I'm even suggesting this. Do you know how hard it was to stare that young girl who believed* she had a chance at living a normal life in the future in the eyes and brutally snap her neck? If I hadn't been overly paranoid and hunted that man down, I never would have had to experience that."

"How was that paranoid? Venik was a threat," Stella said.

"All Venik knew was that Douglas had gotten a lot of wealth from somewhere. He was a weak wind-affinity cultivator who'd escaped his family and ran a brothel. What threat did he pose? How could he even locate Douglas and steal his wealth? The absolute worst case would be if the man somehow got a bigger force involved, but who would listen to the words of a lowly man running a brothel?"

Seeing Stella bite her bottom lip, Diana continued, "Let me give you another example that might help you understand my point. My father wanted to kill you. I was even ordered by him to come here and kill you. If Ashlock had been in the equation back then, you would have sent Larry or Maple to eliminate me, right?"

Seeing Stella frown, Diana offered a weary smile. "Although, on the outside, I agreed to my father's request and even came over here…I never actually intended to kill you." She sighed. "What I am trying to say is that blindly killing anyone who shows the slightest threat is a slippery slope to go down… Where do you draw the line?"

Diana glanced at Ashlock. "If Ashlock gained mind-reading powers, should he exterminate anyone with a single negative thought about him? What about when I lost control over my actions due to my heart demons? If I had been Douglas or one of the Redclaws and tried to chop down Ashlock while in that state with an axe, should I have been killed?"

Ashlock listened to Diana's lecture, and he had to agree. Given the emotional numbness induced by his new biology, it was crucial to establish boundaries to prevent becoming a murderous tyrant. Legitimate threats warranted elimination, but an innocent bystander? Perhaps not…

"But she witnessed the Elder enter the rift!" Stella objected. "If this woman associates the rift with Ashlock upon seeing one of us emerge from a rift in the city and communicates this to her family, we could all die!"

Diana nodded. "That is indeed a possible outcome, and I agree. If she tried contacting her family, we should imprison or kill her."

Stella seemed at a loss. "So…why not just kill her from the start rather than risk—"

Diana raised a hand, silencing Stella. "How do you know she was the *sole witness to the Elder's escape through the portal? I presume this occurred near the Academy, given that the old man rarely strays from the library, right?"*

Ashlock flashed a leaf in agreement. He could already see where she was going with this.

"There are hundreds of cultivators from various families residing at the Academy. Even though most students in Darklight City are discarded heirs or low-talent members of branch families, they possess eyes and may have witnessed the Elder's hasty entrance into the rift. If the Voidmind family were to question any of these people, they could get the same information that woman supposedly has."

Stella frowned deeply, her mind likely racing with thoughts.

"People gossip, and news spreads. No matter our efforts, rumors about the strange events occurring here will inevitably reach the other families," Diana continued. *"What would truly arouse suspicion, however, is if members of the Voidmind family suddenly fell prey to assassinations. Not to mention the risk of an assassination attempt failing, potentially providing them with even more information about us."*

"I just don't like it," Stella grumbled. *"It doesn't sit right with me to leave someone like that alive. If she is the reason Tree perishes, I will haunt you as a ghost."*

Diana chuckled. *"All right, how about this? We keep an eye on this woman, and if she connects the dots, we take swift action. Does that sound reasonable?"*

Both perspectives were valid. Stella's approach may lean toward paranoia and extremity, but Diana's solution bore its own risks. The Voidmind family specialized in void Qi, notorious for eradicating things from existence, making the woman's imprisonment challenging. And there was no way he planned to cram all the Voidmind family members inside his trunk.

Another issue loomed: who would be tasked with surveilling the assistant? He certainly didn't want to spend his day observing her, and his {Eye of the Tree God} couldn't penetrate the Academy walls.

"Larry," Ashlock spoke through the tether to his pet.

"Yes, Master?" Larry replied gruffly.

"Can you control those tiny ash spiders that spew from your mouth from a considerable distance?"

Diana and Stella turned curiously toward the colossal spider engaged in a one-sided conversation with Ashlock.

Larry thought momentarily before replying, *"Some distance, perhaps up to Darklight City at most?"*

"I see..." Ashlock mused. "Could you employ them to spy on someone?"

Larry shook his enormous head. "They lack intelligence."

"Despite their connection to you?"

"I can summon them from other realms for assistance, but they remain infantile ash spiders," Larry replied. *"Their knowledge extends only to killing. I sincerely apologize for my species' intellectual shortcomings."*

"What are they discussing?" Diana whispered to Stella.

Stella grumbled, *"It seems Tree agrees with your suggestion to monitor the woman."*

"That's a relief." Diana smiled. "You should try to curb your paranoid bloodlust a little, Stella." Water began to surround Diana's hand, and she reached up to her head.

"H-hey, what are you doing?"

"You have some Maple blood in your hair." Diana grabbed a few strands of Stella's long, flowing blond hair stuck together with black blood.

Stella looked up as Diana calmly cleansed the blood with water conjured from the humid air, an action that seemed to dissipate Stella's anxiety.

"I'll handle this situation, all right? You said you trusted me. Were those just empty words?" Diana said with a whisper.

Stella huffed, blowing the hair strands out of her face. "Fine."

With Stella's permission, Diana lowered her hands and stepped before Ashlock. "Patriarch, may I handle this?"

After deep consideration, Ashlock assessed the situation as a relatively low risk that would take some time to escalate. The Elder had gone through the portal merely half an hour ago. It would take the assistant several hours, if not days, to begin to worry, and he faced larger, more immediate concerns—like the Elder within his trunk who had just opened his eyes.

Flashing his leaf to show his agreement, he switched his view to his

{Demonic Eye} and glared down at the Elder, who was looking straight up at him while engulfed in void flames.

Time passed, and the Elder finally opened his eyes with a sigh of relief. His Star Core's capacity was above its critical minimum, allowing it to generate enough void Qi passively to resist the spatial Qi of his new environment.

For now, he was safe. Yet a deep frown mirrored his chaotic thoughts. How had he survived an attack from a Worldwalker? They were demi-god beings that wandered the void and stopped void cultivators from freely traversing between the nine realms.

"Could it be realm suppression?" the Elder mused aloud. He had encountered references to it in the archives, explaining why those from higher realms rarely descended to lower ones—the lower realm would stifle their cultivation, and they would struggle to replenish lost Qi.

Shaking his head, he resolved that the wisest course of action was to secure his immediate surroundings before formulating a strategy for the Worldwalker. "Where in the nine realms am I?" Below him was sheer darkness, while around him cascaded waterfalls of spatial Qi, some flowing downward, others rising. When he dared to look up, he saw…an eye that made his skin crawl.

"Am I inside that spirit tree?"

"Yes." An indescribable voice resonated, causing his entire body to quiver. It wasn't a word he directly comprehended. Instead, he sensed pure intent behind it. Soul speech, he concluded—one of the rarest forms of communication.

The Elder swallowed hard, attempting to suppress his excitement. He had just heard the utterance of a divine being trapped within a tree! And its eye was directly above him…ripe for the taking.

16
GIVEN A DIFFICULT CHOICE

Despite the spirit tree's assertions that he was inside its body, the Elder found himself doubting the claim. The environment around him was immense, as if he'd been reduced to an ant's size, and the divine eye overhead appeared to belong to a god-like entity, observing its creation.

His only explanation for this surreal reality was the spatial Qi pervading the area—known to alter the dimensions of spaces. For instance, spatial rings used stored spatial Qi to create a tiny pocket dimension far exceeding the rings' physical size.

Although bewildered by his surroundings, the Elder was certain of one thing: the whispers of the void he had absorbed to restore his cultivation were fading while the spatial Qi around him was accumulating. Over time, despite the spatial Qi being less potent than his void Qi, it would overwhelm him.

So the answer to his predicament was simple: aim for the divine eye glaring him down from overhead. But how? He was suspended in this vast space like a speck of dust, and the eye seemed so far away, like a distant star.

I should have something in my spatial ring for an occasion such as this, the Elder mused. After living and surviving for so long, he had amassed numerous lifesaving artifacts for various predicaments. It had been so long since he started collecting these items, and since he last found himself in such dire straits, he had forgotten what he'd stored.

Feeling the eye's intense gaze on his back that made his skin crawl, he tried to activate his spatial ring, but nothing happened. "What?" Panic set in as he shoved more Qi into the spatial rings that had been on his fingers for centuries, yet in his greatest time of need, they remained dormant, as if they were just glorified lumps of metal and nothing more.

"Those rings use spatial Qi." The Elder paled at the mocking voice. He studied the cold metal encircling his gnarled fingers, frowning deeply. They did indeed harness spatial Qi, so in a place saturated with such Qi, he may be cut off... Then he noticed a crack in one ring, followed by a lilac stream spilling out. Within the stream, he saw miniaturized versions of all his hoarded treasures.

"No!" His panic heightened as another ring cracked, then another. "No, no, no!" He watched in horror as twelve lilac streams filled with his collected items flowed away from him, spiraling past the divine eye.

"I knew wasting points on items was a terrible idea when I can just rob idiots for them." The voice was distant as if it was talking to itself. The Elder struggled to discern the intent behind the soul words, but he felt insulted.

With his face burning red from a mixture of anger and embarrassment, he shouted up at the eye that seemed to be looking at the items swirling around it with glee, "You thieving scoundrel, return those or face the wrath of the Voidmind family!"

"Mhm?" The eye glanced back at him, and he felt an ungodly pressure descend on him. "You should worry about yourself first."

The Elder's eye twitched, and he clenched his fist. No one had dared to speak to him this way in over three hundred years! Drawing void Qi from his core, he directed it toward his missing arm, forming a javelin of pure void.

Aiming was unnecessary, given the eye's colossal size that took up much of the space. Grinning, he hurled the void javelin upward into the vast expanse. The act sent him floating backward for a while. He watched as the eye lazily observed the incoming attack with apparent indifference.

"Foolish," the Elder gloated as the javelin struck the eye. "Void Qi penetrates all defenses—"

Suddenly, the javelin evaporated as if it had hit an invisible wall, leaving the eye unscathed. The eye then turned to him. "Your attacks are powerless against me."

"Impossible!" the Elder bellowed. He was well aware of void Qi's capabilities, and in his centuries-long life, he had never witnessed anything blocking void Qi. Such a feat was only conceivable if the entity in question was...divine.

He had suspected he was contending with a divine being due to the soul speaking, a communication method known only to be used by heaven, but confirming the presence of an actual divine being was another matter entirely.

The Elder felt his entire body lust for power. He may be in a precarious circumstance, but this was likely the greatest opportunity any cultivator had ever encountered. He would be set for life if he could slit that eye open and cultivate within its divinity. Nascent Soul Realm would be a breeze, and Monarch Realm would be a mere stop-off point. He would soar to the greatest heights and then void walk to the higher realms.

"**Elder Voidmind, would you be open to sharing some knowledge with me?**" the voice interrupted his thoughts.

Knowledge? What information could he hold that a divine entity didn't already possess? Was this a ploy to let his guard down? Had his attack inflicted damage and the divine being was buying time to recover?

Regardless, he was running out of time. Spatial Qi was gushing into this vast space at an alarming rate, and he could no longer sense the whispers of the void.

"Tsk. Stop playing with me." The Elder cursed. If long-range void attacks didn't work, he would carve a hole in the eye with his bare hands. Gathering Qi in his hand, he aimed them behind himself and felt his Star Core burn in his chest as he propelled himself forward with void flames.

The eye overhead appeared to be amused by his attempts. Time passed, and the Elder's patience wore thin. No matter how hard he tried, he seemed to make no progress, the eye maintaining a constant distance.

"Why not tell me about your life experiences while slowly depleting your Qi?" the voice proposed, prompting the Elder to halt his efforts and remain floating in the seemingly infinite space.

"Why can't I get closer to you?" Frustrated and feeling toyed with, the Elder questioned the space's peculiar nature. Even before the eye responded, he observed the spatial Qi waterfalls flowing in two directions and had a sudden realization. "You're manipulating the dimensions of this space, aren't you?"

"**What I do is of no matter,**" the eye responded dismissively. "**You'll soon be dead.**"

Gritting his teeth, the Elder swallowed his pride and asked through clenched teeth, "If I answer your questions, will you let me go?"

"**Freedom? After attacking Stella?**"

The Elder winced as he saw the waterfalls of spatial Qi collapse toward him like waves the size of stars. He braced hard as the wave smashed into him, and he felt his Star Core almost bottom out with Qi as it rushed to defend him.

"**You will never be free.**"

As the wave passed, he gasped for breath as if winded.

"But I might propose a deal," the voice offered, reviving a spark of hope within the Elder.

"What is this deal?"

"**I'll allow you to consume some of my divine sap,**" the eye laughed mockingly, "**though I doubt it'll be of much help to you.**"

The Elder didn't know what it meant by that, but even if all he could do was extract some Qi from the sap, he felt it was worth a shot.

The life-saving artifacts he'd been wearing earlier had shattered while defending against the Worldwalker's deadly attack. With his spatial rings, filled with life-saving items, now broken, and his access to void Qi cut off, he was truly running out of time.

"Fine. Deal," the Elder said, trying to regain his composure. "What knowledge are you seeking?"

"**How are you able to communicate with me?**"

The Elder stroked his chin, perplexed. Was this a test of some kind, or was he overthinking things? How could a divine being using such an advanced type of communication not know what they were doing?

"You're communicating with me through your soul," the Elder responded cautiously. "I can sense the intent behind your words."

After a lengthy pause, the voice asked, "**Is that because you are within my soul, or is it due to a particular technique you've mastered?**"

Looking around in confusion, the Elder replied, "I thought I was inside your trunk? How can this be your soul…" Even with spatial Qi manipulation, he was skeptical that he could be shrunk to the size of a Star Core, unless the spirit tree's Star Core was large enough to accommodate a person.

Chilled by the thought of his predicament, he quickly clarified, "If we are indeed within your soul, that would explain it. I don't know any specialized soul communication techniques."

The eye averted its gaze, and the Elder could faintly hear distant mumblings. "If Stella were to enter my soul, could we converse…"

After a while passed and the Elder grew impatient as he looked down and saw a lake of spatial Qi rising, he asked, "Anything else?"

The eye swiveled down to glare at him. "What do you know about alchemy?"

"Nearly everything. I am a master alchemist," the Elder replied. "If you're asking me to relay all my knowledge, there isn't enough time."

"**Can you transfer your knowledge to me?**"

The Elder shook his head. "That's impossible." In truth, it wasn't. He simply chose not to.

"**Mhm, fine, just tell me the basics.**"

The Elder frowned but complied nonetheless. "Alchemy is the art of creating pills and elixirs from ingredients with traces of Qi. These ingredients must be purified and refined by the alchemist before combining them in exact proportions. The alchemist must then burn the ingredients with their soul flame in a specially designed cauldron."

Seeing the eye remain silent, he cautiously continued, uncertain if he was explaining something overly simplistically. "The process tests a cultivator's patience, precision, and understanding of the world's natural rhythms. The cultivator must comprehend the nature of each ingredient and how they interact to produce the desired outcome."

"**Interesting,**" the voice said. "**And is it true that not every affinity is capable of alchemy?**"

The Elder nodded. "That's correct. Affinities without a soul flame find it difficult to perform alchemy. For instance, the Silverspire family in the sect, with their metal affinity, cannot perform alchemy."

There was a long silence as the eye seemed to get distracted by something else. Was it deliberately prolonging the conversation, or was it easily distracted?

"Hello?" the Elder asked. "Are you still there?"

"**Yes, I'm here.**"

"Do you have any other questions?" The Elder felt lost.

"**What are the strengths of void affinity?**" the eye asked.

"Destruction and travel," the Elder replied cautiously, wary of revealing too much about his affinity. "Void Qi violently reacts with all other types of Qi, giving us the ability to overcome those stronger than us. As for travel, we can journey through the void, much like those with a spatial affinity."

The Elder glanced around with fear as he saw the spatial Qi fill up the space. The divine being had already proved he could crush him with a wave of spatial Qi at any time, and he didn't know how much longer his Star Core could hold out with only its passive generation protecting him.

"**I see. Well, you've answered my questions, so I will reward you.**"

A wave of relief washed over the Elder, but he couldn't help but narrow his eyes. This all seemed too easy. What was this divine being scheming?

A solitary drop of black liquid fell gracefully from above, passing the eye and floating before him. He tried to probe it with his spiritual sense but couldn't determine its true nature. It resembled blood, yet it was viscous and so black it appeared almost like the void itself.

It was so obviously a trap of some kind, but did he even have a choice? Maybe the divine being was clueless about how close he was to reaching the Nascent Soul Realm. Perhaps I can consume this, break through to the next realm, and bypass the toxins or whatever is present in this blood by forming an infant soul and escaping.

He knew it was a long shot, but what other option did he have?

Reaching out, the Elder cupped the viscous blood in his hands; it wiggled around as if alive and made him shudder, but without another regret, he consumed it.

A moment passed, and nothing happened...

"**I've always wanted to watch a man transform into a tree.**" The eye's laughter echoed throughout the space.

The Elder recalled the recent demonic tree infestation in Darklight City. His eyes widened as he put the pieces together. Hurriedly examining his body, he saw the blood droplet morph into a black seed that took root in his Star Core.

"**I wonder what type of tree you'll become. Perhaps a void tree?**" the eye joked, and the Elder gritted his teeth.

Ashlock watched with interest as the Elder consumed his cursed sap. It was now dusk outside his trunk, and the feeling of having someone inside his soul drove him nuts. It felt like having a fly buzzing around inside one's empty stomach.

He could have tortured the man for more information, but a few questions answered and several items obtained seemed sufficient, and he just wanted this headache of a person gone.

More importantly, he wanted to witness what happened when a person transformed into a tree.

As it turned out, the process was slow. Over an hour passed, and Ashlock watched as the man meditated desperately, breathing heavily, clearly trying to fight something within.

Eventually, the Elder abandoned meditation, probably due to the lack of void Qi in the environment, and resorted to pleading. "Please! Great divine being, I will be your eternal servant! I can even make an oath of loyalty!"

Ashlock dismissed him. He had no use for a servant, and he suspected oaths were far from foolproof. Also, he would have to let the man out of his soul first for him to say the oath, which was a terrible risk. Seeing the effects of his cursed sap was far more interesting.

"Just perish for me," Ashlock said indifferently to the Elder.

The tormented Elder began to laugh manically, and after a while, he grinned. "Good, good! You dare to treat me like this."

Ashlock observed roots sprouting from the corner of the Elder's mouth and the man's body convulsing. It seemed his Star Core had lost the battle against the cursed blood.

But then something else began to occur—a scene Ashlock was familiar with. Liquid void Qi flowed from the Elder's eyes and mouth as he continued to laugh, indicating he was going supernova.

Ashlock watched with sleep tugging at his consciousness. The sun had set, but the restless sensation caused by the Elder's presence in his soul had kept him awake, denying him much-needed sleep. He wasn't concerned about the Elder going supernova, as the void Qi couldn't harm him.

"I will see you in hell!" the Elder screamed in his final moments, his body expanding until it erupted outward. Ashlock's entire trunk groaned and shook, and the mountain trembled.

Ashlock blinked as he saw the void Qi had eradicated much of his spatial Qi, which he had been amassing throughout the day. Now his Star Core was brimming with void Qi.

The Elder was dead...a ninth-stage Star Core cultivator with centuries of experience. It was almost harrowing how easy it had felt toying with his life. "I guess that's the power of locking someone within your soul, a place you have absolute control."

[Warning: Foreign Qi Detected]
[High Risk of Soul Corruption]

Ashlock looked at the messages and began to panic despite his exhaustion. He knew his body could survive near annihilation and regenerate within days, but to this day, he hadn't found a way to repair soul damage.

[Generating solutions...]
[Convert foreign Qi into spatial Qi]
[Merge void Qi with a system skill to upgrade it]
[Dispel void Qi into the nearby atmosphere]

"Huh?" Ashlock read the options again and couldn't believe it. The first and last ones were ignored as he could generate spatial Qi himself, and dispelling void Qi into the area around him was just stupid.

But to merge the void Qi with one of his system skills?

Without hesitation, he selected the option, and his skill list appeared.

[Demonic Demi-Divine Tree (Age: 9)]
[Star Core: 2nd Stage]
[Soul Type: Amethyst (Spatial)]
[Mutations...]
{Demonic Eye [B]}
{Blood Sap [C]}
[Summons...]
{Ashen King: Larry [A]}
{Infant Grass Snake: Kaida [F]}
[Skills...]
{Mystic Realm [S]} [Locked until day: 3515]
{Eye of the Tree God [A]}

{Deep Roots [A]}
{Magic Mushroom Production [A]}
{Lightning Qi Barrier [A]}
{Qi Fruit Production [A]}
{Blooming Root Flower Production [B]}
{Language of the World [B]}
{Root Puppet [B]}
{Fire Qi Protection [B]}
{Transpiration of Heaven and Chaos [B]}
{Devour [C]}
{Hibernate [C]}
{Basic Poison Resistance [F]}

"Wait…I can select which skill I want to upgrade?" Ashlock was dumbfounded. His system had always been purely random concerning his skills, giving him little control over his progression.

But now he could choose which one to upgrade?

The question was, which skill would work the best when merged with the void affinity?

17
A CONSUMING ABYSS

Despite Ashlock's exhaustion, shrouded by the surrounding cold darkness of night, he refused to squander this rare opportunity.

Cultivation had always been his area of control, where he got to learn and practice his own techniques independently of the system, except for it randomly deciding his spatial affinity.

For the rest of his life on this planet as a tree, he had been prepared to coexist with the system, focusing on his cultivation while hoping it would occasionally provide him with useful skills.

But now, he was granted a choice.

[Select the skill you wish to merge with the void Qi.]

Ashlock scanned the list that had materialized before him. Predictably, his Mutation and Summon sections were grayed out on the screen and unselectable since they were not skills.

"Shame…it might have been cool to give Kaida the void affinity, but forcing a specific affinity on an F-grade snake seems like a bad idea. Evolution will take care of him and make him strong in the future, so it would be a waste to merge the void Qi with him anyways."

Kaida aside, Ashlock would have liked to merge the void with his demonic eye or blood sap, as those sounded useful since, unlike skills, mutations were ever present as they were literally part of his body, so even when the system was offline, they were fully usable.

"All right, if I'm to choose a single skill, let's see... There are two factors in this upgrade I need to consider: the skill's current grade and the outcome of adding void affinity."

Firstly, Ashlock disregarded the production skills. He wasn't certain about the effects of adding void affinity to them, and he certainly didn't want his fruits, mushrooms, or flowers to transform into odd void variants, as that would diminish the appeal of his versatile production skills.

Having mentally dismissed his production skills, he then evaluated his protection skills, such as {Lightning Qi Barrier [A]} and {Fire Qi Protection [B]}.

Defensive skills weren't what he sought currently, even though enhancing his A-grade lightning barrier could result in an S-rank barrier skill post-upgrade that would be hard to penetrate for anyone out here in the wilderness.

So why dismiss defense despite its potential advantages? After witnessing how effortlessly the Elder within his soul was eliminated despite numerous defensive artifacts, Ashlock deduced that if ever cornered, he'd rather neutralize his enemies than merely ward them off.

Also, he was a tree. He couldn't run away. So the best defense was a good offense, especially in a world where if one of his foes escaped, they could inform someone stronger and come back to kill him.

Having ruled out his production and defensive skills, he was left to choose between his utility and offensive skills.

"The system prompt implies that the chosen skill will upgrade a rank. I wonder if I can survive if I choose {Mystic Realm [S]}, as it would ascend to an SS-rank skill," Ashlock pondered. It was a fun thought to have an SS-rank skill, and it did have a lot of capabilities for training his allies.

This was an important point because Senior Lee had advised him to focus on training those around him to be as strong as possible to help make up for his weaknesses... But could Stella or Diana even survive in an SS-rank realm? And a void affinity one at that? There was a fine line between helping his sect members and accidentally killing them.

"I think upgrading my Mystic Realm is a bad idea. Let's see what other utility skills I have..." He scrutinized each of them one by one.

"{Eye of the Tree God [A]} could be a solid contender. It would upgrade to S-rank, and although it achieves neither of the advantages of void Qi that the Voidmind Elder listed, if it could let me see through walls or even peer into the void, it could have untold potential." Ashlock frowned as he realized his lack of information for such a crucial decision.

Noting {Eye of the Tree God} as a good option, he moved on to the next A-grade utility skill, {Deep Roots}.

"Another good option with untapped potential. Just the void Qi alone would allow me to spread out my roots much faster, as the void Qi should help with tunneling, and if I ever turn my roots into tunnels, the void Qi could help protect them from being destroyed or broken into."

A headache began to brew as Ashlock struggled with this tough decision, the fatigue from the sunlight deprivation only adding to his discomfort. "Elevating {Deep Roots} to an S-rank might even allow me to tunnel into the underworld."

If that were possible, {Deep Roots} might overshadow {Eye of the Tree God}, but it was difficult to discern. Scanning the skill list, he managed to eliminate {Hibernate} as it was just a C-grade skill, and he couldn't see how void affinity could improve it much.

"Mhm, what about my cultivation technique, {Transpiration of Heaven and Chaos [B]}?" Ashlock pondered. Promoting his cultivation technique to A-grade seemed like a universally beneficial idea, but how would the void Qi contribute? Would he end up mastering dual affinities of spatial and void Qi? Or could he convert void Qi from below into spatial Qi?

"System, can you really not tell me what the result of the merge with void Qi will cause for each skill?" Ashlock begged the system, only to receive a flash of the skill list in response, pressuring him to decide.

"Becoming a dual affinity would be amazing, but the risk is too substantial. It would be a colossal waste if I failed to attain dual affinity." Ashlock sighed. He was a gambling man, but this was too much pressure and unknowns.

His current cultivation speed was sufficient thanks to the runic formations and his offspring surrounding him. Hence upgrading his cultivation technique seemed excessive, minus the potential dual-affinity idea.

Besides, given the presence of his sect members, the necessity to diversify his Qi was also not a pressing matter.

With that one put to the side, his eyes were drawn to a potentially interesting option {Language of the World [B]}. Upgrading it to A-grade could allow him to talk freely with those around him via telepathy or let him learn local languages super fast.

Communication had always been a limiting factor for him, but how would combining it with void Qi help? Would it let him talk to void monsters or something? It was all speculation, and he felt like he was grasping at straws with his guesses.

"My level of communication abilities is tolerable for now, especially once the Redclaw Elders learn the ancient language so I can communicate with them directly." Ashlock sighed as he added {Language of the World} to his ignore pile.

Ashlock looked at his {Root Puppet [B]} skill and felt like sighing again. This skill had a lot of potential, and he should probably test it now as he'd fully merged with his tree body to see if it was easier to use.

Maybe now he could keep control of a corpse for a lot longer... Alas, the requirement for a corpse to be always available made the skill cumbersome to use, so it was also discarded.

Finally, Ashlock came to the last skill for consideration: his lone direct attack skill, {Devour [C]}. In his view, this skill stood to gain the most from merging with void Qi. However, the bothersome aspect was its current C-grade, making the rare opportunity of upgrading it to a B-grade feel somewhat wasteful.

"It's intriguing that the system has been stingy with direct attack skills. After a decade of drawing skills, I only have one attack skill, which is the one I started with, alongside {Basic Spirit Sight} and {Basic Meditation}. While those F-grade skills have since been upgraded by the system to A and B grades respectively, {Devour} has remained stagnant at C-grade all this while."

Ashlock was beginning to realize something. "The system focuses on giving skills that help me nurture others. Meanwhile, my cultivation depends entirely on how I want to use it."

Recalling the dreams of how the past world trees had perished, he remembered their tendency to provide to the cultivators and cycle the Qi throughout the nine realms rather than lash out and kill those that harmed it.

"Could this be a world tree system? Is it trying to guide me down a particular path?" The only contradictory aspect to this theory was his mutations, like his cursed blood sap that turned people into trees and his demonic eye, which incited fear and prompted others to flee. "However, the system does label them as mutations. An intriguing choice of terminology," Ashlock pondered.

After a while, Ashlock narrowed it down to {Deep Roots} or {Devour}, and after grumbling for a bit, he decided on {Devour} for the simple fact that his system seemed averse to upgrading or providing a single attack skill. In time, he was sure his other skills would either upgrade through draws or he would find cultivation techniques capable of replicating their effects. Whereas he was suspicious if he would ever get another system-granted attack skill, especially one with void Qi.

It had been a hard choice, but in his mind, nothing seemed as valuable as {Devour} in his current predicament. It would grant him a strong attack skill that he could use immediately without training, unlike a cultivation technique.

It also harnessed a different Qi type than his spatial techniques, which would give him a fighting chance if he confronted someone who could counter spatial Qi with their affinity or a monster like Bob immune to cultivators with a single type of affinity.

"Phew..." Ashlock exhaled a nervous breath within his soul as he deliberated over the {Devour} skill.

[Choose system skill: {Devour}?]

Mentally agreeing with the prompt, it flashed with golden light and vanished. His skill list also disappeared, and Ashlock felt the void corruption that tainted his soul begin to gather into a ball due to a mystical force.

[Skill upgrading... 1%]

Ashlock sighed, the tension of choosing a skill remaining unresolved. He had wished for an immediate outcome, but as always, the system was notoriously slow. "I sincerely hope I've made the correct choice," Ashlock groaned, his mind succumbing to exhaustion. "I suppose I'll find out in the morning..."

Basking in the warmth of the sun on his leaves, Ashlock gradually awakened.

"Tree!" Below his shade, Stella voiced her concern. *"Are you all right? The whole mountain was shaking last night. Did the Elder try to escape?"*

Ashlock groaned, channeling his lilac Qi to write on his trunk, 'The Elder went supernova last night. Everything is under control.'

As Stella deciphered the words, she cycled through stages of disbelief. "You're fine? But how? Is the Elder gone? What..." She circled his trunk, seemingly searching for a sizable gaping hole.

Ashlock was about to address Stella's queries, but a sudden system notification snapped him out of his daze.

[Void Qi corruption eradicated]
[Skill upgrade successful]
[Upgraded {Devour [C]} -> {Consuming Abyss [B]}]

Details regarding the skill filled Ashlock's mind, and he concluded that he had indeed made the right decision.

He could still utilize {Devour} as he always had, though with certain enhancements. For instance, the black vines now boasted a substantial spike at their ends that could impale and drag victims backward. Also, the vines moved with astounding speed and could hit moving targets. Furthermore, he could now individually control the black vines instead of merely specifying a target and leaving the rest to the system.

Thus, he had complete control over the skill. He could even retract the vines to avoid consuming someone or use them defensively to shield Stella.

With these modifications, Ashlock presumed this would be the outcome had the system ever upgraded his {Devour} skill to B-grade. However, the integration of void Qi truly set the skill apart.

He could toggle the skill to utilize void Qi, which replaced the black vines with obsidian tendrils of void that moved at an incredible speed and were undefendable. An opponent's only options were to escape his range—the area around his trunk—or be a divine entity immune to void Qi.

However, there was a slight catch that Ashlock didn't appreciate at all. "I must expend a sacrificial credit for every minute I wish to operate the skill using void Qi," he grumbled.

In retrospect, it was reasonable—he was a spatial Qi cultivator, and his Star Core was designed to process and handle spatial Qi, not void Qi. Cultivation and any Qi-related matters were generally his responsibility, not the systems. If he desired the system to perform a Qi-related task, there was a fee—in this case, sacrificial credits.

Interestingly, his daily credits couldn't be used for payment. Did the system perceive them as different? Would more functions appear that only accepted daily credits as payment in the future?

Moreover, the fact that the skill required sacrificial credits to operate made him relieved he hadn't chosen {Deep Roots}. The prospect of expending sacrificial credits to dig deeper was quite upsetting.

"I will need to make sure to have a few monsters trapped in a cage or something down in the mountain that I can consume for emergency sacrificial credits," Ashlock noted.

This was the workaround Ashlock devised since his sign-in system depleted all credits when used, potentially making the system dangerous to use without careful thought. What if he accumulated a hundred points, signed in that day, and a formidable cultivator showed up to kill him because he couldn't use his new void skill?

Whatever the case, Ashlock breathed a long sigh of relief.

{Consuming Abyss} was the answer to his problems. Despite the skill's cost requirements, it sounded darn powerful, and knowing he now had a skill he could employ to defend himself against foes far stronger than himself filled him with confidence.

He recalled how ineffective his spatial Qi–coated vines had been against the Voidmind Elder's void flames. The knowledge that he now commanded such a formidable power gave him hope for his continued survival in the years to come.

Maybe he could even start being a bit more assertive. His gaze landed on Maple, who was peacefully resting atop Stella's head. He pondered if the squirrel was capable of pushing someone as powerful as the Patriarch into his soul, allowing Ashlock to consume them and upgrade another skill with the same affinity as the Voidmind Elder.

Could his soul handle a different affinity, or had he only been able to survive due to his void immunity?

"Actually, didn't the Voidmind Elder mention having a brother slightly more powerful?" Ashlock contemplated the possibility of engaging in conflict with the Voidmind family just so he could capture their members. Frustratingly, this entire plan was contingent on Maple and whether he was inclined to utilize all his strength to trap someone within his soul.

A sudden sensation of a hand made Ashlock look down at Stella, worryingly tapping his trunk. "Hey, Tree? Are you there?"

Ashlock felt like smiling. He could protect her now so long as she was nearby; in other cases, he was sure Maple could lend a hand.

"Speaking of protection, didn't the Elder give me a crazy amount of items?" He excitedly opened his inventory and began to browse. "I wonder how many of these artifacts Stella can wear at once…"

18
TREE SWORDSMAN

After the sweet taste of victory, it was time for Ashlock to enjoy the spoils of his fight. He could now understand why cultivators were so bloodthirsty and prone to killing each other over the slightest grievance. Cultivation was a costly and time-consuming process. Why waste time traveling the realms when he can sit here on his mountaintop and have fools come and offer their lives and treasures to him?

At first, Ashlock had been baffled by the sheer quantity of belongings the Voidmind Elder was carrying, but it made sense. He had observed that cultivators preferred to carry all their personal belongings around in spatial rings rather than leave them in a room or vault.

For instance, Stella and Diana had never claimed a specific room within the pavilion to serve as a bedroom or storage for their belongings. Rather, they would often be found half asleep, cultivating while perched on a runic formation, or on rare occasions, resting on a musty mattress left behind in an old servant's quarters.

It made total sense as in a world where people could teleport through walls or random Dao Storms could come by and rip your pavilion to shreds, leaving anything out in the open was far too risky. It was far safer to keep everything of value on hand at all times within spatial rings.

That was why, when Ashlock looked within his expanded pocket space that functioned as an inventory for the system, he saw a literal mountain of various items that he had extracted from the Voidmind Elder's spatial rings.

Undoing the ninth stage Star Core seal around the rings had been a breeze, and he had even been able to extract the items from the ring's pocket dimensions while they were still around the old man's gnarly fingers. The power one commanded within their own soul was nothing to scoff at. He was practically a god within, especially since he was totally immune to void Qi.

"I'm so glad my inventory expanded when my Star Core grew in size..." Ashlock remarked, eyeing an ornate sword hilt jutting out from the immense pile of artifacts and porcelain pill bottles.

When he had gone on his sign-in spree for low-rank items in the past before his merge, his inventory hadn't been big enough to accommodate all the junk, and items were soon popping out, and he had to stop signing in.

Ashlock went to focus on the sword hilt but frowned when no system notification manifested. "System?" His status screen appeared, but that wasn't what he wanted. "Why isn't it telling me about the sword?"

When he signed in and drew items, the system informed him of the item's name, grade, and potential use. The only other time he had been given an item that he'd stored in his inventory was the SSS-rank Divine Fragment, which was now merged with his soul and might result in a Monarch Realm tree trying to turn him into nutrients.

Impending doom aside, why was his system not helping him?

He tried changing targets to a porcelain pill bottle but still nothing. No matter what item he glared at, he received no information. "Don't tell me I need a stupid appraisal skill or something." Ashlock sighed as he stopped trying after his tenth attempt.

If he couldn't use the system to identify these items, how was he supposed to know what to give out and keep for himself? He could act as a dragon and sleep on his horde of gold, but he was a nurturing tree that wanted to uplift the strength and protect those around him.

"Maybe I should just give them all to Stella and let her handle it alongside Diana?" Unfortunately, he knew almost nothing about any of the items, and apart from controlling some swords with telekinesis, he couldn't see a way he could use these items himself.

"I should definitely start a sword collection," Ashlock mused, spotting more than ten exquisite swords within the pile. A sudden thought struck him. If he correctly understood the potential of his new {Consuming Abyss} skill, he could wield the vines like limbs. Could he curl a vine around the hilt of a sword and fight people with it?

"If you keep ignoring me, I will get mad." Stella's voice made him sigh. He had already told her he was fine! So why was she nagging him so much?

'Hello,' Ashlock wrote on his trunk, and Stella threw up her hands.

"What do you mean hello? Yes, hello, can you tell me what happened? You said the Elder went supernova, and yet everything is all right?"

Feeling good after enhancing his abilities, getting a good night's rest, and finally freeing himself from the invasive presence inside his soul, Ashlock found it challenging to take Stella's distress seriously.

Using telekinesis, he broke off one of his leaves and used it to pat Stella on the head. She let out a yelp, swatting at it as if it were a bothersome fly. "What are you doing?!"

Eventually, the squirrel sleeping on her head reached out his paw while still half asleep, grabbing the spatial Qi-coated leaf and reducing it to dust that floated away in the wind.

Ignoring the horrifying thing Maple had just done to the leaf, Ashlock wrote on his trunk, 'Stop worrying so much. I said everything was fine. The Elder is dead, and I now have many items I was looking through.'

Slumping onto the bench, Stella exhaled a sigh that was equal parts frustration and exhaustion. *"I can tell when you are sleeping by the way your Qi flows, but I was really worried all night that you might have suffered some internal injuries or soul damage because of that bastard Voidmind Elder."*

Looking up at Ashlock's scarlet canopy rustling in the morning breeze, she continued, *"I'm so relieved you're unharmed. You didn't respond to any of us for hours yesterday, and then the entire mountain shuddered at midnight. Finally, you fell asleep without reassuring us you were okay!"*

All right, that was fair. The Elder within his soul had been so distracting that he had mostly ignored the outside world. Glancing around the mountain peak, he saw Stella and Maple on the bench under his canopy. Larry was off to the side, with Kaida coiled around one of his horns. Despite further searching, Diana and Douglas were nowhere to be found.

'I apologize,' Ashlock wrote in lilac flames dancing across his black trunk, 'I was busy interrogating the Elder prior to his demise, then I had to rest to purge the void Qi from my soul.'

Stella tilted her head and mumbled the words to herself as she quickly translated them and then sighed. "Fine, those are pretty fair reasons to be distracted."

While half concentrating on Stella in case she said anything else, Ashlock delved back into his inventory, scouting for a suitable gift for her. Without the system's assistance, deciphering the use of each item was challenging, so he aimed to select something that would suit her, even if it proved to be useless.

Of the ten swords nestled in the pile, he picked out two.

One was a black blade hidden from the world in a black sheath engraved with a gold star pattern—he felt it would harmonize with Stella. Conversely, the dark blue blade in a blue leather sheath seemed a perfect fit for Diana. He felt Douglas didn't quite deserve one of the swords yet, and something about the number seven bugged him.

"Perhaps if I distribute four and keep six, that would work," Ashlock mused. The thought crossed his mind to offer a sword to the Redclaws, but he quickly dismissed it.

These swords had been owned by a very powerful and influential cultivator that had been part of the Blood Lotus Sect for a long time. If the Redclaw Grand Elder began walking around with one of these swords drawn and anyone recognized it, there could be problems.

Another consideration emerged from his past experience with the wooden stick he had drawn long ago. Once he removed items from his inventory, he could not put them back. "But that was before my demonic eye created an opening in my trunk. Perhaps I can find a way to get items back into my inventory now," Ashlock pondered.

Before proceeding further, Ashlock decided to test his newfound theory. He selected a seemingly random gold coin, a currency from a distant empire, and observed as it disappeared from the pocket dimension, only to reappear a meter away from his trunk in the outside world.

Stella eyed the coin that randomly appeared floating in the air with understandable weariness. "Tree, is that yours?"

Ashlock flashed his leaf with Qi to calm her down. He then opened his trunk to reveal his {Demonic Eye}.

"Actually, isn't it quite worrying if people have direct access to my soul by entering the slit in my trunk," Ashlock wondered as he shuddered at the memory of the Elder reaching his hand in and caressing his {Demonic Eye}. Wasn't this similar to how his portals are two-way: if he could attack someone through it, they could attack him back?

Setting aside these unsettling thoughts, Ashlock moved the coin toward the opening in his trunk, his {Demonic Eye} closely observing the approaching object. Stella watched the unfolding scene through her fingers, clearly unnerved by the sight of his eye.

To his astonishment, the coin slipped through the one-meter-long, half-meter-wide gap with ease. It disappeared momentarily before reappearing atop the pile in his inventory.

"The system still won't tell me about the item," Ashlock grumbled but was glad to see he now had a way to get items in and out of his system inventory.

"Tree, was that one of the Elder's items?" Stella asked as she watched the slit in his trunk close. *"Is there anything I could have?"*

Switching back to the pile, Ashlock looked for something to give to Stella. Annoyingly, most of the items were clearly for a man and would be far too big for Stella to wear. She was tall for a girl, but the Elder had been a tall, wide-shouldered man.

Finally, he unearthed a pair of black gloves fashioned from a material resembling leather. The gloves left the fingers exposed, and the inner lining was adorned with a tapestry of intricate silver runes. "These appear small enough to fit Stella's hands," Ashlock reasoned after a thorough inspection. With a mere thought, the gloves disappeared from his inventory, materializing above Stella.

They fell down into her lap, and she gave them a look. "Oh wow, these look expensive. Definitely artifact gear." She then put them on and looked at her hands, turning them around so she could get a good look.

'They suit you,' Ashlock wrote, and Stella grinned after translating the words.

"I think so, too."

She then sprang to her feet and struck a pose, aiming her gloved hand away from him. As Ashlock watched, the gloves pulsed with energy. "Oh! They can absorb the Qi from an attack. Neat!"

"So a defensive artifact, then, although still helpful in combat," Ashlock noted and then went hunting for more stuff to give Stella.

"How can I dig deeper into this pile?" Ashlock had looked at everything on the surface and wanted to see the items buried but wasn't sure how to. He then tried to mobilize his Qi, but it resulted in nothing.

"Stupid system granted space, not letting me use my Qi in here," he grumbled as he resorted to just depositing a load of random stuff outside.

As a mound of items materialized on the mountain peak, Stella, her arms crossed, watched with amusement. *"You truly plundered that old man, didn't you? This is all high-grade stuff, similar to what I saw the merchants in Slymere trying to sell me."*

Ashlock's interest was piqued at Stella's suggestion. Could they exchange some of these items with the merchants for spirit stones to construct more formations? To him, these items were largely superfluous, useful only as gifts for his sect members or as rewards. Moreover, they were now cluttering his inventory.

'Should we sell these?' Ashlock asked.

Stella read his words and tapped her chin. *"I'm not sure. Best to ask Diana when she gets back from observing that Voidmind assistant, as she knows a lot more about merchants than me."*

That seemed reasonable. Ashlock looked back at the pile, and buried under gold coins and many herbs for alchemy, he saw a bit of white cloth poking through. He focused on it, and the garment vanished and appeared outside.

Stella hadn't demonstrated much interest in the accumulating artifacts and items, most likely because unidentified pill bottles and strange devices without instructions were of little use.

But she seemed interested in the newly appeared item, a pair of white trousers with a black snake decor embellished with branches ending in red leaves sprouting from its body, running down their sides. They seemed to be made of a soft material that rustled in the wind as she held them up against her legs for a size comparison.

They didn't quite seem long enough for her figure, but she seemed to love the style. Had these been clothes for the Voidminds' Elder's daughter or something? The end of the trousers seemed to end just below her knees, but due to her slim figure, she was sure to fit in them.

With a flash of gold, her current white leggings and fishnets vanished into her spatial ring. The short white trousers in her hand followed suit, only to reappear fitted around her legs.

She spun around, giggling with delight. *"I love these! Although they don't quite match my top… Tree, did you find the matching outfit among the Elder's belongings?"*

Ashlock revisited the pile, displacing more items to burrow deeper. He successfully excavated a cavity in the center, reminiscent of a volcano, and unearthed additional pieces of women's clothing. It seemed increasingly plausible that these were purchased by the Voidmind Elder for his daughter, or perhaps… "I really hope these weren't intended for that assistant woman Diana is observing."

Whoever they were intended for didn't matter anymore as they were his rightful spoils of war that he could give to Stella as he had no other use for clothes.

Stella smiled as she saw the second clothing piece as it continued the same decor design and was a bit less revealing than her current outfit. She used the same spatial ring technique to instantly swap out her clothes in a flash of gold and grinned as she felt out her new outfit.

Ashlock brought out the black sword, and Stella reached up to catch it. She opened the sheath to reveal the beautiful blade and whistled. "Even my father didn't have a sword this majestic looking. Are you giving it to me?"

'Yes, but keep it hidden for now. Someone might recognize it,' Ashlock wrote, and Stella nodded in understanding, storing the sword away. She then glanced around, seeing the beautiful scenery for many miles.

"We really need to build a pavilion. Doing all this out in the open is risky."

Ashlock had to agree, especially with the Silverspire family staying nearby.

"Do you want these back, or should I hold onto them?" Stella asked while walking over to the mountain of items. She crouched down and began to shift through them but paused when she found a book. It had an odd title: *Journey of Hazel*. Stella flipped the book open, and after reading a few pages, she concluded, "Seems to be detailing a master alchemist's journey through life."

'You can take all of those items,' Ashlock wrote, and Stella quickly stowed everything away between three of her spatial rings. She then sat back down on the bench and hummed while reading the book she found.

While Stella was busy, Ashlock thought over his rather exposed existence up here on the empty mountaintop. He had grown to an enormous size, making him stick out like a sore thumb, even when surrounded by so many other demonic trees. Moreover, the Qi-gathering formation here transformed the location into a potent Qi hub, something that cultivators were highly attuned to.

Entertaining the thought of having Douglas construct an enormous pavilion as a form of camouflage seemed absurd. It would simply draw more attention, sparking curiosity as to why the Redclaws, the apparent lords of this territory, resided in a lesser palace on the neighboring peak. Inevitably, questions would arise concerning the mysterious resident of Red Vine Peak.

When he was a small tree in an abandoned pavilion with nothing but Stella living here, keeping lowkey was a simple affair. But now he had too much influence and had made too much of a scene to stay under the radar.

"Diana's haunted mist worked quite well, but that requires her to be here." Ashlock's gaze landed on his large spider pet. "Larry could produce an ash cloud to shroud the peak, but that would be rather obnoxious and block out the sunlight I need."

Who was always here that could keep the place obscured? "Oh, me..." Ashlock chuckled. "Maybe I should figure out a solution with spatial Qi?"

Ashlock looked at Red Vine Peak through his {Eye of the Tree God}. At a casual glance, the scene appeared ordinary, but a more discerning eye would notice the oddities: the shadows cast by the colossal demonic tree didn't match with the sun's position, and a bird, suspended in mid-flight, seemed frozen in an eternal wing flap.

It had taken a few hours, but Ashlock had succeeded in fabricating a space-time illusion via an altered application of his portals. It required constant upkeep and used a large amount of Qi, but it did the job until he found a better solution.

Basically, he had made a screen around Red Vine Peak that kept replaying a single frame from a few hours ago.

Of course, this weird area of distorted space might attract attention, especially from the Voidminds, if they ask about their missing and now dead Elder, but he felt it would be fine.

Maybe it was misplaced arrogance, but after defeating a peak realm Star Core Elder and unlocking {Consuming Abyss}, he felt a lot more confident about facing stronger foes.

Switching his view back to Red Vine Peak, he saw Stella look up from the book she had been engrossed in and glance around. She furrowed her brows as if confused at what she was seeing.

"Tree, why is everything so...still? The demonic trees aren't swaying in the breeze, and it just all looks so wrong," Stella asked, and he carefully explained what he had done.

"I see." Stella whistled. "I'm jealous. I couldn't even conjure up such a massive spatial technique, let alone maintain it."

She then looked back to her book and continued reading.

With his surroundings now secured and without the risk of someone seeing him testing his new {Consuming Abyss} skill, he mentally activated the skill. Before, he would need a target, and the system would handle the rest by sending black vines relentlessly after the target until they perished or left his range. However, now he could activate the skill freely.

He was careful to avoid the areas with a runic formation to avoid damaging it. A moment later, black vines far thicker than before rose from cracks in the stone or the purple grass surrounding his trunk with sharp spikes gleaming in the distorted sunlight.

They all ended in a single large spike, and he marveled at how he could control each of them independently like extra limbs. They were far more flexible than his roots, and when he then surged spatial Qi through them, he could further shepherd their movements with telekinesis.

Entering back into his inventory, he summoned a sword that materialized outside, and he floated it over to one of his black vines with telekinesis. "Now, let's see if I can hold it."

The black vine coated in spikes coiled around the sword's hilt, digging into and scratching the metal. The hold was a bit awkward, but with the help of telekinesis, he could keep it in place.

Ashlock chuckled, seeing Stella's astonished expression as he waved the sword around.

Was he the first ever tree swordsman?

'Care for a duel?' Ashlock wrote on his trunk, and Stella grinned, summoning the sword he had just given to her hand. She rolled her shoulders and approached the vine, waving the sword around.

"Don't get too angry when you lose!" she declared with a laugh.

Ashlock had no plans on losing, and after testing if this was a viable combat technique, he planned to test the void form of the {Consuming Abyss} skill.

This was going to be a fun morning.

19
RISE OF KAIDA

Within the weird fractured space where the sun never moved and the external world appeared eternally frozen, the sound of laughter and clashing blades resounded.

Sparks flew as a crazed, blond-haired girl with glowing pink eyes blurred as she dashed and weaved through eight black vines coated in spikes, each wielding a sword and trying to chop off her limbs.

Ashlock winced, a jolt of pain flaring as Stella sliced through one of his vines. He sent the now free-floating sword hurtling after her like a guided missile. However, Stella infused her recently acquired leather gloves, which were defensive artifacts, with Qi. Laughing, she easily deflected the sword.

The silver runic formation on the ground glowed with power as spatial Qi drenched the area.

Stella's form flickered as she employed her movement technique. She parried two simultaneous attacks aimed at her head before diving to the side to evade a third. The third blade missed her head by the narrowest of margins.

An hour prior, Ashlock had been taking it easy as it was just a friendly duel, and he didn't want to injure Stella in any way accidentally, but it didn't take long for him to try going all out as Stella seemed unfazed by his attempts.

Although his vines were certainly much more flexible and faster than when the skill had been called {Devour}, their dexterity and speed while wielding the swords left a lot to be desired.

Even when he pumped more spatial Qi into the vines to forcefully bend them faster with telekinesis, Stella could dodge his swings with ease as if they were moving in slow motion to her.

Nevertheless, Ashlock had a strategy up his sleeve. He swung an orange-tinted metal sword toward the giggling girl. As Stella raised her new black sword in response, Ashlock invoked a portal, redirecting the sword slash to emerge from behind her.

The girl's eyes went wide as she realized his genius tactic, but to Ashlock's confusion, a savage grin appeared as spatial Qi surged through her body, and a portal of her own materialized on her back and another on her chest.

Ashlock watched in disbelief as his attack went through Stella's back and came out of her chest, resulting in his own vine being cleaved in half. The portal that created a tunnel through her chest abruptly closed, slicing that vine in two as well.

Eager to maintain the rhythm of the duel, Ashlock launched another attack from the side using a sword-armed vine. Stella seemed to anticipate the incoming assault through her spiritual senses. Without glancing over her shoulder, she leaped into the air to evade the blade, but Ashlock was having none of that.

Call him petty, but he abused his superior cultivation to unleash a wave of gravity from his immense Star Core. Perhaps due to its immense size or Stella's proximity, she was pulled down to the stone below as if chains were attached to her legs.

"Cheater!" Stella shouted as the sword barely missed because she flattened herself against the ground while gritting her teeth, trying to resist his gravity.

Ashlock felt like mentally rolling his eyes. How could she accuse him of cheating when she could practically teleport between his vines, redirect them with portals, and even chop them down? She even had legs, and in his opinion, that was the most cheating of all!

Okay, he had gone a little overboard, but he had tried everything else, and she had triumphed.

"Master, why must you bully your mistress?" Larry spoke gruffly from the side. Kaida seemed to agree with the spider's statement as it hissed toward him.

Ashlock mentally rolled his eyes at the pair and released his gravity, allowing Stella to stand up. She stored her sword away in a spatial ring and collapsed on the bench.

"That was exhausting but fun." Stella grinned. *"Most fights end within seconds, but even when I chop your vines down, you can keep fighting."*

That was actually a rather interesting observation. Ashlock had also noticed that most fights in this world ended nearly instantly through sneak attacks or just because the opponent was a realm higher. Therefore the opposition, who was weaker, never even stood a chance.

Stella and Diana had trained together, and it helped they were of equal strength, but neither could go all out at the risk of killing the other. But for Ashlock? Even if Stella were to try and destroy his trunk, he could regrow from a stump.

"Mhm…maybe I should personally help train Stella and Diana up alongside my Mystic Realm and also all the cultivation resources I can grow?" Ashlock pondered. If he could also provide these benefits to other sect members, or even the Redclaws that were under an oath of loyalty to him, there might come a day when his small Ashfallen Sect was more fearsome than the entire Blood Lotus Sect.

"Although I must say, I never felt very threatened during the fight," Stella said while relaxing. *"The vine's movement is rather predictable and slow. Also, I could always target the vines rather than the swords."*

That was good feedback. If Ashlock wanted to become the greatest tree swordsman—well, he likely already was, but if he wanted to become the best swordsman in the realm—he would need to work on his technique some more.

"What if I used telekinesis to control shields that orbit the vines to protect them?" Ashlock mused. He did coat the vines in spatial Qi, but unlike earth or void Qi, spatial Qi wasn't that great for defense. Or was it…

Ashlock looked around at the distorted space barrier that surrounded him. Raw spatial Qi might not be the best for defense, but what if he put a bit more intent behind the spatial Qi other than simply coating and protecting the vine?

"Distortion or making the space around the vines appear further than it looks could work," Ashlock wondered as he flexed his spatial-coated vine wrapped around a sword. "Oh, wait, I have an even better idea."

Ashlock requested Stella try and fight again, but she rolled her eyes. *"Give me a while to recover. My Qi reserves are almost empty. It won't take long as a lot of spatial Qi is floating around here."*

She then entered a meditation pose, and Ashlock saw the spatial Qi gathered by the runic formation pouring toward her. While she recovered, he spent more time working on his new plan.

Stella's eyes snapped open as she felt that the Qi within her Soul Core had reached a sufficient level to continue the duel.

Getting out of the lotus position and standing up, she stretched her back while glancing around at the surroundings. The way everything seemed frozen gave her a headache. Even the distant clouds hadn't changed position since morning, the sun overhead had paused, but the sunlight's source had moved, casting shadows that didn't make sense.

She tried to pierce the illusion, but even though she had spatial affinity, she could not see through it. Shrugging, she injected some Qi into her spatial ring and felt the cold metal hilt against her fingers and the weight of her new sword.

A thin smile appeared as she approached the waving black vines with the sword resting on her shoulder. "All right, Tree, what are we doing this time?"

Glancing over her shoulder, she waited momentarily, and as she expected, ancient words were inscribed in flickering flames on Ash's black trunk. She quickly translated the words and tilted her head. "You just want me to try and cut the vines?" Her eyes narrowed. Clearly, something was amiss here. Was Ash trying something new?

"Fine." She grinned and got into position, her Soul Core humming in her chest as she mobilized her spatial Qi and techniques she had cultivated an understanding with heaven for at the tip of her tongue, ready to be unleashed at a moment's notice.

Observing the black vines maintaining a careful distance, Stella resolved to seize the chance. A brief surge of spatial Qi enveloped her form, causing her surroundings to blur. She employed a portion of her lightning dao comprehension to amplify the effect, making her legs propel her faster.

Within a single breath, she had closed the distance. Her sword was already mid-swing, and she laughed as she watched it cleave through the vine—except it passed right through as if it was a mere illusion.

Her eyes widened as she was suddenly struck by a heavy, fast-moving object. As her breath was abruptly forced from her lungs, Stella hurtled through the air, pain searing through her side and confusion gripping her mind. How had her sword failed to strike its target?

As she got back on her feet and launched another attack, a similar situation occurred with a different vine. It appeared to be trying to dodge to one side, but she felt no resistance, as if she was cutting air, and then from her blind spot, the real vine hit her.

"I think I see what you are doing here." Stella spat blood to the side and searched one of her spatial rings for a healing pill. Locating the appropriate bottle, she chugged three of them and then wiped the residual blood from her mouth.

Glancing aside, she noted Larry observing her with what seemed like a sorrowful expression. However, it was always challenging to decipher the behemoth's thoughts due to his inhuman features.

"Mistress, is the Master bullying you?" the spider questioned, seemingly detecting her glance.

With a savage grin, Stella shook her head. "No, it's quite all right, Larry. I think I have figured out his little trick, and how am I supposed to get stronger without a little hardship?"

"Why are humans so weird?" Larry muttered, and Stella almost failed to translate it due to his accent.

Deciding to ignore the confused spider, she reignited her sword with her soul fire and dashed in. However, this time she had her eyes closed. She then cycled her meditation technique to connect with heaven and forced her will upon the spatial plane, a vital part of any spatial-cultivator power.

Whenever she wished to cast a portal, she had to consult with the spatial plane connecting all things. In this weird space where only the definitive position of everything mattered, Stella could see the vine in front of her coming from the left side. Opening one of her eyes, she could see in reality that the vine was coming from the right.

"A spatial illusion," Stella muttered as she closed her eye again and went purely by the spatial plane. With a swift slice to the left, she felt the familiar resistance of the thick vine to her blade, but she carved through with the help of her Qi-empowered muscles.

Laughing, she kept her eyes closed and meticulously cut the remaining vines in half. Only when the last of the vines toppled over with a thump did she whip her body around to face Ash and open her eyes to witness the scene.

Eight wiggling vine stumps were next to floating swords, and she could also spot the cleaved-off parts of black vine staying motionless on the stone ground.

Somehow feeling Tree's gaze on her, she felt prompted to provide her assessment of his new technique.

"A massive step up in difficultly compared to last time, and I think those without absolute detecting techniques would struggle." Stella caressed her chin as she watched the vines regrow and grasp the waiting floating swords. "Diana could handle this trick with her mist, but Douglas would struggle as the deception happens above ground."

Stella put her hands behind her head and strolled back over to the bench.

Knowing that even Tree had to practice new techniques and she could help him put a smile on her face. Sitting on the bench and closing her eyes to enjoy the distorted space, she felt the faint whispers of enlightenment caress the back of her mind.

With a surge of excitement, she got into the lotus position and began cultivating. It seemed she had come to a deeper understanding regarding the spatial dao during that duel with Ash, and the heavens wanted to impart new knowledge upon her. Depending on how much it wished to share, she might be able to begin forming her Star Core soon.

While Stella was busy cultivating again, Ashlock retracted his {Consuming Abyss} skill as maintaining those vines and coating them in spatial Qi was draining his resources that he could be giving to the demonic trees surrounding him or contributing to his Star Core Qi reserves.

"Master, I believe your pet wishes your presence," Larry quietly said as he crawled toward him, clearly careful about interrupting Stella's cultivation again.

Kaida wanted him? What for?

Larry raised a limb to his horn, and the tiny black snake reluctantly slithered off the horn and nestled onto the tip of Larry's leg. The spider then raised his leg up, and the moment it came into contact with his trunk, Kaida stuck his tongue out.

[Kaida has accumulated enough Qi to evolve from F to D grade]
[Grass Snake {Kaida} wishes to evolve]
[Yes/No]

"Oh, nice!" Ashlock exclaimed while reading the notification that popped up. It would appear Larry's hunting with Kaida had been a great success and helped the snake level up.

"Wait…to D-grade? What the hell has Larry fed Kaida to give him enough Qi to evolve straight to D-grade?" Ashlock grumbled to himself.

How that had been done, he wasn't sure, but he wasn't one to complain about results, so he rolled with it.

In a way, it did make some sense. An F-grade grass snake was unlikely to ever taste the meat of high-grade spirit beasts that Larry could comfortably hunt and feed him.

Obviously, he replied yes to the system prompt.

[Infant Grass Snake {Kaida} has begun to evolve]
[Please select {Kaida} evolution path…]

While he waited for the system to load, Ashlock was excited to see the potential evolution paths.

Would it just give him a single option? Or would there be a long list for him to choose from? Kaida was going straight from F- to D-grade, so he at least expected some interesting options.

[Infant Shadow Scale Serpent]
A stealthy serpent that can blend perfectly with the shadows. Its scales have evolved to absorb light, providing excellent camouflage.

"Interesting, so does this mean Kaida will have shadow affinity or illusion affinity?" Ashlock mused. He also noted the infant part of the name, suggesting that infants of this snake bloodline started at D-grade.

[Obsidian Terra Constrictor]

Kaida grows in size and strength, becoming a powerful constrictor with scales as hard as obsidian. This evolution greatly boosts his physical strength and defense.

"Noticing a lack of the infant tag with this option. Therefore it is likely a rather late-stage evolution meaning this evolution might even cap out at below S-rank," Ashlock mused.

By the name of the evolution, he could assume this option would give Kaida earth affinity, which could help him out a lot with digging out the mountain or invading the depths.

[Infant Spirit Whisperer Adder]
A mystic serpent that can commune with spirits and even sway them to its will. This would give him a unique power in both offensive and defensive encounters.

"This option is just weird. How am I supposed to know how strong a power like this could even be?" Ashlock hadn't encountered anyone with spirit powers thus far, leaving him uninformed of its potential.

[Infant Moonlight Asp]
This snake's scales radiate soft moonlight, giving it the ability to manipulate illusions and cast confusing mirages.

"Moonlight affinity sounds like it could lead to a higher affinity in the future like celestial or lunar affinity," Ashlock concluded but then ran into another issue. He knew nothing about either affinity, making it hard to decide if this was a good option.

[Infant Ink Serpent]
Kaida evolves into a snake with a body as dark and fluid as ink. His speed increases significantly, and he gains the ability to camouflage in dark environments.

"Ink?" Ashlock wondered to himself. "Does this evolution option give Kaida ink affinity?" Another unusual affinity he wasn't sure about. Why had Larry's evolution options been so much easier than Kaida's?

Was it because this was an earlier choice that would set up later evolutions?

"All right, basically all of these options mention 'infant,' and they also have random snake species names rather than referring to mythical snake-based creatures like Nagas, Dragons, Leviathans, Basilisks, Ouroboros, and more. Therefore, this evolution option is more focused on what affinity Kaida will have, rather than what species he will end up as," Ashlock concluded, but then that raised the question.

Which affinity should he choose for little Kai?

Ashlock looked over the options one last time and noted the various affinities: ink, moonlight, spirit, earth, shadow. They all seemed to have positives and negatives.

20
TENDRILS OF THE VOID

Ashlock wanted to ask Stella or Diana's opinion regarding Kaida's evolution, but one was deep in meditation, and the other was missing from the mountain peak.

"Larry, do you know anything about these options..." Ashlock then read out all of the evolution options through their black Qi tether.

There was a long pause before Larry quietly replied, *"Master, my apologies, but the realm I came from was a place of eternal darkness, fire, and ash. So I lack the insight into many of these affinities, but I would advise against shadow."*

"Oh? What's wrong with shadow?" Ashlock asked, interested in the spider's knowledge.

"Shadow is one of the weaker affinities, and I never struggled against any monsters with such an affinity back in my realm. They relied too heavily on stealth and deception, so when it came to actually fighting, they often lost." Larry snorted. *"They were easy food."*

Ashlock agreed with Larry's reasoning. Out of the options, the Infant Shadow Scale Serpent seemed the weakest alongside the Obsidian Terra Constrictor simply because it lacked the infant tag, suggesting it was an adult at D-grade.

In the wild, where seeing the sunrise was no guarantee, it would make sense for Kaida to subconsciously choose an evolution path that let him be strong now but stunt his future potential.

But Ashlock could power-level Kaida with the help of Larry or the girls, so he wanted to pick the evolution choice that would let him scale the best.

So with those two options off the table, Ashlock was left to pick between spirit, moonlight, and ink affinity.

"With how much death occurs around here, I'm sure there would be plenty of spirits for Kaida to command," Ashlock mused as he looked at the [Infant Spirit Whisperer Adder]. Oddly the part of the description regarding this evolution that turned him off from picking it was that spirit magic was supposedly versatile enough to be useful for both offense and defense.

In Ashlock's opinion, this world was too brutal and unforgiving for someone to consider themselves an all-rounder. "It's far better to specialize in one area, especially because Kaida is part of a sect that can complement his strengths and weaknesses."

Next was moonlight affinity, which Ashlock could also ignore because picking an affinity that was strongest during the night seemed counter-intuitive. He had seen how important it was to have access to an affinity's Qi at all times, so to limit Kaida to only being useful at night was a bad idea.

That left a single, unknown, and possibly foolish option.

Ink affinity.

[Infant Ink Serpent]
Kaida evolves into a snake with a body as dark and fluid as ink. His speed increases significantly, and he gains the ability to camouflage in dark environments.

Its description left a lot to be desired, seemingly giving him the same useless abilities that shadow affinity would provide. But Ashlock could see the future potential. Kaida was only D-grade right now, but in the distant future, he could imagine an S-rank Kaida with some evolved form of ink affinity.

"Worst case, I can use him to transcribe my words to paper." Ashlock chuckled at the idea of the little noodle using his head to write out his profound words.

Ashlock reviewed the options one last time, but the Infant Ink Serpent felt like the best option.

[Evolution path {Infant Ink Serpent} chosen, evolution initiating...]

Kaida's skin became coated in a dark sheen of Qi that matched his obsidian scales. Larry left the snake to rest on one of Ashlock's branches and then crawled backward.

"Master, what should I do now?" Larry asked, and Ashlock contemplated his options.

If he sent Larry away to hunt, he would regret not keeping him close by if another problem like the Voidmind Elder arose. Larry was supposed to be his guardian, so sending him off was potentially foolish, but if he kept the spider around at all times, that would stall his growth.

"Either stay here or hunt nearby if you are still hungry," Ashlock replied after a while. "Once Kaida has finished his evolution, I might send you two out hunting again. I want Kaida to become strong quickly."

"As you wish, my Master." Larry decided to crawl up his trunk and perch himself among his branches. *"I will rest up here then until my servitude is required."*

With some peace and quiet, Ashlock decided to delve back into his inventory and examine his new items some more. "Once Stella wakes up, maybe I should test the void form of my new {Consuming Abyss} skill," Ashlock decided and busied himself as time passed.

Stella's eyes snapped open, and she let out a Qi-filled breath. Her mind buzzed with enlightenment, and she felt only a half-step away from forming her Star Core.

She would try to form it immediately as the surroundings were dense in spatial Qi, but she yearned for the rich spatial Qi environment of the pocket realm Ash had sent her to in the past.

Looking around, Stella felt unnerved. "No way it's still midday..."

Even though she had been in the trance of meditation, the stiffness in her legs and lower back suggested at least a few hours had passed, yet once again, reality lied to her due to Ash's new spatial illusion.

That was part of the heaven-gifted enlightenment she had just experienced. Closing her eyes in accordance with the teachings, she smiled as her surroundings turned into an absolute reality that told no lies.

In this spatial plane of augmented reality, she could see past Ash's spatial illusion that seemed to freeze time. By the sun's now-correct position in the sky, it was late in the afternoon.

Keeping her eyes closed and glancing around the spatial plane, Stella realized just how massive Ash truly was. The spatial plane was divided up into layers in all directions. She took up a single layer. Meanwhile, Ash's canopy extended many layers upward into the sky, and his roots burrowed through the mountain for even more.

Actually, everywhere she looked, Ash's overwhelming presence was there, his canopy lording overhead, and his roots went through the mountain, under the demonic trees, and even extending out into the wilderness.

With her eyes closed while standing on the edge of the mountain peak, she watched Ash's roots sprawling out for many miles in all directions in awe when she saw a sudden pulse of spatial Qi travel down one of the larger roots leading out into the wilderness.

"Did Ash find something?" Stella murmured to herself. But she soon found her answer when she detected another pulse of spatial Qi behind her, right in front of Ash.

In reality, the spatial Qi formed a typical spatial rift. But in the spatial plane, Stella gasped as she saw just how much power Ash wielded. He bent and compressed thousands of layers of reality to make that long-range portal possible.

Then all of the compressed layers of reality sprung back to their previous fixed locations as the rift behind her snapped closed, accompanied by a pop of air and a bestial roar.

As the buzz of enlightenment faded and fear overtook her mind, the spatial plane collapsed, and Stella was returned to reality.

Spinning round, she watched as a demonic beast she estimated to be around the middle of the Soul Fire Realm reared its ugly, mutated head. Stella had never seen this specific type of beast before, but with its hulking form and black fur, it was reminiscent of a bear.

The beast didn't even look her way. Instead, it focused entirely on a floating ball of Qi surrounding a leaf. It furiously tried to swat the leaf and get its maw around it.

Whatever Ash had done to make the beast so angry to bait it through the rift, Stella hoped he had the plan to deal with it.

"What the…" Stella mumbled while stumbling back. Her eyes

widened as a lake of pure darkness that she suspected was void Qi spread out from Ash toward the beast.

Then before the beast could even react, tendrils of void shot out from the spreading void and went straight through the bear. It looked down in confusion at the holes that riddled its body. It then opened its mouth to cry, but there were no lungs to create anything but a pathetic wheeze. It glanced around in desperation, but moments later, its eyes rolled into the back of its head, and it tumbled over.

Stella's hands felt clammy, and her heart pounded in her chest. Since when could Tree use void Qi? Had the Voidmind Elder's soul somehow corrupted or overtaken Tree from within?

She bit her lip as she tiptoed closer to the tree surrounded by a lake of void Qi. She knew that if the Voidmind Elder had overtaken Ash's soul, then her chance of survival was low, even with her speed.

She could run fast and far, but Ash's roots spread out in all directions and could attack her through portals. Her eyes darted to Larry, who seemed to be watching from this side calmly. Was he also being mind-controlled by the Voidmind Elder, or was Ash still in control?

While the corpse lay in a pool of black blood, a portal formed overhead, and the void tendrils attempted to shoot through the newly formed rift, but the rift shattered on contact in an explosion of spatial Qi, as if the void Qi had punched through to the other side.

The void tendrils fizzled out of existence, and the void lake faded away. Then, through cracks in the stone at the sides of the runic formation that Stella had meticulously constructed, many thick black vines coated in spikes shot up and lunged toward the hole-riddled corpse.

Bones cracking filled the courtyard, and Stella marveled at how quickly the vines devoured the large beast. Within a few breaths, they retreated into the ground, leaving bloodstains and tuffs of black fur littering the ground.

Stella's eyes wandered to Ash, and she saw lilac flames begin to take the form of words.

'Good evening, Stella. How was your meditation?' Ashlock wrote out. He had waited until she'd finished her cultivation to quickly test his new void skill as he didn't want to accidentally ruin her enlightenment again.

Luckily, it had been worth the wait, as the results pleasantly surprised him.

The void tendrils had moved at speeds incomparable to his black vines and completely ignored the beast's Qi-coated fur and punched through it like a steel lance to a sheet of paper.

However, if he was to coat his black vines with spatial Qi, he was sure he could achieve a similar result, especially with the spike the vines now had on the end, which was perfect for impaling things.

"The only bad part is that the void tendrils can't go through portals as the void Qi seems to delete spatial Qi, but I had been suspecting that from the beginning." Ashlock sighed. Thankfully, his new-and-improved black vines could still go through portals, but his void tendrils would remain as a trump card he could unleash when enemies were near his trunk.

"My meditation? It was fine…" Stella replied awkwardly as she seemed unwilling to approach. Had his void Qi scared her for some reason?

'Good to hear,' Ashlock wrote, following it up with, 'I waited until you finished meditating before testing my new void Qi technique I stole from the Voidmind Elder.'

Stella nodded. *"Oh, I see. So can you use void Qi all the time now?"*

'No. I only know this one technique, and I need to consume monsters or people to fuel its use,' Ashlock replied through writing.

Stella translated it, and the awkwardness seemed to fade away. *"Well, that's great! Void Qi abilities are a nightmare to deal with, so they are good to learn if you have the capabilities."* She then stepped a little closer. *"Say, Tree, when will you be able to send me to that pocket realm again?"*

That was a good question. Luckily, his system had a timer that he could use to answer such a question.

At the top of his skill list that he summoned with a simple thought was:

|Skills…|
{Mystic Realm [S]} [Locked until day: 3515]

"Now let me check my sign-in system." Another system screen appeared.

> **Idletree Daily Sign-In System**
> **Day: 3510**
> **Daily Credit: 9**
> **Sacrifice Credit: 5**
> **[Sign in?]**

Doing the quick math, Ashlock deduced that it would become available in five days. Relaying that information to Stella, she nodded.

"I see… Will there be any more truffles available by then? I feel at the edge of ascending to the Star Core Realm, and so long as someone protects me in the pocket realm, I believe that I can ascend."

Ashlock realized he had been slacking on the truffle production with all the crazy stuff happening over the last week. So quickly opening the production menu, he set a few more to grow and gawked at the three-day production time. "So fast? And the Qi requirements seem negligible now."

He flashed his Qi once to answer Stella's question regarding the truffles, and she grinned. *"Perfect. With the truffles that purified my spiritual root and undid all the awful cultivation practices I had done throughout my life, I now feel fully confident about forming my Star Core since my foundation is far better now."*

This was fantastic news. A new Star Core Realm person within his sect would significantly increase their fighting potential and give Ashlock more peace of mind sending Stella out on missions or meetings outside of his sphere of influence.

'Sounds great. You must be excited,' Ashlock wrote, and Stella grinned.

"It's every cultivator's dream to form their own Star Core, so of course I am ecstatic!" She then mumbled under her breath, *"And I will be more useful for you…"*

Ashlock pretended he hadn't heard that last part as he was half-focused on the presence he felt coming up the mountain.

Douglas rolled his shoulders as he trudged up the side of the mountain.

He could try and swim through the rock by using an earth-affinity movement technique to reach the peak faster, but a quick glance around at the thousands of demonic trees taking root into the mountain turned him off that idea. He didn't want to try and weave through the dense network of tree roots prevalent throughout the mountain, nor did he feel in the mood to use Qi.

His Soul Core was nearly empty due to finally finishing his work. However, there was a slight anger tugging at the edge of his mind, as his work had been made ten times harder when the Patriarch of the Ashfallen Sect had suddenly stopped helping to move the demonic trees around and left it all to him and the other earth cultivators.

He had been unsure what to do but was still hounded by the city folk to remove the trees blocking the streets. So they had uprooted them and piled up all the trees within the Academy's training grounds.

Now, with all those trees dealt with, he had decided to return to the Ashfallen Sect to see what had happened. Reaching the peak, he furrowed his brows at what he saw. From afar, it had looked a little off, but up close, he could see Stella sitting on the bench, frozen in an odd position as if she was in the middle of getting up from her seat.

The giant tree was also motionless, the leaves mid-sway in a midday breeze that was long gone. Only the cool air of evening was still present.

With a deep frown, he slowly reached out with a Qi-coated finger. Soon enough, he felt it pass through a dense wall of Qi, and he couldn't see the end of his finger anymore, as if it had disappeared.

Distraught, he reeled his hand back and breathed a sigh of relief to see his finger still there. "How bizarre," Douglas muttered as he reached out again—this time putting his whole hand through and then his arm. Eventually, he shrugged and pushed his entire body through the wall of Qi.

It almost made him shriek how everything had changed from what he had seen seconds ago. Stella suddenly stood only a few steps away, looking at him with her arms crossed under her chest.

The giant spider had also seemingly teleported and now nestled between the tree's branches. Whenever Douglas saw that monster, he felt a shiver down his spine.

"Welcome back," Stella said with a fake smile. "You came back just in time. We have some urgent work for you."

Douglas felt exhaustion consume his body, so he replied with the least enthusiasm possible. "And what would that be?"

"To turn the mine down below into an alchemist workshop," Stella replied nonchalantly as she wandered off. "Feel free to get some rest first if you need it, but I suspect the Silverspires will be taking Diana's offer any day now, so it's best we get that sorted out first."

"Funny you say that." Douglas chuckled while trudging over to the personal runic formation. "A Redclaw approached me and requested that I inform someone from the Ashfallen Sect that they wish to meet with you tomorrow."

Douglas hid his grin as he collapsed on the runic formation and tried to ignore Stella's cursing while he meditated.

21
(INTERLUDE) DEMON OF THE MIST

Elenor Evergreen tried to calm her raging emotions as she looked out the pristine glass window, although there wasn't much to see of the vast valley or Darklight City in the distance due to the constant rising smog from the forges at the foot of Slymere City.

In the slight reflection of the glass, she could glimpse the haunted complexion that stared back at her, reminding her of the torment she had faced over the last month or so.

How foolish had she been to not foresee the betrayal of the Patriarch? Everyone in the family knew he'd permitted them to eliminate the Ravenborne family due to their Grand Elder stepping into the Nascent Soul Realm. So what's to say he wouldn't then betray them?

Her hands clenched at her sides. She had traveled to the Nightrose City to tell the Patriarch about her family's downfall, but she was told he wouldn't emerge from his closed-door cultivation. She tried to explain the threat that had befallen Darklight City, but they didn't seem to care, laughing off her claims as those of a lunatic.

"Why should we care about a backwater mining town?" the guard had declared while sneering at her. The humiliation had been so great she had fled and spent a week or two aimlessly wandering the streets.

Eventually, she decided to return to Darklight City to see how the situation had evolved, but an idea entered her mind while on the airship. Why not ask the Voidmind family of Slymere City for help? They should be delighted to learn that Darklight City was without management, and maybe she should convince them to overtake the city.

Just the idea of Tristan Evergreen and Stella Crestfallen ruling over that city together made her skin crawl. Why did they get all the good things in life?

"Elenor Evergreen?"

"Y-yes, that's me." Elenor turned to examine the source of the voice and found a plain-looking woman wearing far too much lavish jewelry that weighed down her ears. She also had brown eyes that seemed to shift to pure black as she examined her.

From the shifting eyes alone, Elenor suspected the woman was a descendent of the Voidmind family, but likely from a side branch as she didn't have all the features that made them famous.

"Perfect, so I found the right person." The woman breathed a sigh of relief as she glanced down at the parchment in her hands. "So just to recap your claims one last time... You say that Darklight City, managed by the Ravenborne family for many decades, has changed ownership to a joint force of the Evergreens and Winterwraths?"

"That's correct," Elenor replied, "although there should be some more—"

"I was getting to that," the woman curtly replied, silencing Elenor. "You also claim that Tristan Evergreen, someone from your family who has somehow recently ascended to the Star Core Realm, teamed up with another girl called Stella Crestfallen—who also somehow ascended to the Star Core Realm—and together they wiped out your family?"

Elenor had to admit that it sounded ridiculous when read in such a suspicious tone. Star Core Realm cultivators were often the Grand Elders of a family or at least a high-ranking Elder. To suggest that two seemingly unknown individuals had ascended simultaneously and then teamed up to wipe out two established noble families sounded farfetched even to her.

"There's a lot more to the story," Elenor quickly said. "For example, the demon with a claw the size of a hallway that crushed and killed the Winterwrath Grand Elder!"

Elenor stopped speaking when she saw the Voidmind woman's judgmental glare.

"Do understand—the only reason we are entertaining your nonsense is because we received some weird reports regarding Darklight City lately." The woman let out a deep sigh seeing Elenor's expectant expression. "Something about a tree infestation and the sky opening up."

Elenor furiously nodded and took a step forward. "Yes, yes! The sky opened, and ash descended upon Red Vine Peak! It was followed by a presence that matched that of the Patriarch!"

The woman snorted. "Have you ever met the Patriarch? I find that hard to believe." She then waved Elenor's protests off as she noted something on the parchment with a quill dipped in ink. "So a giant demon that can crush an elder and ash was coming from the sky…"

Elenor gritted her teeth. She really didn't appreciate the woman's condescending tone.

The woman turned on her heel and began to walk toward two large obsidian doors at the end of the corridor, her shoes tapping on the white marble floor.

She then briefly stopped and snorted while looking out the window toward where Darklight City should be through the smoke. "It sure sounds like you have seen and been through a lot. Which all happened over a month ago? I wonder when these hallway-size demons will make their way over here? They are rather slow, don't you think?"

Elenor barely stopped herself from rolling her eyes at the sarcasm dripping from every word.

The plain-faced woman pouted at her lack of reaction and continued walking toward the doors, waving for her to follow. "You can spout your nonsense to the Grand Elder. He just emerged from closed-door cultivation and is willing to humor you."

Elenor's eyes burned into the woman's back, and she ground her teeth but somehow managed to keep her cool as she followed a few steps behind. Despite being at the peak of the Soul Fire Realm, she had to swallow her broken pride for now as she didn't have a family backing and had been stuck at the bottleneck for Star Core for far too long.

However, she was somewhat surprised that the Voidmind Grand Elder was willing to see her, so even with the humiliation, this was a good result.

Elenor stood within a room of liquid darkness. Only her spirit sight gave her any hope of perceiving anything within. Elenor had no idea how they had created a pocket of void to cultivate within, but the void Qi prevalent throughout the room was suffocating.

"I have already been informed of your claims, scion of Evergreen." A tall, thin man who appeared to be made of the void spoke with a chill in his tone. "My question to you is why here and now?"

"Pardon?" Elenor replied, unable to decipher the man's words.

The Voidmind Grand Elder patiently responded, his voice's chill becoming even more piercing, "You claim these events occurred over a month ago? I find almost all of them hard to believe."

"I understand they are hard to believe," Elenor retorted, "but you have to believe me! You ask why here and now? I went straight to the Nightrose family because of how serious the situation was, but they refused to believe me. Do you think I am so foolish to try and lie to the Nightrose family? Just send a single person to ask the locals of Darklight City or check on Red Vine Peak."

"Hmm..." The Voidmind Elder shifted through the liquid void and came a step closer, looming over her. "And what do you believe we have to gain out of this?"

Elenor gulped at the overwhelming presence. "You are a half step into the Nascent Soul Realm, right? Defeating two Star Core Realm cultivators should be effortless, and then Darklight City is yours for the taking. There shouldn't be a family managing the city right now."

There was a long silence that made Elenor wonder if she had said anything wrong, but eventually, the Voidmind Grand Elder spoke his thoughts.

"I never bothered with Darklight City as mining has never been our interest, and that old bastard of the Ravenborne family was a tricky foe to deal with, but if what you say about his demise is true..." Elenor swore she saw the void grin at her. "Then expanding Slymere's influence couldn't hurt. Although you are either misinformed or lying."

Elenor felt her heart stop beating in her chest. How had she lied?

"The Redclaws now reside in Darklight City as they invited us to participate in an alchemy tournament they are hosting, but I assumed they were working alongside the Ravenborne family..."

The void shifted again, and the Grand Elder's spatial ring, obscured by the liquid darkness of the room, glowed with silver light, and a jade talisman appeared in his hand. "I do not need to send a scout as my elder brother should still reside in Darklight City's Academy. I find it unlikely he would never contact me regarding the affairs you have mentioned, but that man has a dangerous tendency to ignore his surroundings in favor of research."

Elenor waited in anticipation as the jade lit up with a pale green light and then, after a while, dimmed. The communication had failed.

"Strange," the Voidmind Grand Elder muttered. His voice took on a strange, distorted tone. "He usually responds no matter how engrossed in research he is."

Elenor felt a wave of dread and excitement wash over her. If the Voidmind Elder, that acted as the librarian for the Darklight Academy, was to refute her words, she wouldn't be surprised if the Voidmind Grand Elder killed her and stole her cultivation for wasting a single second of his precious time.

"I should have a communication jade for his assistant somewhere here."

Elenor saw a flash of silver from another void-coated finger, and another jade appeared. He inserted some of his Qi, and the jade lit up just like the last one and maintained its brightness, signifying a connection.

"Elaine, are you there?" the Voidmind Elder questioned.

Elaine drummed her fingers on the large wooden desk that took up much of her study. Her head rested on her propped-up arm as she gazed out the window at the scarlet leaves of the demonic tree sprouting up in the garden.

It was late evening, and the Elder had yet to return from his investigation of the rifts. Which was fine, as it gave Elaine some peace and quiet from his constant mutterings about this and that. He was an odd man to deal with.

Her tired eyes drifted from the window and back to the parchments with freshly scribed measurements meticulously transcribed from her apparatus readings. A long sigh escaped her lips as she glared at the numbers and observations that made no sense.

How a demonic tree could alter its biology overnight was a cause for concern, but she needed the Elder's expertise to decipher the cryptic readings she had collected.

"If we can somehow figure out how they did it, maybe we can alter their biology to start producing cultivation resources." Elaine took off her thick glasses, laid her head on the table, and continued looking out the window.

It was a long shot, but maybe they would finally give her the resources she needed to cultivate if only she could discover something that could benefit the Voidmind family tremendously.

She may have been born a genius in research, but what was the point if she died in a thousand years? The Elder had spent centuries on individual problems. Was there any point if she only had a few hundred years to live due to her lack of progress in pursuing immortality?

Elaine breathed in and felt the Qi cycle through her body, only to sigh again as she felt how little she absorbed. The purity of her spirit root was so pathetic that she had been told that the cost of her cultivation journey wasn't worth it. Even at twenty-five, she was stuck at the first stage of the Soul Fire Realm.

Grumbling to herself, she sat up to escape her spiraling thoughts and leaned back in the chair, tapping the end of her quill on her chin as she hummed.

"Elaine, are you there?"

She almost fell backward as a cold voice filled the room.

Quickly opening a side drawer and retrieving the glowing jade talisman, she inserted some Qi and calmed her breathing before replying, "Greetings, Grand Elder."

"As formal as always, I see. You should be more friendly with your father."

Elaine's face scrunched up at the endearing words in such a cold tone. If her father really loved her so much, why deprive her of cultivation resources just because it was a bad investment? At this rate, the old man would outlive her, and she would just be another one of his many children that he forgets about with time.

"Forgive me," Elaine replied. "What is the reason for your call?"

"Your uncle didn't respond. Do you know where he is?"

Elaine rolled her eyes. Of course, he hadn't called to ask about her. Why would he? "Uncle went to investigate something through a rift."

"A rift, you say?" There was a brief pause, and Elaine heard her father move away from the jade and discuss something with someone else. While waiting for a reply, she looked out the window but couldn't see the demonic tree anymore because the window was fogged up.

"That's odd," Elaine muttered as she glanced around the room and realized the whole room was filling with a dense mist. She gulped back her fear as she knew this mist was entirely unnatural.

"Father—" Elaine urgently said into the jade talisman, her fingers going white from gripping it so hard. "Are you there? Father—"

"Silence."

Elaine felt the words die in her throat as a figure appeared from the mist. She was a short woman with black hair, but her features were obscured by a white mask that glowed with demonic Qi.

How a cultivator could wield demonic Qi, Elaine had no idea. Was she facing a demon from the lower realm disguised as a human?

"If you want to live, do as I say." The words tickled the inside of her ear, and she deduced it was Qi-empowered speech being carried through the mist. "Don't make me regret leaving you alive until now."

Elaine's mind raced for a solution. A water-affinity assassin that was potentially a demon was in her room. She was a first-stage Soul Fire Realm cultivator and, although she had one of the strongest affinities, void. She didn't know many techniques, nor was she well-versed in combat.

She did have some life-saving artifacts, but she had been negligent and wasn't wearing them, as the Elder was usually right by her side to protect her.

Reluctantly she nodded very slowly toward the masked woman in the mist.

The Voidmind Grand Elder's words through the jade startled her. "So your uncle went through a rift? That might explain why my jade talisman can't reach him. Elaine, do you know the purpose of the rift?"

"Say no," the voice of the mist insisted.

"No…" Elaine sheepishly replied to her father.

"Hmm…have you heard anything about large demons killing Star Core cultivators, the heavens opening up and pouring ash down onto Red Vine Peak, or perhaps about the elimination of the Evergreen family?"

"Tell him you have heard nothing."

Elaine's throat felt dry, and her hand was trembling. "N-no, Father, I have stayed inside with Uncle all day."

"Elaine, you should go outside more." There was a long sigh, and Elaine hated how casual her father's voice was compared to her situation. "Your uncle is a bad influence on you."

Terrified of answering her father's small talk without being given permission by the demon of the mist, Elaine remained silent.

"Well, good talk as always, Elaine. I will be sending your brother to participate in the ridiculous alchemy tournament those Redclaws are putting on, so make sure to spend some time away from your crazy uncle and show your brother around Darklight City."

Elaine could feel the end of the conversation coming and began to panic. "Why not come right now to see me—" She yelped as the demon of the mist vanished from the corner of the room, and she felt cold metal digging into her neck, drawing a thin line of warm blood that trickled down her neck.

"End the conversation right now," the demon hissed in her ear.

"Haha, I'm far too busy for that Elaine." Her father's voice made her sick to her stomach. Couldn't he tell she had been acting weird? Why couldn't he tell she was in danger? "I can send someone to look after you while your uncle is away investigating that rift, though? It sounds like some weird things are occurring over there, even if you haven't noticed them."

Elaine opened her mouth to reply but felt the cold metal dagger dig a little deeper. "Say you have no need."

"No, Father, I'm quite…all right," Elaine stuttered, tears forming in her eyes. "I have to go now. Goodbye."

"All right, daughter, see you soon." The jade talisman's pale green light dimmed, and Elaine felt all hope drift away.

"What a mess you have caused me." The demon sighed. *"You just had to pick up the call. How unfortunate."*

"Please don't kill me," she whispered, the dagger digging a little deeper as she spoke.

"That's not for me to decide," the demon said, and Elaine felt a powerful blow to the back of her head, making her vision fade to black as she fell unconscious.

22
CRAZY DEMONIC CULTISTS

"Who is this?"

"I believe her name was Elaine?"

Elaine could hear distant voices that echoed as if they were in a large, open space. Her head was pounding, and her mouth was parched as if she had spent days without water.

"But why is she down here? I thought I was supposed to be making an alchemy lab?"

Elaine opened her eyes to a dark cavern illuminated with glowing mushrooms that grew from the cracks in the ceiling.

In the distance, she could make out two blurry figures conversing at the far end of the cavern. A large man faced away from her, a black cloak obscuring his bulky figure. A tall, blond-haired woman stood beside him, facing her. The woman wore a black mask similar to that of the mist demon.

She felt her heart sink in her chest. Had she been captured by cultists? They were crazy people in demonic sects that used human sacrifice to fuel their cultivation.

"Apparently, she is a researcher of some kind," the blond woman informed the man. "Sigh, what a headache. Like I said, we should have just killed her from the start."

Elaine felt a shiver run down her spine, and the cold rock digging into her back felt even more hostile than moments ago. Her eyes darted to locate the source of a breeze she sensed and felt a glimmer of hope by the open passage leading outside. Through the long tunnel, she could see the tops of demonic trees.

Should she run?

Her hands clenched against the cold stone of the cavern. Would she even make it two steps from the tunnel before one of those cultists stabbed a knife in her back?

"Whatever, I have things to do," the blond woman said, turning to leave through a mineshaft. "Just make something basic to show the Silverspires."

"How long do we have?"

"Till they accept our deal? You should have until tomorrow as Diana is in talks with them right now."

A long sigh escaped the large man as he surveyed the barren cavern devoid of anything except a slow-moving stream through its center. His swooping gaze, hidden behind a mask, landed on Elaine, and she panicked, fearing he had caught her eavesdropping.

"Oh hey, she is awake," the man called after the blond woman, but she was already gone. "...Whatever."

Elaine squirmed up against the rock that cut into her back as the hulking man donning a pitch-black cloak and mask advanced toward her. Her eyes darted between her two escape routes; the mineshaft past the man, which seemingly led deeper into the cultist's lair, and the large tunnel to the outside world.

Deciding to take no chances, she lunged forward, breaking into a staggered sprint toward the tunnel leading outside. Her pathetic cultivation cycled through her spiritual roots as her legs burned with power.

Void fire enshrouded her fists as she prepared to fend off the black-cloaked man, but he seemed entirely unbothered by her escape, simply watching her leave with apparent amusement.

Deciding to ignore his odd behavior for a demonic cultist that likely wanted to consume her flesh to advance his cultivation, Elaine charged on ahead without looking back.

The tunnel blurred around her as she dashed with as much speed as she could muster—her entire view became consumed with sunlight, the cloudless sky, and the tips of demonic trees.

She was so close—something surged up from the floor and blocked the exit. It looked like a translucent slime that distorted the light, but it was also filled with black roots. Unperturbed by this obstacle, Elaine reeled back her fist coated in her soul fire and punched forward alongside all her velocity.

There was a brief moment of triumph as the slime recoiled backward from her force, but her face fell as she felt it resist the rest of her force and then rebounded, pushing her back with such power that she was sent flying and tumbling backward.

"Hey, are you all right?" The man's gruff voice was right behind her. Spitting to the side to get rid of the rock dust plaguing her already parched mouth, Elaine looked over her shoulder and saw the masked man trudging up the tunnel.

Elaine sprung back up and shouted through gritted teeth, "Stay back! My father is the Voidmind Grand Elder! If you lay a single hand on me—"

"Whoa, Miss..." The man raised his hands and chuckled. "Where are all these threats coming from? Who said I wanted to lay my hands on you?"

Elaine stood there with her hand raised, the words dying in her throat. What kind of a situation was this? Were these cultists out of their minds? "You kidnapped me!" she shouted again, and the man looked over his shoulder as if she was speaking to someone behind him.

Seeing nobody behind him, the man pointed to himself. "Me?"

"Yes, you!" Elaine slowly walked backward until she felt the weird wall of slime. Then, sensing void Qi from behind, she looked where her hand met the slime and noted it had turned black.

"Never seen you before, Miss." The man shrugged. "Does someone wearing a white mask with black hair sound familiar?"

Elaine's head was cloudy, and she had a terrible headache, but her eyes went wide when she remembered that terrifying demon. "The mist demon?"

The man burst out laughing. "That sounds about right—she does match that name."

Feeling her feeble Soul Core having recovered some Qi, Elaine coated her fist another time and tried to uppercut through the slime blocking her exit, but it resisted her as if it were a brick wall this time, making her stumble back in pain.

"Why are you doing that?" The man tilted his head, his expression impossible to read behind the black wooden mask.

"To escape, of course," Elaine replied while nursing her hand. "Why else would I be punching the only obstacle to my escape?"

"Only obstacle?" The man shook his head sadly. "Oh, you poor soul, if only you knew."

The man then turned to leave. "The name's Douglas, by the way. Feel free to come speak with me once you have given up. We got an alchemy lab to build before tomorrow, after all!"

His weird cheerful tone and nonchalant attitude to a kidnapped prisoner trying to escape perplexed Elaine on a level she couldn't quite describe. Was her chance at escape really as hopeless as the man believed?

Elaine went to push up her glasses that were sliding down her nose and paused in shock as she noticed her spatial ring missing. "Well, there goes calling for help." She hissed in annoyance and turned to face the slime wall again with a vengeance.

Either it was late evening and the sun had long set, basking the outside world in total darkness, or the slime wall had become totally corrupted by the void. Elaine, unfortunately, had no idea as time seemed to blend together.

Her hands hurt, her Soul Core threatened to crack from overuse, and she was fed up. She had tried to punch through the rock instead of the slime with her void Qi, but the slime seemed to move to protect the walls as if it were alive or being controlled by someone.

Or something—those black roots throughout the slime body that wasn't visible anymore reminded her of the demonic trees floating through those portals. It was also very suspicious that the area surrounding this place also had a lot of demonic trees.

What that meant? She had no clue. Did demonic cults usually have a link to demonic trees? Maybe to dispose of the corpses or something?

A long sigh escaped her lips, and she glanced down the tunnel that led back into the cavern. Throughout the hours she had spent pounding away at the slime wall, she had heard that Douglas fellow singing to himself while the whole mountain shook.

"There's no way he will let me walk down that mineshaft tunnel, right?" Elaine grumbled to herself as she trudged down the tunnel, utterly defeated. Her only hope was to last long enough until her brother came for the alchemy tournament and noticed she was missing, or if her father tried to call her jade talisman again and she failed to pick up.

Reaching the cavern, she was surprised to see how different it looked compared to a few hours ago.

Surrounding the river on both sides were dirt banks with a variety of mushrooms and flowers growing. How they had just sprouted up so quickly defied logic. Either they had been brought from outside or Douglas knew the trick that made the demonic trees sprout mushrooms overnight.

Elaine followed a stone path that led her through the garden and crossed over a newly constructed stone bridge. She then walked past many large stone bowls with steps next to them. Incredibly curious, she walked up the steps and peered over the large bowl, finding a weird black plant that resembled a cauldron.

"Alchemy," she mumbled to herself as Douglas's words replayed in her mind. "The Silverspires…Alchemy…" Her brows furrowed. The Voidmind family didn't have a particularly good or bad relationship with the Silverspires, so they were unlikely to ruin their partnership with this demonic cult to save her.

To be honest, the thought that the Silverspires would conspire with cultists wasn't all that surprising. They had a lot of money and influence, so having some cultists on payroll to conduct the dirty dealings behind the scenes made sense.

"Given up yet?" A sudden voice behind Elaine almost caused her to tumble into the weird cauldron plant from shock.

"D-Douglas…" Elaine stammered, feeling awkward, looking slightly down from her vantage point at the large, mask-wearing man.

"That's me." Douglas chuckled while scratching the back of his neck and diverting his gaze from her. "Admiring my handiwork? Please let me know if you have any feedback on how an alchemy lab should be built. I have never even seen one before…"

"Be honest with me, Douglas," Elaine said with the last ounce of strength she had left, disregarding his question about the alchemy lab.

Sensing her tone, Douglas straightened up. "Yeah?"

"Am I a prisoner here?" she said with resolve, and after a brief pause, Douglas shrugged.

"I guess so? The others didn't tell me much about you and your situation, as they are busy right now."

Elaine was rather perplexed. Was that blond woman one of the leaders, then? Clearly, the man was some kind of grunt worker, so he should want to escape from that mist demon, right?

Deciding to shoot her shot, she jumped from the stone steps and grabbed the man's idle hand. "Could you help me escape? W-We could go together!"

Douglas looked down at their intertwined hands and sighed. "Miss, as romantic as that sounds, I don't think either of us would get very far." His spatial ring flashed with golden light, and the black mask vanished, revealing a rather handsome man that seemed a few years her senior. "And who said I wanted to leave? It's rather nice here."

Elaine reeled back her hand, feeling her face getting rather warm. "Please...just open a path out of here for me!"

Douglas shook his head and turned to leave toward the area he had been working on. "Elaine, was it? I admire your courage, but attempting to escape from this place is a waste of time. I need to have this place looking presentable by morning—"

Elaine wasn't listening. With his back turned to her, she took the chance and ran across the cavern toward the mineshaft the blond woman had left through. Clearly, that man was under some mind control technique and was about as useful as the rocks he was moving about.

Sitting around idly might be the best choice for her survival, but the memory of that dagger being pressed into her neck was all she needed to know she had to escape from this prison before that demon returned.

The mineshaft was thinner than the tunnel, with a rusting metal track with rotting wood running through it. Mushrooms lined the walls with a pale blue glow, and black roots were everywhere, threatening to trip her up. Also, there was a bizarre amount of spatial Qi in the air.

The stale air of the mineshaft did little to help her burning lungs as she ran on pure hopes and dreams, with her Soul Core beyond exhausted. Eventually, she reached a fork in the path and decided on the one that seemed to head upward a bit.

Elaine stumbled to a stop as she glanced up at something that had caught her eye. "Is that a hollowed-out root?" There was a very slight draft of fresh air, meaning it was certainly a way out.

With no other choice, she leaped up, trying to find a footing. But, weirdly, the inside of the root wasn't as sticky with sap as she had expected. Instead, this weird, black, viscous blood coated her fingers.

Burning it off with a bit of soul fire, she tried to scale the hollowed root, but her feet and hands kept slipping. Eventually, she tumbled down, falling on her back and looking up at the completely dark tunnel.

"Fuck sake." She felt tears brimming at the edge of her eyes as she felt the despair of the situation fully set in. She was likely far from home, in a weird prison, and they even taunted her with impossible ways of escape.

Soon the tears came, and she began to sob. If only her father had dedicated those resources to her, maybe she wouldn't be so pathetic, and she could have learned a technique like void step that would have let her teleport past that slime.

Her glasses began to cloud up through her tears, and she felt completely miserable. Why had this happened to her? All she had done was answer a stupid call from her father, and then a demon had attacked her? "I never made trouble with nobody, and this is what I get?" she muttered and gulped back the mucus that was gathering in the back of her throat.

She was just a researcher. What had she done to deserve imprisonment?

After sobbing for a good ten minutes, she wiped it all away on her sleeve as she didn't have access to the supplies in her missing spatial ring. Then, getting herself together, she wandered the mineshafts for a long time, never finding anything else of interest.

"Oh, you're back?" a voice she was now familiar with echoed through the cavern.

Elaine hadn't even intended on finding her way back here, too lost in her doomed thoughts to care about where she was going. "Guess I am," she replied with a sigh.

Wandering over, she sat on a rock and watched Douglas hard at work for a while. Then, to her surprise, he came over after pouring some soil from a spatial ring into a hole he had made and handed her some cloth to wipe her tears.

"Don't sit here all night sniffling behind me," he said somewhat endearingly. "Although you might have been kidnapped, they are good people. Stop stressing so much."

That was a lie. Had this man never met the mist demon? And hadn't the blond woman literally threatened her life earlier?

Elaine reluctantly accepted the cloth, wiped her face, and then almost choked in shock when Douglas moved to the side and showed the previously barren soil now sprouting all sorts of foliage.

"How is that possible?" she couldn't resist asking, the curiosity getting the better of her.

"The plants?" Douglas shrugged as he always seemed to. "They come from the immortal that rules this place."

Elaine pouted, unsure if Douglas was messing with her. "Seriously?"

"Yeah, he has total control over this place. That's why I told you fleeing isn't worth the effort."

"If you are so sure of this supposed immortal's power, why can't you let me try and escape?"

Douglas leaned on the shovel he was holding and stared at her for a few seconds, and then a cheeky grin appeared. "All right, Elaine, how about we make a bet?"

"A bet?"

Nodding, Douglas gestured to the far wall with the shovel, and Elaine felt the cavern shake as the rock crumbled away. "I will give you a chance to escape. If you succeed, you earn your freedom. But if you lose and are brought back here, you have to help me with this project—no more sitting around and feeling sorry for yourself. Deal?"

Was that even a question? "Deal," Elaine said as she brushed herself off and ran toward the opening. It took a while, but eventually, the rocks fell away to reveal the dead of night.

The twinkling stars overhead illuminated many miles of demonic trees, the cool night air rustled her hair and clothes, and she breathed in with relief. Then, glancing back, she saw Douglas leaning on his shovel with an amused expression.

"Good luck, Elaine!" he shouted after her with a grin. "And if you meet Larry out there, tell him I said hi!"

Elaine furrowed her brows. Was Larry a guard for this demonic cult or something else? Either way, she had been given a chance at freedom and planned to grasp it.

Without another thought, she dashed out into the night.

23
A BET

The chilly night air rushed past Elaine's ears as she scampered down the mountainside. Her breathing was ragged, and her lungs burned. She couldn't remember the last time she had felt this weak as she had to resort to her mortal body—her Soul Core was utterly depleted.

"Being...so...weak...sucks," she said between gasps as she reached up to clean her glasses. She was still in the first stage of the Soul Fire Realm, so she wasn't that far from a mortal, especially when she was out of Qi. One day, she could be freed from her thick glasses when she advanced her cultivation.

Feeling her burning muscles due to a lack of Qi, she debated sitting down and spending a few minutes meditating but concluded that staying in place was an unwise decision.

The dense forest of demonic trees that unnaturally clung to the steep mountain face she was rushing through was eerily silent—devoid of any people or animals.

It would have been impossible to navigate this treacherous environment at night without her Soul Fire illuminating the way as the scarlet-leaved canopy blocked the moonlight overhead.

But to her surprise, there was a warm orange glow from these fire Qi plants growing on the demonic tree's trunks, providing light so she didn't trip on the exposed roots underfoot.

She honestly had no idea where she was going, but she figured that following the steep slope downward was for the best. Once she was as far from the cavern and demonic cultists as possible, she could quickly meditate and figure out things.

Her mouth was beyond parched from all the running she had been doing without the assistance of Qi, but without her spatial rings, she felt almost naked. No weapons, life-saving artifacts, or even spare clothes to replace her sweat-drenched ones.

A quiet rustling overhead broke Elaine from her thoughts. Glancing over her shoulder at the canopy, she saw nothing but the scarlet leaves illuminated by the fire Qi plants rustling in the wind.

"Ah—" She felt her left foot get stuck under a root, and she stumbled forward, barely catching herself in time on a low, protruding branch from a nearby demonic tree to stop herself from tumbling a thousand meters down a cliff.

Having to take a longer route to the side to avoid the cliff, Elaine proceeded downward at a good pace. Although the rustling seemed to follow her, there were no other signs that anything was amiss. So without incident, she reached the mountain base many hours later.

Collapsing against a tree with shaking legs, burning lungs, and a pang of hunger, she took a deep breath of the damp air. Then, looking around, she noticed a dense mist flowing between the trees that sent chills down her spine as it reminded her of the dreaded mist demon that had caused all of this misery.

Trying to ignore the constant rustling overhead, she closed her eyes in a vain attempt at meditation. Eventually, the noise stopped, and she breathed a sigh of relief as she cycled her Qi a few times.

As she entered the perfect state of meditation, she felt a waft of foul breath that startled her. Opening her eyes in a hurry, she came face to face with many red eyes that seemed to stare into her soul.

Many giant legs cast a looming shadow, and she couldn't even see the forest past the monster's body. It was that enormous. The two stared at each other for a while; Elaine swore her heart had ceased beating in her chest from fear, and every muscle in her body had seized up as if making a single move would lead to her demise.

Seemingly amused by her state, the enormous spider crawled a little closer with an eerie silence that didn't match its colossal size, and Elaine was ashamed to admit she totally freaked out.

"S-Stay back! Ah!" she shouted as the little bit of void Qi she had cultivated moments earlier engulfed her fist, and she waved the soul flame–coated hand in front of the spider as if trying to deter it.

The weird ring of floating ash that seemed to rotate around a crown of horns on the monster's head sped up, and Elaine paled as she felt a mere hint of the monster's true cultivation press down on her—making her legs buckle slightly and her arms fall to her side.

It then looked at her with an expression she could only describe as curiosity and backed away, seemingly unbothered by her previous threats.

Elaine didn't move, wondering if the monster was messing with her.

She then turned to leave very slowly, keeping the spider in sight as she ensured not to trip on the tree roots by feeling them with the back of her foot as she retreated.

This stare-off continued as the spider crawled closer with every step she took backward—always stopping when she did. Eventually, she couldn't take it anymore and did something potentially foolish: she turned her back to the monster.

Cycling the little bit of Qi she had cultivated, Elaine rushed through the dense, misty forest and was relieved to see some typical green trees for once rather than the ominous demonic ones that made the place reek of death.

Unlike the demonic forest growing on the mountain, this forest did have some wildlife, as Elaine could hear birds chirping, signifying the coming of morning. Through the tree line, she could glimpse the vast walls of the Darklight City in the distance, illuminated by the rising sun.

She couldn't hear anything else besides the rustling of trees in the early morning breeze and the cheerful birds. Had the monster given up? Glancing over her shoulder, her heart almost jumped out of her chest when she saw the spider behind her, moving with creepy silence through the foliage.

Not seeing where she was going and with no Qi to utilize for spiritual sight, Elaine ran straight into a low-hanging tree branch—knocking into the back of her head. Her strengthened body and speed meant it was torn off the tree and sent flying in a shower of splinters, crashing into another tree and exploding.

Elaine suffered a similar fate to the branch as she spiraled through the air until her exhausted body failed to smash through a sizeable, green-leafed tree. Her head spun, and she wanted to cry as her entire body was in pain.

If things weren't already terrible enough, an ash-coated spider limb loomed over her, ready to squash her to the next life. She winced and closed her eyes. "Screw you, demonic cultists. I will meet you in hell!" she cursed under her breath.

But the crushing death never came. Instead, the limb nudged her, and she had the unsettling feeling of all the hairs on the spider leg seemingly searching her skin for something. Elaine knew from her research that spiders tasted and smelled through the hairs on their limbs; was it trying to smell her or something?

Whatever the monster was searching for, it seemed to have found it when the beast paused as its limb was pushed up against her neck, where the mist demon's blade had left a scar.

Elaine watched wide-eyed as the sun crested the mountain range, basking the back of the ashen spider in warm light, casting a looming shadow over her.

Maybe she was insane, but watching the spider curiously poke her made her feel it was domesticated somehow, and if there was someone who could tame such a beast, it would be the immortal Douglas had mentioned earlier. That man's cheeky grin when she had left and he had told her to say hello to someone...

"Are you...Larry...?" The words half died in her throat due to the absurdity of it. What kind of name was Larry for a spirit beast of this capacity?

The spider seemed taken aback by her words as it crawled backward to give her some space.

There was a brief moment as they stared at each other, the silence only broken by birds chirping. "So your name is Larry?" she questioned again, unsure if it had understood her.

Instead of answering, it raised its limb again, and rather than stepping back like every instinct in her body told her to, Elaine raised her hand and met the tip of the limb.

Elaine wasn't sure why, but a small smile manifested as she held the limb of a creature that could obliterate her with a mere thought. She then broke into a small chuckle as all the exhaustion she had bottled up overtook her while shaking hands with a spirit beast.

No wonder Douglas had been so confident she couldn't escape with a beast like this roaming around. All those hours of punching the slime wall until her hands bled and wandering the mineshaft until she was reduced to tears...a fucking waste of time and effort.

As Douglas had said, escape had been pointless from the start. Instead, she should have just listened and relaxed while helping him design the alchemy lab.

Elaine knew that was twisted logic, as only an insane person wouldn't have tried to escape that prison run by demonic cultists that threatened her life, but she was so tired from running and fighting a pointless fight that thinking was the last thing she wanted to do right now.

As Elaine let the exhaustion consume her, she leaned on the limb, and the spirit beast kept her standing by giving her a limb to rest against, like a fluffy tree. She almost wanted to snuggle up to it and sleep...

But then she felt an explosion of spatial Qi behind her, and before she knew it, the limb she had been resting on pushed her through a newly formed rift that instantly closed with a pop of air.

The forest's damp, misty air and morning sunshine were replaced with the blue glow of mushrooms and stale air.

"Oh, you're back."

She was back in the cavern, and Elaine heard those same accursed words she'd been told hours ago before all the running for her life with false hopes and dreams of escape.

Turning around while gritting her teeth, Elaine saw Douglas leaning on his shovel implanted in a patch of dirt next to the slow-moving stream running through the cavern's center.

"Y-You fucking bastard! You knew all along that I never had a chance!" Elaine didn't know what she was saying and understood it wasn't wise to accuse the only person that hadn't threatened her life so far...but she couldn't care less right now. She was mad.

Douglas shrugged and grinned. "I tried to warn you many times, but some people refuse to listen to reason. Especially the smart ones, they always think they know everything."

He then picked up the shovel and gestured toward the half-constructed alchemy lab. "Now a bet's a bet. We only have a few hours until the Silverspires arrive. So come and help me with this."

Elaine wanted to scream and shout, stomp her feet, and punch the smug bastard in the face. It was clear he had taken some entertainment in her antics. He could have explained everything to her and avoided all of this, but he hadn't done that!

But all her anger vanished as Douglas swiftly walked toward her with a cup of cold water and food. His smug grin was replaced with one of concern, and her body reacted before her mind, reaching out for the water and food her body so desperately desired.

"I still hate`you," she muttered as she took the food and water to a nearby rock and collapsed against it.

Douglas chuckled to himself and wandered away, leaving her to wallow away in peace.

Ashlock hadn't expected to wake up to a prison escape. Last thing he remembered while succumbing to sleep was setting some mushrooms and flowers to grow within a flowerbed.

As his mind had slowly awoken at the crack of dawn, he'd heard Larry informing him through the tether of a suspicious person wandering the forest.

Curious, Ashlock had used {Eye of the Tree God}, and after locating Larry's position, he found him confronting the Voidmind woman they had captured.

Without delay, as they weren't that far from Darklight City's walls, Ashlock had Larry push Elaine through a portal that led back to the cavern. While Douglas and the woman conversed, he checked the cave for ways Elaine could have escaped.

"Bob is still guarding the tunnel exit, and by his color, it's clear Elaine gave the slime a real beating, and she certainly hadn't escaped through my root as Stella is meditating on the bench under my canopy and would have noticed her escape…"

Ashlock was perplexed. There were no other noticeable exits she could have taken. So had Douglas let her out? Stella had definitely told Douglas to not let her escape, so there was no way he would create a path, as that would break his oath of loyalty to the Ashfallen Sect.

Or would it? He had some suspicions that the oath wasn't a very airtight contract. What was loyalty anyway? If Douglas let her escape with good intentions for the Ashfallen Sect even though it went against Stella's orders, would that breach his oath?

"What a headache," Ashlock muttered. "Diana brought the woman back yesterday, claiming she was the daughter of the Grand Elder of the Voidmind family, so killing her would be dangerous. I took all her items and verified her cultivation was barely in the first stage of the Soul Fire Realm. So how could she escape a mountain shrouded in my spatial Qi via my roots and with Douglas watching over her?"

Ashlock let out a long sigh. So early in the morning, and already there were problems. But he made a mental note that Douglas was a very lousy guard and shouldn't be trusted with prisoners in the future.

As for Elaine, he wasn't sure what to do with her.

According to Diana, she had worked as a research assistant to the Voidmind Elder that he had consumed within his soul, so she might be an excellent addition to the Ashfallen Sect with her knowledge.

But they hadn't exactly gotten off on the best foot.

You know…the kidnapping and her traumatically encountering Larry in the forest while being so close to escaping. The poor girl looked like a miserable mess as she slowly ate the food and water Douglas provided her while half asleep against a random rock.

Ashlock didn't exactly plan to torment her or anything, but he needed to decide his method of approach with her. Should he force her to take an oath of loyalty like Douglas had? Or take it slower and let her ease her way into living here?

Why keep her around as a glorified prisoner in the first place? Despite his immunity to void Qi, he didn't wish to take his chances against a ninth-stage Star Core Grand Elder or fight their allies, such as the merchants. Keeping her alive but out of sight allowed Ashlock to avoid or delay a conflict.

But that relied on her not escaping and causing a scene.

"Larry, if Elaine escapes again, I will leave it up to you to bring her back," Ashlock declared through the tether, and he felt the spider's acknowledgment.

The rest of the morning passed without incident.

After moving all the remaining demonic trees that had piled up in the Academy's colosseum out to the wilderness and expanding the wall, he spent the rest of the morning observing Elaine and Douglas as they worked on the alchemy lab he had instructed Douglas to build in anticipation of the Silverspires' visit.

There was a chance a deal wouldn't be signed, but he was hopeful. It had only been a few days, and Diana's negotiation tactic of offering a higher percentage in the business the faster they agreed to a deal was paying off. They seemed desperate if they were already asking for a meeting with Diana.

Ashlock was rather happy to see how well Elaine and Douglas seemed to get on as they bantered and half messed around. He could see a future with Elaine being part of the sect.

"Wait, she doesn't even know anything about the Ashfallen Sect or me. We kept that all hidden from her," Ashlock mused as he saw Stella finally awaken from her meditation and stretch her back.

"Good morning, Tree!" She yawned and snacked on one of his low-hanging fruit that he had decided to grow to match the summer mood. "So how's the prisoner?"

'Go and see for yourself if you wish,' Ashlock wrote. 'She could make a good addition to our sect, so be kind to her.'

He didn't miss the small pout on Stella's lips. *"Fine. Open a rift for me, then. I needed a break from cultivating anyway."*

Ashlock happily opened one for her and watched as she put on her black wooden mask and stepped through. He was curious about what she would say to Elaine, but then he felt something lightly hitting Bob.

Shifting his view, he saw Diana knocking on the slime wall as if it was a door. She then stepped back and waited outside the cavern's tunnel alongside Ryker von Silverspire and his butler Sebastian.

"Now is really not a good time to arrive…" Ashlock sighed as he saw the half-finished alchemy lab and its three occupants conversing. Wait…Elaine was still down there.

Should he let her stay or get Stella to hide her before the Silverspires entered?

24
DEAL WITH THE SILVERSPIRES

Stella stepped through the rift in a good mood as her Soul Core was filled to the brim with rich spatial Qi, and she felt on the edge of forming her Star Core and ascending to the next realm.

With the pop of the rift closing, Stella felt the sudden change in environment from the mountain air and sunshine to the dusty darkness of the mineshaft. She looked up and noted the end of the hollowed-out root that led to the surface.

Having been down here before, Stella strode down the mineshaft with measured steps, making sure not to trip on the roots and random bits of rotting wood or rusty metal minecart tracks.

The pulsing Soul Core in her chest made her body feel warm, and she couldn't help but place a hand on her chest as she walked.

I just need to solidify my foundation and absorb as much spatial Qi as possible before going into Ash's pocket dimension again, and then I will have no problems forming my Star Core.

Her musing was interrupted by a distant conversation between Douglas and the prisoner.

But until then, I have to deal with these people.

Stella sighed as she emerged from the mineshaft a while later into the expansive cavern. The overwhelming smell of flora took her by surprise as it starkly contrasted with the previous dusty and stale air of the mineshaft.

On the banks of the stream in the cavern's center were many

soil patches housing various flowers, mushrooms, and even spirit grass. Stella didn't plan to pretend she knew all their names or purposes, but she wasn't totally clueless after reading that alchemist's journal she had retrieved from the deceased Voidmind Elder's belongings.

Those should be valuable ingredients for making pills.

Her eyes drifted to the large stone bowls on the opposite bank across a stone bridge.

And those stone bowls should house alchemy cauldrons required to form the pills with the alchemist's soul fire.

"Oh Stella, welcome," Douglas called out to her as he stepped into view from behind one of the stone bowls.

"To what do I owe the pleasure of your esteemed visit?" The man was dust-covered, and his face suggested exhaustion from his hunched posture, so his sarcastic tone was understandable.

"I came to check on our prisoner," Stella said as she strode over the stone bridge and used the slight vantage point to glance around. "Where is she?"

"Elaine is right here," Douglas replied dryly as he reached to his side and gently pulled the woman to stand beside him.

Stella hadn't gotten a good look at the Voidmind assistant yesterday, so she took her time scrutinizing her.

Elaine was clearly older than her due to her more defined bust and figure, perhaps in her mid-twenties. Rose-gold hair messily sprung from her head and somewhat obscured her face. And oddly, she wore thick glasses.

Have I ever seen a cultivator wear glasses before?

Stella pondered, but it didn't take long to conclude that the answer was no. Actually, she hadn't interacted with that many cultivators. Her list of people was pathetically small...

Realizing she had been staring for too long, Stella questioned Douglas. "The Patriarch told me he believes Elaine could make a good addition to our sect. What do you think?"

Stella had deliberately chosen the word "Patriarch" to refer to Ash as it helped build some confusion, and she didn't ignore Elaine's look of shock and distress and the relief on Douglas's.

"Despite the situation surrounding her, I believe we require more members here." Douglas looked down and smiled at Elaine. "And I believe she would make a great addition. She has been a great work partner, and her insights were invaluable."

In truth, he wasn't wrong. The Ashfallen Sect was far too small and lacked skilled individuals to cover all the fields a sect needed.

But why did I hope he would say she was useless?

Stella frowned behind her mask; deciding to confront these weird emotions another time, she spoke directly to Elaine. "We killed the head librarian."

For the first time, Elaine stopped looking straight at her shoes, and her head practically snapped up, her eyes wide behind those thick glasses coated in a thin layer of dust. "What—"

The words died in her throat as she was reduced to pure confusion. Her mouth opened and closed like a fish gasping for air as she tried and failed to speak.

Douglas didn't have his mask on, so seeing his look of shock was rather amusing. Perhaps she had been too rash in spilling the truth to Elaine, but quite frankly, she had a few days until she went to form her Star Core in the pocket realm, so she didn't have time to waste on slowly explaining the situation with this new person—she had cultivating to do.

Deciding to continue the lie she had told the Redclaws, Stella continued, "You are currently in a cavern under the Ashfallen Sect, a secret group that controls the Blood Lotus Sect from the shadows."

"So you aren't a demonic cult?" Elaine blurted out but then clasped both hands over her mouth, clearly terrified that she had misspoken.

"Where did you get that?" Stella inquired. "We don't participate in those rituals or demonic techniques."

"But…but…" Elaine stammered, her voice shaking and dropping to a whisper. "I overheard…that you wanted to kill me?"

"Yeah?" Stella said flatly and tilted her head in confusion. "All cultivators eliminate threats, not only demonic cults. I suggested to everyone that we kill you, but Diana insisted we give you a chance."

Elaine shrank back from Stella, which she found amusing. But then she remembered Tree had told her to be friendly, so she quickly added, "Although there aren't any plans to kill you now that you are here."

Elaine breathed a small sigh of relief. "Who is Diana? I need to thank her for giving me a chance…"

"She's the mist demon," Douglas whispered from the side and laughed when Elaine yelped.

Are they calling Diana a mist demon? Stella thought and felt it fit her quite well.

There was a moment of awkward silence until Elaine gathered the courage to ask, "So the Ashfallen Sect rules the Blood Lotus Sect? Is the Patriarch you refer to Lord Nightrose? Or is it the immortal Douglas keeps referring to? Also, what makes me a threat? Why did you kill my uncle? What am I doing here—"

"Whoa, whoa." Stella raised her hands. "There's no hurry. I can answer your questions, but please remember to breathe."

Elaine had frantically asked all her questions without pause and was now panting.

"But to answer your questions...the immortal is the true Patriarch of this land. The Patriarch you've known about all your life is merely a puppet." Stella almost felt like the heavens would smite her down any moment for sprouting such lies. "As I said before, we operate from the shadows and eliminate anyone who discovers our existence."

A look of realization dawned on Elaine's face. "So my uncle discovered this Ashfallen Sect when he went through a rift?"

Stella nodded. "Yeah, the rift led to a project we were working on. He then got aggressive and tried to fight the immortal, so he paid for his ignorance with his life."

"But Uncle was so strong." Elaine seemed perplexed, but eventually, she slowly nodded. "I see... So what makes me a threat?"

Stella had to admit even though she was clearly a little older than her, the woman was incredibly innocent looking, and coupled with her low cultivation, even she found it hard to see her as a threat to their continued existence.

Maybe I had been rather rash to call for her execution without even giving her a chance.

Discarding those thoughts, Stella had to be honest with her. "It's your family that makes you a threat, as the immortal noted that you witnessed the Elder going through the rift in the sky. We hoped to hide our activities as much as possible and avoid conflict, and you bringing the Elder's disappearance to light would hinder our plans."

Elaine needed a moment to compose herself. All of this information was a lot to take in, so Stella asked Douglas, "Is the alchemy lab ready? The Silverspires should be arriving soon."

"What do you think, Elaine?" Douglas asked the distraught woman.

"We have done a rather good job considering how much time you spent trying to run away."

Stella smiled, seeing Elaine's embarrassment. "Douglas, don't tease her so much. Although I have to say, the place does look quite good."

"Yeah," Douglas looked around with a proud grin, "not too shabby for a night's work."

"Err, excuse me, Miss…" Elaine glanced at Stella and pushed up her glasses. "What do you want from me, then? Do I have to stay here forever as a prisoner?"

Stella honestly didn't have a definite answer to that question, as the whole situation surrounding Elaine was chaotic.

"For at least the next three weeks, you must remain out of sight and away from your family. After the alchemy tournament we are organizing, we can reevaluate your position here. You may become a full member if you do a good job, giving you massive benefits."

"Benefits?" Elaine seemed intrigued. "What type of benefits?"

"Well…" Stella tapped her chin, debating how much to reveal.

I have already told her a little too much, but isn't the best way to win someone's trust to disclose secrets? It's not like she can escape or contact her family, right? So it should be fine?

Stella raised her palm, and her high-purity soul fire sprang to life. Elaine took an understandable step back, showing she didn't trust her yet.

"We can offer the greatest cultivation resources ever discovered to you." Stella gestured to the cavern with her aflame hand. "We have remained in the dark for so long to cultivate our strength, but we are finally about to expose the quality of our cultivation resources to the world through alchemy."

She then leaned forward and whispered for dramatic effect, "Have an impure spirit root? What about heart demons that plague you at night? Heck, forget about cultivation. What about a pill that improves your skin?"

Stella swore she saw stars in Elaine's eyes with everything she mentioned. A feeling of pride for Tree's capabilities swelled in her chest, making it impossible not to brag on his behalf.

"You really have such profound resources?" Elaine was barely concealing the excitement in her voice.

Stella chuckled. "Why would I lie? Look at my soul fire's purity for proof. Of course, the good stuff isn't grown down here, but even these mushrooms and flowers are bound to carry amazing effects."

To hopefully solidify some more trust, Stella's spatial ring flashed with power, and she fished out two wooden masks that Diana had given her. One was black and the other white.

They were cheap wooden masks, but giving a prisoner the illusion of choice and the feeling of inclusion would go a long way. "Pick which color of mask you want."

Elaine looked between the options and then up at Stella and then Douglas. Eventually, she hesitantly reached out and grabbed the end of the black one.

I bet she picked it because Douglas also wore a black one. Also, these two have a weird relationship going on. Why is Douglas being so sweet to her, yet he was so rude to me?

"Good choice." Douglas gave Elaine a thumbs-up as she tried to fasten it to her face.

After some struggle, she gave up and sighed. "I can't fasten it with my glasses in the way."

"Give them to me. I can store them away in my spatial ring," Douglas said as he offered an open palm.

Taking him up on his offer, Elaine took off her glasses and handed them to Douglas.

"You will be able to see fine?" Stella asked, worried Elaine might walk into walls or trample the plants. The idea of a cultivator needing glasses was ridiculous to Stella. How bad had her sight been in the Qi Realm as a child for the affliction to follow her into the Soul Fire Realm?

Elaine looked around with the mask attached to her face and hummed. She even raised her hands and looked at them. "Yeah, I can't see anything."

Stella was about to offer solutions, but she heard Diana's voice echoing down the tunnel at the cavern's end beside the stream.

Ashlock had tried to devise a way to notify Stella about Diana and the Silverspires waiting outside, but a good opportunity never arose, and keeping them waiting outside began to get awkward.

After seeing Stella provide a mask to Elaine, he deemed that good enough, so he used his {Root Puppet} skill to move the void-tainted Bob to the side, allowing the curious Silverspires to enter the tunnel leading to the cavern alongside Diana.

"We are still getting things together," Diana said to Sebastian. "It should be all up and operational by next month after the tournament."

"But we get fifteen percent, right?" Ryker shouted excitedly. "That was the deal!"

Ashlock wasn't sure how the profit share had jumped to fifteen percent from the originally agreed upon ten percent, but whatever Diana had managed to wrestle out of them was likely valuable as Sebastian looked exhausted and far from thrilled about the fifteen percent cut.

"Yes, you do!" Diana patted the Silverspire heir on the shoulder. "You will beat your siblings and get that silver core."

"To be honest, if everything goes at least somewhat to plan, that isn't an empty promise." Ashlock laughed to himself. He planned to be among the richest in the entire sect, surpassing even the Silverspires.

"What's this about a fifteen percent share?" Stella stood before the trio with her arms crossed below her chest. Douglas and Elaine stood beside her on either side, their black wooden masks obscuring their features.

Ashlock was worried Elaine would speak out and ask for Sebastian's help, but she thankfully remained quiet, although a bit nervous by her shifting her weight from one leg to the other.

Sebastian was the one to answer Stella's question with exhaustion dripping from every word. "We spent a few days surveying Darklight City for other business opportunities, but none of them seemed lucrative enough to give the returns we require to win the inheritance war. With that in mind, we planned to take up your offer and invest in your business, but a ten percent share seemed too low due to the high level of risk we are taking."

Stella sighed. "So Diana gave in and offered a higher share?"

Sebastian snorted. "Absolutely not. We had to offer the Silverspire name as the official backer of the alchemy tournament for the extra five percent. If nothing goes wrong with all the families coming here to participate, it would be a miracle from the heavens, but Ryker was insistent that it was a good idea, so I shall let him learn from his mistakes."

Ashlock couldn't believe how great of a deal they had just gotten. After the incident with the Voidmind Elder, the safety of himself and his allies weighed greatly on his mind. There was a reason a small family like the Redclaws couldn't usually put on such a tournament, as what if a competing family used it as an opportunity to seize control of the city? Or a brawl broke out between two larger families at the tournament?

But with the Silverspires backing? He could be bolder and live without fear of repercussions, as he could always cower behind the banner of the Silverspire family and let them take the heat until he got stronger.

"Ryker has no idea the mess he has just caused his family." Ashlock felt like grinning. "Maybe I should taunt the Voidmind family a little more..."

Sebastian surveyed the cavern and honestly seemed too tired to care. *"Looks good to me, although I know nothing about alchemy."* He then took off a silver spatial ring and held it out for Diana. *"As promised, here is the payment of a thousand high-grade spirit stones and fifty thousand Dragon Crowns."*

As Diana took the ring, Ashlock felt the pressure of heaven as if it was taking note of the deal's completion. Had they taken an oath regarding the payment?

"Thank you for your patronage, and I hope for a fruitful partnership." Diana then handed the ring to Stella, and Ashlock knew she was super excited to use all those spirit stones to make more formations.

"All right, that will be all. I'm exhausted—" Sebastian turned to leave but stopped when he saw Ryker dash over to Elaine.

"Big Sister, I haven't seen you before," he said with childlike innocence while trying to shake her hand. "What's your name? Where are you from?" He then looked between all the people standing before him. "Are you friends with Stella?"

"Oh, this little shit," Ashlock cursed.

25
A RELAXING SUMMER DAY

To Elaine, the world was a blur without her glasses, so she planned to stand beside Stella and Douglas and keep quiet while listening in on their conversation. Of course, she had debated asking the Silverspires for help, but without her vision, she couldn't tell how powerful the Silverspires were.

Her hopes of salvation had been squandered when she overheard that only two people from the Silverspire family had shown up, and one was a child. She had experienced the mist demon's killing intent before, and with the presence of the immortal that supposedly lorded over this place, she didn't want to hedge her bets on a Silverspire brat and a tired butler.

If I could guarantee a route out of here back to my family, I would take it. Her hands clenched at her sides as her mind raced. *But if there's no opportunity, it's best to stay on my captor's good side and maybe reap those promised rewards.*

Elaine didn't fully believe Stella's claims of such miraculous cultivation resources. If they truly existed, the Blood Lotus Sect would be the most powerful demonic sect throughout the wilderness, and they would have no reason to fear the beast tide.

Lost in her thoughts, Elaine felt startled when someone tried to reach for her hand.

"Big Sister, I haven't seen you before," the Silverspire child said with childlike innocence while trying to shake her hand. "What's your name? Where are you from?"

Elaine was unsure what to say. Her body had completely frozen up as she couldn't see the child before her. Other than handing her a mask, Stella had told her to keep quiet about anything she had told her, so what could she even say?

"Are you friends with Stella?"

Elaine almost screamed no into the child's face, but she refrained.

Fumbling to find the child's shoulder, she patted it and answered, "I'm no big sister. I just work here."

"Come on, Ryker." The butler spoke with exhaustion. "We can sit back and cultivate for a few weeks while we wait for the tournament to start."

Elaine almost frowned at how quickly Ryker let go of her hand, losing all interest in her. *Does he love cultivation that much? What a weird child. Although I'm rather jealous. I felt his cultivation was superior to mine, yet he sounded so young!*

"Nice job, Elaine." Douglas's gruff voice broke her from her depressing thoughts. She then felt a warm hand lightly grasp hers. "Hold my hand so you don't trip and fall," he whispered into her ear.

Elaine hated to admit it, but she liked his presence, and soon enough, her hand had intertwined with his, and he thoughtfully led her deeper into the cavern. However, once the distant conversation between the Silverspires and Diana faded, Elaine felt slightly sad when Douglas unlinked their hands and paused beside her.

"Here's your glasses." He held them out for her. She happily took off the mask and put them on, the blurry world becoming crystal clear.

They were near the stone bridge that went over the slow-moving stream, and Elaine enjoyed the view of the grinning Douglas standing beside the soil patch overflowing with flora.

"I had expected you to beg the Silverspires for help," Douglas said, and Elaine felt her blood run cold. "Glad you didn't. I have no doubts you and the Silverspires would have died today if you had said anything."

Elaine couldn't believe how off-handed Douglas had mentioned the murder of a Silverspire heir. They were beyond powerful, and their standing within the sect was second to none. Was this mysterious Ashfallen Sect really all Stella had made them out to be?

The Silverspires had even handed over such a large sum of Spirit

Stones and Dragon Crowns for a small profit share... Who else could demand such a good deal from a Silverspire other than an immortal?

Elaine feared she was making leaps in logic to justify all the nonsense she had witnessed over the past day, but things were starting to add up, no matter how ridiculous they seemed.

"Douglas, come with me!" Stella shouted from the entrance to the mineshaft. "I need help with some runic formations."

"Coming!" Douglas yelled back and gave a reassuring smile to Elaine. "You stay here, all right? I will be back before you know it."

Elaine nodded and watched Douglas leave with an odd feeling of abandonment in her chest. Then, with a long sigh, she sat on the stone bridge, watched the stream slowly flow by, and decided to try cultivating.

"Brother, please come and save me soon," she murmured as her body drifted off into a state of deep meditation.

Ashlock sighed in relief as he opened a portal for Stella, Douglas, and Diana to return to the mountain peak. That meeting with the Silverspires had many chances to go completely wrong, so for it to have ended without much incident was a blessing in his books.

With the meeting that had been hanging over his head for the last few days now in the past, he felt a similar sense of relief to what he had experienced when he left job interviews back on Earth when he had been a man of flesh and bones, doomed to work an endless nine-to-five job in software development.

An exhaustion he didn't know that had been plaguing his body and mind was expelled all at once, and all he wanted to do was turn into a couch potato and sleep.

"Wait...aren't I kinda close to that right now?" Ashlock chuckled to himself.

The point was he felt fantastic and free of worries. So he cleverly decided to pretend the upcoming tournament that was guaranteed to be a massive headache at the end of the month wasn't quickly approaching.

For now, he was chilling. Basking in the glorious afternoon sunshine, he allowed Stella and Douglas's conversation regarding array formations to play in the background as he listened to the chirping birds.

"Say, Tree, what type of formation should we make?" Stella was tapping his trunk with a look of excitement.

"Ugh…" Ashlock groaned. He really didn't want to use his brain right now.

By late afternoon, Stella had settled on using the thousand high-grade spirit stones provided from their fruitful partnership with the Silverspires to create a concealment array, which had been his suggestion.

There were many varying options for array formations to choose from, but since the spirit stones provided were all high grade, a smaller-scale but highly Qi-intensive formation was the best decision.

Of those, Ashlock could pick between a shield or concealment array as they were the only two Stella felt confident at trying.

He had gone for the latter for the simple reason that the current technique he was utilizing to obscure Red Vine Peak from outsiders with spatial Qi was consuming around half of his Star Core's passive Qi generation.

With the many truffles he was growing for the girls and his plans to let his Star Core fill up so he could advance his cultivation, he could not continue that non-stop high-cost technique. It needed to be replaced asap.

He had the system-granted skill that gave him a shield against his arch nemesis, lightning, so he felt a concealment array was of more importance for now.

"I don't quite want to announce my presence to the world just yet, so concealment is ideal."

Ashlock couldn't wait to finally start throwing his weight around and stop cowering on his mountain peak. "Once Stella and Diana return from the Mystic Realm even stronger than they are now, and with my new void ability and the Silverspires' name behind me, the Ashfallen Sect should rival the other mid-size families here in the Blood Lotus Sect."

"Patriarch, may I return to my duties down below?" Douglas asked with a hint of impatience below his trunk. Ashlock was a little confused about his rush to get back down into the dark, dusty cavern below as his job had been satisfied for now, and didn't Douglas want to rest?

Seeing that Stella was busy drawing out the runes on the ground for the concealment formation that went around the rim of the mountain peak, Ashlock also couldn't see much reason to keep Douglas up here, so with a mere thought, he created a portal and let him leave.

"Thank you," he said with a cheery wave as he vanished into the depths.

"What an eager worker," Ashlock noted as he looked for something to do.

Diana was cultivating on top of the personal runic formation, and Stella was happy at work. So much had occurred over the last few weeks that it almost felt weird to have a moment of calm.

No immortals were appearing out of nowhere, cultivators knocking at his door wanting to fight with Stella, or Dao Storms hellbent on his destruction. Just a peaceful summer day.

Ashlock felt oddly restless, so he decided to get some hunting done.

"System!" he called out to his eternal friend that lived in his head, and soon enough, the words he was familiar with materialized in his mind.

Idletree Daily Sign-In System
Day: 3511
Daily Credit: 10
Sacrifice Credit: 5
[Sign in?]

Obviously, he didn't plan to sign in with so few credits. Being too preoccupied, time had slowed to a crawl, and he had little opportunity to go out and hunt. The few SC he had accumulated were from testing his void skill {Consuming Abyss}.

"Time to go check on my traps." Ashlock had been building the wall of demonic trees in the wilderness for various purposes. One was obviously for it to serve as an early warning system so he wasn't caught so unaware as he had been with the Dao Storm. But another reason was a place to draw in monsters he could hunt efficiently.

The last time Ashlock tried hunting in the wilderness, he had wasted hours searching for a few chicken monsters that gave almost no sacrificial credits. It wasn't until the incoming Dao Storm sent a wave of monsters his way did he finally have a decent amount of monsters to hunt for credits.

So like a cast-out fish net, the wall of demonic trees had flowers and mushrooms releasing attractive smells and Qi into the surrounding area to attract any wandering monsters. The stronger ones would feast on the weaker ones that wouldn't give him many credits anyway, and then he could swoop in and consume the biggest fish!

Or at least that had been the idea.

Ashlock's vision blurred across the vast, grassy plains and rolling meadows of the wilderness until he arrived at the wall of demonic trees. He was disappointed to not find the large gathering he had been hoping for, as he had felt a large presence of Qi near the trees, but he had a reason to suspect the cause.

A grotesque, worm-like creature that reminded Ashlock of a train from Earth spanned the entire length of his demonic tree wall. Toxic pus coated its body like a slug's slime, and Ashlock noticed the trees bending toward the worm as if it had its own gravity.

It was, without a doubt, a Star Core–level monster. At one end was an abyssal maw of razor teeth, while at the other was the torn-up ground from which the worm was still emerging. The hole was so large he questioned if it was an open-air coal mine. "How fucking big is this thing? It has to already be miles long, and there's still more of it below ground?"

The Dao Storm had been terrifying due to its sheer looming presence, but this monster was scary to Ashlock for a different reason. What's to stop a Star Core monstrous worm that was miles long from burrowing through the mountain and emerging within the cavern? Or even eating away the entire mountain and him included?

The worm was that big. Its maw could have enveloped him and his canopy without a problem.

If the beast tide was supposed to force all monsters, no matter their strength, to charge along the path of a leyline below the surface that the Blood Lotus Sect had built itself upon. How was he supposed to keep his allies safe if sheltering underground wasn't an option?

Ashlock observed the grotesque monster some more and wanted to look away due to the way it moved. Seeing its segmented body ripple and convulse as it slowly lumbered forward irked him.

"I wonder how I should go about killing this big boy," Ashlock mused to himself. As a Star Core–level monster, it would be worth many sacrificial credits. "What about blasting it with spatial rifts?"

Ashlock's Star Core pulsed with immense power as he directed an obscene amount of spatial Qi down his roots that linked his mountain and the wall of demonic trees many miles away.

The roots coiling around the planted demonic trees' trunks lit up with spatial Qi, and the enormous worm seemed to notice something was amiss as it began to try to shift away.

"Shit, it's going underground." Ashlock worked quickly as he wasn't confident in ways to kill something below ground, despite his vast network of roots down there. Spatial Qi didn't bode well underground due to the abundant earth Qi present, so fighting above ground was his best bet.

"I need to keep it above ground somehow. Mhm, I can control the black vines of the {Consuming Abyss} skill as if they were my own limbs now." Ashlock suddenly had an idea. Even if this monster was of equal strength to him, it relied on its enormous body and giant maw to fight. But how could it fight against being dissolved from afar?

Without much time to waste, as the worm was about to dive underground, the sky rippled and cracked as hundreds of rifts opened above the worm. Ashlock felt a large quantity of nutrients he had been storing vanish as he activated his {Consuming Abyss} skill hundreds of times.

He had obtained this vast amount of nutrients because, over the last week, the residents of Darklight City had noticed that the Qi-enhanced demonic trees were very eager to absorb their…bodily waste and were terrific at absorbing it quickly due to their acidic soil.

Of course, Ashlock had told most of his offspring to cease production of their corrosive fluid, and in exchange, he gave them Qi and nutrients. But those nutrients had to come from somewhere, and as it turned out, becoming the waste disposal manager of the city was lucrative.

Absorbing people's shit aside, it gave Ashlock access to a disturbing amount of nutrients that he could utilize to quickly create black vines that surged out of the ground and through the hundreds of portals.

"What in the nine realms!" Stella yelled from the side of the mountain peak where she had been carefully drawing out runes as she looked up at the sky above the mountain and witnessed Ashlock going to war.

'I'm killing a pest,' Ashlock wrote on his trunk in spatial Qi before focusing his full attention on controlling all the black vines.

Like a ship trying to hunt a whale, the black vines ending in sharp spikes shot forth with Qi-empowered speed and burrowed deep into the worm's soft, slimy flesh. A feral screech escaped its titanic mouth, and

Red Vine Peak trembled slightly as the worm thrashed against the vines. Earth Qi rippled across its exterior, but it was already too late. The black vines had penetrated deeply, all the way to its organs, so he had a direct route to try and burn the thing alive with his soul fire.

His pure soul fire shot down the vines, and the creature screeched some more, its flesh boiling on its skin, and a toxic gas cloud rose upward and outward, blanketing the entire area.

Ashlock didn't care much for the toxic cloud as he didn't have a nose, but he soon heard a shout from Red Vine Peak, where he noticed the poisonous cloud had leaked through his portal and was now blanketing the mountain peak.

Stella had thankfully gotten away mostly unharmed, having been already up and moving. But Diana had been deep in meditation and unaware of his battle.

Quickly closing the hundreds of portals that had torn the sky apart, the thick vines that were cut fell to the ground with a thump, and Ashlock worriedly looked at Diana, chugging pills from her spatial ring while stumbling away.

[Upgraded {Basic Poison Resistance [F]} -> {Poison Resistance [E]}]

A system notification briefly distracted him and showed how truly potent the poison really was—

[Upgraded {Poison Resistance [E]} -> {Greater Poison Resistance [D]}]

Ashlock began to worry as he saw the purple grass surrounding him begin to wither and die, and he even began to feel a burning sensation on his bark.

[Upgraded {Greater Poison Resistance [D]} -> {Superior Poison Resistance [C]}]

Wasting no time, Ashlock opened portals next to Diana and Stella, quickly relocating them below ground, away from the toxic cloud.

"I really need to be smarter with my portal usage." Ashlock cursed to himself. It always felt like the obvious way to fight, but he needed to remember it was two-way. His foes could fight back.

Confirming that Diana was indeed okay after chugging many pills, he quickly opened his {Qi Fruit Production} skill and chose fast-growing fruit to have his newly acquired {Superior Poison Resistance} skill.

He wasn't sure how widespread of a disaster this poisonous cloud would become, so he decided to get prepared, as even with his Star Core, his body and skills were still slow and required preplanning.

With that headache of a problem to think about, Ashlock's vision blurred as he checked on the giant worm.

But it was gone. A large hole laced with poisonous sludge was all that remained. If that was all, Ashlock wouldn't be too worried, but the huge tremors below ground concerned him.

The monstrous worm was on the move.

26
SKILLS, SKILLS, AND MORE SKILLS

Ashlock hated to admit it, but his idea of an early warning system had only half worked. Through his connection with the demonic trees forming a vast wall out in the wilderness, he had felt that something deserved his attention—hence he had decided to go out and hunt, but this worm monster had been beyond his expectations.

"Ugh, how can I even improve the early warning system? My body, which includes my roots, is so vast that it's impossible to pick up on things unless something directly hurts me or I focus my attention in its general direction."

Basically, he wouldn't notice a fly perched on his toes unless it bit him.

If the worm had gnawed on one of the demonic trees, he would have felt instant pain as he had a root coiling around their trunks. He also had his roots growing in the middle of mushroom clusters in hopes that monsters would have come by and feasted on the mushrooms, therefore alerting him to their presence, but the giant worm had scared them all off and hadn't tried to eat the trees.

That issue aside, he could feel through the massive tremors in the ground that the titanic worm was on the move. Oddly, he had been half expecting the worm to be heading toward him, but luckily it seemed to be heading southwest rather than directly south, where he was.

The worm had quickly traveled outside his root network's range, likely by abusing its earth affinity to swim through the ground at tremendous speeds, so he could not discern its position. Other than the missed opportunity for sacrificial credits, the worm's existence had raised many concerns.

Returning his view to Red Vine Peak, Ashlock had much to reevaluate. He had dedicated a lot of time and resources to people recently without thinking about the monsters as the beast tide appeared so far away, and other than the Dao Storm, the monsters hadn't seemed so strong.

On reflection, it made sense since human cultivators were a more immediate threat to his existence, and they could be reasoned with and bribed—whereas monsters could only be answered with overwhelming force, so he had ignored them for now with the mindset of, "I can defeat them so long as I get stronger."

"But that's the wrong mindset," Ashlock mused. "With my biology being so slow and many of my skills reflecting that, I must prepare for threats in advance rather than being purely reactionary."

The poisonous gas cloud had reminded him of his ability to impart skills to his fruit. There was a good reason his {Qi Fruit Production} was an A-grade skill.

"Talking of the poisonous cloud…" Ashlock glanced around and noticed it was still lingering.

The wind wasn't too strong today, so it was slowly dissipating. "Hmm, I can't bring the girls back up here as it's still lingering. I guess I can check my Qi Fruit Production menu in the meantime."

"System, show me my skills," Ashlock said, and words materialized in his mind.

[Demonic Demi-Divine Tree (Age: 9)]
[Star Core: 2nd Stage]
[Soul Type: Amethyst (Spatial)]
[Mutations…]
{Demonic Eye [B]}
{Blood Sap [C]}
[Summons…]
{Ashen King: Larry [A]}
{Infant Ink Serpent: Kaida [D]}
[Skills…]

{Mystic Realm [S]} [Locked until day: 3515]
{Eye of the Tree God [A]}
{Deep Roots [A]}
{Magic Mushroom Production [A]}
{Lightning Qi Barrier [A]}
{Qi Fruit Production [A]}
{Consuming Abyss [B]}
{Blooming Root Flower Production [B]}
{Language of the World [B]}
{Root Puppet [B]}
{Fire Qi Protection [B]}
{Transpiration of Heaven and Chaos [B]}
{Hibernate [C]}
{Superior Poison Resistance [C]}

{Qi Fruit Production} had been one of the first skills he had ever unlocked with his system, and back then, it had taken months to grow fruit with his pathetic F-grade poison resistance. Because of this, he had left fruit production on the wayside in favor of his new, shiny production skills that had offered potent effects.

"I know I have been really busy recently, but I still can't believe I forgot to regrow fruit with skills after the Dao Storm wiped me out." He had grown some delicious summer fruit for Stella to enjoy a few days ago but hadn't thought to add skills to them.

In fairness, his Qi Fruit Production skill hadn't been the greatest in the past due to its high cost and the fact that he could only add skills he had, and back then, his skill list was far shorter than it was today.

Turning his attention back to the production menu, he couldn't see a way to add his summons or mutations to any fruit. "Heh, well, that was to be expected. At least it looks like I can add any skill I want without a problem."

Curious how a fruit with his {Mystic Realm} skill would look, he tried adding it, but a system notification came up:

[Cannot add skills that are higher grade than Qi Fruit Production]

"Mhm, so I can't add anything higher than A-grade. I don't know why, but it relieves me that I haven't been wasting this skill's potential for that long, as I only upgraded it to A-grade a few months ago."

Even so, it was unfortunate that he couldn't add skills higher than the {Qi Fruit Production} skill's grade, as Ashlock was incredibly curious about what biting into a fruit with the {Mystic Realm} skill would do.

"What about adding my other production abilities to a fruit? No way that will work, right?" Ashlock selected his {Blooming Root Flower Production}, and as expected, another error appeared:

[Cannot add production skills. Do you wish to alter the skill?]

"Huh?" Ashlock hummed as he thought back to the past. He had only ever added poison resistance to his fruit before, and it had provided a temporary poison resistance buff. But more importantly, he had been able to alter the skill {Basic Poison Resistance} into poison that he used to kill birds.

Since altering skills had worked in the past without a problem...

"Yes," Ashlock told the system, and he watched as his {Blooming Root Flower Production} was morphed into a brand new skill called {Florist's Touch}. His flower production skill remained intact in his skill menu, so his system had created a brand new skill that he could temporarily grant people who ate his fruit but couldn't use himself.

In a way, didn't this make his {Qi Fruit Production} one of his strongest skills so long as he was surrounded by powerful and capable allies he trusted? Senior Lee's words about uplifting those around him for his survival became more and more true with every passing day.

He checked the {Florist's Touch} skill description and concluded it gave a temporary buff that allowed someone to harvest flowers without contaminating them or killing the stem.

"Huh, that's actually pretty neat." Ashlock honestly hadn't been expecting much from trying to add one of his production skills, as how could humans even use such a skill? It wasn't like Stella could start growing flowers out of her ears or something.

Scanning the list, he selected his other production skill, {Magic Mushroom Production}. He watched it transform into {Mind Fortress}, which significantly increased a cultivator's resistance to mind-altering effects, and unsurprisingly he couldn't add his {Qi Fruit Production skill} to itself.

"The {Florist's Touch} could be a great temporary buff to provide Elaine and Douglas when they try to harvest the flowers and mushrooms I have grown down in the cavern. Meanwhile, {Mind Fortress} has more practical uses in combat or could maybe even be used while cultivating." Deciding to try his other skills, he just ran down the list. Not like he had much else to do while waiting for the poisonous cloud to pass.

{Eye of the Tree God} had to be changed into {Clairvoyance}, and the production time and Qi requirement for fruit involving clairvoyance were ridiculous, but even he could see the massive benefits, so he set a few to grow.

{Deep Roots} was another tree-specific skill, so the system transformed it into a more human-friendly skill called {Root Control} that made Ashlock shudder. It let people take control of his roots. "Yeah, let's pretend this one doesn't exist. No way I am letting anyone control me."

{Lightning Qi Barrier} was added to a fruit without issue, and Ashlock was curious how that would work. "Will they eat the fruit, and then a lightning barrier will manifest around them? Or will it appear only when they are about to take damage?"

Unsure and deciding to wait and see, he saw the next option in his skill list and felt a hint of excitement. {Consuming Abyss} was one of his weirdest skills and deeply tied with being a tree and consuming a Voidmind Elder. How could it be transformed into a temporary skill a random cultivator could utilize?

The system's apparent answer was to transform the B-grade skill into one called {Vampiric Touch}. The name alone impressed Ashlock, and the skill description only furthered that feeling. Those with the {Vampiric Touch} buff could forcefully absorb Qi from others through physical contact.

"That would be amazing for a body cultivator if they exist in this world." Ashlock hadn't run into any yet as even the earth-affinity cultivators whipped out swords, but if someone out there relied solely on their hands, this would be a formidable technique.

"Although it does give demonic technique vibes." Ashlock chuckled. Elaine had thought they were a demonic cult, and he wanted to avoid that image if possible, as it was bad for business. The fact that a demonic tree ruled the Ashfallen Sect was already bad enough. "But this skill is far too good not to use. I will definitely have to grow a few of them."

Ashlock sighed as he saw his immense Star Core Qi reserves dip a little lower as Qi traveled down his branches to slowly growing stalks that would soon house his new fruit.

"Anyway, what's next? Oh." Ashlock looked at the next skill and felt like a potential idiot. With apprehension, he put {Language of the World} into the menu and was a little disappointed it didn't transform into telepathy but became {Language Comprehension}.

"Mhm, this gives a buff that lets people understand and learn languages faster." Ashlock sighed with relief that he hadn't overlooked such a potentially fantastic avenue of communication, although this skill was still beneficial. "I feel bad for the Redclaw Grand Elder now. His experience of learning the ancient language would have been far easier with this buff. Hell, if it's powerful enough, maybe even Diana will be willing to learn the ancient language."

It was a blunder on his part, but it had only been a month or two. "If anything, he will be extremely grateful for this fruit now rather than if I had given it right at the start."

Ashlock then paused as a thought drifted by. Why hadn't he considered selling these fruit to linguists, formation masters, or using them for alchemy? One look at his diminishing Star Core that he had planned to let fill up so he could progress to the next realm gave him the answer. This skill was too darn expensive to use on a mass scale.

"It's fine. I may use up a lot of my Star Core of Qi to produce all these fruits now, but I can always enter hibernation for a few months over the upcoming winter to focus on advancing a stage or two in the Star Core Realm."

Checking that the poisonous cloud was still swirling around his trunk, Ashlock sighed. "Still here...although my poison resistance skill hasn't improved from C-grade." Since the cloud was still prevalent, he tested his last few skills.

{Root Puppet} was another skill that was specialized for trees, so it was altered by the system to {Neural Root}.

"This skill feels like something out of a sci-fi movie."

Ashlock couldn't believe root puppet would transform in this way, as he had expected something in the field of necromancy as {Root Puppet} had let him control corpses.

"Let's see... {Neural Root} is a temporary buff that lets someone control their body perfectly and greatly boosts their reaction speed. This would be amazing in combat."

Ashlock was actually rather jealous as this skill sounded helpful for him, too! Why couldn't he get the good stuff?

Meanwhile, {Transpiration of Heaven and Chaos} was also special to him as a tree, so the system replaced it with a more human-friendly skill, {Enlightenment}, that helped a person establish a connection to heaven. Other than {Fire Qi Protection}, which obviously gave a fire Qi resistance buff, the only skill left was {Hibernate}, which morphed into {Deep Meditation}.

"Phew, I hate having to go through so many skills like that. Sleep is far better." Ashlock let out a long sigh.

That had been a lot to process, but he was excited to see how strong he could make his sect members with all these skill fruits combined with the psychedelic truffles and Mystic Realm.

"So to recap, other than the truffles I have promised Stella to grow for her trip into the Mystic Realm, I have created delicious apple-size fruits with the following skills set to grow over the next few days: {Deep Meditation}, {Enlightenment}, {Neural Root}, {Language Comprehension}, {Vampiric Touch}, {Lightning Qi Barrier}, {Clairvoyance}, {Mind Fortress}, and finally, {Florist's Touch}. How the hell am I supposed to keep track of all these?"

A few hours later, the poisonous cloud had finally dissipated. Thankfully, the slow-moving wind had sent the cloud away from the city, so he didn't need to worry about a toxic rain shower killing all the mortals he needed for…nutrients.

The mortals may not provide him any system credits. Still, their bodily waste allowed him to sustain his forest of demonic trees up on the mountain, giving him a higher Qi generation.

It was a wonderfully balanced ecosystem where everyone needed each other. Alas, he was only one man…person…tree…and his realm of expertise regarding topics like alchemy, formations, and cultivation was limited. Also, as proven by the worm, he lacked the firepower to handle all threats himself, so the development of the Ashfallen Sect would have to continue.

Talking of the sect, he should probably let Stella and Diana out of the cavern…

"Oh, she's mad," Ashlock noted as he saw Stella's expression when she stepped out of the rift; her arms were crossed, and she had a deep frown.

"Hunting a pest, you say?" She raised a brow. *"One that releases a poisonous cloud that almost killed Diana? What in the nine realms were you thinking? Are you trying to get us killed?"*

Ashlock could understand their anger. He got them poisoned and then shoved them into a dark cavern for a few hours without explanation.

'My apologies, Stella and Diana. I didn't realize the worm monster would emit such a potent airborne poison,' he wrote on his trunk. It was only fair for him to admit when he had made a blunder that put his weaker sect members at risk. Not everyone was as immune to things like poison as he was with his system and unique biology.

Stella let out a long sigh and gripped her nose. *"You know if Diana didn't have demonic Qi in her body to fight the poison, she would have died today? What if Douglas had been up here? There's no way he would have lasted even a few minutes before perishing."*

Ashlock fell silent. Although it had been an accident, he needed to be more aware of those around him. "I really need to get Douglas to carve out this mountain and turn it into a runic fortress to keep everyone safe as there's very likely to be situations in the future where I have to use my {Consuming Abyss} skill again, and I don't want my sect members to be caught in the crossfire…"

"It's fine," Diana said flatly as she walked back to the runic formation and sat down. "If I had died in such a pathetic way, I deserved it."

"Don't humor him," Stella said as she rolled her eyes.

Diana shrugged and got back to cultivating.

'Can you tell Douglas to carve out rooms in the mountain? It's too dangerous for you all to stay above ground constantly,' Ashlock wrote, and after translating his words, Stella nodded.

"Sure, but first, help me finish outlining the concealment array I was working on. I want it finished before sundown, and I am behind schedule."

Huh? How did she expect him to do that?

Stella pointed off to the side. *"Just summon your black vines and use something to carve runic words into the stone. It's not that hard."*

Ashlock wanted to protest and say she was a genius and that it actually was hard, but he decided to humor her. Using {Consuming Abyss}, he summoned a single black vine from the ground. Now he just needed to find something to use as a giant pencil.

"What about that oversize sword I got as a system draw?" Ashlock mused. Looking through his inventory, he soon found it. Summoning it to the real world and floating it to his waiting vine with telekinesis, he was soon wielding the stupidly big sword.

"*Perfect. Now come over here,*" Stella said, gesturing his sword-wielding vine to follow. "*You see these runes? Just copy them in the same pattern over and over around the entire circumference of the mountain. I will go this way, and you go the other way. We will meet at the other side in a few hours, okay?*"

It felt ridiculous being ordered around by Stella, but after a while, he soon got the hang of it.

"Haha! I'm a runic array master now!"

Although he doubted Diana appreciated the constant scratching noise of a sword against the mountain rocks.

"It's fine. Cultivators meditate to the point they can be poisoned without noticing...right?" That thought aside, Ashlock enjoyed the peaceful flow of scratching out the runes on the rock that Douglas would later widen with his earth affinity.

Alas, even in this state of peace, he couldn't help but worry about that giant worm. Although it hadn't been heading directly for him, it was still heading in his general direction, and unless he focused all his attention on his roots, he wouldn't see it arrive until it was too late.

"I should probably check on my roots." Ashlock paused his runic work for a moment as it required all of his focus and gave a brief look around through his root network.

At first, he didn't detect anything around him for many miles. It wasn't until he checked on his roots deep under Darklight City that he began to pick up slight tremors that were getting closer.

"Oh, you have to be joking." Ashlock began to panic. What if the worm emerged in the center of the city?

27
(INTERLUDE) DISTANT TREMORS

The sound of fingers drumming on wood in an irate rhythm filled the study.

Grand Elder Redclaw sat hunched in his seat while mulling over a series of reports he had been putting off for a while. Yet, even while engrossed in his work, he subconsciously breathed in and out in a controlled manner, circling fire Qi throughout his body, slowly pushing the boundaries of his Star Core.

He could feel its warmth in his chest. Despite being in the center of a forest, practically overnight, the place had become drenched in fire Qi. Of course, it wasn't as dense or pure as the Qi back in the volcanic region, but it had been a blessing after weeks without any fire Qi to cultivate.

His brows furrowed when he saw the latest report at the top of his pile that had come in just hours ago. The Ashfallen Sect had provided additional funding of ten thousand dragon crowns for the event. A rather inconsequential sum to a large family, but for the Redclaws, which lacked much value to the Blood Lotus Sect, it was a significant sum.

The Grand Elder let out a sigh. All fire Qi cultivators had going for them was firepower and an edge in alchemy, but they didn't have the resources to train up their trainee alchemist any further.

Why couldn't I rule over a family of earth or metal cultivators? Then I would live a rich and comfortable life under any demonic sect Patriarch rather than being kept in reserves for any potential wars.

As the Blood Lotus Sect was somewhat notorious for being one of the strongest sects out here in the wilderness, his days of fighting were long in the past. A warm orange flame sprouted from his open palm, illuminating his face with dancing shadows. This flame had burned to death thousands in past centuries, but now he felt like a forgotten old man.

Grumbling to himself, he extinguished the flame and leaned back in his wooden chair, rubbing his chin while reminiscing. This went on for a while until a flash of Qi caught his attention.

A communication talisman hanging from a hook on the wall had lit up, but rather than it being one with an Elder's name written on a plaque above the hook, it came from one off to the side with the words council written haphazardly on a block of wood nailed to the wall.

The Grand Elder raised a brow. It was very rare for the mortal council to dare send a message straight to his study—as to potentially disturb a Star Core cultivator from their work or meditation was enough to lose one's head.

Rising from his chair and strolling across the room, he fished the communication talisman from its plaque and inserted a sliver of his Qi.

"Grand Elder Redclaw, this is the council's representative speaking. Please forgive us for the spontaneous communication, but the situation is potentially urgent."

The Grand Elder could hear chatter in the background beside the representative's voice. It would appear the mortal council was engaged in a furious debate regarding something.

Mortals are constantly arguing over pointless things. Although I suppose living for a few fruitful decades at most puts more importance on the mundane things in life.

Rolling his eyes, the Grand Elder suppressed the urge to ignore the mortal's request as he was terribly busy, but in the end, he decided to humor the man on the other end of the communication talisman.

"Tell me, councilman, what terrible travesty has befallen you?"

There was a brief pause as the man on the other end seemed to be listening to the developing situation being relayed to him by the others in the room.

"Esteemed Grand Elder, the city is experiencing tremors."

"Tremors, you say?" The Grand Elder spread his spiritual presence toward the city but couldn't pick up on these tremors. "Tell me more."

"They were occurring in the southwest of the city and were faint to begin with but have been getting more severe over the last hour." The man paused to catch his breath as he had spoken very quickly. "We originally believed them to originate from earthquakes as the beast tide is expected to come from the north, but due to the weird pattern of the tremors, we believe a titanic creature may be lurking below the ground."

There was a long pause as the Grand Elder mulled over the councilman's words. "I see. That is indeed concerning."

"Which is why—"

"Although I don't see what you want me to do about it," the Grand Elder cut the man off, "Until this lurking monster rears its ugly head above ground, I'm unable to offer much assistance."

It was shameful for him to admit, but these tremors could go on for weeks, and considering he could fly to the site of the monster within minutes should it surface, he was unwilling to idly stand around the city to give fake reassurance to the mortal council.

The councilman's tone lost a hint of respect. "Esteemed Grand Elder, the people of Darklight City have put up with a lot of nonsense in recent weeks, ever since you took over. We hardly complained when half the city was transformed into a foul-smelling forest or the mine was mismanaged for weeks. We pay hefty taxes to you for security, a duty I implore you to conduct—"

There was a loud crack as the Grand Elder's shaking hand crushed the communication talisman. A flame of anger flashed past his eyes, and he felt his body heat up.

Who in the nine realms does that puny mortal think he's talking to? He implores me to do something? Me? I have lived through ten generations of his pathetic lineage, and yet he dares to lecture me?!?

His teeth ground together as he paced the room, desperately trying to calm his raging spirit. The last thing he wanted was for his heart demons to flare up over a foolish argument with a mortal that would perish to the grasp of time by the end of his next secluded meditation.

Ten minutes later, his rage finally subsided, and he opened his palm. In his anger, his fire Qi had run rampant across his skin, reducing the cracked artifact to nothing more than ashes that fell to the floor, forming a neat little pile. The room was also sweltering hot, and the air shimmered with heat.

He breathed in once and cycled his Qi, and the room's temperature plummeted and returned to normal.

"Tsk, what an awful day." The Grand Elder rolled his shoulders as he glanced at the pile of work still sitting on his desk. Due to his foul mood, the mere thought of returning to work irked him, so he decided to leave his study for the courtyard.

Through the corridors of the White Stone Palace, he briefly passed a few Silverspire servants that were chatting away with his own family's servants. It seemed they were on their way to replenish their master's mountain of metal.

What a weird form of cultivation—terribly expensive but also with the advantage of being possible anywhere so long as a steady supply of metal can be brought in.

The Redclaw Grand Elder was especially envious of the location part. Although fire Qi was now available to him, the shock of being without it for weeks still plagued his mind.

As he exited the front door and strolled into the courtyard, his long crimson hair fluttered in the mountain breeze. Many of his family members were nestled within the windbreak provided by the tall walls, diligently cultivating the ambient fire Qi.

He wished to join them, but his Star Core would overpower everyone else, and all the Qi would be drawn to him, so he had to refrain. Walking with quiet steps, he strode through the courtyard and emerged at the peak of the steps that led down to the mountain's base.

From up here, he could survey the expansive forest—a sea of lush greenery broken up by the occasional splash of red—between him and Darklight City. But, even from up here, he could see a white mist swirl between the trees, giving it a haunted feel.

Breathing in the fresh air, he expelled the last remnants of rage and achieved inner peace. He hadn't got that furious in a long time, and if not for the Ashfallen Sect that loomed over him, he might have acted rashly.

To be fair, it's not my fault. Cultivating fire Qi turns even the most placid youth into a raging, hotheaded idiot. Sometimes I feel we spend more time and effort cooling our emotions than advancing our realm.

It was the fate of all cultivators to be altered by the affinity they filled their souls with. "I would still choose rage over the madness of heart demons, though," the Grand Elder muttered as his spatial ring flashed with power.

The sword he had used to ride into battle versus the Dao Storm materialized in his hand. Despite his words earlier, he did plan to check out the city as it had been entrusted to him by the immortal of Ashfallen, and he knew his time was less valuable than his.

Although I hadn't lied. I really can't do anything unless it comes above ground.

He could expend a vast amount of his Qi to turn the ground into a molten wasteland, but that was both counterintuitive if the monster wasn't lurking below the city and a terrible waste of the Qi he had spent weeks meditating for. Ideally, he would avoid fighting at all costs and wasting his Qi as he was on the verge of the next stage in the Star Core Realm, which would boost his power significantly.

Alas, he refused to travel on foot, so his Star Core pulsed with power as his waiting sword became sheathed in crimson flames and floated before him, inviting him to step on.

However, the spiritual sense he had tapped into earlier alerted him to a pulse of spatial Qi to his left.

"Ah, Grand Elder." A woman he was very familiar with stepped through a rift beside him. Her blond hair gleaming in the sunlight, flowed down her shoulders, and a white wooden mask obscured her features.

"Stella," the Grand Elder replied respectfully, "to what do I owe the sudden visit?"

Stella tilted her head, looking at the floating sword he had been about to board to fly to Darklight City.

"Heading to Darklight City?" she replied coldly.

He calmly nodded, ignoring the frigid tone as he was used to it from her.

"Great, we can speak on the way." She gestured to the sword with her chin. "Get on and take me. I can't fly."

The Grand Elder felt the wind rustle his dark-red robes as he soared through the clear sky on his flaming sword. The forest below was a blur, and soon enough, he had passed over the city walls and was making his way to the southwest, where the councilman had reported the tremors.

He had taken a journey like this many times before, but he had never had such an important person on the back of his sword and clutching his shoulders so…aggressively.

She's in the Soul Fire Realm, so maybe…

"Never flown before?" he asked casually, careful not to disrespect one of Ashfallen's leaders.

"N-no…not on a sword," Stella replied, loosening her grip slightly. "I usually use rifts to travel around."

The Grand Elder gave a hearty chuckle to dispel some tension. Although he had to admit it was odd for someone of her caliber to have never flown on a sword before. Didn't she have Elders at her beck and call to take her around?

"Well, you might not notice due to your own Qi," the Grand Elder said calmly, "but the sword is enveloped with my fire Qi. Don't you see that I have no need to hold anything while standing here?"

He felt Stella shift behind him as if peeking over his shoulder to check he really wasn't holding onto something.

Sometimes I forget she is pretty young for such a powerful cultivator. It's the wooden mask and haughty attitude that makes her seem older than she really is.

"Yes, I see," Stella said sheepishly.

"My Qi will keep you rooted to the sword. If you believe me, then release your hands from my shoulders." He chuckled. "It's not like you would die from a fall from this height anyway."

He slowly felt the grip loosen and then a gasp of amazement. He briefly checked over his shoulder and saw Stella leaning side to side, clearly testing if she really would fall, and her masked face looked down at the burning sword.

The Grand Elder returned his sights to the distant southern section of the city. "Anyway, with that out of the way, I was informed by a councilman of tremors below the city. Hence I am heading there to investigate."

I'll just keep the whole fact I tried to ignore it to myself.

Awkwardly clearing his throat, the Grand Elder continued, "So why did you come to see me?"

"Oh, for something similar," Stella said over the roaring wind. "The immortal casually fought with a Star Core worm monster deep in the wilderness through some rifts, but the worm emitted a poisonous cloud that wafted through the rifts and ended up becoming a problem."

There was a long sigh until she continued. "Anyway, that's beside the point. The worm monster, clearly enraged at being attacked, retreated underground. The immortal thought nothing of it until the demonic trees he is linked to picked up its vibrations under Darklight City."

The Grand Elder's face paled. An earthquake was one thing, but a Star Core–level monster was another.

When they become that strong, they reach an intellect closer to an animal or human rather than a bloodthirsty monster hellbent on consuming prey for power. Although not as aggressive, these intelligent monsters are far harder to deal with because they know when to escape a losing fight.

"That's a concern," the Grand Elder eventually said, rubbing his chin as he watched the horizon. "Especially if the monster can travel underground, it will be tough to pinpoint its location—"

"That won't be an issue," Stella said in her usual cold tone. Seemingly some of her confidence had returned.

He felt her hand brush past his arm, then saw her hand point into the distance. "Through the tree roots throughout the city, the immortal always knows the worm's location. We just have to follow the signs."

"Signs?"

"Yes, signs," she insisted. "Look where I'm pointing. Don't you see the demonic tree on that building's roof glowing with spatial Qi?"

The Grand Elder was a fire cultivator, so his body wasn't as in tune with the surrounding spatial Qi as Stella's, so he had to focus his spiritual sense on the area she was pointing before he noticed that there was indeed a single demonic tree lit up with spatial Qi like a beacon.

Wait, why did it stop?

The purple flames had extinguished a mere moment later, but before he could ask Stella why, he noticed another tree that was further away light up with spatial Qi.

Oh, I see what's going on here.

That tree then extinguished, and another lit up a few hundred meters further. "It's moving away from us very fast," he noted, and Stella hummed in agreement.

But then something weird happened. The distant tree remained lit with purple flames for quite a while, enough time for him to close the gap.

"Why is the monster waiting there?" Stella asked from the side, but her question was soon answered when the distant tree dimmed, and one much closer to them suddenly exploded with spatial Qi.

Then another and another. Many trees in a direct line toward them lit up all at once. Even though they were hundreds of meters in the air, the Grand Elder pushed some more Qi into his sword to make it ascend slightly higher, just to be safe...

The ground exploded in a surge of rock.

To say his heart jumped in his chest was an understatement. He had expected something big, but this was *enormous*. An entire city district had been obliterated as the monster rose from the earth, shaking everything.

The rock and dust cloud was shoved aside as the worm's abyssal mouth of razor-sharp teeth encompassed his entire vision. He could feel Stella panicking behind him because her hands suddenly clasped his shoulders again, but he paid it no mind.

His centuries of experience in combat that had lain dormant for far too long flared up to the surface. His mind became a still lake as it logically processed the situation.

He knew the worm would catch him if he tried to fly over it, and he couldn't fly under or risk being crushed to death. In a split second, his sword, enshrouded in flames, was moving to the left, but the worm was far faster than he expected. Its sheer size meant it took seconds to escape the circumference of its mouth.

He aimed to the right with both hands, and his Star Core burned brightly in his chest as a javelin of deep crimson flames sprang from between his fingers and bolted, leaving a trail of fire and superheated wind in its wake.

The worm appeared oblivious to the attack but clearly felt it as the javelin of crimson fire containing Qi from a week's worth of meditation tore a hole in the side of its mouth.

Black blood spurted from the wound, painting its nasty yellowed teeth and causing a shrill scream to escape the depths of the creature's body that was loud enough to make the Grand Elder fear it was a sound-affinity attack.

With the worm recoiling slightly to the right, the sword-riding duo could barely evade the worm's body, dropping down to the city below. The Grand Elder could see mortals fleeing like ants trying to avoid being crushed in the shadow of the creature's titanic body.

Screams were accompanied by chaotic bells that began to ring throughout the city, signifying that it was under attack. The Grand Elder couldn't do anything for those who perished under the monster, but he could try and kill it so their souls may rest peacefully in heaven.

His Star Core pulsed with power once more as he dived down toward the worm's grotesque, slime-covered body. Wrathful flames appeared around his fingers and—

"Stop!"

Startled, the Grand Elder shot off his attack a little too early, but it still impacted. However, earth Qi coating the worm's body easily absorbed the attack.

The fact my attack didn't even scratch it suggests it is at least a mid-stage Star Core monster.

"Why did you tell me to stop?" the Grand Elder asked through gritted teeth. That attack had consumed days of meditation and had been wasted by her shout.

"Don't you remember about the poisonous cloud?" Stella quipped back, clearly angered. "If you attack it like that, it will release it!"

"Oh..." The Grand Elder looked back at the grotesque thing. Its head was hardly out of the ground, yet its giant body had eliminated such a massive area. Sure enough, he saw a dense mist floating into the air from the area he had struck.

"What should we do?" he quickly asked, but Stella gave no helpful reply.

Where's the immortal? Why doesn't he attack it? Oh yeah...the poisonous cloud. What a tricky foe this worm will be.

The ground then rumbled, and the monstrous worm reared its ugly head before slamming it back into the ground, vanishing below. The earth churned and moved to fill in the enormous gap left, and if not for the line of destroyed buildings, it would be hard to convince anyone that such a monster had really been here.

"Look! The trees are lighting up again. The worm's on the move..." Stella pointed off to the east, toward the Academy, the forest, and then the demonic tree–covered mountain range. And also Red Vine Peak, where the immortal resided.

28
HE WHO FIGHTS WITH WORMS

Ashlock felt a tinge of dread as he tracked the worm's titanic body moving swiftly toward him at an impossible speed. It had delved deep beneath the earth, so the tremors on the surface were minimal, but it was a different story through his roots.

"Shit, why is it heading straight for me all of a sudden?" Ashlock panicked. He kept lighting up trees to show its path to the Redclaw Grand Elder and Stella flying overhead on a sword of crimson flames, but he had to admit they were rather useless here.

Unfortunately, so was Ashlock. Unless he could fight the worm on the mountain peak near his trunk, he had few options for combat against an earth-based enemy. His roots were used for resource management and intel gathering rather than combat.

"And my spatial Qi is beyond useless underground due to the earth Qi stopping me from making portals." Ashlock cursed.

It was why he couldn't conjure a portal inside someone's stomach or in the earth below their feet. A person's or environment's Qi interfered with other types of Qi, and when the earthworm could surround itself with soil drenched in earth Qi, it almost acted like armor it could use to shield itself from most enemy attacks.

While half distracted, Ashlock shoved a little too much Qi into the demonic tree above ground and noticed the worm's direction briefly change as if it was a moth attracted to a flame.

"Hold on…" Ashlock was starting to realize why the worm randomly went after the Redclaw Grand Elder and Stella. The worm must have sensed a tasty snack flying in the air. "I forget that monsters get stronger by eating and absorbing the cultivation of others. Basically, just like how I get stronger."

With that realization in mind, Ashlock checked his Star Core Qi reserves. Due to the large number of fruit and truffles he had growing, over half of his reserves were gone, and his passive Qi regeneration from his pulsing Star Core was also being wholly consumed.

"This is going to be hella risky… Shit." Ashlock had taken a gamble he didn't even consider, and it hadn't paid off. Since the Mystic Realm opened up in a few days, and it took around that long to grow all the fruit, he had gone all in and produced them all at once while not considering that the worm would return with a vengeance.

A rather big oversight on his part, but this was the trade-off. Suppose he had not spent any Qi on fruit and instead kept all his Qi in reserve for a rainy day. Then, when Stella wished to enter the Mystic Realm in four days, she would go in without his produce.

Ashlock wasn't entirely fearing his death at this point as he still had his {Consuming Abyss} and his guardians, Larry and Maple, as trump cards. The problem was Larry undoubtedly lacked a way to fight the worm underground, and he was unsure about Maple's true capabilities.

"Ideally, I want to divert the worm away so it doesn't destroy Red Vine Peak or eat me somehow," Ashlock decided. "I will make sure to keep a little Qi in reserve for some rifts if needed, but hopefully, this will work…"

Spatial Qi surged through his root network, and a line of trees leading away from Ashlock and Darklight City was ignited in lilac flames. It was a rather haunted sight and seemed to spook the nearby residents, who suddenly watched the trees catch fire with an almost ghostly flame. Nevertheless, his plan worked.

He could feel the worm diverting and following the long line of trees that led away from him and the city. The problem was that when the worm reached the end of the line a while later, it paused as there was no reason to continue.

Without a way to pump spatial Qi that far away, as it was beyond the limit of his roots, the worm seemed to lose interest. Noticing the worm's behavior change, Ashlock cut the supply of spatial Qi through the roots and watched silently, hoping it would go away.

His Star Core was a flicker of its previous brilliance, so he had little to do besides tracking the worm's movements.

The worm seemed dormant for a while, remaining in the same location.

Just when Ashlock had a glimmer of hope that the worm was far enough away and that he had emptied out his Star Core enough that it couldn't detect his Qi anymore, the worm slowly began to slither through the earth toward him, gradually picking up speed, and very quickly, it was rocketing straight for him.

"Larry, get ready. There's a Star Core–level earthworm on the way that's large enough to gobble this mountain peak whole." He called through the black tether, "You, too, Maple. We got incoming."

Maple was resting on his branch and let out a long yawn as he rolled over, falling back asleep. Meanwhile, the ever-diligent Larry stood ready in the courtyard's center.

"Master, what should we do?" Larry asked gruffly. *"I await your guidance."*

Ashlock had forgotten that neither Larry nor Maple had witnessed the monster as he had fought it through rifts the first time and then out in the city the second time.

As for Larry's question…what should he do?

"All right, let's evaluate. The monster is attracted to the largest source of Qi. Its mouth is large enough to gobble me up in one bite, and none of us have any capabilities to fight it while it remains underground —except Douglas, but he is an entire realm below the worm, so his value here is questionable."

This thought trail made Ashlock realize again how fights worked in this world.

"Swarm tactics aren't advantageous. No matter how many weak Redclaw cultivators I throw at the worm, it will never falter, as its body and Qi can easily resist attacks from those below its cultivation," Ashlock mused as he felt the worm rapidly approach. "Therefore, it's the heavy hitters on my side that matter, and they need to be varied in skillset and affinity; otherwise, I risk losing to a weaker foe due to them having a counter affinity."

Ashlock hummed to himself as he looked at the mountaintop. The worm was still a way out despite its speed. Ideally, he wanted to make this the final battleground so he could unleash his trump card, {Consuming Abyss}, and penetrate the worm's defenses with void Qi.

"If swarm tactics don't work, I should draw it to a spot where all my heavy hitters can strike it at once," Ashlock mused while Larry patiently awaited his orders.

"Larry, stand as far from me as you can while still being at the edge of the runic Qi-gathering formation and unleash as much Qi as possible."

Larry crawled backward, away from him, and perched himself at the very edge of where the silvery runes lay. Cocking his massive head, he asked, "Here?"

"Yeah, just there is perfect. The worm will arrive soon, but it's drawn toward Qi. I want it to emerge away from myself by using you as a distraction," Ashlock slowly explained to his loyal pet. "So you must jump out of the way at the last second. Do you understand?"

Larry grunted in agreement, and the ashen halo orbiting his crown of black horns began to spin faster. An immense pressure descended as Ashlock felt the full force of Larry's cultivation. Then, as if unable to stay contained, the ash halo rapidly expanded until it was like the rings of Saturn and orbited around Larry's enormous body.

The rapidly moving ring of ash generated a whirlwind that violently rustled Ashlock's leaves, making his thick black branches waver slightly. In times like this, he was thankful that Larry was an ally rather than a foe. If he could train Kaida up to this level of strength, he would feel much more secure. What would an ink affinity serpent at the A-grade be capable of? Ashlock looked forward to it.

The silvery lines of the runic formation suddenly began to glow with power as the formation got to work, trying to absorb the suddenly abundant Qi in the air and transfer it down into Ashlock's roots, which he resisted by pumping the last remnants of his Star Core Qi into the formation.

He didn't want Qi to be transferred toward him. Ideally, he would like to appear as a random tree of little interest so the worm would target Larry and the formation rather than him.

This whole plan was risky and heavily relied on the worm targeting the greatest source of Qi. If he miscalculated, he would find himself in the maw of a mountain-size worm that could crush him with a single bite.

"You know, it's in times like this that I wonder how the hell the world tree in the center of the celestial empire ever reached the Monarch Realm without being mauled to death by monsters or chopped down for spirit wood by greedy cultivators."

While mumbling to himself, he almost missed seeing Maple open an eye and snap his paws, making the runic formation go from glowing silver to a blinding beacon of Qi.

In fact, so much Qi was being forced into the runic formation that the silvery metal began to liquefy and boil.

"If the worm ignores all this and still aims for me, then it's not my fault. It's just blind," Ashlock joked with himself, trying to stay optimistic. If he could survive a Cloud Titan crushing him to death, why shouldn't he survive a stupid worm?

"Come on, Ashlock, what tree has ever feared worms?"

The mountain began to tremble as the worm drew closer.

Ignoring the fear gnawing at the back of his mind, he went through his mental checklist one last time and suddenly remembered something.

His vision blurred, and he eventually arrived in the cavern deep within the mountain. The place was already faintly shaking due to the rapidly approaching worm with bits of rock tumbling down from the ceiling and splashing into the slow-moving stream or flattening the flora.

Douglas stood behind Elaine, using his large body to shield her from the falling debris. The falling rocks broke into dust as they impacted his head and back.

Without further hesitation, he sent a flash of Qi through the mountain and summoned a portal right before them. Elaine's eyes went wide, and Douglas cracked a smile. "Seems salvation has arrived."

Ashlock didn't know why he was acting so dramatic. He could always have used his earth affinity to tunnel out of the cavern or just walked out via Bob. "There should be no reason Douglas felt the need to stand and protect Elaine here. He could have just left with her."

He felt suspicious of Douglas's overly heroic actions, but he had bigger things to worry about, so he dismissed it for now. The duo held hands, stepped through the portal, and emerged in the courtyard of the White Stone Palace with matching black masks obscuring their features. The Redclaws naturally welcomed them with respect as Ashfallen members, and Ashlock hoped that Elaine wouldn't run her mouth and ask questions.

Moments later, the rift back in the cavern collapsed, and despite his roots being so intertwined with the structure, the whole place trembled as the worm began to shoot upward.

Until now, Ashlock had just felt the distant tremors of the worm's movement, but now he felt its progress toward the mountain's peak in a very unpleasant way.

Pain as if he had shoved his foot into the rotating blades of a combine harvester overwhelmed him. "Holy shit!!!" he screamed in his mind space as he reeled back his consciousness. Now all he could feel was a distant, dull ache and the intense shaking of the entire mountain.

Unable to track the monster's movements without experiencing the excruciating pain again, Ashlock waited patiently for its emergence on the surface. Then, as the dull ache got louder and louder, he shouted through the tether, "Larry! It's here!"

Larry curled in his legs before jumping to the side just as half the mountain peak exploded in a surge of rock. A great shadow loomed over Ashlock as the grotesque, slime-covered body that looked like a skyscraper-size, diseased intestine eclipsed the sun.

Its body then curved in the air, and its abyssal mouth of razor-sharp, yellowed teeth, dripping with molten spirit ore that had made up the now destroyed Qi gathering formation, turned toward Larry. Seeing so far down the monster's throat was harrowing as its body convulsed and globs of poison dripped between its teeth and melted the stone below.

After a brief hesitation due to the pain of his roots being torn through and literal tons of rock raining down on his branches, Ashlock activated his {Consuming Abyss} skill and mentally selected the void affinity option.

A timer appeared in the corner of his eye, ticking down. He had five sacrificial credits stored up, so he could use his skill for five minutes.

"That's all the time I need!" Ashlock shouted as the mountain peak became enveloped in a lake of pure void. Tendrils of void like an abyssal kraken emerged from the lake and shot toward the worm's body. As much as its size gave it many advantages, it also made it unable to even try to dodge the impending void attack.

The worm, intelligent enough to notice a threat, tried to swivel its giant maw away from Larry and toward Ashlock.

Its skin shimmered with dark brown flames as earth Qi coated its skin for protection and pressure so immense he thought a literal star had been dropped on top of him, causing half of Ashlock's branches to snap in half as they couldn't resist the excessive gravity from the worm's Star Core, which was undoubtedly a few stages higher than his.

"I see that size doesn't only work well for me." Ashlock cursed as he identified that this monster likely had a Star Core that wasn't fist-sized. It might even be larger than his trunk-size Star Core.

A screech that blew off all of Ashlock's remaining scarlet leaves escaped the monster's mouth as the void tendrils from his {Consuming Abyss} skill impaled straight through the thick earth Qi flames as if they weren't even there and skewered the creature's body.

It was fascinating to see how different a void-affinity attack had been compared to the fire lance the Redclaw Grand Elder had unleashed only minutes ago.

Ashlock's guardians weren't idle, either. Larry opened his maw and sent a powerful ball of ash into the worm's gaping mouth; it burst, and soon enough, the worm had millions of spiders crawling around inside it.

Things were looking good until the mountain shook even more, and the worm began to fall forward…toward Ashlock. Now he was one strong tree, but having a monster that likely weighed about as much as a skyscraper falling on him when his Qi reserves were near empty was far from ideal.

Maple, who had remained sleeping on his branch this entire time, seemed annoyed that the worm was blocking the sunshine as he slowly got up. Then there was a shudder in reality as Maple vanished into the void realm and reappeared, standing defiantly in the air beside the falling worm.

He reeled back his tiny paw and thrust out.

There was the briefest moment as the worm's body rippled, the immense energy from the punch desperately trying to find somewhere to go. Then, after rippling a few times, the worm's flesh seemed to give way to the tremendous energy flowing through it, and like a popped water balloon, it burst.

A plume of poison accompanied a literal surge of grotesque black blood and pieces of worm. Like a building experiencing a demolition, the explosion traveled down the worm's body until it paused just below the surface.

With pieces of worm skin draped over his bare branches, black blood trickling down his trunk, and with no soul fire to burn it off, Ashlock felt genuinely disgusted. But he did his due diligence and checked on his foe.

"Is it dead?" Ashlock wondered as his spiritual sight drifted across the mountain peak, and he cautiously stared down the giant hole with streams of poison and liquid silver pouring down into the darkness below.

Confused, Ashlock looked a little closer and saw that the darkness was alive—it then tore open, revealing thousands of freshly grown teeth. It let out an awful screech, and then the mountain rumbled.

Ashlock still had his {Consuming Abyss} skill running, so he commanded the void tendrils down into the hole, but to his surprise, the worm wasn't interested in revenge; instead, it retreated downward and back into the depths of the earth below.

There was a long silence as Larry, Maple, and Ashlock just stared down at the giant hole that went through the center of the mountain. The tunnel did cut into the cavern but had mainly avoided it, so his alchemy farms were fine, but the runic formation they had spent so many spirit stones on had been gobbled up.

"At least we hadn't started on the concealment array yet, so those high-grade spirit stones haven't been wasted yet." Ashlock didn't know how to feel about all this. Neither side had explicitly won.

They had destroyed its head, but it had somehow cut its losses and regrown its head.

Although Ashlock hadn't died, the monster had taken away all of his Qi, significantly damaged his mountain, and eaten the formation Stella had spent so much effort on.

Looking around the mountain peak, he saw massive chunks of flesh and teeth everywhere, so he quickly turned off his {Consuming Abyss} skill and then unleashed his black vines to devour what was left.

"Got to get something out of this mess…"

The sound of teeth snapping and large chunks of flesh being dissolved filled the courtyard. To his shock, he also noticed some of the chunks of flesh slowly turning to wood… It seemed his cursed blood had started morphing the head of the worm into a tree.

Then, finally, a system notification brought Ashlock out of his sour mood.

[+100 Sc]

"Huh?" He was surprised by the rather large sum. He hadn't been left with much to absorb after the explosion, and he estimated he had only devoured a small part of the worm's overall length.

"That entire monster should be worth well over a thousand credits... enough for another S-rank skill draw." Ashlock suddenly felt hunting down that monster might be a good use of his time and resources.

As he looked around, Ashlock breathed a sigh of relief. His concealment technique was flickering and still active—

The frozen space shattered as a man on a flaming sword crash-landed and barely missed the enormous hole, landing near Larry in a heap. Stella was also sent flying from the back of the sword and caught herself on one of Ashlock's branches.

"Tree!" she whisper-shouted. *"Are you okay?"*

Without Qi to answer her, he opened his trunk and revealed his Demonic Eye that glared up at her. Stella gulped as she let go and dropped to the blood- and flesh-splattered rock below.

"I'm sorry I brought the Grand Elder here..." Stella's eyes begged for mercy. *"I was just so worried as I saw the whole mountain tremble from afar but couldn't see through the spatial concealment and feared the worst."*

Ignoring Stella's pleas for now, he turned his Demonic Eye to glare at the Redclaw Grand Elder that was brushing the blood and guts off his robes. He froze when he felt Ashlock's gaze on him.

The man instantly knelt despite the condition of the floor, splashing black blood on his face. He then clasped his hands. "This useless one greets the esteemed immortal."

Ashlock let out a long sigh. Despite the seemingly doomed situation, perhaps this was a golden opportunity. Through his roots, he could feel the injured worm retreating out into the wilderness and back toward his wall of demonic trees.

That worm was worth far too many credits to let it leave so peacefully.

"But there's no way it's dumb enough to come back here after discovering I have void affinity." Ashlock's gaze drifted between his sect members, whom he considered heavy hitters.

He had grown an abundance of cultivation resources, enough for everyone, even the Grand Elder, Douglas, and Elaine. So maybe it was time for him to send everyone into the Mystic Realm for a teamwide power-up.

And then they could go worm hunting. Nobody messed with his peaceful mountain peak and got away with it.

29
AN UNEXPECTED REJECTION

Ashlock needed to take a moment to let his body recover, as trees didn't handle having their branches and roots ripped off very well.

Closing his Demonic Eye so he could ignore the outside world, he reeled in his spirit sight and retreated into the refuge of his mind. Slowing his thoughts and entering a state of deep meditation, he cycled his cultivation technique {Transpiration of Heaven and Chaos} and relished in the pleasant feeling.

Chaotic Qi surged up and poured into his dimmed Star Core through his roots buried deep within the world. Meanwhile, nutrients were also pulled up through his roots and redirected toward the bare stalks that once housed his lush scarlet leaves in an attempt to regrow them.

Luckily, the fruit he had spent so much Qi on had survived the turbulent winds from Larry's ash and the worm monster's screech. Which he was incredibly thankful for as the {Qi Fruit Production} skill took a large amount of Qi initially to create a unique seed imbued with one of his skills from which the flesh of the fruit would grow around. Once this initial Qi cost to develop the seed had been paid for, the fruit could grow with minimal resources from him.

As Ashlock cycled his cultivation technique, his connection to the heavens was restored as his leaves rapidly regrew. Once his Star Core had filled a little, he expended some Qi to burn his trunk and branches in soul fire to remove the ick he felt from the blood and guts of the worm that still caked his bark.

With his leaves regrown within minutes, he could fully utilize his cultivation technique as heaven and hell were connected through him. In this deep state of meditation, he could feel his profound connection to all the demonic trees surrounding him. Waves of emotion traveled through the mycelium and root network he shared with them.

Usually, he blocked them out as the constant surges of emotion from thousands of trees were a lot to take in.

"Don't worry, my children. Dad is all right," he transmitted through his roots and felt warm at the wave of happiness he received back. "Maybe I should talk to them more often."

Ashlock took a moment for himself for an unknown amount of time. He knew people were awaiting his guidance beyond his bark, but he was at peace in the darkness of his mind. He felt like there had been drama or fighting for every waking moment recently, and sometimes the need to just breathe and relax became too overbearing to ignore.

Stella failed to decipher Ash's mood as his trunk reclosed, hiding away his unsettling eye, and she felt his very weak Qi retreat deeper inside his trunk as if he were going to sleep. She knew she had messed up bringing the Redclaw Grand Elder here, but she wasn't willing to risk being away from Ash as he got attacked again.

Last time I had been in Darklight City, Tree was attacked by that brutal storm that reduced him to a smoldering stump. And today, I left to deal with the worm, and after getting hit once, it ignored me and went straight for Ash instead!

Stella pouted as she felt the world was unfair.

Keeping up our facade is important, but I felt coming to save you with the Redclaw Grand Elder's assistance was the best course of action. Stella let out a sigh. *If only I could have entered the spatial plane to peer through the concealment and check on you. Alas, ever since the buzz of enlightenment wore off, I have been unable to return there at will.*

She shook off her thoughts, and her eyes drifted across the mountain peak that smelled of rotting blood and guts. The black blood that painted the rock stuck to her shoe like paint, making her nose scrunch.

Stella then heard a cracking and felt movement behind her. Looking over her shoulder at the looming tree, she noticed the stumps of the weaker branches that were torn off during the fight begin to rapidly regrow like spindly fingers, and scarlet leaves sprouted from the other branches.

He's recovering, thank the heavens.

She stood there for a while, watching the fascinating scene of regrowth, but then stumbled back when the whole tree suddenly lit up with lilac soul fire. An awful stench wafted from the tree, smelling like burned, rotten blood.

Slowly backtracking away from the tree, Stella carefully sidestepped the massive hole and met with Diana and Larry, patiently waiting off to the side. The Redclaw Grand Elder was also there, still clasping his hands toward the recovering tree with a hint of awe in his aged eyes.

Stella ignored the man, half out of embarrassment and also because she had nothing to say to him, until Ash decided how to handle this situation. So instead, she stood beside Diana, who was humming to herself while letting Kaida lick her finger.

The snake appeared much larger than before, at least a few feet long, so his body was draped on Diana's shoulders like a scarf. Kaida's golden eyes were much the same, but his black scales had an almost liquid-like shimmer as if they were dripping in ink.

"Kaida seems to love you," Stella noted, trying to distract her mind from how awkward she felt due to the Grand Elder's presence.

"Well, I sure hope so." Diana flashed a thin smile. "He finished his evolution right as the worm arrived. Everyone was so busy fighting that he was forgotten about, so I swooped in and saved him."

Stella narrowed her eyes. "You didn't help with the fight?"

"How was I supposed to?" Diana shrugged, earning a hiss from Kaida as his body shifted. "The monster was in the mid-stage of the Star Core Realm. So even if I empowered my daggers with Qi, they couldn't penetrate its defenses. Also, the monster was so large that my mist technique would have hindered everyone more…and not to mention the poison that coated its skin."

She then glanced around. "Although I think I can help now that the… tree has finished its meal." The air suddenly became arid as a large ball of water manifested above Diana's palm.

Stella noted Diana's odd choice of wording as the Redclaw Grand Elder was still standing nearby, listening to their conversation.

Oblivious to Stella's thoughts, Diana splashed the ball of water on the ground, and it spread out with a viscous consistency like slime, collecting all the blood and guts left over from the decimated worm.

The awful smell that had been prevalent subsided, and Stella watched as the slimy water pulled all the black blood off her shoes and returned to a ball floating above Diana's palm.

"What are you going to do with that?" Stella asked, eying the swirling ball of blood and guts.

Diana answered her question with her golden spatial ring flashing with power and the water ball vanishing with a pop of air. "I'll store it in here for now and deposit it out into the wilderness the next time I go training out there."

"I see..." Stella said, tapping her chin. An awkward silence continued for a while. Then, finally, her eyes darted between Ash, still regrowing, and the Redclaw Grand Elder. Just as she was about to say something random to break the silence, the lilac soul fire consuming the tree vanished.

Has he woken up from his sleep?

Moments later, a rift formed, and two people she was familiar with stepped through, both wearing black masks.

"Holy friggin' shit!" Douglas shouted as he saw the enormous hole in the center of the mountain peak. He dashed over to the edge of the hole, practically dragging Elaine with him as he went as she was holding his hand.

Stella couldn't help it, but attention was drawn to their interlocked fingers. She flexed her own and then subconsciously looked over to Ash's branches. A frown formed on her face.

Douglas, oblivious to Stella's stare, cautiously leaned over the edge. His earth Qi channeled through his legs, and the now-clean stone surged up around his feet, locking him in place and allowing him to stare down into the abyss. "This has to be over a hundred meters wide and goes all the way to the base of the mountain!"

"Why do you sound so excited?" Stella said—the words coming out a little harsher than she expected.

Douglas cocked a brow at her attitude, and then he looked between her and Tree and seemed to come to his own conclusion. Which only made her mood sour further.

I'm not mad about Tree being hurt. He's fine...

Douglas shook off the stone around his feet and turned to face her with a grin. "I'm thrilled because I can turn this hole into the most awesome spiral staircase on this side of the continent!"

Stella looked between the excited Douglas and the hole large enough that she wasn't sure she could jump its length.

Does this idiot want to make a spiral staircase for a titan?

Realizing her mood was affecting her, she let out a single controlled breath and, behind her own wooden mask, offered a smile. "That does sound like a good idea, Douglas."

Stella then noticed that Ash was writing something in his soul fire on his trunk. "'Stella, translate my following words to everyone,'" she murmured to herself and then nodded.

Everyone quieted and watched as mystical words were written in soul fire on the demonic tree.

"'First of all, Douglas, I agree that is a great idea, but I have bigger plans for now,'" Stella read and saw Douglas clench his hand in glee. "'Things are moving faster than I would like. It's clear we need an immense amount of spirit stones to build a place of safety for everyone.'"

"Immortal, if I may," the Redclaw Grand Elder spoke respectfully, and Stella gave him a nod to continue. "Darklight City is a frontier region that borders the most active part of the wilderness. As the beast tide approaches, things will only get worse. I felt the deep desire to take this opportunity to apologize to your esteemed self that my family has not lived up to the expectations this city requires and have placed a heavy burden on your shoulders in recent weeks."

Stella didn't say it out loud, but she silently agreed with the Redclaw Grand Elder. All of these recent problems could have been dealt with by the old Ravenborne Grand Elder, who had been at the peak of the Star Core Realm and even stepped into the Nascent Soul Realm before his death.

Even with the Ravenborne gone, the Evergreens and Winterwraths could have defended this frontier region with the Evergreen's strong affinity for the area...but the Redclaws only have a single Star Core cultivator who is weakened due to the environment. Maybe I am being harsh due to seeing how useless he had been against the worm earlier today, but I see where he is coming from.

Stella patiently waited for Ash's reply, curious to see his thoughts as words materialized on his trunk.

"'I planned to wait until after the alchemy tournament for this, but if you all struggle this hard against a single Star Core monster, I will need to move up the schedule,'" Stella translated, her eyes going wide behind her mask as she suspected where Ash was going with this, yet she was still surprised as she glanced between Elaine and the Grand Elder.

The Grand Elder clasped his hands and bowed. "What does the great immortal advise?"

"'Including you, gather your five strongest members and come back here in two days at the crack of dawn. Prepare for a month-long excursion into a very hostile land with the goal of advancing your cultivation. Tell your family you will be gone for a week,'" Stella slowly translated, momentarily getting stuck on a few of the words.

He is referring to the Mystic Realm, I'm pretty sure...

"As you wish." The man bowed, and Stella saw a rift open beside him. Through the slightly distorted view, she could see the courtyard of the White Stone Palace. The Grand Elder gave one final bow and swiftly left through the rift.

Stella had never mentioned it, but either she had spent so much time around Tree, or her cultivation had improved enough that she could feel when his spiritual sight moved around ever so slightly. Her eyes wandered to where she guessed his gaze was and landed on Elaine.

"Prisoner, decide now. Do you wish to join our sect or remain in the cavern?" Stella translated and was glad the mask obscured her smirk, which then subsided.

Was she really this much of a vicious person? She quite liked Diana and tolerated Douglas for the most part, but something about Elaine just irked her on a primal level.

Elaine and Douglas had removed their masks once the Grand Elder had left, and the girl stared at her with wide eyes as if she had just handed her a death sentence.

Hey, don't look at me. I'm just the messenger.

"W-what does joining your sect involve?" Elaine stammered out while quaking like a leaf.

There was a long pause before Ash wrote, "'An oath of loyalty. In return, you will be provided freedom, unimaginable cultivation resources, and status.'"

Douglas looked down at Elaine, who was gripping his hand so hard that her knuckles were going white. "It's a pretty good deal—"

"I...refuse," Elaine said, her voice dying to a whisper at the end.

Stella hated to admit a gasp of surprise escaped her lips. It was insanity to turn down such an offer! Ash seemed equally confused because it took him a while to reply through Stella's translation. "'May I ask why? Your void affinity would be of great value to us, and we will take good care of you.'"

"An oath made out of fear or greed...is not an oath made from the heart," Elaine said. "In my opinion...y-your need for an o-oath of loyalty from m-me is a shallow attempt for c-control. If everything you say about this A-ashfallen Sect is true, then I w-would have no reason for betrayal."

By the end of her passionate speech that she had clearly practiced many times over in her head, the mountain peak was dead silent. Only the sound of the wind rustling Ash's leaves accompanied Elaine's ragged breaths, likely from nerves.

Anger brewed in Stella's heart as Elaine had directly insulted Ash, calling him a shallow manipulator. If only she could cut open that empty head of hers and shove all of Tree's greatness in there so she could see. Before she knew it, she had taken a few subconscious steps closer, and Douglas glared her down, making her pause.

"Her words were harsh, but they carried some truth." Douglas shrugged. "I understand the need for secrecy, I really do. But forcing oaths onto people isn't the way forward."

"Oh, really?" Stella crossed her arms. "Have you not benefited a lot since joining and taking the oath? Was my kindness on you wasted? Why are you taking the side of a prisoner rather than ours? Mhm?"

"Whoa, whoa." Douglas raised a hand, showing her his palm. "Stella, whenever something involves the tree, you get a little too confrontational."

"I do not—"

"Relax, Stella," Diana said flatly while patting her shoulder. "At least hear the girl out."

Elaine gave an appreciative nod toward Diana, which made Stella curse quietly under her breath.

The terrified girl seemed to gain some confidence with Douglas offering her support, so she continued with less stammering, "Great Immortal, I truly appreciate your invitation to join your sect. B-but you did kill my uncle, who had taken care of me for the last d-decade, and although my family doesn't treat me as well as I would like due to my i-impure root, I do not despise them enough to swear an oath to someone who k-killed one from my bloodline. To do so would be an insult, and I would be ashamed to call myself a Voidmind."

Douglas patted her shoulder and smiled warmly, making Stella's skin crawl.

I still don't understand why he treats her so much better than me unless something deeper is happening here. Stella squinted her eyes, trying to make sense of their body language, but she still couldn't put her finger on it.

Her wandering thoughts were interrupted by Ashlock writing with his soul fire. Reading the words, she relayed them to the others. "'The potential for diplomacy between myself and the Voidmind family is likely impossible with your knowledge of the Head Librarian's death. Without an oath of loyalty, you are too risky to waste resources on.'"

Elaine bowed and said to the floor, "Immortal…I am not o-opposed to working together in the f-future. But, if you wish to go to war against my family, I cannot, in good faith, work with you."

Despite her strong message, she was a stammering mess, which dulled her message somewhat.

Stella crossed her arms. "Well, then, we have no need for you."

We should have just killed her from the start, then we could have avoided all this nonsense. Ugh, I hate dealing with people. Can't we return to when it was just me, Tree, and maybe Diana?

Douglas shot her a glare, but Stella didn't care. Why was so much care and consideration given to this random woman who was a significant risk to their existence?

Dead people tell no tales.

"Stella…" Diana said flatly from the side. "You know deep down that the Ashfallen Sect needs to expand. Maybe in the future, we can delegate all of this work to others and hang around here in peace."

That does sound rather nice.

"Now, I don't know what the immortal thinks, but I see a lot of value in Elaine," Diana continued. "Void affinity alone will help us tremendously, and she has much more knowledge than us on many topics."

"Exactly," Douglas piped up. "There has to be a solution here."

There was a long pause. Everyone remained quiet as the wind rustled the decision makers' scarlet leaves. Eventually, Ash began to write Elaine's fate in his lilac soul fire.

Everyone turned to Stella, eager for her to translate the words. Instead, she glared at the ancient text that did not provide a solution she liked at all.

30
REVEALING THE TRUTH

Ashlock knew there was a slim chance of getting denied by Elaine. Hence he had offered her two options, but it was a little unexpected that she had openly stated her support for her bloodline while standing before her uncle's killer.

"I obviously know almost nothing about Elaine, but I had been under the assumption that most cultivators in the demonic sects were willing to backstab family in favor of power," Ashlock mused as he glanced over everyone standing before his trunk, awaiting his decision. "Perhaps she is this against saying an oath because she hasn't actually seen my cultivation resources yet?"

Either way, she was stupidly stubborn, overconfident in her value, or incredibly naive. To speak in such a way to someone so much more powerful than her while surrounded by foes truly baffled Ashlock.

"Unless..." His gaze shifted to Douglas and Elaine's hands. "Is Douglas giving her the confidence to defy me?"

If so, wasn't Douglas technically defying his oath of loyalty indirectly? Shouldn't the heavens be striking him down? Or were oaths more subjective to the individual than he had first thought? If Douglas believed in his heart and soul that he was not betraying him by trying to win Elaine over to the sect, then what was he to do?

Ashlock honestly found this whole situation a massive headache and a great annoyance. He had just survived a near-death attack by a Star

Core worm, and he needed strong, reliable people around him to prevent more incidents like this from occurring in the future.

Yet, sect politics were getting in the way, and he couldn't have Stella fully manage the sect as some of her worldviews and ideas were still immature due to her unique upbringing and young age. And to put Diana in charge would infuriate Stella and strain their relationship.

"I'm getting off topic." Ashlock sighed. "All right, let's take this one step at a time. Elaine is valuable as a sect member. She has a lot of knowledge I greatly lack, and void affinity is one of the most fearsome things I have ever encountered. If I wasn't immune to it due to my divinity, I would have had my eye ripped out and been chopped up into logs by that Voidmind Elder."

With Elaine established as valuable, Ashlock needed to figure out a way to bring her over to his side without excessive force, as that would strain his relationship with Douglas, who had been a relatively loyal and hard worker thus far.

"Although she is only valuable to me if she is loyal and doesn't speak about me to her family. Eventually, I will become strong enough to have no fear of the Voidmind family, but until then, I must sadly rely on oaths, as disloyalty is far too risky."

Ashlock knew he acted rather paranoid, but as a tree that could not move, he already had enough things trying to kill him without having his existence known to anyone outside his tight circle. He would eradicate loose ends until the end of time. Arrogance was the greatest killer in a world like this.

"Since oaths are not as secure as I had first thought, it's best to try and win her over through rewards and kindness, although I will still request for an oath of secrecy," Ashlock mulled. "Unlike Douglas and the Redclaw Grand Elder, which have rather replaceable skill sets, Elaine has both useful knowledge and a super-strong affinity, so it's worth going the extra mile to reel her in."

Ashlock sighed once again as he came to a decision. He would need to figure out a better chain of command and a way to bring new talent to the sect. There was no way he would interact personally and try to win over hundreds or thousands of people like this.

He glanced at Stella and ruled her out as someone who could handle that task. Diana also wasn't fit for the job, nor was Douglas, Elaine, or any of his guardians.

"Oh...I should get the Redclaws to manage this in the future."

The answer had been so obvious. Elaine was a special case, but he would definitely make the Redclaws handle sect recruitment in the future. "Anyway, time to give my decision. Let's hope she agrees..."

―――

Elaine felt sick.

She put on the strongest facade she could, but this was the most stressful situation she had ever faced in her entire life. Her father had warned her about oaths. They were basically slave contracts usually used by cultists or shady individuals who didn't want information leaked, as those with a true purpose or the strength to back up their words did not require heaven's interference.

Although she didn't say it out loud, she was beyond skeptical about this whole thing, especially once this supposed immortal that wasn't even showing himself brought up an oath.

Yes, she may die here due to her arrogance, but in her opinion, that was far better than betraying her family and being a slave to the person who had murdered her uncle.

They said my uncle paid with his life because he tried to fight this supposed immortal. If he really is dead, there's a good chance there is someone inside or below that weird tree more powerful than my uncle, but there's also a chance my uncle is still alive, trapped somewhere, or was caught by surprise. So all I have is their word that he is dead and deserved it.

What Elaine needed was time.

She needed to find a way to somehow delay being forced into saying an oath of absolute loyalty. With time she could uncover the truth behind this Ashfallen Sect to deem whether it was worth betraying her family and pledging her eternal loyalty for.

And if the whole thing turned out to be fake, as she suspected, there was the upcoming tournament where she could get her brother to save her.

She just needed time. Only fools signed a one-sided deal.

They said you were valuable. Otherwise, they would have just killed you earlier.

Elaine squeezed Douglas's warm hand. His looming presence gave her a thin strand of hope.

A moment passed, and a wave of anxiety washed over her as she saw that stupidly pure spatial Qi write words she couldn't understand.

"The immortal wishes to avoid a war with your family," Stella slowly read out. Clearly, she wasn't fluent in the mysterious language and had to translate the words one by one.

"Therefore, he believes reciting an oath of secrecy regarding your involvement with us and what happened to your uncle is reasonable. In exchange, he will give you a cultivation resource and welcome you into the sect."

Elaine bit her lower lip and flexed her fingers. An oath of secrecy was much better than one of loyalty.

If my family can somehow figure out what happened to Uncle without my help, then I won't be forced to fight my family alongside my uncle's killer. This gives me a lot more flexibility and options while still allowing them to cover their backs. Smart. I must be missing something here...but I can't figure out what.

Her mind raced, and she debated asking to be given a day to mull over her thoughts, but on the other hand, she felt like she was about to pass out from stress and nerves. Although they had been more hospitable than expected to a prisoner, she was still pushing her luck.

This oath gives them peace of mind while also giving me more time. It should be fine...

"Immortal, I accept your oath of secrecy." Elaine stepped forward, releasing her hand from Douglas. "Tell me the exact terms of the oath and to whom I should recite it."

Her heart was pounding so hard in her chest that she could hear it in her ears as soul-fire words manifested on the black trunk of the tree.

"'You will not mention or try to convey anything regarding the Ashfallen Sect, including its members and activities, to anyone not recognized as an Ashfallen Sect member,'" Stella slowly read out. "'Furthermore, you will never disclose what you know about your uncle's disappearance.'"

There was a short silence as the words vanished and new ones materialized.

"'As an oath done under the heavens, failure to abide by the sworn oath will result in the crippling of your cultivation.'" Stella then gestured toward the enormous spider that had hunted her down. "'And Larry will be sent to dispose of you.'"

Elaine gulped, and to make matters worse, the trunk of the tree suddenly cracked open like an accursed maw, and through the darkness peered an eye that was incomprehensible to her mind. It made her feel like there was a soup of eyes invading her mind, as they superimposed on each other in an eternal cycle that made her dizzy.

A shadow loomed over her, dispersing the visions plaguing her mind and giving her a moment of salvation. She felt vomit rise up her throat, but she barely managed to keep it down. Her breath was shaky, and sweat dripped from her forehead and clouded her glasses.

The shadow loomed closer, casting her in darkness. Apprehensively, she looked up, wiping her glasses with quivering hands, and came face to face with Stella, the blond-haired girl. Her mask was removed, and she could see her perfect skin and crazed pink eyes that seemed to glow with power.

"You have gazed upon the immortal and know the terms of the oath," Stella said with a smirk. "Now recite the oath to him so we may move on from this nonsense."

Elaine looked past the crazy person taking up the majority of her view at Douglas, who was standing off to the side. He seemed apprehensive about stepping in to help her here.

He must fear this girl somewhat. If I don't recite the oath, I really fear she will stab me in the throat.

Elaine stood up on shaking legs and looked straight at the tree. She slowed her breathing and thought back to that unsettling gaze.

"I, Elaine Voidmind, pledge secrecy to the immortal of the Ashfallen Sect. I will not mention or try to convey anything regarding the Ashfallen Sect, including its members and activities, to anyone not recognized as an Ashfallen Sect member. I will also not disclose any information I know about my uncle's disappearance to anyone."

As the final word left her mouth, she felt a pressure from above gaze down on her as if heaven had taken an interest in the oath. She had never heard of any mention of this phenomenon before.

She then felt as if phantom chains had wrapped around her Soul

Core, and she instinctively knew in the back of her mind what would happen if she broke the oath.

Her death would be inevitable.

Ashlock let out a long sigh of relief. Of course, it wasn't the perfect outcome, as he would have much preferred an oath of loyalty, but this should be good enough for now. He wanted allies that would cultivate immortality and surround him for eternity, so creating a divide between his sect members this early on by forcing Elaine with an ultimatum of loyalty was a terrible idea.

"Larry," Ashlock said through the tether. "Continue to keep an eye on her."

He thought about adding that Larry should kill Elaine if she betrayed him, but he didn't trust the spider to discern what counted as a betrayal.

Receiving a grunt of agreement, he watched as everyone surrounded the newest member of the sect. With the reciting of the oath, as agreed, she was now a member just like Douglas.

Diana also removed her mask and patted Elaine on the shoulder while appraising her with her dull eyes.

"D-Diana, right?" Elaine asked as Douglas moved in to stand beside her.

"Yeah, that's me," Diana said flatly. "Welcome to the Ashfallen Sect."

She then raised the snake. "This is Kaida. He is one of the immortal's pets."

Elaine apprehensively patted the large snake on the head, earning a hiss.

"Wait...since when did Kaida finish his evolution?" Ashlock only now noticed the large snake coiled around Diana's shoulders.

While Diana spoke with Elaine, Stella sneaked over to stand beside Ashlock and whispered while distorting her voice with spatial Qi, "Should we tell Elaine about the truth? That you are the Patriarch? If we have Elaine hanging around us all day, one of us will inevitably let it slip by accident."

The paranoia in the back of his mind wanted to lock Elaine up in the cavern and tell everyone to ignore her to keep that information secret, but he acknowledged that wasn't possible.

"Best to get it out of the way," Ashlock grumbled and flashed his leaf once to tell Stella it was all right to proceed. Of course, he expected Elaine to become skeptical, but hopefully, offering her a skin improvement truffle would convince her that almost everything else wasn't a lie.

Stella strode over to Elaine. *"I have a confession to make, Elaine."*

Elaine shrank back into Douglas's side, clearly quite terrified of Stella.

"Yes...?"

"The Ashfallen Sect is ruled by its Patriarch, Ashlock." Stella gestured to the demonic tree lording over the mountain peak. *"Although we tell everyone there's an immortal that rules the sect, that's technically not true...although the tree is sort of immortal."*

Elaine tilted her head, a frown forming on her face. "So what are you implying?"

Douglas laughed heartily as he patted Elaine's back. *"It means these nutters take orders from a fucking tree!"*

Stella crossed her arms and glared at Douglas. "You do as well."

"I know!" Douglas wiped a tear from his eye. *"It's still hilarious to me, but I have to admit, he is one bloody good Patriarch."*

"I don't understand!" Elaine tugged on Douglas's arm but became distracted as the stone cracked open nearby her foot, and a root poked out. Growing on its tip was a single truffle.

Stella plucked the truffle and handed it to the confused Elaine. *"Go back down to the cavern with Douglas and consume this truffle. It will make your skin as perfect as mine and Diana's."*

Elaine's eyes went wide as she glanced between the maskless girls. She then clutched the truffle close to her chest and gave Stella a small nod.

Ashlock was curious to see her reaction and enthusiasm regarding the Ashfallen Sect once she had consumed that truffle. However, in the meantime, he needed everyone to do things while they waited for the Mystic Realm to open up again.

"I need Douglas to integrate Elaine into the sect and explain things to her, and then I need him to help Stella with the formations. Ideally, I want both the concealment and Qi-gathering formation completed within the next three days."

Ashlock wrote out his orders on his trunk in lilac flames, and Stella relayed them to everyone.

Opening a rift to the cavern below, Elaine stepped through without delay, and Douglas gave Ashlock a hearty grin and thumbs-up before following.

"At least he's happy." Ashlock chuckled and watched as Stella wasted no time returning to work on the concealment formation, which was by far the most important right now, as he didn't have the Qi spare to maintain the spatial distortion technique.

"I must keep some Qi in reserve and refill my Star Core in case I get attacked again. As for the worm..." Ashlock shifted his view to the wilderness, and sure enough, the monstrous worm was loitering below the wall of demonic trees, likely for the same reason it had been there the first time.

It was hunting to regain its strength.

As within just an hour or so, there was already a small gathering of monsters. All of them were weak and unlikely to provide many sacrificial credits, so Ashlock left them alone.

"Best to leave the bait out to keep the worm happy and away from me," Ashlock mused. He was still excited to capture and kill the monster for all those juicy sacrificial credits, but that would have to wait for now. He needed his sect to become stronger first.

"Tree!" Stella hollered from the side of the mountain peak. *"I need your help with the runic formation!"*

"Oh yeah, I was helping her before the whole worm incident." Ashlock found the giant sword dumped off to the side, picked it back up with a black vine from his {Consuming Abyss} skill, and returned to work.

31
(INTERLUDE) LACKING PERSPECTIVE

"I knew something was off about all this," Elaine grumbled as she collapsed against a rock and rotated the truffle in her hand, frowning at it.

Douglas, who was leaning against a nearby wall, shrugged. "You got far better treatment than I ever did. They practically bullied me into an oath of loyalty."

An oath...

Elaine reached up and touched her chest, feeling the cold phantom chains around her Soul Core constantly reminding her of the lifelong commitment she had so foolishly accepted.

I knew I should have rejected them and asked to remain a prisoner in the cavern. How couldn't I have seen the immortal was fake and they were all crazy people worshiping a talking tree?

She clenched her fist and asked Douglas, "The oath of loyalty, how does it feel?"

"Feel? Hmmm... If I have thoughts of betrayal, the cold chains around my soul tighten," Douglas said. "And I know if I were to act on one of these thoughts, the chain would burn holes in my soul, allowing the heart demons to overwhelm me."

"Do you regret it?" Elaine asked. It sounded awful to her. Would she experience the same if she tried to contact her family and tell them about the Ashfallen Sect?

Douglas shook his head with a faint smile. "I would do it a hundred times over if I could. After being kicked out of the Terraforge family due to a lack of talent, I became a wandering rogue cultivator of Darklight City, struggling under a crushing amount of debt with nowhere to go. Yet despite all that, they took me in, paid off my debts without another thought, and have treated me well ever since. Kindness is hard to come by out here in the wilderness, so it should be cherished when given."

"They didn't seem very kind to me," Elaine mumbled.

Douglas laughed. "They get very defensive when something threatens the tree, but they are great people once you get to know them. From what I've heard, your uncle caused quite the commotion and almost killed them, so it's no wonder they are apprehensive about you."

"Why am I being punished for what my Elder did, though?" Elaine sighed as she leaned back and looked at the cavern ceiling. Her prison.

"I would say you are fortunate, and this is one of the greatest opportunities you will ever encounter," Douglas said confidently. "To call this a punishment means you lack perspective."

Elaine snorted. "What about this is fortunate?"

"Say, Elaine," Douglas said seriously, his joking tone gone, making her look up and meet his eyes. "You were a rather sheltered child, weren't you? Perhaps a scion of your house? I remember you shouting about being the daughter of the Grand Elder when we first met."

Elaine didn't answer. *Why is he asking me such a question?*

He let off a short laugh and walked over, crouching before her. "You are too naive. You could have been turned into a pill furnace where alchemy is performed in your stomach, and they use your own fucking soul and flesh as part of the pill-making process. Or how about feeding you to a caged monster so it could further its cultivation? My point is there are a million ways to treat a prisoner, and you weren't treated like that."

Douglas leaned over and tapped the truffle in her hand. "You think your family cares that fucking much about you? What cultivation resources have they dedicated to you, a supposed daughter of the Grand Elder? Even I have a better spirit root and cultivation stage than you, and I was kicked out of my family due to a lack of talent. It's pathetic."

Elaine was taken aback by Douglas's shift in tone. "They do care about me…" she whispered, trying to retreat up against the rock.

"Let me guess, they discovered you lacked talent in cultivation and told you some bullshit about it being too expensive?" Douglas snorted.

"But then they discovered you weren't totally useless and sent you to live out your near-mortal life while being a glorified slave to your now-dead uncle. Right?"

Elaine felt her heart sink in her chest. She didn't want to believe his words, but she started seeing through her family's lies when he framed it like that.

Douglas let out a long sigh. "Sorry, Elaine. But to hear you badmouth the Ashfallen Sect after you took an oath nauseates me, and that's straight from my fucking heart, not the oath talking. They are a bit insane but otherwise generous people and have offered you an opportunity many like me would kill for. The fact you put your family, that would have abandoned you, over them is crazy to me. You simply lack perspective. Eat that truffle, and then we can talk."

Without another word, Douglas stood up and strode off to somewhere within the alchemy lab, and a while later, she heard the familiar rumbling of rock as he got to work, likely on that staircase he was talking about.

Elaine looked down at the black thing they called a truffle. At first, she had been against eating it, but Douglas's passionate speech had filled her with curiosity. Did she really lack perspective?

I cultivated at home with my family, and once they discovered I had no talent, they sent me to study under my uncle. I suppose you could consider me sheltered. Am I really missing something here?

Elaine rotated the truffle in her hand one last time, feeling the rough surface between her fingers. She'd always wanted to be a cultivator over a researcher.

The first time I met Stella, she mentioned they have cultivation resources that could improve spirit roots, remove heart demons, and even improve a person's skin. So if this truffle makes my skin look as good as theirs, then there may be a chance for me to pursue the long journey of cultivation here with the one that improves my spirit root.

"Lacking perspective, huh?" Elaine sighed before opening her mouth and chucking the truffle in. It had an earthy, almost nutty taste, and she chewed for a while and eventually swallowed.

Almost immediately, she felt ecstasy flow through her body, her skin became warm, and she suddenly felt refreshed. The experience was so overwhelming she barely managed to force herself into a lotus position and begin to cultivate, trying to cycle the truffle's power that felt like liquid honey throughout her body.

Elaine's eyes fluttered open, and she let out a pleasurable groan. Her body felt ten years younger as the stiffness in her lower back was gone. Looking around the sunlit cavern, she realized she still needed her glasses, which was a shame.

Her nose then scrunched up when a foul stench overwhelmed her. She looked down at her body and saw her clothes drenched with yellow-and-black sludge.

"Is this gunk impurities expelled from my body?" Elaine gagged as tears filled her eyes. The smell was truly vile. She went to rip off her clothes but paused. Searching around, she couldn't see Douglas anywhere, but the distant rumbling of earth suggested he was still hard at work.

Peeking around one of the large earthen bowls that housed an alchemy fruit, Elaine noted that sunlight poured down the enormous hole in the side of the cavern.

It was late afternoon when I ate the truffle, but the sunlight's intensity suggests it's midday now. Did a day pass since I went into meditation?

Elaine glanced back at the rock she had been leaning against and saw a white towel, a black cloak, and a spatial ring in a neat, folded pile.

Who left this here for me? Was it Douglas?

While trying to hold her breath to resist the vile stench, she rubbed the gunk from her hands on her clothes and then slid on the spatial ring, eagerly searching through its contents.

This is my spatial ring. Almost everything is still in here…except the communication jades.

Unable to bear the smell, Elaine waved her hand while her ring flashed with power, and the towel and cloak disappeared into the spatial ring. She then made a beeline for the sound of rushing water.

Within minutes, she had made it to the entrance of the tunnel that led outside, blocked off by that slime door. Next to the tunnel was a hollow black root poking out of the wall with crystal-clear water gushing out.

Doing one last check to see if anyone was around, she ripped off her clothes and tossed them to the river bank as if they were cursed.

"Ugh, this is so disgusting." Elaine cursed as her arms were glued to her sides from the gunk. Without wasting any more time, she dashed into the freezing cold water and tried to wash the gunk off.

The sunlight was dim, and the glowing mushrooms overhead didn't offer the best lighting. However, Elaine's eyes still went wide as the gunk was washed away, revealing skin so smooth and unfamiliar that she felt like she was inhabiting someone else's body.

"How is this even possible?" she muttered as her hands moved faster, eager to see the results. By the end of her cleaning session, she was shivering from the freezing water, but a smile bloomed.

Exiting the water and walking barefoot on the rough stone, she summoned the towel from her spatial ring, quickly dried herself, and then wrapped the towel around her waist. "I should have a mirror somewhere in here."

Digging through the heap of unchecked belongings in her spatial ring, she soon discovered a mirror that had not been used in a long time. Ever since her path in cultivation stalled, she hated how her face clearly aged faster than her peers, so she had ignored it.

"Gosh, I don't look twenty-five at all," Elaine murmured as she stared at the beauty looking back at her in the mirror. The bags that had always been under her eyes due to forgoing sleep in favor of meditation or research were long gone.

Wait...I haven't looked at my reflection in a long time, but did my bone structure change?

Elaine squinted as she traced her jawline and general facial structure. She wasn't certain, but had the truffle also altered her bones? If so, this wasn't the work of a mere cultivation treasure but a gift from the heavens themselves.

This is freaky. It's like I am a different person.

Elaine reached up and felt the strands of her rose-gold hair between her fingertips. It was silky smooth, and the ends weren't frayed anymore.

"You done checking yourself out?"

Elaine almost dropped the mirror as she yelped at the sudden voice. Spinning round, she crossed her chest with her arms, but they failed to obscure her bust from the newcomer.

There was a blond-haired girl she was familiar with standing there.

Stella appraised her for a moment and then pouted. "I see you took the truffle the Patriarch gave you."

"Y-yes?" Elaine replied, unsure of what to make of this situation. *Why is she here?*

"I almost couldn't recognize you for a second. It didn't have this profound of an effect on me." Stella stopped, appraising her body, and laughed awkwardly. "Sorry, I am staring a bit too much. I came here to hand you this. I think someone from your family is trying to contact you."

Stella opened her palm, revealing a communication jade with a subtle green glow.

"I can take the call?" Elaine felt puzzled. Why would they return her spatial ring without the communication jade and then allow her to take a call anyway?

"Sure," Stella replied. "Although I will stay here to listen in."

"Can I get dressed first?" Elaine asked, hushed, as she felt the breeze against her bare skin. Stella nodded, turning her back and looking in the other direction, which for a cultivator was basically pointless with spiritual sight.

Deciding she didn't have time to fully dress, she summoned the cloak that had been left alongside the towel, hung it over her shoulders, and secured it around her chest. Since it was rather tight-fitting, she kept the towel around her waist as a skirt substitute.

"All right, give it to me," Elaine said, and Stella turned around and handed her the glowing jade. Inserting a sliver of her Qi, the connection was made.

"Sister? What took you so long to answer?" a voice she hadn't heard in years echoed out of the jade.

"Forgive me. I was preoccupied, Brother," Elaine answered while shooting glances at Stella, who had her arms crossed. "Why are you calling me?"

"What's with that tone, Sister? I took time out of my cultivation to talk to you, yet you have the nerve to leave me waiting?" There was a haunted laugh. "Were you too busy following Uncle around like a lost dog? Or lost in research about nonsense?"

"No, Brother..."

"Anyway, Sister, I will arrive in Darklight City in two weeks. You will show me around that backwater city and accompany me. Do I make myself clear?"

Since when did he speak to me like this? Actually, when was the last time we spoke? Before I was kicked out of the family to this city... Ah, I see.

"I'm not sure, Brother," Elaine replied while looking at Stella. "I might be preoccupied when you plan to visit."

There was a long pause before the voice coldly asked, "Doing what? Cultivating? Don't make me laugh. Where are you right now?"

Elaine was about to tell her brother she was in a cavern, but she felt the phantom chains coldly wrap around her Soul Core.

So Heaven sees that as leaking information about the Ashfallen Sect to my family, which triggered my oath... I see.

Without being able to disclose anything to her brother about her whereabouts, she couldn't see a viable way of continuing the conversation.

"I'm very busy, Brother. Please call back another time. Goodbye." Elaine ruthlessly cut off her sibling, and before he could reply, she cut the call.

Elaine returned the communication jade to Stella. "That was rather embarrassing. I didn't expect him to talk to me like that."

Stella took the jade back and shrugged. "My human family is all dead, Diana's were also eradicated, and Douglas's family kicked him out to the streets. Compared to that, it seems you have it easy."

"Human family?"

"Yeah," Stella nodded, "Tree and I have been together since I was a child, and he was nothing but a sapling. So I consider him my family now."

"I'm sorry..."

Stella tilted her head in confusion. "About what?"

"I don't know...everything." Elaine sighed. "Douglas said earlier that I lacked perspective, and it's true. I have eaten a few cultivation resources in the past, and they were just some Qi-enhanced grass and leaves mashed together in a disgusting pill that did nothing substantial. I looked down on the truffle your tree provided me as a token of friendship because I was skeptical, but it's hard to deny the results... Your tree is amazing."

"You should call him Patriarch," Stella quipped back but grinned. "Although I do agree that Tree is amazing."

"Would it be all right if I apologized to the Patriarch? Or should I remain down here in the cavern?"

Stella glanced at her hardly put-together outfit and laughed. "Well, two days have passed since you recited the oath, so the Redclaws should be arriving soon. You might want to put on some real clothes."

"Oh yeah…" Elaine noted with a smile. "Thank you, Stella, I genuinely mean it. If my uncle really did the things you claim, I apologize on his behalf and hope you don't hold it too much against me."

Stella shrugged. "Tree clearly seems to see some value in you, so you better not let him down and get to cultivating."

"Cultivating…" The word felt so foreign to her. Would she really be allowed to cultivate to her heart's content here?

"If you think that truffle you ate was impressive," Stella smugly grinned, "just wait until you experience the spirit-improving one or get hurled into the Mystic Realm. Then you will be in for a real treat."

32
MYSTIC REALM PREPARATIONS

Elaine, Douglas, and Stella stepped through a rift Ashlock had conjured up.

It was almost creepy how much Elaine had changed from two days ago. Before, she had been a perfect example of an overworked researcher, with a hunched-back, reserved presence and the plague of sleep at the edge of her eyes.

However, now she looked full of life while laughing with Douglas. She had a slightly more mature demeanor than Stella and Diana, but it made sense as she was almost a decade older than Stella.

Elaine stopped chatting and glanced around in confusion, likely at the distorted view that enshrouded the mountain peak. Stella had successfully created the concealment array over the last two days, but it was nowhere near as good as his personal technique.

Neither Stella nor Douglas was an array master, so the concealment array was an amateur's work at best. But it got the job done by attempting to mimic his previous technique. Ashlock actually had to divert some of his attention and Qi into the array to make it function, but it was far less than before.

The Qi-gathering array was also almost completed, and Stella had been in the middle of finishing it up when the communication jade in her spatial ring that she had confiscated from Elaine's lit up. Deciding this was a perfect opportunity to test how her oath functioned, Ashlock had sent Stella to meet Elaine down in the cavern.

It had been unfortunate timing, as Elaine had been in the middle of bathing, but even after seeing her bare bust, Ashlock had felt nothing. Even with his slightly human mind, his tree biology made seeing naked humans feel the exact same as seeing a naked animal. However, even he had been just as surprised as Stella at Elaine's drastic change.

For Stella and Diana, the truffle had made their skin smooth and their hair silkier, and that was about it. Whereas for Elaine, it had made her a different person. Maybe Ashlock hadn't noticed how different cultivators and mortals looked in this world, as he never really paid much attention to mortals, but after witnessing Elaine, he realized the drastic difference in appearance between the two.

"You can cultivate with us up here if you want, Elaine," Stella said nonchalantly. *"The Redclaws will be here soon, and then we will head into the mystic realm."*

"What is the mystic realm?" Elaine asked. Douglas also seemed curious.

"Tree will create a weird mist, and when you walk through it, you will find yourself in a pocket realm full of Qi that matches our Soul Cores. Although we have only gone there once, so that may change."

"A pocket realm?!?" they both said simultaneously, and Stella grinned, seeing Douglas and Elaine gobsmacked.

"That's right." Stella pointed her nose to the sky. "Isn't Tree awesome?"

Ashlock wished she would stop flattering him over a system-given skill. It wasn't like he got the skill out of his own hard work, unlike his cultivation techniques that required hours of meditation for him to reach a mutual understanding with the heaven's will.

"Will I be entering this pocket realm?" Elaine asked curiously.

"Sure, we all will—"

"Hold on," Diana cut off Stella as she walked over. *"We know little about the mystic realm, so allowing someone with little cultivation and combat experience to enter may lead to their death."*

Ashlock had to agree that was a good point.

"I wanted to use the mystic realm a few more times to gauge its capabilities before sending more people in, but I don't have time to waste months on testing," he pondered.

His current plan was to send everyone in and try to get Maple or someone else to somehow end up in the same pocket realm as Stella so she could ascend to the Star Core Realm with less risk.

"Patriarch, do you mind if I test Elaine's capabilities?" Diana asked, and Ashlock replied with a flash of his leaf.

"I don't plan to bring the Redclaw Grand Elder and his chosen people over for a few hours, so testing Elaine's capabilities is a good idea, as I am also rather curious," Ashlock mused.

"Go do it over there." Stella pointed to the area behind Ashlock. *"I need to finish up the Qi-gathering array and don't want you accidentally damaging it. Douglas, come and help me."*

"But…" Douglas glanced between Elaine and Diana. "Will she be all right?"

Diana snorted as she summoned a sword to her hand and walked past Ashlock. "I won't go too hard on her, don't worry."

Elaine gave Douglas a reassuring smile before running after Diana. On the way, she stopped before Ashlock and gave a short bow. "Patriarch, I just wanted to apologize for not seeing the greatness of your gift earlier."

Ashlock appreciated the apology, and since she didn't know the ancient language, he flashed his leaf to show he accepted the apology.

Elaine pointed at the leaf and shouted after Diana, *"The leaf flashing once means the Patriarch is happy, right?"*

Diana didn't turn to look but still chuckled before calling over her shoulder, *"If it flashed once, it means yes, twice for no. You can talk to him directly if you learn the ancient runic language like Stella."*

"Oh!" Elaine said. *"I'm good at languages. Maybe I can learn it quickly."*

That reminded Ashlock of the skill fruit he had been growing. "I will give them to her later alongside the truffles," he decided as he watched her walk away and stand opposite Diana.

"Draw your sword," Diana said, and Elaine gave her an awkward smile.

"Err… I was never given one."

"You have never held a sword?" Diana furrowed her brows.

"No, no!" Elaine waved her hands. *"I held a sword…back when I was fifteen."*

Diana let out a long sigh. *"So, what? A decade ago? How haven't you held a sword since? You are a cultivator, right?"*

Elaine seemed to suffer emotional damage as she recoiled. *"I...I was a cultivator until my family said I was better suited as a researcher at the Academy."*

Ashlock also couldn't believe Elaine hadn't even been able to practice with a sword in the evenings or something. In a world like this, being smart was pointless in the face of overwhelming might. The beast tide wouldn't care about how many hours you spent memorizing textbooks or advancing the primitive science of this world.

"That's likely why civilization hasn't advanced that much, even with the modern-style stuff they find from rifts. The cultivators are too focused on meditating to care about research, and those conducting research are either looking for ways to overcome a bottleneck or developing demonic techniques. Cultivators care little about fashion trends or new dishes, and the mortals are too busy trying to get through their day-to-day lives to invent new things."

That aside, Elaine needed a sword. "Would it be too morbid of me to give her one of her dead uncle's swords? Or would that prove to her I did kill him and increase her respect for me? Hmmm."

Ashlock delved into his collection and picked out one of the Voidmind Elder's swords with a flowery pattern embroidered on the hilt. It also looked the lightest of the swords and was made from a weird black metal that he was curious about, so he decided to give it to her.

"Oh, looks like you are in luck," Diana said as Ashlock took the sword out of his inventory and floated it over to Elaine with telekinesis.

"That's," Elaine frowned as she gripped the sword from the hilt and inspected it, "one of my uncle's swords."

Diana remained mute as Elaine traced the hilt with her finger, a mixture of emotions flickering across her face. "So you really did kill him, huh?"

"It would seem she still harbors some doubts about Stella's words," Ashlock mused, "which makes sense as a lot of what comes out of that sly girl's mouth is bullshit."

"Can I keep this?" Elaine asked Ashlock, and he flashed his leaf. He still had seven other swords.

"Oh, wait, I never gave Diana her sword. I only ever gave one to Stella."

Digging through his inventory, he fished out that dark blue blade in a blue leather sheath he had reserved for Diana and floated it over to her.

Diana gripped the sword out of the air and whistled. "Wow, this is an expensive-looking sword." She then traced her finger along its blade and exclaimed, "It's made from water Qi-infused metal!"

Dark blue flames with a hint of demonic Qi shot out of her hand, curled around the sword hilt and down the blade. The metal seemed to ripple as if it had turned into a liquid substance like mercury. She then slashed it at the other sword she was holding, and Ashlock marveled at how the blade harmlessly passed through as if it was made from water.

Diana then sliced through again but this time solidified the blade halfway through, which caused the other sword to crack in half.

"So this was one of the Voidmind Elder's swords? He had quite expensive tastes. This could cost hundreds of thousands of spirit stones." She then eyed Elaine's black metal sword. *"That one must be made out of a metal that harmonizes with void Qi."*

Elaine eyed her own blade and frowned. *"I don't know how I feel about all this."*

Diana shrugged. "He deserved it. He tried to turn the Patriarch into firewood and also kill Stella." The words came out so monotone and cold that even Ashlock was surprised.

"I see..." Elaine shook her head as if trying to stop her spiraling thoughts. "Okay, enough with sentiments. How can I use this thing?"

What followed was Diana explaining at length to Elaine how to insert her Qi into an object as Elaine had only recently made it into the Soul Fire Realm, which was the first realm where a cultivator could manipulate their Qi outside of their own bodies, and Elaine had never had any practice imbuing objects with her Qi before.

"Whoa!" Elaine exclaimed as the black metal sword looked like it was made from a starless night sky.

"Don't wave it around," Diana scolded. *"Even at the first stage of the Soul Fire Realm, your void Qi is dangerous for the rest of us. I'm not even certain I could fully resist it with my own Qi."*

Elaine seemed to struggle with wielding the sword and accidentally swung too low, making the blade carve effortlessly through the rock like a hot knife through butter. Shocked, she reeled in her Qi and looked at the gash in the rock.

"Ah...I'm sorry," she muttered while scratching her head.

"I don't think you would survive even five minutes in the mystic realm," Diana ruthlessly claimed while depositing her sword in her spatial ring, signifying the end of the assessment.

Elaine let out a tired sigh. "That's unfortunate."

Diana shrugged. *"Don't worry too much. There should be another chance in the future. But between now and then, you must advance a few stages in the Soul Fire Realm and learn to fight and wield a sword."*

That gave Ashlock an idea. He would have a week to kill while waiting for everyone to return from the Mystic Realm. He could totally have sparring matches with her.

"Fear not, Elaine! The greatest sword tree on the continent is here to train you!" Ashlock chuckled to himself. He still found it rather funny that he could swing swords around as a tree.

While he had been thinking, the pair walked past him and over to Stella, who was working alongside Douglas to complete the Qi-gathering array. It was smaller scale than the previous one, but it utilized only high-grade spirit stones, so it should have a similar level of performance.

Stella was trying to get rid of the ink that was all over her hands while Douglas melted the spirit stones into the grooves.

"Let me help you with that," Diana said as water from the air coiled around Stella's hands like snakes and washed away the ink.

Stella smiled in response and asked about Elaine's sparring session. Meanwhile, Douglas finished his work, and the array was operational moments later with a flash of power.

Everyone breathed in a Qi-filled breath, and Ashlock felt like he had dipped his roots into warm water as Qi surged through the transfer arrays and into his roots.

With the extra Qi and Elaine having completed her assessment, Ashlock decided it was time to bring over the Redclaws. The mystic realm wasn't opening for two more days, but all of them would need time to prepare and consume the truffles.

Relaying that information to Stella, she turned to everyone. "All right, everyone, put on masks. The Redclaws are arriving soon."

"Is everyone here?" the Redclaw Grand Elder asked the ever-scowling Elder Mo.

"Amber will be here any second now, Grand Elder," Elder Mo replied.

"Mhm, good." The Grand Elder surveyed the mostly empty courtyard of the White Stone Palace. He had made sure the place was cleared out to avoid any chance of angering the Ashfallen Sect's immortal.

He then suddenly felt a surge of spatial Qi as a rift opened. Through the wobbling view of the rift's destination, he saw four people wearing black masks standing in a row with Stella in the center.

"I'm here, Grand Elder!" Amber called out and stumbled across the courtyard to stand beside Elder Margret. "Sorry I'm late."

The Grand Elder gave a disapproving glance before turning toward the portal and gesturing for everyone to follow him.

There was a pop of air and a sudden temperature drop as he emerged on the higher mountain peak. The wind rustled his robes and hair as he waited for his family to follow.

"Welcome, Redclaws," Stella announced once the Grand Elder felt the rift collapse behind him.

The Grand Elder managed to resist looking around and gawking at everything. But the Elders to his side, especially Amber, could not hide their curiosity as this was the first time they had seen the infamous Red Vine Peak in person.

Without missing a beat, the Grand Elder bowed. "As per the immortal's request, I have brought the four strongest of my family."

He then straightened up and eyed the four people in front of him and was surprised to see a woman with rose-gold hair that he hadn't seen before standing beside the Underlord, the hulking man that wore the black cloak.

"Douglas, if you will," Stella said to the man he knew as Underlord, and the earth-affinity cultivator cycled his Qi, causing the mountain to rumble and an earthen table to rise from the stone.

Stella then walked up to the newly formed table. Her spatial ring flashed with power, and a variety of freshly picked fruit appeared—none of which the Grand Elder recognized.

"All right, in two days, the immortal will allow us to enter the Mystic Realm, which allows cultivators to travel to Qi-rich pocket realms that match their affinity, allowing their cultivation to increase quickly." Stella waved off their questions. "I will answer your questions later, but first, let me tell you about these fruits and truffles that I am going to give you."

Who cares about some fruit!?! the Grand Elder shouted in his mind while keeping a stoic expression. *What do you mean the immortal can send us to a pocket dimension? Only Monarch Realm cultivators can create a single pocket dimension, yet you say he can send us to multiple? Just how powerful is this Ashfallen Sect?*

Clearly oblivious or uncaring for the Elder's pleas for more information, Stella pointed at each fruit individually. "Deep meditation, enlightenment, neural root, language comprehension, vampiric touch, lightning Qi Barrier, clairvoyance, mind fortress, and finally, florist's touch."

"What?" The Grand Elder didn't understand what he was hearing. He was still stuck on the Mystic Realm part. Are these fruit special as well?

Stella cocked her head to the side. "What's wrong? I am just listing the temporary effects these fruits give when you eat them."

"Temporary effects…" The Grand Elder pointed to a random one and asked, "What does the language comprehension fruit do?"

"It lets you learn languages super fast," Stella replied as if it was the most obvious thing in the world. "Anyway…"

"Wait—" The Grand Elder felt a headache creeping into his mind. Not that he blamed them for not giving him such a precious fruit earlier, but he had spent weeks learning the ancient language to converse with the immortal and save his family, yet there had been a fruit that could help him with that all along?

"Questions later, please," Stella replied with a huff. "Every time you interrupt me, I lose my place. Now, where was I?"

"Truffles," the black-haired girl to her side answered flatly.

"Ah, yes, thank you," Stella said cheerfully, pointing at an unassuming black ball with a stubbly surface. "This truffle, when consumed, improves the purity of your spirit root permanently."

The Grand Elder felt ashamed to admit he shouted, "WHAT?!?" alongside his family members, but he couldn't hold back anymore.

"Yeah?" Stella replied with that same dismissive tone. "See? I used to have an impure spirit root."

A light purple soul flame flickered to life in her palm, and all of the Redclaws stepped closer, gawking at it.

What in the nine realms is going on? the Grand Elder cursed. He hadn't mentally prepared himself for these gifts. Would they really give them these cultivation resources? Each one could sell for thousands or even cause wars between families.

"Anyway," Stella pointed to the next one, "this one devours your heart demons and lets you overcome a bottleneck."

The Grand Elder saw Elder Mo stumble forward, his eyes glued to the truffle. "C-can it really?"

Elder Mo had been stuck at the same bottleneck for so long that he had accepted his inevitable death and turned to teach the younger generation, turning him into a bitter old man that cursed the heavens and barely kept his festering heart demons at bay.

"Sure." Stella deposited the truffle in his open palm. "Give it a try."

Elder Mo didn't even take a second to inspect the truffle. As if afraid the opportunity would be seized from his grasp, he desperately devoured the black ball and swallowed.

Everyone waited in silence, anticipating the result of the mysterious truffle.

33
VANQUISHED HEART DEMONS

Grand Elder Redclaw watched Elder Mo collapse to his knees, grasping at his throat while he choked. His balding head was on full display as he threw his head back, and his eyes stared wide-eyed at the distorted sky.

Is this supposed to happen? It looks like he is dying.

Unsure of the situation, the Grand Elder remained stoic as he watched with worry gripping his heart. Elder Mo may be a bitter old man, but at the eigth stage of the Soul Fire Realm, he was one of the strongest in his family and an excellent teacher to the younger generation. To lose him here would not only be a massive blow to his family's current strength but also its future prospects.

"Elder Mo!" Amber, the youngest Redclaw present, couldn't hold back her worry and stepped forward, but the ever-stern Elder Margret stopped her advance with an iron grip on the young woman's shoulder.

"Trust the process," Elder Margret hissed under her breath. "Elder Mo is already near the end of his lifespan."

Upon Elder Margret's words, Amber fell silent and stepped back. It was a silent truth among cultivators, but once someone reached the end of their lifespan due to a bottleneck, it was expected for the cultivator to go insane while furiously searching for a way to overcome their impending mortality.

Basically, if Elder Mo died here, it was worth taking the chance. His death was a few decades away at most, so taking a gamble, no matter how foolish, was all Elder Mo could do at this point, and trying to "save" him right now would only backfire in more ways than one.

"Ahhhhh!" Elder Mo screamed as something from within his body pried his mouth open. Grand Elder Redclaw watched in horror as a shifting black mass that he recognized as demonic Qi by its feeling of wrongness crawled out of Elder Mo's mouth.

Like void Qi, demonic Qi was difficult to deal with because it reacted violently to natural types of Qi. So the Grand Elder, despite being in the Star Core Realm, wasn't confident he could defeat this seemingly sentient mass of demonic Qi.

Nevertheless, his Star Core burned in his chest as he directed his crimson soul fire to his hands, ready to try obliterating the abomination leaving the screaming Elder's mouth.

Elder Brent, Margret, and Amber followed suit, stepping forward with various degrees of crimson flames enshrouding their hands.

"Don't worry. I'll handle it." The Grand Elder didn't need to look toward the masked individuals of the Ashfallen Sect to know who was speaking. With about as much enthusiasm as a Qi-less sloth, Diana stepped forward with blue soul flames with a hint of darkness flowing from her fingers.

She reached toward the demonic Qi phantom and blasted it with her soul fire. It screeched as it was burned alive, and everyone stood watching as the blue soul fire traveled down the length of the demonic Qi phantom body and into Elder Mo's throat.

The phantom was slowly corrupted, turning into a black drool that leaked down the sides of the Elder's face.

Elder Mo violently coughed and staggered to his feet. A while passed, and eventually, he managed to get himself together.

He began to howl with laughter, making the Grand Elder concerned about his sanity.

"I can feel it! Haha!" Elder Mo shouted to the heavens more joyfully than he had seen out of the old bastard for centuries.

"Elder Mo," the Grand Elder questioned, concern dripping from his tone, "are you all right? Did the truffle work? What can you feel?"

His voice had a hint of urgency, but curiosity was getting the better of him.

"It's gone! It's really gone! Haha!" Elder Mo half ignored his words as he shouted nonsense.

Walking over with embarrassment, the Grand Elder gripped the shorter man's shoulder. "Elder Mo, get a hold of yourself. We are in the presence of an immortal."

Elder Mo froze, fear flashing across his aged face. "Forgive me… I was overwhelmed with emotion and lost my composure."

"It's fine, Elder Mo. Now tell me what happened," the Grand Elder pressured. If that truffle really worked, it would be one of the most valuable things a demonic cultivator could ever lay their hands on. In pursuit of rapid power, most demonic cultivators cultivated with the demonic Qi from beast cores. So long as they did it in moderation, it was possible to resist the heart demons that would fester.

But if a truffle emerged that could purge heart demons from a cultivator, then the cultivators of demonic sects could rapidly rise in power from overconsumption of beast cores and mitigate its downsides.

"It worked," Elder Mo said with a hint of awe. "It really worked. My body is free of heart demons. I believe overcoming my bottleneck is now just a matter of time."

The Grand Elder recoiled a little when he saw tears at the edge of the centuries-old man's eyes. "Grand Elder, I'm not fated for death anymore! My life is worth living again…"

"Right…" The Grand Elder released his grip and stepped back.

Best not to associate with this nutcase too much until I see the Ashfallen Sect's reaction.

Glancing over, he mentally groaned. It wasn't fair they got to hide their expressions with masks. For all he knew, they were just as surprised as him that the truffle actually worked, or maybe they were all bored as they had seen this scene before. He sadly had no way of knowing.

"Ashfallen Sect," Elder Mo said as he gave them a deep bow, "as the generous people that have given this old man hope, I would once again like to express my deep loyalty toward you."

"That was actually going to be my next point." Stella's voice drew everyone's attention. "The Ashfallen Sect will not be leaving with the Blood Lotus Sect and escaping the beast tide. That truffle you just ate and these special fruits can only be grown by the spirit tree behind me on this mountaintop. To move the tree is impossible."

"But the merchants that have seen the gathering of beasts up north claim this will be the largest one yet," the Grand Elder countered. "It could be to the point where even the immortal may struggle to keep all of us alive."

Cultivators can only operate as long as they have Qi. Even an immortal may struggle to fight against the largest beast tide to date alone, especially since he hasn't shown himself to us he might be injured or half dead. To put my entire family and my own safety in an unknown immortal's hands is far too risky.

At those thoughts, the Grand Elder felt the phantom chains of his oath tighten slightly around his Star Core.

Stella tapped the truffle on the table. "As mentioned before, this truffle can permanently improve your spirit root, allowing you to absorb and cycle Qi faster. With this cultivation resource alongside the others and access to the Mystic Realm, it should be enough to allow everyone here to rapidly rise in cultivation."

She then surveyed all of the Redclaws and continued. "You have all pledged your loyalty to the Ashfallen Sect, and we choose to stay. The beast tide is still a few years away. We have time to become strong enough to fend it off."

Elder Mo was the first to break the silence, stumbling forward, collapsing to his knees, and kotowing toward the spirit tree. "My life is for the tree. If I must remain here until my final fleeting breath and my Qi runs dry, then so be it."

"Thank you, Elder Mo," Stella said as she looked toward the Grand Elder. "We aren't giving you these precious cultivation resources for free. Your strength is for the Ashfallen Sect."

The Grand Elder reached up and felt the cold phantom chains around his Star Core that signified his eternal oath of loyalty. So long as he drew breath and the tree stood tall, he was bound to this land.

This is all crazy, but if the claims of this pocket realm and those cultivation resources are true, then surviving the beast tide might be possible.

The Grand Elder hated to admit it, but a sliver of greed slipped into his consciousness. At the end of the day, he was a cultivator in the pursuit of immortality. When he reframed this demand as a trial sent by the heavens to test his resolve, he couldn't help but smile.

When was the last time he had been needed by someone? The Blood Lotus Sect hadn't been at war for a long time, and his days on the battlefield were nothing more than fleeting dreams. He was an old man living out his last centuries peacefully and quietly.

Perhaps it was time to fight again.

Stella patiently waited for the Redclaw Grand Elder's acceptance. At the end of the day, if she ordered something on behalf of the Ashfallen Sect, the oath would be activated, and they had no choice but to agree.

Why did Ash tell me to approach the negotiations like this? He even told me to let them see and try his precious fruit? I thought we would just chuck them into the Mystic Realm and see if any of them managed to crawl out alive.

Stella ground her teeth behind her mask. She found having to act as the representative infuriating, but Diana had insisted she take the role for practice.

Glancing to the side at the culprit who had forced her into this role, she saw Diana reaching down and picking up Kaida, who had been coiling around her leg for the last few minutes. The inky snake happily licked at Diana's neck as he took his rightful place on her shoulders.

Stella reached up and didn't feel Maple on her head. Looking to the side, she noticed Maple relaxing in the sun on Larry's back. The large spider's eyes were glaring at Elaine, never leaving her for a moment.

I bet Tree asked his pet to keep a sharp eye on Elaine.

Stella felt her mind wandering, totally bored and irritated with her current role. If not for the mask, she feared her ability to maintain a presentable facade would overwhelm her.

"Stella, I believe your proposal has merit," the Grand Elder eventually answered. "We need to get stronger. I couldn't even leave a lasting impact on that worm monster from a few days ago, and the beast tide will comprise thousands of monsters far stronger than that worm was. But if you have such rare cultivation resources and access to pocket dimensions, it may be possible to train us all up to a point we can fend the beast tide off."

Stella honestly didn't care about the Grand Elder's speech. She would remain here with Tree whether she had the strength to fend off the beast tide or not, as she trusted that Tree would take care of her somehow.

"Perfect. With your help, I believe we can overcome the looming threat," Stella said with as much fake enthusiasm as she could muster.

"Please step forward and retrieve all of the cultivation resources we have designated for you. I assume you all remembered what each one does from earlier?"

They all nodded.

Even though Tree had provided her with skin-improving truffles, she had deliberately kept them in her spatial ring. They weren't necessary for advancing cultivation, and she didn't like the idea of these old men suddenly turning into handsome teenagers. The drastic change in Elaine had been disorienting enough.

The Redclaws formed a line based on authority, so the Grand Elder was the first to step up to the table and receive his bundle of fruit and truffles. Waving his hand over the stone table, his spatial ring flashed with power, and the pile vanished.

"Should I use any of them now?" the Grand Elder inquired, and Stella realized she hadn't explained that part yet.

"Listen up! Before entering the Mystic Realm, you should consume the truffles as they provide permanent effects that will help with your cultivation inside." She then looked down at the pile of fruits, trying to remember the names that Tree had told her earlier.

Wait, did I forget one of the truffles? I know the beauty one is taken out, but there's still one missing. Ah! The dao enlightenment one that I took and then Larry distracted me in the past. Should I also not give it to them because they were the ones that caused me to waste it? That's maybe too spiteful.

Stella's ring flashed, and another truffle appeared on the table, earning a raised brow from the Grand Elder.

"I forgot one. This truffle lets you understand the language of heaven. It's the only one I would save for using in the Mystic Realm."

The Grand Elder picked it up as if it was the most precious treasure and deposited it into his spatial ring. "If these truffles are capable of even a fraction of what you claim, they are undeniably precious, so you have my eternal gratitude."

Stella shrugged. It wasn't like she grew these truffles and fruit, so the praise was wasted on her. With the Grand Elder still standing there, she remembered his previous question and pointed at the fruit.

"Where was I? Ah yes, you asked what fruit to consume now and which to save for the Mystic Realm. I would say that fruits providing deep meditation, enlightenment, and mind fortress might be ideal to consume in the pocket realm to boost your cultivation speed as you will only remain there for a month, so every second counts." Stella then pointed at the other fruit in another neat pile. "Lightning Qi barrier and neural root may also be useful, depending on the situation. However, I would save the language comprehension and others for when you return."

The Grand Elder slowly nodded, walked off to the side, and found a nice spot within the Qi-gathering formation to sit cross-legged. While Stella handed out the fruit and truffles to the other Redclaws, she kept the Grand Elder in the corner of her eye.

He was inspecting the truffle and running his finger across its surface. He even tried sniffing it. Eventually, he chucked it into his mouth and seemingly disliked the taste as his face twisted.

That's certainly the spirit improvement truffle.

Stella was very curious to see how the truffle would work on someone in the Star Core Realm. She had absolute faith in Tree's cultivation resources, but even she knew to keep her expectations within reason.

The stronger a cultivator got, the less impact the same resource would have. It's likely why the skin improvement truffle did little for her but altered Elaine so much, as she was many stages in the Soul Fire Realm weaker than her.

The rest of the Redclaws sat down one by one in a circle.

Elder Mo, still giddy after ridding himself of his heart demons, sat down a few meters from his Grand Elder and gingerly consumed the spirit root improvement truffle alongside Amber.

Meanwhile, the other two Elders chose to start with the truffle that removed heart demons, so Diana had to step in and vanquish the demonic Qi phantoms that tried crawling out. Surprisingly, Elder Margret had an even more vicious heart demon crawl its way out of her throat than Elder Mo's.

"All right, Douglas, you should join them as well," Stella said to the large man, handing him a handful of fruits and truffles. "You will be entering the Mystic Realm alongside all of us."

Douglas excitedly took the provided cultivation resources and scurried off to sit in the circle.

"What about me?" Elaine asked quietly, her head slightly drooping.

"Well, since your skills are lacking too much to enter the Mystic

Realm, you will stay here with Tree," Stella said as her spatial ring flashed and a bundle of parchments appeared in her hands. "Take these and learn the ancient runic language so you can converse with Tree, as it will just be you two for the next week."

"What about…errr, was his name Larry?" Elaine gestured to the giant spider that was still glaring at her.

Stella nodded. "Yeah, he will be staying here to watch over you and protect Tree while we are gone."

"Right…okay." Elaine took the parchments and was surprised when Stella also put a heap of fruit and truffles on top.

"Don't forget to eat the language comprehension fruit while studying." Stella left with those departing words as she turned her attention to the circle of people cultivating. She also planned to join them and push every bit of Qi she could into her Soul Core before entering the Mystic Realm that would open in two days.

I'm going to reach the Star Core Realm no matter what. Nothing can stop me from being the most useful for Tree.

A cold smile bloomed on her face behind the mask as she eyed her competition.

34
MAKING FATHER PROUD

As the warm sunlight cascaded over the horizon and shone onto Ashlock's scarlet leaves, his mind slowly kicked into gear. As always, his system appeared in his mind, reminding him that yet another day had passed in this new world he now called home.

Idletree Daily Sign-In System
Day: 3515
Daily Credit: 11
Sacrifice Credit: 103
[Sign in?]

Upon seeing the day, Ashlock became excited as today was a special day. The timer for the Mystic Realm skill, his one and only S-rank skill, was gone, meaning an entire month had passed since he had last used it, and this time was different.

The last time it had been activated, his sect members had gone in unprepared and thankfully made it out alive. However, this time, they were going in fully prepared to make the most of the pocket realms.

On the mountain peak sat the strongest of the Ashfallen Sect. On one side were three masked women and a large man. Various Qi, including earth, water, and spatial, swirled around them like a dense fog.

Meanwhile, on the circle's opposite side were five Redclaws. Their Star Core Grand Elder sat proudly in the middle, crimson flame spiraling around him and being siphoned off by the others to further their cultivation.

Over the last day or so, Ashlock had watched their flames take on a lighter shade as their spirit roots improved due to the truffle. He also noticed the sheer intake of the surrounding fire Qi had drastically increased, another boon of pure spirit roots.

All was calm as the cultivators meditated in complete silence. However, that was broken by a sudden explosion of crimson flame. As if a rocket engine was facing upward, a pillar of roaring fire rose to the heavens as all the fire Qi for miles poured toward a single man.

Elder Mo gritted his teeth as he went through a stage advancement.

The Grand Elder's eyes snapped open, and a wide grin formed on his aged face. Raising his hands, pure fire Qi poured out from his Star Core toward Elder Mo, taking the pillar of fire to new heights.

An immense pressure briefly blanketed the mountain peak as the pillar of fire collapsed on top of Elder Mo and was absorbed into his Soul Core.

"Elder Mo," the Grand Elder smiled, *"congratulations on your advancement to the ninth stage."*

Letting out a deep breath of flames like a burping dragon, Elder Mo grinned. *"Thank you, Grand Elder. I feel like the clutch of death on my weary soul has been slapped away, and I may live for many more years."*

"That's good news. The Redclaws would struggle without your exceptional guidance and strength, Elder Mo."

Elder Mo laughed heartily, his permanent scowl and foul mood long gone. *"What's with the formal speech, old friend? Too comfortable up there in the Star Core Realm to see me as an equal?"*

The Grand Elder rolled his eyes. *"Hard to see you as a friend when you have been nothing but a grumpy old fart for the last century."*

Elder Mo burst out laughing. *"All right, that is fair enough. I have been a bit of a grumpy bastard."*

"Now be quiet. The others are still meditating" the Grand Elder said in a forced whisper as he gestured to the masked Ashfallen Sect members.

Ashlock felt like informing them that the Mystic Realm was ready, so he wrote on his trunk and was surprised when the Grand Elder translated his words and relayed them to the group.

"The immortal has spoken. The Mystic Realm awaits us."

Everyone awoke from their meditation and got to their feet.

Stella seemed to glance at the Grand Elder, who had made the announcement for a while, but with her mask obscuring her face, it was impossible to tell her mood.

"Is she jealous someone else translated my words?" Ashlock mused as he saw her hand clench at her side. She then let out a long sigh through the mask and addressed the group.

"Assuming the Mystic Realm acts the same way as last time, a sudden white fog will appear. Shards will be within the fog, each showing a glimpse into a pocket realm. Reach out and touch the one you feel the strongest connection to. Any questions?"

Amber was the first to speak up. "How long will we be in the Mystic Realm?"

"Well, last time we were in there for a month, but only a week passed in real-time," Stella replied. "So prepare to survive there for a month."

Elder Mo then piped up, "Can we travel into the same pocket realm?"

Stella shrugged. "We have only used the Mystic Realm once, and two of the immortal's pets ended up in the same realm. So I would say it's possible. Maybe try holding hands or something when you enter the fog, as all of you would benefit from a fire Qi realm, so traveling together would be ideal."

The Grand Elder chuckled as he left a hand out to Elder Mo. "Consider this gesture a rekindling of our century-old friendship."

Elder Mo snorted and took the hand. "Yeah, right."

Soon enough, the Redclaw family stood side by side, holding hands and ready for the Mystic Realm.

Ashlock was very curious to see if Stella's theory of them holding hands was correct. If true, they could take turns meditating and guarding, making the whole experience safer and more beneficial.

"Maple, come sit on my head," Stella called to the lazy squirrel.

Maple didn't even open his eyes as his body vanished from Larry's back and reappeared through a hole in reality onto Stella's head, still asleep.

"All right, Ash. We are ready," Stella called out.

Ashlock took a deep breath. After hearing the horrors they had endured last time, it felt like he was sending his family and friends into a warzone where the chance of death wasn't low.

"Come back safely, you hear me?" Ashlock whispered in his mind as he activated his only S-rank skill, {Mystic Realm}. "Especially you, Stella."

From the very moment he activated the skill, everything changed. A dense white fog filled with bizarre celestial flakes swirled around the mountain peak, swallowing his sect members, and before Ashlock knew it, everyone was gone once again—except for him, Larry, and Elaine, who stood beside his trunk.

A moment passed, and he sighed once he confirmed that nobody was stumbling back out. The sudden silence was unsettling, so he turned his attention to Elaine.

She had removed her black wooden mask and looked at the fog with a longing expression. Eventually, she shook her head and looked up at his canopy. "P-patriarch, is it all right if I sit here on the bench?"

He flashed his leaf to say yes, and Elaine smiled and relaxed on the wooden bench. She then brought out the stack of parchments Stella had provided detailing how to translate the ancient runic language.

Her spatial ring flashed a second time as a fruit similar to a small apple appeared in her hand. She took a hearty bite of the fruit, and her eyes went wide as they began to glow with a blue hue.

Quickly picking up the parchments with the enthusiasm of a kid on Christmas day, Elaine scanned Stella's notes, and a gasp escaped her lips. "This is incredible! I can feel the information burning into my brain."

That was a rather worrying description, but Ashlock assumed she meant the information was being permanently burned into her memory.

"Interesting…the language comprehension buff seems to give the user perfect memory retention for languages." Ashlock hummed to himself as he watched for a little longer. Her eyes seemed to take in the information incredibly quickly as she replaced the parchment she read every few seconds.

Ashlock was beginning to feel worse and worse for not having thought of his {Qi Fruit Production} skill earlier and giving one of these to the Redclaw Grand Elder.

"Oh well, I'm sure he will be appreciative once he leaves the Mystic Realm a stage or two stronger." Ashlock began to grow bored. What should he do for the next week?

Stella reached up and made sure to keep one hand stroking Maple's furry head. The little rascal was her ticket to successfully reaching the Star Core Realm, so she wanted to make sure he traveled with her to whatever pocket realm she ended up in.

Her eyes darted around the shard-filled white fog like a huntress searching for prey.

Brief glimpses of inhospitable worlds, filled with fire and ice, floated past her vision. Panic began to set in as she had been wandering for a while and hadn't encountered a pocket realm with spatial Qi.

Eventually, she closed her eyes and felt out with her spiritual sense. A smile appeared on her lips as she noticed a distant hint of spatial Qi. Moving in that direction, she soon hunted down the shard, and still keeping her eyes closed, she reached out and grasped it.

Her eyes snapped open as a violent and freezing wind smashed into her, causing her to almost lose her footing on the jagged black rock that lay underfoot. Glancing around, she found herself at the peak of a mountain surrounded by an ocean of liquid metal.

A ferocious storm system of glowing blue clouds swirled overhead, flashing brightly as thunder roared loudly in her ears. Maple shifted around on her head, seemingly glancing around in annoyance.

"Sorry, Maple, any pocket realm with spatial and lightning dao is going to be a nightmare to try and sleep in."

Maple snorted and rolled over, somehow falling back asleep.

With the squirrel asleep, Stella looked around for a place to conduct her ascension. "There's spatial Qi all around this place, so maybe a cave or something?"

A frown appeared. Other than sharp black rocks pointing out the metal ocean-like abyssal spikes reaching for the heavens, there was nowhere else to stay.

Her heart almost lunged out of her chest when the world suddenly lit up, and as if she was a lightning rod, the glowing clouds overhead deemed her a target.

Lightning lashed out at her. Stella enshrouded her fist in lightning dao and managed to punch one of the bolts away, but the other was a little off the mark and hit the rock below her feet, exploding the thin shard of rock she had been balancing on and sending her tumbling down the sheer rock face toward the liquid metal ocean below.

Snapping her fingers, a wobbling rift manifested below her, and she fell through, reappearing back on the mountain peak.

All right, this is going to be more challenging than I thought. The abundant spatial Qi here makes traveling around by rift easy, but how can I ascend to the Star Core Realm when lightning keeps trying to blast me?

Stella cast her mind back to when Tree had ascended to the Star Core Realm. His soul had left his body and taken on the golden lightning to rapidly grow to a truly monstrous size.

I don't think human souls can leave their bodies like that. I may have lightning Dao, but that doesn't mean I will survive being struck by lightning repeatedly while trying to form my Star Core...

Stella still found Dao comprehension a weird concept. It wasn't affinity, as she couldn't cultivate lightning Qi, but due to her deep understanding of the natural laws behind lightning, she could utilize lightning to empower her body and also knew how to punch it away.

But unlike spatial Qi, her body couldn't deal with being overwhelmed with lightning Qi, so it was still lethal to her in large amounts.

Didn't Tree give me one of his fruit that could help with this?

Stella went through the mental list of fruit in her mind and remembered the Lightning Qi Barrier fruit. Looking down, she decided this bit of rock seemed flat enough, so she sat cross-legged, trying to ignore the harshness of the jagged rock on her butt, and bit into the fruit.

Almost immediately, she felt a foreign but comforting power envelop her. A weird purple energy enshrouded her body like an extra set of clothes and stuck to her arm as she waved it around.

"How weird," Stella muttered.

The sky overhead flashed again, a lightning bolt heading straight for her. Holding out her palm, she was surprised to see the purple energy surge outward and meet the lightning bolt, effortlessly absorbing its power.

After the initial awe, a sense of urgency followed as Stella remembered Tree telling her it was a temporary effect, which made sense since she didn't feel any of her own Qi being used to fend off the lightning, so this purple energy must have come from the fruit.

"All right, time to form my Star Core." Stella grinned as she summoned multiple fruit and truffles. "I hope my body can handle all these resources Tree gave me."

For some reason, Stella felt warm and happy, feeling the weight and texture of the fruit and truffles in her hand, knowing that Tree had been the one to carefully grow them for her. It almost felt like a graduation present or a parent's love. Other scions received their first swords for getting into an academy or maybe a bunch of pills to help them reach the next realm.

But those were gifts bought with coin rather than meticulously grown and nurtured with love like these fruits and truffles. Stella looked up at the ferocious storm system of glowing clouds swirling overhead with great determination.

Tree, as your daughter, I will follow in your path and cultivate the purest and largest Star Core the world has ever seen. I want to make you proud.

Without another thought, Stella bit into each fruit she held. First, the Neural Root fruit, which suddenly made her hyperaware of every nook and cranny of her body, and she could control everything at will without a problem.

"Being able to control each lung individually is freaky," Stella mumbled with her mouth full of fruit. Next up was the mind-altering fruit such as Deep Meditation, which, upon eating, made the outside world vanish with ease, and she found herself in the darkness of her mind.

However, with the help of the Neural Root, she was still able to control her body while in this state of meditation. Stella manipulated her body to eat the Enlightenment fruit next, which flooded her mind with wispy streams of spatial Qi, with a few other streams of Qi sprinkled in.

The benefit of being in a spatial Qi–rich pocket realm. Not many other Qi types here to distract me.

Stella then switched it up and gobbled down the truffle she had told everyone to save for the pocket realms, the language of heaven truffle. The one that had allowed her to understand heaven's whispers a while ago.

As she felt the truffle travel down her throat, the confusing whispers from the streams of spatial Qi within the darkness of her mind almost all at once became a chorus of crystal-clear shouts.

The problem was there were too many competing for her attention, and she hadn't come here for enlightenment but rather to form her Star Core, so she needed them to be quiet in order to have a clear state of mind.

That's where the Mind Fortress fruit came in that apparently made cultivators immune to mind-altering effects. After biting into it, Stella felt her mind grow numb, and the insistent shouts that plagued her mind became distant whispers unless she wanted to focus on them.

Stella let out a deep breath of relief. All was going well so far. With her mind tranquil and her body a fortress of purple energy from the outside world, it was finally time to form her Star Core and make Tree a proud father as his daughter was finally growing up and reaching the next stage in her life.

35
(INTERLUDE) SPIRIT FORGE MASTER

Amber clenched Elder Mo's hand harder than she felt comfortable, but it was hard to ignore the pain of having such dense fire Qi flowing through her spiritual roots.

Other than holding hands, they had mutually agreed to exchange Qi to try and guarantee they ended up in the same pocket realm, and there was no way Amber planned to end up lost and alone in an alternate world filled with danger. She hadn't even left the sect all that much except for the occasional excursion into the wilderness near the volcanic region she used to call home.

"Everyone hold tight. I found a shard with immense fire Qi coming from it." The Grand Elder's calm voice reached her ears, and Amber gripped Elder Mo's hand tighter.

There was a sudden flash as the white fog with drifting shards vanished and was replaced with a scorching wasteland. Extreme heat she hadn't felt in months blasted her in the face, and the dry air burned her lungs. She cycled her Qi, and the uncomfortable environment soon became hospitable.

"You can let go of my hand now, Amber." Elder Mo chuckled at her side, and Amber released his hand with a hint of embarrassment.

All of the Elders had their eyes closed as they stood in silence. Amber was confused but didn't dare disturb whatever they were doing. After a while, the Grand Elder's eyes snapped open and looked behind them.

Oh, they were searching around with their spiritual sight. Just shows how clueless and out of my depth I am that I didn't even think of that.

"We really are in a pocket realm," the Grand Elder said calmly. "I can't detect any immediate threats or lifeforms. However, there is an immense gathering of energy in that direction."

Amber followed his finger but couldn't see or sense anything. The fire Qi in this place was so overwhelming that she wanted to sit down where she stood and cultivate. A day of meditation here would equal weeks back in the White Stone Palace courtyard where the only source of fire Qi was those plants growing on the demonic trees.

Well, that's rather ominous. What could be causing such a gathering of fire Qi?

"Should we investigate?" Elder Mo pondered while stroking his chin.

"I vote we remain here," the usually silent Elder Brent offered his opinion. "With no threats detected within the Grand Elder's range, we should be able to cultivate here safely."

"I will have to agree with Elder Brent here," Elder Margret said. "The fire Qi all around us is many times denser than back home, and any time we spend traveling over to the gathering of fire Qi is time we could have spent meditating."

The Grand Elder looked over his shoulder. "Elder Mo? What are your thoughts on this?"

Elder Mo grinned. "No pain, no gain—we already sat on our butts cultivating for the last few days, and did you all forget about the cultivation resources the immortal gave us? What if that is a one-time deal? Do you want to waste those resources cultivating the Qi here rather than closer to that immense gathering of Qi?"

The Grand Elder nodded, and then his calm eyes met Amber's. "What do you think?"

He's asking for my opinion?

Amber was baffled. She searched the faces of her Elders. Was this a type of test? Why would they care about the opinion of a younger generation? They were the ones that fought in wars, not her.

"Uhm..." Amber clenched her fist. She saw the logic in Elder Margret and Brent's words, but Elder Mo also had a really good point. She already felt like she was behind the two Ashfallen Sect girls as their cultivation stages were a few higher than hers.

It's not like I am trying to compete with them, but I have been heralded as the genius of my generation since I was little, and compared to them, I feel like a failure.

"I agree with Elder Mo," she said as confidently as she could, and her facade almost cracked when she saw Elder Margret and Brent's deep frowns.

The Grand Elder glanced at everyone. "Well, I believe we should maximize this opportunity, so I am with Elder Mo and Amber here. We can reach the location within a few hours by flying sword."

He then smiled thinly. "However, I can only support three people at most, so Elder Brent and Margret, you can remain here."

The two had looks that could kill, and Amber felt their glares to her core, but what could she do about it? Call her young and reckless, but she was bubbling with excitement, and the thought of sitting around here on a small mound of red sand for the next month and meditating when there was something out there of interest didn't sit right with her.

Cultivators should seize every opportunity given to them. Who knows when we will be next allowed in this Mystic Realm? If Stella's words are correct, we only have a month in here, so we should make the most of it.

The Grand Elder snapped his fingers, and a broadsword appeared floating before him, wrapped in crimson flame. "Come on, Amber and Elder Mo, let's go and see what lies on the horizon, shall we?"

Amber felt the burning wind rush through her hair as she stood on the back of the Grand Elder's sword and soared through the orange sky. Down below was an endless desert of red sand dotted with random outcrops of rocks and molten rivers.

Eventually, even Amber could feel the immense pressure of fire Qi from a building in the distance.

"Monsters are guarding that temple up ahead," the Grand Elder commented from the front of the sword without turning his head. His words were crisp in her ears as if he was beside her. "They seem to be at the peak of the Soul Fire Realm. Elder Mo and I will handle them. Amber, you stay back and observe."

A while later, the sword began to descend and touched down. Amber hopped off the sword and felt her feet sink slightly into the scorching red sand.

She didn't even have time to take in the colossal sight of a black stone temple that reached for the orange sky before them as prowling around the pillared entrance were three-headed dogs the size of buildings with a ghostly blue flame as fur.

"Spirit Fire," Elder Mo commented as he shrouded himself in his own crimson flames. "Best to cut through it with soul fire–coated swords."

"Indeed, I'm surprised you remembered." The Grand Elder smirked. "Let's go. Whoever kills the most wins."

What followed was a slaughter as Elder Mo and the Grand Elder displayed the remarkable teamwork fostered through centuries of standing side by side on the battlefield. Amber had heard stories of their feats against other demonic sects, but seeing it in action was fascinating.

Fire Qi flowed into her eyes in a vain attempt to follow their swift movements. Flashes of flame followed blurred swords coated in crimson fire, easily beheading the seemingly helpless dogs.

Before long, the final groan left the head of the last standing monster, and Amber hesitantly went to join her elders at the entrance to the temple, carefully sidestepping the pools of blood, decapitated heads, and swamps of organs.

"Enjoy the show?" Elder Mo grinned. "Not every day I get to stretch myself that much."

"You could say that again," the Grand Elder said, shaking his blade once to remove the blood. "And I believe I won."

Elder Mo went to retort, but Amber cut in to hurry things along. "It was awe-inspiring," she admitted, still finding it weird that she was invited alongside these old monsters to join them on this expedition.

Elder Mo's spatial ring flashed, and one of the corpses disappeared. "Secured us some food, and it should have a beast core that will be rather valuable." He surveyed the rest of the carnage and shook his head. "Will take too long to dig out the beast cores from these monsters. Their meat is fire resistant, so burning the corpses to reveal the beast cores won't work."

The Grand Elder strode past Elder Mo. "Don't worry about those corpses for now. The fact they wielded spirit fire makes me eager for what we may find within these stone walls."

So that weird ghostly flame is called spirit fire. What makes it so unique compared to the soul fire I can control? Amber kept her thoughts to herself as she followed her elders deeper into the temple.

It took many more hours, but eventually, the trio had slaughtered their way into an expansive room. Although a trail of death lay behind them, her Elders appeared relaxed as they looked around.

That was until the entire temple began to shake, and the tunnel they had used to enter the room collapsed. Amber desperately looked around and then noticed an altar rising in the center of the room.

"Grand Elder, look," she said, and the two men followed her gaze.

"A hammer?" Elder Mo asked, and sure enough, a metal hammer coated in that same ghostly spirit fire sat proudly on the altar, dominating the room with its presence.

The trio walked up and looked at it from all angles.

"Looks like a blacksmith's hammer." The Grand Elder broke the silence. "Could this be a hammer that once belonged to a spirit forge master?"

"What's a spirit forge master?" Amber couldn't hold back her curiosity any longer.

Elder Mo did his signature humming while rubbing his chin as he contemplated how to answer her question. "I haven't seen a spirit forge master in a long time, but if my memory serves me correctly, they are people able to use a special type of fire to imbue intent into objects."

Amber nodded in understanding, and her gaze landed back on the hammer.

So the person who left this here was some type of ancient blacksmith?

"All right, my spirit sense cannot penetrate the black stone of this building, nor can I detect a way out," the Grand Elder said seriously. "There is also not much fire Qi in here, surprisingly, so if we want to make the best of this situation, we need to get out of here and soon."

Elder Mo grunted in agreement. "Are you thinking what I'm thinking, old friend?"

"I sure am," the Grand Elder replied, and the two engaged in a contest of spirit stone, two swords, and palm strike. Glaring at one another, they raised their hands and shouted, "Draw!" at the same time.

Elder Mo went for the classic opening of spirit rock with his hand in a fist, whereas the Grand Elder went with a riskier two-sword opening with his two fingers out.

"Spirit stone beats two swords." Elder Mo grinned and patted the Grand Elder on the shoulder. "Unlucky old fool."

Sighing, the Grand Elder lowered his hand and looked long and hard at the blacksmith's hammer.

What were they fighting over? Oh.

Amber's question was answered by the Grand Elder reaching out and grabbing the hammer handle. Clearly, they had deemed the hammer the answer to escaping here and had been competing on who had to try grabbing it first.

Elder Mo and Amber tensed as the Grand Elder's fingers wrapped around the handle coated in Spirit Fire. Everything seemed fine briefly until the Grand Elder's eyes suddenly exploded with ghostly flames. He released his grip on the hammer and stumbled back into Elder Mo's arms.

"Are you alive?" Elder Mo asked, and the Grand Elder nodded, clearly shaken by the experience.

"What happened, Grand Elder?" Amber asked as respectfully as she could without her deep curiosity and fear becoming too obvious.

A wide grin formed on the Grand Elder's aged lips as if he had gone insane. "It's a technique! An inheritance!"

"What?!?" Elder Mo roared, dropping the Grand Elder to the floor and dashing over to the hammer. Without a second thought, he grabbed the handle and suffered the same fate as the Grand Elder, with Spirit Fire roaring from his eyes.

He managed to stay standing by catching himself on the altar edge and began to laugh manically. "It's true! An inheritance from a Monarch Realm expert is really here!"

Amber knew it might be foolish, but she didn't dare hesitate and dashed past the Elder, grasping at the cold handle of the hammer.

Spirit Fire has no heat? Amber frowned. The metal was far colder than expected, and the ghostly flame wrapped around her hand.

As that thought drifted through her worried mind, a sudden force slammed into her body as the Spirit Fire from the hammer surged up her arm and into her brain.

The Spirit Fire carried the knowledge and life experience of someone that had lived thousands of times longer than her. Naturally, so much information was impossible to grasp within a single moment, so the Spirit Fire carrying the vast knowledge was expelled from her eyes.

As she stumbled back and felt the cold stone hit her butt, she was too overcome with everything that she could not form words. Her eyes flickered to the hammer, and a realization from the memories made her overcome with greed.

Whoever can comprehend the technique to wield the hammer first can claim the inheritance to become a spirit forge master and wield the hammer freely.

Her eyes flickered to the Grand Elder, who had a grave expression. Would he kill her and Elder Mo here to guarantee ownership of the spirit hammer?

A cough from Elder Mo drew her attention. "I believe we have all realized the seriousness of the situation before us?"

Amber and the Grand Elder nodded.

"Now, you may both have some...nefarious thoughts, shall we say, going through your mind, but I ask you two to see the bigger picture."

"Whatever do you mean, Elder Mo?" the Grand Elder questioned. "This is the opportunity of a lifetime. In all my life, I have never even heard of someone encountering a Monarch Realm inheritance, let alone being given the chance to actually obtain it."

Elder Mo snorted. "And who gave you this opportunity? An immortal. Do you think you can escape here with our blood on your hand without facing repercussions from an immortal? Stella said that they needed us all to get stronger for the Ashfallen Sect. That is why they gave us such precious cultivation resources and allowed us access to this Mystic Realm."

Amber nodded in agreement, mainly because she wasn't the one with any power here. The Grand Elder could defeat her with the gravity of his Star Core alone.

The Grand Elder frowned and didn't seem convinced, so Elder Mo pressed on. "There were thousands of pocket realms within that mist. Who is to say this is the only one with an inheritance? What if every time we get to venture into this Mystic Realm, we stumble upon an inheritance? Do you plan to seize every single one for yourself by killing everyone around you?"

The Grand Elder looked at both of them briefly, and the hostility in his eyes lessened. "So what do you suggest then, Elder Mo?"

"We all compete against each other for the inheritance," Elder Mo said without missing a beat. "From my understanding, it's not an inheritance that's based on your affinity or talent, but rather sheer determination and concentration to learn the ways of Spirit Fire and the forge."

Amber saw the Grand Elder's thoughts wander. "Grand Elder, don't forget that there's still a pocket realm of rich fire Qi out there that Elder Brent and Margret are enjoying."

The Grand Elder snorted. "Fine. We will compete for the inheritance. Don't get angry when you lose!"

His spatial ring flashed, and a bundle of fruit and a truffle appeared. Without hesitation, he ate them all in one gulp and quickly dropped into a lotus position with his eyes closed.

Elder Mo gave Amber a thumbs-up and a cheeky grin before following in the Grand Elder's steps, consuming all his fruit and truffles before focusing on the inheritance.

Amber took one last look at the forge hammer shrouded in a ghostly flame with a grim determination. If she could obtain the inheritance of a Monarch Realm cultivator, her life would be set.

She could become the realm's only spirit forge master. A cultivator capable of granting intent to their creations.

36
QUALITIES OF A SMITH

What were the qualities of a forge master?

Amber raised her arm and struck down on the piece of metal, making sure to strike the spot of ghostly flame that danced along its surface. The cold handle in her fingers vibrated in the process, making her hand numb, and upon striking the spot, a sliver of information entered her mind.

Reappearing, the spot of ghostly flame on the metal shifted position again, and Amber tried to strike it but missed slightly and felt that sliver of information she had previously gained expelled from her mind.

She gritted her teeth and tried again, but in her impatience, she missed again as the ghostly spot changed location last second and lost another sliver of information.

"Ah! This is so frustrating." Amber cursed. While the buffs from the fruit had been in effect, it had felt like cheating. For a day straight, Amber's mind had been tranquil and focused, her body had been in complete control, and her patience was manageable.

But slowly, the effects of the fruit and truffles wore off, and as the days rolled by with her stuck striking this same piece of metal with a hammer, her resolve began to waver.

I need to hurry up. I'm sure the Elders are ahead of me by now.

Amber knew it was a toxic cycle. The more she felt behind, the more she rushed the process and messed up, which then caused her to lose more and more information regarding the inheritance.

What were the qualities of a forge master? Amber had realized the answer to this question during this grueling task. It was a test of patience and willpower.

She had to keep her hand steady, her pace perfect, and her mind calm. If anything was out of balance, she fell back a step. Who knew being a forge master was so grueling? She had assumed it would be easy from the first few days: just hit the piece of metal repeatedly on the correct spot until she gained all the knowledge.

Amber let out a long sigh and looked around. There was nothing but darkness beside the anvil with a single piece of unchanging metal and the hammer in her mental hand. Some streams of fire Qi flowed near the edge of her consciousness, and the hushed whispers of knowledge tempted her to throw the hammer down and concede to her Elders.

She hated herself—such a seemingly simple task lay between her and glory, yet she couldn't do it. It was frustrating beyond measure.

"Come on, Amber, you can do this," she muttered to herself as her mental grip around the hammer within her mind tightened. "Just calm yourself and take it one step at a time."

She raised her arm and struck down, hitting the ghostly spot perfectly. It fizzled out and granted her a sliver of knowledge regarding the ways of becoming a forge master. The problem was not all of the titbits of information were helpful. This was an inheritance of a person's life, meaning they passed down all their life knowledge, no matter how mundane or ridiculous.

It's part of what made this seemingly tedious task so frustrating. Strike a few times successfully, gain a portion of the technique, and then acquire a recipe for fried rice and the vulgar memories of a one-night stand.

It was distracting and sometimes downright gross. How was Amber supposed to keep a clear mind and try to impart her will through the hammer when she had this Monarch Realm's sex life playing in her head? These weren't memories suitable for someone like herself, leading her to question many things.

The sound of metal on metal struck her ears. She missed the ghostly spot. A force seemed to rip that tiny part of the inheritance she had just comprehended from her consciousness as if it had never been there, but the silence was deafening—impossible to ignore.

The Grand Elder was unperturbed by the memories as he slaved away at the anvil in his mind. The steady beat of the hammer calmed his soul and fed his brain with information. Slowly, he grew closer to his goal.

But he was still a little impatient, causing him to miss every now and then, much to his subdued frustration. He had never been a man known for patience, always rushing into battle head first, so to keep completely still and repeat the same repetitive task over and over was driving him insane.

He just had to press on...

A year within his mind had seemingly passed, and Elder Mo felt at peace.

The hammer beat down with a consistent rhythm, never missing its mark. Years of patiently teaching the younger generation the ways of cultivation and meditation allowed him to put up with a lot of nonsense.

To him, the intrusive memories containing aspects of this Monarch Realm's life were of unimportance, simply noise in the background like the constant chatter of his students.

If he could teach, he could learn. Years of frustration at trying to chip away at the bottleneck had strengthened his resolve, and resisting the heart demons that ate away at his sanity had steeled his mind into an impenetrable fortress.

Facing this trial a week ago would have been impossible. Back then, only a grim determination had kept him going, whereas now he was lifted by a second wind, and his hopes for his life were reignited.

In all honestly, Elder Mo didn't even care for the inheritance. He felt at peace just being able to live for a few more centuries, nurture the Redclaw family's younglings, and perhaps reach the Star Core Realm.

The battlefield had been his home, a place of chaos where a quick-thinking mind was key. But he had left that life of slaughter behind long ago for days of peace and quiet, away from the screams of the dying.

With a faint smile, he kept hammering away, enjoying the peaceful rhythm and hints of knowledge that gave him some perspective on a longer life. Perhaps similar to one, he may get to live due to the tree's truffles.

Amber sat in the silence of the black stone room.

Her eyes were open and looking longingly at the hammer shrouded in ghostly spirit fire perched upon the altar. Perhaps it was rather immature of her, but she had given up and put the hammer down within her mind in frustration.

Deep down, she knew she wasn't worthy of wielding the hammer. Either it was due to a lack of life experience, or she lacked the quality needed in a master forge master.

Stop being a brat. The world doesn't owe you the inheritance.

Amber huffed the strands of red hair out of her face and curled up into a ball, clutching her knees to her chest. Resting her chin on her knees, she continued glaring at the hammer.

What was I thinking? I'm no forge master, happy to sit inside by an anvil all day making weapons. I want to explore the world, see new things, and get stronger.

Maybe she was just trying to make herself feel better, but her thoughts held some profound truth that was hard to ignore. She was not worthy, nor was she suited for the hammer.

Perhaps her talents lay elsewhere?

I never gave alchemy a go. I heard the Redclaws are naturally good at alchemy due to our fire affinity, but I always skipped the lessons to advance my cultivation.

Amber was startled from her thoughts when Elder Mo let out a satisfied sigh, and his eyes opened.

He turned to look at her with an uncharacteristically warm smile. She was so used to seeing a permanent scowl on his face that she almost feared that some haunted spirit had overtaken him.

Relax. Elder Mo has been a changed man since overcoming the bottleneck.

"No luck?" Elder Mo asked calmly as he got to his feet and stretched his back, seemingly in no rush.

Amber reluctantly shook her head. "I just couldn't keep it together.

Kept getting...frustrated and rushing, which only made things worse. I figured I was too far behind at some point, so I quit."

Elder Mo nodded. "I see. Young with a lot to learn. This was an interesting test of patience, willpower, and resistance."

"Resistance?" Amber asked.

"Indeed, resistance. To be unbothered by outside forces and pressure. One of the hallmark truths of being a smith is to hammer away, rain or shine. Never rush a job or leave one unfinished. See it to the bitter end."

Amber felt her heart clench. She had done everything wrong. What use was a smith that constantly let the world affect their work and then quit halfway through a masterpiece?

But wait, why isn't he stepping forward to claim the inheritance?

"Elder Mo," Amber asked cautiously, "why don't you pick up the hammer?"

The man chuckled. "I have no need. I know the Grand Elder well enough. We fought side by side for many years. Just like you, he never had a chance."

Amber tilted her head. "How so?"

"Everyone has their own strengths in life, Amber." Elder Mo lectured as he always did. He had been the one to teach her how to cultivate when she could barely walk. "You can't teach a fish to fly or a tree to walk. That is what this inheritance test was all about: finding someone worthy. A person with a perfect match to the original owner."

For some reason, Elder Mo's words made Amber feel better. She had been beating herself up over it, but maybe they weren't compatible.

The Grand Elder's eyes snapped open a while later, and he immediately groaned when he saw the smug Elder Mo leaning against the altar.

"You could have just woken me up, you bastard." The Grand Elder huffed as he got to his feet and stretched out his weary joints.

"You wouldn't have forgiven me." Elder Mo smirked. "I knew you would spend the rest of our lives claiming you were mere moments away from enlightenment. You're a sore loser after all—always have been."

"Just grab the darn hammer and be done with it." The Grand Elder didn't even want to glance at the majestic hammer on the altar that had provided him so much grief. The closer he got to the truth, the more impatient he became, leading to him losing more and more knowledge.

And the idea that the other two Elders are meditating in such rich fire Qi outside made me feel like a fool for wasting my time here. I hate that darn hammer with a passion.

The Grand Elder had lived long enough to know when something didn't suit him. He belonged on the battlefield blasting monsters with his flames, not holed up in a cave crafting weapons. He was a wielder of swords, not a creator.

"As I said before," Elder Mo said as he reached out to touch the hammer, "I'm sure this is the first of many such opportunities under the gracious Ashfallen Sect. So long as we stay loyal, I'm sure future opportunities will arise."

"Stop trying to sound wise and claim your prize, you smug bastard," the Grand Elder said while tapping his foot impatiently. He didn't want to be consoled by his old friend right now. He wanted out of there to meditate and advance a stage in the Star Core Realm so he could blast that worm in the face.

Elder Mo laughed as his fingers wrapped around the handle, and he easily picked the hammer up. An explosion of spirit flame from his body sent a plume of dust and rustled the Grand Elder's clothes.

Elder Mo turned to face them, his eyes glowing a ghostly blue, and the hammer seemed almost fused to his hand as it was hard to tell where his hand ended and the handle began. It was just a blur.

Elder Mo then raised the hammer above his head, a miniature sun of ghostly fire formed on the hammer's head, and he then struck down on the anvil, sending a sonic boom throughout the temple that made the entire building crumble around them as if it was a glorified sand castle.

Idletree Daily Sign-In System
Day: 3520
Daily Credit: 16
Sacrifice Credit: 103
[Sign in?]

Ashlock dismissed the system notification and welcomed a brand new day.

"Five days have passed since the Mystic Realm was deployed."

Ashlock sighed as he did his morning check. His vision blurred as he activated {Eye of the Tree God} to appear out in the wilderness.

As usual, the grotesque worm had emerged from underground, feasting on the weak monsters gathered around the wall of trees overnight and munching happily on his sweet-smelling mushrooms.

It was tragic to watch so many monsters being taken away from him, but as long as it kept the darn worm that should be worth over a thousand sacrificial credits around, he felt it was worth it.

Casting his view back to Red Vine Peak, he saw Elaine wipe the sleepiness from her eyes.

Over the past few days, she had rotated between learning the ancient language, practicing her sword-fighting skills, and consuming truffles. The root improvement truffle had been uneventful as her void Qi looked much the same, and the expelling of her heart demons had gone much the same with her own void Qi obliterating them.

Elaine yawned. *"Good morning, Patriarch. Up for more sword fighting today?"*

Unlike Stella, who usually spent hours lazing around under his shade and talking nonsense, Elaine was always straight to business first thing in the morning.

"How does she have so much energy when the sun has barely even risen yet?" Ashlock grumbled.

Back when he had been a human, he was a self-diagnosed night owl that would regularly stay up till five a.m. even if he had work the next day. "I wonder if some of my degeneracy has carried over to my life as a tree. Or maybe my body is slow in the morning since it's cooler and there's no sun."

Alas, Elaine's enthusiasm to improve her sword skills was infectious, and Ashlock greatly enjoyed flexing his new limbs and being the teacher rather than the student for once. It had felt unwinnable when he tried fighting Stella, but Elaine was so garbage at combat that he had to hold himself back.

Within his inventory, Ashlock had arranged the swords he had looted from the dead Voidmind Elder into a neat pile so he could grab the one he wanted at any time.

"I will use these three today," Ashlock mused as the swords vanished and appeared outside.

Carefully placed holes in the stone that avoided any of the Qi-gathering arrays let his black vines emerge, and soon enough, he had equipped them with the beautiful swords.

'What do you want to practice today?' Ashlock wrote on his trunk, and Elaine effortlessly translated his words. The language comprehension fruit and multiple days and nights of studying had done wonders for her ancient runic language capabilities.

Ashlock had to admit it felt freeing to not rely on Stella to translate everything; soon enough, he expected all of the Redclaws to understand him alongside Douglas and Diana.

"Let's do parry practice today," Elaine said as she raised her sword. Ashlock complied as he sent three of his black sword-wielding vines to strike at her with nonthreatening speed.

The sound of Elaine's sword parrying his to the side filled the courtyard. Since the speed was so slow, he could let his mind wander. For some reason, seeing Elaine so earnestly learning the sword reminded him of when he had spent hours watching Stella and Diana spar in the training courtyard that no longer existed.

"Man, I miss them… I hope they come back all smiles and stronger," Ashlock lamented as he looked at the mystical white fog encompassing most of the mountain peak. "I wonder how the Redclaws are doing. If they didn't make it into the same realm, then I think Amber might struggle to survive. Actually, on that point, how the hell is Douglas going to make it through?"

Sadly all Ashlock could do was sit there and pray that his sect members made it back safely.

Before he knew it, dusk had arrived, and Elaine collapsed where she stood. Her rose-gold hair was drenched with sweat, and she gasped for breath.

"I probably…shouldn't have become…such an unfit potato…" Elaine sadly laughed to herself as she lay on her back.

Ashlock chuckled at her statement, and before he fell asleep, he watched Elaine stagger to her feet and collapse again in a hunched-over sitting position on the Qi-gathering array.

The world rippled slightly as she cultivated void Qi, and he soon felt the coldness of sleep envelop him.

However, when he awoke the next day and dismissed his system notification, he immediately felt like something was…coming his way.

His mind kicked into gear far faster than even Elaine, who was stirring awake, and his vision blurred as he went to look at the tree wall.

"Oh shit." Ashlock panicked.

The worm was heading toward him, but there was more than one. There was an entire family of the grotesque things.

37
FEAST AND SLAUGHTER

Red Vine Peak trembled as many enormous worms circled its base below the surface.

After a week of doing nothing but meditating and training with Elaine, Ashlock's Star Core had been brimming with Qi. Annoyingly, this Qi was now being shoved down his roots and into the mountain to stave off the worms.

"Why the fuck is that worm back here?" Ashlock cursed. "And where the hell did it get friends?"

Although the other worms weren't as large or powerful, there were far too many to count, and they were still in the Soul Fire Realm, meaning they were still a threat if they attacked all at once.

"It's fine. They seem unable to dig up through the mountain so long as I keep pumping it full of spatial Qi. I have so many roots throughout this lump of rock I call home that it's an impenetrable fortress for these worms so long as I have Qi on hand," Ashlock mulled as he tried to mentally calculate a way out of his situation.

Things were okay for now, but there was still a full day and night until the Mystic Realm disappeared, and everyone came back out.

However, he didn't even know if they could make a difference. Even with powerups, he suspected they would struggle to deal with the Star Core worm just like last time due to its ability to stay underground.

"If only Douglas was stronger…or Elaine. Her void affinity would be beneficial here." Ashlock's gaze drifted to Elaine, who was cluelessly swinging her sword around. She didn't even seem to notice the trembling of the mountain, or perhaps she assumed it was his doing?

Sighing deeply at the useless ally he was stuck with, Ashlock kept his vision below ground and tracked the worm's movements. They were like sharks circling a wrecked ship.

There were multiple problems. Ashlock only had enough Qi to keep the eight-thousand-meter-tall mountain full of spatial Qi for a day at most, and that wasn't even the biggest concern.

"The White Stone Palace is mostly undefended with all the Elders gone." Ashlock could open portals to get the Redclaw youngsters to safety, but who was to order them around? All the Elders had gone into the Mystic Realm.

"Maybe I should have suggested the Grand Elder leave one of the Elders behind…" Ashlock realized that had been a slight oversight on his part, but that was something to keep in mind for the future. Right now, he needed solutions.

Red Vine Peak was safe for the next few hours due to his spatial Qi, but those worms were totally free to attack the White Stone Palace or even ignore the mountains completely and go gobble up all the people in Darklight City.

"All I have on hand to fight is Larry and myself. Everyone else that could fight is in the mystic realm for another day…shit." Ashlock tried to keep calm, but it was hard. If he ran out of spatial Qi and the Star Core worm traveled up the massive hole it had made last time, it could aim for him this time and eat him in one bite. Only a mile of spatial Qi–filled roots under the mountain kept it at bay.

Hours of stress passed, and by late evening something had changed. The worms had stopped circling the mountain, perhaps because they deemed there would be no end to the spatial Qi, and they began to target something else.

His children.

Ashlock felt a wave of pain and fear through the mycelium network as the mountain range between Red Vine Peak and the peak with the White Stone Palace became the hunting grounds for the worms.

He watched in horror as a worm surged up through the rock like a great white shark and swallowed up a demonic tree as if it was a tasty fish. Other than the immense pain Ashlock felt through the network as his child was ripped from the network, shivers ran through his mind hearing his child's bark cracking as it was devoured by the monster's thousands of teeth.

"You fucker." Ashlock's mind grew deathly cold with fury. The air around his swallowed child became drenched in spatial Qi as he unleashed spatial blades that tore through the exposed worm whose mouth was still enclosed around the tree with only its scarlet leaves poking out of the top.

As this worm was only in the Soul Fire Realm, its earth Qi that rippled across its body did little to block the sliced space. As if attacked by a hundred invisible blades, large wounds opened up on the worm's body all at once, and blood spewed out, covering the nearby demonic trees.

A wave of happiness spread through the mycelium network due to the shower of blood, and seeing the worm reduced to a bloody pulp restored some emotion to Ashlock's mind. Quickly, he checked his Qi reserves and cursed, seeing how much that stunt had cost him.

"Shaved about half an hour off my Qi reserves. I can't do that for every worm that surfaces and tries to eat my children. Fuck." Ashlock hated it as he felt the mountain range tremble again, and more worms surged up through the rock and enveloped helpless demonic trees in their jaws.

As this scene played out, Ashlock saw a bunch of Redclaws standing at the entrance to the White Stone Palace and watching the carnage unfold with fear in their eyes.

Weak was his only thought. They were nothing but cannon fodder and an irritant for him to think about while watching his children get slaughtered. If they were stronger, maybe they could step in and help.

Ashlock decided, perhaps against his better judgment, to kill the worms but tried to keep it as Q_i-efficient as possible. His idea was that if he could portal the corpses back to his main body, he could use {Consuming Abyss} to convert them into sacrificial credits and Qi.

"Larry," he said through the black tether, and his ever-faithful spider perked up.

"Yes, oh gracious master? Your will is my command."

"Go out there and slaughter the worms that are feasting on my offspring. But make sure to stay close and keep your senses open. I may need you to return here quickly if the Star Core Worm somehow gets through my spatial Qi–filled roots and aims for my trunk," Ashlock rattled off quickly while half distracted with dragging the corpse of the first worm he had killed through a newly formed rift.

"As you wish, master—"

The worm corpse fell through as the rift materialized overhead with a thud, but so did something else he hadn't been expecting. The corpse exploded open, and a smaller worm wiggled out and tried to lash at Ashlock.

Elaine screamed and uselessly raised her sword. Luckily, Ashlock had been half expecting some nonsense when he opened the portal, as he had learned from the last few times that portals opened him up to counterattacks, so he had his mind ready to activate the void version of {Consuming Abyss} at the first sign of trouble.

The worm didn't even make it a few meters before the stone surrounding Ashlock turned black as a lake of void spread out from his trunk, and a hundred tendrils of void shot out and impaled the worm. A screech escaped its body as it deflated like a pierced balloon and died.

With two corpses to consume for Qi, Ashlock wrapped them in black vines, and within moments, he saw the familiar notification of sacrificial credits.

[+280]

"That's not too shabby," Ashlock mused, noticing he had recovered all the Qi he had wasted by devouring their corpses.

With the immediate threat dealt with, Larry scurried through the concealment array and into the demonic tree forest growing on the mountainside to fulfill his master's orders.

Almost immediately, the giant spider seemingly felt a rumbling below and managed to impressively leap to a nearby tree. The worm that had missed its prey screeched as Larry sunk his two fangs into its side, easily shattering any pathetic earth Qi defenses it had tried to muster up.

"Once out of the ground, they are quite weak," Ashlock noted. The problem was getting the Star Core worm to come above ground without him being the tree in its mouth. Last time he had baited it with a large gathering of Qi off to the side, so it missed him, but he feared that cheap trick wouldn't work again.

Putting those thoughts aside, Ashlock tried to ignore the waves of fear and misery through the mycelium network. He knew his children were suffering for his gain.

Screeches rang out as Ashlock sliced another five worms to death—his spatial Qi blades easily cut through their own Qi defenses and their slimy, poison-coated skin.

There wasn't much wind today, so the poison from the slain worms lingered more than Ashlock would like as they burned the bark and killed the leaves of his children as they didn't share the same poison resistance that he did.

If he didn't kill the worms, they would chew his children to shreds, and if he did, their poison burned them alive. It was a truly fucked-up situation.

"Why are the worms even targeting my children?" Ashlock wondered as he opened portals and deposited the fresh corpses on the mountain peak to be consumed. "Is it because they noticed my children were feeding me Qi, and they think if they kill my children, then they can reach me?"

If so, that was terribly concerning. Not because killing a few hundred of his children would make a huge difference on his Qi supply, but because that level of planning suggested intelligence, and the last thing Ashlock wanted was to face a wave of powerful beasts all smart enough to find ways around his defenses and kill him.

[+570]

Ashlock's eyes went wide at the system notification. Despite all the suffering around him, it was hard to ignore the monumental gains.

He had been hoping to devour the Star Core worm for a thousand credits, but after eating just seven of the smaller ones…

"System! Show my credits."

Idletree Daily Sign-In System
Day: 3521
Daily Credit: 17
Sacrifice Credit: 952
[Sign in?]

"Holy shit, that's nearly enough for an S-grade draw already."

Ashlock turned his attention back to the mountain in search of more prey. This felt like some special event in a game where he could harvest a stupid amount of exp.

Alas, real life wasn't a game. It seemed the constant rumbling had awoken someone he really didn't want getting involved.

Standing on the wall of the White Stone Palace was Sebastian. His silver hair shone in the evening sunlight as a stream of silver liquid orbited his body. He coldly appraised the situation, and when a worm got a bit too close to the White Stone Palace's entrance and looked like it was aiming for the Redclaws, the stream of liquid shot out and skewered the worm straight through and came out bloody on the other side.

It then cycled back and returned to orbiting around Sebastian. The butler then waved his hand covered in many silver rings, and the body vanished.

"Fucker is stealing my credits," Ashlock grumbled. On the one hand, he was glad to have another ally that could protect the Redclaws so he could focus on saving his children, but on the other…his precious credits.

What followed was a hunting contest between man and tree.

Their target? The hundreds of worms hellbent on eating any human they caught a whiff of, the Redclaws and Sebastian included, or committing the most heinous crime: deforestation.

Being in the Star Core Realm, Sebastian could whizz around on a blade of pure silver and slaughter the worms faster than Ashlock could see. There was a constant whistling noise as the stream of silver flew through the tree's canopies, skewing the vile creatures.

Ashlock didn't even have a chance to try and open a portal and steal the corpse as they kept vanishing into the butler's spatial rings to stop the poison from spreading. So leaving the worms closer to the White Stone Palace to him, he focused on working with Larry to kill as many closer to Red Vine Peak as possible.

|+170|
|+335|
|+237|
|+115|

Sacrificial credits were flying in faster than he had ever seen before, and he was so distracted he didn't notice until he felt a sudden pain that something was wrong.

Blinded by his greed and the seemingly free lunch before him, he hadn't been keeping track of the Star Core worm as much as he should have. For hours, the worm had remained seemingly dormant below the range of his roots and uninterested in trying to eat its way through his spatial Qi–coated roots.

With everything going on and the worm's inactivity for the last few hours, he had ignored it until it was too late, and it was already on the move.

The mountain shuddered to the point even Elaine became concerned.

"Patriarch! What's happening? I can't see through the concealment array."

"Wait, she has been standing there this whole time feeling the mountain shake and seeing giant worms fall through a portal in the sky and only now felt the need to ask what's going on?"

Finding the source of the shaking wasn't hard as the titanic Star Core worm surged up the side of the mountain, its body completely exposed. Dense earth Qi rippled across its body that could rival an ocean liner as it effortlessly traveled up the mountainside.

Ashlock hurled blades of spatial Qi in a vain attempt to slow its advance, but its earth Qi easily absorbed his attacks. Obviously, he began to panic. "Larry, come back! Help!" he shouted through the tether while preemptively casting {Consuming Abyss}.

He debated signing in to his system for an S-grade draw as he had over 1800 credits, but it was too late. He didn't want to be distracted by the knowledge of a new skill entering his mind when something that could kill him would arrive in a few seconds.

Right as the concealment array shattered due to the worm swallowing a large chunk of it, Ashlock cast a portal right behind Elaine that led to the cavern below.

As expected, she stumbled back in fear from the sudden appearance of an abyssal mouth of human-size teeth that took up her entire view. "What the—" Her words were cut off as she walked back through the portal, and it snapped closed.

With Elaine out of the way, there was nothing between the worm and Ashlock apart from his {Consuming Abyss} skill and Larry, who had just arrived. The worm let out a violent screech that made Larry stumble back a few steps, and even Ashlock felt his branches creak under the force.

Ashlock felt an immense shadow loom over him as the worm blocked out the sun. Even though Red Vine Peak was over eight thousand meters tall, Ashlock still couldn't see the end of the worm as it lay against the mountainside.

The worm charged at him, and he sent out his hundreds of void tendrils to intercept. Larry also hurled a wave of ash at the monstrous being, but they met nothing.

There was a thunderclap as air rushed to fill in the sudden vacuum. The worm had literally vanished as if deleted from the world.

"What the fuck? Oh. Oh no." Ashlock realized what had happened.

Compared to the worm's colossal size, the Mystic Realm looked like a tiny fart cloud, but the worm had made contact with the fog still floating around the mountain peak when it vanished.

"The worm was sent to the Mystic Realm…but the skill will deactivate by tomorrow morning and automatically bring everyone back if they are still alive." Ashlock felt both relief and fear. What if all his allies returned injured and immediately had to face the Star Core Realm worm?

"Shit…should I sign in now? I don't want to rely solely on my void affinity skill to kill the worm and protect my allies."

Ashlock opened his system and stared at it.

Idletree Daily Sign-In System
Day: 3521
Daily Credit: 17
Sacrifice Credit: 1809
[Sign in?]

It was enough for an S-rank draw, that was for sure. But should he wait, kill all the remaining worms, and attempt an SS- or SSS-rank draw? He knew they existed due to the shard Lee had given him.

"Fuck it. I don't know if I can handle something in the SS- or SSS-grade bracket with my current cultivation." Ashlock gave one final moment of thought but caved in.

"System…sign in…"

38
EMPEROR OF THE SPIRIT TREES

Sebastian Silverspire flicked his wrist to guide his manifested silver core to impale yet another monster that dare threatened his peace. Recalling his silver stream to orbit around himself, he put his hands behind his back and felt the air rush through his robes as he rode his sword through the sky above the sea of demonic trees.

All the worms dealt with over here. How is the Ashfallen Sect handling their side of the mountain range?

His spiritual sense was spread wide to ensure nothing snuck past him and attacked Ryker, who was still meditating without worry back in the White Stone Palace.

Glancing over at Red Vine Peak to sate his curiosity, he noticed a surge of earth Qi followed by a distant rumbling. Moments later, he saw a titanic worm surging up the side of the mountain.

He was about to rush over to help kill the monster but paused mid-flight. His objective was to keep Ryker safe and earn some trust from the Redclaws by keeping their youngsters alive while the Elders were gone somewhere unknown.

To leave Ryker's side to chase a distant threat was too risky, and this was the perfect opportunity to witness how the Ashfallen Sect dealt with threats. Alchemy wasn't just about finding alchemists and securing ingredients. It was a ruthless industry full of sabotage.

Since arriving here, he hadn't been idle. Information got leaked here and there, and his Star Core spiritual sense was able to help him listen in on conversations happening within the White Stone Palace. Few details slipped, but sometimes they did.

That's where he had confirmed the group he had done the deal with called themselves the Ashfallen Sect and apparently was run by an immortal. Whether this immortal was a different person from the nature affinity cultivator capable of growing any type of plant Diana had mentioned had yet to be discerned.

I also failed to detect any defensive formations when I last visited or the lingering auras of any hidden masters. I'll let the worm test it for me.

Sebastian stood silently, his sword motionless in the air as the entire mountain range trembled beneath him. His face was stoic until the distant Red Vine Peak suddenly changed. It was as if a distorted veil had been shattered, and everything altered.

A concealment formation on such a grand scale? How peculiar.

All of a sudden, he saw the large demonic tree on the bare mountain peak surrounded by void Qi. Tendrils of pure void surged upward. At first, he had assumed it would be that masked girl he had met earlier in the cavern as he had detected void Qi within her, but she was nowhere to be seen.

There was just a tree and a giant spider.

Is that a spirit beast? There's also no sign of any Ashfallen Sect members nor any of the Redclaw Elders. So who is fighting?

Squinting his eyes, the only other thing he saw was a dense white fog staying mysteriously motionless as if contained by an invisible force.

The giant worm reeled back its head and then went to gobble up the lone tree or perhaps the spider. It was hard to tell who its target was due to its size. It could swallow the entire mountain peak if it so wished—

It vanished.

Sebastian blinked his eyes and then went to rub them in confusion. Was it an illusion array? What had happened to the massive worm?

He hadn't been hallucinating as the ravine carved out by the monster all the way up the side of the mountain was still there, yet its entire body was just…missing.

Sebastian didn't like to admit it, but his hand began to tremble. Assuming the worm had really vanished like that, the implications were horrifying. Either there was an array around that mountain capable of deleting a Star Core abyssal worm out of existence, or there really was an immortal residing in the mountain that could remove something from reality with a snap of their fingers.

Without delay, Sebastian turned and flew back to the White Stone Palace. His mind was a mess of chaotic thoughts, and he didn't wish to be seen, having not offered a hand.

The Ashfallen Sect is far more terrifying than I thought.

"Sign-in," Ashlock confirmed and watched as his credits dropped to zero and a new system message popped up.

> [Sign in successful, 1826 credits consumed...]
> [Unlocked an S-grade skill: Progeny Dominion]

The entire mountain range and the surrounding lands began to tremble, and the sea of demonic trees violently rustled as if alive. Birds fled to the skies in droves, and distressed howls of animals cried out from the misty forest far down below.

Ashlock felt the system's power pulling on his roots, forcing them to grow in ways and directions he couldn't control. However, it felt like all his roots had an intended destination.

Content with letting the system handle whatever monumental task it was performing, he sat back and waited to witness its magic. Although he didn't understand how that could cause such violent trembling.

Suddenly, Ashlock felt a small surge of Qi coming up through his roots. It was as if someone had gone from drip-feeding him water to suddenly turning on the hosepipe. It came like a flood alongside a wave of intense happiness, and Ashlock soon realized what was causing the trembling.

His thousands of roots were moving to meet the roots of all his offspring and fuse. It was that sheer amount of movement that was causing the trembling. He no longer had to exchange nutrients and Qi through thin strands of mycelium with his children and instead could connect with them directly.

A while passed, and Ashlock watched his Star Core fill up faster and faster as his roots fused with more trees. Even the volume of nutrients cycling through the network between all the trees had become immense.

"It's like going from dial-up internet to fiberoptic." Ashlock chuckled as he felt the warmth of emotions and excitement from his offspring. They were happy to be fused with their dad.

"I will pay all of you guys back soon enough. Just let me defeat the worm first," Ashlock reassured his children, and he felt a wave of acceptance back. He couldn't wait for all of his children to develop their egos further so he could have more in-depth conversations with them in the future.

As the trembling finally stopped, Ashlock noticed his Star Core suddenly glow exceptionally bright and then collapse, losing most of the Qi he had gathered.

But that was trivial. Ashlock's trunk cracked and bulged, growing upward as his Star Core forcefully expanded, and he went up a stage.

[Demonic Demi-Divine Tree (Age: 9)]
[Star Core: 3rd Stage]
[Soul Type: Amethyst (Spatial)]

"Oh! I'm now in the third stage. I was worried I would never advance at this rate with all the bullshit I have to waste Qi on—" Ashlock's rant was cut off as he felt information regarding his new S-grade skill flow into his mind, and it felt as if a veil at the back of his consciousness had been lifted.

To his surprise, fusing with his offspring was simply the beginning of his new skills capabilities.

Ever since he had gained the ability to spread his offspring via seeds in his fruit, he had felt a compulsion to do so. It felt as natural as breathing to want to spread his seeds around far and wide.

But he had never stopped to ask why.

Why did he want to spread his seeds around so badly? Was it something trees just naturally did, or was there a higher purpose? Ashlock wasn't sure, but this new skill made him glad he had made efforts to spread his seed around up until now.

"No way. I can control one of my offspring now? As if it was an extension of myself? Like an avatar? Holy shit…does this mean I can fight people without risking my main body? Fighting the worm would have been a piece of cake if I didn't have to waste so much Qi baiting it to miss me."

Ashlock ran over the skill's strengths and limitations and concluded that the skill allowed him to temporarily impart his will on any of his children with an ego and wield all his abilities and powers at full capacity through that tree. However, it came with many restrictions.

First, the demonic tree he was overtaking had to be linked to him through its roots and must have a formed ego. So he couldn't plant a seed randomly and immediately overtake a tiny sapling. It was the type of ability that required preplanning and setup.

Second, his mutations, such as his demonic eye and cursed sap, weren't carried over, nor was his Star Core. He would have to provide the demonic tree Qi to fuel his skills through his roots by using his main body as a power station, or he could utilize the soul core of the demonic tree he took over. "It should be fine to use my own Star Core to power the skills if the tree is within a few hundred miles of my main body. Otherwise, I will probably need to use the demonic tree's own soul core."

Third, although the skill didn't have a cooldown like the Mystic Realm, repeated use within a week could result in permanent soul damage. This was because the skill used a fragment of his soul to impart his will on the tree, and it needed time to recover. So it was best to use the skill sparingly rather than all the time.

And finally, he could only impart his will on one tree at a time as it would take up all of his focus. However, this wouldn't be a limitation if he found a way to split his brain in two.

"But this is crazy… This skill gives me so many more options than I had before despite its limitations. Even with my minimal arsenal of attack skills, it's already practical, as the void tendrils from {Consuming Abyss} can't go through spatial portals."

Ashlock hummed to himself as he thought of all the potential of his new {Progeny Dominion} skill.

"Isn't this the closest I can get to walking or traveling around?" Ashlock mused, "Wait… Couldn't I enter the Mystic Realm with this skill? It says I have to be linked with the tree via my roots, but I was able to send my roots into the Mystic Realm before. I just couldn't see anything through them. So I was basically just fumbling around in the dark, but if I can use a demonic tree as my proxy, maybe I can also go in?"

Ashlock let out a sigh. He was bubbling with ideas, but the Mystic

Realm was less than twenty-four hours from closing, and he didn't want to risk permanent soul damage from testing the skill for now.

"But I should at least check on my offspring to see if they have upgraded since I last checked on them."

Casting {Eye of the Tree God}, Ashlock set out to search the sea of demonic trees on the mountain range for the one with the most developed ego.

Some time had passed since the Dao Storm was transformed into trees due to his cursed sap. However, besides bringing his offspring nutrients in exchange for Qi, he mostly ignored them in favor of other things that demanded his attention.

They were trees, after all. Even with Qi, they grew very slowly and were about as interesting as watching paint dry for the most part. But feeling their pain and suffering from being devoured by worms made Ashlock realize that almost every demonic tree around him had developed infant egos.

Before, it had just been the demonic trees he had planted himself months ago that had egos, but now all the demonic trees for many miles were developing into spirit trees capable of emotion.

"It would seem the ones from the Dao Storm are developing faster than the ones I planted. They must be using the residual Qi left over from their rapid growth to further their cultivation," Ashlock concluded. From what he had been told about spirit trees, they cultivated at a glacial pace and took many years to move up a single stage within a realm. So the fact his offspring were developing so fast was likely due to their abnormal upbringing.

"Ooh! This young lad is in the late stages of the Qi Realm." Ashlock had discovered a ten-meter-tall demonic tree slightly taller than all the trees surrounding it because it grew atop a boulder.

"You're stealing all the sunlight from your siblings. How selfish." Ashlock chuckled as he opened a portal right next to it. "Now, let's take a better look at you." He then used his {Demonic Eye} to peek through the portal at his offspring.

With his {Eye of the Tree God}, he could only get a vague sense of something's cultivation realm, but with his {Demonic Eye}, he could see everything.

"Ninth stage of the Qi Realm, and it appears to have...fire affinity." Ashlock watched as some of the fire Qi coming from the Blaze Serpent

Rose was absorbed through the demonic tree's leaves and cycled through its body.

Weirdly, Ashlock identified various Qi types competing for dominance within the tree's body. Although fire Qi was the current winner, there were traces of spatial, water, wind, lightning, and nature Qi within its trunk that had yet to form a soul core.

Ashlock spent a long time observing the tree and then switched to look at a demonic tree at the mountain's base in the misty forest between Red Vine Peak and Darklight City. He noticed this offspring had no fire Qi and was instead dominated by water Qi due to the Serene Mist Camellia.

While searching the misty forest some more, he was shocked to find one of the demonic trees had actually broken through the Qi Realm into the Soul Forge Realm, where it would try to forge a soul core of a particular affinity.

Within the trunk of the demonic tree, he saw water Qi slowly filling up the inside of its trunk and forcing out all the other Qi types.

Ashlock couldn't believe it! This was proof that he could undoubtedly steer his offspring into a particular affinity by altering their environment.

"Hold on…what happens if I use {Progeny Dominion} on one of my offspring with a different affinity from me? Would I be able to wield their affinity?"

Ashlock's inspection of his offspring sadly had to end as he felt the chill of the setting sun. Tearing his sights away from his tree inspection, he saw the sun was dipping below the horizon, meaning he would fall asleep within the hour.

"Shit. Is there anything I need before tomorrow?" Ashlock looked through his system screens and noticed his sacrificial credits were empty. "The void version of {Consuming Abyss} is unusable without sacrificial credits, and I will need that skill to kill the worm if it comes back out of the Mystic Realm. Should I quickly go out to the wilderness and hunt chickens, or perhaps I can get those worm corpses from Sebastian?"

Deciding that the latter option was a good idea as those worm corpses would be worth hundreds of credits. Ashlock created a portal to the cavern and brought Elaine back up to the mountain peak.

He would have sent Larry to handle this task, but Sebastian didn't understand the ancient language.

'Elaine, I will send you over to the White Stone Palace. I need you to get the worm corpses off the Silverspire butler, Sebastian,' Ashlock wrote on his trunk, and Elaine took a while to translate it. Simple instructions she could handle with no problem, but even with the language comprehension fruit, some words or phrases still tripped her up.

"I think I understand, Patriarch," Elaine said seriously as she retrieved her wooden mask from her spatial ring. "Should I just demand he hand them over? Or offer payment?"

Ashlock wasn't sure how Sebastian would react as he didn't know the value of those corpses. To him, they were valuable due to the sacrificial credits they were worth, but to Sebastian? There's no way the worms had much value other than their beast cores and the slime coating their skin that could be used to make potent poisons.

'Tell him the Redclaws will offer compensation when they return,' Ashlock wrote, and Elaine nodded in agreement.

Ashlock created a portal with a mere thought, and Elaine hesitantly stepped through. Because Elaine didn't know her way around the palace, he had created the portal through a root in the White Stone Palace's ceiling to lead her directly to Sebastian, pacing around the corridor outside his room.

The butler seemed to pause his pacing and slightly freak out like a child caught stealing cookies when a portal manifested right before him, and a masked woman stepped through.

"To what do I owe the visit?" Sebastian gave a short bow toward Elaine, and his tone carried a hint of unease, which felt odd for him as he was in the Star Core Realm and a member of the elusive Silverspire family. What had given him the feeling of inferiority that caused this action? Ashlock wasn't sure...

"I-I have come," Elaine was a bundle of nerve behind the mask, "to collect the worm corpses."

Sebastian blinked, and a smile bloomed. It seemed some invisible weight or pressure had been lifted from his shoulders. "Oh, the worm corpses? Absolutely, here take this. I have broken the seal."

He pulled off a silver spatial ring and skillfully threw it to Elaine, who fumbled to catch it. "Uhm...thank you? Do you need some compensation—"

"No need." Sebastian waved her off and turned to leave. "Those *corpses belong to your leader anyway. I was simply helping out to protect Ryker."*

Ashlock was stunned into silence by how awkward and confusing this entire conversation had been. Meanwhile, Elaine watched Sebastian's departing back for a while until he rounded a corner and went out of sight. Only then did she gather her senses and step back through the still-open portal.

"What a reasonable guy," Elaine said as she held out the silver spatial ring. Ashlock took the ring from her hand with telekinesis, and since the seal was broken, he could extract the corpses from inside.

The silver ring flashed with power, and a small mountain of corpses materialized. Elaine stumbled back and almost vomited in her mask from the awful stench of dead worms.

Ashlock teleported her back down to the cavern with a well-placed portal that she stumbled back into and then cast {Consuming Abyss} to devour the corpses for sacrificial credits.

"I won't be able to sign in for a while as I need to have sacrificial credits on hand for my void skill," Ashlock mused as he watched the credits flow in. He couldn't wait for tomorrow when everyone returned from the Mystic Realm, and he could finally delve into the mysteries of his new S-grade skill.

39
(INTERLUDE) DEMONESS

Diana finally felt free within the Mystic Realm as she could be herself away from prying eyes.

Last time she had chosen a world of pure water Qi as she desperately tried to suppress the darker side of herself that she wanted to keep hidden away.

However, things had changed since her last visit to the Mystic Realm a month ago. The darkness within her soul was becoming harder and harder to suppress. The monster within was trying to claw its way out, and she couldn't hold it back anymore.

It wasn't until she saw the Redclaws take the heart demon truffle that she realized she was different from them. When she had taken the truffle, she had been able to beat down and suppress the demonic Qi within herself, subduing it with dominance. Whereas for the Redclaws, the truffle forced the demonic Qi outside their body like some cursed-looking creature.

Luckily, the mask had hidden it, but when she saw the demonic Qi crawling out from their throats, she had licked her lips and felt hungry. Perhaps foolishly, she had given in to her primal desires and stepped forward, offering her "assistance."

She destroyed the first few with her own demonic Qi, but for the last one, she had absorbed it and barely managed to suppress the sudden increase of demonic Qi within her soul for a few minutes.

So when the Mystic Realm shrouded her in celestial fog, like a starved beast, she ran through the dense fog in search of a pocket realm overflowing with demonic Qi where she could run wild.

She had chosen hell. A realm of scorched earth shrouded in a haunted fog. If one looked closely, one could see red eyes and shifting shadows within the fog accompanied by the occasional howl.

Diana's eyes of pure darkness snapped open, and she exhaled a breath of demonic Qi. "Ninth stage of the Soul Fire Realm." She grinned, showing her newly grown fangs.

I wonder if I will be stuck in this demonic form when I reach the Star Core Realm?

A sudden tickle on her cheek made her look down to the side. "You hungry, Kaida?"

The inky black snake had grown during their month together, and Diana reached up her clawed hand of shadows to scratch him on the head. She had done extensive testing, and all her demonic features seemed to be a step up from illusions. She liked to call them manifestations, as they looked like shadows but were solid enough to tear into the flesh of monsters.

Although she looked like a demon, Kaida didn't shy away from the sharp claws her fingers had become and happily closed his eyes while sticking out his tongue.

"Kaida, do you think Stella will see me differently if she sees me like this?" Diana wondered aloud, and Kaida seemed to look at her curiously. Sometimes she wondered if the snake was actually very smart and could understand her.

I mean, just look at me... I have feathered wings sprouting from my back, my eyes are pure black, and I have claws. Even my body has changed shape. I almost look like a succubus. What if she gets jealous of me? I've seen how jealous she gets of everyone around her.

Kaida nudged her on the cheek with his head.

"You're right, Kaida. I shouldn't worry so much." Diana sighed deeply as she stood up, looked around the haunted mist, and spread out her improved spiritual sight. "Now, where can I find you some food?"

Picking a random direction, she began to walk. Even though she had large feathered wings almost identical to a raven, she could not fly despite her best efforts.

Maybe once I reach the Star Core Realm, I can fly. I mean, it only makes sense... It would be silly if I could fly around on a sword but not with these massive wings.

Even without flying, she could move through the pocket realm's haunted fog with immense speed due to her water affinity. She could also detect anything alive for a thousand miles in all directions.

Where is everything? I know I have feasted on the flesh of one too many demons over the last month, but for there to be none around me is bizarre... Oh!

Right on the edge of her spiritual sense was a demon she detected around the fifth stage of the Soul Fire Realm. Switching her direction, she headed straight for it. Once she got within a few miles, it seemed to sense her incoming presence and turned to escape.

A savage grin appeared on Diana's face. Something about being in her demon form made her enjoy the thrill of the hunt. Within seconds, she had arrived right behind the demon.

It reminded her of a hideous fish as it seemingly swam through the haunted fog. Spikes jutted out from its purple-skinned body. It turned to face her with a malformed mouth of sharp teeth. Diana coated her manifested claws in demonic Qi, gripped the fish between its teeth, and held it in place.

There was a brief moment where the demon seemed to realize it was about to die and let out a screech. Ignoring it, Diana grunted as she ripped the fish in half down the middle. Its clump of organs slid out of the carcass and dropped to the scorched ground alongside a beast core, which Diana grabbed and chucked into her mouth.

While absorbing the beast's core, she tore off bits of flesh from the carcass and fed them to Kaida, who greedily gobbled them down.

As Diana cycled the demonic Qi from the beast's core through her body, her mind drifted to something that had been bugging her.

My family name is Ravenborne, and my claws resemble that of a demonic bird, and my wings also match that of the birds that used to hang around in our courtyard full of scorched trees. There's a good chance this is all a coincidence, but what if it's not? What if I was always supposed to turn into this demon?

If that was true, she would feel more comfortable revealing her transformation to Stella and Ashlock. Whenever she remained in her "human" form, she felt the need to suppress her emotions or risk showing this side of her.

My memories are vague, but didn't I turn into a version of this form when Ashlock gave me the heart demon truffle the first time, and I fought down in the cavern with that slime? There's no way Ashlock didn't notice me then…right? I mean, I was hidden within my haunted mist technique, but at least a shadow of my monstrous form should have been visible.

Diana shook her head to clear her thoughts. It wasn't an ideal situation. If the Ashfallen Sect deemed her a monster and kicked her out, she would have to retreat to the wilderness, as no demonic sect would accept a demon, and neither would the Celestial Empire.

Demonic cultivators would hunt me down and devour my soul core to further their cultivation. I would become the ultimate prize for them.

A shiver ran down her spine at the thought. She didn't feel in the mood anymore to eat the demon's meat, so she gave a few more chunks to Kaida until the snake was satisfied and tossed the carcass to the side.

As Kaida finished his final bite, Diana detected something suddenly appearing within her spiritual sense as if it had been teleported into the realm.

"What the…" she muttered as she closed her eyes and became one with the mist to try and figure out more about the new threat. "Earth Qi and I can't detect its cultivation realm? But why does it feel so weak?"

One of the features of her demonic form was the ability to gauge an opponent's threat level. It seemed to be a survival instinct of all demons as Diana had noticed some demons gave off the feeling that they were much more threatening than they actually were, almost like animals that colored themselves to seem poisonous.

"Kaida, there's some weird earth Qi monster in the mist. Should we go and fight it?" The snake tilted his head and flickered his tongue at her nose.

Diana chuckled. "I'll take that as a yes."

Without wasting any more time, Diana began to dash through the mist, which swirled around the large, manifested raven wings on her back that was thrice her size.

Within a few minutes, she arrived a few meters from the target. Up close, she could see the grotesque thing was like a segment of a giant worm as if it had been cut on both sides. It didn't appear conscious as it kept convulsing and spewing out blood.

Diana cautiously approached and noted the foul-smelling slime that coated its skin.

"That's definitely the worm Ashlock had fought before we entered the Mystic Realm, but why is it here?" Diana ran through some scenarios in her head, and none were good. Ashlock had been left alone with only Larry for protection, so if a part of the worm had ended up in her pocket realm, had Ashlock cut it up and thrown it into the Mystic Realm?

Was the Patriarch fine? Or was she about to leave the Mystic Realm and see the Ashfallen Sect gone?

With a bloodthirsty rage rising in her chest, Diana summoned a ball of water above her palm. She then loaded it up with demonic Qi to the point it turned pitch black and then hurled it at the motionless piece of worm.

To her surprise, the segment of worm that still towered over her by many times seemed to react to the incoming threat as earth Qi rippled across its surface.

The slime coating its skin then began to boil and rise off its flesh as a poisonous cloud. Diana snapped her fingers, and the mist swirled around her, directing the toxic cloud away from herself.

I doubt this segment has a beast core, so it's just a large chunk of flesh making use of the latent Qi leftover to defend itself. Therefore I should win in a battle of attrition...

Diana collapsed to the scorched earth, out of breath. Her ninth-stage Soul Core was near empty, yet a grin arose on her face, followed by exhausted laughter.

"Haha...what a tough bastard." She groaned as she flipped her body over onto her back so she could rest. Beside her, Kaida was slowly pulling off chunks of the Star Core Realm worm meat and gobbling it down.

"You're such a glutton, Kaida." Diana petted the top of his head, but the snake was too preoccupied with his meal to pay her any attention.

The worm corpse looked like an archery target board with how many holes had been made by Diana's claws and thrown balls of demonic Qi. "I don't see how any of the others could have even put a dent into this thing. Except maybe Elaine with her void affinity."

After a short rest, Diana staggered to her feet and put her hand on the worm's side. All the poisonous slime had long boiled away, so it was safe to touch. She then closed her eyes and let the demonic Qi from the corpse flow into her system and cycle through her purified spirit roots, thanks to Ashlock's truffles.

She breathed in and out, slowly cycling her Qi, and debated whether to suppress the demonic Qi within herself and try to return to "normal" or remain a demon.

"You know, Kaida, I'm feeling like the end of the Mystic Realm is coming," Diana said over the sound of munching. "Should I emerge from the Mystic Realm as a demon or a human?"

The snake sadly didn't offer his opinion. Diana left him to his meal. She was excited to see what he evolved into after eating so much monster meat.

"Guess I will figure it out myself."

Douglas felt incredibly lucky with his choice of pocket realm. Although he would have appreciated if it wasn't quite so hot.

After finishing a round of deep meditation, he breathed out and opened his eyes. He summoned his earthy soul fire to his hand and marveled at how powerful it looked. "Sixth stage of the Soul Fire Realm. I can't believe I have progressed three entire stages in a month."

Honestly, it felt like cheating to him. A frown appeared on his lips as he surveyed the endless flat plains of gray rock that had remained the same since he arrived and wiped the sweat from his brow.

It was so hot due to the five suns in the sky that cycled on a constant rotation. Douglas had feared that he would have lost his feet once his Qi ran out when he had first arrived in this desolate realm. Luckily, he had discovered the giant turtle he was perched on the shell of before that happened.

The turtle was so giant it was like a moving island, and it didn't seem to care about his presence on its back as it munched on the rock as if it was tasty.

Douglas was busy feeling a sense of achievement from his advancement that he almost didn't notice when the giant turtle changed direction for the first time in a month. Until now, it had continued a constant slow march toward what he expected was north.

"What happened, buddy?" Douglas asked aloud and then felt the whole island-size shell shudder and tilt to the side. The shell rumbled as the giant turtle roared in pain. "Whoa! What the fuck is happening?"

Douglas stumbled across the shell for a few minutes due to its ridiculous size and eventually could look down at the ground below. The turtle's legs, which were thicker and taller than Ashlock, were trembling, and Douglas could see something emerging from the ground and tearing massive chunks of flesh from one of the turtle's legs, dyeing the ground below in crimson.

"No fucking way." Douglas couldn't believe what he was seeing. How had the worm followed him into this pocket realm? Looking closer, he noticed it was injured but was rapidly absorbing the earth Qi in the area and healing itself.

Douglas began to panic as he stood up. The horizon in all directions was nothing but burning-hot gray rock. If he got down from the turtle and tried to run, there was no way he could survive if the worm switched targets and went for him…or if there were more worms.

The turtle's shell continued to vibrate, throwing him off his footing as the turtle roared in pain and tried to move its leg to crush the worm underfoot.

"That won't work, you dull creature," Douglas shouted. "The worm doesn't care about the rock. It can swim through it. There's no way you can crush the fucking thing."

Looking back under the shell, Douglas watched in horror as the worm had enclosed the entire turtle's leg within its body, and its ring of freshly regrown, razor-sharp teeth suddenly clamped down around the top of the turtle's leg where it met the shell.

The following roar of pain was earthquake-inducing as the turtle collapsed to the side, sending a landslide of rock out for a few miles. Douglas dug his hands into the deep grooves of the turtle shell to avoid slipping down and tried to think about what to do. Should he run while the worm was busy with its meal? Would he even get very far?

It had been two days, and Douglas was facing death.

The turtle was long dead. The worm had eaten its way inside its shell and devoured it from within. He could hear the poor turtle being consumed through the shell beneath him.

Glancing over his shoulder, he could see more segments of the worm. For whatever reason, these had taken longer to regenerate as they still remained as lumps of worm meat, but earth Qi still rippled across their surface, so he didn't want to take his chances jumping down and trying to dash past them.

Suddenly a terrible crunch, like a bone snapping into pieces, drew his attention, and Douglas's face paled. The turtle's shell that was buried deep into the stone below caved in, and something emerged from the hole.

Douglas didn't even need to look at the grotesque abyssal worm that came out the hole like cursed pus and blocked out the sun as it loomed over him.

He slowly pushed himself up the shell, digging his feet and hands into the grooves as he went, but soon enough, his hand met the air. He was hundreds of meters above the gray rock as he sat at the peak of the turtle shell.

All around him was endlessly flat rock and regenerating segments of worm. And before him was a somehow still hungry Star Core worm that he swore he would have nightmares about if he managed to live through this somehow.

"You don't scare me, you fucker!" Douglas shouted as the worm seemingly stared him down. "I'm the great Douglas Terraforge. The greatest builder of the Ashfallen Sect!"

The worm reeled back and let out an ear-shattering screech that almost pushed him off the edge of the shell. Douglas gripped the shell tightly to hold on and wasn't very proud of the words that escaped his lips.

"Mommy, save me…"

40
END OF THE MYSTIC REALM

Ashlock awoke to birds chirping and the warmth of the morning sun. As always, his body took a while to slowly wake up.

"Why can't I drink coffee as a tree? Being so sluggish in the morning is annoying," Ashlock grumbled as he looked around. Like every other morning, the sign-in system popped up, signifying yet another day had passed.

Idletree Daily Sign-In System
Day: 3522
Daily Credit: 1
Sacrifice Credit: 871
[Sign in?]

"Huh, those worms from Sebastian gave me more credits than I had expected."

Ashlock debated signing in, as it should be enough points to guarantee at least an A-grade draw, but he decided against it. "Since I should eat some more worm today, I should wait for the main course and get the best rewards."

He did have plans to sign in for lower-grade rewards in the future, but being only a few hundred off from another S-grade draw made him hesitant to spend. What if he drew a fantastic new A-grade skill when it could have been S-rank instead?

Dismissing those thoughts, Ashlock glanced at the Mystic Realm fog. "Today's the day that I see my sect members again. I wonder how much they have grown in our short time apart."

He hoped the answer was a lot. Tensions were rising, and he feared an all-out war between him and another family like the Voidminds or perhaps the entire Blood Lotus Sect was only a single tiny slip-up away.

There were simply too many loose ends mounting up and people witnessing his absurd feats. A city with millions of people suddenly found themselves living alongside demonic trees with bizarre mushrooms growing on their trunks and pink flowers on their branches. If that wasn't bad enough, they had appeared seemingly overnight.

Then there's the sudden disappearance of the Voidmind Elder and his assistant, the death of three entire cultivator families, heaven opening up and dumping ash spiders everywhere, and even his ascension to the Star Core Realm.

"There really has been a lot of nonsense going on, hasn't there?" Ashlock chuckled. "There were even floating trees through portals and a giant worm that attacked the city. The fact Darklight City hasn't revolted and demanded answers is already a miracle."

Ashlock wasn't delusional. He knew all his activities were bringing him increasingly into the spotlight. But what was he supposed to do? He couldn't grow strong enough to fend off the beast tide in time if he wasn't a little daring. Opportunity came to those who sought it, and as a tree that couldn't move, he was limited in how to stumble across treasures.

"I got my void skill by being obnoxious with my activities, for example."

While Ashlock was thinking to himself, he briefly checked on Elaine, who he had deposited into the mine the night before. She seemed a little nervous as she paced around the cavern, seemingly aimlessly, only occasionally glancing up the large hole through the center of the mountain.

"Best she remains down there. I have no idea what will emerge from the Mystic Realm today, and her fighting and survival instincts are about as sharp as a panda. Which is to say, I am surprised she hasn't died already." Ashlock switched sights back to the swirling fog seemingly trapped within an invisible snow globe.

The last time the Mystic Realm had been activated, he had sent in his roots, but this time he activated {Consuming Abyss} and sent his black vines into the fog as they were faster and easier to control.

For a brief moment, he debated activating the void version but decided against it because he concluded it could only end badly. What if the void tendrils destroyed any pocket realms they came into contact with? Not a risk worth taking while his sect members were still inside.

The fog of the Mystic Realm hindered his spiritual sight, just like the mountain's rock or walls. However, he could feel things; environments of the pocket realms flooded his mind as one vine ended up in a scorching hot climate. Meanwhile, another was up against ice.

It was incredibly unsettling, and he debated whether this was even necessary. Last time he had done this out of fear for an entire week straight as he was trying to find where Stella had gone like a crazed parent fearing the worst for their child.

Ashlock numbed the varying sensations—one of the many advantages of becoming a tree. He didn't pick up sensations like pain the same way humans did.

The sun slowly rose over the horizon, and the sunlight made Ashlock feel rejuvenated. Nothing truly made him happier than a beautiful day of clear blue skies and warm sunshine.

An hour passed, and Ashlock suddenly felt a pair of hands grabbing the tip of one of his many black vines. "Why does it feel like claws, though?"

Curiously, Ashlock told Larry through the tether, "About to bring someone back from their pocket realm. Or at least I think it's a person…"

The giant obedient spider crawled into position, and without further ado, Ashlock pulled on the black vine, and Diana came tumbling out. Ashlock swore he caught a glimpse of wings through the fog, but Diana emerged from the fog looking like usual.

"Strange…" Ashlock usually felt proud of his vision capabilities despite not having eyes, yet this time he started questioning things.

Diana picked herself up and brushed off the dust and dirt. Kaida hissed with annoyance around her neck as she looked around, patting his head. "Am I the first one back?" she said with even less emotion than usual.

Ashlock flashed his leaf once to confirm her thoughts, which earned a shrug from Diana as she walked over and perched herself on the bench below his canopy.

"Has she ascended to the ninth stage? She almost seems ready to form her Star Core with how much Qi is swirling within her." Ashlock then mentally frowned. "There's also a lot of demonic Qi being suppressed in her Soul Core."

Kaida slithered off from around her neck and curled around a low-hanging branch.

[Kaida has accumulated enough Qi to evolve to C-grade]
[Infant Ink Serpent {Kaida} wishes to evolve]
[Yes/No]

Ashlock obviously selected yes.

[Infant Ink Serpent {Kaida} has begun to evolve]
[Please select {Kaida} evolution path...]

The system flickered and soon displayed all of the evolution options at once.

[Shadowcall Scriptor Serpent]
This evolution emphasizes the serpent's ink and stealth attributes, allowing Kaida to blend seamlessly into shadows and manipulate darkness to his advantage. His golden eyes glow ominously in the dark, unnerving any potential enemies.

[Golden-Eyed Ink Mystic]
In this evolution, Kaida's golden eyes become even more striking, enabling him to see through illusions and perceive the truth of the world around him. His ink affinity deepens, allowing him to cast complex ink-based techniques and illusions, confusing his opponents and giving him an edge in battles.

[Ebonflow Serpent Sovereign]
As an Ebonflow Serpent Sovereign, Kaida's ink affinity merges with water and darkness, giving him fluid control over his surroundings. His scales become jet black, and his golden eyes gleam with newfound

authority. This evolution boosts his offensive capabilities, allowing him to attack with torrents of ink and water.

[Inkborn Nether Viper]
This evolution allows Kaida to tap into nether- or death-related energies, adding a deadly edge to his ink-based abilities. The golden eyes take on an otherworldly glow, and his presence becomes even more fearsome. This evolution makes Kaida an intimidating opponent, especially against those who fear darkness and death.

Ashlock read through the options.

They seemed more interesting than the ones he had been given for Larry. This also meant he had to think harder about which to pick, as the best option wasn't as obvious.

"Shadowcall Scriptor Serpent can be ignored as it focuses on stealth abilities. Although I don't have someone specializing in stealth in my group, I have {Eye of the Tree God} to spy on people and can always evacuate Diana or someone else if they get caught with a portal. An evolution in stealth feels pointless compared to the other better options."

Crossing out the first option, he contemplated the second. "Golden-Eyed Ink Mystic sounds very fancy, but it basically boils down to looking through illusions and fighting with illusions. This would force Kaida into the support role, as illusions are great if he's alongside someone else that can provide the firepower."

Ashlock hummed as he contemplated. It certainly had a lot of potential, but wouldn't Kaida's power be rather limited if he fought someone who didn't use illusions or, even worse, a cultivator that could also see through illusions?

"Personally, the next option, Ebonflow Serpent Sovereign, seems the most promising to me, for the simple fact it gives Kaida the ability to work with water Qi, making him the ideal guardian for Diana as they will work perfectly together."

Ashlock still had the idea to group his summons up with those most important to him. Maple for Stella, Kaida for Diana, and Larry for him. He could imagine it now, Kaida around Diana's shoulders as she dashed through her haunted mist and attacked foes.

He gave the last option a brief look but didn't like it. Something about turning the cute snake into a death affinity–wielding monster didn't sit right with him. Also, the fact it mentioned a snake species in the name made him fearful that it was a dead-end evolution.

"All right, I will pick…" Ashlock felt a sudden pain through his black vines as he pondered his options. "Ow, what the fuck?"

He tried to dismiss the system notification, but it wouldn't budge. The words flashed, prompting him to make his decision. Meanwhile, the pain only got more extreme. He focused on the source and felt two large hands gripping the vine. It felt like someone was trying to climb up his vine despite its large thorns.

"Ah, what the hell. I will pick Ebonflow Serpent Sovereign!" Ashlock shouted at his system.

[Evolution path {Ebonflow Serpent Sovereign} chosen, evolution initiating…]

Ashlock ignored the snake as the system message vanished, and he could focus on the strange pain through his vine. Without delay, he pulled that particular vine back and watched Douglas fly out of the Mystic Realm…screaming like a little girl.

His clothes were shredded and bloody as he collapsed in a heap on the ground. He groaned as he tilted his head, and his eyes seemed to go wide with relief as he saw Diana staring at him weirdly while sitting on the bench.

Before Douglas could even open his mouth to explain, the end of the Ashlock's vine whipped out from the Mystic Realm, dragging the all-too-familiar Star Core Realm worm with it.

Although far smaller than its full size, the enormous worm was still a few hundred meters long and gnawing on his vine. Ashlock sent a surge of spatial Qi down the vine and straight into the worm's body, causing it to screech and try to reel back, but the spike on the end of the vine was deeply entrenched inside its body's inner wall like a harpoon.

With the worm somewhat under control, Ashlock didn't delay as he toggled the void version of his {Consuming Abyss} skill. The usual lake of void Qi spread out from his trunk, and hundreds of tendrils shot out, impaling the worm gnawing on the end of his vine, causing it to let out another ear-piercing screech before falling to the ground beside a terrified Douglas, which made the mountain tremble.

Once on the ground, that sealed the worm's fate. The void lake flowed against its body and washed away any feeble defense. The worm segment released a final cry as it became blanketed in void Qi.

"It almost ate me!" Douglas shouted as he hauled his bloodied self away from the worm-turned swiss cheese from all the holes leaking blood.

Ashlock wanted to call him a drama queen, but his body did suggest a life-or-death battle. "It's a good thing that I decided to send in my vines. Otherwise, Douglas might have become worm food."

Diana stood up and went to Douglas's side, offering him help. Meanwhile, Ashlock got to work on devouring the corpse for sacrificial credits.

[+543 Sc]

Stella's eyes snapped open as a burst of power emanated from her chest, traveling for hundreds of miles throughout the vast pocket realm. The violent tempest of spatial Qi and lightning encircling her began to die down as her ascension had concluded.

She took a deep breath, and the surrounding storm flowed into her mouth and cycled throughout her body and her newly formed Star Core, invigorating her with a level of power she had only dreamed about.

A massive grin manifested on her face as she stood up and stretched. Her bones cracked, and her muscles protested the stretch as she had been sitting perfectly still for the last month, but it was finally over. She had successfully formed every cultivator's dream—a Star Core.

Something her biological father had failed to do. Perhaps if he had access to Tree's amazing cultivation resources, he wouldn't have perished and left her alone for those early years...

Stella reached up and placed her hand on her chest as she sighed. It was a spatial Star Core, the last remnant of her biological father, as it had been passed down to her through blood. In a way, he would live on through her, and that was all she needed.

"Mother...Father, don't worry about your daughter. I'm in good hands...err, I mean branches..." The image of Tree flashed through her mind, and a warm feeling spread throughout her.

Shaking her head, she focused back on the feeling in her chest. It felt so weird for the burning star in her chest to constantly supply her body with a stream of spatial Qi without any need for meditation.

Although I will still have to meditate to push my Star Core to grow and eventually reach the Nascent Soul Realm. Only then can I relax as I will have escaped the shackles of a finite lifespan and become a semi-immortal.

But that was a long way away. Stella surveyed the silver metal ocean surrounding the tiny spike of obsidian rock she was standing on. Over the last month, the relentless lightning had often missed her, hitting the black mountain and eroding it to almost nothing.

Closing her eyes, the world was reduced to its rawest spatial form. Everything was outlined by grids. Stella spread her spiritual sense further than ever before and found a flatter piece of black rock jutting from the metal ocean.

Her Star Core flared up in her chest as she summoned a portal at the tips of her fingers and designated that distant flat rock as the anchor for the portal's destination. As the entire pocket realm was saturated with spatial Qi, she easily compressed the grids to shorten the space between her and the distant flat rock to almost nothing and…stepped through.

Opening her eyes as she heard the portal snap closed behind her, she grinned. "It really worked! Hahahaha! I finally figured out the spatial plane. Woohoo!" She giggled and glared at the metal ocean below, eager to try something else.

Her Star Core pulsed in her chest, and she saw the metal ocean compress and flow away as if an invisible force was pressing down on it.

The pressure of a Star Core cultivator… I always wanted to be able to crush people with my mere presence.

She still remembered the feeling of when she had made Tree mad when they were being invaded by the Evergreens and Winterwraths, and he had unleashed his Star Core pressure on her.

Satisfied with her new power level, she reached up and gave Maple tummy rubs while looking around. "What should I do now?"

An entire day later, as Stella stood there throwing rocks into the metal ocean, procrastinating instead of doing any more meditation after doing it for a month straight, she suddenly felt something surfacing.

Drawing her sword from her spatial ring, she watched as a half-formed abyssal worm she was all too familiar with tried to escape the molten metal ocean.

Furrowing her brows in confusion at the presence of the worm, Stella aimed the sword at the worm. It crackled with golden lightning as she unleashed all of the lightning Dao stored up in her body after being struck by lightning for a month straight.

A concentrated bolt of golden lightning arced out the tip of her sword and slammed into the worm halfway out of the ocean. The sheer force of her attack nearly pushed it back under, but its scorched, malformed head remained on display.

The smell of cooked worm meat mixed with decay and poison made Stella reel back. Even after ending her attack, the lightning arced on the metal ocean's surface, further cooking the worm alive.

Does it not have any earth Qi left to defend itself?

Stella wasn't sure, but she had no intention of sticking around to find out due to the rancid smell and poison. Closing her eyes and entering the spatial plane again, she picked a location near where she had initially landed in this pocket realm and exited there.

To her surprise, moments later, a black vine coated in spikes she was familiar with appeared seemingly out of nowhere.

"Tree! Is it really time to leave? Have you come to get me?" The vine offered no words or signs of hearing her, so she grabbed it. The vine rapidly pulled back, causing her to yelp in surprise.

It brought her through a tear in reality, rushed her through the dense white fog of the Mystic Realm, and threw her out onto the mountain peak.

Landing gracefully, Stella glanced at Douglas, who was crawling away from her in tattered rags, and Diana, standing over him. The black-haired girl offered her a genuine smile, which made Stella pause.

Since when did Diana have fangs?

41
NECROFLORA

Stella carefully sidestepped the encroaching lake of void Qi originating from Ash as she walked over to Diana.

The black-haired girl appraised her with her usual dull-gray eyes devoid of emotion. She seemed to stare straight into her soul. "You got stronger," she said with her customary dry tone.

"So did you," Stella replied, her attention still fixated on Diana's lips, trying to peer past them to see the fangs. Eventually, she just decided to ask straight up to break the awkward silence caused by her staring. "Since when did you have fangs?"

Diana's eyes widened a little, and she sealed her lips shut. Stella squinted her eyes at the girl's odd behavior.

What's up with her? Why is she acting like this?

Stella then noticed Diana running her tongue along her teeth behind her sealed lips.

Once she had finished, she grinned, showing a distinct lack of fangs. "What fangs? Is there something on my face?"

Stella rolled her eyes. "Diana, I'm not delusional. I saw your fangs."

Diana pouted.

"Just tell me, okay?" Stella sighed. "When have I ever left you in the dark before?"

Diana seemed to think for a while and then awkwardly scratched the back of her neck. "I'll show you later." Her eyes seemed to dart between

Douglas, looking up at them from the ground while taking deep breaths, and the Mystic Realm.

Stella genuinely smiled at Diana. "If it's uncomfortable, you don't need to tell me. Just let me know whenever you are ready."

But I really want to know right now... Look at me being considerate. I hope Diana doesn't shy away from me now. Please say yes, please, please...

"Sure." Diana nodded. "Thank you, Stella. I have a lot on my mind right now, but you will be the first to know."

Yes! Stella gave herself a mental pat on the back.

Ashlock listened in on the conversation between Stella and Diana and felt a sense of relief. "So I hadn't gone crazy. She really did have fangs."

Since nothing drastic had occurred since Diana last fought her heart demons, it had gone to the back of his mind, but there was a lot of mystery surrounding Diana.

First, she manifested a demonic form obscured by her haunted mist when she fought with Bob to expel the demonic Qi from her system. Secondly, Larry had said there was something ancient smelling about Diana and Stella.

"But if she doesn't want to share, that's fine, too." Ashlock wasn't worried. Even if Diana turned out to be a crazed demon unable to resist slaughter, he would just transport her to the wilderness and keep an eye on her occasionally. Diana was very important to him and was also one of Stella's only friends. So he wished the best for her.

Ashlock was broken from this trail of thought by feeling multiple pairs of hands gripping one of his many vines. "Are these the Redclaws?" He sure hoped so. Otherwise, he was about to bring out some undiscovered alien species.

When he pulled back that particular vine that felt very dry, as if all moisture had been sucked out, three Redclaws came flying out.

The Grand Elder, Amber, and Elder Mo landed with varying degrees of gracefulness, but Ashlock wasn't paying attention. He was more concerned about where the other two Redclaw Elders were.

Standing up and brushing himself off, it seemed the Grand Elder shared his concern as the aged man glanced around. *"Where are Elders*

Brent and Margret? We searched for them throughout the pocket realm but couldn't find them anywhere, so we assumed they arrived before us."

Stella shook her head. "We haven't seen them."

Ashlock quickly sent his black vine back into the Mystic Realm and tried to return to that fire Qi pocket realm and search for the missing Elders. He had no control over which pocket realms his vines ended up in as he had sent in over a hundred vines, and there was no way there were that many pocket realms with people in them, so it was totally random and dependent on his luck if he managed to get a vine to someone.

Or so he thought…but that theory didn't make sense, considering he found and pulled out his sect members within a few minutes of each other. "This Mystic Realm sure is a mystery…an annoying mystery if it kills my people."

Focusing on that black vine, he suddenly felt a damp climate. "Nope, not this one…" He pulled it out and then ended up in a cold environment. He repeated this process a few more times and eventually felt a dry climate, but it felt different from the one where he had found the Redclaws.

While this was happening, the Grand Elder was getting restless on the mountain peak due to his missing Elders.

"Don't worry. The Patriarch will find a way to save them," Stella reassured them. *"He is very reliable."*

The Grand Elder let out a nervous breath. *"I…have full faith in the Patriarch's capabilities."*

Ashlock certainly didn't have the situation under control and really wished Stella wouldn't put him on the spot like that. Sometimes, her almost zealous faith in him became dangerous to his reputation.

While he continued searching the Mystic Realm, he felt the sun slowly climb the sky overhead, and the second the sunlight snuck past his canopy and hit the Mystic Realm, he saw the celestial glitter that represented the shards to the pocket realms within the fog begin to vanish as if they were reactive to the sun.

"On the dawn of the seventh day, the Mystic Realm closes," Ashlock murmured as he tried to send more black vines into the Mystic Realm and desperately searched around but had no luck.

Looking into the fog closer, Ashlock watched as each pocket realm vanished under the sunlight and was surprised when a giant worm segment popped out from the Mystic Realm, followed by another and then another.

"What the fuck?" Ashlock couldn't help but swear as everyone stumbled back at the sudden appearance of the worms. Some were frozen solid in ice, and others seemed charred like they had been deep-fried in lava.

Ashlock sent in his void lake and tendrils as he had kept the skill active this time. Some worm segments were still alive as he saw earth Qi ripple across their skin upon sensing a threat, but most were utterly unmoving and devoid of Qi, making them easy to devour. However, they were each around a hundred meters long, making them hearty meals.

[+280 Sc]
[+263 Sc]
[+127 SC]
[+198 SC]

"Not much Qi compared to the worm that had been attacking Douglas," Ashlock noted as he saw the sacrificial credits flow in, "but still a substantial amount. I believe it's due to all of these being nothing but Qi-filled meat, as any semblance of a Star Core in any of these is long gone."

"Hey, that's the worm I encountered right before I returned here," Stella said while pointing to a worm coated in a silver metallic sheen. It didn't seem to be moving, and the charred flesh within its malformed mouth seemed like something had fried it alive.

[+134 Sc]

Ashlock devoured it and then was about to move on to the next one when the Grand Elder stepped forward. "Patriarch, please wait."

Pulling his void lake and tendrils back, Ashlock watched as the Grand Elder drew his sword and approached the worm. This one was more active than the others and had a semi-formed mouth filled with half-broken, brittle teeth. The thing seemed to be convulsing as if trying to throw something up.

Surrounding his sword in crimson flames, Ashlock felt the weight of the Grand Elder's heightened cultivation as he slashed down against the worm's side. The attack was blocked by earth Qi, but the Grand Elder didn't relent. The attacks kept coming until the earth Qi rippled away by the tenth overhead slash, and he cleanly sliced through.

To Ashlock's surprise, two humans with fire Qi blazing around their bodies emerged from the hole. They looked haggard as they gave the Grand Elder a grateful bow.

"What in the nine realms happened to you two?" The Grand Elder looked between the almost unrecognizable visage of Elder Brent and Elder Margret.

Elder Brent staggered a few steps before collapsing to his knees and seemed to kiss the ground with tears of joy.

"We were both cultivating back where you left us," Elder Marget said, *"but then this worm came out of nowhere and ate us. We cut ourselves out multiple times, but every time we escaped, it would heal and chase us down. Without our fire Qi keeping us safe from the digestive fluids and poison, we would be dead."*

Elder Brent added while lying on the floor, *"We are both in the Soul Fire Realm. We never had a chance against a Star Core threat while running across a seemingly endless desert. We tried heading toward you but never made it in time."*

The Grand Elder crossed his arms and frowned. *"I should apologize then as it was my idea to split up. I searched the entire area with my spiritual sense and couldn't even detect a fly, let alone a Star Core Realm worm."*

Elder Margret looked like she was about to say something but then refrained. Elder Brent, on the other hand, shook his head and laughed. "No, Grand Elder, we were simply too weak. This was our fault."

Ashlock was certain they were trying to help the Grand Elder save face, as they were currently in the presence of the Ashfallen Sect. The trio continued to speak for a while, and eventually, they got to their feet and went to talk with Elder Mo, who was holding a very impressive hammer surrounded by ghostly flames.

"You got an inheritance?!? From an immortal smith?!?" Elder Brent looked like he had eaten shit by his facial expression.

"That's right!" Elder Mo chuckled while showing off the hammer. *"I can now utilize spirit fire to imbue my will into weapons! Imagine my vigor and battle spirit living inside your blade!"*

"All right, I take it back." Elder Brent glared at the Grand Elder.

"You should have come back to get us. You really left us to almost perish in a desert because you were greedy for an inheritance?"

The Grand Elder blinked and seemed to find the sudden change in Elder Brent's opinion on spending the last month or so being chased down and inside a worm's stomach rather hilarious as he burst out laughing.

While the Redclaws were conversing, Ashlock resisted asking about the inheritance as that could wait for later and kept an eye on the Mystic Realm.

It was rapidly shrinking as the sunlight made the pocket realms vanish. "If I built a hut to shade the Mystic Realm from the sun, would it always stay open? Actually, even better idea: I should plant a tree right in the middle of the Mystic Realm to provide shade, and then I can overtake it with {Progeny Dominion} and enter the pocket realms, too. That should work, right?"

But that would have to be for next time. For now, Ashlock let the Mystic Realm fade away as he wanted to ensure all worm segments were brought out. The last thing he wanted was for one of the worm segments to remain in the pocket realm, grow super strong over time, and then kill one of his sect members the second they stepped foot in its territory the next time he used the Mystic Realm.

Just as the Mystic Realm was about to fade away, he was glad to see three more worm segments suddenly appear. Seeing a colossal-size worm that could rival the size of a whale materialize out of thin air was a bizarre sight.

Moments later, the Mystic Realm ceased to exist, and he saw in his skill list that it had gone on cooldown for a month once again.

"So these are the last few segments of that giant worm," Ashlock noted as he identified the two most active worm segments. "I should eat these two and then sign in. Best to keep some sacrificial credits on hand to fuel my void skill."

After attacking the two worm segments, which Ashlock suspected had come from an earth Qi realm as they were far more reformed and full of Qi than the last few, he also devoured the worm that had swallowed the Elders.

[+430 Sc]
[+390 Sc]

[+398 SC]

"System, sign in!" Ashlock said with excitement.

Idletree Daily Sign-In System
Day: 3522
Daily Credit: 1
Sacrifice Credit: 3630
|Sign in?|

"Holy shit...three thousand credits?" Ashlock gawked at the number for a long time. Was this the highest number he had ever seen? "I won't get an SS-grade draw, right? I don't know if my body could handle it with my current cultivation realm."

He refused to believe a single Star Core Realm threat could result in this many sacrificial credits. "Actually, it's also strange that the Mystic Realm pulled the worm apart and sent it to different pocket realms. Was the worm not one creature but multiple working or attached together?"

Each worm segment seemed to have the ability to be cut off from the others and still thrive. Humans and other monsters Ashlock had encountered had a single soul core or beast core within their body that provided them with Qi converted into their affinity. Yet each part of this worm seemed capable of producing Qi independently.

While pondering these ideas, Ashlock killed the last worm segment left with his void tendrils as he knew the void part of his {Consuming Abyss} skill would vanish the second he signed in and ran out of sacrificial credits.

Wrapping his black vines around the corpse just to make sure it didn't suddenly come back to life somehow and kill him while he was briefly distracted, Ashlock finally said the words...

"Sign in."

[Sign in successful, 3630 credits consumed...]
[Upgraded {Root Puppet [B]} -> {Necroflora Sovereign [SS]}]

Ashlock read the system notification and was at first glad to see that one of his more outdated skills was getting an upgrade as he couldn't even remember the last time he had a use for root puppet, but then his brain froze when he saw the [SS] beside the upgrade.

Within moments, knowledge of the {Necroflora Sovereign [SS]} skill flooded his mind.

"Wow...this sure is quite the upgrade." Ashlock whistled in his mind as he reviewed the knowledge. Rather than spend all day thinking about his newest skill, he decided to try it since there was a corpse right before him.

Activating {Necroflora Sovereign} caused a black root to emerge from the ground, much to the interest of everyone watching. The root then entered the worm's mouth just like with {Root Puppet}, but this time it was different.

There were no hair-thin roots to take control of every inch of the body. Instead, the root tip opened up and deposited a single pitch-black seed.

Both the Grand Elder and Stella instantly drew swords from their spatial rings and pulsed their Star Cores as if on instinct.

"Tree, what in the nine realms was that?!?" Stella asked urgently as spatial flames coated her sword. *"The feeling of imminent death washed over me."*

The Grand Elder nodded at her side. *"Me too. It felt like death itself had a grasp around my neck."*

'I'm testing a new technique,' Ashlock wrote on his trunk.

Stella and the Grand Elder translated his words aloud for the others to hear. Everyone exchanged a wary glance as those weaker than the Star Core Realm seemed to shiver in fear rather than feel the instinctual need to fight something. As if their bodies instinctually knew they could only cower in fear.

'You're welcome to go down into the mine if you don't want to stay and watch,' Ashlock offered as he felt the {Necroflora Sovereign} skill move into its next phase...the reawakening.

Everyone shook their heads, clearly eager to see the result of an immortal's new skill.

Ashlock had debated sending them away, but he had already let them try his fruit and truffles and even enter the Mystic Realm. At this point, the only secret he wanted to keep from the Redclaws was that the immortal they idolized was actually the demonic tree right behind them.

"Anyway, now comes the fun part if my knowledge of the skill is correct." Ashlock laughed evilly as the seed emitting pure death Qi bloomed within the worm.

Restrained by his black vines, the worm corpse began to metamorphose into black wood. Before his spiritual sight, the worm's corpse began to fight against the black vine restraints, so Ashlock released them and allowed his new creation to stand up.

At first, it looked like a tree, but slowly it split up, and two thick legs and arms became apparent, and then finally, a maw and two empty eye sockets that ignited with his lilac soul fire.

He had created a twenty-meter-tall Ent—a humanoid tree monster from the worm corpse—and by the looks of it, the titan was in the Star Core Realm. It loomed over everyone, only almost matching Ashlock in height.

An immense pressure suddenly blanketed the area, causing everyone but Stella and the Grand Elder to struggle to stand. The Ent lit up with spatial flames roaring from every gap between the twisted roots that made up its body, making it look like an aflame demon lord about to take its throne.

Ashlock noted that his root remained connected to the monster but knew he could disconnect it and let the Ent roam free. However, its body would decay slowly over time depending on the realm of the corpse used to make the Ent.

"But for a Star Core Ent...it should be able to roam around for a month at least without my Qi."

That aside, the Ent could always return to him or one of his offspring under this {Progeny Dominion} skill to reverse the decay.

So if managed well, Ashlock now had an eternal Star Core servant that he could dispatch into battle without worrying about it dying, as it was nothing but a mindlessly reanimated corpse.

"The immortal never ceases to impress me," the Grand Elder muttered under his breath as he lowered his sword. *"This is truly a servant befitting one such as him."*

42
GOODBYE, OLD FRIEND

Ashlock excitedly tried to send a command to his new Ent, but it refused to move no matter how much effort he put into it.

"Huh? Why isn't the skill working? Is my realm not high enough to command it?" Ashlock glanced around in confusion and noticed it wasn't only his Ent stuck in place and refusing his commands. His leaves were stuck, and none of his sect members were moving.

Everything was perfectly still, as if time had been frozen, but if he looked closely, he could see the eyes of his sect members still moving around in their eye sockets, and the spatial flames burning within the Ent were still flickering.

"My friend, we need to have a talk." A voice Ashlock was all too familiar with drew his attention.

Senior Lee stood on the edge of the mountain peak, his back facing Ashlock as he gazed at the distant Darklight City. His long white hair flowed down his back like a cape, and his simple white robes rustled in an invisible breeze.

"Senior Lee? Why are you back so soon?" Ashlock questioned the back of the man. "I thought you said you would meet me at the top."

Turning to face him, Senior Lee glanced up at the Ent's maw and lilac flame-filled eyes. *"Well, I felt a sudden wave of death Qi near an old friend, so I came to check up on you before I entered my final meditation."*

"Final meditation?" Ashlock asked.

"Indeed, what may be an entire lifetime to you is but a passing moment for me. Yet my time is running out. I have but one last eon of meditation left in this fleeting spirit of mine." Senior Lee's eyes flickered, and Ashlock swore he saw galaxies within his pupils. "Now tell me, friend, what is this creature of death you have manifested?"

"Ah, this thing." Ashlock relaxed a little. Whenever Senior Lee arrived, he feared he was about to dump some bad news on his plate. "This is an Ent I made with a new technique. It's completely under my control."

"Impressive. I knew my gift wasn't wasted on you." The man circled it once, his eyes closed as if appraising it with his spiritual sense. "What a bizarre and fascinating mixture of death's decay, the nature of life, and absolute control. It's as if you have compressed all that governs the life and death of this universe into a single abomination."

Senior Lee then opened his eyes and began to walk over to Ashlock's sect members. "Hello, Stella and Diana, long time no see. You both have grown so much in our little time apart. Star Core Realm already?" He offered them a warm, grandfatherly smile as their eyes followed his movement. "I just need to have a little private chat with my friend here, so you will all need to go for now."

Stella's eyes widened as Senior Lee snapped his fingers, and everyone vanished as if they were never there. Ashlock was about to panic, but he felt their presence reappear in the mine alongside Elaine.

Time wasn't frozen down there, so they all burst into chatter, and Douglas ran over to Elaine, and the two hugged. Ashlock wanted to listen in on what they had to say, especially regarding Elder Mo's inheritance and ghostly spirit flames, but he had a more important person to pay attention to.

Senior Lee perched himself on the vacant bench. His visage was that of a friendly elderly man—the facade he had employed the first time they met. The old monster in human skin had taught Ashlock to never rely on appearances when discerning the true nature of someone in a cultivation world where at the peak stages, the body was nothing but a vessel that could be warped and changed into a person's will.

"I believe the first time we met, I spoke of visiting an old friend." Senior Lee's voice took on a stern tone, and his warmth was replaced with a cold and unreadable face. "A sworn brother of mine, in fact. One from the Voidmind family..."

Ashlock felt his mind freeze as he took in Senior Lee's words. *"So, spirit tree, care to explain why I feel the lingering soul of my sworn brother trapped within your trunk and detect his niece in the mine below our feet?"*

"Well…" Ashlock didn't even know where to begin. He felt like every word could be his last as an aura of pure rage lurked below Senior Lee's unreadable face. "After the Dao Storm got turned into demonic trees, the people of Darklight City demanded the trees blocking roads and crushing houses be removed. I took it upon myself to move these trees through rifts. That's when I seemingly caught the attention of the Voidmind Elder as he entered through the rift and ended up here."

Senior Lee clicked his tongue. *"I told that old bastard to remain within his library and ignore what happened around him no matter how interesting it seemed."*

Ashlock let Senior Lee finish his mumblings before he added, "He then spotted my eye and tried to pull it out. All the while claiming he needed it to finally ascend his cultivation."

"I've told him time and time again that his bloodline is cursed to never step into the Nascent Soul Realm." Senior Lee sighed. The man summoned a teacup to his hand and leaned back on the bench, taking a long sip of the steaming tea. *"Spirit tree, tell me more."*

"Well, the Voidmind Elder threatened to kill Stella and my other sect members, so Maple compressed him in the void and trapped him within my body."

Senior Lee shook his head. *"He pulled that nonsense in the presence of a Worldwalker? What a fool."*

"Worldwalker?" Ashlock asked.

"Worldwalkers are powerful creatures that guard the void to stop those unworthy from crossing the space between realms, and I believe that squirrel is one," Senior Lee replied. *"Not sure why, but there's a Worldwalker trapped in that tiny form. I'm surprised it hasn't exploded."*

So Maple really was the Worldwalker, yet in a tiny form? So his S-grade summon all those years ago hadn't exactly failed but hadn't succeeded, either.

"He does sleep a lot," Ashlock chuckled, "and often collapses after a single big technique."

Senior Lee hummed in agreement while taking another sip.

"Also, if you don't mind me asking, what is a bloodline, and why is the Voidmind family cursed?" Ashlock couldn't contain his curiosity.

Senior Lee shook his head. *"Bloodlines belong to those of the higher realms. To speak about them down here would earn heaven's wrath. You will learn more about them when you initiate the Era of Ascension and escape this place."*

Standing up from the bench, he added, *"However, I can tell you that only those worthy can cross the void, and having void affinity does not give you that right."* He reached over and tapped his trunk. *"You should know that well as a Demi Divine being that's immune to the void."*

There was a long pause.

Despite the man answering his questions, Ashlock felt Senior Lee was still suppressing some rage over his sworn brother's death. "I'm sorry for killing your sworn brother. I didn't really have another option."

"Have I taught you nothing, young spirit tree?" Senior Lee stepped forward and placed his palm on his trunk. *"A body is nothing but a vessel for the soul, and a fragment of my sworn brother's soul still lingers within you."*

Ashlock felt a foreign presence, as if a ghostly hand was within his trunk, grasping at a whisp of something invisible to him.

"Death is merely a state of being that can be ignored, reversed, or inflicted by those that stand at the top of creation." Senior Lee drew his hand back, a visible black whisp following his fingers like a translucent black tar.

It squirmed as Senior Lee trapped it within his closed fist. A green crystal appeared in his other hand, and he then merged the two, seemingly trapping the black tar whisp inside the green crystal.

"Don't worry, I will punish this foolish man for his sins against you," Senior Lee said as the green crystal vanished. *"However, now I must leave. His soul is already too weak, so I must find a vessel."*

He turned to leave, but his eyes landed on the looming Ent. *"Actually, talking of vessels for the soul, could you make another one of these?"*

Ashlock mentally checked the skill description in his mind and confirmed that so long as he had a corpse, there were no problems. "If you can provide me with a corpse, I could."

Senior Lee rubbed his chin and grinned. *"Interesting, very interesting. Why don't we give it a try?"*

Although Ashlock was a little mad about Senior Lee wanting to bring the Voidmind Elder back to life, as that old bastard had tried to kill everyone he loved and even blew himself up in a vain attempt to kill him, alas, Senior Lee was some kind of godlike being, and it wasn't worth arguing with someone that had given him so much help over something that had occurred in the past and given him a void-based skill.

A sudden pressure descended on him when a corpse materialized on the stone between him and Senior Lee. The man wasn't wearing rings, so Ashlock had no idea where he was summoning things from.

Ashlock simply couldn't describe what he was even looking at. It was as if his mind wasn't supposed to comprehend this corpse, even in death. It had a similar shape to a giant squid, but its body was overwhelmingly bright, while its tentacles were like the night sky.

"This is a Celestial Void Leviathan corpse, something you can find in the upper realms of creation," Senior Lee helpfully explained. "Use this to make a vessel for the Voidmind Elder. I care not for what shape it takes on nor how it looks."

Ashlock resisted the urge to devour the corpse with {Consuming Abyss}. Just the thought of how many sacrificial credits he could gain...

"Don't eat it. You will die," Senior Lee said as if he had read his thoughts. "Any corpse I bring out from the higher realms will overwhelm your pitiful Star Core like trying to shove an ocean into a teacup."

As if to demonstrate, Senior Lee made the tea in his teacup suddenly boil and then explode outward. None of the tea ever reached his spotless white robes as it vanished someplace else with a wave of his hand.

"Anyway, I digress." He seemed excited. "Now show me what you can do!"

Ashlock was starting to wonder if displaying his new SS-grade skill in front of Senior Lee was a good idea. He really should have told him that he could not create another vessel for some arbitrary reason.

Alas, he had no plans to let the crazed demi-god in human form down now, so with a mental thought, he activated {Necroflora Sovereign}. Once again, a thick black root emerged from the ground and approached the Celestial Void Leviathan. Luckily, the skill handled everything for him as he could not even see where the mouth was due to the blinding light.

The sudden wave of death Qi suggested the seed had been successfully planted within the Celestial Void Leviathan's stomach.

Senior Lee stood off to the side with his eyes closed and his hands behind his back, but the thin smile on his lips suggested he was enjoying the show.

The corpse began to convulse as its celestial flesh was twisted into wood. Very quickly, a tree sprouted between them, shooting up toward heaven. Its bark looked like someone had condensed the star-filled night sky into paint and smeared it on a tree. Ashlock looked up and saw its celestial leaves glowing like streetlamps.

Within seconds, the tree was taller than him, and a minute later, Ashlock swore it was touching the clouds. A loud crack resounded as the tree began to split into a more humanoid form, with two legs and arms breaking away. At the top, a maw opened wide, and Ashlock swore he saw a galaxy within. Its eyes also ignited with two small blue stars that looked down at him from above.

"What the..." Ashlock was speechless. He had thought his Star Core Ent was impressive, but it looked so small and pathetic next to this hundred-meter-tall titan that seemed to lord over all creation.

"Magnificent!" Senior Lee exclaimed. *"In all my years, I have never seen a Star Core Realm cultivator perform such a tremendous feat! Even those on the first layer of creation would struggle to make something like this so quickly."*

Ashlock was certain if he could get an Ent anywhere near as powerful as this one under his control, he could easily fend off the Beast Tide. Even the Patriarch and World Tree couldn't stand up against this.

He was about to ask Senior Lee if he could spare him another one of these Celestial Void Leviathans, but then he saw a crack in the sky.

"We need to move quickly. Heaven has taken notice." Senior Lee stopped looking relaxed. *"All right, first of all, this form is far too big."*

The white-haired man clapped his hands, and an immense crushing force descended on the titan. Ashlock heard the wood cracking as the towering giant was compressed and shrunk. Within a minute, the titan had been reduced to the equivalent of a tall human of about two meters tall.

Ashlock knew Senior Lee was powerful, but this was just unnecessary flexing at this point. How could he reduce his Ent, made from the corpse of some mighty creature, into such a pathetic form with just a clap of his hands?

The world trembled as the sky opened, and Ashlock saw thousands of eyes glaring down at Senior Lee. They seemed to push against each other as if they wanted to be the first to squeeze through the gap in the sky.

The man met their glare with a frown. "This was not a good use of my energy. Let's wrap this up." He summoned the green crystal from an unknown space to his hand and reached up to shove the crystal into the heart area of the Ent.

Senior Lee then said some words Ashlock couldn't understand, and the black tar whisp spread out from the green crystal wedged between the night sky wood.

Like corruption, the Voidmind Elder's remnant soul spread out, and Ashlock suddenly felt his connection and control over the Ent cease, and it began to move without his command.

"Old Lee?" the Ent questioned. His voice sounded like ten people speaking at once. It was disorienting yet understandable at the same time.

"Brother Void," Lee replied with a light smile.

The Ent acknowledged him with a weird nod and then looked at Ashlock. "It's you. I remember you... You killed me."

It was clear the Voidmind Elder was still adjusting to his new form, as his speech was sluggish and confused.

The Ent's two glowing blue suns for eyes slowly turned black as if the void was corrupting them. The Ent then raised his arm and tried to reach up to tear one of Ashlock's branches off.

Senior Lee lightly slapped the Ent's arm, and with a loud crack, it was obliterated in a shower of splinters. The Ent slowly looked at where his arm should be, and Ashlock was amazed at how fast the roots of liquid night sprung forth to form a new arm.

"Why...stop...me?"

"Brother Void, we must leave this place before heaven traps us here for eternity. I will explain everything to you later." Senior Lee snapped his fingers, and the Ent vanished.

"Spirit tree, I will have to leave you to fend for yourself for the next eon or so. If you survive and meet me once again at the peak of creation, then fate smiled upon you."

By now, the sky had become a sea of golden eyes with perfectly white pupils that spread to the horizon.

"See you at the top, old man," Ashlock replied, and Senior Lee grinned before he took a step forward and also vanished. The sky returned to normal at once as if it had all been a nightmare, and the world resumed as everything became unfrozen.

Ashlock felt the warm wind rustle through his leaves and enjoyed the chirps of birds. "How does Senior Lee freeze time in an area around him like that? Maybe I could learn how, too?"

On the topic of unanswered questions, Ashlock looked up at his Ent and came to a realization. "Why didn't my Ent take on the properties of the worm corpse like the poison coating its skin?" Humming to himself, he went through a mental checklist of the differences. "All I can think of is that the worm corpse had little Qi left in it, so it was just a slab of monster meat, whereas the corpse of the leviathan still had Qi."

Whatever the reason, he would discover it with more testing. Senior Lee had given him a glimpse of his SS-grade skills potential. All he needed was to ascend in his cultivation and go out and seek strong monsters to turn into Ents.

Excitedly, Ashlock gave his Ent a command to sit, and the lumbering titan collapsed onto its wooden butt before him, causing the entire mountain to rumble under its immense weight.

A sudden portal appeared on the mountain peak, and Stella ran through. "Tree! Are you okay?" She glanced around as if trying to find Senior Lee.

Ashlock was about to reply but paused. "Wait, since when could Stella create portals by herself like that?"

43
RECHARGING ENTS

While Ashlock questioned Stella about her newfound ability to make portals via writing in soul fire, everyone else stepped through the still-open portal behind Stella.

She ignored them as if they weren't even there as she walked over, sat on the bench, and patiently explained, *"Because of your enlightenment truffle, I was able to grasp the basics of the spatial plane before entering the Mystic Realm, but it wasn't until I ascended to the Star Core Realm that I was able to fully comprehend its secrets. That's how I can make portals so freely now!"*

She then explained how she could close her eyes and see the world in grids. Ashlock knew of the spatial plane's existence as it had been mentioned in *Spatial Techniques of the Azure Clan* technique book, and he had been utilizing it himself for his portals and other spatial techniques like telekinesis.

But it appeared Stella comprehended the abstract concept more profoundly than even himself, to the point that she could open short-range portals across a vast distance without having a tree body.

"Interesting," Ashlock mused as he listened to Stella rambling on. "Maybe I should spend more time learning techniques and practice with my spatial Qi. I feel like I have been neglecting meditation and improving my techniques in favor of system skills recently."

"So yeah, that's about it," Stella said while swinging her legs off the side of the bench. *"The Mystic Realm was a lot more pleasant this time,*

despite being struck by lightning for a month straight while sitting atop of spike of rock jutting out of a molten metal sea."

Ashlock found cultivators' concept of what was pleasant to be so far removed from any logic that it was hard to comprehend. How could sitting still in an alternate dimension surrounded by molten metal while being attacked by lightning be considered pleasant? Just how bad had the previous time been?

That aside, Ashlock was confused about why the mountain peak was dead silent except for Stella's ramblings. Diana was off to the side, playing with little…well, big Kai now. The inky snake was going through his evolution and was already two meters long and looked barely small enough for Diana to have draped over her shoulders. It certainly didn't help that Diana was short, so Kai's tail almost touched the floor.

Diana aside, seven other people were present, but they were all kneeling toward him with the Grand Elder at the front. Looming behind them was the motionless Ent that cast a flickering shadow due to the spatial flames.

"What are they doing?" Ashlock was baffled. Had he done something weird without knowing it to cause them to kneel before him like this? Deciding to break the awkward atmosphere, as he had no idea what was happening, he asked Elder Mo a question that had been on his mind.

'Elder Mo, tell me more about this inheritance,' Ashlock wrote, and Stella relayed the message.

Elder Mo stood and had an almost fanatical demeanor. *"Due to the immortal's infinite generosity, this humble one was able to obtain the inheritance of a spirit forge master!"* He then raised the mighty hammer that almost seemed glued to his hand. *"With my ghostly spirit fire, I can imbue weapons with my will, turning them into spirit weapons."*

Upon hearing that, the only thought that went through Ashlock's mind was if he should ask Elder Mo to make the swords he stole from the Voidmind Elder more tree-friendly somehow. After all, he was the most extraordinary tree swordsman on the continent.

"He could also turn Stella and Diana's swords into something special. Ah, actually, I will wait until he has had more practice first before requesting anything from him."

Other than that, the fact there were inheritances of ancient cultivators within the pocket realms made Ashlock even more enthusiastic about sending his sect members in whenever possible. "Maybe I should even send in the entire Redclaw family next time. Although what happened to the two Elders concerns me regarding safety."

While he was lost in thought, Elder Mo kept rambling on.

"Of course, such an insignificant inheritance pales compared to you and your delectable fruits and...creations..." Elder Mo added as he looked up at the Ent.

"Okay..." Ashlock wasn't sure where this sudden off-putting flattery was coming from. He had given them overpowered cultivation resources and even sent them into pocket realms, and they hadn't been this enthusiastic. They hadn't even seemed this enthralled when he demonstrated his SS-grade skill, which had been impressive enough to impress Senior Lee... "Are they flattering me in hopes of getting closer to Senior Lee?"

It was hard to know for sure, but he understood it must have been a humbling experience being frozen in time and then removed with a finger snap from a cultivator that suddenly appeared and called him a friend.

Whatever the reason, Ashlock wasn't interested in speaking with them when they were acting weirdly like this. "Let's get this over with so I can send them away. Having so many people up here on the mountain peak makes it feel crowded, and the giant Ent over there isn't helping. However, before I wave them off, I want to see their progress."

Ashlock had already felt the difference in the Grand Elder's cultivation when he had sliced the worm apart, and Stella naturally had reached the Star Core Realm.

'I will now check everyone's progress, and then you can leave,' Ashlock wrote as he opened his demonic eye. All of the kneeling people shivered slightly and kept their eyes glued to the stone to avoid eye contact.

Ashlock looked at them one by one. "The Grand Elder is now in the fifth stage of the Star Core Realm, and Amber is in the seventh stage of the Soul Fire Realm, although I can't remember what she was before."

He glanced at the Elders and was somewhat disappointed. "Although Elder Mo got the inheritance, he is still at the peak of the Soul Fire Realm. Meanwhile, Elder Brent and Margret seemed to have made some progress, each going up a single stage in the Soul Fire Realm to the eighth. Perhaps their lack of talent is holding them back. Actually, to be fair, they had been running away and burning their stored-up Qi to survive the worm segment hunting them down."

Ashlock had learned through a lot of observation and testing that combat was a great way to refine and learn techniques but an awful way to advance cultivation stages as it was a waste of Qi.

"Elder Mo had advanced right before entering the Mystic Realm and was likely too busy learning the secrets of his newfound inheritance to sit down and meditate to gather Qi. So his lack of progress also makes sense." Ashlock watched as the ghostly flames filled Elder Mo's entire body. It would seem the inheritance had somehow altered his affinity, a concept he had never seen before.

Ashlock then glanced at Douglas and noticed he had gone up three entire stages. "That's almost a stage a week. That cultivation speed is absolutely insane. Is Douglas secretly a genius cultivator? Or did he just get lucky with his pocket realm?"

Whatever the reason, Ashlock was delighted with Douglas's progress and was also glad to see that Diana was at the peak of the Soul Fire Realm and on the cusp of ascending to the Star Core Realm like Stella.

He studied Diana's Soul Core—a light blue storm tainted black due to the prevalent demonic Qi that was barely being suppressed. When his eye focused on her, the demonic Qi seemed restless, as if trying to escape and overtake Diana.

Seeing her pained expression and heavy breathing, Ashlock looked away as he wasn't interested in causing unnecessary discomfort. He skipped over Elaine as she still hadn't progressed from the first stage of the Soul Fire Realm, and he moved on to the final person here, Stella.

Unlike the others, she didn't shy away and openly accepted his gaze as if trying to show off her new power. Within her was a pulsing lilac star, much like he had before turning fully tree. Except hers was special as lightning arced between the star and the rest of her body.

It was to Ashlock's understanding that once Stella used the lightning Qi stored within herself, her Star Core wouldn't generate any new lightning Qi, only spatial Qi, as that was her affinity.

With his demonic eye still open as he had one last thing he wanted to check, he summoned a portal in the White Stone Palace's courtyard and ordered the Redclaws to return home.

The Redclaw Grand Elder relayed his ancient words to his family, and they all gave deep bows and expressed their gratitude before stepping through and leaving the mountain peak.

"*Elaine and I would also appreciate being excused if that's all right with the Patriarch,*" Douglas humbly requested.

Ashlock actually had something he wanted to tell Elaine, so he wrote on his trunk, 'Elaine, did your uncle ever mention someone by the name Senior Lee?'

Elaine translated his words and tapped her chin. *"Lee...mhm, that name does ring a bell. My uncle often said Lee had cursed him to die and had told him not to go outside. I also heard my uncle ranting that this Lee person was supposed to show up months ago yet never visited."*

Ashlock suspected that was his fault as Lee had stopped by his mountain on the way to visit the Voidmind Elder and left after saving Stella.

'Well, Senior Lee stopped by earlier, and I passed him a fragment of your uncle's soul,' Ashlock wrote, and Elaine seemed confused.

"So my uncle...isn't dead?" She scrunched up her face as if deep in thought.

'He did perish,' Ashlock replied. 'However, a part of him will now live on, so in a way, he is still alive.'

Elaine readjusted her glasses and seemed rather flustered. "Well... that's good, then? I think?"

'That's all I had to say. You may leave now,' Ashlock wrote and summoned a portal down into the mine. Douglas led the bewildered Elaine through the portal, which snapped closed behind them.

Ashlock breathed a sigh of relief. With everyone except Stella and Diana gone, it was much quieter. A lot had occurred in the last few hours, and he needed time to test and process everything; to do that, he needed peace of mind.

His demonic gaze drifted to the impossible-to-ignore Ent that almost rivaled him in height, as this was the first thing on his list to investigate.

For this titan of a monster, he couldn't look down or even straight ahead with his demonic eye. He actually had to look up toward the creature's maw.

To his surprise, Ashlock felt intimidated by his own creation as it was at the fifth stage of the Star Core Realm. Searching the information in his mind about his {Necroflora Sovereign} skill, he realized the skill would always produce an Ent of equal strength to the corpse, assuming the monster still had enough Qi left in its body to fuel the seed's growth.

The corpse of choice impacted the Ent's features, size, and capabilities. However, if the corpse didn't have enough Qi to fuel the seed for all those additional features like the corpse Senior Lee had provided, it would turn out as a basic demonic tree Ent like the one standing before him.

"I see, so the skill hardly uses any Qi or nutrients from me to form the seed as it feeds off the Qi leftover within the monster's corpse." As great as that sounded, Ashlock knew this world had no free lunches. Something had to be powering this Ent that was two stages above him.

Following the flow of Qi throughout the Ent's body, he confirmed that, just like himself, the Ent's own Star Core provided enough Qi to function independently. However, it was nearly empty right now, and it was drawing on his Star Core through the link to fill itself up.

Which was a big problem. Ashlock was two entire stages below the Ent, and its Star Core wasn't exactly small. Furthermore, Ashlock felt a significant strain on his body's nutrient and water reserves as the Ent had another problem.

It was a walking tree; even magical trees needed a steady stream of nutrients and water to live. But because the Ent was designed to always be on the move, its body hadn't come equipped with roots to acquire nutrients and water.

"Hmm, so no upfront cost other than losing out on potential sacrificial credits by not devouring the required corpse, but the maintenance cost of an Ent, especially of one stronger than me, is rather high."

Ashlock ordered the Ent to remain still and detach itself from him. The root connected to its leg fell to the ground with a thud, and Ashlock suddenly felt his Star Core begin to fill back up instead of being drained.

With his demonic eye, he continued to track the changes occurring within the Ent's body post-detachment. "Okay, the Ent's Star Core is still working and producing Qi, but it's not filling up or depleting. Just remaining perfectly stable."

Ashlock's Star Core naturally produced Qi by itself without needing to cultivate, but it was a minuscule amount compared to what he gained when meditating with his cultivation technique or drew in from the thousands of trees he was linked to.

"But the Ent doesn't seem to have a cultivation technique, nor is it attached to my network of demonic trees." Ashlock was starting to understand what he was working with. The Ent was powerful, but like an electric car, it needed to be charged or plugged in to function without depleting its reserves and rotting into nothingness. Although the Ent's Star Core produced some Qi, it wasn't enough to support any more than its massive body just standing there.

"So charge it up and then send it to war," Ashlock mused. "Wait, if I nurtured hundreds of trees to the Star Core Realm, couldn't I use them as charging stations like those that charge electric cars back on Earth? That way, the Ents won't use my Qi reserves."

It was a ridiculous-sounding idea. Ashlock could already imagine out in the wilderness a massive hub of Star Core trees all protected by a concealment formation with them charging up hundreds of Ents, which he could then transport anywhere within his root network at a moment's notice through portals.

Despite the ideal vision in his mind, it had some problems. Trees cultivated very slowly, and even his offspring were only around the peak of the Qi Realm.

He had to make some sacrifices here. Either he continued consuming a large portion of Qi from all the thousands of offspring around him to fuel his activities and advance his cultivation. Or he could reroute some or all of that Qi to a small group of trees to power-level them up to the Star Core Realm.

"Hmm, I think that's a good idea, but what group of trees should I pick?" Ashlock took to the skies with {Eye of the Tree God}. There were many options. For many reasons, it could be good to keep them close to home on the mountain range between Red Vine Peak and the White Stone Palace.

"Easy to protect as I won't get distracted and not see them get killed." Ashlock hummed. "But…keeping all my eggs in one basket by having them so nearby could also be bad."

His next port of call was naturally the trees within Darklight City, but he decided against there as it was too out in the open and close to a major civilization hub to keep his activities somewhat on the down low.

He then thought about the wall of trees in the wilderness but shot that idea down quickly. It was so far away that unless one of the trees was literally bitten, he wouldn't be alerted of any threats nearby, and his offspring were too weak to defend themselves.

"I could have Ents guard the place, but I only have one for now. And if I take on too many new Ents, I might not even have the Qi on hand to charge them up to the point they could run for a few days on their own,"

Ashlock lamented. Until his offspring were actually at the Star Core Realm and able to charge the Ents up without his help, he would have to limit the number he had.

"Actually, I have an idea." Ashlock had planned to eventually build some type of pavilion around himself, and he also planned to grow an offspring where the Mystic Realm spawned so he could use {Progeny Dominion} and enter the pocket dimensions alongside his sect members.

The mountain peak was large enough that it had once had a pavilion built upon it with multiple courtyards and enough space for thousands of people. So to plant some trees around the circumference to form a sort of tree wall and place one opposite himself where the Mystic Realm spawned seemed like a good plan.

"In the future, I could always have Douglas uproot them, and then I could move them all out into the wilderness through portals, so it's best to grow and nurture them close by."

Ashlock debated growing trees from scratch but decided it would be far faster to uproot around twenty carefully selected demonic trees and replant them around him in a wide circle. For this task, he needed Douglas.

'Stella, can you get Douglas for me? I need his help with something,' Ashlock wrote and then went to find Douglas down in the mine. The man was talking with Elaine, but it seemed they were nearing the end of their conversation, so he created a portal next to him, which Stella poked her head through.

"The Patriarch wants you for something."

Douglas groaned but followed Stella through the portal. "I will be right back, Elaine. Think about what I said."

"I will," she replied with a smile and wave. "Have fun."

Douglas rolled his eyes but was soon up on the mountain peak.

"I wonder what they were talking about…" Ashlock mused as he was about to change his view, but then he noticed the end of the tunnel that led outside and came to a realization.

He had forgotten about Bob, the slime under control with his {Root Puppet} skill that had since upgraded.

What would happen if he turned Bob into an Ent?

44
TITUS

Ashlock focused on Bob, the slime acting as a door to the tunnel that led from the cavern deep within Red Vine Peak to the outside world. Bob's body was a dark shade as there was still Void Qi left over from when Elaine had tried to punch her way out, but it seemed the Void Qi had dissipated over time, and Bob was slowly turning back to his Qi-less gray state.

Bob was an interesting specimen. A slime without a soul core, but rather had a cloud of nodes serving as its consciousness. Because of this, the slime had no affinity and absorbed whatever type of Qi it was hit with and slowly grew stronger the more it got hit with the same kind of Qi.

It was neither alive nor dead, some bizarre state in the middle. So Ashlock was curious how his new {Necroflora Sovereign} skill would affect him.

"Bob proves I can still use {Root Puppet} just like before, as my hair-thin roots still control the slime." Ashlock was glad that the system didn't strip away old functions of skills when they upgraded. "How weird is it that Bob consumed a large portion of my Qi output and was one of my strongest weapons against the rats at one point, but nowadays, I have forgotten about him?"

Ashlock sighed. Thinking about how far he had come in a few short years was nostalgic.

"Well, let's give it a go. I don't see much reason to keep Bob the way he is right now as a simple door." Ashlock focused on the root that linked him and Bob and activated his new SS-grade skill.

The hair-thin roots spread throughout Bob's body, retracted back into the black root, and then the tip split open to reveal a seed before Bob could wrestle back control from Ashlock as his conscious nodes were freed from {Root Puppet}'s control.

"What the?!" Elaine shouted from within the cavern, her head practically snapping to look straight at Bob when the seed bloomed within the slime's body.

Ashlock didn't worry about Elaine; his focus was entirely on Bob. The void Qi within the slime's body was pulled toward the blooming seed as if it was a black hole, greedily devouring all Qi within the body.

The viscous gray slime that made up Bob's form began to harden slightly and turn into a wooden shape, yet it kept that slime consistency. Within moments, Bob morphed into an Ent that was too big to walk down the tunnel as he ballooned in size vertically to around five meters tall.

Elaine was at the bottom of the tunnel and looked up its slope to see Bob the Ent obstructing the exit. A sword was summoned to her hand, and she assumed a battle position.

Ashlock didn't blame her. Compared to the Ent on the mountain peak that was obviously related to him in some way with the black bark, red leaves, and purple flames, Bob looked like something that had crawled straight out of hell. He was a smooth gray thing resembling an Ent but was faceless and constantly looked like he was melting like an ice cream.

Bob honestly looked like a thing of nightmares, but Ashlock didn't want Elaine attacking the slime Ent, so he tried to order Bob to wave at her. Through the root still attached to Bob, spatial Qi pulsed through the gray form and gave the slime Ent a lilac glow.

Only then did the slime seem to acknowledge his command and eventually turn very slowly to give Elaine a wave. The woman only frowned at the slime tree thing.

Luckily she didn't seem confident enough to launch an assault, so Ashlock could take a moment to better grasp what made Bob different from the other Ent.

"Actually, I should give that nameless Ent a name since Bob has one... Hmm, what about Titus?" Ashlock pondered. It seemed like a good fit, so he rolled with it. "Right, let's see. Titus is in the fifth stage of the Star Core Realm and, therefore, can produce Qi independently. Whereas Bob doesn't really have a cultivation stage at all."

It had always been a point of interest for Ashlock regarding Bob. The slime seemed near invincible once it absorbed its attacker's Qi. Even now, he couldn't exactly say what cultivation stage Bob was at.

However, if he had to guess, he would put Bob at the peak of the Soul Fire Realm, as Bob didn't have his own gravity field around him or the capability of generating Qi passively without cultivating.

Ashlock then decided to test what would happen if he detached from Bob. Would he cease functioning? Return to a slime? Or was he not giving Bob enough credit?

Pulling the root free, nothing happened straight away. Ashlock could still give Bob commands, but the lilac hue from the spatial Qi within his gray body slowly dimmed until it ceased entirely.

"The rate at which Bob burns Qi is concerning," Ashlock mentally frowned. While the spatial Qi had remained within the slime, he could give Bob commands without problems, but once it ran out, Bob remained motionless and as motivated to listen to him as any ordinary puddle.

Which was to say not at all.

"Mhm, so when Bob's Qi runs out, I lose control, but Bob has no control over his own body anymore, either, so we enter a stalemate where nothing has control of the slime, and he just sits there."

Meanwhile, even when Titus was detached, Ashlock could still order him to move around due to the spatial Qi coming from his Star Core.

"Well, this is annoying," Ashlock grumbled as he kept trying to make Bob do anything at all.

"Losing control over my own minions is dangerous. Maybe I should only focus on getting Star Core and above Ents to avoid this issue," Ashlock mused as he regained control over Bob via his root and felt a significant tug on his Star Core for Qi.

"Fucking hell, Bob, you are a greedy bastard, aren't you?" Ashlock couldn't believe Bob took over ten times the Qi to charge up compared to Titus, a fifth-stage Star Core.

"All right, this isn't going to work out." Ashlock ordered Bob with the Qi he had just pumped in to block the tunnel's entrance like before.

The gray slime lumbered into position while making squelching sounds and crawled into the tunnel. Ashlock was somewhat surprised that despite Bob's wood-like appearance, he was still just as flexible as before.

Once Bob was in place, Ashlock ordered him to stay in place and then cut the connection. Slowly, the lilac hue of the spatial Qi radiating within the gray slime dimmed, and Bob eventually returned to a dull gray.

Elaine had watched everything, and once she saw Bob return into a much larger and thicker door, she seemed to figure out what was going on and lowered her sword.

Ashlock ignored her for now as Douglas was waiting restlessly in front of his trunk on the mountain peak for his job. "I think I will use Bob in the future when needed, but keeping him constantly pumped with Qi is pointless because he dispels Qi from his body too fast. It's just a waste."

Returning his sights to the peak, Ashlock wrote on his trunk, 'Douglas, I need you to uproot twenty-one demonic trees that I pick out.'

Standing beside Douglas, Stella translated the words, and the impatient Douglas nodded. "Sure thing, Patriarch, just lead the way."

Ashlock took to the skies with {Eye of the Tree God} again and felt through the fused root network he shared with his offspring to identify the ones that were the farthest along in their cultivation. He found a few at the peak stage of the Qi Realm and then sent Douglas to dig them up through portals.

A few hours later, Ashlock finished placing down the twenty-first tree exactly in the middle of where the Mystic Realm had spawned the last few times. He wasn't sure if the Mystic Realm would open there again now that a tree was in the center of it, but that was an experiment for later.

Removing these trees from the mountain had been more challenging than before. Ashlock had to mentally detach from the trees due to the fused roots, which caused them a lot of stress. However, they seemed much happier once they were planted closer to their dad.

"Okay, with that done, I just need to fuse my roots with them again to test {Progeny Dominion}." Ashlock wrapped his roots just below the rocky surface with the freshly planted trees in a perfect circle around him and felt their waves of happiness, yet the roots weren't fusing.

"Fuse! Come on, fuse with Dad!" Ashlock tried to encourage his unruly children; as expected, he only got waves of simple emotions back. "Sigh...what am I to do with you lot if I can't fuse my roots?"

Ashlock then spent the next few hours until dusk trying to figure out a solution. Meanwhile, Douglas went back down into the cavern to be with Elaine, and the girls were happy to cultivate under the shade of one of the new trees.

Idletree Daily Sign-In System
Day: 3523
Daily Credit: 1
Sacrifice Credit: 0
[Sign in?]

Ashlock awoke the next day to the usual sign-in message. He had spent all of yesterday trying to fuse with his children but had been unsuccessful—

[Fused with nearby offspring]

Ashlock mentally blinked at the system message and then groaned. Of course, the system had been the one to conduct the fusing the last time, so why wouldn't it handle it again?

"Can I only fuse overnight while I am asleep?" Ashlock contemplated but didn't have an answer, so he swiftly moved on.

Red Vine Peak was no longer a desolate peak with a single demonic tree and a bench. Now Demonic trees—his offspring—encircled him in a sparse ring so they each had plenty of room to grow upward and outward without impacting one another.

"Best to plan ahead. I could have easily fit a hundred trees in a tight ring around me to the point they formed a literal wall with their trunks, but then their branches would be intertwined, and that would cause problems if they start to develop at different rates."

Besides the distance between them, Ashlock had made a conscious effort regarding the locations of the demonic trees. Those trees about to form a fire affinity and covered in the Blaze Serpent Roses were placed on the northern flank to face the White Stone Palace.

Then on the western flank facing the misty forest that lay between Red Vine Peak and Darklight City were trees about to form water affinity. Diana sat below their shade and enjoyed the water Qi from the Serene Mist Camellias.

Ashlock was also enjoying the mist as the wind blew it toward him.

Meanwhile, Stella was cultivating on the southern flank under the shade of trees that weren't affected by a Qi-producing flower, so they were developing spatial affinity due to the thick amount in the air around the mountain because of him.

These spatial affinity trees were also on the eastern flank facing the farms, villagers, and the large wall flattened by the Dao Storm.

Ashlock did have plans to build groves on the mountain around him that were little pockets of trees that created perfect pockets for cultivating different Qi types, but he would get around to that another day. As for now, his mountain peak alongside the Qi-gathering formation was ideal for fire, water, and spatial cultivators.

Fire and water due to the Qi-producing flowers growing on their trunks, and spatial because he naturally radiated spatial Qi with his activities that drenched the area.

With that aside, Ashlock's mind was finally awake as he basked in the fresh morning sunlight. "Now, what should I do first? Ah yes, the system message."

With a quick check, he confirmed without a doubt that he was fused with all the trees around him.

"I can provide them all with Qi, nutrients, and water, but I should be careful pumping too much spatial Qi into the trees attempting to form fire or water affinities. I don't want to force them all into becoming spatial affinity trees."

Slowly increasing the amount of Qi, he was sharing through the local root network, he felt his offspring's excitement.

However, his focus was on the tree opposite him, as it was his firstborn.

Ashlock had found and located the first demonic tree that had ever bloomed from his seed and felt it only fitting that he brought the eldest child up onto his mountain peak to be the one that would help him explore the Mystic Realm.

"Eldest, are you ready?" he asked through their fused roots. "You will be the first tree I test {Progeny Dominion} on."

As expected, the tree just sent waves of happiness back. The Eldest was just delighted that its father was speaking to him. Ashlock ran through a mental checklist to make sure he had everything ready to use the skill as unlike a lot of his other skills, {Progeny Dominion} had a lot of requirements that had to be met first due to how overpowered it was.

"All right, let's see... Fused with offspring, check. Offspring has a formed ego capable of emotion, check. I haven't used the skill for a week, so there is no risk of soul damage. What else? Ah yes, it's the start of a brand new day, so I will get the most out of the skill as it will cut off on sundown. And I believe that's it?"

Ashlock ran through the list one last time, but he was convinced there was nothing to go wrong. "Okay, let's do this." Focusing on his eldest child, he cast {Progeny Dominion}.

There was a brief pause before he suddenly felt a divine force pulling on his soul—it wasn't painful per se, but it also wasn't pleasant. A moment later, a fragment of himself was torn away. This fragment then traveled seamlessly through the fused roots and into the eldest tree.

Ashlock felt that horrible sense of loss he had experienced when Tristan Evergreen sucked away one percent of his soul, but this time it was ten times worse. It was a sense of despair and loss that was hard to describe to a mortal mind.

And then that feeling vanished as if it was a fleeting memory, and he felt whole again with a special connection with the tree in front of him as if he was staring into a mirror of himself.

"Oh, this is so weird," Ashlock muttered. He felt both disconnected and complete with the tree before him. "Now let's see if I can cast {Consuming Abyss}."

Black vines surged out of the ground, not just from around his trunk, but also the rock encircling his eldest offspring cracked as thinner black vines emerged and met with his black vines in a tangled dance.

Was he holding hands with his son...or himself?

Stella awoke from meditation under the shade of a spatial tree and wandered over in a confused daze. "Why are the trees fighting?" she muttered while glancing between Ashlock and his eldest surging black vines at one another.

Ashlock saw her coming over and had a sudden idea. 'Stella, do you want to duel again?' he wrote on his trunk, and she grinned upon translating it. A sword—the one he had gifted her—materialized in her hand.

"Sure, who am I fighting?" she questioned while looking at the tangled mess of Ashlock's black vines.

'Both of us,' Ashlock replied. 'We are one and the same.'

Stella seemed confused, but as the black vines untangled themselves and parted. Ashlock brought out his swords from his inventory and floated three of them to be held by his eldest's vines. Stella then seemed to see the hundred-meter gap between the two trees as the battleground.

Walking forward, she stood between them. Her back was turned to Ashlock's offspring as she seemingly decided he was the threat. Raising her sword into a battle-ready position, she gestured for him to bring it on.

Ashlock's trunk split open like a maw and revealed his {Demonic Eye}, which made Stella shiver only slightly. However, Ashlock had suspected that. He hadn't activated his eye to intimidate but to observe.

"My demonic eye is great for seeing the flow of someone's Qi within their body, but due to the red hue I see the world in and its limited perspective, it usually inhibits my ability to fight...but the {Progeny Dominion} skill says I can use all my skills at full capacity through my offspring, and that doesn't only include attack skills."

Through his eldest offspring he was now soul bound with, Ashlock activated {Eye of the Tree God}. His vision became split yet joined at the same time. Surprisingly, even without two brains, he had no issue analyzing Stella through his {Demonic Eye} from his main trunk and tracking her from the sky overhead with {Eye of the Tree God}.

With this, he had no blind spots. He then sent all the sword-wielding vines after Stella in varied attack patterns that he could orchestrate perfectly by utilizing his two different visions. He attacked from the left when he noticed through his {Demonic Eye} that Stella had mobilized the Qi within her Star Core to travel down her right arm.

Her eyes went wide as she tumbled to the side to avoid the attack from her weak side, but from the skies above, Ashlock had already seen this coming and had a sword bluntly smack her from below, sending her tumbling.

Stella staggered to her feet with a wild grin. "Now, this is a real challenge. How could you get so much better in only a week?" She tilted her head, and her blond hair obscured her expression.

There was a sudden burst of spatial Qi, and Ashlock was surprised to see Stella vanish through a portal and reappear behind the surge of vines heading toward her, and she effortlessly chopped through a few of them. She then tried to suppress the vines with her own Star Core's gravity.

Ashlock responded in kind with his own gravity from both his main trunk and also his offspring after sending a load of spatial Qi through their fused root, and despite the tree only being in the Qi Realm, the {Progeny Dominion} let him ignore this and use his full power by transferring his Qi.

Stella groaned as she stood between two trees unleashing a Star Core gravity two stages higher than her own. Yet even in this situation, she laughed and teleported again through the spatial plane.

"I wonder if there is a way I can stop her doing that," Ashlock wondered. He could track where her portal led to before she exited it but couldn't move his vines fast enough to attack her.

"Hold on, I can make portals, too." Ashlock laughed evilly as he waited for Stella to take another portal. She got cornered again by his vines, so when she vanished—

"There!" Ashlock spawned a rift right before Stella's portal and sent the blunt sides of three swords right into Stella's face before she could even react.

The force was more than he had anticipated, as Stella was sent flying across the mountain peak and even flew between two of the demonic trees and off the side of the mountain.

At this point, Diana had left her state of meditation, and her gaze followed the flying girl without a hint of concern.

Stella zoomed down the side of the mountain with her arms crossed, a frown on her face, and a small red mark on her forehead. "Stupid tree and his cheap tricks," she muttered as the space warped around her, and she reappeared back on the mountain peak.

"Fighting you is no fun." Stella put her hands on her hips. *"Can't I fight that thing instead?"*

Ashlock followed her gaze, and it landed on Titus, the looming twenty-meter-tall Ent with four stages in the Star Core higher than Stella. He wanted to say no…but even he was a little curious.

Diana wandered over and seemed interested. *"How about we both fight this monster? I think it might be fair then."*

Ashlock contemplated momentarily but eventually sighed as he flashed his leaf once.

It was time to test the limits of Titus.

45
BLOOD OF A RULER

Stella stood beside Diana on the rolling meadows of the wilderness.

Standing between her and the distant Red Vine Peak, which looked so small on the horizon, was a true titan of wood.

"Did Ashlock call him Titus?" Diana questioned from the side. Dark blue flames corrupted with demonic Qi flickered across her skin and down the length of the sword that hung loosely in her hand, with the tip aimed at the grass.

"Yeah, Ash also said Titus was in the fifth stage of the Star Core Realm." Stella frowned and bit her lower lip. That meant this behemoth was on par with the Redclaw Grand Elder, a man that had cultivated for centuries and had likely fought in more wars than years she had been alive. The fact that Ash had created such a thing within seconds from a corpse was something only a god should be capable of.

Stella tightened her hand around the grip of the sword Ash had gifted her. She needed to get stronger, faster. When she was the only one around, Ash gave her all the tasks. Then others arrived, and fewer jobs found their way to her.

And now Elaine and the Redclaw Grand Elder know how to translate the ancient language. What's my purpose, then? I can't negotiate as well as Diana, I don't have as much knowledge as Elaine, and I can't build things like Douglas. Even this stupid titan of wood has spatial Qi and is in a higher realm than me.

"You always make that face when you have pointless thoughts," Diana said flatly.

Stella sighed and hit the tip of her sword against the lush grass underfoot. The breeze out here was warm and refreshing, and the expansive blue sky overhead devoid of clouds did help to lift her spirits somewhat.

"I know," Stella absentmindedly replied, her thoughts still spiraling. She knew her anxiety wasn't logical, but it was hard not to feel inferior and fear losing the respect of the one she looked up to when she fell behind her peers.

Diana glanced around as if searching the distant horizon for something and whispered, "Want to see something freaky?"

"Errr…" Stella blinked. "Yes? Do I? I don't like that face you're making. Why are you smiling like that?"

"Oh, I am only getting started." Diana grinned as mist cascaded off her body and blanketed the area. A moment later, Stella couldn't even see the looming titan anymore; it was just the two of them surrounded by a dense, swirling fog.

"Remember when you saw my fangs? And I told you I would tell you about it when I was ready?"

"Yeah…oh." Stella's eyes widened as she noticed Diana's teeth took on a sharper edge, and there were now two prominent fangs.

"Like them?" Diana ran her tongue across their tips. "I didn't want to show them off in front of Ashlock as I wasn't sure how he would respond, so I thought of showing you first."

Stella tilted her head and realized something. "So that's why you suggested we fight Titus out here."

"Well, that and other reasons." Diana shrugged. "I mean, just one look at the thing, and it's obvious why fighting it on the mountain peak was a bad idea. Also, I know Ashlock somehow sees through my mist, but at least this way, I am near the wilderness and can run away if needed."

"Run away over some fangs?" Stella squinted. "There's no way you thought some fangs would even faze Ash. He eats people, Diana. Why would some elongated teeth bother him?"

"Ah," Diana chuckled, "this is just the beginning."

As those words left her mouth, she blinked her gray eyes away and replaced them with liquid darkness that seemed to stare into Stella's soul.

Demonic Qi rippled through the surrounding mist and seemed to pour toward Diana and swirl around her fingers, forming inch-long claws of shadow around her hands. Stella thought that was it, but then two large, feathered wings sprang from her back and fanned out, showing off their glory as they towered over Diana.

Taken by surprise, Stella stepped back. The extreme transformation had occurred so quickly she was baffled. What the hell had happened to Diana in that Mystic Realm? Stella thought she had emerged from that realm of liquid metal and wrathful storms as a new person, but Diana... Was she even the same species anymore?

Diana had always been pretty, but now she looked seductive, which made Stella a little uncomfortable.

It's the stark difference that's making me freak out. Just calm down. It's the same old Diana you always knew. You can grow used to this form with time. But darn, why is her bust like that? And that hourglass figure... Nope! I can't get used to this.

"So?" Diana said in the same flat voice that didn't match her body. "What do you think?"

"Have you become a succubus?"

Diana pouted. "No, I'm a demon."

Stella snorted. "Succubus is a type of demon."

"I'm not a succubus." Diana groaned in annoyance. "I have no plans or capabilities to go around seducing men or women and sucking out their souls."

"Succ—" Stella leaped backward just in time as the mist parted to reveal a massive black wood fist that barreled downward and smashed into the ground with enough force to send out a shockwave of wind and rock that Stella had to raise her hands and cycle her Qi to avoid being turned to meat paste by.

Stella closed her eyes, and the world transformed into grids; she quickly compressed the spatial plane and tore open a rift through the stacked grids. The air popped into her ears as she reappeared on the titan's shoulders.

"Aren't you curious about how I became a demon? No questions at all?" Diana's head came into view past the titan's nose as she asked from the other shoulder of the titan. Her eyes of liquid darkness unnerved Stella.

How did she get up here so fast? Stella wondered as she diverted her gaze and looked down at Titus's arm, coated in a haunted mist. Ah, I see now... She must have dashed through the mist.

"Questions, you say?" Stella said as she coated her sword in soul flames and raised it overhead, readying to strike the Ent's head. Diana mirrored the action, and with a mutual nod, they both hit the wooden skull simultaneously.

Stella's blade bit into the thick, twisted black wood that made up Titus's form but only a fingernail deep. Meanwhile, Diana's blade completely bounced off, her peak Soul Fire Realm flames unable to pierce Titus's defenses.

Titus roared, and Stella and Diana met each other's gazes and exchanged a plan without words. Stella blinked, returning to the spatial plane, and created a portal behind her. Diana charged into her, pushing both of them through the portal right as fifth-stage Star Core flames erupted from the gaps in the black wood, turning the titan's shoulders into a death trap.

"I guess I do have a few questions." Stella laughed as they observed the raging titan a mile away from within a nearby forest. "Such as why you turned into a succubus."

"Don't worry, I can change my looks to an extent." Diana rolled her black eyes. "What part do you have an issue with? Do you think this would scare away a future husband?"

Stella looked her up and down. "Eyes are a bit creepy, wings and claws could be toned down a bit, and your changed figure is way too much." She then tapped her chin as an idea came to mind. "Actually, you can switch between that and being human, right?"

"Yes..." Diana replied skeptically. "What are you scheming, Stella?"

"Initially, I was in shock because of how drastic the changes were, but in a way, that's a good thing."

"How so?"

"Well, Elaine referred to you as the mist demon. And now that I see you like this. Why not embody that title?" Stella laughed. "Turn into this form when you need to conduct some murder on behalf of the Ashfallen Sect and then appear as an innocent human the rest of the time."

"So you're saying this form has a purpose?" Diana said over the rumbling of Titus striding toward them with lumbering steps that shook the earth. "Kind of an odd approach, but I like the sound of it."

While Diana was mulling over her words, Stella wandered over and couldn't resist touching Diana's wings. Up close, she could tell they weren't solid but a manifestation of demonic Qi in the shape of raven wings.

She reached over and could feel Diana's gaze as she tried to touch the feathers. "I wouldn't if I was you—"

Stella ignored her warning but paid for it as she winced in pain with a hiss while nursing her hand. "Ow, ow, ow, that hurt way more than expected."

Diana chuckled. "What did you expect? It's pure demonic Qi."

"Can you fly...ow...with these?" Stella asked through gritted teeth as she cycled her Qi to rid her fingertips of the lingering demonic Qi. Expelling it was a simple matter with her Star Core Realm Qi, but that just made Stella more concerned about how powerful Diana would become in the future.

The shadow wings flapped, but nothing happened. "Nah, I can't. Maybe when I reach Star Core, I will be able to. Actually, speaking of that, have you tried to fly around on a sword yet?"

Diana then gestured over her shoulder at Titus, who was a few steps away, glaring at them with wrathful eyes of lilac flame. "Could be useful to fight this big guy."

Stella threw her sword to the floor and flexed her Star Core to reach out and make it float. It wasn't quite something that came instinctually, but it wasn't that hard, either.

"Want to go for a ride?" Stella gestured to the floating sword but then glanced at Diana's claws. "But no claws. We will be going through rifts, so you will need to hold onto me."

Diana shrugged, and the manifested claws of demonic Qi retracted, revealing her usual petite human hands. They looked so harmless compared to the claws she had just seen...

Ashlock was overseeing Titus from afar, but he was half distracted by what he had seen from Diana. Had Larry meant this demonic form when he claimed he smelled something ancient on Diana?

Either way, he thought her new form had potential, as Stella had pointed out. Demonic Qi acted a lot like void Qi in its destructive capabilities, so the fact Diana could wield its power and even manifest it gave her a massive leg up on everyone else. She basically had a dual affinity and a whole separate form to make use of.

"But Larry claimed he smelled the same thing on both Diana and Stella. Therefore, will Stella have some type of form like this one day?" Ashlock wondered. He couldn't imagine Stella as a demon, so what would she become? Something to do with lightning, perhaps?

That aside, he noticed the golden sun nearing the horizon. It had taken hours for him to charge Titus with enough Qi to operate independently for a while, as he wanted to test the Ent's battle capabilities without his help. So the day was almost over.

From overhead with {Eye of the Tree God}, Ashlock witnessed Stella step onto the sword, followed closely by Diana, who perched on the back. Due to the sword's length being so short, Diana had to wrap her arms around Stella's waist to avoid falling off.

Ashlock could see a sheen of spatial Qi leave Stella and wrap around Diana, and then the two vanished. Ashlock had commanded Titus to try and restrain the girls with any means necessary but not to kill them as he wanted to test the creature's intelligence.

Which so far seemed relatively high. If he had told Titus to kill them, they likely would have died when they had been talking in the mist, as they had been distracted, and Titus missed on purpose—showing that he understood Ashlock's command of restraint.

Titus sent out a pulse of spatial Qi like an EMP, and Ashlock was surprised to see the Qi wave seem to travel through reality and smash into Stella and Diana, who had been briefly traversing the spatial plane.

Reality snapped, and they were thrown out of a half-formed tear. As they were spiraling through the air, Titus's eyes glowed with power, and even from this far away, Ashlock could feel the immense pressure exerted by a fifth-stage Star Core Realm monster that was twenty meters tall.

The sheer size of Titus's Star Core gave him an immense gravitational field and overall power. Still, the downside was how fast he burned through his Qi reserves, which in turn was terrible for Ashlock because he was the one who would need to charge him back up while having a Star Core of a similar size and two realms lower.

Stella and Diana had crash-landed with some grace and now stood defiantly on the ground as the titan's black wood fist descended, casting a shadow so large it was as if there was a solar eclipse.

Ashlock was confused why they were just standing there and became concerned when Stella tried to activate her spatial technique to escape, but it didn't work as a concentrated pulse of spatial Qi left the titan's fist and slammed into them, shattering the forming portal.

Luckily, Titus had been ordered not to kill, so rather than crush them like a person killing a fly by slamming a hardcover book on its head, Titus opened up his fist and surrounded the girls with his fingers as if trying to trap them.

Diana felt the ground below her churn as the space around her gradually constricted. Sunlight streamed in through the small gaps between the Ent's fingers buried deep in the earth and its palm overhead, acting as the roof of the prison they found themselves in.

The air seemed to wobble and distort as it became suffocated with spatial Qi. Clearly, the titan had decided to entrap them both physically and with Qi, as Stella couldn't use her techniques when Titus lorded over all of the spatial Qi in the area.

"Stella, come with me," Diana shouted to the girl. She was staring absentmindedly at her fingers, covered in a flickering spatial flame that was likely her own.

Diana knew exactly how she felt because she had experienced the same whenever her father had decided to flex his power to teach her a harsh lesson. It was known that those in higher realms could suppress those in lower ones, but it was also possible for those within the same realm to achieve the same to a lesser effect if the gap in stages was big enough.

Glancing up at the closing-in palm dead set on crushing them, Diana felt the impending doom from the Ent with a Star Core so large that it was incomparable to a human one because they were merely fist-sized. This size difference gave it a tremendous advantage. Stella simply never stood a chance in a contest of spatial Qi.

"Stella, we need to leave." Diana gripped her shoulder, shocking the girl from her dazed state. "I can break us out of here."

"Oh...all right." She seemed depressed, but now wasn't a good time. Diana led Stella through the closing space toward the largest gap near the thumb.

Feeling within herself for her Soul Core that felt like a tiny and useless pebble compared to Stella and Titus, Diana let the demonic Qi being suppressed by her water Qi be fully unleashed.

She gritted her teeth as her muscles rapidly expanded and felt like they were cooking in hellfire, her vision became a hazy red, and her mind became chaotic with wrathful thoughts. The usual wall to her emotions she had built up crumbled, and much of the misery she had bottled up rushed throughout her body.

She just wanted to scream, rage, punch a wall, and snap someone's neck. Diana funneled this insanity all toward a single goal: break through the black bark of a Star Core monster.

Something inconceivable for someone in an entire realm and many stages below, but that was the one upside of being overwhelmed with demonic Qi...

Destructive power.

Coating her hands in the darkness of her soul, she brought her fist back and struck out at the thumb, alongside both of her demonic Qi wings that thrust forward. A large chunk of the titan's thumb was disintegrated into nothingness as if a projectile from a god had smashed into it.

Escaping into the sunlight, Diana manically laughed as she finally felt physically and spiritually free.

Ashlock brought Stella back to the mountain peak, and the girl slothfully collapsed onto the bench. She was alone as Diana was still...busy being crazy. Titus and the demon girl were having a lovely brawl out in the wilderness and going wild.

This was actually an excellent test for Titus as he would need to face the beast tide in the future, which may include monsters that wielded demonic Qi. So far, Titus's defenses and regeneration seemed to be significantly affected by attacks inflicted via demonic Qi.

Which made sense. Titus was a tank, and the counter to anything tanky was true damage. Basically, damage capable of ignoring or piercing defenses easily...usually at the cost of something else.

In this case...sanity. Ashlock wasn't sure when Diana would regain her senses and leave this berserk state, but he hoped it would be before Titus ran out of spatial Qi and could no longer regenerate or fight back.

"Hey, Larry," Stella called out to the behemoth spider that had happily settled in the canopy of one of the demonic trees.

"Yes, mistress?" Larry said gruffly as he crawled down the trunk of the tree. His many red eyes were set on her as she lounged on the bench.

"You said that Diana and I smelled ancient, and now Diana has awakened as a demon. So tell me, what smelled ancient about me?" Stella said impatiently. *"Was it because of that pill Senior Lee gave me? Did that make me special?"*

Larry shook his head. *"It has nothing to do with the pill. Like Diana, you likely have a dormant ancient bloodline. She treads the path of a demon because that had always been dormant within her."*

Stella frowned as she processed the spider's words. "But I have never felt any dormant thing within me."

"Mistress, your bloodline may still be dormant for a good reason."

"Which is?"

Larry crawled closer and flexed the ash around his crown of horns. "The blood of a ruler takes longer to bloom."

46
ASHFALLEN COURTYARD

"Bloodline of a ruler, you say?" Stella tilted her head. *"What do you mean by that?"*

"Mistress, I know little about bloodlines. I merely offered a thought of mine," Larry gruffly replied. *"I know I have the bloodline of a king within me, and it was only due to my master's eternal benevolence that I could awaken the dormant potential within me."*

"I did such a thing?" Ashlock wondered and chalked it up to being system shenanigans. It had given him a list of options when Larry had asked to evolve, and he'd picked the evolution that sounded like it had the most future potential.

"Hold on. Senior Lee may withhold information regarding bloodlines due to his fear of heaven, but I have two data points to build upon now." Ashlock entertained a few ideas. "Diana was able to awaken her bloodline by herself, which allows her to take on the form of a demon. Whereas Larry is still an ash spider but carries the blood of a ruler, granting him immense authority over the Dao of ash and his own species. So would Stella be the same as Larry? I could see her gaining authority over a Dao rather than transforming into another form."

While Ashlock was brooding, Stella furrowed her brows at Larry's words. "So you're telling me that I might have royal blood running through me?"

"Mistress, it was just a guess from my humble self," Larry clarified. *"As mentioned before, I know little about these mythical bloodlines."*

Stella groaned in annoyance as she flopped back onto the bench and closed her eyes. Larry seemed to take this as an opportunity to crawl away and retreat back into the canopy of a tree.

Ashlock didn't blame his loyal servant. Talking to Stella when she was moody was always a bad idea.

"She is only sixteen this year, so it makes sense she is moody sometimes." Ashlock couldn't believe how fast the years had passed.

It felt like only yesterday that Stella had been barely ten years old and fighting off those Ravenborne assassins that had snuck their way into the pavilion's staff. "She will mature with time and experience. A few more rounds in the Mystic Realm and a bit of practice with politics, and she will grow into a fine lady."

Ashlock wasn't worried about Stella. She had the talent to outshine other scions and a great work ethic. She had always been hyper-competitive, which led her to rival those many years her senior.

"She is already in the Star Core Realm before age twenty. That might even be a cultivation record." Ashlock chuckled. "Although I'm sure she doesn't see it that way."

Maple took this as an opportunity to appear on top of Stella's head and relax in the shade. As if on impulse, Stella reached up and gave the fluffy white squirrel that likely housed an S-grade void creature a head pat. The squirrel leaned into her touch and gleefully closed his eyes to enjoy the affection.

Ashlock left the two to enjoy the evening breeze as he went to check up on Titus and Diana. His vision blurred as he traveled a thousand miles and arrived at a peculiar scene.

Titus lorded over the wilderness as he brought up his two wooden fists, and the land shuddered as he slammed down, creating yet another crater. The impact briefly dispersed dense smog that blanketed the area, but it soon returned and swirled around Titus's legs and up his torso.

Ashlock could see Diana's devilish form dashing through the smog from his aerial view. The woman shot up Titus's legs, and with her demonic Qi claws, she carved out a deep tear into the Ent's body.

Titus roared and brought both his hands toward his chest in a vain attempt to capture Diana, but she was already on the move, having disappeared back into the fog with a manic laugh.

Ashlock inspected the injury on Titus and could see the demonic Qi spreading like corruption, which not only caused more damage but stopped Titus from regenerating.

"Mhm, so long as Titus doesn't use many Qi-intensive attacks, he should last until the morning." Ashlock saw the orange sun setting on the horizon's edge and knew he would soon fall asleep.

Deciding he had one last thing to do before he slept, Ashlock returned to Red Vine Peak and saw Stella playing with Maple on her lap. He still wondered if the squirrel was really a Worldwalker, it just didn't match up to his cute form, yet so many things pointed to it being the truth.

Ashlock interrupted their little play time by dropping one of the many fruits he had growing from his branches onto Stella's head.

"Ow!" she yelped in surprise and then caught the red fruit as it bounced off her head. While holding the fruit, Stella smiled at his canopy and laughed. "Tree, why did you do that?"

'You know I will always be proud of you,' Ashlock wrote on his trunk.

"Huh?" Stella's eyes widened in surprise. *"Why would you suddenly say such a thing? I...I..."*

A single tear appeared at the edge of her eye, and she quickly looked away, her gaze focused on the fruit in her hand. "Do you really mean that?" she murmured into her knees as she curled up into a ball.

'Of course, why would I not be proud of everything my talented daughter accomplishes?' Ashlock wrote, and he meant it. Someone needed to tell her how great of a job she was doing through life, and a few comforting words could go a long way.

Stella glanced back, read the words, and buried her head between her chest and knees, but Ashlock swore he saw her smile. A comforting silence ended the conversation as Stella was lost in her thoughts, and Ashlock felt exhausted as the sun dipped below the horizon, so he drifted off to sleep.

Idletree Daily Sign-In System
Day: 3524
Daily Credit: 2
Sacrifice Credit: 0
[Sign in?]

Ashlock awoke to another beautiful day with his sign-in system in his mind, reminding him once again that he was a tree in a cultivation world. A life he wouldn't trade for anything in all the multiverse.

To his surprise, people were already awake, and some work was already occurring on the mountain peak. "Wait, can I refer to this as a courtyard now that there are trees around acting as a wall?"

Seeing the gap between the trees, he felt that stretched the definition of courtyard a little too much, so he stuck with mountain peak for now. That aside, he was surprised to see Douglas and Stella working together to repair the arrays, as the Qi-gathering formation and the concealment array had been damaged.

"*Morning, Tree!*" Stella said as she leaped out of a hole. "*I couldn't sleep or meditate last night, so I got Douglas here to help me upgrade the arrays.*"

How had she known he was awake from all the way over there? Ashlock had no idea, but Stella's words caught him by surprise. Upgrade? Not repairs?

'How are you upgrading them?' Ashlock wrote.

"*We can incorporate the demonic trees into the arrays. Or at least I think we can. Everything I do regarding arrays is trial and error, after all,*" Stella patiently explained.

"*What Stella says is correct,*" Douglas chimed in. "*Usually, array formations are built into structures like buildings, walls, or caves for the horizontal and added vertical surface area.*"

He then pointed down into the hole Stella had just jumped out of. "*There were no buildings here when I originally arrived, so I advised we build deeper into the rock.*"

Douglas then glanced longingly at the massive hole in the mountain peak that led all the way down. "Once we have enough spirit stones, we could even turn that entire hole into a runic formation."

They were too poor to build such a massive formation like that, so Ashlock focused on the more important part for now. 'So how do you plan to use my children as part of the array?' he wrote in flickering lilac flames.

"*Simple, really.*" Stella pointed up at the canopy of the demonic tree beside her. "*Turns out trees are really good at capturing ambient Qi, so by incorporating them into the Qi-gathering formation, they can share the Qi between everyone!*"

"*And for the concealment formation,*" Douglas added, "*instead of throwing out Qi into the surroundings by force, we can use the trees as focal points for the array to function, making it far more efficient.*"

Ashlock was impressed. It seemed his words last night had brought on some motivation and inspiration for Stella. Arrays were a perfect outlet for her intellect and helped calm her overactive mind. Even he could tell the arrays she could currently make were inefficient and likely used far more spirit stones than necessary, but at least they worked, and she would get better with time.

Perhaps she could get hold of an immortal's array inheritance or something like Elder Mo got in the future. Or he could even hire one of those formation masters to teach her.

All of that aside, their idea was a great one, and he was excited to see the results. His spatial Qi distorting the air around Red Vine Peak and their distance from the white stone palace weren't enough to guarantee that Sebastian hadn't seen their activities. Ashlock could only hope the man was either too busy cultivating to care what was happening a mountain peak away or would keep his mouth shut in favor of future profits for his young lord.

That aside, he needed to give his feedback.

'That's a great idea,' Ashlock wrote and saw Stella beam with pride.

"I'm glad you like it." Stella turned to scramble back down into the hole. He could only see the top of her blond head. "It will be ready later today. Just a bit more work to do."

Chuckling to himself, Ashlock saw no reason to stick around watching them work, so he cast his vision out into the wilderness with {Eye of the Tree God} as he was curious to see if Titus had survived Diana's crazed slaughter.

To his surprise, he found Titus collapsed on the ground like a felled tree. Blissfully sleeping against his shredded leg was Diana. There were no signs of demonic traits like fangs or wings—her body had returned to the usual petite form he was accustomed to.

Most curious was the fact there were the corpses of a few monsters sprawled around them, and he was pretty confident they had traveled many more miles deeper into the wilderness during their scuffle throughout the night.

Ashlock never said no to a free meal, and he wanted to bring them back through portals, but they were just outside the range of his roots.

He felt like a man standing on the edge of a cliff and seeing a ship out at sea.

Maybe this was his fault for letting them fight so close to the edge of his roots, but he wanted them as far out as possible to avoid the interest of the Silverspires or any other cultivators.

"Mhm, this reminds me, I should really work to expand my roots out further in all directions and plant demonic trees everywhere I can."

Ashlock then began to ponder on how to solve his current situation. He wanted those corpses and a way to bring Diana and Titus back.

Growing his roots out far enough to open portals above them would take hours, so he wanted a more immediate solution.

"Titus is out of Qi, and his Star Core only gives him enough to very slowly repair his wounds. So commanding him to drag himself and Diana toward me won't work."

If Ashlock looked closely, he could see the black wood that made up Titus's body slowly fighting off the demonic Qi corruption and mending back together, but that might take weeks at the rate he saw.

"I could ask the Redclaw Grand Elder to fly out there, but how would he even move Titus into the range of my portals? What about Larry? Nah, I don't see how he could, either. Not even his millions of spiders working together could move Titus. They aren't magical ants able to lift far above their weight class, after all."

Ashlock was sure Maple could handle the situation, but he wanted to find another solution, as the squirrel was unreliable. The scenario of one of his Ents being outside of his portal range and running out of Qi was bound to occur again, so he needed to figure out what to do in advance, and this was a good time for this to happen as there was nothing else going on.

"Let's see...I need something I can command that will be reliable and have the strength to drag Titus into the range of my portals." Ashlock hummed to himself as he mentally ran through the list of those that met his set criteria and eventually landed on Bob.

It was unknown if the slime Ent had the strength to lift Titus, but it was worth trying. Ashlock's Star Core blazed with power as spatial Qi poured through the mountain and converged toward the root in Bob.

The gray slime began to glow brightly as spatial Qi poured into him. An hour later, Bob was as bright as a light bulb with a lilac hue—Elaine wandered over in confusion due to the bright purple light shining down the tunnel.

Deciding he had pumped enough Qi to operate Bob without issue for a few hours, Ashlock unplugged his root from Bob and mentally commanded the slime to walk forward and out of the tunnel.

The five-meter-tall Ent lumbered out of the tunnel with wet sounds that didn't match his wooden appearance. Ashlock then spawned a portal right in front of him, which wobbled slightly due to the sheer amount of spatial Qi that Bob was expelling into the surroundings.

After he stepped through with a pop, the portal collapsed, and Bob was now a thousand miles away, out in the wilderness at the edge of Ashlock's root network. In the distance was the half-dead Titus and peacefully sleeping Diana.

"Go and bring the Ent, Diana, and the monster corpses back here," Ashlock commanded, and Bob trudged forward to fulfill his command. It was nice to finally have some servants that mindlessly followed his orders without question.

While Bob slowly made his way over to Titus, Ashlock checked back at the cavern and was somewhat surprised to see Elaine sitting at the tunnel exit and enjoying the rising sun. She seemed to make no effort to run away, which made sense. She was rather integrated with the Ashfallen Sect at this point.

Even the reason she had to hate them wasn't entirely valid anymore, as the Voidmind Elder had been given a new body and left with Senior Lee to the upper realms. The fact such scum was brought back to life still left a sour taste in Ashlock's nonexistent mouth, but it was good to have friends in high places, and he wasn't about to offend Senior Lee over something so trivial compared to their friendship.

Switching back to the wilderness, Ashlock watched Bob for a while. The Ent seemed to move slower than Titus, even with the size difference factored in, and it was rather funny to see leaves and bits of dirt get stuck to the slime's body—slowly turning the glowing Ent into a walking leaf ball.

Over an hour later, Bob arrived at the site and began trying to pick up all the monster corpses. The dead bodies just stuck to the slime's body like the leaves had, and then Bob went to pick up Diana, who was still fast asleep somehow.

With her secured in his palm, Bob wrapped his other arm around

Titus's head. The slime's hand split up and slithered between the gaps in Titus's body, seemingly trying to get a better grip.

Ashlock then watched the comical display of a leaf blob with dead monsters stuck to it dragging a twenty-meter-long Ent body through a forest. Fellow trees were carefully avoided as Bob soldiered on and displayed impressive strength.

"Well, it's not strength in the normal sense, as Bob doesn't even have muscles."

As Bob glowed brighter and Ashlock saw the immense amount of spatial Qi pouring out of his body, he realized that Bob was basically a being of pure Qi that grew stronger depending on the amount of Qi stored in his body.

Sadly, no amount of Qi would make Bob move any faster.

Ashlock waited patiently, and once Bob was within range of his roots, he created portals overhead.

"Good job, Bob. Drop everything," Ashlock ordered, and the slime expelled everything attached to his body. Leaves, soil, random shrubs, rotten branches, corpses, and a snoozing Diana fell to the floor. Finally, his slimy arm snapped back from Titus's body with a squelch.

Ashlock activated {Consuming Abyss}, and black vines emerged from his body back on Red Vine Peak.

Stella poked her head out of the hole in the ground and frowned with concern at the portal's opening overhead, seeing Ashlock's black vines shooting through and latching onto things on the other side.

"Is that Diana?" she wondered aloud as she squinted at the wobbling rift.

The black vines returned, bringing with them the brutally killed monster corpses that were unrecognizable. Ashlock got to work absorbing them for a few credits while Stella dashed through the still-open portal and arrived beside Diana.

"What the hell did you do?" Stella gasped as she saw the state of Titus. Noticing that Diana wasn't responding, she grabbed her by the arms, flung her over her shoulder, and carried her back to Red Vine Peak.

Once they were back and the rift snapped closed behind them, Stella laid Diana down on the bench and gave her a once-over. She then nodded to herself. "Qi deprivation. She will be fine in a day or two."

The mountain peak trembled a little as Ashlock dumped Titus nearby and linked up to him with a root. The immense pull on his Qi reserves was a shame, but it had to be done. Maintaining a fifth-stage Star Core Ent was no cheap affair.

Stella glanced briefly at the Ent but then returned to her work. "Douglas, I believe it's time to activate the formation."

Douglas nodded. *"I agree. Everything seems in order."*

Ashlock watched in anticipation as Douglas sealed up the hole Stella had been in and created a podium on top of it. The final touch was a marble-size spirit stone exposed like a trophy.

Stella stepped up to it and placed her finger on the spirit stone. Her Star Core flared up in her chest, and Qi flowed into the spirit stone, making it glow briefly. She then stepped back as the silvery lines weaving through the rock of the mountain peak lit up with a soft glow.

Qi began to pour in from the surroundings, and as if the encircling trees were the walls of a snow globe, the gathered Qi rushed around within their confines. It was a fantastic display of power that lasted for a few moments as Stella's Qi reached every part of the formation, and finally, everything stabilized.

The gap between the trees seemed distorted, and a perpetual mist seemed to slowly orbit around the edge of the trees, acting as the perfect wall to keep out prying eyes.

Ashlock finally had something he could consider a courtyard and was eternally grateful for it. Now all he had to hope was that no darn monster would come and ruin it again.

"Douglas, go ask him," Stella whispered into the man's ear and nudged him forward.

The man gave her a betrayed look. *"Didn't you say you would ask him for me? That's why I helped you all night long with your project."*

Stella glanced away and acted clueless.

Douglas sighed and walked to stand before Ashlock, a look of grim determination on his face.

Ashlock was really curious about what the man had to say…

"Patriarch…" Douglas gulped as he stared up at his towering form. *"Would it be possible to take Elaine on a date into the city today?"*

47
LEARNING NEW THINGS

A date?

Ashlock's initial thought—seeing Douglas standing before him and asking for such a thing—was how sad this was. Why did a grown man feel the need to ask a demonic tree whether or not he could go on a date? Of course, Ashlock could see the concern surrounding this request and why Douglas had felt the need to ask him, but it still felt wrong. He firmly believed that people should be able to do their own thing and follow their dreams, yet now that he thought about it, he almost had everyone around him on a leash.

It was for a good reason, and he didn't exactly regret his odd relationship with the Ashfallen Sect members. The way he saw it, this was a two-way street. He provided cultivation resources, and in return, he expected them to fulfill whatever duties were given to them and maintain the status quo of the Ashfallen Sect.

"All of that aside, I don't see a big reason not to let them go on a date. In fact, now is the perfect time for such an activity as the alchemy tournament is still a week away, so the other families shouldn't be arriving for a few days. It's the calm before the storm."

Ashlock saw Douglas shifting nervously below his canopy, anxiously looking up at his leaves. His eyes darted around as if afraid he would miss the answer to his question.

Naturally, Ashlock flashed his leaf once to confirm going on a date was fine. The overwhelming look of relief on Douglas's face felt ridiculous to Ashlock. He wasn't some crazed tyrant that wished to deprive his followers of basic human needs.

"Actually, if the only Patriarch they have experienced is a demonic sect Patriarch that is fine with turning their followers into pill furnaces and nocturnes, I must be a respectable leader!" Ashlock consoled himself. He wasn't the most benevolent ruler due to his unique circumstances that resulted in paranoia, but there was no way he was worse than the alternative.

"*Thank you, Patriarch.*" Douglas gave a deep bow. His voice was full of emotion. "*This means a lot to me, so I am most grateful.*"

"*Congratulations, big guy!*" Stella shouted from the side and gave him a grin. "*You managed to attract a girl with that ugly face of yours.*"

The tension vanished, and Douglas glared at Stella. "*Brat, watch your mouth.*" His shoulders sagged. "*You have no idea how hard it is to date when you are lagging behind in cultivation and start to age.*"

Stella laughed. "*That's true, but you don't have to worry about that anymore, you oaf.*"

"Why not?" Douglas frowned and squinted as her skeptically. "Are you calling me handsome—"

"*Absolutely not,*" Stella ruthlessly shot him down. "*But you could be handsome with the skin improvement truffle that Diana, Elaine, and I took.*"

Douglas wasn't convinced, so Stella's ring flashed with golden light, and a small truffle appeared in her hand. "Consider it my present to you," she said while forcing it into Douglas's open hand.

He looked at it for a moment before storing it away. "*You are never this nice. Why do I feel you are trying to poison me?*"

"*How am I never nice?*" Stella rolled her eyes. "*And why would I try to poison someone gullible enough to work all night for something useless?*"

"Eh?"

"*Seriously, did you really think Tree would say no to your date idea? You didn't really need my help at all.*"

Douglas's eyes widened. "*You tricked me! You said there was no way he would understand why humans would even need to date!*"

Stella whistled to herself and walked past Douglas to check on Diana, who was still sleeping on the bench.

Douglas let out a long sigh and then composed himself. "*Well, thank you for the gift. I may make use of it in the future."* He then turned to Ashlock. *"Would it be possible to bring Elaine up here? She had something to ask you, too."*

Ashlock was curious about what Elaine had to say, so without delay, he created a portal, and with a pop, the familiar Voidmind girl appeared. She glanced at Douglas and saw the man nod and smile.

"He said yes?" She walked over and embraced him. *"That's great! What about the other thing?"*

"You should ask him about that," Douglas whispered back. *"Sounds more sincere coming from you."*

Ashlock was genuinely curious if they thought he couldn't hear them. Even if they were a thousand miles away, so long as they were within the range of his roots, he could listen to anything and everything he wanted.

Assuming they didn't mask their voices with Qi, that was.

"Patriarch, I was wondering if it would be possible for me to return to work in the Academy?"

'Why?' Ashlock wrote on his trunk.

If some precautions were put in place, he didn't hate the idea, but it seemed like a headache waiting to happen. A date was relatively harmless, but having Elaine return to work after being absent for so long and with the Voidmind Elder gone could cause problems.

"I don't want to stay in the cavern all day with nothing to do. Meditation does help pass the time, but I still have some research I was working on back at the Academy I have been longing to get back to, and I miss my students," Elaine passionately replied. *"I...I could look for new recruits for the sect, so sending me back there won't be a total waste!"*

Ashlock found that reasoning dubious at best. Elaine was one of the most socially awkward people he had met in this world, and the idea of her approaching students with a beaming smile and trying to manipulate them into joining an elusive sect that promises seemingly impossible cultivation resources was hard to picture.

Elaine paused for a while, but seeing Ashlock's silence on the matter, she added, *"My brother is also visiting in a few days, and he will be looking for me. I don't want him to end up like my uncle if he tries to locate me..."*

That was a good point.

Ashlock had almost forgotten that call she had shared with her brother not long ago. The Voidmind family, alongside many other families, was sending people here. This was an issue because Ashlock didn't want rumors regarding the Voidmind Elder's whereabouts circulating among the students and their families that came to visit.

It was risky to allow Elaine to return to the Academy, as this could be a scheme planned by the two of them. But for what? He had provided a good life here...right?

"Actually, Douglas wouldn't be able to scheme with Elaine even if he wanted to due to his oath of loyalty," Ashlock mused. "So this would have had to be a plan made by Elaine, but I can't see a reason she would use this as an opportunity to run back to her family."

Ashlock wasn't a gambling man, so he agreed on two conditions to make this a safe bet.

'Elaine, you may return to your life in Darklight City at the Academy, but you must first swear an oath of loyalty to the Ashfallen Sect and return to working here part-time after the tournament.'

She had, after all, been integrated into the sect on the understanding that she would be a pillar of the alchemy division of the Ashfallen Sect. She may not be the most knowledgeable or capable at performing alchemy, but with his cauldron fruit doing most of the work, he just needed intelligent people willing to learn.

Elaine translated his words at a speed comparable to Stella's and relaxed in apparent relief. "An oath of loyalty? I have no qualms with that." She glanced around and smiled at everyone. "I like the people here. It's a good place."

Ashlock wasn't sure what had changed her mind regarding the oath of loyalty. The fruit and truffles, the Mystic Realm, him training her one-on-one in a vain attempt to improve her sword skills. It was likely a combination of all these things that had occurred in recent days.

Elaine stepped forward, placed her hand on her chest, and closed her eyes.

"I, Elaine Voidmind, pledge my loyalty to the Ashfallen Sect. If my loyalty is to falter, may my cultivation be forever crippled and my heart demons unleashed upon my unfaithful soul."

The sky seemed to tremble as immense pressure descended on the courtyard. Ashlock felt the oath bond between him and Elaine strengthen as her hair fluttered in an invisible breeze.

Within moments, everything settled down, and Ashlock felt heaven's intense glare subside. Initially, he was confused about why heaven seemed to pay so much attention to him, but it made sense when he thought about it some more.

He was a demi divine being on a lower plane, making oaths of loyalties to mortals. He did it without much thought and had multiple oaths with his sect members now, but it likely wasn't something that other demi divines had abused this much in the past.

"I wonder if the World Tree ever gives out oaths to those in the Celestial Empire?" Ashlock could picture a cult of people surrounding a thousand-meter-tall Monarch Realm tree reaching for the heavens and begging it for a blessing.

While Ashlock had been lost in his thoughts, Elaine and Douglas were embraced in a hug. To be nice, he created a portal behind them that led them to the edge of the misty forest just outside Darklight City.

'Have fun, and don't forget to come back,' Ashlock wrote, and Stella waved them off.

With a joyous bow, they both turned and left through the portal, hand in hand.

Diana awoke with a pounding headache. She tried to massage her temples, but it did little to help. She took a deep breath and was surprised at how dense the ambient Qi was.

"Where am I?" she croaked out as if dying of thirst and glanced around. Her vision was a little blurry, but soon she saw the demonic trees and wall of mist.

"Oh, you're awake," Stella said from above.

Diana looked up and saw Stella perched on one of Ashlock's branches and swinging her legs. She was humming a pleasant tune and seemed overall in a great mood.

What the hell happened? Weren't we getting crushed by Titus just a moment ago? Oh.

Her gaze caught the Ent lying motionless on the ground nearby. His body was like a savage animal had ripped him apart, with deep cuts oozing demonic Qi covering almost every limb.

"Feeling better?" Stella asked. "I wouldn't be surprised if you needed another day or two to regain your senses. After all, you were a crazed demon for a day and night."

Wait, that means Ashlock saw my demon form, and his half-dead creation is because of me.

"I'm sorry, I really am," Diana said. "I didn't realize I would lose total control like that... I had practiced extensively in the Mystic Realm, but it's different out here."

She then felt a presence behind her. Turning her head, she saw lilac flames dancing across the black bark of Ashlock, spelling out something in that strange language she had failed to learn in the past.

"Stella, what is he saying?" Diana asked in a small voice, dreading the answer.

"Mhm?" Stella glanced down and read the words while she continued humming.

"Father—ahem, Tree said that he doesn't care whatever form you take on Diana, and he can always repair the Ent, so it's no big deal."

Phew, it's good to know Ashlock accepts me... Wait.

"Don't play that off." Diana felt her headache subside. "You said 'Father.' Didn't you?"

"So?" Stella giggled. "What's the problem?"

"The fact your father is a tree aside, didn't you say Ashlock was planted after you were born? So how could he be your father if he is younger than you—"

Stella's swinging legs paused. She looked down and glared at her. "Tree is my father. Stop speaking nonsense."

She's gone crazy, Diana thought. *Completely crazy.*

"Anyway, I wanted to ask you something." Stella switched topics and returned to her good mood. "Since when did you know there was something different about you?"

Diana frowned. "Different? Do you mean my demonic bloodline?"

"Yeah. When was the moment you were like, 'There's a demon inside me'? Or when did you know you had an ancient bloodline?"

Diana felt the headache making a vicious return, and her entire body felt out of balance. She needed—no, she hungered—for demonic Qi. Standing up, she trudged over to the Ent while feeling Stella's curious gaze on her back.

"I would say the moment I knew I was different, as you say..." Diana ran a finger along one of the cuts oozing demonic Qi, and breathing in, she felt it lurch out of the cut and leap down her throat. "... was when Ashlock gave me the truffle to expel heart demons. I could just tell how my body reacted to its power was unnatural."

"I see. I wonder when I will feel that way..." Stella hummed to herself and seemed lost in thought, so Diana continued recovering the demonic Qi off the Ent corpses, and she was sure that Ashlock would appreciate not having to expel the nasty stuff.

After finishing up, Diana returned to the bench and crossed her legs to cultivate. Within herself, her body was in turmoil. While in "human" form, she had to suppress the demonic Qi within her Soul Core or risk turning part or fully demon.

An hour or so passed, and Diana's eyes snapped open. Stella was still overhead, relaxing against Ashlock while sitting on his branch and enjoying the summer breeze.

Seemingly noticing her gaze, Stella met hers and smiled. "Seems Kaida has found his rightful place again."

"Huh?" Diana felt something lick her chin and weigh down her shoulders. "Oh, hello, Kaida."

The inky snake gave her a little hiss in reply.

"We have a week or so until the alchemy tournament," Stella said. "What do you think about trying to teach Kaida some techniques for his ink affinity while we wait?"

"What?" Diana was confused. Why was that the logical thing to do?

Stella chuckled. "Well, with Elaine and Douglas off on a date, there is nothing else to do other than meditate. So don't you think now is a good time to learn some new things?"

Diana didn't like where this was going. "New things you say..."

"Yeah, like, I think you should give learning the ancient language another try." Stella's face suddenly appeared in Diana's view as she hung upside down from Ashlock's branch. "Don't you agree? Elaine learned it in a week, and I'm tired of translating for you."

Diana huffed. "Fine...but let's start with Kaida first. I have always wanted to try combination attacks with our affinities."

48
ODD LOOKS

Diana placed Kaida down on the ground. The snake glanced back at her with deep golden eyes, and his pink tongue flickered out. It was obvious to Diana that Kaida didn't like being on the cold stone ground and would prefer to be wrapped around her shoulders, but it wasn't convenient anymore.

He was far too big to comfortably wear around her neck like a scarf.

After all, Kaida had completed his evolution and wasn't so small anymore. Diana had spent a long time with Kaida in the Mystic Realm, but he had been a little ink snake unable to do anything but eat and nibble on her hair back then.

Diana glanced to the side and saw Stella intently reading the flames flickering on Ashlock's trunk in the ancient runic language that she was sure Stella would force her to learn later.

"Mhm, I see. How impressive sounding," Stella said as she turned to face her. "All right, according to Tree, Kaida is now an Ebonflow Serpent Sovereign. He also mentioned something about Kaida's ink affinity merging with water and darkness. Errr…supposedly, this evolution also seems to boost Kaida's offensive capabilities, allowing him to attack with torrents of ink and water. Sounds pretty menacing, if you ask me."

Diana nodded and looked down at the snake trying to coil around her leg. Crouching down, she patted Kaida on the head and tried to think about his rare combination of affinities.

Actually, even with Ashlock's power, there's no way that Kaida could access three affinities simultaneously. Diana placed her palm on Kaida's head and closed her eyes. She confirmed her suspicion by sending a pulse of Qi into the snake's body, which made Kaida hiss.

"Kaida has a Soul Core with ink affinity and is somewhere near the bottom of the Soul Fire Realm." Diana opened her eyes and stood back up. "But he likely has a strong Dao comprehension of water and darkness."

"That was my thought as well," Stella said. "Three separate affinities sounded unlikely." She then tapped her chin as she looked at the two-meter-long snake. Kaida looked between them curiously, his tongue flickering out nervously.

"Diana, do you know anything about ink affinity?"

"Not a lot, to be honest. Nobody in the Blood Lotus Sect has the affinity. But there are some merchants and tales about ink affinity cultivators." Diana crossed her arms as she tried to scrape her mind for those distant memories she had picked up through stories and books over the years.

"Let me see… I believe ink affinity is very similar to water, except it has a magical ability to alter reality and manifest things."

Stella stared at her, confused. "What does that even mean?"

"For example, I could create an elemental out of the water Qi to fight for me, whereas Kaida could draw creatures with the spiritual ink, and these creatures would then come to life as manifestations and fight."

"Isn't ink just a better version of water, then?" Stella asked. "No offense, of course. But if ink can act just like water and even manipulate reality…"

Diana chuckled. "No offense taken. The simple answer is the environment." A ball of swirling water condensed into a cloud and, finally, into a ball above Diana's palm. "Water is all around us. In the air, rivers, oceans, and even your body. But where is ink?"

"Oh… Yeah, I see now." Stella frowned. "So Kaida has to conjure all of this spiritual ink straight from his Soul Core?"

"Yeah, and that's not the only problem. Cultivating ink Qi is impossible as it doesn't exist around us, so he has to convert the ambient, chaotic, untamed Qi into ink Qi inside his Soul Core, making cultivation ten times slower." Diana sighed.

Stella still didn't seem convinced entirely that ink was worse than water, so Diana felt the need to add, "Rare affinities, although powerful, have so many downsides that most sects prefer to populate themselves with basic affinities like earth, water, fire, and air."

Diana then gestured around. "You can only practice and use a rare affinity like spatial as much as you do because Ashlock is passively releasing spatial Qi everywhere."

"Mhm, that's true." Stella nodded. "Anyway, we are getting off-topic. Ink affinity… What else can it be used for besides drawing creatures and having them come to life?"

You're the reason I got off-topic! How can you think ink is better than water affinity? Diana paused her thoughts. Why was she getting so mad over Stella accidentally insulting her affinity? Ugh, whatever.

With a sigh, Diana replied, "As I said before, the spiritual ink can bend reality to make anything possible. One of the greatest legends regarding an ink affinity cultivator was when a man went insane and painted heaven's gaze with his own blood. Upon the final stroke of his bloody brush on the white canvas, it glowed with power as the spiritual ink manifested into a giant golden eye that obliterated him with lightning."

"Right…" Stella eyed Kaida with a dubious look. "That does sound ridiculously strong. Do you have any ideas for a more basic skill, perhaps? One we could try and coax Kaida into learning?"

"Sure, I would say anything to do with calligraphy would be his best place to start. If he could write something in his spiritual ink like a runic word, something might happen?" Diana shrugged. "This is all speculation, though. I did some background research regarding ink affinity because it's so close to water affinity, and I thought the stories about it sounded interesting. Still, I only spent a few hours reading a few books."

Stella crouched down and tried to pat the snake, but it swerved its body to avoid her hand. "Little guy, let me pet you…please? Sigh." Lowering her hand in defeat, she continued, "Well, if we get stuck, I'm sure we can ask Elaine to sneak some technique manuals out of the Academy for us, assuming there are any for ink affinity."

Standing back up, Stella took a few steps back and arrived under the shade of the nearby demonic tree. "Kaida seems to only like you, so I will stand back here and observe. Maybe try to get him to write something in the ancient language."

"Will he know it?" Diana asked.

"Perhaps." Stella leaned against the tree. "Larry seemed to be able to understand it, so I don't see why the snake wouldn't be able to, either. They are both pets of Tree, after all!"

Diana turned and eyed the snake. "Can you?"

Kaida tilted his head and flickered out his tongue. His black scales already appeared to have a sticky texture, making Diana think if she placed her hands on Kaida, they would return covered in black paint. This staring contest went on for a while until Kaida brought his tail between them.

He slowly scraped his tail across the bare stone, and Diana saw ink left in a trail behind. Kaida was really using his tail as a brush to write!

There was a silence only broken by the sound of Kaida scratching his tail against the stone. Diana and Stella exchanged surprised glances a few times, but neither dared to disturb the snake.

Eventually, Kaida withdrew his tail, gave his work a once-over, and then glanced back at Diana with his golden eyes as if asking her to read it.

Diana tried deciphering the black squiggles but couldn't make heads or tails of their possible meaning. "Hey, Stella, what does this say?"

Stella snorted. "If you bothered to learn the ancient language instead of sleeping and reading random history books, then maybe you could read it."

"Don't use this opportunity as a way to make fun of me." Diana rolled her eyes. "Just come and translate it already."

"Fine..." Stella pushed herself off the tree and walked over. "But this should be a good reason to actually sit down and learn it! You can take the language comprehension fruit. It will be over before you even know it."

"Yeah, yeah." Diana stood back to give Stella space. "Whatever you say."

"Now let's see..." Stella leaned over the runic words. "This translates to...explosion?"

Kaida tapped the words with his tail, and Diana saw a rush of Qi spread throughout the ink, causing it to briefly glow and then...explode upward.

Right into Stella's face.

Stella stumbled back, more surprised than hurt. Her hair was all over the place and drenched in sticky black ink. "What the…" she mumbled as she blinked away the confusion.

Diana glanced back at Kaida and saw the snake having the time of his life. He slapped his tail excitedly against the floor while hissing in a way Diana interpreted as laughing.

"Tree, your pet is bullying me!" Stella glared at the snake as she tried to pull out the ink that drenched her hair. Diana gave the snake a playful wink and then turned to Stella. "Come here. Let me help you with that."

As Diana had expected, ink was close enough to water that she could manipulate it without much issue. With a mere thought, the ink was pulled from Stella's hair into a swirling ball above her palm. Diana then passed the ball of ink back to Kaida as she knew how hard it must have been to cultivate that amount of ink Qi.

I can easily gather water Qi from the air, but any ink Qi Kaida uses on techniques sets his cultivation progress backward. So it's best to return it to him when possible.

Kaida stopped his happy hissing and opened his mouth to gobble up the tiny floating ball of ink.

Diana approached the snake with a smile. While playfully scratching his chin, she whispered, "You're a little troublemaker, aren't you? Don't be so mean to Stella. She is a nice person…sometimes."

Kaida returned a blank stare that made Diana softly laugh.

Stella tapped Diana on the shoulder. "Yeah?" Diana asked over her shoulder, and Stella handed over a stack of parchments with a single fruit placed on top.

"Since you want to take that rascal's side," she smiled, but it wasn't a sweet and kind smile at all, "then you can practice the ancient language with him!"

Diana took the parchments with a sigh. Even she could see the immense value of learning the ancient language now. Not only to communicate with Ashlock directly but also to be able to translate Kaida's ink.

Hopefully, the language comprehension fruit will make this more tolerable.

Lowering her arm so Kaida could coil himself around it, Diana took off to the corner of the mountain peak to pick a demonic tree within the high water Qi area so she could cultivate and learn the ancient language simultaneously.

"Come on, Kaida, we got some work to do."

Ashlock couldn't believe it. His little pet snake had really used his powers for the first time!

"Wow, ink affinity is far more versatile than I first thought if Diana's story about the guy who painted heaven's eye is true. Can it really manifest anything? I assume there are limits to its power, but what are they?" Ashlock was fascinated.

Of course, he could already identify the many drawbacks of ink affinity.

"The amount of ink that Diana managed to gather from Stella's hair was a mere fraction of the total ink he expelled to create that…array? Would array be the correct term? It acts like an array but more of a one-time thing."

Ink affinity's high cost aside, just the fact that it took Kaida a few minutes to draw out the ancient runes for such a harmless effect was concerning.

"Obviously, he will get faster with time, but what if the opponent can read the ancient script from afar? He got lucky this time because Stella was careless, but I doubt he could catch Stella with a prank like that again."

However, downsides naturally came with upsides. Ashlock had picked the ink affinity for Kaida over the others because he believed it had great future potential and how well he would work alongside Diana.

"The fact Diana was able to gather the expelled ink into a ball like that and return it to Kaida is already proof that maybe Kaida could use Diana's mist as a canvas for his spiritual ink." Ashlock could already picture the scene of Diana dashing through her haunted mist with Kaida wrapped around her demonic form or slithering through the mist beside her and filling the mist with floating arrays of spiritual ink that do a wild variety of things.

While Ashlock was lost in his fantasies, Stella returned to sit on the bench and closed her eyes to cultivate. With nothing to do other than watch the sun traverse through the sky, Ashlock also decided to get some cultivating done for once, as repairing Titus was really straining his Qi reserves, and he hadn't conversed deeply with heaven for a long while.

Elaine awoke to the birds chirping and warm sunlight on her face. "Ugh…it's morning already?" She groaned as she turned over and buried her face in the fluffy pillow.

She had slept like a log as she had yearned for a comfortable place to sleep ever since arriving at the Ashfallen Sect.

They were all good people, but they were also cultivators. They could ignore the temptation of sleep for days, weeks, or even months. But Elaine was barely a cultivator. She still had many mortal needs.

Actually, Stella should be able to stay up indefinitely now that she is in the Star Core Realm. And she is so young, too… I'm jealous.

With a sigh, she rolled over a little more, and the sudden feeling of warm skin next to her shocked her slowly awakening mind. Her eyes shot open, and she saw Douglas's hulking form sleeping peacefully beside her.

They hadn't done the deed last night as she hadn't felt ready after a single date. But she still felt terribly embarrassed to sleep half naked with someone else for the first time. Carefully exiting the blanket one leg at a time, Elaine tried to sneak over to the corner of the room where her clothes had been tossed, but the floorboards of the inn they were staying in creaked underfoot.

"Morning," Douglas said as his eyes sleepily opened.

Elaine was frozen in place, her arm reaching to grab her dress. To her relief, Douglas seemed to take even longer than her to free himself from the drowsiness of sleep, so she quickly got dressed.

"Leaving so soon?" Douglas said with a yawn as he sat up in bed, causing the poor bedframe to creak loudly.

"I need to get to the Academy before morning registration," Elaine replied with a weary smile. "And it's already late morning. You are welcome to come and see me at lunch, though."

Douglas grinned. "Sounds good. I always wondered what the Academy was like from the inside."

"Cool," Elaine said, feeling awkward standing there. "Well…see you later, then."

Turning to leave, she made it halfway out the door when Douglas shouted after her, "This inn does killer sandwiches, so don't forget to grab one on your way out. Wouldn't want you to go hungry."

Elaine wasn't sure why, but Douglas's care warmed her heart.

"Thanks, will do," she replied with a smile and then closed the door carefully behind her.

Elaine strode through the campus grounds with a sandwich in hand. Honestly, she wouldn't describe it as "killer," but it wasn't bad at all. Perhaps she had been spoiled with high-grade cultivator food made from powerful beasts her whole life, so much so that a genuinely good sandwich like this made from mortal ingredients tasted so...bland.

There was also the chance that her appetite was being soured by all the stares she was getting. Every group of students she walked by seemed to pause in their tracks to gawk at her as if she was some caged animal on display for their pleasure.

Initially, she thought it was because she had been away from campus for a while, and they were amazed to see her return, but then she reality-checked herself.

You spent every waking hour, every day, in that study with Uncle. There's no way even half these people know of me, and my disappearance for a few weeks shouldn't warrant this type of reaction.

Was there something on her face? Had Douglas left a mark on her or something? She decided to soldier on and check herself out in the mirror in her office.

Alas, as Elaine rounded a corner to cut across the gardens to get to the library that dominated the skyline, she bumped into someone she didn't want to see.

"Cousin?" A man she knew all too well was standing before her, and his jaw was practically on the floor.

"Hey, Jasper," Elaine replied with a tired smile, still not knowing what made everyone freak out. "Long time no see. Where's my brother?"

Since they were little, Jasper had been her brother's friend, and the three would often hang out. However, once Jasper was found to have lackluster talent in cultivation, he was sent off to the Academy here in Darklight City alongside Elaine.

If I remember correctly, Jasper is supposed to graduate this year. But despite being older than me, he is only at the third stage of the Soul Fire Realm.

"Gosh, I hardly recognized you." Jasper schooled his expression and straightened up. "Funny you should mention your brother... I was just on the way to meet up with him. The Voidmind airship should be arriving within the hour. Do you want to come with me to meet him?"

Elaine felt a terrible sinking feeling brewing in her chest. She knew her brother would be arriving soon. But now that the moment was here, she didn't want to face him.

"I have something to check up on in my study." Elaine weakly brushed off the request and shuffled past Jasper. "But I will be right behind you."

"Oh...okay." Jasper ran a hand through his pitch-black hair, a trait many of the Voidmind family had. "Well, see you later, then."

Elaine breathed out a sigh of relief as she saw Jasper leave. Now more than ever, she wanted nothing more than to reach her study and find out what the hell was wrong with her face.

49
DANTE VOIDMIND'S ARRIVAL

Elaine stood before a mirror hanging in her study with a frown.
She had made a window in the thick dust coating the mirror with her sleeve and now stared at her reflection.
"How?" Those words left her lips. She could see her mouth moving, so the mirror wasn't playing tricks on her. This was really her reflection. There were no odd marks or anything exactly weird about her face unless you considered her otherworldly beauty as something strange.
I saw my reflection in a hand mirror back in the cavern right after I had taken the truffle.
Elaine traced her face with deep confusion. Had the dim lighting in the cavern caused this mismatch between what she remembered seeing in that mirror and what she was staring at right now?
"Oh, this is bad news," Elaine groaned. No wonder Jasper and all the students had reacted like this. Her skin was lustrous with life, her eyes seemed to glow, and her hair looked so silky it could be woven into a garment befitting a goddess as it draped over her slim shoulders.
"What the hell did that truffle do to me! I hardly even recognize myself. Where are my baggy eyes, hunched back, and depressed air? People will actually notice me now." Elaine felt anxiety rise as she began to panic. She could not face her brother while looking like this, right? "What should I do?"
Elaine glanced around the dusty study in a panic. The lack of human

activity here in recent days was apparent. Even her open notebook filled with details regarding the demonic tree outside was left open on the desk after she had been kidnapped by the mist demon.

"Never before did I think my appearance would become such a problem," Elaine muttered as she paced up and down the dusty room. "Nobody ever looked my way before. I was just another person… I have no idea how to deal with this!"

Elaine paused and glanced at the door. "What if I just run away back to the Ashfallen Sect, never to be heard from again?"

It was tempting, but she eventually shook her head. "That would cause even more problems. Jasper and all the students already saw me."

Elaine returned to the mirror and gave herself one last hard look. "What if I just…own it? Say I started looking after myself for once or something." Her smile quickly faded. "No. Nope. No way. I can't handle those stares anymore. What if I wore a mask instead?"

She still had that black mask that Douglas had given her, but wasn't that for sect activities?

I should only wear that particular mask when I am trying to keep my identity hidden. Agh, what the hell should I do, then? I don't have any makeup, and even then, how could I hide all of this? Even my bone structure has changed.

Elaine collapsed into the chair behind the desk and stared out the window at the demonic tree. It was only now that she noticed the window was slightly ajar, and a black tree root was poking through. Had it been open when she arrived?

Whatever, so long as nobody heard my crazed ranting.

A while passed, and she just sat there, exhausted. She had been in this exact position when her entire life had changed…for the better. It felt weird to sit here now that she knew how vast the world was outside these four walls that had surrounded her for the last few years.

"I'm a changed woman," Elaine muttered, "both mentally and physically. To shy away from my new self in fear of my brother is nonsense."

She smiled weakly. Those words sounded bold, but she really didn't have that level of confidence.

"I don't want to have to go outside again…"

As those words left her mouth, there was a ripple of spatial Qi.

Ashlock had completely ignored Elaine and Douglas during their date, as he trusted them as they had both signed oaths of loyalty, and he had little interest in what humans got up to in their free time. However, when it came time for Elaine to meet up with her brother, he needed to watch over her to ensure nothing bad happened to his sect member.

After seeing the students' and Jasper's reaction to Elaine and overhearing her rant in front of the mirror, Ashlock realized he might have made a huge mistake in giving the girls, especially Elaine, the skin improvement truffle.

Unlike a sudden jump in cultivation, which could be handwaved as stumbling upon a treasure or sudden enlightenment, improving your looks was much harder to explain—especially to those that knew you as well as a sibling.

Ashlock hadn't really noticed as he spent all day watching his sect member, so a steady change of their appearance went unnoticed, but now that Elaine also pointed it out, he was sure of it—the truffle kept working overtime. There was an initial drastic improvement right after taking it, but it seemed to rewrite a person's DNA, so as their cultivation progressed and they grew up, it kept improving.

This was a problem. A big one. Ashlock had forgotten that his sect members might conduct negotiations or talk to old family members because Stella and Diana didn't have that issue with all their family dead. But Elaine and Douglas likely still had ties to people, and it would be weird for them to wear masks when talking to these old acquaintances.

"She might have been able to justify wearing the mask due to some facial disfigurement or something if only Jasper hadn't already seen her face." Ashlock cursed. The worst part about this situation is he had no idea how to predict how serious it was. For example, what if the Voidmind family desperately needed someone to marry off, and they had forgotten about Elaine due to her lackluster talent?

"Should I send someone to kill Jasper?" Ashlock thought briefly but dismissed that idea as nonsense. So many students from various families had seen her just moments ago, and he was sure Elaine's brother would ask about Jasper's whereabouts. It was already a big enough headache with the Voidmind Elder gone.

Ashlock tried to think of a solution. Jasper couldn't be killed, and

Elaine could not wear a mask without seeming like she was trying to hide something, and it was pointless as others had already seen her change in appearance.

"All right, she will meet her brother with her face exposed. So what now? She can't say anything about the Ashfallen Sect or what happened to the Elder due to the oaths she took, but she could lie." Ashlock glanced into the study room and saw Elaine sitting in the chair, biting her lower lip and looking to be having a minor panic attack.

"I need to come up with a lie for her. She won't be able to make up one on the fly," Ashlock mused as he tried to formulate a foolproof lie.

"Before Elaine had been kidnapped by Diana, she had mentioned on a call with her father, the Voidmind Grand Elder, that her uncle had gone through a rift to investigate something. What if I spin that into the Elder going into a secret realm like the merchants, and he had returned with treasures…one of which had been the thing that turned Elaine beautiful?"

Ashlock felt like he was onto something here. He dived into his inventory and searched for suitable items for Elaine to help with the lie. Those that had belonged to the Elder were ignored, so he was left with those trashy items he had signed in for ages ago.

"Just like the stick I gave Stella, which she turned into daggers, any system-created items have an unusual perfectness to them. Therefore even something like this F-grade 'Ordinary Pebble' could be seen as mysterious for how unnatural it looks."

Ashlock ignored a few items like the Energy Depleting Tea, Leaky Water Pouch, and Fake Spirit Stone as they wouldn't provide that sense of instant confusion he was looking for as the tea would need to be brewed, the water pouch filled, and the fake spirit stone inspected to decipher what made them special.

With those aside, he narrowed down his selection of F- and E-grade items to give to Elaine alongside a perfectly crafted lie.

Elaine looked at the sudden ripple of spatial Qi and saw words manifesting on the wall in lilac flames. She blinked multiple times, confused by the spectacle.

"I thought the Patriarch could only write on the tree's trunk." Elaine furrowed her brows as she squinted at the words and started translating their meaning.

You need to lie to your brother regarding your new appearance's origin.

Well, that much was obvious. The flames flickered, and new words appeared.

I have devised a lie for you to tell.

There was another ripple of spatial Qi throughout the room, and suddenly a tiny rift materialized above her desk. Half scared to death, Elaine almost fell from her chair when multiple items cascaded out of the rift and clattered onto the desk.

The rift snapped closed, sending a gust of wind throughout the room, which created a dust storm. Elaine went into a coughing fit. It wasn't until a bit later that the dust finally settled.

"What the hell..." She wheezed while wiping her glasses clean on her dress. "These items are for?" she questioned the wall, and once again, magical words appeared in lilac flame.

The lie is that your uncle went through a rift and ended up in a secret realm. He then returned and handed these items to you alongside a pill that removed a curse that had been plaguing your soul.

Elaine stroked her chin as she mulled over the lie.

Cursed, huh? That's an interesting approach. I did take all the truffles the Patriarch provided me, including a spirit root–improving and a heart demon–expelling one. It would make sense for all these changes to occur to me if some terrible curse had been lifted, allowing me to become my true self... The only problem is this new version of myself is superior to even my brother.

At that thought, a small smile crept onto her lips. Just imagining his face made her want to laugh, but her smile quickly faded. The Patriarch was speaking to her; now wasn't the time to mess around.

"I assume you want me to say my uncle is still in the secret realm?" Elaine asked.

Yes. Your uncle isn't dead, his soul has ascended to a higher realm with Senior Lee, but they won't buy that story. This lie gets us the time we need and explains your sudden change.

Elaine massaged her temples. This was all a lot to take in, and translating the ancient runic language she had only started learning a week ago was more challenging than she thought.

"Okay, so what are the descriptions of these items?" Elaine said. "Let's start with this one…"

She then pointed at each one as the words on the wall flickered to provide a name and short explanation.

"So an unhatchable spirit beast egg, ordinary pebble, bamboo sword, weighted training gear, low-grade detoxification pill, low-level barrier token, and meditation mat?"

Once Elaine got a confirmation that she had remembered the name of each item correctly, her spatial ring flashed, and all but one of the items vanished inside.

Picking up the pebble, she just couldn't make sense of it. The rock looked way too flawless, as if a god had descended and crafted the perfect pebble. The existence of this rock alone further cemented the image of the Patriarch as an untouchable existence in her mind.

As the pebble followed the rest into her spatial ring, she felt another ripple of Qi as a portal manifested in the corner of the room. She could see a distorted view of the airship station at the end of an alleyway through the rift.

Letting out a long sigh, she stood up and strode through the portal. The moment she felt the sudden wave of city noise assault her ears and the nasty smell of the alleyway, all the confidence she had built up vanished.

After all, in the sky above the grand station was a giant black airship with the Voidmind family insignia plastered on the side.

Much to everyone's confusion, a station employee shouted at the crowd, "Move out of the way. Make way! Don't stand around. Move!"

Mortals about to board their airship muttered words of complaint, but they were drowned out by the noise of more station employees moving the crowd.

Elaine stood off to the side with a twist in her stomach as she knew why the employees were making such a massive deal. Her brother, the direct heir to the Voidmind family, had arrived.

"What is the meaning of this?" A large man with more muscles than any human should possess crossed his arms while towering over the mortal employee. "I have planned a day trip to Slymere, and I'm already running late."

The man flashed his cultivation, and earth Qi rippled across his body, giving him a murky brown sheen.

"Sorry, sir cultivator, but there is nothing I can do," the mortal employee replied while trembling. "It's an order from the Azurecrest family."

It was a well-known fact that cultivators could use the airship industry however they wished. Hence, the Azurecrest family would only order rogue cultivators around if someone of higher importance had arrived.

"Tsk. Those noble bastards always causing a fuss." The man clicked his tongue in annoyance. He didn't pressure the mortal any further, but he didn't exactly move, either. He just stood there with a scowl and his arms crossed.

The mortal eventually gave up trying to move him and went off to fulfill his duties of moving the crowd back. Soon enough, the employees held back two perfectly formed lines of people on either side of the station with their arms spread out to indicate a line not to cross.

Everyone was trying to peek over the shoulders of one another to see who had caused the temporary shutdown of the largest airship station in Darklight City.

Elaine sighed in a vain attempt to calm her nerves when she saw two people wearing long, flowing black robes flanking a man she knew all too well in the center.

Unsurprisingly, Dante Voidmind had changed little over the years they had been apart. Like their father, Dante was even taller than the earth affinity cultivator and the two that flanked him by an entire head. Yet he was as thin as a bamboo shoot, with sunken features that made him look like a ghoul.

His shifting black eyes glanced around from his vantage point, only partially obscured by his coal-black hair that fell over his face like a waterfall.

"A Voidmind brat?" The earth Qi cultivator snorted, drawing Dante's unamused gaze. "Don't you know shutting down an airship station like this for no other reason than to stroke your ego is rather pathetic?"

One of the black-robed men tried to step forward to deal with the rogue cultivator but paused when Dante's spindly fingers gripped his shoulder.

Without another word, the two attendants hung back and let their lord walk forth to challenge the rogue.

"Something like an ego has no use to one such as I," Dante spoke, his voice carrying a piercing chill that reminded Elaine of her father and made her unintentionally shiver.

The rogue cultivator stood his ground as earth Qi of the late-stage Soul Fire Realm solidified into a barrier over his body.

Elaine shook her head. All cultivators were affected by the properties of the Qi they altered their bodies with. And earth Qi cultivators happened to have an almost suicidal tendency to want to test their defense against anything. Basically, they became muscle-brained idiots.

At least Douglas isn't too bad. But he is rather outspoken at times.

"Everyone has heard about the upcoming alchemy tournament." The rogue snorted, looking at Dante's slim build with disdain. "What right does someone like you, who plays with herbs all day, have to mess with my weekend?"

Dante cocked his head. "You see me as weak?" His eyes stopped shifting color and settled on an impenetrable abyss that seemed to swallow everything within their sight.

An immense pressure pulsed out, flooring all the mortals standing nearby and bringing the cultivator to one knee. His muscles bulged as he staggered back onto two feet, but his arrogance was gone—replaced with a mixture of fear and anticipation of a fight.

The poor Soul Fire cultivator realized his folly in challenging a Star Core.

Dante sauntered over with unnerving tranquility. His unhurried strides were marked by an understated elegance, each step landing as though perfectly choreographed. Elaine had always hated this uptight demeanor of her brother that had been carefully nurtured since childhood.

"You aren't from a side branch, are you?" The cultivator seemed to have realized his grave mistake. Even if he managed to win the fight, he would be hunted to the end of the realm for killing a scion.

And he likely also knew scions didn't take insults personally but saw them as an insult to the noble house they represented. To offend Dante was to insult the Voidmind family.

"No, I don't hail from a side family." Dante spoke as if that was a slur. "You are talking to the heir."

"Then let's dance, your majesty." The cultivator discarded all reason and sneered. Then in a vain attempt, he tried to pour his earth Qi into the floor to make it rupture, but Elaine saw the entire building light up as the intricate defense formations activated. It was almost impossible to damage this building.

Realizing his attack wasn't working, the cultivator tried to lunge forward and punch Dante in the face with an earth Qi–empowered fist, but Dante met the punch with his void-coated palm.

There was a loud thunderclap as Dante effortlessly stopped the strike. It was almost surreal to watch a man who was more muscle than human get his attack stopped by Dante, whose arm looked like it could snap any moment.

"I never was one to accept a dance with brutish men," Dante said nonchalantly. "Now perish."

The earth cultivator let out a brief wail as his earth Qi barrier was shattered and void Qi rippled through his body, devouring his flesh, and within moments all that remained was his pearly white skeleton.

Dante stepped back and summoned a white handkerchief to wipe the blood from his fingers as the cultivator's skeleton disintegrated to the ground and joined the soup of organs and blood staining the floor.

The entire station was pin-drop silent. Nobody dared to move as they lay on the floor, even after the Star Core pressure from Dante had subsided.

This was the power of cultivation. No matter the outward appearance, nothing could topple the strength of a superior cultivator. Elaine didn't want to admit it, but she felt excited. Due to the resources provided by the Patriarch, maybe by the end of the year, she too could display this kind of godlike power.

Sadly her excitement died out when she realized she was the only person still standing among a sea of mortals sprawled around her.

Naturally, their gazes met once Dante had finished cleaning his hand of an inconvenience.

"Sister?" he half whispered to himself, as if worried about mistaking someone but still loud enough for everyone to hear. "Is that really you? You look so…different."

Every pair of eyes in the entire station turned to stare at her.
She really wanted to dig a hole and die in it.

50
DELUDED SCION

After fusing with his children's roots, Ashlock could peer into many buildings by sneaking a root through a window or a doorway. With so many demonic trees throughout the city, people didn't really pay much attention to them anymore and wouldn't find it suspicious seeing roots growing into places they shouldn't.

Besides a few rooms in the Academy, including Elaine's study, Ashlock also had roots sneaking into the airship station. With the tournament only a few days away from starting, he had long anticipated a rush of new people and potential problems arising in the vicinity of the airship station, so he had made sure that all the demonic trees nearby had roots in and around the station.

Due to this foresight, Ashlock could watch Dante Voidmind's arrival.

"So scions are treated like celebrities in this world?" Ashlock pondered as he saw Dante Voidmind saunter toward Elaine while flanked by two escorts.

His first impressions of the Voidmind scion were mixed. Despite what he claimed, it was clear Dante had a sizable ego that he felt needed to be protected. But at the same time, unlike the rogue cultivator, Dante had this air of calmness around him, even when he obliterated someone into nothing but dust. It was all so effortless that it made it impossible to determine his mood.

Which made Ashlock fearful for Elaine. Her appearance had caused a small crack in Dante's facade, and Ashlock saw a look of genuine confusion on his face for the first time since he arrived.

"Sister, is that really you?" he asked Elaine, who opened her mouth but could not form words.

Dante frowned, and Ashlock felt his mind tense up. He was mentally prepared to open a portal at any moment to save her. Losing Elaine would be a massive loss for the Ashfallen Sect, and he had no interest in entertaining this Dante fellow.

"You haven't seen me in so many years, and you have nothing to say to your brother?" Dante's voice took on that chill again. *"Come with me. We need to have a talk away from prying ears."*

Ashlock did not like the sound of that one bit. Luckily he had made Elaine swear an oath of loyalty and secrecy, so the chance of her managing to find a way to reveal the Ashfallen Sect's existence to the Voidmind family was unlikely.

Elaine didn't even get a chance to react as the two escorts urged her toward the station's exit, and she reluctantly followed her brother's back while fidgeting with her dress and biting her lower   lip.

"Lead me to the house," Dante instructed one of the escorts, and the man gave his lord a bow before taking the lead.

"What house?" Ashlock wondered as he followed them from above with {Eye of the Tree God}.

Even though his roots had slithered their way into many places, the further they walked from him, the less coverage of the city he had, so hearing of a house put him further on edge.

"Should I send Larry or Diana to follow them?" Ashlock estimated Dante Voidmind to be around the same stage as him in the Star Core Realm.

Meanwhile, Larry was near the peak of the Star Core Realm, but he wasn't that adept at espionage with his enormous size and lack of stealth capabilities. On the flip side, Diana was simply far too weak to not be detected by Dante's spiritual sense.

While Ashlock was lamenting his lacking abilities in intel gathering, the Voidmind group arrived at a house in the noble district. Rich mortals wandered the paved streets with their hired rogue cultivators in tow. They all sent one look at the group and smartly steered clear.

The house they stood before was a manor of decent size. Strangely, its windows were bricked up so no light could get in, and Ashlock noticed faint silver lines indicating the entire building was acting as a formation for something.

Obsidian-colored doors swung open, and a few maids and a butler walked down the steps onto the manicured front lawn that flanked a gravel pathway.

"*My Lord,*" the butler bowed, "*preparations for your stay have been concluded. Please come inside and make yourself at home.*"

The butler then glanced at Elaine and skillfully hid his surprise behind an awkward cough. "*Lady Elaine, it's a pleasure to see you again as well. You should visit more often. Taking care of an empty house brings rust to my knives.*"

"Sorry…I have been rather busy recently." Elaine spoke for the first time since Dante's arrival.

"So Elaine knew about this house?" Ashlock mused. Now that he thought about it since Slymere was the closest city and multiple Voidmind family members were staying here in Darklight City, it only made sense that they had purchased a residence. It wasn't weird for nobles or affluent families back on earth to have homes in multiple countries to make traveling more comfortable.

"*Enough with the pleasantries, Clive.*" Dante hurried the conversation along. "*Prepare the chamber. I have some discussions to conduct with my sister here.*"

"As you command, My Lord." Clive bowed and clicked his fingers at one of the maids. She didn't even need to be told what to do as she vanished into the house.

"Right this way." Clive led the group down the gravel path and into the house. With a resounding thud that showed the thickness of the doors, Ashlock was left helpless. All nearby demonic trees had been removed, and guards patrolled the manor's grounds.

He wouldn't even know how to get a root into the building so he could eavesdrop, as it was more a fortress than a manor with bricked-up windows and tightly sealed doors.

"I will wait for a while, but if I don't see Elaine emerge by sundown, I will send the Redclaws to go and investigate," Ashlock vowed as he maintained his surveillance on the building, ensuring to not miss a thing.

Unlike Clive, the maids of the Voidmind residence openly gawked at Elaine as she timidly followed her brother through the corridors. She hated how awkward she felt, but how could she not? Dante hadn't made a big fuss of it yet, but she had made the very occasional visit back here over the years to make use of the void chamber. So the staff was used to her old appearance.

The doors up ahead at the end of the corridor opened with a resounding click, and Elaine felt the coldness of the void wash over her as the corridor was bathed in darkness. It was as if the doorway led to an endless abyss. She always felt nervous walking in as there was no visible floor in the void chamber, and she felt like she would fall into the realm of hell below.

Dante strolled in without worry, and Elaine saw him stand impatiently in the abyss as if floating. "Come in."

Elaine glanced around one last time before gathering the courage and stepping in. She didn't bother looking down as her brain would fail to comprehend how she was walking on nothingness and would cause motion sickness.

Oh, the joys of being a weak cultivator.

While Elaine lamented her fate, Dante snapped his fingers and summoned two chairs of liquid void. He gingerly sat and crossed his legs as he gestured for her to follow his action.

Elaine perched herself on the seat, and the two silently looked at each other.

Dante sighed. "Sister, you already know the question on my mind."

Elaine felt her stomach twist into a knot as she tried to replay the carefully crafted lie in her mind. What if she slipped up? Would she bring the Ashfallen Sect to its demise?

No, don't be stupid. They defeated Uncle like it was nothing. What would my father or brother be to them? Nothing but a nuisance.

Elaine sighed and regained some semblance of confidence. "No need to hold back, Brother. What's on your mind?"

"Being coy, are we now, dear sister?"

Elaine returned a blank expression.

"Some changes appeared to have occurred while I was sealed away in cultivation." Dante smiled ever so slightly as if amused. "Since when did my dear sister begin to care for herself?"

Elaine blinked. That had not been the exact phrasing she had been expecting. Also, why was his tone so different from when they spoke through the talisman?

"Whatever do you mean, Brother?" Elaine replied while trying to keep the nerve out of her voice.

"You look gorgeous now, just like our mother. Dare I say you are an improvement! Which would only make sense, as you are the product of the two greatest cultivators to bless our Voidmind family."

Elaine almost rolled her eyes. Her mother was indeed beautiful, but that was only due to her high cultivation. Compared to the girls on Red Vine Peak, she was nothing special.

Her thoughts then paused on one of the words Dante had mentioned. "What do you mean product?" she asked. "I am a child of our parents, just like you."

"I will be frank, Elaine: when I saw you last, you reminded me of a failed product. I mean, just look at myself. Tall, handsome, talented, and with the etiquette of a distinguished gentleman. Meanwhile, you were anything but that."

Dante then scowled at her. "Whenever myself and Father had the displeasure of having to gaze upon you, all we could see was an imperfect reflection of ourselves."

Elaine wanted to vomit. This was the brother she knew—a narcissist that saw people as nothing more than products of the Voidmind family—not the weirdly kind one from moments ago. He hadn't been this vile years ago, but it seemed years apart had completely changed both her and him.

The way he spoke of her was truly sickening. As if her mere presence had brought about a great inconvenience for him.

Holding back her rage, she tried deciphering the truth from her brother's insane delusions. She would never understand whatever image of himself and their family he had crafted in his twisted mind. In her opinion, other than their affinity, there was nothing special about any of them, especially her brother.

With her saying nothing, he continued speaking, and Elaine started to wonder if he just liked the sound of his own voice.

"Once we discovered your lack of talent for cultivation, we decided to send you away. Out of sight, out of mind." Dante grinned. "And it seems we made the right choice! Do tell me, my dear Elaine, how did this transformation come about?"

Did he just take…credit? Does he truly believe that his conspiring with my father and sending me here to live with my uncle somehow resulted in my transformation? Although I wouldn't have joined the Ashfallen Sect without being here, the fact he is patting himself on the back for my years of neglect is disgusting.

Dante then reached over and grabbed her wrist with his spindly fingers, causing her to jolt. A pulse of void Qi then traveled throughout her body.

"And your Qi has become as pure as mine," he muttered as he withdrew his hand and leaned back in his void chair. "You have truly bloomed into the purity of our bloodline. How marvelous."

His cold gaze drilled into her soul as he commanded once more, "Now tell me. How did this happen?"

"I…I was cursed." Elaine choked out the words. All she wanted to do was strangle this deluded bastard to death. But she lacked the power to do so. He was king in this void chamber, and she had no option but to obey.

"Cursed?" Dante leaned forward. "Tell me more."

Elaine nodded, trying her best to sell the lie. "Yes…well, Uncle recently discovered a rift that led to a secret realm. He was gone for a few days before returning and giving me various items."

Her spatial ring flashed with power, and the items the Patriarch had provided her appeared floating between them. Dante reached for the bamboo sword first and then discarded it. He then meticulously checked each item, turning them in his hand and running his fingers across their surface.

When he reached the pebble, he finally looked up and met her eyes.

"What do these items have to do with your transformation?" he said while frowning. "Other than this pebble, none of these could lift a curse. Unless you are trying to suggest that you utilized this meditation mat?"

Elaine shook her head. "Most of the items Uncle discovered were useless like these, but don't you notice an unusual perfectness to them all?"

Dante turned his attention back to the pebble in his hand and hummed to himself as he traced its flawless surface. "I see what you mean."

Elaine suddenly saw a chance to add on top of the lie. "Flawless like our Voidmind blood." She winced slightly as Dante looked up again with a cold stare.

Just before she blurted something out to try and claim it was some type of joke as she couldn't take any more of his stare, Dante's gaze softened slightly, and he smiled. "Yes, exactly. All descendants of our great family are flawless, like this rock here and now you."

Sighing with relief, Elaine then realized she needed to continue the lie. Her eyes darted across the items before landing on the pebble in his hand. "When Uncle originally gave me that pebble, it was coated in void Qi."

"Void Qi, you say?" Dante held the pebble a little higher and inspected it further. "Where is the Qi now?"

"The void Qi on the pebble helped eat away the curse festering inside me. Without this curse, I would not have sullied the Voidmind bloodline and brought shame to you and Father." Elaine really wanted to strangle herself rather than play to his twisted ego, but what choice did she have?

"Interesting, how very interesting. So you are claiming a mere pebble was capable of such a feat?" Dante continued humming as he leaned back and rubbed the pebble with his thumb, clearly suspicious. "And where is Uncle now? I wish to ask him about this secret realm."

Elaine tensed up slightly. "Uncle went back into the secret realm moments after returning. He found a lot of fascinating things there he wished to study. I wouldn't be surprised if he didn't come out for months or even years."

"Do you know the whereabouts of this secret realm?"

Elaine shook her head. "Sadly, I do not, as he used void step to reach it. Uncle couldn't trust me with the knowledge of its location."

"Why not?" Dante raised a brow. "Merchants discover secret realms all the time."

"Dante, there was a pebble in that secret realm coated in void Qi that could free me of a curse that nobody even knew I had. That is no normal secret realm, but rather one that may hold an inheritance for our family." Seeing Dante's shock, she felt the need to calm him down. "Or at least that is my guess. Be patient; Uncle is strong and will be back in due time."

"I see." Dante nodded slowly. "That would explain why we couldn't reach Uncle despite calling multiple times. In truth, one of the reasons I came here to attend this amateur alchemy tournament was to inquire more directly about Uncle's whereabouts."

"Oh? And what were the other reasons?" Elaine asked.

Dante leaned a bit too close for her comfort. His ghoulish face was mere inches away. "You see, Sister, I'm glad you asked…" he whispered. "I came to conquer."

"Conquer? What do you plan to conquer here, Brother?" Elaine asked while clenching the seams of her dress.

"Everything. First, I will start with the alchemy tournament to spread our family's good name, and then I will rid Darklight City of the Redclaws." A look of pure disgust accompanied his outrageous claims. "You want to be rid of that vile filth that prances around claiming to be cultivators like us. Don't you?"

Elaine was about to reply with "Yes" to maintain the lie but felt the cold chains of her oath tighten around her soul at the thought.

So a lie that could cause harm to the Ashfallen Sect will be denied by the oath. What should I say?! Why is this bastard such a creep? Can't he stay over there in his chair and keep his weird fantasies to himself? Why does he feel the need to lean over and whisper in my ear?

"How will you deal with them, Brother?" Elaine decided to deflect the question while showing agreement in a roundabout way.

A burst of haunted laughter escaped his lips. "By slitting their throats, of course, like the pigs they are!"

Honestly, Elaine was struggling to take this lunatic seriously. Even for a scion, he was utterly insane.

"Father has tasked me with overtaking Darklight City now that the Ravenborne Grand Elder is gone and has given me full control over the family's forces." Dante leaned back and drummed his fingers on the liquid-void armrest, lost in thought.

Elaine bit her lower lip as she tried to find a way to reason him out of it. She disliked her brother and father, but her mother and some of her cousins, like Jasper, were nice, so she would rather not watch her family be humiliated and wiped out.

"What about the Patriarch?" Elaine reminded Dante. "Won't he be furious with you for killing another family?"

Dante snorted. "The Redclaws? Didn't you hear the Winterwrath, Ravenborne, and Evergreen families were killed off recently?"

"Yeah?"

"All of that death, yet there was no word from the Nightrose family. That's because they are all replaceable." Dante smirked. "The Patriarch could grab two random rogue fire cultivators off the street and have them start a new Redclaw family if he so pleased. Fire cultivators are abundant and serve little purpose other than war and alchemy."

Elaine hated to admit it, but Dante had a point. If the Blood Lotus Patriarch had to choose between punishing the Voidmind family, which held a rare affinity and a solid political standing, or the Redclaws, which helped fight in wars many decades ago but have fallen into mediocrity in recent years...the choice was obvious. He would pick the Voidmind family every darn time.

The problem lay in the fact that the Redclaws were no longer mediocre due to the Ashfallen Sect. In fact, Elaine would go so far as to claim the Ashfallen Sect was superior to the entire Blood Lotus Sect.

"Now let us cultivate the whispers of the void," Dante said as he ended the conversation and entered deep meditation.

While Elaine was busy cultivating the void Qi around her and lost in thought about how Dante was leading her entire family to its demise, there was a resounding knock throughout the void.

Dante snapped his fingers, and the doorway to the void chamber behind Elaine opened—revealing a distressed Clive.

"My Lord." The aged butler bowed. His forehead was sweating profusely, and he seemed to be panicking.

"Spit it out, Clive," Dante replied with a chill. "You are disturbing my conversation with my dear sister here."

"Right, my lord, I will be brief then." Clive straightened up and coughed. "The Redclaws...they are outside."

Clive then turned to look at Elaine. "And they demand Elaine's presence."

51
DOUBLE AGENT

Elaine reluctantly left the void chamber with Dante.

He was insane, and she felt sick listening to his nonsense. But it wasn't often that she was allowed access to the void chamber, which was one of the only places she could get access to a substantial amount of void Qi to cultivate with. While they talked, she had been cycling the abundant void Qi in the chamber throughout her body and filling her Soul Core.

If only I could cultivate like this without the help of an array. Dante may believe our affinity is superior to everyone else, but that's because he can ignore the massive downside I have to live with daily. The scarcity of naturally occurring void Qi made reaching even the first stage of the Soul Fire Realm at twenty-five years old a struggle.

Elaine sighed as her steps echoed through the corridor with pulsing silver lines interwoven in the walls. They all led back to the void chamber fed by an enormous and expensive array throughout the manor.

It took weeks for the chamber to accumulate void Qi, so its use was restricted to those in the family that the Grand Elder had deemed worthy. People like Jasper, the Elder, and maybe others from her family that were attending the Academy.

Not her. Elaine had been cut off from the family's resources due to her supposed lack of talent—which she now realized was a translation for having an impure spirit root. Ever since taking the truffles from the

Patriarch, her mind and body felt in perfect harmony and clean from impurities, making cultivation a breeze.

If only I could have unlimited access to a void chamber like my brother. Maybe then I could reach the Star Core Realm like he has.

"Do you have any idea why they are here?" Dante asked Clive, who was walking quickly beside them.

"The Redclaws said that Elaine was expected at an important meeting," Clive replied, "although they refused to mention what for."

Clive's words helped bring Elaine's thoughts back to the present. Now that she thought about it, why would the Redclaws be here? She hardly ever interacted with them, and she had no planned meetings as far as she knew.

Even from behind his tall figure, Elaine could hear Dante grinding his teeth in annoyance. "Vile scum, coming in here as if they own the place," he muttered under his breath as they continued through the manor.

"My Lord, please remember to keep your composure," Clive mentioned, which surprised Elaine. "Your father expects results. Which includes spreading the wonders of the alchemy technique you have been practicing."

Dante snorted. "We could achieve that without attending their little tournament. I don't know what Father is thinking—"

"My Lord, did he not inform you about the Silverspires?"

Dante paused mid-stride, causing all three of them to come to a halt. He looked down and glared at Clive. "Come again?"

"The alchemy tournament is being sponsored by the Silverspire family," Clive explained. "Rumors are that the Silverspire Grand Elder's children have entered some type of competition where they compete for profits. One of them has settled here in Darklight City and decided to pour their money into the tournament."

"Doesn't this hamper our plans? If we mess with the Silverspires, we risk angering the Nightrose family."

Elaine could barely contain a smile. Seeing Dante in such distress over the Silverspires while she had the image of the seventh son in her mind made the whole thing rather comical.

"Fret not. We had informants learn that the heir to grace Darklight City was the seventh son."

"Since when was there a seventh?" Dante asked.

"He's only a few years old, so he was likely birthed during your closed-door cultivation," Clive replied as they began walking again. "And since he's so young, we doubt that the Silverspire family expects much from him, nor does he hold much power over the Silverspires' forces."

"I see…" Dante mulled as he stroked his chin. "So I must still attend the tournament to show face and not mess with the Silverspire brat's investment. But once the tournament has finished, we can get away with taking over the city?"

Clive nodded. "That's the current plan, although we will continue intel-gathering operations in the meantime. There is always the possibility that we may need to postpone our invasion until after the Silverspire scion has left."

"What a waste of my precious time," Dante cursed, and the trio continued in silence until they reached the entrance hall. Waiting in the middle of the hall was a woman with crimson hair and a stern expression.

"Elder Margret, sorry for the wait." Clive switched his tone to that of a friendly host. "Lady Elaine was in discussions with Lord Dante."

"Sorry to interrupt, then," Elder Margret replied while studying their faces with her sharp gaze. "However, Elaine had previously agreed to a meeting, and it would disgrace the Voidmind name to break promises with fellow cultivators. Wouldn't you agree, Dante Voidmind?"

Elaine saw the corner of Dante's eye twitch, his hand clench and then unclench at his side. It was clear the way a Redclaw was speaking to him in his own home was angering him, but the gentlemanly demeanor he had honed over the decades won out—much to Elaine's relief.

"That is quite right, Elder Margret," Dante replied with a fake smile. "Elaine failed to inform me of such an arrangement, so please pardon my actions resulting in you having to waste your precious time coming to retrieve her."

Elaine stood in silence, but her brain was whirling the entire time, trying to decipher what this meeting could be about. Had she truly agreed upon a meeting and forgotten about it?

I said I would meet Douglas for lunch, but I doubt that warrants an Elder to collect me. So what is Elder Margret on about?

"Well then, we will leave without delay." Elder Margret gestured for Elaine to follow as she began to walk toward the ajar obsidian doors.

"Wait a minute," Dante said, pausing her steps.

"Yes?" Elder Margret had a blank face.

"What is the meeting for?" Dante glanced down at Elaine. "I have yet to conclude my conversation. So I hope she will be returning soon."

"Elaine is on the planning committee for the alchemy tournament," Elder Margret declared, and Elaine managed to hide her surprise.

Planning committee? What nonsense is this...unless...

Elaine began to connect the dots. The Redclaws worked for the Ashfallen Sect, so they may be here on the orders of the Patriarch. Did he want information out of her or something?

Other than that, all she could think was they had come to save her. But even that felt far-fetched. Her brother may be a creep and a bit insane, but he would never go too far against her as they shared the same parents...right?

Elaine bit her lip as she watched Dante and the Elder face off. Now that she thought about it more, maybe she should seize every opportunity to escape from her brother. If not for the allure of the void chamber, she would have tried to leave herself the moment their conversation had concluded.

Locking eyes with Elder Margret, Elaine finally broke her silence. "Oh, how foolish of me! I was on the way to the meeting when I was informed that my brother was arriving, so it completely slipped my mind."

Dante glanced at her with a look of doubt.

Elaine brushed off his gaze and stepped forward, leaving his side. "I will see you later, Brother. We can talk some other time."

"I will come with you." His cold voice sent a shiver down her spine. "You have yet to show me around, so this is a good opportunity."

Elaine barely contained a frustrated groan.

Why did I have to eat that darn truffle? If I hadn't, he would have treated me worse than a maid and demanded I leave his sight.

"That would be rather inconvenient, as I assume you are here to participate in the tournament?" Elder Margret's words gave Elaine a glimmer of hope. "Participants shouldn't be seen dabbling with the organizers. Otherwise, you may be accused by the other participating families of foul play."

"Where is the meeting being held?" Dante asked.

"The Academy," Elder Margret replied after a brief pause.

"Perfect." Dante's smile grew wider. "The academies across the Blood Lotus Sect are fully open to scions."

Elder Margret frowned. "Fine, you can come with us, but you must remain outside the meeting."

Elaine began to feel anxious. How were they supposed to conduct a meeting for a society that didn't even exist while Dante was waiting outside?

Trying to ignore those thoughts, she followed Elder Margret outside, surprised to discover it was late evening. A substantial amount of time had passed since she met her brother at the airship station.

Her gaze then lowered and paused on the tall, blond-haired girl wearing a black mask standing at the end of the pathway, being eyed cautiously by the manor guards.

"Who is this?" Dante asked Elder Margret.

"This is a cultivator hired by the Silverspire family to help the committee members get around." Elder Margret effortlessly lied straight to her brother's face. "Darklight City is one of the biggest cities in the Blood Lotus Sect in terms of size, and the Redclaws are a small family, so we required some assistance to keep everything running."

"Right…that makes sense," Dante nonchalantly replied. "And how does she plan to assist us exactly?"

Stella clicked her finger, and a portal manifested right behind her. Through its distorted view was the Academy that Elaine was very familiar with.

"A Star Core spatial cultivator," Dante muttered beside her, and Elaine could feel the mixture of awe and terror in his voice. "The Silverspire family never fails to impress me."

"The portal can only take one at a time," Stella said, gesturing for Dante to step forward. "Why don't you and Elder Margret go first?"

Elder Margret stepped through with a pop of air, and her distorted body became visible on the other side.

Dante followed suit, giving the portal a dubious look before stepping through.

"Elaine, are you okay?" Stella quickly asked. Clearly, she was using Qi to mask her voice, as none of the nearby guards reacted.

Elaine gave a slight nod.

"Phew, that's a relief. You had us all worried that your family would do something to you." Stella gestured for Elaine to go through the portal but kept speaking. "The meeting is entirely made up and was just a chance for us to catch up. If you want to say anything, just write it out in ancient runes on the table, and we will pretend you are our runic expert. Also, we are considering conducting the meeting in the dining room with Douglas so Dante can see that you are involved with us."

Elaine gave another slight nod as she felt warmth in her heart. It was nice to hear they had been looking out for her.

And their idea of doing it out in the open could be good. Dante will see me as even more valuable for making his invasion work as he can use me to gather insider information.

A thin smile appeared on Elaine's lips as she stepped through the portal and felt the sudden change in environment from the quite noble streets to the bustling noise of the Academy campus.

If I can orchestrate this perfectly, I might be able to seize the leftovers of my family for the Ashfallen Sect.

Moments later, the eye-catching group was strolling through the Academy grounds. Men and women of indecipherable ages, due to cultivation slowing down the aging process, walked by while chatting with one another. As Darklight City was one of the less desirable locations where mainly delinquents and talentless heirs were sent, there was a more casual air about the place, which Elaine appreciated but Dante seemed to despise.

His gaze roamed the groups with a look of disgust deepening on his face. One group consisting of three women returned his glare, but the presence of Elder Margret, a cultivator hailing from the current ruling family, helped to defuse the situation before someone got killed.

Death on Academy grounds was rare, as the perpetrator was often kicked out and then denied the cultivation resources provided at the Academy, which was, in turn, a death sentence. Not to mention the Academy grounds were also treated as politically neutral grounds where students from all families could unite and further the strength of the Blood Lotus Sect.

Elaine glanced up at the white stone buildings bathed in the late evening sun surrounding her. Atop their roofs were cultivators hired by the Academy to ensure the security of the students while also there if someone tried to steal cultivation resources.

All their eyes were glued on their group, and Elaine couldn't blame them for the looks Dante gave all the students that passed by.

Is he just glaring at them because he feels superior, or is he doing that to protect me?

Elaine did feel numerous people staring at her specifically, but they all shifted their gazes when Dante caught sight of them.

As they approached the dining hall, which wasn't so far from the massive oval building that served as the library, Elaine caught sight of a familiar black-haired man running toward them.

"Dante, is that you?" Jasper shouted down the hallway. "I went to the airship station, but you were already gone! I hear you created quite the scene, though."

"Jasper…so we meet again," Dante replied without a hint of warmth at seeing his childhood friend.

While the two talked, Elaine took the opportunity to sneak ahead into the dining hall with Elder Margret and Stella. Glancing around, she saw Douglas sitting in the corner alone at a table and picking idly at his food with a fork.

Joining the queue, she grabbed some food for herself from the self-service area as she felt a little hungry even after eating a sandwich this morning. She didn't have to eat, but there was a lack of food options on Red Vine Peak, so she planned to make the most of the food available here in the Academy.

The Ashfallen Sect really needs to hire some chefs.

Making her way over to the table and desperately trying to ignore the stares and whispers, she finally placed her tray on the table, causing Douglas to jolt from his trance.

"Elaine?" He glanced at her and smiled. "Glad to see you could make it. How's your brother?"

"He's fine…" Elaine's eyes darted to the doorway as she saw him wander in, half ignoring Jasper, who was hounding him with questions.

I can't talk about anything here. Dante's spiritual sense will easily pick it up. Oh yeah…Stella said I could pretend to be a formation expert and draw out runes.

Elaine pulled back the chair and sat down. Stella did the same and sat beside her. Her tray surprisingly had food on it, and Elaine wondered how she planned to eat the small mound of purple meat sausages and dark yellow potatoes.

Her answer came in the form of Stella picking up a sausage and then summoning a small rift that led inside her mouth behind the mask and passing the sausage through.

I should have seen that coming. Elaine sighed as she noticed Elder Margret gesturing for Dante and Jasper to sit a few tables away before she took the final seat at the table.

"Right, on behalf of the organizer who fell asleep by the tree," Elder Margret said, and Elaine immediately picked up on the fact she was referring to the Patriarch, "could you please draw out a runic formation for preserving the ingredients for the contestants?"

Elder Margret's spatial ring flashed with power, and a parchment, ink pot, and quill appeared beside Elaine on the table.

Without hesitation, she picked up the quill, dipped it in ink, and wrote out in the ancient runic language, which she only had a week of practice with:

End of the tournament, Voidmind invasion. Brother is the leader.

52
ALCHEMY EMPIRE

Ashlock observed the meeting occurring in the dining room from above. As he had planned, Elaine began to write on the parchment in ancient runes, which he and Stella could read without problem.

It was almost like a secret language, allowing them to communicate without looking suspicious.

Dante Voidmind sat a few tables away, and despite Jasper's constant attempts at starting a conversation with the scion, Dante's solid black eyes were set on Elaine's every move. Ashlock could also see ripples of Qi emanating from him as if he was a stone dropped into a calm lake.

Ashlock waited patiently for Elaine to write out three pretend attempts at an array. Clearly, she had zero knowledge about arrays, but Ashlock's {Language of the World} skill effortlessly translated the ancient runic language in his head.

"At the end of the tournament, there will be a Voidmind invasion led by my brother," Ashlock read, filling in the gaps where he deemed necessary. The message wasn't that shocking, as the reason for the scion's participation was dubious at best.

In a world where power was gained through closed-door meditation, why would a scion dare stray from the safety of their cave and waste time at some small-time alchemy tournament hosted in a backwater city by a small cultivation family?

For this very reason, they even advertised the tournament as having meager rewards and being open to rogue cultivators. Ashlock expected a few families to show up with maybe an aspiring alchemist or someone they were training just to show some face to the Redclaw family but to send a scion? An heir to the entire family? That was just nonsense.

It was another reason Ashlock had been so eager to rescue Elaine from that suspicious mansion. Not just for her own safety, as he had no idea what problems her improved looks and spirit roots could cause, but also because he wanted information. What was the real reason Dante Voidmind was here? He hadn't expected her to get such juicy details so quickly...

"An invasion, huh?" Ashlock mused as he eavesdropped on the meeting for a while longer. An hour passed, and the only other thing Elaine felt the need to write out in ancient runes translated to her being fine with watching over her brother as she also wanted access to something called the void chamber.

Ashlock wasn't sure what this void chamber was exactly, but he could make an educated guess. It was well known that cultivators needed to meditate in areas with Qi of their affinity floating around if they wished to advance. So this void chamber was likely a place of concentrated void Qi.

"Come to think of it, Elaine has been basically unable to cultivate the entire time she's been at Red Vine Peak as there's no void Qi around, and I didn't let her enter the Mystic Realm this time." Ashlock felt bad about this revelation. And it made him feel even worse, knowing that she was willing to stay with her brother just to have the opportunity to surround herself with some void Qi for once.

"Maybe I can build her a cultivation room." Ashlock sighed. "I still need to get Douglas to build that staircase and hollow out the mountain with rooms for everyone."

It had been so busy recently that none of them had found the time.

"After the alchemy tournament and defeating this Voidmind invasion, I will take a week off and get all hands on deck to turn this mountain into the greatest cultivation abode this realm has ever seen! I just need to find a way to somehow survive many Voidmind cultivators coming here hellbent on taking over my beloved shithole of a city."

Which was going to be no easy feat. Killing the Voidmind Elder had been a mixture of luck and Maple coming to the rescue. Neither of those were very reliable solutions or ones that could be utilized at scale against a full-on invasion. Maple—for all the power shoved in such a tiny body—got exhausted after just a few attacks.

"I do have {Consuming Abyss} this time 'round, which will let me fight void with void. But if the Voidmind Grand Elder makes an entrance, then we might run into problems." Ashlock hummed to himself as he thought of scenarios. None of them looked too good.

"Why do they even want to invade? Would there be a way to call it off? Reach a peace deal, perhaps?" If all they wanted was a chunk of Darklight City or access to the mines, Ashlock didn't mind letting them have some control for a while if it bought him enough time to get strong enough to steamroll them.

"Ah, whatever. Why can't they let us have our little tournament in peace?" Ashlock let out another long sigh in his mind. Alas, his wandering thoughts were interrupted by the sound of multiple chairs being pushed back on the dining room's tiled floor.

Stella, Douglas, and Elder Margret stood up from the table.

"Since the tournament is so soon, we must meet regularly," Elder Margret said as per the script he had told her earlier in the day. *"The dining room is too noisy, so let's meet in your study next time."*

Ashlock would raise his concerns and ask if peace was an option away from Dante's prying eyes at this next meeting.

"That's a great idea, Elder Margret." Elaine gave her a sweet smile. *"I will look forward to it."*

Elder Margret nodded, looked over to Dante's table to see his irritated expression, and then back to Elaine. *"Just because your brother is here doesn't mean you can skip out on attending the lectures you promised the Academy to teach due to your uncle's absence. It will be a good experience for you."*

Elaine bobbed her head in agreement. *"You're right—with Uncle gone for the last few weeks, I am sure the students have suffered greatly and fallen behind in their studies."*

"Will you be fine teaching them?" Douglas asked.

"Sure." Elaine was obviously refraining from showing Douglas any affection in front of Dante. *"I used to sit in on his lectures occasionally, and he left his lecture notes in my study so I could stand in as a substitute for a while without problems."*

"Perfect! Well, we must be on our way." Elder Margret bid farewell and led Douglas and Stella out of the dining room. Ashlock's gaze lingered in the room as he saw Dante stand up and then sit on Elaine's table.

Elaine only seemed slightly bothered and uncomfortable in her brother's presence as they exchanged words while eating.

"Since when did you learn about runes?" Dante questioned.

Elaine effortlessly answered, *"Dante, do you think I was idle these last few years? You would be surprised how much time I have to study random topics such as runes when I don't get to spend any of it cultivating."*

Dante opened his mouth to say something but then shut it. Elaine had seemingly answered numerous of his other questions with that one statement. A few minutes later, they concluded their meal, and the three Voidminds stood and exited the dining hall while drawing many stares and whispers.

Ashlock watched them walk back to their house, and once he saw they were all safely inside without incident, he sighed in relief. He had half expected Dante to kill someone for looking at him funny the entire way home.

With the sun beginning to set, signifying the coming of dusk, Ashlock returned his sights to Red Vine Peak. People were waiting for him.

Stella had brought the group back to the peak via a portal, and they were idly chatting while waiting for his presence. The moment he deactivated his skill and used his spiritual sight to look at the group, Stella seemed to somehow notice his attention.

"All right, the immortal is present. We can begin the real meeting." Stella clapped her hands and drew everyone's attention. *"With only a little over a week to go until the tournament, and while we have you here, Elder Margret, can you give us a summary of the tournament preparations?"*

"Certainly," Elder Margret said as she summoned a parchment to her hand. *"Other than the Voidmind family that has already arrived, the Starweaver, Terraforge, Skyrend, and Azurecrest families are still planning attendance and will arrive shortly."*

Switching out the parchment for another, she continued, *"Along with them, over a hundred rogue cultivators have sent in applications, so we will have a preliminary round where we will filter them out with a quick test."*

"A single testing round?" Douglas asked. "Seems rather harsh."

"Well, that leads to my next point..." Elder Margret said. "Cultivation resources used in alchemy are expensive. However, in this rare case, funding isn't the issue but rather the sourcing. We aren't sure if one of our political rivals caught wind of the tournament or if one of the other Silverspire scions wants to screw over their little brother, but there's simply no market out there for the amount of resources we need for the tournament."

That didn't sound good. How did the Redclaws plan to run an alchemy tournament without any ingredients to perform alchemy with?

"That is why we have a single testing round where we mainly test people's knowledge and give them a single low-grade herb to refine in front of a few judges to see their practical skills." Elder Margret sighed as she tapped the parchment in her hands. "But even with this odd formatting, we still might not have enough resources for a single round due to the hundreds of rogue alchemists attending."

Ashlock had many dragon coins and various artifacts and things he could sell if money was the problem. But according to Elder Margret, money wasn't the issue. Instead, it was a scarcity of resources—likely caused by a rival that wanted to see the tournament fail—that was the problem.

"Hold on. I have an idea..." Ashlock mused as he wrote on his trunk in lilac flames, 'Do you have a complete set of ingredients on hand?'

Stella translated the words.

Elder Margret nodded, and her ring flashed with golden light. A wooden box filled with porcelain bottles appeared between them.

"Everything an alchemist could need to make a low-grade Body Strengthening Pill is within this box."

"Why low grade?" Stella inquired as she crouched down and inspected the bottles.

"Cheap ingredients," Elder Margret replied. "Either they were grown in imperfect conditions leading to impurities, or they are easier to find alternatives of the ingredients required to make a high-grade pill."

Ashlock was glad they had one complete set of ingredients, as that was all he needed. He planned to create an alchemy empire with his system-granted production skills.

So a shortage of ingredients was no issue for him. He just needed to add the ingredients to his systems database to grow them with his

{Blooming Root Flower Production} skill or even create mushrooms and fruit that mimic or replace the ingredients.

Blanketing the area with his Qi, he began to use telekinesis to lift up the porcelain bottles and extract the ingredients from them. This was so he could analyze them for his system.

'Explain each one, Elder Margret,' Ashlock wrote, and she raised a brow, likely confused about his ignorance, but she obeyed anyway.

"The Body Strengthening Pill is an easy-to-make pill that has a few key ingredients. First is the Qi Flowing Grass." She pointed to some plain-looking grass with yellow tips. *"This grass is known for its properties to facilitate the flow of Qi through the body's spirit roots, so it's an essential ingredient for most pills."*

Ashlock had brought up his {Blooming Root Flower Production} menu and saw the Qi Flowing Grass added to his list of analyzed flowers. It did surprise him to learn that grass counted as flowers, but he wouldn't complain.

"Then we have the starlight lotus." Elder Margret pointed at a beautiful light blue flower that looked like it had twinkling stars growing on its petals. *"Despite how beautiful they look, they aren't too rare. They can be easily grown in lakes exposed to the night sky. This is important as they only bloom under starlight and absorb cosmic energy. Once plucked, they begin to degrade within days."*

"What is the effect of the starlight lotus?" Stella asked in awe. It was clear that Stella was interested in the flowers as she greedily absorbed all of the information. Was it due to that book about alchemy he had given her previously from the Voidmind Elder's stash?

"It's known to enhance the potency of pills by unblocking muscle tissue," Elder Margret said. *"This makes the starlight lotus vital for the Body Strengthening Pill as it will primarily target the muscle tissue."*

"I see." Stella crossed her arms as she contemplated. *"How do you know so much about alchemy, Elder Margret?"*

A look of nostalgia overcame the stern-faced woman. *"Back when the beast tides were less frequent and weaker, and war between the demonic sects raged, we were at our peak. Our versatility in providing firepower on the front lines while also being alchemists and smiths made us invaluable to the Blood Lotus Sect. Very few other affinities could do all that at once, so we thrived in the war era. But once the beast tides became more frequent and stronger with every wave, we had to start* moving. Not every location the Blood Lotus Sect moved to had good access to abundant fire Qi, and the demonic sects saw less need to wage war over territory as that land would have to be conceded to the beast tides anyway."

Ashlock felt his mind freeze. It had been mentioned in the past about how this was the strongest beast tide yet. But now that Elder Margret laid it out, he became concerned. Senior Lee had told him the world was dying. And during those flashbacks of previous world trees, he distinctly remembered the feeling of the realms around his roots turning into hellscapes overflowing with demonic Qi. By a dying world, was this what Senior Lee meant?

"Oh, look at me rambling away about the past..." Elder Margret sighed as she looked up at Ashlock's canopy that blocked the setting sun. *"To answer your question, we have a long history in the art of alchemy. But training up new alchemists is expensive, so as we faded into obscurity in this post-war era, we had to let go of alchemy and smithing to focus on keeping our firepower high just to survive out here."*

Ashlock had pushed his concerns about the world to the back of his mind and listened to the old woman's tale. He felt sorry for them. In peaceful times like now, those families specializing in something like the Silverspires with their spatial rings will thrive. It was only in times of war when resources and manpower were limited that the all-rounders were preferred.

"Most of our knowledge has been lost or sold throughout the many times we have moved," Elder Margret said as she tapped her head with her finger. *"But I still remember a lot of it—which I try to pass down to those who will listen to me."*

Stella grinned. *"Well, tell me all you know!"*

Elder Margret lightly chuckled. *"All right, let's see... The main component of the pill is the Dragon Marrow."*

She pointed to a bottle with white jelly streaming out of it. *"Despite its grand-sounding name, it can be found in most mammal-type monsters in the Soul Fire Realm or above. However, the problem lies in the fact it can only be harvested from monsters that are days away from ascending to the next stage in their cultivation. Otherwise, the bone marrow won't have enough Qi to be considered Dragon Marrow."*

Stella nodded her head. *"That makes a lot of sense. We draw all the*

Qi lying around in our bodies into our cores to push them over the edge to reach the next stage."

"Indeed, it's a hassle, and with the increasing strength of the monsters out in the wilderness due to the incoming beast tide and with the cultivators having to travel in larger groups and be better equipped, it's driving up the cost."

Ashlock looked at the bone marrow and mentally frowned. That was definitely an ingredient he could not grow, as it had to come straight from a monster.

"But I can drag many monsters through portals without sending out a group of cultivators, so it shouldn't be too hard to source enough of the stuff." Ashlock was starting to realize just how much of a cheat his existence was. He may not be able to move, but that was a small price to pay for the skills of the system.

"And that's it." Elder Margret sighed again. "These are the three most basic ingredients needed for the Body Strengthening Pill, which was the pill we planned to get the contestants to concoct for the final round. The Qi Flowing Grass is the ingredient we have in abundant supply. It's the Starlight Lotus and Dragon Marrow that's the problem."

Ashlock wrote, 'Elder Margret, please return tomorrow with two aspiring alchemists from your family. I have a solution to this problem,' on his trunk after confirming he had added the Qi Flowing Grass and Starlight Lotus to his production menu.

It was time to expand the farm in the cavern, as producing thousands of these resources was a simple affair for Ashlock.

And after listening to Elder Margret's tale, he decided there was no need to wait for the tournament's conclusion to start production. Even after unlocking the cauldron fruit, he had refrained from using the Redclaws as he hadn't trusted them.

But times had changed, and the Redclaws were now an irreplaceable part of the Ashfallen Sect. He no longer had any qualms about going all out to improve and level them up.

It was about time he returned the Redclaws to their former glory, one flower, fruit, and mushroom at a time.

53
CELESTIAL MONOLITH

Douglas looked over his shoulder as he saw the distorted sunset on Red Vine Peak through the shimmering portal. Stella gave him a little wave before the portal snapped closed behind him with a pop of air that ruffled his short hair.

With a sigh, Douglas surveyed the large cavern that encompassed his view. His wandering eyes were naturally drawn to the sound of moving water. Built along the stream's banks that ran through the cavern's center were farms with mushrooms and flowers. Stone bridges connected the two sides over the slow-moving stream, and on the far side were earthen bowls that contained a large, open-top black fruit that resembled a cauldron.

The whole place was dimly lit by the mushrooms sprouting from cracks in the ceiling and walls, emitting a soft blue glow. However, there was a recently added light source. Looking to the left, Douglas saw the massive opening that led to the hole that ran throughout the entire mountain, all the way to the peak.

It was almost nighttime, so only a slight orange glow made it this far down.

"Time to get to work," Douglas grumbled as he trudged into the cavern's center. He had made good progress on setting up something to impress the Silverspires last time, but now that he looked at it again, it was half-assed at best.

Well, I was given the entire night to prepare the place for the alchemist tomorrow. I should be able to turn this into a place I am proud of by then.

After all, he was now a few stages higher in the Soul Fire Realm. He flexed his Soul Core, and light brown flames manifested on his fingertips. Just weeks ago, his soul flame was murky, full of impurities. But now, it was clear and flowed effortlessly through his body.

Dropping to one knee, he placed his aflame fingers on the ground and closed his eyes. Humming to himself, he felt his earthen Qi easily penetrate the rock, and soon he had a mental map of the entire cavern in his mind. Every nook and cranny became crystal clear to him, as if the cavern had become an extension of his own body.

With a grin, he forced his sixth-stage Soul Fire to overwhelm the rock around him and mold it to his will. The entire place began to shake as the hard rock softened like clay and shifted around to fulfill the changes he willed upon the world.

Thousands of meters of rock above him began to weigh down on the now-softened stone ceiling of the cavern. Luckily, with a combined effort of his own Qi and the thousands of roots from the Patriarch holding the whole place together, Douglas managed to prevent the cavern from collapsing on his head.

Bridges sprouted from the ground like worms of rock over the river and farms. Despite the cavern's grand size, he planned to have a multi-layered farm as the cavern had limited floor space. So the bridges over the farms were the first step to this plan.

The mushrooms could grow on the lower layer, and then plants could bloom on the upper level. Douglas wondered how the Patriarch made flora grow underground when he was clearly a spatial affinity cultivator. But he wasn't going to complain.

As the rumbling of the cavern finally stopped, he reeled back his Qi and stood up. Glancing around, he felt satisfied. He had created a second layer of stone like a massive bridge over the existing farm held up by pillars. Many gaps allowed for stone ramps that led up to the higher level.

He had even created an aqueduct to carry water between the plants on the higher and lower levels. Douglas let out a tired breath as he noticed the absence of the orange light cascading down the hole that led to the surface, signifying it was night.

His soul core felt half used, and it was clear a few hours had gone by while he had been shaping the cavern to his plan. Going for a walk around the place, he followed a pathway that led him through a mushroom farm. Stone pillars marked the corners of each soil patch, holding up the structure overhead.

Reaching a ramp, he wandered up to the upper layer. As far as the eye could see, there were hundreds of bare patches of soil with pathways between them.

"The Patriarch should populate these with plants in the morning," Douglas said aloud, stroking his chin. His voice echoed around the cavern, and sudden loneliness overtook him.

His hand dropped to his side—it felt cold without the warmth of Elaine's hand. This cavern also felt far emptier without her bright company.

Feeling his shoulders sag, Douglas remembered the face of Elaine's brother. Something about his ghoulish appearance and air of superiority irked him. It was hard to believe they were related at all.

His ring flashed with power, and the black truffle Stella had gifted him materialized in his hand. He couldn't tell if this was a roundabout way of her calling him ugly. "Heh...that's definitely something she would do." Douglas stowed it away again, chuckling to himself. He didn't feel a need to use it just yet.

"Now, what should I do for the rest of the night?" He hadn't expected to finish his plan for the cavern so soon. The difference between his past and present power was unbelievable. Not only had his stage gone up, but his purified soul fire allowed his Qi to easily penetrate the rock and move it to his will with a fraction of the effort.

A brief flicker of pride and perhaps arrogance clouded his mind.

Should I try and challenge one of the girls to a duel?

Douglas slapped himself. That was stupid. They would beat him with their eyes closed and one arm behind their backs. He knew all too well how earth Qi corrupted his mind, as did all Qi types. It was especially noticeable after a sudden leap in power.

He decided the best way to stave off the loneliness and quell his muscle-brained thoughts was to empty out his Soul Core on something. Anything. He glanced around for a distraction, and his eyes eventually landed on the giant hole leading to the mountain peak.

"The hole is far too big for a staircase, but what if I create a vertical garden in the center?" His fingers itched to get started, so he waltzed over with a grin.

Ashlock tossed off the grogginess of sleep like a warm blanket on a Sunday morning and spread his spiritual sight in all directions to catch up on what he missed while asleep.

After sending Elder Margret back to the White Stone Palace last night, he'd told Douglas to prepare the cavern for many more plants he planned to grow once the sun rose. Not that he needed sunlight to grow plants, but he didn't want to tell Douglas that he was sleeping while the man was working hard.

Looking around, he saw Stella and Diana cultivating quietly under their chosen trees on opposite sides of the courtyard. A hazy mist of water Qi swirled around Diana, and the air around Stella seemed slightly distorted due to the spatial Qi.

Meanwhile, Douglas was nowhere to be seen.

"Is he still working?" Ashlock wondered. "I only asked for him to add a few more farms. It shouldn't have taken him that long."

A sudden rumbling from the giant hole in the courtyard's center drew Ashlock's attention. "What the…" Ashlock's vision blurred as he followed one of his roots that poked into the hole.

Surprisingly, he saw a pillar of gray stone rising in the center. Its diameter was less than the hole through the mountain, leaving a wide gap.

Ashlock could cast his sights down into the depth of the hole as he had roots running down its side and estimated that the freshly raised pillar was a few thousand meters tall, which only brought it slightly past the cavern area.

Red Vine Peak was many thousands of meters tall, after all, and Ashlock would have been amazed if Douglas had the Qi on hand to create a ten-thousand-meter-tall pillar that was fifty meters in diameter.

Through his spiritual sight, Ashlock caught sight of Douglas, who looked so small from up here as he climbed up a spiraling staircase he had begun building into the outer wall of the hole.

Ashlock was confused. Why was he building the staircase along the wall of the hole that was very wide instead of on the pillar?

Douglas stood on the staircase, his arm resting against the hole's wall and breathing deeply as if he had just run a marathon. Clearly, creating such a structure had taken a lot out of him.

Ashlock then noticed empty stone troughs built into the pillar, and everything became clear.

"Elder Margret claimed the Starlight Lotus requires starlight to bloom. I haven't grown that many flowers yet, so I assumed I could grow flowers wherever I needed...but maybe that's not the case." Ashlock knew he could provide nutrients and water to flowers through his roots from elsewhere, so he was confident in keeping most plants alive underground. But if a flower required something like a starlight? How could he provide that through roots? Unless Qi somehow made it work anyway.

"Something to test, then," Ashlock mused.

It was clear Douglas had built the pillar as a place for him to grow the Starlight Lotus in more ideal conditions, so Ashlock sent his roots to begin crawling up the side of the pillar and start emptying water into the stone troughs. Lotuses needed to grow in ponds, so this was a good substitute.

A while went by, and Ashlock had finally filled most of them with water that he had pumped from a lake at the mountain's base. However, as he opened his flower production menu to populate them with the Starlight Lotus, he felt something through his connection with Bob the Ent.

Closing the menu, he cast {Eye of the Tree God}, and sure enough, three cultivators with crimson hair were at the entrance to the cavern tunnel guarded by Bob.

"Elder Margret, are you sure we are at the right place?" a teenager standing beside the stern woman asked in a small voice. The boy clearly had doubts but was too scared to question the strict Elder with any confidence.

"Of course we are," Elder Margret snapped, causing the boy to shrink and stand beside a girl who looked almost identical to him in every way.

Were they twins? They really looked far too similar to be merely brother and sister. That aside, it was time to welcome them in. It would be rude to keep them waiting.

Returning his sights up to Red Vine Peak, Ashlock debated waking

Stella out of her meditation to deal with the visitors, but her peaceful face deterred him from such action.

Diana also seemed busy, and her ancient language studies were only partly done, leaving him with Larry.

"Larry, go lead Douglas to the tunnel. We have visitors."

A nearby demonic tree shook as the monstrous spider crawled out, his spindly legs hitting the ground one at a time as his many red eyes glanced around.

To make things faster, Ashlock summoned a portal that would lead Larry straight to Douglas.

Elder Margret stared at the weird wooden wall that blocked off the entrance to the cavern she had been informed about. After a few minutes, doubt began to fester at the back of her mind.

Despite her confident response to one of the twins she had brought with her, she had only been informed of this place via vague instructions and was unsure if she was supposed to stand here, knock on the door, or just walk straight through.

The only reason she played with the ludicrous idea of walking straight through was the wall's slimy texture, making her think she could push her hand through.

Just wait a few more minutes, Elder Margret reassured herself as she tapped her foot. *We did arrive a little earlier than expected. Or maybe this is a test of our patience, as that is one of the many virtues of alchemy—*

Her thoughts were silenced as the wall began to shift—toward them. Elder Margret hated to admit she took a few steps back alongside the twins.

The gray wall pulsed with a lilac hue as if a flickering candle was nestled somewhere deep within. There was a squelching noise as the wall morphed and freed itself from the tunnel. The gray mass surged forward, formed limbs, and then stood up.

Moments later, the sun was blocked out by a towering five-meter-tall Ent made from gray slime resembling wood.

Between its legs was a dim tunnel illuminated with a blue glow. Elder Margret was about to take a cautious step toward the now-exposed tunnel, but her Qi-empowered eyes noticed something big moving in the shadows.

And then she saw a second figure also emerging, this one smaller and humanoid.

Elder Margret felt Olivia's hand grip her robe when an ashen-furred leg the size of a small tree emerged from the tunnel, followed by another leg and then a head with many scarlet eyes that looked curiously around.

"Yes, yes, I'm coming," a gruff voice echoed out of the tunnel, and then a hulking man wearing a black robe with a large hood and mask emerged into the morning sunlight beside the monstrous spider.

"Relax, it's just the Underlord and the spirit beast of the Ashfallen Sect," Elder Margret whispered to Olivia and Oliver, the twins she had brought with them. They were both young, at fourteen years old, and had shown a lot of promise and interest in alchemy.

Elder Margret knew of Douglas's real name and face as they had met in the dining hall a day earlier, but he clearly wanted to keep his identity hidden, so she used the title he had been introduced with previously.

"Why did you lead me here?" Douglas asked the spider in an annoyed tone and then glanced around. His masked gaze eventually landed on her. "Elder Margret? Is that you?"

Elder Margret could tell this man was exhausted, even with the mask and hood, from his tone of voice and slumped shoulders. She gave him a nod. "Yes, it's me, and I brought along the two aspiring alchemists the immortal asked for."

"Oh!" Douglas seemed to wake up, gesturing for them to follow him. "Come in, come in."

He turned, and his form vanished back down the tunnel. Elder Margret began to walk and noticed Olivia and Oliver exchanging a nervous glance before falling in line a step behind her.

A thin smile appeared on her lips as the tunnel's darkness enveloped them, and they descended into the cavern. Reaching the base, Elder Margret only saw Douglas standing there. The spirit beast had clearly gone off somewhere else.

"Welcome to the cavern." Douglas's voice drew the attention of Olivia and Oliver, who curiously glanced around at the sea of mushrooms growing in neat plots of dirt.

Elder Margret glanced up at the five-meter-high ceiling and wondered where the rest of the vast cavern had gone. After all, they had taken shelter down here to escape the Dao Storm a few months ago.

"Before I show you around, what are your names?" Douglas asked the twins.

"Oliver."

"Olivia." They answered at the same time.

"Err, right. Your parents have a good sense of humor." Douglas chuckled, drew back his hood, and removed his mask. "My name is Douglas. I manage most of the Ashfallen Sect's construction projects and will be your tour guide today."

Both of them nodded.

"We will be working a lot together in the future, so let me know if you have any problems. Anyway, onward with the tour. Please follow me, and don't stray off the paths."

Douglas then led them down the darkened path. Elder Margret summoned a fireball to her hand to help light the way so the youngsters wouldn't accidentally stray off the trail and crush the mushrooms underfoot.

Elder Margret was surprised to feel the path curving upward into a ramp, and soon enough, she was on an upper level and looking out across a vast flatland of bare soil patches that reached all the way to the cavern walls.

Douglas gestured around. "This is where the Qi Flowing Grass—"

A sudden wave of power blanketed the area, sending a shiver down Elder Margret's spine. She blinked and then blinked again—unable to register what she saw.

The numerous soil patches exploded as thousands of yellow-tipped grass stalks sprouted all at once. The vast barren land had been transformed into a lush grassland within seconds.

Elder Margret stood witness to this unfathomable miracle, her jaw hanging in disbelief, the mechanics of closure forgotten in the face of an incomprehensible domain over nature.

"—will grow." Douglas finished his sentence with a smirk.

"How…" Oliver murmured.

"So this is the power of an immortal." Olivia mirrored her brother's disbelief.

"Come on, a bit of grass isn't that exciting." Douglas began to wander toward a large hole in the cavern off to the side with sunlight pouring down it.

Elder Margret had to disagree, but she followed along anyway—grateful that the twins had been too busy being shocked to catch sight of her shameful face of awe.

Calm yourself. You have seen things as ridiculous as this before. You went into a pocket realm, for heaven's sake!

Shaking away the nonsense plaguing her mind, Elder Margret mindlessly followed Douglas until he stopped.

"Whoa," Olivia said as she glanced over the edge into the abyss below.

They were currently standing on the steps of a staircase and looking at a stone pillar covered in black vines that seemingly led all the way into the darkest depths of the earth.

"And this is where the Starlight Lotus will grow," Douglas declared with a smile.

Elder Margret uttered a disbelieving, murmured, "Impossible." Her eyes, however, remained unwaveringly riveted on the pillar. She was skeptical, resistant to accept the potential for the same miraculous spectacle to unfurl again.

Despite her doubt, the impossible unfolded once more before her as that same godly pressure descended.

The stone pillar pulsed with life, bursting into a breathtaking spectacle as innumerable Starlight Lotus blossomed from the water-filled crevices. Their magnificent petals, a celestial blue, unfolded like a million stars had descended from the heavens to bloom, decorating the pillar as if it was a cosmos rising up from hell and challenging the heavens.

A once-unremarkable stone pillar had transformed into a stunning canvas of floral brilliance, a monolith shimmering with the cosmic beauty of the night sky—an ethereal celestial garden.

Elder Margret collapsed to her knees as she realized the event's gravity. To the immortal, an inconvenience as minor as sourcing Starlight Lotus could be solved with nothing more than a wave of his hand.

She had never felt so small yet full of hope in all her long life.

54
A PROFOUND PILL

Ashlock felt a little prideful watching Elder Margret's and the twins' reactions to him growing cultivation resources in the blink of an eye. The system may refrain from giving him many powerful attack skills, but it didn't shortchange him regarding production skills.

He was a tree, after all. A being that was here to nurture the world and those around him as well as kill those that threaten his existence. Luckily, even with his system being frugal with attack skills, he could use his spatial Qi in any way he pleased, and as his cultivation realm increased, so did his ability to chop things in half with half-formed rifts.

Those thoughts aside, and with his feeling of pride fleeting, Ashlock could finally take in the entire situation as he had only just woken up, and already so much had occurred.

The hundred-meter-wide hole that went through the entire mountain and into the depths below now had a fifty-meter-wide pillar of stone blooming with Starlight Lotus rising in its center. Neither the pillar nor the stairs built into the outside wall of the hole reached the peak yet. But Ashlock was sure Douglas could reach those heights in due time.

"He did completely renovate the farm to the point I can hardly even recognize the cavern anymore, so he must be exhausted." Ashlock's sights shifted through his vast root network, and he looked at the farm from various angles.

The lower floor was a sea of mushrooms that thrived in the darkness. However, these mushrooms only grew on the west side of the river that ran through the cavern, as on the east side, there were the cauldron fruits inside earthen bowls. Then over both sides was a second floor held up by pillars with the Qi Flowing Grass growing in many soil plots.

"Wait...I now have some aspiring alchemists and someone who knows about alchemy here. And I even have access to most of the ingredients I need to make a pill." Ashlock began to get eager. He finally had a way to use the cauldron fruit he had unlocked when his {Qi Fruit Production} skill was upgraded to A-grade all those moons ago.

"I might have been able to mess around with it or have Stella try alchemy after killing the Grand Elder, but I decided to just leave it be for a while as we were all busy with other things." Ashlock sighed. It had been a very hectic few weeks, and keeping track of everything demanding his attention was getting hard.

"Let's see... I must prepare for the imminent Voidmind invasion and the alchemy tournament. I should probably expand my roots in all directions, advance my cultivation, kill monsters for credits, practice spatial techniques, build up Red Vine Peak..."

Ashlock sighed again. Those all sounded like great uses of his time, but with alchemists finally here in the cavern, the wonders of alchemy were calling to him. He had complete confidence in his ability to perform alchemy with his overpowered production skills to grow the best ingredients and the cauldron fruit that allowed him to produce the highest-grade pills from the provided ingredients due to his soul flame's purity.

The only things that had been holding him back were a lack of knowledge about pill recipes and actually getting his nonexistent hands on the cultivation resources so he could grow them himself.

But with Elder Margret's presence, who seemed to be an encyclopedia of knowledge regarding the art of alchemy, he felt confident creating some fantastic pills.

"If only I had trusted the Redclaws sooner," Ashlock mused as he switched views back to Elder Margret and the twins, who had only just recovered from their shock. "Maybe then I wouldn't have needed to conduct the alchemy tournament."

Although the primary purpose of the alchemy tournament had been to find a talented alchemist to live on Red Vine Peak, the tournament did have some other goals. Such as establishing the Redclaws as the powerhouse over Darklight City, and he also wanted to form some contact with the merchants as he would need someone to sell the pills he made. After all, Darklight City was too poor to afford the top-grade pills he planned to create.

"I also wouldn't have formed a business relationship with the Silverspires if not for the tournament. That alone makes all of this worth it."

Ashlock naturally didn't know the full extent of the Silverspire family, but from what he could gather, they were one of the top dogs here in the Blood Lotus Sect, and if anyone could afford his pill supply, it would be them.

"And for just a fifteen-percent cut, they are allowing me to conduct business under the Silverspire name. Even the tournament is protected by their name." Ashlock hummed as his mind drifted down a rabbit hole of thoughts.

He was brought back to reality a while later when he heard Elder Margret speak.

"Can I inspect one?" she asked Douglas with a slight tremble in her voice.

"A Starlight Lotus? Sure, that should be fine." Douglas turned and then paused as he realized something that Ashlock also noticed at the same time.

The hole was a hundred meters wide, yet the pillar was only fifty meters in diameter. Although the stone steps that jutted out of the hole wall were wide enough for many people, there was still a considerable gap between the pillar decorated in Starlight Lotuses and them.

Ashlock was about to use telekinesis to save Douglas from embarrassment but paused when he saw the man close his eyes. Earth Qi rippled out, traveling all the way into the depths of the mountain and then rocketing up the pillar.

The nearest stone trough on the pillar suddenly broke away like a desk drawer. It wasn't terribly fast, but it eventually arrived beside them. The stone stretched out many meters and defied gravity, but with Douglas's earth Qi rippling across its surface and giving it immense strength, there were no issues.

Elder Margret stepped forward after a nod from Douglas and began to harvest all of the Starlight Lotuses growing within the trough with utmost care. It was almost mesmerizing watching the stern woman cycling her Qi and carefully burning the lotus with her soul fire just below the bud so the stalk was left behind.

After the third one, she paused and stood back. Her spatial ring flashed with power, and a red fruit appeared in her hand. Without hesitation, she bit into the fruit, and Ashlock came to a realization.

"Isn't that my fruit with the {Florist's Touch} skill?"

Sure enough, a subtle glow formed around her hands, and she got back to work on clipping the Starlight Lotus buds with her soul fire that now looked like blades. It was all so effortless compared to before. The Starlight Lotuses practically leaned into her hands as if wanting to be freed from their stalks.

To Ashlock, they had looked like typical plants other than their starry petals. However, after seeing the difference between before and after Elder Margret ate the fruit, he realized just how difficult harvesting Qi-filled plants was.

It was as if the Qi within their bodies gave them a sliver of survival instincts. When Elder Margret had chopped the first two, the plant's Qi had gone to fight off the soul flames attempting to burn through its stalks.

A while later, the glow faded from Elder Margret's hands; she had a satisfied grin as she inspected the flower buds in her hand. *"I don't know how the immortal did it, but these Starlight Lotuses are of the highest quality. It's like they were grown on a Qi-dense lake under constant moonlight for centuries."*

Elder Margret's words confirmed something at the back of Ashlock's mind. He had just bloomed these Starlight Lotuses within seconds during the early morning sun—yet she had claimed earlier that these flowers could only bloom under starlight and supposedly absorbed cosmic energy.

Ashlock didn't have cosmic energy as far as he knew, nor did he grow these flowers under starlight. Therefore the only explanation was that he could grow them anywhere—even underground.

"They did take a stupidly large chunk of Qi to grow, though," Ashlock mused. Spending Qi was getting increasingly annoying as he wished to advance his cultivation stage, but that would never happen with him spending Qi like this.

"Cultivating can wait until the winter. This is too important to skip out on for now. The fact I can grow spiritual plants this easily is beyond a cheat. Can't I lay my eyes on any plant and grow as many of them as I want?" Ashlock doubted it. These were the most basic type of plants possible. One was even glorified grass, yet they had taken half of his Qi reserves to spawn.

If growing simple Qi Flowing Grass was this costly, what about some plants that the gods liked to put in their tea? Would he even have the Qi reserves to grow a single petal?

"If there wasn't a sudden shortage of spiritual plants due to rival families wanting to mess with the tournament, I would take out a loan and buy as many plants as possible. Actually, couldn't the Silverspires help me here?"

It was worth a shot, but that could wait. For now, he wanted to try alchemy or at least watch someone else perform it.

While he had been thinking, the group had moved on to the Qi Flowing Grass, and once again, Elder Margret was harvesting the grass by wrapping her hand in soul fire and pulling out the grass in fistfuls.

Beside her were the twins, Oliver and Olivia. They were copying the Elder's movements and harvesting the grass. However, unlike the Elder, who effortlessly pulled out many grass stalks at once, they struggled a lot more and resorted to focusing on one stalk at a time.

It was rather amusing watching the two youngsters wrestling with an overgrown grass stalk as it fought back and strengthened itself with its Qi.

"They appear to be in the first stage of the Soul Fire Realm, meaning they successfully formed their Soul Cores only recently." Ashlock looked a little closer and noticed their crimson flames were very pure. "I can see why they were interested in alchemy with spirit roots that pure. However, they will struggle with a soul flame that weak."

Luckily, Ashlock had a solution for almost any weakness in a cultivator. Whether it was heart demons, impure spirit roots, or overall weakness, he knew a cure. He mentally prescribed meditation near the fire trees and entry to the next Mystic Realm for the twins.

"What do we do now, Elder?" Olivia asked while her brother wrestled with a grass stalk behind her and fell onto his back with a huff.

Elder Margret looked to Douglas. *"I assume there are cauldrons somewhere?"*

"Sure there are." Douglas nodded and gestured for them to follow him. *"You can take any ramp down to the lower level and then, if you need to, cross the river and head toward the earthen bowls."*

Elder Margret raised a brow while following Douglas but didn't comment further. The group of four didn't end up needing to cross the river, as the nearest ramp led them down to the east bank of the river.

"*Here we are.*" Douglas paused beside one of the bowls. "*There are small stairs beside it that you two might wish to use to get a better view as the cauldron is rather large.*"

Oliver and Olivia exchanged a glance before they curiously climbed onto the step and glanced over the side.

"*What is that?*" Oliver blurted. "*Is this really a cauldron?*"

"*It does kind of look like one, though...just more natural?*" Olivia tilted her head. "*Elder Margret, is there a way to grow a cauldron?*"

"*Not that I know of.*" The stern woman shook her head as she approached the bowl and peered over its side. "*They are usually made of Qi-infused metal, so I can't see how you could grow one... What is this?*"

All pairs of eyes looked to Douglas, but he just shrugged. "I have no idea."

Elder Margret returned to scrutinize Ashlock's cauldron fruit. He hadn't realized it was that weird, but now that he thought about it, he understood their reaction.

"Should I wake Stella and send her down there to explain?" Ashlock grumbled. He really needed to make it mandatory for every Redclaw to learn the ancient language. There was literally no excuse why they couldn't with the help of the {Language Comprehension} fruit.

"In fact, I will do that right now." Ashlock's vision blurred, and he soon overlooked the study in the White Stone Palace, where the Redclaw Grand Elder sat back in his chair with his eyes closed.

Ashlock flooded the room with spatial Qi, which made the Grand Elder's eyes snap open. Ashlock ignored him and used telekinesis to pick up a fountain pen that seemed very expensive and began to scribble on a blank piece of parchment left on the desk.

The Grand Elder had jumped up, sending his chair crashing behind him and crimson flames surrounding his body. He eyed the floating pen with suspicion and tracked its every movement.

By decree from the Ashfallen Sect:

All Redclaw family members must learn the ancient runic language within the next month. Make use of the fruit provided to you and come and collect more if needed.

Upon finishing his message, the pen fell to the side with a thud, and

Ashlock withdrew his presence back to the cavern as he didn't want to miss what was happening there.

"*Why not give it a try?*" Douglas said. "*It's not like we have a limited amount of plants to experiment with.*"

"*I guess I could try,*" Elder Margret said. "*Do you have any Dragon Marrow?*"

This was an area of alchemy that Ashlock didn't have total dominion over. Basically, any ingredient that could be grown wasn't an issue. But something like the Dragon Marrow, which had to be sourced from a monster that was on the cusp of ascending to the next stage or realm, would require some effort on his part to gather.

"*I don't believe so,*" Douglas replied.

"All right, I will only create one batch of pills, as we have a very limited supply of Dragon Marrow." Elder Margret ushered the twins to pay attention as she gathered all the ingredients on the edge of the earthen bowl.

"*Oliver and Olivia, pay attention, okay?*" The pair nodded, so she continued. "*The first step of alchemy is to know the recipe for the desired pill. In this case, we have gathered the three ingredients needed for a Body Strengthening Pill.*"

She then picked up the jar containing the Dragon Marrow and poured the jelly into her hand. "Second step is to purify the gathered ingredients. I will start with the Dragon Marrow."

Crimson soul fire blanketed her hands and the jelly. Everyone, including Ashlock, watched in anticipation as Elder Margret closed her eyes and then explained, "*The art of purification takes a long time and practice to master. Essentially, I must push my soul fire into ingredients to remove the impurities. This is difficult because if I am not careful, my fire Qi will react with the residual Qi left in the ingredient that makes it useful for alchemy in the first place and corrupt it. The moment my Qi taints the ingredient, it becomes useless.*"

Ashlock could see tiny beads of sweat accumulating on her forehead as she guided her Qi through the jelly with expert control. Looking closely, he could see a black substance, almost like soot, carried away from the jelly by the flames.

A tense minute passed, and eventually, Elder Margret let out a sigh of relief and opened her eyes. Her soul fire receded back into her body, leaving an almost translucent blob of bone marrow behind.

"I could have done a better job as the speed of purification also affects the quality of the ingredient. But overall, this was a good result." Elder Margret carefully reached down and placed the jelly in the cauldron fruit.

"Next up would be the Qi Flowing Grass. The order isn't that important for this particular recipe, but I have personally always followed this order, so remember it well." Elder Margret picked up the grass in question, and her flames reappeared.

A tense ten minutes went by as Elder Margret kept her eyes shut as her crimson flames danced up and down the grass stalk. Eventually, Ashlock saw the green stem begin to turn black and then disintegrate shortly after into a pile of dust.

"Elder...what happened?" Oliver whispered, worried she would snap at him.

"Amazing. I simply can't believe it," Elder Margret muttered while looking at the pile of ash.

"Was there something wrong with the Qi Flowing Grass?" Douglas asked. He had a look of concern as he studied everyone's faces.

She shook her head. *"Nothing wrong. If anything, the ingredient is so perfect that I struggled to improve it. Only the slightest hint of corruption was present within the grass stalk."*

"So, Elder, why did you turn it to dust?" Olivia asked while inspecting the pile of soot.

Elder Margret ruffled the young girl's hair. *"I let my competitiveness overwhelm me. It's the fate of all alchemists to see the slightest imperfection in something as a direct challenge, and I sadly lost the duel. Remember when I mentioned that the time spent purifying an ingredient mattered?"*

Olivia bobbed her head under the Elder's palm. "Yes, I do."

"Well, this is what happens if you take too long," Elder Margret said. *"No matter how careful I am, my soul fire carries its own impurities and slowly corrupts the ingredient I am trying to purify. It's an odd balancing act, and it's why those with the purest spirit roots fare best in alchemy."*

Removing her hand from the girl's head, she summoned another one of Ashlock's homegrown Qi Flowing Grass from her spatial ring and tossed it into the cauldron fruit. She then also threw in the Starlight Lotus without even attempting to purify it.

"With the top-quality ingredients, I have no need to waste time puri-

fying them and can get onto the main event: unification!" Elder Margret summoned crimson fire to her hands and filled the cauldron with her soul fire.

Ashlock noticed that he couldn't feel anything. Likely because the cauldron was a fruit rather than directly connected to his body like a branch or root.

"Just like cooking a meal, you can't shove all ingredients into the same wok and blast them at the same temperature and expect anything but a burned clump of mismatched ingredients to come out."

Elder Margret lectured while her eyes were closed. *"Alchemy is much the same. We must know how each ingredient reacts with one another and how to combine them in the correct order. If I mess up at any stage, I will either waste the ingredients or form a low-grade pill that is no more useful than just chewing on a random bundle of the ingredients."*

While Elder Margret created the pill, Ashlock felt the slightest pull on his Qi reserves toward the cauldron fruit. As he was inspecting the cause, Elder Margret seemed to have noticed something was off by her expression, but she kept going.

Eventually, she finished, and her flames died out. Reaching into the cauldron, she retrieved a pill resembling a translucent marble with twinkling stars and strands of green throughout it.

The pill was beautiful.

Twirling it around, Elder Margret muttered, *"There's no way I could create a pill of the Profound tier out of these simple ingredients with my soul fire."*

Ashlock finally figured out what had happened. His pure soul fire had helped with the process, allowing Elder Margret to create a pill above her capabilities.

But now he was really curious. Just how good was a Profound-tier pill?

55
STELLA'S NEW TALENT

Stella let out a deep breath as her consciousness returned to reality. Her eyes fluttered open, and she squinted briefly as she was blinded by the warm midday sun.

Feeling within herself, she couldn't help but sigh. Even with the help of Ashlock's truffles, fruits, and residual Qi blanketing the mountain peak, it would still take at least a few months to move up a single stage in the Star Core Realm.

Yet despite the disappointing realization regarding the monumental amount of time it took to advance through the Star Core Realm, Stella wasn't so worried.

With the existence of the mystic realm, it almost feels pointless to waste time meditating out here, even with the help of the Qi-gathering formation and the resources Ash provided me.

Stella shook her head and stood up. Her ass ached as the ground was rough stone, and she had been sitting far too long.

I should really buy a cushion or something for when I meditate. Stella's eyes drifted across the mountain peak and settled on the bench under Ashlock's canopy. *Or I could meditate on the bench. Not like there's a massive difference in Qi over there compared to here.*

Stella glanced up at the canopy of the demonic tree she had been meditating under and saw it rustle in the wind as streaks of sunlight poured through the gaps. It was beautiful, with its striking resemblance to Ash.

Wait...if Ash sees me as his daughter, then are these my siblings?

Stella chuckled to herself and patted the tree on the trunk. Her hand then paused on its bark as she felt something tingle at the back of her brain.

Did I just feel a tiny hint of happiness?

She removed her hand, and the distant feeling faded. Placing it back on brought it back. The tree was happy.

Stella withdrew her hand and stared at it. "Since when can I talk to trees?"

Sadly, her hand didn't seem to have the answer, nor did she. "Mhm... weird." Shrugging, she walked across the sunlit mountaintop with a spring in her step. She glanced briefly at the far end of the courtyard, where she could see Diana's silhouette, barely visible through the swirling mist around the group of water affinity demonic trees facing the forest between them and Darklight City.

She also noticed Kaida, who was curled around Diana. The snake had grown rather large, which reminded Stella of Maple. Instinctually, she reached up and was only half surprised to feel the soft fur of the white squirrel that claimed her head as his throne.

Maple sleepily rubbed his head against her fingers, which made her smile.

Eventually, Stella made it to the bench under Ash's canopy. Before doing anything else, she used telekinesis to pull a few low-hanging fruits down to her as she needed replacements for the fruit she had eaten before meditating.

"Let's see. I ate two deep meditations and an enlightenment one." Stella pulled down the required fruit and stowed them away in her spatial ring. She was then about to ask Ash about today's plans when she noticed his attention was elsewhere.

Stella couldn't quite explain it, but she could sense when Ash was asleep or focused on something else.

What could be drawing his interest this time? Stella pondered while tapping her chin and glancing around. Her gaze eventually landed on the large hole in the center of the mountain peak, and she suddenly remembered that the Redclaws were supposed to be arriving today.

Closing her eyes, she entered the spatial plane, and with a click of her fingers, she materialized a portal before her and walked straight through. As the portal snapped closed behind her, she suddenly felt everyone's gaze on her, including two teenagers with crimson hair and eyes she had never seen before.

It had been quite a while since she had to introduce herself to new people, and it was made even worse as they were teenagers. Stella found adults easier to converse and connect with compared to children. Perhaps it was because she didn't have a normal childhood, but she never felt she could connect with those younger than her.

Relax…you can do this, Stella. Just politely introduce yourself to the newcomers. There's no need to worry. You won't make a fool of yourself. It's not like they can see your face—

A slight breeze originating from the hole in the side of the cavern brushed her hair over her eyes, making her blink as it itched her eye. Blink. Stella could feel her hair. Which could only mean one thing: she had forgotten to wear her mask.

Stella felt her stomach sink. She had finally started getting comfortable ordering people around for Ash, but that required the mask that could obscure her expressions. Unlike the Elders of the Redclaw family, she hadn't been brought up with etiquette lessons, nor did she have centuries of life experience to pull from to navigate conversations.

She had a facade as the face of the Ashfallen Sect and the descendant of an immortal. How was she supposed to keep that act up without the darn mask?!

Elder Margret suddenly stopped staring at her and became flustered. She put her hands on the back of the twins' heads and forced them into a bow with her. "Greetings, Stella. I hope our early arrival didn't disturb you or the immortal's meditation."

Stella wanted to respond, but nothing came out of her mouth. She replayed every word in her head, but nothing sounded right. Suddenly a small paw smacked her on the forehead, bringing her out of her daze.

"You did no such thing, Elder Margret," Stella said as she felt Maple roll over on her head into a better sleeping position. "And who might these two be?"

All three Redclaws straightened up, and Elder Margret helpfully introduced her to the twins. "These two are Oliver and Olivia. They have some of our family's purest crimson soul flames and took an early interest in alchemy. We have trained them the best we could over the years, but our resources are limited. We have also taken a conscious step away from alchemy, so I could never provide them the education they deserved."

Elder Margret gestured to Stella. "Oliver and Olivia, this is Stella. She represents the Immortal and the Ashfallen Sect that lords over us."

Stella gave them a brief nod and then walked over while trying to ignore the stars in their eyes. She wished she remembered her mask, but it would be odd to wear it now.

It's fine. These two should be spending a lot of time in the cavern, and I don't want to wear a mask every time I come down here to speak to Douglas. I should get used to their stares.

"So, Elder Margret, were you able to conduct alchemy with the cauldron the immortal grew?" Stella asked while leaning over the earthen bowl and inspecting the massive black fruit.

She furiously nodded. "It is actually the best cauldron I have ever had the pleasure of using. Look here at the pill I was able to create."

Stella turned to face the stern woman and was handed a pill that looked like a glass ball. It was cold to the touch and incredibly smooth.

So this is a freshly made pill. It feels high quality, but besides reading that book I got from the Voidmind Elder's stash, what do I know about alchemy?

Humming to herself, Stella side-eyed the Elder and debated if she should ask about the pill. Would the Elder judge her lack of knowledge? Deciding her acting skills were only so good and her knowledge too shallow to continue the lies, Stella took the risk.

"I must admit, Elder Margret, although I have dabbled in some old literature that speaks highly of alchemy's great mysteries, I am not well versed in pill creation." Stella carefully handed the pill to the Elder. "Could you tell me about the pill?"

To Stella's relief, none of the Redclaws showed any adverse reaction to her admittance of ignorance, and Elder Margret explained the entire process from start to finish in one long lecture that didn't bore Stella in the slightest.

So Ash can produce such amazing cultivation resources in mere moments. As expected of him. And Elder Margret created such a supposedly amazing pill with the help of the cauldron fruit.

"So this is a Profound-tier pill? What does that mean?" Stella asked.

"Well, you see..." Elder Margret caught her breath and continued.

"There are eight tiers of pills that exist in our realm: Mortal, Spirit, Profound, Earth, Sky, Divine, Celestial, and finally the Heavenly tier."

"So you created a third-tier pill?" Stella frowned. "That doesn't seem very impressive considering what you told me about the amazing ingredients and how the cauldron assisted your soul fire."

Elder Margret shook her head. "You misunderstand. The body-strengthening pill is a Mortal-tier pill. Yet due to the high-quality ingredients and pure soul fire, I could turn such a simple pill with only three basic ingredients into one with a similar effect to a Profound-tier pill."

Now that she worded it like that...Stella could see how miraculous the whole thing was. She had turned a tier-one pill into a tier three.

"To create higher-tier pills, the rarity and number of ingredients required increases exponentially," Elder Margret lectured. "Also, the time it takes to create the pill increases quite quickly. It gets to the point where an alchemist doesn't have the cultivation realm, skill, or ingredients to create higher-tier pills, and they become ever stuck at a certain tier of pill creation."

"I see..." Stella contemplated. "What is the highest-tier pill you can make?"

"As an eighth-stage Soul Fire Realm cultivator with centuries of experience, the best pill I have ever created was an Earth tier." Elder Margret had a hint of nostalgia in her voice. "But I will never create something so high tier again."

"Really?" Stella tilted her head. "Even with the immortal's cauldron, ingredients, and access to the Mystic Realm?"

Elder Margret seemed to pause, and then her eyes widened. "You're right. With his assistance, I should be able to make an Earth-tier pill before I die."

"Miss Stella, have you ever performed alchemy before?" the male twin, whom Stella believed was called Oliver, asked her with awe in his eyes.

Stella wanted to shy away from the enthusiastic gaze but gathered some courage. "No, I have never tried before."

"We can learn together!" Olivia piped up.

"Uhm..." Stella wanted to turn down the offer and learn away from prying eyes, but their enthusiasm rubbed off on her. "All right, fine, show me how it's done."

After an hour lecture that she swore was half nonsense, Stella stood before the fruit cauldron with the three ingredients needed for the Body Strengthening Pill laid out before her.

The twins were on either side of her, standing in front of their own earthen bowls. Somehow they had turned this into a competition, and unable to say no, Stella had agreed to their challenge on who could create the best pill.

Elder Margret stood behind them and acted as the judge. "You may now begin."

Stella let out a breath as she focused.

Okay, first, I need to purify the Dragon Marrow... How hard can it be?

Picking up the weird jelly substance, she surrounded it in her spatial flames and closed her eyes. In the silence of her mind, she finally found some peace.

Now what do I do? Remove the impurities?

Stella frowned. Her soul fire wasn't actually hot, so it wasn't like she could burn the impurities away. But spatial affinity wasn't listed in the book as an affinity unable to perform alchemy, so there had to be a way...

What about the spatial plane?

Her entire reality shifted, and everything became outlined in grids. The lump of bone marrow in her hand seemed like nothing special, but as she focused closer, she noticed the tiny traces of impurities floating about as they were outlined in faint grids that were easy to miss.

Stella interjected her spatial Qi into the bone marrow through tiny gaps in its jelly-like surface. She then carefully followed shifting pathways to avoid messing with the crystalized Qi within the bone marrow.

Then as she snaked her Qi toward the marked impurities, she noticed the walls of the shifting pathways slowly erode away from her Qi.

I need to hurry up. Stella cursed as she felt sweat accumulating on her forehead. Her heart pounded in her chest, and her Star Core lightly pulsed with power. Never before had she needed to be this precise and delicate with her Qi control. It was a totally new experience for her.

Luckily, despite her lack of experience, her pure Qi glided through the pathways effortlessly, and she managed to isolate the impurities moments later.

Okay, good job, Stella. Now what? Think. You can't just shatter them with your Qi, as that will corrupt the rest of the Dragon Marrow... Hmmm.

Her mind raced as she slowly noticed the corruption of her Qi on the pathways. Rather than panic, the time pressure helped her focus. Eventually, she settled on a potentially stupid idea.

What if I just teleport the impurities with tiny rifts?

Since the impurities shifted around like fireflies, all she had to do was open a rift the width of a hair right in front of where she predicted they would move, and with a tiny pop, it was gone!

A minute went by, and Stella meticulously removed every trace of impurity she could spot. However, as she was nearly done with just a few to go, she could already see hints of her own Qi beginning to corrupt the Dragon Marrow as the pathways were eroded away.

It's too risky to continue pushing to get every last impurity out. I should withdraw here.

She wasn't happy about it, but it was important to know when to retreat and take the small victories.

Opening her eyes, she saw the Dragon Marrow in her hand was more translucent than before and almost mirrored that same glass-like appearance as the pill Elder Margret made.

Glancing to the side, she saw Olivia sniffling as she held a blackened blob of Dragon Marrow in her hand.

"Olivia, you took too long to remove the impurities, and your own Qi has ruined the Dragon Marrow," Elder Margret said from behind with the voice of a stern teacher. "Therefore, you are disqualified."

"Can't I try again?" Olivia begged. "Please...I was so close."

Elder Margret shook her head. "You got arrogant, and this is the price you pay. We have a limited amount of Dragon Marrow, so I can't waste any more on giving you a second chance." She then walked over and looked between Stella and Oliver.

"Stella, yours is near perfect, and Oliver...did you even remove any impurities?"

"Y-yes, Elder Margret, look here..." Oliver pointed at a tiny pile of ash on the earthen bowl's rim.

Elder Margret snorted. "That is a poor attempt, but at least you didn't ruin the precious Dragon Marrow like your sister."

Stella felt a pang of sympathy for the twins, but she could do little for them.

I never realized alchemy was this brutal. No wonder most people just focus on cultivation and ignore this path in life.

Her eyes wandered across the other two ingredients.

If I had to also remove the impurities from both of these, I don't think I would have any patience left to actually make the pill. And yet Elder Margret said all this is for a tier-one pill? Wouldn't preparing all the ingredients for an Earth-tier pill take days?

Stella didn't know how to describe it, but knowing how steep the path to becoming a master alchemist was made it all the more appealing.

If I became an alchemist capable of crafting pills of the Heavenly tier, Ash would be even more proud of me, and I could help him so much more. I know he loves and cares for me now as his own daughter, so I'm not worried he would throw me away...but that doesn't mean I should get complacent! Nobody likes a lazy daughter.

With the fire of passion burning in her chest...or was that her Star Core? Either way, she gathered the three ingredients that were all prepared and threw them into the cauldron she bathed in her soul fire.

Honestly, this was the stage she had absolutely no idea what to do. Elder Margret had described it as cooking a meal, but she had never cooked before. Ash always provided her fruit, and sometimes she feasted on birds that were prepared for her by Diana.

Closing her eyes, the spatial plane did help with manipulating the ingredients more precisely, but the actual combining of them was a mystery to her.

Do I wrap the Qi Flowing Grass around the Dragon Marrow like a dumpling?

Stella did that, and all she noticed were hints of corruption seeping back into the ingredients, which made her panic a little. However, right as she was going to try and unravel them and try again, she felt something lovingly embrace her soul fire.

Lilac flames, far purer than her own that could only belong to Ash, blanketed the clump of ingredients and helped keep the corruption at bay.

"Thank you, Tree," Stella muttered under her breath and smiled. The sensation of a caring parent helping her while learning something new warmed her heart as it wasn't a feeling she was used to.

The sudden help allowed Stella to try different combinations of the Starlight Lotus, Qi Flowing Grass, and Dragon Marrow without worry.

Soon she was getting the hang of it, and ten minutes later, a pill rose from the cauldron.

Stella retrieved it and frowned. It was clearly a lot worse than Elder Margret's, with a dark cloud overshadowing the sparkles of the Starlight Lotus and the lush green of the Qi Flowing Grass within the glass marble.

She was disappointed but also proud. This was her first-ever attempt at trying alchemy, after all.

Turning around, she handed the pill to Elder Margret and the three Redclaws, and even Douglas stared at it in awe.

"Have you really never performed alchemy?" Elder Margret asked skeptically. "Even with the hints of corruption, this is a high-grade Mortal-tier pill, or perhaps even a Spirit-tier pill!"

So definitely a high-grade tier one and might even be a tier two. Got it. I think I'm fine with that as a first attempt.

"That's amazing, Stella!" Olivia gave her a bright smile despite the redness in her eyes from tears.

Oliver also nodded in approval. "Mine was a dud. I corrupted the ingredients in the cauldron." He then scratched the back of his neck. "Even with the help of some mysterious lilac flames, I still messed it up."

Elder Margret let out a long sigh. "You two have really disappointed me today—"

"Don't be too harsh with them, Elder Margret," Stella interrupted the woman. "They are still young and have a lot of time to grow and improve."

The two twins looked at her as if she was their guardian angel. For some reason, she felt no need to shy away from their gazes. Perhaps it was because they had gone through a trial together.

Elder Margret was about to reply when she suddenly paused. Her spatial ring flashed, and a talisman appeared in her hand. It glowed with power.

Stella noticed a sliver of the Elder's Qi enter the talisman, and then it seemed like she was listening to something.

Everyone waited patiently, and eventually, Elder Margret furrowed her brows. "The Grand Elder has called an emergency meeting. Apparently, the Ashfallen Sect has given us a decree. Stella, you wouldn't know anything about it, would you?"

Stella thought long and hard, but nothing came to mind, so she shook her head. "Must have come straight from the immortal. I could go and ask him for you?"

"No, it's quite all right." Elder Margret waved her off. "I will head back now to hear what the Grand Elder has to say. Can I leave the twins here?"

Stella glanced between the teens and sighed. "I guess so."

"Great, see you all later." Elder Margret turned and was surprised when a rift manifested before her, showing the courtyard of the White Stone Palace. Without hesitation, she stepped through and vanished.

Stella let out another sigh as she saw the two eager teenagers gaze at her.

What am I supposed to do with them? Should I take them to the mountain peak and let them cultivate under the fire trees?

And what the hell was that decree Elder Margret was going on about?

56
HUNTING WITH TITANS

Grand Elder Redclaw frowned as he gazed out his study's window at the distant Red Vine Peak. A perpetual mist swirled around the mountain, obscuring everything but the tips of the demonic trees from his curious gaze.

I wonder what goes on over there...

His wandering thoughts were interrupted by frantic footsteps that echoed beyond the thick wooden doors of his study. He turned to face them just in time to watch a worried-looking middle-aged man push them open.

"Elder Brent, welcome."

"Grand Elder...what has the Ashfallen Sect decreed of us?"

"Calm down and wait for the others." The Grand Elder smiled reassuringly. "It's not that serious, so calm yourself."

"Oh, thank the heavens." Elder Brent let out a breath and respectfully stood beside his desk. But his crossed arms and drumming fingers showed his impatience.

Moments later, Elder Mo strode through the ajar doors with his spirit flame hammer still in hand. The Grand Elder looked at it with slight envy for a moment, but alas, he could only blame himself for not being deemed worthy of the immortal's inheritance.

So long as we keep on the good side of the Ashfallen Sect and the immortal continues to grant us access to that Mystic Realm, there will be a next time for me. I'm sure of it.

"Grand Elder, you called?" Elder Mo asked and also gave a friendly nod to Elder Brent.

"Once Elder Margret arrives, I will explain everything, but until then...how goes the forge, Elder Mo? Enjoying life as a smith?"

Elder Mo grinned. "Of course I am. If anything, I lament the fact I didn't pick up the hammer sooner."

"Any progress with making weapons containing your will?" Elder Brent asked from the side.

"Aye, I have." Elder Mo approached the desk, cleared aside some papers, and with a flash of power from his spatial ring, a sword manifested on the desk.

"Still a work in progress, but I forged this thing myself from scratch." Elder Mo awkwardly scratched the top of his balding head. "I'm having to learn smithing on the job, so it's rather amateurish in quality."

The Grand Elder had been holding back his opinion out of respect for his lifelong friend but had to agree with Elder Mo. It was the work of a beginner smith at best. The blade wasn't straight, the edges were dull, and it looked like a basic steel sword that even a mortal might sneer at.

"Elder Brent, try picking it up." Elder Mo had a mischievous grin that made Elder Brent raise a brow.

"Is it cursed or something, Elder Mo? Why are you grinning at me like that?"

"Just pick up the darn sword. Do you really believe I would try to harm you, my good friend?" Elder Mo chuckled. "If you don't dare, perhaps the Grand Elder will?"

The Grand Elder studied Elder Mo's suspicious demeanor; he had to admit he was curious now. What could make his old friend act like this? Eyeing the ordinary-looking steel sword with a dubious gaze, the Grand Elder finally gave in to his curiosity and reached over to grip the sword's hilt.

The moment his fingers curled around the bare metal hilt, a dormant feeling he was all too familiar with washed over him. War. The unending brutality of war consumed him.

His heart pounded in his chest as memories of horrific, century-old battles flashed through his mind. The sky was dyed crimson from blood —the wails of the anguished screamed in his ears. A chaotic storm of Qi swirled around him as the clangs of swords reverberated across the hellscape as two sides fought under the laws of heaven.

He reeled his hand back from the cold steel—the sword clanged on the desk like a gong freeing him from the mental torment of a distant past.

Elder Mo stood there, his grin holding an eerie meaning.

"Do you remember now, old friend?" Elder Mo said. "The darkness of war laid dormant in your bones."

Elder Brent looked curiously between the two and then back at the sword. He made no move to follow in the Grand Elder's footsteps in grasping the sword hilt.

"I see…" the Grand Elder murmured as he calmed his pounding heart. "So this is what it means to imbue your will into a sword with spirit fire."

Elder Mo nodded thoughtfully. "With every impact of my hammer on molten metal, another memory was imbued. I might have gone a little overboard, but the idea was to have a sword that, when held by someone, would give them the overpowering feeling of being on the battlefield. I thought it would make a good training weapon."

"I can see the direction you were going for, but perhaps lock that one away." The Grand Elder's gaze lingered on the sword hilt. He felt his fingers itch as if wanting to grasp it again—to relive those glorious, death-filled days—after all, he was a retired man of war who still craved his enemies' blood.

Elder Mo's ring flashed, and the sword vanished.

The brief moment of thoughtful silence was broken with Elder Margret entering the study. The Grand Elder gave her a nod to welcome her and then clapped his hands.

"All right, with everyone here, we can begin." He pointed toward the parchment on his desk with the ancient runic language scribbled in half-dried ink. "Who here can read this?"

All three Elders crowded around the desk and scrutinized it.

"I know this is the ancient language. Sadly, I haven't gotten around to learning it yet," Elder Margret said. "What does it say, Grand Elder?"

It was such a perfect reaction that he couldn't help but chuckle. "It's a decree straight from the immortal. He wrote it himself with that fountain pen."

All of their gazes landed on the fountain pen as if it was some divine artifact.

The Grand Elder cleared his throat and then translated to the best of his ability. "The immortal wants us all to learn the ancient runic language within the next month."

Then after a pause to let everyone digest the words, he continued, "With the help of those language comprehension fruits, I bet you can all learn it within days."

"Was that it?" Elder Brent furrowed his brows. "I can see how learning the language could be useful, but did you really call the meeting just for that?"

The Grand Elder chuckled. "Of course not. We are all so busy that we haven't had a spare moment to catch up, and I thought this was a fitting occasion."

He smiled at Elder Margret. "You took two promising alchemists from our family over to the Ashfallen Sect today. How did that go?"

A sigh escaped her lips.

Did something go wrong? The Grand Elder studied her disappointed expression and felt a hint of worry fester in his stomach.

"Mixed results, to say the least. Ugh, I'm just so…embarrassed."

"Why? What happened?"

"I don't know if they got nervous or I had high expectations, but both failed to create a pill." Elder Margret frowned.

"Well, that's only to be expected," the Grand Elder said calmly as he drew back his chair and sat down. "They have only been practicing for, what, a year now? Most alchemists take a decade before they can produce pills on demand like that."

"That's true, but look at this." Elder Margret summoned a beautiful pill and handed it to the Grand Elder. All the other elders also curiously leaned in to inspect it.

"Is this a Profound-tier pill?" Elder Brent frowned. "Wait, a Profound-tier body-strengthening pill? Did you make this? Why would anyone waste such high-grade resources on such a basic pill? You know we are short on resources for the alchemy tournament already, so to go around wasting—"

"Elder Brent, be quiet," Elder Margret snapped. The man grumbled and stepped back. "It wasn't a waste. The resources to make this pill weren't even ours. I know you will find it hard to believe, but I saw the immortal grow thousands of Qi Flowing Grass and Starlight Lotuses within seconds. It was the most magical experience of my life...even better than the Mystic Realm."

The Grand Elder's eyes widened, and he looked back at the Profound-tier pill in his palm. "So you're telling me the ingredients for this pill were grown in seconds by the immortal? If you aren't lying, then that Silverspire brat has signed the deal of a lifetime."

"Indeed, they have," Elder Margret replied seriously.

"So why were you upset with the twins again?" the Grand Elder asked, steering the conversation back to the original topic.

Elder Margret's ring flashed with power, and a less impressive but still very well-crafted pill appeared. "This was made by Stella." She placed the pill onto the desk. "She has never done alchemy before."

"Impossible," Elder Brent blurted out as he scooped up the pill and inspected it. "That's simply impossible. Even if the ingredients are devoid of impurities, it would still take godlike intuition to merge them into a Spirit-tier pill on their first try."

The Grand Elder seized the pill and ignored Elder Brent's protests as a wide grin formed on his aged face.

Knowing someone like the immortal was one thing, but having a connection to a master alchemist was another.

It would appear his fortune kept rising the longer he was associated with the Ashfallen Sect. He couldn't help but reminisce about the day he encountered Stella and the spirit beast and surrendered his family to them via an oath, a decision that in previous months had brought him great misery. Nothing in his long life brought him more despair than seeing his family trapped in a palace of white stone on a mountaintop as glorified slaves to an unknown force and unable to cultivate due to the lack of fire Qi.

Yet, recently, his family's perseverance had begun to be rewarded.

Ever since that worm attack led me to Red Vine Peak with Stella, my family has been blessed with reward after reward by the immortal. At this rate, under the enriching shadow of the Ashfallen Sect, my family will rise to heights unheard of in the history of my bloodline.

The Grand Elder slammed his hand on the desk as he stood up—causing everyone to shut their yappers and stare at him.

"Enough nonsense. Listen here, if you were respectful to Stella before, now imagine she is a master alchemist in the making. If I hear anyone has caused her problems, I will deal with them personally. Do I make myself clear?"

"Yes, Grand Elder," all three of his cherished Elders responded in unison.

"Good. Now tell me, how goes the tournament preparations?"

Elder Brent coughed. "Ahem, well...the noble families will be arriving within the next few days, so we have put the airship station on a temporary lockdown to avoid another incident like the one with the arrival of the Voidmind scion."

"I see, and who do we believe is arriving next?"

"The Skyrend family should arrive tomorrow morning," Elder Margret said.

Everyone groaned, and the Grand Elder gripped the bridge of his nose. "Those overzealous, heaven-worshiping bastards are always a handful to deal with. All right, make sure nobody, and I mean nobody, is present in the airship station to mess with them on arrival."

Everyone nodded, and the Grand Elder sighed. "All right, that is all I wished to discuss. You can all return to your duties now. However, Elder Margret, please stay behind. I have something else to discuss with you regarding the tournament…"

Ashlock found it amusing listening in on the Redclaw's conversation—it was interesting to see the reactions of ordinary people to his and Stella's shenanigans as he lacked a frame of reference—but got bored as the Grand Elder and Elder Margret spent a while discussing logistics for the tournament. He had left the running of the tournament to them for a good reason—logistics and pandering to noble families weren't his forte.

Anyway, he was in a good mood as the whole day had been rather full of surprises.

Despite their young age, he hadn't expected the Redclaw twins to be so…meh at alchemy. However, that disappointment had been washed away by Stella's capabilities. He had given Stella and Oliver nearly the same level of help during the competition to keep things fair, but Stella had approached everything with a calmness and skill that seemed alien to him.

In his mind, Stella was a hotheaded, think-later type of person who acted on her instincts far too often. But put her in front of a pill cauldron, and she completely changed into someone with a calm and calculative demeanor.

"Perhaps this mindset is what allows her to excel in cultivation compared to others as well," Ashlock mused. He had no way to crack open her skull and see how she meditated compared to others, but after observing her approach to alchemy, he was convinced she could concentrate and hyper-focus on tasks.

Regarding focusing, Ashlock was finding it harder to keep up with things. There was just so much going on recently that he felt scatterbrained.

Instead of being a fleshy human with two legs and a limited perspective that would have the intelligent idea to delegate things to others as there was no chance in hell they could monitor so much at once, he had decided to abuse his new biology to its limit and do most of the things himself.

"This is why I want everyone to learn the ancient language. That way, I can order people around more efficiently," Ashlock grumbled. "I need to learn to focus my efforts on the things I am best at and let the others do the rest. I don't have to do everything myself anymore. I got a lot of people around me to help."

Ashlock felt the way the sun hit his leaves and determined it was mid-afternoon—meaning he still had half a day left before he fell asleep and then had to oversee the welcoming of the Skyrend family. So what should he focus his time on?

His thoughts were interrupted when there was a sudden pop of spatial Qi, and a girl he was all too familiar with stepped through and collapsed straight onto the bench with a sigh.

"I'm exhausted, Tree…" Stella sulked. *"And it's all your fault."*

"My fault?" Ashlock was taken aback. "How could it be my fault?"

Stella naturally couldn't hear him but continued talking to the air as she always did. *"Why did you give the Grand Elder a decree and cause Elder Margret to leave the twins in my care? I have no idea what to do with them!"*

"Ah…that was kind of my fault." Ashlock chuckled. He hadn't foreseen the Grand Elder calling an entire meeting over it, but he could see why Stella was mad.

"Hey, Tree," Stella patted his black bark, *"what was the decree anyway?"*

'I told them to learn the ancient language so I can speak with them and not bother you so much,' Ashlock wrote in lilac flames on his trunk, and she quickly translated it.

"That's not a good reason to leave me with two darn teenagers!" Stella grumbled. *"Why must I take care of them anyway? Can't you do it?"*

'Why not practice alchemy with them?' Ashlock asked through writing, and she rolled her eyes.

"Tree, we only have two ingredients to make pills from. How can we make Body Strengthening Pills without the Dragon Marrow?"

That was a good point.

"I still need to find a solution to that ingredient shortage. Hmm, it comes from monsters, right?" Ashlock's vision blurred as he crossed many miles through his roots and appeared far out in the wilderness near the demonic tree wall where he first spotted the worm.

It had been a while since the worm disrupted the place, so it made sense that there was a large gathering of monsters in the vicinity. None were super strong, which was ideal because Ashlock just needed their bone marrow.

Ashlock's vision blurred back to the mountain peak where Stella was still ranting about being a glorified babysitter, so he gave her an outlet.

'There is a group of monsters out in the wild. Why not go and kill them?' Ashlock wrote, and then after a moment of contemplation, he added, 'You could also collect new plants while you are out there.'

Even if he didn't know the pill recipes, it would be great to amass a database of as many plants as possible.

"I don't know anything about plants, though," Stella said while standing back up. She then stretched her back with an audible crack and rolled her shoulders. *"But I could go for some good old punching monsters in the face after concentrating so hard on that pill. Douglas can look after those terrors for me."*

Alas, Ashlock needed Douglas to work on extending the staircase and pillar. He also required him to add rooms throughout the mountain, so sadly, the man couldn't be left looking after the twins.

'Douglas needs to work and rest. Why not take the twins with you?'

Ashlock wrote, and the face of pure betrayal Stella pulled after reading it was priceless.

"You want me to look after two weaklings out in the wild? All while I hunt monsters and pick up plants for you?" She crossed her arms and huffed. *"I don't want that type of responsibility!"*

'Titus can look after them,' Ashlock wrote as he mentally commanded the twenty-meter-tall Ent to stand up. The towering creature of black wood loomed over the annoyed Stella with two eyes of lilac soul fire glaring down at her.

"Fine! If the big guy is responsible, then I don't care anymore," Stella grumbled as she clicked her fingers, and a portal manifested before her. *"I will tell the twins what's happening. So please open a portal down there once you've gotten Titus near the monsters...and be quick about it!"*

And with that, she was gone. Some peace and quiet returned to the courtyard, but Ashlock always enjoyed having a little fight with her. Anyway, now wasn't the time to sit around and think. He had to get this lumbering giant out into the wilderness to avoid Stella getting really cross with him.

His Star Core pulsed with power, and a portal over ten meters high wobbled into existence. Diana cracked open an eye at the scene but soon returned to meditating.

Titus bent down and took a lumbering step through the portal. A moment later, he passed through with a massive pop as air rushed to fill the void left behind. The portal then collapsed, sending another blast of air that briefly disrupted the mist wall and rustled the scarlet leaves of every tree in the courtyard, including Ashlock's.

"Right, now to open a portal onto his shoulder." Ashlock easily set the anchor point as Titus was a blinding beacon of spatial Qi. With that done, he could open a rift in the cavern, connecting two locations many miles apart.

Ashlock then watched as Stella led the two bewildered twins through the portal onto Titus's shoulders.

"S-Stella..." Olivia stuttered as she looked off the side and saw the ground far below. "What are we doing here?"

"Well, Elder Margret said I needed to keep watch over you." Stella grinned. *"And we had no more Dragon Marrow, so why shouldn't I bring you hunting for some monsters?"*

At this point, the two twins huddled with one another and gripped the twisted black roots that made up Titus's body for dear life as the behemoth strode forward.

"How does that make any sense!" Oliver shouted over the roaring wind as Titus moved toward the sea of monsters surrounding the wall of demonic trees.

Stella shrugged as her blond hair blew in the wind. *"Titus, protect these two at all costs, but listen to their orders."* She then addressed the confused twins. *"I will be busy down there fighting monsters, but feel free to order this big guy around if you want to join in the fun.*

"Anyway, see you two later!" Stella spread her arms and fell backward into a freefall down the side of the Ent, causing the two twins to scream and lean over the side. However, before she had even fallen halfway toward the lush grass of the wilderness, a portal manifested below her and teleported her off somewhere else with a resounding pop.

The two twins exchanged a glance, and Olivia muttered, "She's insane…right?"

57
SELF-REFLECTION

Stella felt wild and free as she swung her sword and brutally slashed a mutated beast in half—the sheer force of her attack sent the two halves of the corpse hurtling through the air in opposite directions. One half took out a small gathering of monsters nearby—while the other shot off toward one of the towering demonic trees forming a wall and splattered a chicken-looking monster against the tree bark, turning both into nothing but meat paste and making the tree shake.

She was wholly unconcerned by the shower of blood she ran through as a single pulse from her Star Core reversed the blood's trajectory. This was the first time since exiting the Mystic Realm that she could go all out with her new cultivation stage, and she loved it.

Having a Star Core made life incomparable to before. It was hard for Soul Fire cultivators to truly let loose without worry as every drop of Qi they spent would have to be meditated for later, whereas the warm Star Core pulsing in her chest was a beacon of self-sustaining power that flooded her body with boundless energy.

She could slaughter without worry, as once the killing was finished, she could flop down and sleep on the rolling lush meadows and regain all of the spent Qi without effort.

The monster's screams were music to her ears as she manically laughed. Having to maintain such a perfect mask of excellence was the least of her concerns out here. Even with the twins perched on Titus's shoulders far away, she could be herself out here.

A few more sword swings finished the monsters around her—they were terribly weak, so they offered little to her besides stress relief. Stella paused as her area became devoid of anything living and glanced around while breathing in the fresh air tainted with death. It was beautiful. The scent of death oddly brought a sense of comfort to her.

If everything was dead, then I could be left alone with Tree. Stella sighed and tapped the tip of her bloody sword on the stained grass. A few flashes of old memories surfaced at the forefront of her mind.

She could still recall the heaviness of the decapitated head hidden away in that coarse bag she had clutched in her tiny hands while being stared down by those servants sent to kill her.

"Tsk." Stella clicked her tongue as she tried to shake away the memories of the screaming mortal servants fleeing her and how she had survived the Ravenborne murder plot. She had lived through it all with Tree by her side. Why would she need anybody else?

"Stella, you're being weird again," she muttered to herself as she kicked a nearby monster's head in a daze, causing it to explode from just a tap. "Mhm, I need to rein in my strength when dealing with these weaklings."

A sigh escaped her lips as she flicked off the brain mush from her shoe and was about to teleport to a distant grouping of monsters near the demonic tree wall when she felt a familiar wave of spatial Qi blanket the area.

Rifts manifested overhead, tearing through the peaceful blue sky. Stella cranked her neck to see black vines ending in a spike coated in thorns wiggle through the rifts and descend on the meal below.

"Oh yeah, Ash wanted Dragon Marrow," Stella realized as she saw the vines try to skewer and wrap around the pieces of corpses leftover from her rampage. "Maybe I shouldn't have attacked with such force. Sorry, Tree."

A vine diverted from the corpses and carefully nudged her with the tip of the spike in an almost endearing way.

"I know, I know." Stella patted it. "I messed up. I will get you some good food."

The vine slowly moved away and then slammed down into the stomach of a wolf-looking beast with enough force to crack the earth. The spike dug deep between the monster's rib cage, allowing the vine to effortlessly reel back into the rift overhead with the corpse dangling from the end.

Stella stepped back to avoid the dripping blood from the corpses being dragged away and because she wanted to try something new, which she needed some space away from Ash's influence to do.

Raising her sword so the blade was perfectly between her eyes, Stella observed the distant group of monsters crowded around the demonic trees. For this crazy idea of hers to be executed flawlessly, she needed to be lightning-quick.

She had learned from Ash's previous mistake: portals were a two-way affair. If she could stab the monsters in the face, they could rip hers apart with their claws.

Stella closed her eyes, the world became grids through the spatial plane, and she began setting multiple anchor points as she planned to open numerous portals in quick succession.

"This is going to be fun."

While Ashlock was half distracted with dragging the corpses through his rifts, he watched Stella's odd actions in confusion.

"Why is she standing still like that?" he wondered. The group of monsters wasn't that far away. She should be able to teleport and make short work of them, so why hesitate?

His questions were answered when the sword she was holding suddenly lit up with purple flames concentrated at the tip. Her eyes snapped open, and a second later, a portal manifested right in front of her, providing a distorted view of a monster's back.

The ape-like monster seemed to notice the sudden portal behind it and turned to look over its shoulder in confusion. Stella didn't give it a chance to foresee its death as the flaming sword struck through the portal and decapitated the ape in one clean arc.

A shrill scream came from all the other ape monsters as they watched the headless corpse fall forward with a thud, and the head rolled down the slope. They all began to ignore the mushrooms they had been gingerly munching on and searched around for the unknown foe. Some even sniffed the air, and one leaped up to a low-hanging branch and tried to use the vantage point to spot the killer.

However, before the apes could even get a chance to fathom what had occurred, death already came knocking. Ashlock watched in amazement as portals rapidly popped into existence around Stella one after another, always showing an unguarded side of an ape. With her eyes closed, she mercilessly slashed at the portals, the spatial Qi coating her sword, allowing it to pass through without affecting the rift.

A swoosh marked the end of the spectacle as Stella flicked the blood from her blade and opened her eyes. "How was that, Tree? Are the corpses in good enough condition to be snacks for you?" She then twirled around with a smile. "Also, I got no blood on my clothes! Aren't I a genius?"

Ashlock sent some spatial Qi through his roots and wrote on the ground in lilac flames, 'Show off.'

Stella laughed. *"Honestly, I got the idea from you! You always attack through rifts, so I thought I could, too. Although I opened and closed them quickly to avoid an incident like the worm poison."*

She then began to hum to herself as she glanced around, so Ashlock took the opportunity to open rifts above the new ape monster corpses and drag them back to the mountain peak. He planned to go through them individually and harvest any corpses with Dragon Marrow.

He would then eat the rest for some sacrificial credits, even if he didn't expect great returns from these Soul Fire monsters.

After dragging the ten ape corpses through rifts, including their heads, Ashlock returned to find Stella staring at Titus in the distance. The twins seemed to be having a blast, but he felt they could do with some supervision, so seeing as Stella had finished up with this area, he asked with flames on the ground, 'Why don't you go to the twins?'

Stella frowned as her hair fluttered in the breeze. There was a long pause as something seemed to be on the tip of her tongue. Eventually, she sighed. *"Tree, am I weird? Is it strange that I don't want to talk to them or anyone? Sometimes I feel like I am the odd one out. Like...I don't see the world like all of them do."*

Ashlock could tell that question had been bothering her by her fidgeting with the sword hilt while staring at the ground where he had been writing.

As someone that had seen her grow up, he knew what had caused her deep-set issues. Her entire family had died when she was young, leaving her abandoned in a massive pavilion, all alone except for servants wanting to kill her. Once they were dealt with, she didn't speak to another human for almost a decade.

Who wouldn't come out from a rough childhood like that as a little weird, even by cultivation world standards?

In recent times, especially as he tried to expand the sect and Stella was his main form of communication, he had deemed her inability to communicate a significant issue that needed resolving. But honestly, he was starting to realize that it was just part of what made Stella…Stella. If she improved slowly over time, then great, but he wasn't so concerned anymore.

'You are perfect the way you are,' Ashlock wrote in flames. 'Behave in a way you deem fitting and do whatever makes you happy.'

"*Mhm.*" Stella didn't seem convinced at all. "*Fine, if you say so. But how do I get more people to like me? Whenever it comes to sect decisions, everyone treats me like a crazy person.*"

Ashlock had to admit she could be unhinged at times, but to demand she alter her world views without the life experience to reach those conclusions herself was nonsense. Everyone saw the world through their own tinted lens.

'You're not crazy. You just have a unique viewpoint,' Ashlock wrote. 'As we all do, so don't worry about it.'

She seemed lost in thought for a while and then shook it off and strode toward Titus in the far distance. Her speed increased as she became wrapped in soul flames, and moments later, she was shooting across the landscape through a tunnel of portals.

Titus raised his titanic arm, and under the excited shouts of Olivia, he struck down a group of fleeing monsters, pulverizing them into the ground.

"Sigh…it seems they are also getting carried away like Stella did. How can I extract any Dragon Marrow from bones crushed to dust?" Ashlock lamented as he watched the twins cheer and Stella suddenly appear beside them.

"*Having fun?*" she asked. "*How are we supposed to get anything if you kill these monsters like that?*"

The twins yelped at the sudden voice.

"*Sorry…*"

"*We were just…*"

They let off a flurry of half-completed excuses—Stella waved them off.

"I'm going to relax on the other shoulder. You two kill the monsters while leaving their corpses as intact as possible, and if you see any interesting plants down below, let me know, and I will go get them."

Without hearing their answer, Stella leaped over Titus's head, landed on the opposite shoulder, and sat down. It seemed she had a lot on her mind, so Ashlock left her to it.

The next few hours consisted of Titus flattening all monsters in the vicinity with his fifth-stage Star Core gravity and then squishing their heads with his giant fingers—leaving the corpses mostly intact.

Ashlock would then drag the corpses away, much to the twins' excitement.

"Stella!" Olivia shouted over the head. *"Down below, toward the setting sun, there's a grove."*

Ashlock looked in the direction of where Olivia was pointing and could see the aforementioned grove. It didn't look like anything extraordinary, except it seemed a bit out of place. It gave the vibe of an oasis surrounded by nothing but lush grassland.

Stella stood up with a yawn and glanced toward the sun. "What about it?"

"It's just a guess, but Dreamweaver Orchids might be there."

"What are those?" Stella inquired, and Ashlock also wanted to know.

Olivia squinted at the grove. *"Dreamweaver Orchids aren't that special on their own, but when grouped up in a cluster, the illusionary Qi they release can create mirages."*

"Interesting." Stella tapped her chin. *"And you think that grove is an illusion?"*

"Maybe." Olivia shrugged. *"I've only read about them in dusty old books. It could just be a random grouping of trees."*

"All right, well, we can go check it out before heading back," Stella said as she patted the Ent on the head. *"Titus, go grab one of those trees."*

The Ent wordlessly obeyed the command and trudged toward the grove. Ashlock was somewhat surprised Stella didn't dash in alone and instead used Titus to test the waters.

Titus got close enough to reach down, and his hand passed through the tree like a projection. Ashlock didn't have time to be surprised as a flurry of tiny, orange-feathered birds exploded from the illusionary grove in all directions.

Ashlock commanded Titus to pulse his fifth-stage Star Core, and all the birds plummeted to the ground like hail as the immense gravity robbed their ability to fly.

Titus then sent a tidal wave of spatial Qi that smashed into the grove and washed away the illusion Qi. The fake trees were replaced by a giant bush of light pink orchids.

"You were right, sis!" Oliver shouted in awe while pointing at the bush.

Olivia pointed her nose to the sky and chuckled. "Haha, as expected!"

Ashlock began to open rifts and deploy vines to secure the birds. Even though they were weak, they should be worth a hundred credits together, which was no small amount.

Diana had long given up on meditation for the evening. It was rather hard to concentrate when corpses were raining from the sky. The place reeked of death and stale blood.

She couldn't help but raise a brow when hundreds of fluffy orange birds impaled on vine spikes were brought through and added to the ridiculous pile that had grown in the courtyard's center.

Kaida was coiled loosely around her legs, and his head rested on her shoulder. His tongue kept flicking out while eyeing the mountain of food. It was likely heaven to him, but it was nothing but an eyesore for Diana.

A sudden enormous portal blocked the setting sun, and the Ent stepped through. It strode a few steps before sitting down. A root emerged from the ground and connected to the titan that became dormant in the corner of the peak.

There was no sign of Stella, which confused Diana. She was about to look for the girl when she appeared beside her.

"Phew, finally got rid of them. Oh hey, Diana, how's it going? Did you miss me?"

"Hi...?" Diana frowned. "Why do you sound so friendly?"

Stella snorted and shook her head. "Whatever, at least I tried."

"Right... May I ask what the meaning of all this is?" Diana gestured to the mountain of rotting meat.

Stella gazed at the pile and whistled. "Wow, I didn't know we collected so much. To answer your question, my dear friend, this was all in an attempt to get Dragon Marrow!"

"Dragon Marrow?" Diana searched her mind and had a vague idea. "Are you talking about an alchemy ingredient? Also, stop talking like that. It's not like you."

"Fine, fine," Stella grumbled. "Yes, I was talking about the alchemy ingredient. Apparently, it's found in the corpses of beasts on the cusp of ascending to the next stage or realm."

"Huh, that's odd. Why is that?" Diana inquired while letting Kaida gnaw on her finger. The little guy was clearly getting restless for some of the food.

"Something about the Qi in the body being the most dense while on the cusp of ascension."

"Makes sense," Diana said as she walked over to the corpse pile surrounded by shifting vines coated in spikes and picked up one of the skewered bird corpses, which seemed bite-sized for Kaida.

Diana then felt an all-too-familiar chill run down her spine. Glancing up, she caught a glimpse of that mysterious eye that glared through a jagged slit in Ashlock's black bark.

The vines shifted faster, making Diana stumble back despite the eye's presence. She could even feel Kaida hiss quietly as he slithered off her shoulder and retreated backward.

Like some accursed octopus checking out its prey, the vines brought the corpses one by one in front of the mysterious eye as if inspecting them. Most corpses got chucked to the side into a new pile and began to be dissolved, while a select few were placed in a separate pile. From a glance, Diana could tell those were the corpses with the most demonic Qi still wafting from their bodies.

Are those the corpses with the Dragon Marrow? Diana wondered, and then an odd thought crossed her mind.

Wait...as a demon, do I also have Dragon Marrow? I hope the alchemists won't start hunting me down.

58
ABYSSAL WHISPERS

Through his Demonic Eye, Ashlock could see through the mortal flesh and gaze upon the spiritual nature of the corpses he had acquired. Rather than black fur sprouting from leathered skin, he saw the dormant underlying spirit roots that had once served as the passageways for Qi that had fueled the dead monster's power.

Holding one of the headless ape corpses by the spike of his vine in front of his Demonic Eye, Ashlock scrutinized it. The passageways were devoid of the demonic Qi—which made sense as the monster had died. Without the Soul Core in their chest consciously directing the flow, the demonic Qi had nowhere to go except two places: into the rotting flesh or back to the outside world.

This ape had a lot of muscle tissue that had greedily absorbed the uncontrolled Qi. However, through his Demonic Eye, Ashlock could also see demonic Qi rising off the corpse—like smoke into the surrounding atmosphere.

It's why he preferred fresh corpses. They always provided the most sacrificial credits and had worked best for root puppets due to the Qi still present in the body.

Ashlock tossed this ape corpse to the right into a giant pile doused in corrosive fluids. It showed no signs of having been near ascending to the next stage or realm, which was what he was hunting for—he wanted Dragon Marrow.

"I can see why alchemists charge so much for pills now," Ashlock grumbled as he picked up another corpse to inspect it. "I'm going through all this effort for a single ingredient used in a tier-one pill, and I'm cheating with my Demonic Eye! Hell, I even grew the other two ingredients, so this should have been a breeze. Right? Am I missing something here? Why is sourcing ingredients so darn hard?"

Ashlock's grumbling was cut short as his eye pulsed with interest—this ape monster seemed more promising than the last few he had inspected. The demonic Qi smoke was denser, and the muscles were also packed with demonic Qi. It was all a guess at the end of the day, but Ashlock felt confident that this ape may have Dragon Marrow, so he carefully lowered it into the smaller pile to his left side and retracted his vine.

He still hadn't figured out how to get the Dragon Marrow out of the corpses, but he decided to deal with that later. Sorting through this monstrous pile came first.

As Ashlock picked up yet another corpse, he heard Larry gruffly ask, "Master, may I eat some?"

"What?" Ashlock's eye turned to glance at Larry, who had crawled down from his resting tree and stood beside the corpses that he had been busy absorbing.

"I can't?" Larry said, his head dropping a little.

"Of course you can. You just startled me." Ashlock obviously wanted as many sacrificial credits as possible, but he wasn't going to deny his summons a good meal.

"Thank you, Master, your generosity is as boundless as the stars in the sky!" Larry said as he opened his maw wide to devour a nearby corpse, but then Ashlock had a sudden idea.

"Wait!"

Larry comically froze mid-bite as if time had stopped.

"Don't eat from that pile. Come eat these ones instead." Ashlock pointed a vine at the pile of corpses that should have Dragon Marrow. "However, you must leave all the bones behind. Only eat the flesh."

Larry slowly withdrew his fangs and closed his maw. He then crawled past Ashlock, careful not to step on the hundreds of vines that slithered around his feet and made his way to the smaller, more tasty-looking pile.

To both of their surprise, Kaida had also made his way over to the pile and flickered his tongue at Ashlock as if asking for permission to also feast.

"Yes, yes, you can have some, too, Kaida. I need you to grow up big and strong, after all. Just remember not to eat the bones. I need them," Ashlock reassured the snake and earned a gleeful hiss.

He hadn't forgotten about the ink snake's unique power to bend reality to the words written in his ink. But he needed the snake to get to the Star Core Realm so that he could slowly produce ink Qi to use his powers without setting his cultivation backward.

Kaida's current Soul Core was like a tiny ink pot inside his body. He needed to fill the ink pot up to advance his cultivation but would drain the ink pot if he used his powers. This was why reaching Star Core would be so monumental, as the ink pot would automatically refill itself over time without Kaida even needing to cultivate.

Ashlock watched in interest as Larry reopened his maw, and thousands of tiny ash spiders tumbled out and latched onto the corpses. Then just like worker ants, they started tearing off bits of flesh with their fangs and carrying it back to Larry.

"A rather suitable way to eat for a royal spider." Ashlock laughed as he returned to work. An hour passed, and the final corpse had been checked as the courtyard was bathed in the orange glow of the setting sun.

Of the hundreds of corpses, only twenty had been deemed by him to potentially have Dragon Marrow. All of them had been devoured to the bone by Kaida and Larry. After having their fill, his two pets were relaxing off to the side with stuffed bellies.

With night approaching, Ashlock wanted to quickly confirm if any of these bones contained the alchemy ingredient they were after.

'Stella, can you check for Dragon Marrow?' Ashlock wrote on his trunk.

The girl chilling on the bench below his canopy and playing with Maple noticed his spatial Qi. She sat up and translated his words. With a sigh, Stella got up and walked over.

Diana was already crouched over and touching the bones with her finger.

"What are you doing?" Stella asked while crouching down beside her friend.

"I'm checking which one has the most demonic Qi," Diana replied in

her usual monotone voice while pointing between two sets of bones. *"I think this one will have Dragon Marrow while this one is a dud."*

"Well, let's find out..." Stella trailed off and frowned. *"How do we find out?"*

"I don't know? Aren't you the alchemist?" Diana snorted. *"You just spent the last hour telling me how easy you found alchemy, and now you are stumped."*

Stella crossed her arms and grumbled, *"I didn't lie. I'm good at alchemy—much better than those brats the Redclaws sent."*

"Oh? You didn't tell me they were young." Diana snorted. *"And yet they knew about the Dreamweaver Orchids? Impressive."*

"There's nothing impressive about memorizing plants from some dusty old books," Stella retorted.

"Didn't you learn the ancient runic language from some dusty old books?"

Stella glared at Diana. *"Will you shut up? Whose side are you on?"*

"We were picking sides?" Diana rolled her eyes. *"Why don't you go and get one of them to tell us how to do it?"*

"But I just dropped them off with Douglas," Stella protested. *"Surely we can figure it out without their help. Can I try something, Ash? I think I have an idea."*

Ashlock would rather get the twins' advice with the sun setting and the somewhat limited number of carcasses, but it wouldn't hurt to let Stella quickly try her idea, so he flashed his leaf once.

"It's rather funny how motivated she gets in an attempt to avoid having to rely on others," Ashlock mused. "Hopefully, she will be willing to work with others more as the sect expands and she gets used to those around her. But if she doesn't, that's fine, too."

Stella pulled a single bone free from two of the corpses. "You said this one was a dud, right?" she asked Diana, and the black-haired woman nodded.

"All right then, let's do this—" There was a snap as Stella cleanly cracked the bone in half down the middle with her Star Core strength. Inside was normal solid bone marrow.

She then cracked the bone Diana had identified as likely containing Dragon Marrow, and sure enough, a more jelly-like substance oozed out.

"Ha! Dragon Marrow!" Stella cheered as she tried to stop it from falling onto the floor. "Told you we didn't need the twins."

"But why would the Dragon Marrow be more jelly-like than regular bone marrow?" Diana tilted her head in confusion. *"That doesn't seem to make much sense."*

Stella shrugged. *"Why would I know? Go ask the twins or read the answer in a dusty book."*

Ashlock listened to them bickering for a while longer before deciding to fall asleep. He would finish absorbing all the corpses overnight, and then he could spend his points in the morning.

Ashlock awoke to another pleasant day. In fact, he was starting to get worried that there hadn't been rain in weeks.

"Actually, has it rained since the Dao Storm?" Ashlock wondered as he yawned in his mind. There was something about sleep that seemed to revitalize his soul and make him more motivated to tackle the day.

That was, of course, after his biology had finished kicking into gear. He had never been a fast riser, even when he had been human, but now it wasn't his laziness that held him back from starting his day but rather a wrestle with his tree body every morning.

Idletree Daily Sign-In System
Day: 3527
Daily Credit: 5
Sacrifice Credit: 821
[Sign in?]

"Morning, system," Ashlock mumbled at the familiar notification but then realized he had accumulated a surprising number of credits from the corpses.

"It would have been more if Kaida and Larry didn't eat a portion of them, but it would never be loads as they were all Qi Realm or low-stage Soul Fire Realm monsters." Ashlock hummed to himself as he debated whether he should sign in.

"Eight hundred points. Should be enough for an A-grade draw." Ashlock could wait around and farm more points for yet another S-grade draw, but the tournament was starting soon, and he had killed literally everything alive for miles around his demonic tree wall.

And if Dante Voidmind's plans were anything to go by, he was sure many sacrificial credits were on the horizon in the form of arrogant Voidmind family members.

"System, sign in for me."

[Sign in successful, 826 credits consumed...]
[Unlocked an A-grade skill: Abyssal Whispers]

Ashlock tried to hold back his excitement and relax as the information was shoved into his memory as if it had always been there. However, he was unable to stay calm for long...

"Is this telepathy? No fucking way—wait, no, not quite. It is telepathy, but the system lists it as an attack skill. Why?" Ashlock ran through the information in a half panic one last time and complied as a sort of ability description in his mind.

"The skill lets me project my consciousness outward, infiltrating the minds of those nearby with an insidious whisper. This isn't ordinary telepathy; the whispers are an invasive force that disrupts the mental and spiritual equilibrium of those with the misfortune of listening. I can use these whispers to sow confusion, fear, or paranoia through hallucinations by essentially assaulting the target's mind and spirit from within."

Ashlock sighed. This was too much excitement and confusion for so early in the morning. He had been practically dying for telepathy as a skill, and although this sounded similar, it was most certainly an attack skill meant to overwhelm a target's mind so he could impale with his vines and devour them.

"So {Abyssal Whispers} shouldn't be used on the weak-minded as I effectively invade their mind with my entire presence, and my words cause hallucinations and instill fear..."

Ashlock glanced around and saw Stella stirring awake from her meditation on the bench. As her eyes fluttered open to the rising sun, he decided to write her a message in his lilac flames.

If there was anyone he wanted to test this skill with first, it would be her.

Stella stretched her back as she cycled the Qi she had just absorbed throughout her body. It was a pleasant sensation, and she didn't notice a massive difference between cultivating on the bench or under the demonic trees lining the mountain peak.

"I think I will cultivate here from now on," she said aloud while leaning back and enjoying the sunrise.

However, she soon felt a small burst of spatial Qi behind her, so she turned to see lilac flames manifesting on Ash's black bark.

"'Stella, I want to talk to you,'" she translated and then smiled. "What's up, Tree?"

There was a pause, and Stella started to wonder if she had translated the meaning wrong, but the flames soon changed to clarify. 'I have learned a form of telepathy.'

Stella's eyes widened. "Speak to me? Directly? Will I finally hear your voice after all these years?"

'Yes,' Stella read from the flames. 'However, it may frighten you or make you mad. So relax and don't worry. Is that okay?'

Stella grinned. "I'm already mad! Hit me with it—" A chill throughout her body forced her to blink. When she opened her eyes, the courtyard was gone, the sky was black, and all around her was a mystical fog that reminded her of the Mystic Realm.

But most importantly, there was a familiar tree before her. It was alone in this abyssal world, its bare branches spreading to the starless sky above and fading out of view.

"Is this a dream?" Stella called out. Her voice sounded normal and didn't seem to match the space she was in. She desperately glanced around; things weren't adding up. She could still feel the constant cool wind of Red Vine Peak, and the way it brushed against her skin didn't match how the mystical fog rotated around them.

"This is a mental projection of me into your mind. You are still on the bench."

Stella felt her Star Core quiver as Ashlock's strange words echoed in her mind. She couldn't write out his words nor recite them. But she understood them on a fundamental level.

"Can you understand me? Am I speaking in the ancient runic language?"

As if it was listening to its master's whims, the mystical fog began to morph and change into a mirage of vibrant silver runes that floated around her, tempting her to read them, but if she focused on one for too long, it vanished as if scared of being seen and understood.

"Yes...no." Stella shook her head. She was getting disoriented. "It's not the ancient runic language, but I understand your intent."

"I see. It must be Soul Speech, then."

Stella had no idea what Soul Speech was, but she was far too distracted by the leafless tree. "Your form, why do you look like that? I am still on the bench, right? So you should be just behind me?"

"It's all an illusion..."

The tree suddenly grew larger and more menacing as it loomed over her. Even though she knew Ash wouldn't try to harm her, she couldn't help but gulp and feel fear festering on the outskirts of her mind.

"So this is Tree...no, Father's voice," she said in a small voice. "A bit more haunting than I imagined in my mind."

"These are not my words—I speak to you through the whispers of the abyss," Ashlock said. *"Now tell me what you see."*

Before Stella could respond, the fog morphed again into a sea of ghostly eyes that all glared at her, their pupils pulsing as if daring her to speak.

"I...I see a black barked tree, bare of any leaves or features," Stella hesitantly replied as the eyes moved in closer. "And thousands of creepy eyes glaring at me. I think every time you talk, it gets worse."

"Gets worse?"

Stella shivered as the eyes began to scream and wail, the starless sky cracked and shook, and a terrible feeling washed over her, making her stomach twist.

"Stop talking!" Stella snapped as she clutched her head. A moment passed, and the wails died down just enough for Stella to hear herself think.

I need to block out the mental torment somehow... Ah!

An idea struck—her spatial ring flashed with power, and a fruit materialized in her hand. Without delay, she bit into the fruit that should have the {Mind Fortress} effect Ashlock said would protect her from mental attacks.

A calming wave washed over her, banishing the horrors surrounding her and freeing her mind from the nightmare.

"Tree, I can think now!" she yelled, but her smile faded as the illusionary world cracked and crumbled around her. Streaks of morning sunlight cascaded through the gaps, and the next time she blinked, the world was back to normal.

Glancing back, Ash was there just like always. His scarlet leaves rustled in the morning breeze. His words felt like distant whispers in her mind that she struggled to recall as the calming wave continued to flow through her mind.

She leaned back on Ash's bark to enjoy the wonderous feeling of tranquility. "Mhm…I think the fruit was too powerful. It completely cut you out, Tree. I'm sorry."

After a while, as the numbing tranquility passed, she had a sudden realization.

What if I turned that fruit into a pill to lessen the effects? That way I can listen to him without the nightmare. However, I don't know any recipes using Ashlock's fruit, but we have Dragon Marrow, Qi Flowing Grass, Starlight Lotus, and even Dreamweaver Orchids to work with! I'm sure I can create something with those ingredients. To hell with old dusty books. I'll just make it myself.

Stella sprung up from the bench, grabbed a few of the {Mind Fortress} fruit growing from Ashlock's branches, and after consulting the spatial plane to set her anchor point many thousand meters below, she snapped her fingers, and a portal manifested.

"Tree, I will be right back!" she hollered before stepping through the rift and feeling the sudden shift in pressure and air quality.

Douglas was chatting away with the two twins, but they all turned to look at her when she arrived. She disliked their gaze but was getting used to it with time. The twins weren't so bad after spending most of yesterday with them.

"Have either of you ever created a new pill recipe?"

The twins both shook their heads as if it was obvious.

"That's impossible," Oliver replied respectfully. "It would take a master alchemist their whole life to create a new pill recipe that hasn't been discovered before."

"What if I had ingredients that have never existed before?" Stella grinned as she strode over to the cauldron. "Just sit back and watch if you don't believe me."

The twins looked to Douglas, who was grinning ear to ear as he watched Stella bring out an assortment of fruits onto the rim of the earthen bowl.

59
TALKATIVE TREE

Elder Margret tapped her foot in annoyance while waiting in the empty airship station. The midday sun streaked through the windows and doorways, which could only mean one thing.

The Skyrend family was late...as usual.

"They always do this," Elder Brent grumbled beside her. "Pretentious bastards that make everyone wait on them."

"Careful. What if their god strikes you down for the insult?" Elder Margret joked, and Elder Brent snorted.

"Good one."

A moment of silence passed between them with nothing but Elder Margret's impatient tapping. Eventually, Elder Brent spoke up. "You're heading straight to Red Vine Peak after greeting House Skyrend, right?"

"Yeah, got to check up on the twins and ensure they haven't offended the Ashfallen Sect somehow." Elder Margret sighed. "Especially Stella. That girl is hard to predict, which makes it all the more troublesome that one word from her could ruin us."

"She holds that much power?" Elder Brent cocked a brow. "I haven't interacted with her all that much, so I wouldn't know."

Elder Margret nodded. "Not only is she the descendent of the immortal, but she can command around a spirit beast capable of killing two families singlehandedly. And if that wasn't enough, she is one of the most talented alchemists I've ever seen."

"Scary stuff." Elder Brent whistled. "I guess I did know of all those things individually, but when you list it out like that... And her cultivation stage is what? Star Core?"

Elder Margret nodded over a bell ringing through the large lobby and a single mortal calling out, "House Skyrend has arrived!"

Both elders sighed deeply as pressure descended on the empty airship station.

"Did the scion come as well?" Elder Margret wondered aloud as she began to walk deeper into the station while cycling her own Qi to resist the pressure. "What a showoff."

A while later, the airship of House Skyrend had docked, and they began to walk into the large lobby, which would usually be overflowing with mortals buying tickets, saying goodbye to family members, or rushing to get on their flight. Yet for House Skyrend, it had been kept clear.

Around twenty men and women that were easily seven feet tall began to saunter into the lobby. These were the servants to the important members of the family, which was evident due to their gray robes.

Two people stuck out like sore thumbs within the group of servants. Not only were they a head taller than the servants, but their robes were a silky white that glowed in the sunlight.

The group walked across the desolate lobby and soon arrived before the two Redclaw Elders. The servants parted and made way for their masters, the Skyrend scions.

"Elder Margret?" A man almost twice her height glared down at her. His eyes had no pupils and were a pure glowing white. The white cloth he wore for clothes barely concealed his ripped muscles that looked inhumanly perfect, and his golden hair was combed back and ran down his shoulders and back.

This was, undoubtedly, a young man Elder Margret had met before.

"Theron Skyrend? It's been years since I last saw you or your father." Elder Margret offered a smile that Theron mirrored.

"Indeed, it has been far too long. We were wondering where you fire-loving lot had snuck off to, and it turned out to be so far east!"

Elder Margret held back her frown. She'd wondered why Theron had visited when he was a Star Core cultivator and one of the Skyrend Grand Elder's eldest descendants. However, from his words, it was now clear. He was here to gather information.

"Well, we felt like having a change of scenery," Elder Margret joked and then switched topics. "I see you are here with your sister. Come to support her in the tournament? I can't imagine you participating."

Theron's smile turned into a predatory grin like a shark. "Of course, I'm here to support Kassandra. She wanted to put her alchemy skills to the test against what the rest of the Blood Lotus Sect had to offer. Isn't that right?"

Kassandra Skyrend, whose eyes glowed a pale blue, smiled and nodded. "That's right, Brother." Her voice was soft and calm, matching her face that, much like her brother's, looked chiseled out of marble.

There was a reason the Skyrends called themselves heaven's children. Other than their inhuman looks, they were also called that due to their affinity, which was lightning. Their Grand Elder could wield heaven's lightning and was often hired to help elders from other families survive their heavenly tribulations.

"Obviously, she doesn't even need my support." Theron's laughter boomed through the expansive space. He then rested a hand on his sister's shoulder. "She could win with her eyes closed, after all."

"Brother, stop." Kassandra giggled. "That's giving the others far too much credit."

And there it is. Elder Margret sighed in her mind. *Their arrogance knows no bounds, to the point even the heavens would feel humble.*

"Well, we have quite a lot of talented people coming for this tournament—" Elder Brent coughed awkwardly when the two Skyrends glared at him. "But I am sure Kassandra will excel beyond our expectations."

Theron snorted. "Of course she will. Nothing this side of the continent compares to my dear sister's alchemy skills."

"Kassandra, if you don't mind me asking…"

The extremely tall woman tilted her head. "What is it, Elder Margret?"

"When did you begin to learn alchemy?"

Kassandra's glowing eyes pulsed briefly, and she smiled. "A month ago. But that's all the time someone like me needs to master such a primitive art form."

Elder Margret felt her blood boil as her field of expertise was insulted but kept her calm facade. It was tough to control the hot-headed nature of cultivating fire Qi. Still, she was determined not to end up like the earth-affinity cultivator that was obliterated by the Voidmind Scion a few days earlier.

She hadn't lived for centuries for nothing.

"As expected of someone from the prestigious Skyrend family." Elder Margret fake smiled as she summoned a parchment to her hand. "Before you go, let me just repeat the itinerary for the next few days."

"You can tell our servants such meaningless information." Theron waved her off and pulled his sister away. Half the servants moved to encircle them, and then they were gone in a flash of white lightning followed by a thunderclap.

Elder Margret's smile cracked slightly as she looked up at a stern-looking giant of pure chiseled muscle that gazed down at her with those same glowing eyes. "My name is Alexandros. I will manage the young master's and mistress's stay here in Darklight City."

Too exhausted to comment on the disrespect two youngsters from the Skyrend family had shown an Elder, she nodded and read off the parchment.

"In two days, we will organize an evening feast at the Immortal Gourmet Pavilion in the noble district. All families participating in the event are invited. Then the following morning is the preliminary round, where contestants will be expected to purify an ingredient and answer a simple question. The following afternoon will host the finals where those that passed the preliminary round will battle it out."

Elder Margret then handed the parchment to the man, who took it graciously with a slight bow. Even though they were members of the Skyrend family with unparalleled arrogance, the servants still knew not to disrespect an Elder of another noble family.

"We will be off, then." Alexandros ushered the other gray-robed servants to follow, and soon they were gone in a flash of lightning.

"I hate it when they do that," Elder Brent grumbled as he picked at his ears due to the constant thunderclaps that could kill a mortal child. "Are you off now?"

"Yeah, see you later."

"Tsk, leaving me here to greet the other families arriving today."

Elder Margret waved him off as she walked away. "Azurecrest and Terraforge should be a piece of cake. It's House Starweaver that will be unpleasant."

"Yeah, whatever," Elder Brent lamented. "I just hope one of those Terraforge hardasses doesn't try to punch my face for fun."

Elder Margret chuckled a little imagining the scene as she left the airship station and began to walk through the crowded streets back toward Red Vine Peak in the distance.

Stella felt like collapsing against the earthen bowl housing the cauldron fruit. Her hair was glued with sweat, and her legs felt like Dragon Marrow as they wobbled.

In her hand was a pill. Would it work? She sure hoped so, as she didn't know how much more torment she could handle.

"I feel like this could be the one!" Olivia said for the tenth time. Every attempt was the one in her eyes, but Stella found her optimism encouraging, so she refrained from calling it out.

Opening her mouth, she chucked the pill in and almost recoiled from the awful taste. The {Mind Fortress} fruit did little to overshadow the intense flavor of the Qi Flowing Grass. The previous versions with more Dragon Marrow and even the Starlight Lotus had been better tasting than this, but they hadn't helped.

Her aim was to create a pill with some juice from the fruit to help negate the awful effects of Ash's telepathy. Without the {Mind Fortress} fruit, she had no hope of lasting more than a few moments in that nightmare illusion, but eating the whole fruit closed her mind to everything, including his voice.

If possible, she wanted to find a balance—where the fruit numbed her mind just enough to ignore the wailing eyes but not enough to block out Ash.

"Ugh, so bitter and grassy…" Stella said while half choking on it. Eventually, she managed to swallow the ball of grass and cycle the pill's effects. The Qi Flowing Grass doused in the fruit juices was vital as the grass was known for its properties to facilitate the flow of Qi through the body's spirit roots, which Stella needed the most.

Dragon Marrow enhanced muscle tissue, whereas Starlight Lotus was known for unblocking muscle tissue. Both were useful for strengthening a body but had no use for a mental defense pill, so she hadn't included them in this iteration.

The only difference between this pill attempt and the last was the addition of the Dreamweaver Orchids, which according to Olivia was helpful with things involving illusions, so it sounded like the perfect plant to throw into the recipe as Ashlock had mentioned his new skill invoked illusions.

Very quickly after ingestion, Stella felt the familiar tranquility of the fruit creep into her mind, but it wasn't an overwhelming wave this time. Instead, it was like a mist clouding her consciousness.

"Okay, Patriarch, you can hit me with it again!" Stella shouted to the ceiling and then stumbled back against the bowl as she felt Ash's presence push its way into her consciousness.

If the sensation of a demonic tree trying to grow inside her mind wasn't weird enough, the strange looks the twins and Douglas gave her every time didn't help.

"I still haven't figured out what's wrong with her," Oliver whispered in his sister's ear as if she couldn't hear them loud as day due to her spiritual sense.

There's nothing wrong with me, Stella grumbled in her mind. *Blame Tree for sending creepy things at me while he's talking!*

Stella blinked as she noticed that same mystical fog swirl on the edge of her vision. However, the ceiling remained cold rock rather than all-encompassing darkness, and there were no wailing eyes. All good so far.

"You can speak now," she said mentally, as this was a telepathic connection. A moment passed until that same feeling of not quite words being imposed on her soul as pure intent hit her.

"Can you see me?"

"No—" Stella caught her tongue as she saw black roots begin to twist and grow along the cavern walls toward her and merge into a malformed tree. "Well, yes, I can sort of see you now, but I think the drug is reducing your presence."

"That's fine, so long as my words don't hurt you…"

Stella felt a pinprick of pain as cuts superimposed themselves on her skin.

"Let's not use the words hurt and pain again, okay?" Stella said as lovingly as she could through gritted teeth. If this had been the first time she had tried to talk with Ash today, she would have tolerated the pain, but with so many failed pills that had actually enhanced the illusions rather than reduced them, she was mentally exhausted.

"Okay…how's the pill?"

Stella ignored the sudden man-eating illusionary plants that spawned in the corner of her eye and replied, "I think this is the best one so far.

The Dreamweaver Orchids were a good addition. Thank you for growing them for me."

"*That's great news. A few more trials and you will have created a new pill.*" Ash's voice became a distant murmur as if he were mumbling to himself but came back in full force. "*This is amazing. You know, I'm so proud of you. I never knew you would be this talented at alchemy.*"

Stella couldn't help the grin that appeared on her face, but then she scowled at the twins. "Can you two stop looking at me like I'm crazy? It's ruining this great moment."

"Oh...sorry." Oliver scratched the back of his neck awkwardly and looked away, which only made Stella feel more awkward.

"Stella, I have good news for you." Ash laughed, which made the mist flash with different colors.

"What is it?" Stella wondered.

"*Elder Margret is outside the tunnel and is about to enter.*"

"Yesssss!" Stella shouted in her mind. "Freedom!"

She didn't even wait for the woman to enter the cavern. "Your Elder is back, so I will take my leave. See you two another time."

"Wait!" Olivia blurted. "At least explain your new pill to Elder Margret."

"No, thank you." Stella clicked her fingers, and a portal to the surface materialized. "You want to come with me, Douglas?"

The man shook his head. "No, I'm fine down here. I will try to relay your findings to Elder Margret when she arrives."

Stella shrugged and stepped through.

Only once the portal snapped closed behind her could she finally relax. She practically collapsed onto the bench as the mystical fog gathered around her, showing the telepathic connection was still working.

"Tree?"

"*I'm here.*"

With every word, she felt the mystical fog draw ever closer as it ate away at the mist enveloping her consciousness. Soon the awful-tasting pill would wear off, but until then, she could talk to Tree!

"This is so convenient! Sure, your words make my Star Core ripple from pressure, and I keep seeing things manifesting in the corner of my eye, but apart from that, this is great!"

Stella lay down and closed her eyes. Sadly the visions didn't stop just because she closed her eyes as they were being superimposed straight into her mind. They weren't real, after all.

"It is indeed convenient... I can talk to you even with your eyes closed now." Ash chuckled. *"It's funny what you're willing to put up with just to talk to me."*

"I spent a year hunched over books in a library trying to decipher how to read a language that was clearly designed by raving lunatics that have no concept of basic grammar rules. Not to mention so many words were missing that I have to guess based on context what you are saying half the time." Stella snorted. "Compared to that, this is nothing."

"I just wish I could have spoken to you sooner. I was always here, watching over you as the seasons passed. Actually, let me tell you about this one time when I woke up after being struck by lightning. Do you remember? You must have been only thirteen at the time. Gosh...where did the time go? You used to be so small, haha. Do you remember when I dropped fruit on your head when you got annoying? Wait, I am getting off-topic... Anyway, as I was saying, when I first got struck by lightning, I fell asleep for a long time, and when I woke up, you had grown up into this ice-cold beauty—"

Stella's eyes snapped open. "What?!?"

"And you strode into the courtyard while twirling your daggers, trying to look all cool..."

"Shut up, la, la, la, I'm not listening." Stella covered her ears and tried to drown out the embarrassing story.

"I was so sad. I thought I had slept too long and you had forgotten about me, but then the most humorous thing happened. This ice beauty devolved into a kitten and leaped across the courtyard to hug me while shouting, 'Tree!' It was adorable."

"Ugh..." Stella collapsed on the bench as her face heated up. "You're going to kill me."

"And then there was that time you thought trying to punch lightning would be a good idea. You went against Senior Lee's words and ran up my trunk while shouting some nonsense—"

Stella's ring flashed with power, and the last {Mind Fortress} fruit appeared in her hand. She scarfed it down as if it was life-saving medicine and then let out a satisfied groan as the mist in her consciousness morphed into a wave and drowned Ash's words.

"Ah...peace at last. Who knew he would be so talkative?"

60
DARKLIGHT CITY ACADEMY

"That will be all for this lecture on how to overcome the limits of your affinity. Are there any questions?" Elaine scanned the lecture hall for any raised hands or confused faces, but all she got back was bored looks or lecherous stares.

She stood on a raised wooden platform surrounded by rows of benches curved around the circular lecture hall. This was so all students, no matter where they sat, could get a good view of her, and the wall behind her that was painted in a thin sheen of low-grade spirit stones so she could draw and write things with her Qi.

Written on the silvery wall in glowing black lines were the fundamental truths that her uncle had taught her, and since she was relatively familiar with this topic due to her own research in an adjacent field, she decided to memorize her uncle's left-behind lecture notes and give the talk today.

A small sigh escaped her lips. The students had come from far and wide across the Blood Lotus Sect to attend this academy. Most were from noble families, but a few mortals that awakened their spirit roots were sprinkled here and there in their little clusters. They were easy to spot due to their lack of majestic robes and fingers weighed down by golden spatial rings.

Without a noble family to provide the cultivation resources and facilities needed to advance, these cultivators raised by mortals had to spend every Golden Crown they could work for on those resources that the nobles got for free.

Elaine would pity them if not for their and everyone else's utter lack of interest in her lecture. She knew she was partly to blame as she had never been the best at public speaking. However, she wasn't the sole reason for their disregard, as it was also known throughout the sect that Darklight Academy was where the talentless, delinquents, and descendants from side branches came to study.

Why would anyone willingly attend Darklight City's academy when Slymere was a quick airship ride away? Darklight was known for its mining and farming industries. In contrast, Slymere was known for its creative sector and top-tier academy attended by all noble families, including the Nightrose family.

Comparing the two was like night and day.

"Seriously, no questions?" Elaine glanced at the top row, wholly occupied by those from the Redclaw family, unmistakable due to their crimson hair, dark red robes, and similar features. Even they seemed a little bored, which hurt Elaine's pride a tad.

It's not my fault that Uncle is gone, and you're stuck with me. I wonder how the Redclaws' attitude would change if they knew I was with the Ashfallen Sect. That's a funny thought...

With nobody engaged or asking questions, Elaine checked her internal clock. Qi followed the will of the realm, so it was easy to estimate the time by checking the density of various Qi types floating around, such as light.

Mhm, around half an hour before midday. If I end the lecture early, I could stop by the study on the way to the dining hall to meet Douglas.

Elaine touched the silvery wall behind her and pulled the Qi back into her Soul Core. It was teacher etiquette to remove one's Qi from the spirit stone wall, and there was no way Elaine would waste the precious void Qi she had managed to accumulate by leaving it here.

"Well, since nobody has any questions, I shall end this lecture a little earlier than planned. Have a good day, everyone... Oh, and don't forget about the alchemy tournament happening in two days. Everyone from the Academy is allowed free entry."

Elaine's words were drowned out by the sudden chorus of students standing up and gathering their things before leaving the room. Only a few cultivators—mainly from the Redclaw family—gave her a short nod as they walked out. As the region's ruling family, they had been told by their Elders to respect the teachers at the Academy.

With another sigh, Elaine gave the now-empty lecture hall a quick glance to make sure nothing was left behind, and then she followed the tail end of the students down the corridor.

Her mind wandered as she walked alone through the hallways.

Ugh, what do I do about Douglas? He is handsome and kind, but I thought I would end up with a bookworm like me rather than someone from the Terraforge family.

Elaine frowned as she imagined her father's face if she told him she had almost slept with someone from the Terraforge family. Raised as a scion of the Voidmind family, she had been taught that the Terraforge family were no better than the beasts that howl beyond the walls.

Why should I care what my family thinks anyway? They abandoned me, so I owe them nothing. But I do have to admit Douglas is rather rough around the edges, with a very down-to-earth personality.

But it was nowhere near as bad as the stigma her father had drilled into her head.

Should I just commit to the relationship and stop leading him on? We already slept in the same bed, so the jump to the next step feels a little easier, but still, I want to take things slowly to make sure he is the one for me. My world has been flipped upside down since that fateful night when Diana pressed a dagger to my neck, and it's taking some time for me to readjust to the absurdities of the Ashfallen Sect.

Elaine rounded a corner. Her eyes followed the floor as she mulled over her thoughts; however, her brain recognized the changing floor pattern to mean she had entered the teacher's area. So she glanced up and was taken aback when she saw someone leaving her study. Even worse, it was a man with an all-too-familiar silhouette.

She only caught a brief glimpse of Dante shutting the door behind him before he used Void Step to vanish. The runes engraved in the walls and doors of the corridor flashed with power as they attempted to suppress the influx of Qi, but there was very little in this world that could stop Void Step—the famed movement technique of House Voidmind.

He shouldn't have detected me coming because of the runes in the walls. Did I catch him leaving because I ended my lecture early? What the hell was he doing in my study?

Technically, it was a joint study between her and Uncle. And it wouldn't be peculiar for the scion of the Voidmind family to enter a study run by his Elder and sister, but it still struck her as odd.

Elaine approached the study's door with bated breath. The bland wooden door looked normal, like always. It clicked open when she inserted her Qi, and the insides looked as disorderly as ever. The central desk was still covered in parchments.

What could he possibly want from here? Elaine tapped her chin as she walked around. Every shadow or corner she passed made her heart race. She knew deep down that Dante wouldn't directly harm her, but that didn't mean she wasn't a little terrified. What if he discovered her secret and tried to force her to tell him about it? The oath would kill her before he could.

We did plan to have our next meetings here. Should I tell Douglas to move them someplace else?

With the tournament so close and all the noble families arriving today, she saw little need for more meetings, so maybe she could just tell Douglas to call them off. The stage was already set, and they all knew chaos was on the horizon.

I do want to figure out the real reason Dante is here. His nonsense about overtaking Darklight City doesn't make sense. Why would the scion of House Voidmind, one of the most powerful and influential families, deem it necessary to overtake Darklight City? A backwater mining city with little going for it?

Elaine wasn't buying it, but she couldn't find a way to get to the truth without confronting Dante about it, and that was an interaction she wasn't eager to participate in.

There were many ways to die in this ruthless world, but asking too many questions was one of the best to find a sword through one's back.

Elaine sighed as she left the lecture notes on the desk and ran a hand through her silky hair. What was she to do? Why was everything so stressful now?

I must be careful what I say here. There's a chance Dante left a recording artifact. Should I still go to see Douglas now and confront him about our relationship? Or should I head back to the mansion and confront my brother?

She found herself pacing the messy room. All that lay before her were twisted paths without clear results—something she hated.

Just relax, Elaine. The Ashfallen Sect knows of Dante's invasion and should be able to handle any other nonsense he's got hidden up his sleeve.

She stopped her pacing and glanced out the window.

I should get a move on. Douglas is likely waiting for me.

"Not enjoying the soup?" Douglas looked at her with those warm brown eyes. Elaine just stared and got lost in them. Her mind told her this was illogical and that she was only enthralled with him due to the circumstances surrounding their meeting.

Yet after a few days apart and spending them alone meditating in the Void Chamber or reading research notes, she felt the same warmth she had the first time they met.

Perhaps I'm really in love...

"Is there something on my face?" Douglas started licking his lips as if trying to remove nonexistent food from his stubble.

"No, I was just enjoying the view." Elaine smiled, glanced away, and decided to hide her shamefulness by dipping bread in her soup.

Douglas snorted. "Bold today, are we?"

"Perhaps," Elaine tapped his shin under the table with her foot, "but wait till after the big day."

Telling Douglas to wait until after the tournament to avoid blowing their cover had been her tactic to delay things so she could get a better feeling for the relationship. She was now more sure than ever that this was a relationship she wanted to pursue after spending time apart. The problem was she had zero experience in dating as she had been moved out of the family before she could be used as a marriage pawn.

This lack of experience had been fine when she felt her life was at risk if she didn't latch onto Douglas. But now it was different. She could approach it with a calm mind, and that just made it all the more stressful.

"Stop teasing me, then," Douglas grumbled.

Elaine continued smiling, lost in her own little world.

Idletree Daily Sign-In System
Day: 3529
Daily Credit: 2
Sacrifice Credit: 0

[Sign in?]

Ashlock awoke to his system notifying him that yet another day had passed. Honestly, the last two days had been rather dull.

"Isn't the meal at the Immortal Gourmet Pavilion happening tonight?" Ashlock slurred to himself as his mind kicked into gear.

Other than watching the various noble families arriving, he had spent his days overseeing Stella in the cavern, trying to improve the Mind Fortress pill.

On the topic of noble families, he had expected all of them to turn up with big-shot scions after the Voidmind and Skyrend family, but that was not the case. Azurecrest, Starweaver, and Terraforge all showed up with people from side branches or low-ranking scions if the grumbles of Elder Brent were anything to go by.

However, this information didn't put Ashlock at ease. Instead, it made him even more worried. Dante Voidmind's reason for being here was discovered by his sister, so why was Theron Skyrend here with his sister?

"No way he plans to invade, too? I still don't understand why Dante needs an alchemist tournament to justify his invasion." Ashlock felt a headache coming on so early in the morning. He needed more information, but the mansions controlled by the various families throughout the noble district were heavily guarded, just like the Voidmind mansion had been.

While mulling over his options, a portal appeared.

Stella and Diana strode through and glanced around.

"Okay, after a few days, I think I have perfected the ratios as best I can," Stella said while holding up a purple-and-green pill with spots of yellow. *"You can speak to Tree with this."*

"I can?" Diana's eyes widened a little. *"You're not trying to poison me, are you?"*

"I..." Stella blinked. *"I'm not even sure how to feel insulted by that. Are you suggesting I would backstab you or that I am so incompetent at alchemy that I would accidentally kill my friend?"*

Diana snorted. *"It was a joke, Stella. Just give me the darn pill."*

"Oh...sure." Stella frowned and placed the odd-looking pill in Diana's palm. "I don't see how that was funny."

"Shhh, now tell me what to do." Diana held the pill and inspected it.

"Just eat it?"

"Wait a moment. This pill is the strongest one yet, so Tree may need to start the connection first. Once you see the white fog appear, then eat it."

Honestly, that was unnecessary. {Abyssal Whispers} was an A-grade mental attack skill, it could force its way past even the {Mind Fortress} fruit if he put his full power into it, but he hadn't, as hurting Stella had never been the intention. When he saw her struggling, he'd pulled back his presence and tried to avoid sending any mental attacks her way.

Diana stood there glancing around as if trying to find the white fog Stella was talking about, so he activated the skill and targeted her. He only used a fraction of its full force as she was a realm weaker than Stella. Within a second, he had smashed through her mental defenses and weaseled into her consciousness.

It was a surreal experience, even for him. The sensation of his voice actually being able to leave through his trunk and travel down the mental link through the skill was magical to him in a bizarre way.

"I see the white smoke!" Diana shouted and then ate the pill.

Immediately, Ashlock felt a force try to push him out, like a hot blast of air. He could resist it by dialing up the power of the skill, but he did so in a way that focused on telepathy rather than all the hallucinations.

"Can you hear me?" Ashlock asked, and Diana practically jumped out of her skin.

"Yes, I can. Wow...this is so weird." Diana's monotone voice came straight into his mind and didn't sound slightly distorted like usual.

"Why are there floating ears with wings near the Patriarch?" Diana asked Stella.

The blond girl laughed. *"They are all illusions. Just ignore them."*

"I see...and it was worse than this before the pill?"

All the color drained from Stella's face as she shuddered. "Yes...yes, it was."

"Sorry, Patriarch, I am just a bit distracted," Diana said through the mental connection. "I didn't expect your voice to sound like this."

"Does my voice sound weird?"

"It's hard to describe, but it's like a chorus of a thousand tortured souls all shouting at once past my ears and straight at my soul." Diana laughed. "Meanwhile, I thought you would sound like an old grandpa. No offense."

"None taken," Ashlock replied. It was unfortunate to learn his voice was so hard to listen to, but with a skill named {Abyssal Whispers}, it made sense that he wouldn't have the voice of an angel.

"I can feel a pressure on my soul that's making it hard to stand here," Diana admitted, "as if your words are direct attacks wearing away the barrier on my consciousness from the pill Stella gave me."

She then looked back at Stella. *"How did you survive this without the pill?"*

Stella shrugged. *"No idea. I'm unsure if my brain is still in one piece."*

"How many pills did you make?"

Stella counted on her fingers. *"Maybe thirty? It's been a long two days. Actually, on that note, I used up quite a lot of Dragon Marrow practicing the Body Strengthening pill alongside the twins. Elder Margret says there's still enough for the tournament, but I was going to ask how we plan to acquire it in the future."*

This was actually a topic Ashlock had some ideas for but hadn't had a chance to bring it up.

"Diana, you see that pile of bones over there?"

She turned around and saw the pile. "Yes, Patriarch, I see them? Aren't these the bones left over from the hunt a few days ago?"

"Yes, they are the ones Stella didn't snap in half because they didn't have enough Qi to be Dragon Marrow. I had a thought. Would either you or Kaida be able to artificially create Dragon Marrow with demonic Qi?"

Diana was nursing her head after his words, but she slowly nodded. "It's possible, but I wouldn't advise it."

"Why not?"

"Well, if you order me to, I can force my demonic Qi into a single bone, and it may transform the insides into Dragon Marrow. But then I would have wasted weeks of cultivation and thrown off my body's harmony between demonic Qi and water Qi." Diana paused to massage her temples and close her eyes. "Kaida is much the same. It just doesn't seem worth it to me."

Interesting. So it was, in fact, possible, or at least Diana thought it was. But it was such an inefficient method that it was basically off the table.

"Sorry, Patriarch, do you mind retracting from my mind?" Diana half begged. "My soul is trembling."

Ashlock said nothing to avoid inflicting further pain and turned off the skill.

Diana stumbled forward and collapsed on the bench while breathing heavily. "Stella...I have...no idea...how you managed to survive...making this pill."

"I have no idea. Just rest easy and recover." Stella sat beside her. "I need you well rested by this evening."

"Why?" Diana slurred as she massaged her forehead with her eyes closed.

"I didn't get a chance to tell you yet, but the Redclaw Grand Elder requested we attend the feast tonight at the Immortal Gourmet Pavilion."

Diana's eyes shot open. "What? I thought only I was going. Why would you come as well?"

"The Grand Elder told me through Elder Margret earlier today that with Dante Voidmind and Theron Skyrend there, he needs another Star Core cultivator beside him to avoid being looked down upon. So he asked if I could attend the event."

"And you agreed to that?!? Ow, ow..." Diana clutched her head and fell backward again.

"Well, not initially, but after some thought, I decided it would be a perfect opportunity to practice socializing with other cultivators. Also, I can wear my mask and just stand in the corner if it's too much."

"That has to be the worst idea I have ever heard." Diana groaned, and Ashlock had to agree. There was no way Stella could navigate such a political gathering and not cause problems.

"I'm not that bad at socializing." Stella pouted. "Come on, trust me! I have been speaking with the twins all day without a problem. And remember all the times I talked to the Redclaws?"

There was a long pause before Diana replied, "Fine...but we got a lot of work to do to get you ready."

61
IMMORTAL GOURMET PAVILION

Stella sat on the bench with her back straight. Her gaze was dead set ahead on the demonic tree offspring in the courtyard center in a vain attempt to ignore the perpetual mystical fog hanging at the edges of her consciousness due to her open telepathic connection with Tree.

Her new pill may provide a decent amount of mental protection, but half-formed horrors still lurked beyond the fog begging for a single look so they may inflict nightmares.

Diana was behind her, leaning against Ash while she wrestled with her hair to try and get it into a ponytail. Apparently, her wild hairstyle wasn't noble enough for tonight's feast, and Diana seemed determined to style it for her.

"I still don't think this is a very good idea," Diana muttered in her ear, and despite the Mind Fortress pill soothing her mental state, Stella still had a knot in her stomach.

She agreed with Diana that attending such an event was questionable as she had grown up alone since childhood and had never participated in noble parties nor been taught the correct etiquette.

Still, the Grand Elder had requested her presence not only for his own protection but also to bolster the presence of the Redclaw family. It would be an embarrassment if the Redclaws were to turn up with a single Star Core cultivator when a family like the Silverspires used them as bodyguards.

And she felt this was a rare opportunity to jump into the deep end and face her fears. *Whether I like it or not, the Ashfallen Sect will continue to expand. If I can't even stand in the corner at an event, how can I be helpful to Tree? I have spoken numerous times with the Redclaw family in the past, and more recently, I held conversations with the twins without too much issue, so I should be able to pose as a wallflower and hide in the corner.*

That was her grand plan: turn up, locate the quietest corner, and silently convey her presence so the other families wouldn't think to look down on the Redclaws and the tournament.

"Stella, are you sure you will be all right?" Ashlock asked. His voice somehow calmed her soul despite its power and chaotic form.

"Will you be watching over me?" Stella replied. "I have plenty of pills to maintain our telepathic connect all night."

"Won't the horrors of my technique throw you off?"

Stella shook her head, earning an annoyed huff from Diana as she moved her hair. "No, your presence brings me a strange peace rather than fear."

"Well, I am always watching over you... I just sometimes get distracted...or fall asleep." Ashlock chuckled. ***"But if you want my focus, I will always give it. Not like I would miss my daughter's first social event for anything."***

"Then I have nothing to worry about with your support." Stella sighed with relief, but the knot in her stomach remained. However, she didn't want her indecisiveness to be known as she wanted to reassure Diana that she would handle herself properly tonight at the Immortal Gourmet Pavilion.

"Yes, you do have things to worry about." Diana lightly yanked her head back and placed a hairclip to keep it all in place. "Even with your hair done, you still need to change out of those comfortable trousers you are wearing into a dress."

"I don't really like dresses, though." Stella pouted. "They feel so formal, and I can't run around in them as easily."

"Tough luck, you're wearing one." Diana paused. "Wait, do you have a suitable dress?"

"No..."

Diana groaned, drummed the bench's backrest in annoyance for a moment, and then seemed to have an idea. "Patriarch, can you portal me over to the White Stone Palace?"

There was a noticeable movement of spatial Qi through the ground and up through the Qi-gathering formation, and a moment later, an almost perfect portal formed.

Diana dashed through, and the portal closed behind her.

With nothing else to do, Stella sat there and watched the evening sun while thinking up scenarios for tonight in her head. What should she do if one of the scions approached her and tried to strike up a conversation? Should she develop a new identity, or would she forget it during a crucial moment and blow her cover?

"Be honest with me, Stella. Are you doing this for yourself or in an effort to please those around you?"

"Both," Stella replied without hesitation. "I understand I had an odd start in life, and I don't want to be that weird girl that feels uncomfortable around people forever."

A breeze rustled Ashlock's leaves overhead, and Stella could hear distant birds chirping as the mountain peak was bathed in the orange glow of the setting sun. Stella could feel the winds of change in the air and knew tonight would be a memorable one, that was for sure.

"It makes me sad you feel that way. Are you suggesting my parenting wasn't good enough?" Ashlock grumbled. *"Kids these days have no appreciation of how hard it is to raise an unruly child when I had no mouth or arms."*

Stella touched the red maple leaf earrings she had worn since childhood and laughed. "Tree, don't be sad. You did the best you could. It's not like it was your responsibility in the first place. If not for the Patriarch pressuring my father, he would have still been around to raise me."

Her eyes narrowed. "It seemed like an impossible dream, but with every passing day, I feel closer to the day I may be able to create a pill from the Patriarch's cold corpse."

"He will die." The surrounding mystical fog flashed crimson, and the power behind Ashlock's voice made Stella's Star Core tremble. *"He cannot escape me. My roots will spread across the land and then throughout the nine realms. Not even heaven would save him from me."*

"I trust you, Tree." Stella leaned back and rested her head against his bark. "You wouldn't lie to me."

There was a sudden surge in spatial Qi, and a rift manifested.

Diana stepped through with a grin and said flatly, "Miss me?"

"No."

"Well, now I am even more glad with my dress choice, knowing you can't hate me any more than you already do!" Diana walked over, her ring flashed with power, and a very sleek black dress appeared in her arms.

"There's no way I would wear something like that," Stella said, glaring at the dress.

Diana shrugged. "Then you can't come."

"But the Redclaw Grand Elder said he needed me to save face," Stella protested, but Diana wasn't budging.

"There are two Star Cores from other families there," Diana said. "And we have the Redclaw Grand Elder and Sebastian attending from our side, so that's two on two."

"Why does he need me, then? I didn't know the Silverspires were going when I agreed to attend."

"Because cowering in the Silverspires shadow is a bad look, and Theron Skyrend would also need two Star Cores to hold him down if something were to go wrong."

Stella gulped. "Fine, I will wear the dress. Wait, why are you going to the party, then?"

Diana handed over the dress. "It's noble etiquette to host a gathering before an event as it gives a rare chance for the families to mingle. I'm going there alongside the Silverspires to talk to the merchants about a potential trade deal."

"Oh, I see." Stella's ring flashed, and a small bottle of pills manifested. "You should take these, then. They will help in the negotiations."

"Thank you." Diana took the pills and then frowned when she saw Stella's apprehensive look at the dress. "These pills change nothing. You still have to wear that."

"How did you even get this?" Stella asked while standing up and holding the dress before her to get a better look.

"I asked Amber for it," Diana replied. "You two have a similar body type."

Stella pouted. "We do not…"

"Yes, you do. Now put on the darn dress, the sun is setting, and we still have things to do."

"Fine." Stella sighed. Her ring flashed with golden light, and her current clothes vanished. The dress in her hands briefly entered the ring and then materialized on her body.

Why is it so tight? Stupid parties and their impractical dresses. Maybe I should just stay home and tell the Grand Elder good luck...

"You look great," Diana said with her usual utter lack of enthusiasm, which made Stella somewhat doubtful that she was telling the truth.

Stella shivered as the cool breeze tickled her bare back. "Can I wear a jacket or something? This feels far too exposing."

"No, that would ruin the look," Diana said resolutely. "Absolutely not."

She then summoned a black mask that was different from the others. It was made of a soft cloth material that would only cover her mouth and not her eyes.

"I know you want to hide your face, but a wooden mask is too obnoxious to go unnoticed, so you will have to do with this instead."

"Is it really fine that I wear a disguise? Won't people look at me weirdly?"

Diana shrugged. "They will anyway. To them, you are an unknown. You don't have the features of a Redclaw or a Silverspire, yet you will be introduced as working for both. Your looks are eye-catching, and your high cultivation realm at such a young age is very impressive."

"So they are going to stare at me?" Stella looked at the mask in her hands, the knot in her stomach only worsening.

"Yeah, which is why I suggest you don't go."

Stella took in her words and stared at the floor, her mind racing with thoughts.

I understand her concerns, but nobody ever achieved anything by being comfortable. I have always learned the most by putting myself in new and frightening situations, and I feel I have gotten too comfortable under Tree's canopy lately.

Stella put on the mask—the soft material obscuring her lips reignited her confidence, but the dress was still far too much. Most of her back was exposed, and so were her arms and shoulders. It was simply too much skin for her.

Diana stood there, tapping her chin while looking at her. "Your disguise is good, but I feel we could go a step further somehow."

"Why? Will people recognize me?"

"Gods, no, very few know of your existence. But what if you make a fool of yourself? It would be best to obscure your true self as much as possible as insurance."

Stella's mood soured. She really didn't appreciate Diana treating her like some mischievous child that would spoil the party.

"What is it, Kaida?" Diana looked down to her side to see the snake hissing happily about something. She reached down to pat the snake on the head, but Kaida dodged and then pointed at Diana's hand with his tail glistening with ink.

Diana crouched and held out her hand. "Why do you want my hand?"

Kaida placed his tail's tip against Diana's palm and drew a small X, which made her pull back her hand with a slight hiss of pain.

Diana tried to wipe the ink off, but it stayed under her skin. "A tattoo?"

Her eyes widened. "Can you take the ink back?"

With a swish of his tail against her palm, Kaida reclaimed most of the ink Qi, but he did leave around a third behind, which seemed infused in Diana's skin. She inspected the faint X still on her palm—a quick burst of demonic Qi and the ink Qi evaporated away, leaving no mark behind.

"Fascinating." Diana stood up and grinned. "Kaida, would you be able to give Stella some tattoos? Especially one on her back?"

Kaida let off a low hiss as he slithered closer to Stella and joined her on the bench.

The two locked eyes for a while, neither saying anything.

What does he want me to do? Stella wondered.

"Haha, why didn't I think of this? Kaida becoming a tattoo artist makes so much sense!" Ashlock's voice boomed in Stella's mind. **"Anyway, Stella, Kaida is asking what type of tattoo you want."**

"A demonic tree!" Stella said without pause as she looked straight ahead at Ashlock's offspring.

"No. That's too risky." Ashlock shot down her dreams and felt herself deflate on the bench. "Why not?"

"The whole point of all this is to give you an identity you can throw away if needed. Branding yourself with a tattoo you might want to keep in the future is a waste. Pick something similar if you want. How about my black-thorned vines?"

Stella didn't feel like arguing with people anymore. The social event hadn't even begun yet, and she already wanted to retreat into the cavern and do alchemy alone.

"Fine, I will settle for that." Stella straightened and turned her back to Kaida. "Just cover my back and arms in them— Ow!"

Stella felt a pinprick of pain wherever Kaida moved his tail. It likely would have been much worse, but the Mind Fortress pill helped protect her mind from the pain.

"Is it usually this painful?" Stella questioned while trying to look over her shoulder at the half-drawn design.

"Considering Kaida has to forcefully inject his ink Qi into your skin, I'm surprised your body isn't reacting more violently."

An hour later, dusk had arrived, signaling the start of the gathering.

"Aren't we going to be late?" Stella worried as she stood on the mountain peak while inspecting her new tattoos. She liked how the black vines covered in menacing thorns curled up her arms and bloomed on her back. It gave her a weird sense of confidence, and she looked forward to when she could get a demonic tree one.

"No, the host always arrives last to these kinds of events." Diana chuckled as she looked to the sky. "But we should probably get going. Patriarch, can you portal us over to the Redclaws?"

A moment later, a portal manifested, and Stella went to walk through but stumbled. "Stupid heels. Who invented these abominations?"

"Language, Stella. They were discovered in the rifts, and just like the dress, they were designed to make our lives as difficult as possible."

Stella scrutinized Diana, who was wearing a similar black dress and high heels to her and had copied the black vine tattoos. A black cloth mask also obscured her features, leaving her eyes partially hidden behind her short hair.

"Less staring and more walking." Diana strode through the portal, and with some difficulty, Stella soon followed.

With a pop, they arrived in the courtyard of the White Stone Palace. Already waiting was the Redclaw Grand Elder alongside Elder Margret and Brent. Standing off to the side were Sebastian and Ryker.

"Big Sister!" Ryker perked up and dashed over. "You look so pretty!"

Stella was baffled and tried to stumble back from the kid. "Is he really coming with us?"

The Grand Elder chuckled. "Who are we to tell a scion of House Silverspire what to do and where to go? If anything, bringing him with us will give us more face."

Ryker balled his fists. "The adults are scared of my might!"

"Ahem, anyway…" The Grand Elder drew everyone's attention. "Tonight is a big night for us all. To our surprise, two Star Core scions have decided to attend our little tournament, and some merchants from Slymere are also present. Our goal is simple: show that we, the Redclaw family shadowed by the Ashfallen Sect, rule over Darklight City with an iron fist and that it cannot be seized from us. We already know that nefarious plots are afoot, with more lurking in the darkness. So keep your wits about you and don't show a hint of weakness."

Everyone nodded, and Stella felt anticipation rise within her. It felt like she was going to war rather than a feast between supposedly friendly families of the same sect.

The Grand Elder stepped toward the gate, his silky crimson robes fluttering in the breeze. "When we arrive, the Silverspires, alongside Diana and I, will confront the merchants present at the venue. The rest of you may get a head start on socializing with the other families."

Stella whispered in her mind, "Tree…can you portal us over? I can't walk very well in heels."

"You want a grand entrance?" Ashlock laughed. *"Then I can give you one."*

The air in the courtyard trembled as spatial Qi gathered and formed a truly enormous portal so clear it was like staring through a lilac-tinted window to the other side.

"So that's the Immortal Gourmet Pavilion," Stella muttered as she scrutinized the majestic establishment through the portal. While she was busy staring, the others had already begun to walk through, and before she knew it, she was one of the last ones.

You can do this, Stella. Just walk through, find a corner, and stay quiet.

You are nothing but a pretty wallflower, here to observe and threaten with your presence.

Stepping through, she was greeted by a wide, serpentine path lined with ancient, flowering green-leafed trees. Inferior plants, was all Stella could think as she clumsily followed the others down a trail illuminated by lanterns adorned with intricate carvings of mythical beasts that cast a warm, inviting glow over the polished jade pavement. Up ahead was the entrance, a colossal gate of vermilion and gold, upon which the name of the pavilion was elegantly etched in glowing calligraphy.

[Immortal Gourmet Pavilion]

Stella gulped as she carefully walked up the jade steps through the colossal gate and into the entrance area.

A man wearing a suit off the side puffed up his chest and shouted, "Now entering, the tournament's host House Redclaw alongside the tournament's main sponsor, House Silverspire!"

Stella felt numb as a wave of applause shook the building. She stood alongside the others on a raised balcony overlooking everyone. Two grand staircases led to the restaurant below, and a terrible realization hit her as her eyes darted around the dimly lit space.

There were no corners to hide in. There were tables everywhere, even in the corners, and at least one person was sitting at each one. Before she knew it, the others descended and went off to the side to meet with a group of masked individuals that were likely the merchants.

"Shall we go and greet the guests?" Elder Margret offered her a reassuring smile and took her hand. Everything felt like a blur as Stella was led through the tables, receiving various glances.

Eventually, they came upon a mostly empty table, apart from two giant people that loomed over the table and looked like they had been chiseled from marble.

"Those two are from the Skyrend family." Ashlock's voice rumbled in her mind. ***"Be careful of them, especially Theron Skyrend. He is a stage higher than the Grand Elder in the Star Core Realm."***

Stella felt her mind blank as Theron looked her up and down with his glowing eyes, and a smile appeared on his lips. "I don't think we have ever met before, young miss. Which family are you from?"

62
THE SIN OF PRIDE

Which family was she from?

Stella stood there, unsure how to respond. Her true identity would be easy to discover if she admitted to being a Crestfallen. Ashfallen was out of the question as it wasn't a known family or sect yet, and she didn't have the facial features of someone from the Redclaw or Silverspire family. So what should she even say?

Sensing her hesitation, Elder Margret stepped slightly forward. "She is currently with us."

"The Redclaw family?" Theron Skyrend narrowed his glowing eyes and grinned. "Come take a seat, miss."

His massive hand was gesturing to the empty seat before her, and in the dim lighting of the restaurant, she feared it would either eat her or chains would spring out and strap her down.

A part of her wanted to turn around and walk away, but even she knew that would be incredibly discourteous after being offered a seat at someone's table.

Why did I think this was a good idea? was all Stella could think as she pulled the seat back and carefully sat in its confines. A large ornate wooden table may separate her from Theron, but his giant body made the table feel smaller than it was.

Elder Margret pulled out the chair beside her, offering some reassurance. Elder Brent had gone off to another table nearby with members from a family unknown to her, but from their cosmic-looking hair, she could guess they were the Starweaver family.

Theron took charge of the conversation and decided to do a round of introductions. "My name is Theron, and this is my dear sister Kassandra Skyrend. I already know of Elder Margret. I believe we last met a decade ago at the Silverspire economic summit?"

"That is correct." Elder Margret nodded. "You were a teenager back then."

Theron's laughter boomed across the table. "That's right! I wonder if there will be another event hosted by the Silverspires." His voice dropped slightly as he glanced across the room at Sebastian's back as he talked with the merchants. "You know…because of the whole silver core inheritance thing."

"It's possible. I just hope they don't announce another drastic increase in the cost of their spatial rings." Elder Margret sighed. "They were already expensive enough."

Stella listened in silence, eager not to draw any attention to herself. However, she had to keep her eyes on one of the people's faces to avoid seeing the horrors lurking in the mystical fog at the edge of her consciousness.

Finding Theron hard to look at, she ended up glancing at Kassandra. She returned the glance, but it didn't come off as friendly. Almost as if she was looking down at her…which she was due to her height, but it still made her feel looked down upon. Unlike Theron, Kassandra's eyes glowed a light blue.

Eventually, the exchange of pleasantries between Theron and Elder Margret dried up, and Theron turned to Stella and asked the dreaded question. "And your name was?"

"Roselyn," Stella answered calmly. This was a name she had thought up after getting the tattoos.

"No family name?" Theron was really hung up on finding out which family she was from, which irked Stella. Why was he so darn persistent?

Stella remained silent, so Elder Margret chimed in. "She is just here to observe rather than engage in discussion."

"A lesser should learn to keep quiet," Theron snapped at Elder Margret. "I was asking Mistress Roselyn here, not you."

Elder Margret's eye twitched. She opened her mouth and then closed it. Her eyes darted briefly to the Grand Elder, who was engaged in an intense discussion with the merchants.

"Tree, I don't like this guy," Stella whispered in her mind. "Should I fight back for Elder Margret?"

"Hold on, let the conversation develop a little more."

Theron crossed his arms and leaned back with a grin. "I thought it was rather bold for a lower-tier family to dare host an event like this, so after hearing it was sponsored by the Silverspires, I came to see what's up." He gestured with his chin to Ryker, standing quietly next to Sebastian. "But it seems that a mere child was behind the sponsoring due to the inheritance event."

Kassandra snorted. "And to think I bothered spending a month to learn alchemy for this. What could a lower-tier family teamed up with a child offer us for our time and attendance? Do you think our time away from cultivating to show you face is cheap?"

"We provided very reasonable rewards considering the low barrier to entry for this tournament," Elder Margret snapped back. "It's you who decided to attend. We were just being courteous and sent you an invite."

Theron laughed. "Would you dare not send one?"

"Yes, we would," Elder Margret said without pause. "We actually hoped you wouldn't even attend."

Theron frowned. "Since when did the Redclaws lose sight of their place in this sect? Just because you have the Silverspire kid backing you doesn't mean you can show such disrespect to me."

"I fear neither the Skyrend family nor you," Elder Margret retorted.

"So confident, Elder Margret. Is it because your Grand Elder is almost on par with me? Or perhaps the Silverspires' bodyguard is giving you confidence?" Theron sneered. "I am sitting here right now in front of you, and I could spit in your face, and there's nothing you, the Redclaws, or even the Silverspires can do about it."

"I dare you to show such disrespect—" Elder Margret's eyes widened as Theron spit a lightning-infused ball of saliva straight at her face.

Stella's eye twitched as she created a portal that redirected the spitball at Theron's face. It all happened in an instant, and Stella didn't even have time to think about what she had done.

Theron reached up with a trembling hand and slowly wiped off the spit from his cheek. His eyes pulsed white as he seemingly contained his rage.

Kassandra seemed to be holding back a chuckle as she shifted away slightly from her enraged brother.

"Nice shot," Ashlock commented, which made Stella smile behind the mask.

Theron let out a long breath and then leaned forward. Both elbows were on the table, and his hands crossed beneath his chin. "Tell me why a spatial Star Core Realm lady with no family name is willing to defend the honor of a lesser and, in turn, make an enemy of the Skyrend family? How much are they paying you?" It was clear from his overly calm speech that he was holding back a flood of rage.

"I don't even know who you are," Stella replied calmly.

Kassandra burst out laughing, which made Theron frown.

"What's so funny, dear sister? Or do you find humor in shaming our family name?"

"I have never…seen someone…dig their own grave like that," Kassandra said between wiping away her tears of laughter. "It would make sense if she had just arrived from a distant demonic sect to not have heard of us…but outsiders should be killed on the spot. And if she is from this sect, she is courting death."

"I've lived here my whole life," Stella retorted. "Yet I have never heard of your family. What's so great about it? You can shoot some lightning? A bunch of random clouds in the sky can achieve the same thing."

Kassandra fell silent, staring at her with bewilderment. Theron also seemed baffled, and Elder Margret could only offer her a weary smile.

"I think you shattered their fragile egos, Stella. Weren't you coming here to make friends?"

"I'm here to empower the Redclaws and our sect. They have done nothing but insult Elder Margret at her own event while throwing around the weight of their stupid family that nobody cares about," Stella replied. "I feel cowering before them right now would only lead to more issues down the road."

"Hmmm, maybe, but he looks pretty angry now. What's your plan?"

Stella's mind froze at Ashlock's words. "Plan? I thought you were going to protect me?"

"I said I would watch over you, not help you. This is supposed to be a learning experience for you. I can't hold your hand all the time."

"Can't you fill his mind with your telepathic technique and tell him to leave?" Stella began to panic a little. She had only dared to act so pridefully as she thought Tree was backing her up!

"No, I can't do that. My technique can only be cast near my trunk."

"Why can I still hear you, then?" Stella asked.

"It acts like a curse. Once cast on someone, I can maintain the link so long as they are within the range of my roots."

"Will you really not help me?" Stella pouted behind her mask.

"Of course I will if you really need it, but I would rather not. I need to save my special technique for the finals when the Voidmind family invades."

Stella wasn't sure what Tree's secret technique entailed, but if she would inconvenience him and condemn the sect to the Voidmind invasion due to her actions, she needed to fix this situation somehow.

"Good! Very good!" Theron drummed the table with his fist as he laughed. "This has to be the most interesting meeting I have ever attended!"

Stella tilted her head. "Why?"

"I like you. Come work for me." Theron grinned. "I could always use a spatial affinity cultivator to help transport my servants up the mountain and carry my things."

"No, thanks. I will remain here." Stella politely declined while holding back her rage from the insult, but that seemed to be the wrong answer, judging from Theron's pulsing eyes.

"I advise you take my offer." Theron leaned in. "I don't know why a pretty little thing like you is out here in this backwater city working alongside lessers when you could come and work for me."

"I said no, thank you. Do you not have ears? And don't call me a pretty thing. You're vile."

"You intolerable woman!" Theron shouted as he stood up and slammed the desk. His Star Core pulsed, and white lightning crackled across his skin. "Working for one such as me would be an honor."

Everyone in the room turned their heads, and Stella could even see the Redclaw Grand Elder begin to run over in the corner of her eye, but it was too late.

Stella felt an immense pressure descend on her, and before she could even blink, a tremendous bolt of lightning shot out from Theron's hand at her, illuminating the entire room in a bright white.

Her Star Core flared up and coated her body in purple flames. The lightning slammed into her, almost throwing her off the chair and onto the floor. Her body became flooded with lightning Qi that she managed to just about get under control due to her dao comprehension.

It was clear that the attack hadn't been intended to be lethal, but it had still come from a cultivator many stages above her, so it was obvious he intended to humble her.

As Stella blinked away the bright light, she inserted some Qi into her spatial ring and summoned a lightning Qi barrier fruit into her mouth. Quickly chewing it behind her mask, she escaped the chair and stepped away from the table. She could only walk under Theron's pressure because the Redclaw Grand Elder was combatting it with his own gravity.

"So much arrogance...all for that?" Stella crossed her arms and raised her brow. "I expected a bit more firepower."

Stella could feel every pair of eyes in the entire restaurant on her. It made her skin crawl and also made her feel extremely anxious. Clearly, she had messed up somewhere to end up in this position...

You were supposed to remain low-key, Stella! Like a wallflower! Why did you have to run your mouth like that?

"Stella, do you need my help?"

"No, I caused this mess, Tree. Let me handle it," Stella replied mentally.

"What seems to be the problem?" the Redclaw Grand Elder said as he strode over.

Theron Skyrend's face was twisted in anger, his eyes glowed, and his chiseled, almost stone-like muscles bulged. "Your hired rogue cultivator dared to disrespect me, Grand Elder. I don't know how you found her, but I demand she is presented on my doorstep after the tournament, or you will face the wrath of the Skyrend family."

The Grand Elder looked between the two before clearing his throat with an awkward cough. "Theron. I am far more scared of her than your father."

Total silence shrouded the room as everyone absorbed those words.

"Interesting...such bold words, Grand Elder." Theron sneered. "Do you dare tell me this woman's family name or origin so I may also know to fear her?"

"Why are you so obsessed with me?" Stella tilted her head.

Theron snorted. "I would never be obsessed with a talentless country bumpkin like you."

"You called me pretty and tried to make me your servant just a moment ago." Stella took a fearless step forward. "Yet now I am a talentless country bumpkin? What makes you better than me?"

"Just look at me—"

"Yes, I'm looking. I see nothing but unearned arrogance." Stella scoffed. "All you do is throw your family name around and call others lesser to feel important. I have no need to bend the knee to a man child such as you."

Theron threw his head back and laughed manically for a while. Eventually, he looked back at Stella with pure wrath. "You dare compare yourself to me? I'm a descendant of a god! To disrespect me is to defy the heavens!"

He raised his hand, and the ceiling exploded as lightning tore through it and collected into a bolt he held like a javelin. Through the shower of splinters, as the building almost collapsed upon them, Theron hurled the lightning bolt alongside roaring thunder.

Under everyone's shocked gazes, Stella surged the power of the fruit to her palm and effortlessly slapped the lightning bolt away.

"I defy the heavens at every turn!" Stella shouted as she kicked the table that separated them into splinters. "I care not for your weak god."

"Heretic!" Theron's massive fist plummeted toward Stella, but she activated her earrings. Her eyes became abysses as she sidestepped the fist with lightning-enhanced speed.

Meanwhile, Kassandra hurled lightning bolts from the side, but Stella easily shrugged them off with the power of the fruit and her comprehension of the lightning dao. She had punched heaven's lightning. How could Kassandra compare?

Theron was disoriented and shrieked as if terrified of what he saw in her eyes. The eight-foot-tall giant stumbled to the side and ended up crashing into a table with a very calm man and an all-too-familiar woman sitting at it.

Stella glanced at the man whose eyes were as black as his hair. His figure was lean and almost ghoulish.

"Dante Voidmind," Theron said through clenched teeth. "This bitch crawled out from hell and dares to protect the lessers and offend me. Will you not show some face and help?"

Dante sighed and stood up from his chair. "Grand Elder Redclaw. Squabbles between families can be overlooked, but I hope for your sake that you agree this hired woman of yours has taken it a step too far?"

His voice sent chills down Stella's spine. Lightning she had no issues against with the help of her dao comprehension and Ashlock's fruit, but a void-affinity cultivator was a whole different beast. Dante could likely delete her from existence if he so wished, so she reluctantly stepped away from Kassandra and spared her from a similar beating.

The Grand Elder ignored Dante and asked Stella, "How do you wish to handle this?"

Stella glanced between the two Skyrend siblings. Every ounce of her being wished to tell them to leave and not even bother with the tournament, but she didn't know if Ash wanted to go to war with the Skyrends over her personal grudge.

"Tree, what should I do?"

"Whatever you want, Stella. I trust you. Since when did we fear a bit of lightning?"

Stella smiled behind her mask. "I will formally apologize to them if they can prove they are better than me at anything."

"I don't want your worthless apology," Theron snapped. "I want you chained on my doorstep."

Stella shrugged. "Fine."

"Who picks the challenge?" Dante asked.

"They can. I will beat them at anything," Stella said nonchalantly and loved the scowls she received from them. It was clear getting a taste of arrogance was unnerving for them, and she had confidence that she could prevail over any challenge with Tree's cheat fruit and truffles.

"Were you planning on attending the alchemy tournament?" Kassandra asked, and Stella shook her head.

"No, I was not."

An unsettling grin appeared on the woman's face, and the two siblings nodded to one another.

"Then you will enter the alchemy tournament and compete against Kassandra." Theron grinned, seemingly convinced of his victory. "That is our challenge to you."

"I accept," Stella said as she turned to leave the building because the stress was beginning to overwhelm her, and she didn't wish to stay any longer. "I will see you all tomorrow."

A portal manifested with a snap of her fingers, and she was gone, leaving behind a shocked group of spectators and two very angry Skyrend siblings.

63
RISE OF THE TYRANT

Ashlock watched as Stella entered the alleyway behind the half-destroyed restaurant through her conjured portal. She looked understandably distraught, so he quickly opened a rift for her that led straight to Red Vine Peak.

"Thanks, Tree," she said in a low voice through their telepathic link as she walked through. The moment the portal snapped closed behind her, she reached down with a grunt, hastily tore off her high heels, and hurled them through the air. Before they could hit the stone, her spatial ring flashed with power, and they vanished.

Then with a frustrated huff, she marched across the stone while barefoot. Her ring flashed again, and the dress briefly vanished, only to be replaced with her usual comfortable wear.

She then sat on the bench, lay down, and closed her eyes angrily. A few moments passed, and her eyes snapped open. "Ugh! I just had to mess it up, Tree. I just couldn't keep my darn mouth shut!"

Sitting up, she tore the hair clip off and gripped her head in her hands while shouting in her mind. "Stupid Skyrends and their arrogance. Why are most cultivators such assholes? Ugh, I'm sorry… I'm so sorry. I ruined everything."

"What did you ruin?" Ashlock asked through the telepathic link.

"I was gone for what? Ten minutes? We spent all day dressing me up and getting me ready to speak with the other nobles, and here I am crying to you only ten minutes later!" Stella smacked her forehead multiple times. "I. Just. Can't. Do. Anything. Right."

"Stella, calm down. Relax. It's okay."

She took a long breath and sat back on the bench, her conflicted gaze settling on his leaves that rustled in the early night breeze. "Is it really okay? I didn't ruin everything?"

"Silly girl, you did great out there." Ashlock chuckled as he saw hope reappear in her eyes. **"Do you not remember the entire purpose of this tournament and the feast?"**

Stella furrowed her brows, and a sudden realization seemed to bloom. "The point was to establish the Redclaws as the rulers of this land and to find an alchemist. Oh, and something about making a deal with the merchants."

"Exactly, and what did you achieve tonight? You saw how Theron treated Elder Margret. He thought so low of her and Redclaws' family that he would spit in her face. But now, after your fight, I think everyone in that room sees the Redclaws in a different light."

"I see…" Stella nodded to herself. "So what you are saying is I did a good job?"

"Well, no…not exactly. You went with the intention of learning how to converse with the other cultivators…"

Stella's face fell.

"And yet, within minutes, you were fighting them, and then you arrogantly offered them a chance to choose a challenge and even agreed to become his slave if you lost."

"I did?"

"You don't even remember?"

Stella frowned. "I just really wanted to get away from there, so I just agreed to whatever they said so I could leave quickly. Did I even have the option to negotiate the terms? I mean, I fought someone from a supposed higher-tier family within the Blood Lotus Sect. The fact he didn't tell Dante to kill me there and then surprised me."

"You might not have felt like it, but I believe you had the upper hand in negotiations. You had utterly crushed their pride, so you could have been more demanding."

"Well, it's fine." Stella waved him off. "I didn't want anything from those bastards anyway, and they picked something I should win at easily."

"But imagine if they hadn't. You got lucky that you picked up alchemy a few days ago and seem to have an immense talent for it, but even then, you have only made a few pills. You keep getting away with it, but one day your arrogance will catch up to you and become the downfall for us all."

Stella was mute as she mulled over his words.

From the seriousness in her expression, it was evident that she knew she had fucked up.

What if she had sat at Dante Voidmind's table and infuriated him? There was no way Stella could shrug off a void-affinity cultivator a few stages above her as she did with the Skyrends due to her dao comprehension.

"You're right, Tree. I hear you. I really do. I just find being all diplomatic like Diana and the others so hard... Ugh, I should go practice alchemy for tomorrow." Stella stood up. Her shoulders sagged as she clicked her fingers, summoning a portal, and a moment later, she was gone—down into the cavern below.

With the darkness of night enveloping him, Ashlock felt weary. He didn't like to fight with Stella or scold her like that, but with his newfound telepathy, it was about time he set things straight with her.

As she was trying to focus on her alchemy, he withdrew his {Abyssal Whispers} skill. He couldn't talk with her while asleep, and he didn't want to keep haunting her all night.

"Before I sleep, let me check back on the restaurant." Ashlock's vision blurred, and he soon returned to the restaurant. He had naturally infiltrated their wine cellar below the building with a root a few days ago and was poking its tip up through a gap in the floorboards so he could see what was happening within.

If Stella had faced a problem he didn't feel she could deal with, he was prepared to go all out to protect her through this root. Thankfully, he could keep his presence from the families hidden for a while longer due to Stella navigating the hectic situation surprisingly well.

She may be bad at casual conversation, but she was great when it came to throwing hands and hurling insults. "I think it's about time Stella realized that being a noble that bends the knee to others for benefits and relationships isn't her forte. Which is fine. She can be a tyrant that lays down the law when needed instead. She would serve that role so much better."

Ashlock hoped tonight would lead to that realization for her. It was obvious a few hours ago that she was actually convinced she could keep her words and hands to herself when confronting someone who would naturally look down on both her and this backwater city she had called home her entire life. But alas, the reality had been far different.

"Anyway, that aside, before I go to sleep, let's see what's happening over here." Ashlock used his spiritual sight to glance around the restaurant. To his pleasant surprise, members from the Starweaver, Terraforge, and Azurecrest families were crowded around the Redclaw Grand Elder and the other Elders.

They were, of course, mostly asking about the mysterious Roselyn, but there were other questions and pleasantries thrown around for a while.

However, that wasn't of interest to Ashlock. What did draw his gaze was Dante Voidmind and Theron Skyrend sitting at a table far away from the hustle and bustle around the Redclaw Grand Elder.

Unfortunately, ripples of void Qi surrounded them, so although their lips were moving slightly, suggesting an occurring conversation, no sound escaped the confines of their table.

Ashlock wasn't too worried, as Elaine was sitting right there next to Dante, so anything said within that void bubble that could harm him should be relayed to him or the Redclaws somehow before it became a problem.

"So tired… I should sleep. Tomorrow is going to be a hectic one," Ashlock mused as he began to retract his gaze. The feast was rather dull with Stella gone, especially with the Qi bubbles everywhere preventing him from eavesdropping on any exciting conversations.

However, on his way out, he noticed Diana bidding farewell to the merchants.

"Thank you for your interest, Nox." Diana's words drifted into his mind after the bubble surrounding them collapsed.

"We will speak again soon," the woman called Nox replied and then walked off.

Diana watched the mysterious merchant leave and then turned to Sebastian and Ryker. "I'm going to head back and check on…you know who. Are you two staying here?"

Sebastian nodded. *"I want Ryker to have a chance to interact with some of the families here. This is one of his first-ever social events, and I want it to be at least somewhat normal for him after her antics."*

"All right." Diana bid them farewell, and a moment later, she left the restaurant that had moonlight pouring in through the hole in the roof. She began to walk down the tree-lined, lantern-lit, serpentine path, but Ashlock saved her the trouble and sent a portal her way.

Ashlock waited a moment to see if any Redclaws would also leave, but they seemed content to stay for the rest of the night by their grinning faces. Stella may have caused a scene, but it had greatly elevated the Redclaws to this odd status they seemed to enjoy.

"The fact that Theron was so convinced he could spit in Elder Margret's face and not face any repercussions whatsoever shows the vast difference in status between these noble families," Ashlock mused. "No wonder the Nightrose family has never even shown a hint of interest in the deaths of the Winterwrath or Evergreen families. They must be like bugs to them."

Ashlock was curious about what standing the Skyrend family had. It was clear they were on a similar level to the Voidmind family, but he wasn't sure why. The Silverspires were easy to understand. They produced one of the sect's most lucrative exports, the spatial rings. Meanwhile, the Voidmind family had one of the most powerful affinities and ran Slymere City, a center for education and creativity.

But what could the Skyrend family provide the Blood Lotus Sect? Ashlock couldn't figure it out.

"Whatever," Ashlock sighed as his vision blurred back to Red Vine Peak. "Let's see how Diana is."

Diana was glancing around frantically. "Stella? Where are you?"

Since Ashlock didn't want to overwhelm her mind with his telepathy and she wasn't good enough to translate his ancient runic words, he made a portal and sent her down to the cavern where Stella was standing over the earthen bowl with a deep frown on her face.

"Diana?" Stella said as she saw the frantic black-haired girl appear next to her. "Why are you back so soon?"

"I should be asking you the same thing!" Diana strode over and poked Stella in the chest. *"I. Told. You. It. Was. A. Bad. Idea."*

Stella slapped her hand away. *"Yes, yes… I admit I might have overestimated myself. I'm really sorry."*

Diana sighed. *"It's fine. Despite your antics, you made that the most entertaining social gathering I have ever attended, so I don't know whether I should laugh or cry."*

"Eh?" Stella tilted her head. *"What do you mean?"*

"Stella, you basically told Theron what everyone was thinking straight to his face and got away with it!" Diana giggled. *"Almost every family hates the Skyrend family, but since they wield lightning and can be crucial for facing heavenly tribulations, everyone puts up with their nonsense."*

"But Tree faced a heavenly tribulation, and he got through it fine." Stella shrugged. *"I don't see what's the big deal. It's just some lightning."*

"Are you forgetting that time you tried to punch heavenly lightning and almost died if not for Senior Lee's healing pill?"

"I have a selective memory..."

Diana rolled her eyes. *"Of course you do. The heavenly lightning is a trial sent by the heavens to test those who are worthy. You may look down on it after encountering it so many times to the point you can slap it away so effortlessly like you did earlier, but that is not true for most people."*

Stella shrugged. *"I could do the same thing as those Skyrend bastards. There should be no need to hire those arrogant assholes. I will do it for free if it takes business away from them."*

"That's actually a good idea..." Ashlock mused. How valuable would his lightning Qi barrier fruit be if Theron could throw his weight around like that just because his old man could fend off a few lightning bolts?

Diana laughed. *"That would be great. You should do that."*

There was a brief silence between the two.

"I was so worried, Stella," Diana said seriously. *"You might not have noticed, but Dante Voidmind almost intervened earlier, but Elaine whispered something in his ear that made him sit back and watch. There's a reason I say that was the most fun social gathering I have ever attended because usually, it's a quiet exchange of small talk and pleasantries. Nobody would dare fight at them. That's suicide."*

"I know." Stella sighed. *"Tree already told me... I messed up. I won't go to gatherings like those again. Or at least not until I am strong enough to defy anyone who runs their mouth like that."*

Diana chuckled. *"Never change, Stella. You are just what this dull world of arrogant young masters needs."* She then wandered off. *"I will leave you to your practice. I know you have a tournament to win tomorrow."*

"Thank you…" Stella said quietly as she watched Diana's departing back and then returned her focus to the ingredients laid out before her.

Idletree Daily Sign-In System
Day: 3530
Daily Credit: 3
Sacrifice Credit: 0
[Sign in?]

Ashlock awoke bright and early the next day. He quickly glanced around and didn't see any angry Skyrend family trying to smite the place down, so all in all not a terrible start to the morning.

Diana was cultivating under the mist-shrouded trees, and Stella was still slaving away in the cavern. Ashlock was about to go check on some other things when he felt the presence of a group outside the tunnel.

"Oh, thank god, it's just a Redclaw." Ashlock breathed a sigh of relief as he instructed Bob to move to the side and allow Elder Margret to enter. She walked down the tunnel purposefully and soon crossed the desolate cavern to Stella.

The twins had left sometime yesterday back to the White Stone Palace, and Douglas was busy working on his staircase in the hole, so it was just Stella slaving away over the earthen bowl.

"Morning, Elder Margret," Stella said while wiping sweat from her brow. On the earthen bowl's rim was a neat line of tier two body strengthening pills that Elder Margret eyed with appreciation.

"You caused quite the commotion last night."

"Yeah, I know—"

"Thank you." Elder Margret gave a short bow. *"To stand up for one as lowly as I was more than I ever anticipated."*

"What are you saying?" Stella seemed bewildered. *"You are part of the Ashfallen Sect. When they insult you, they insult all of us, especially the immortal. I will not stand for it."*

Elder Margret's lip quivered slightly, and the image of the stern woman shattered. *"To be treated as a lesser at every social gathering…*

to be looked down upon as if I was some useless old hag and treated as such by the more favored families by the Patriarch...I don't know how, but I became numb to it—accepted my fate as a pawn others used to disrespect to feel superior. We all did..."

Ashlock saw Elder Margret's fists clench at her sides. He could understand her feelings. This world was a dark and cruel place where powerful people treated those below them as nothing.

"But I feel we have been reborn under you and the immortal. Last night was the first time I felt listened to and valued in so long. I know it's silly, as they only wanted to talk to us about you, but I was so happy." A single tear ran down Elder Margret's cheek. *"I tried so hard for so many years to revive our family name that has been stamped and spat on. But we were crushed at every turn...just like this tournament, how the families banded together to keep us down by restricting the sale of ingredients."*

Stella stood there, stunned, clearly not knowing what to say.

"I..."

"Sorry, ignore my ramblings." Elder Margret wiped away the tear and regained her composure. *"I don't know what overcame me. The purpose of my visit was to tell you that the tournament's preliminary round starts in a few moments, and everyone eagerly anticipates your attendance."*

Stella let out a long sigh as she stepped down from the step and offered Elder Margret a sincere smile. "I think it's time those bastards learned who the true tyrant of this tournament is."

64
A SIMPLE TEST

As much as Stella wished to leave immediately, she was unprepared for the day ahead.

"I wasn't planning on attending, so I'm not caught up on what the preliminary round entails," Stella said while cleaning her face off with a towel she had summoned from her spatial ring. "Can you tell me before we go?"

Elder Margret had thankfully returned to her usual self after taking a moment to regain her composure.

"Sure, but first, let me give you this." Elder Margret brought out a black robe with a fire insignia that all robes worn by the Redclaw family had on the chest area. "You will be participating on behalf of us. By wearing this, the guards at the entrance will recognize that you are a member of the noble houses, so you should be waved in without having to queue up or pay the entrance fee."

"There's an entrance fee?" Stella raised a brow as she took the robe and secured it around herself. A small smile appeared on her lips when she realized the robe hid her comfortable clothes, so she wouldn't need to wear that revealing dress anymore.

Elder Margret sighed. "We didn't plan for one initially, but far too many people were showing interest, so we had to add another barrier to entry. Any rogue cultivator out there actually able to create tier-one pills should have no issue paying the Golden Crown entrance fee, whereas those frauds or people trying to cause trouble won't be willing to sacrifice a golden crown to do so."

"I see. That makes sense." Stella nodded thoughtfully. "But why would people not planning to participate or who aren't even alchemists want to attend?"

Elder Margret gave a weary smile. "The immortal may be able to grow alchemy ingredients with a wave of his hand. But the rest of us have to either risk our lives out in the wilderness to harvest the ingredients ourselves or choose between saving up for beast cores to advance our cultivation or buying a tier-one ingredient that will likely be ruined during practice."

"So they are really willing to travel all the way here just to have a chance at trying to remove impurities from a plant?" Stella couldn't believe it. Was it really that hard for someone to become an alchemist?

Elder Margret chuckled. "They would do far more for less. Everyone is convinced they are one opportunity away from their big break. I bet some imagine that today is the day they discover they have some hidden bloodline that allows them to effortlessly perform alchemy."

"Bloodline?" Stella latched onto that word. "What do you know about them?"

Ever since Diana's transformation, trying to discover her own bloodline had weighed heavily on her mind. Why hadn't she grown wings yet? What had Diana done to unlock her bloodline?

"Not much. They are mostly a legend popular among the common people as it gives them a ray of hope." Elder Margret waved it off as if it was a nonsense fairy tale. Her dismissive attitude toward bloodlines annoyed Stella.

Why did nobody know anything about these bloodlines when she saw Diana change her race right before her eyes? It wasn't some nonsense myth or legend. It was real.

Grumbling in her mind, Stella decided to put the issue of bloodlines aside and focus back on the tournament ahead of her. "So it's the preliminary round today and then the final round tomorrow?"

Elder Margret nodded.

"So how is the round today structured?"

"I was about to get to that," Elder Margret replied. "It's a rather simple test. As the purpose of today is to reduce the number of participants by at least ninety percent, we don't have the time or resources to do anything that in-depth."

Stella nodded in understanding, so the Elder continued. "You will be asked a simple random alchemy question. After that, you will be requested to remove the impurities from a tier-one ingredient to show a basic level of alchemy capability. Most won't pass this part."

Wait, a question? I don't know much about alchemy. Stella began to panic slightly, and Elder Margret seemed to notice.

"What's wrong? You should handle removing the impurities with ease."

"The question is what I'm worried about. How simple is it?"

"Oh, don't worry about the question." Elder Margret chuckled. "Even if you don't know the answer, so long as you remove the impurities from the ingredient, they will let you through."

Stella frowned. "The Skyrend and the other noble families will be watching me closely. If I failed to answer a simple question, it would reflect badly on me and the Redclaw family."

"That's true." Elder Margret rubbed her chin in thought. "This is where the fact we hired teachers from the Academy to be the judges will cause issues. If they had been family members, I could naturally set up a question ahead of time and give you the answer…"

"Are you able to stay here today?" Stella asked, and Elder Margret nodded.

"I'm not needed at the tournament today. Why, you ask?"

Stella summoned one of her carefully made Mind Fortress pills. Each one took half an hour of intense focus to create, so she was somewhat reluctant to hand it over, but if it let her pass the test with flying colors, then it was worth it.

"Take this pill. It will help protect your mind."

Elder Margret seemed confused as she reached out and accepted the pill. "What is this?"

"A pill I created." Stella shrugged off Elder Margret's stare. "I used one of the immortal's effect-giving fruits, you know, the Mind Fortress one that you likely used in the Mystic Realm?"

"Right…and you made a pill from it?" Elder Margret eyed the pill like a treasure. "Why would you give me something so precious?"

"As I said, it will protect your mind. I will take the test, and if I get stuck on the question, I will relay it back to the immortal and have him ask you for the answer."

"What am I protecting my mind from?" Elder Margret tilted her head in confusion.

"The immortal's voice comes with rather unpleasant hallucinations. You will thank me later, trust me." Stella offered her a reassuring smile. "Anything else I should know before I go?"

Elder Margret shook her head. "Nothing comes to mind. All I can offer you is good luck."

"Thanks." Stella then pointed to the side. "Portal, please!"

There was an immense ripple of spatial Qi throughout the cavern as the world twisted and bent to Tree's will, creating a doorway through space that led to an alleyway near the colosseum.

"See you later." Stella waved to Elder Margret as she stepped through. The stale flora-rich air of the cavern was replaced with the stench of Darklight City. Stella's nose scrunched up behind the cloth mask as she strode out of the trash-filled alleyway.

"How are there so many people?" Stella murmured as she saw a shifting wall of people between her and the colosseum up ahead. The usually sparsely populated grand square used as a casual meeting place for students was now packed with cultivators and mortals.

Darklight City was already a densely crowded mega-city, but Stella had never seen it like this.

With her interest piqued, she tried to slip past the hordes of people to get a look at the trinkets, food, and clothes the mortals were selling from wooden carts, but trying to peek over people's shoulders made her skin crawl, and the screams and shouts of the people around her were disorienting.

"Ah, this is too annoying." Stella's ring flashed, and one of her old swords appeared. She didn't want to bring out the one taken from the Voidmind Elder in case Dante somehow recognized it.

She then pulsed her Star Core, and everyone around her stumbled back to give her space as she threw the sword to the ground and used her Qi to make it levitate there. She hopped on, and everyone cheered as she pulsed her Star Core again and rose up into the air.

Stella could have used a portal to skip the crowd, but using techniques was frowned upon in the city, and she also wanted to get a better view of her surroundings from the sky.

She saw from above a sea of brown-and-black robes shifting between the maze of stalls. The sound of deals being made and the people's joy lifted Stella's spirits somewhat.

Looking toward the colosseum, she noticed a single massive entrance. Instead of a door, there was a line of cultivators collecting entrance fees and generally controlling the flow of people.

What baffled Stella was just how long the packed line was. It ran through the maze of carts in the grand square and all the way down one of the nearby streets.

"Yeah, right. As if all of you could perform alchemy." Stella snorted. "Now I can see why Elder Margret introduced an entry fee."

Stella laughed as she felt the wind flow through her hair. "There must be thousands of you! I don't even think all of the flowers in the cavern would be enough to give all of you a single ingredient to show off your skills."

Stella hadn't had great respect for alchemists in the past simply because she was ignorant of how hard it was to become one. If not for Tree's truffle improving her spirit root and the various fruit that helped boost her concentration, she never would have been able to make even a tier-one pill.

"Wait...if we ever open the Ashfallen Sect to new cultivators, will the turnout for entry look like this?" Stella felt all the blood drain from her face, and she decided to look away. The thought of so many cockroaches crawling their way up Red Vine Peak in an attempt to join their sect made her shudder.

To distract her mind while she slowly flew toward the colosseum that dominated half her view, Stella surveyed the skyline of Darklight City and then saw something rapidly approaching her.

She squinted at the flying dot, and as it got closer, she groaned in annoyance.

Oh god, not these assholes again.

Within moments, a small, ornate wooden boat carrying two giant people with marble-like skin began flying beside her. The bare-chested Theron Skyrend was busy controlling the flying ship. Meanwhile, Kassandra was free to put one foot on the boat's rail and sneer at her. "Roselyn, I'm surprised you showed up after the insanity you pulled last night. If I were you, I would have run away—"

"Of course you would have," Stella retorted. "Because you are a coward that hides behind your family name with no redeeming qualities. Why would I have any reason to run from someone as pathetic as you?"

Kassandra's face twisted in anger, which brought Stella great joy.

However, she had no desire to hear another word out of the annoying woman's mouth nor engage in a conversation, so she shoved more Qi into her sword to speed up and began descending toward the entrance.

"Vile bitch!" was all Stella heard behind her as she looked for a suitable place to land. The cultivators in the line below seemed to notice her presence as they all gazed up and began pointing.

Remembering Elder Margret's words, Stella put her hands behind her back, soared past the line of cultivators collecting entrance fees, and touched down in the much quieter area inside the entrance.

Now where do I go? Stella wondered as she hopped off her sword and stowed it away. She scanned her surroundings for a clue, which was more challenging than she thought, as there were no signs.

"Mistress?"

Stella spun around and faced a short woman with the familiar beautiful crimson hair of a Redclaw. The woman also wore the same cloak as her with the fire insignia, confirming she was likely part of the Redclaw family.

"Yes?" Stella replied, confused why the woman just stood there studying her face.

"You look familiar yet different..." The woman narrowed her eyes but then, noticing Stella's annoyed glare, she became flustered. "Oh, sorry, I'm staring too much. What is your name?"

"Roselyn."

"No family name?" the woman asked with some concern. Clearly, a random Star Core cultivator flying in was a big worry.

Stella rolled her eyes and pointed at the fire insignia on her robe.

The woman relaxed slightly and then looked at the parchment in her hand. She read until the bottom of the second page before her eyes lit up. "Ah, here you are, Miss Roselyn. You were added to the list last night, so I wasn't briefed about you. My apologies. Please follow me to the testing area—"

Stella was about to follow when a shadow loomed over them, followed by a small explosion. Stella sighed as Kassandra dropped from the flying boat and appeared beside her.

"Roselyn, you should go back and pay the entry fee." Kassandra gestured with her chin to the line of tournament workers. "Only those with a family name have this privilege."

Stella looked up to meet the towering woman's glowing blue eyes. "Really? Why am I on the list to be shown in without paying, then?"

Kassandra snorted and walked past. "Ha! Who cares about a list? I go where I please."

To Stella's slight annoyance, the woman wasn't lying. Unlike her, who had been questioned by this Redclaw family member, Kassandra could just walk straight through with nobody daring to even look at her for more than a mere glance.

"Right this way, Mistress Roselyn. We will conduct your test in a quieter area along with the other nobles," the short woman said, pulling Stella out of her mood.

With a wordless nod from her, the woman turned and led her deeper inside the colosseum. To Stella's surprise, they spent some time walking along a corridor with glassless windows showing the stands and fighting area.

"The rogue cultivators will take their test out there." The woman gestured to the sandy pit that had been converted into a testing ground with tables and examiners. "Whereas you will conduct yours just through here."

The woman gestured to an ajar side door with a Redclaw family member standing guard. The man gave Stella an odd look as she walked past and into the room.

Stella gulped as she felt many pairs of eyes belonging to all the nobles turn to stare at her. She couldn't even look at the floor to escape their gazes as nightmares lurked in the mental mist from Ashlock's telepathy.

The room she found herself in was rather lavish, with a high, vaulted ceiling and decorated walls. If she had to guess, this was the relaxation room for nobles when they came to the colosseum for any reason, as the place was well furnished with various lounge chairs surrounding small tables.

However, at the far end was a large, ornate table that looked rather out of place with three gray-robed, middle-aged people standing behind it.

Those must be the Academy people Elder Margret was talking about, Stella concluded as she took a mentally hesitant but physically confident step into the room—she had the persona of the prideful Roselyn to portray, after all.

Although the room was large, the furniture was mostly occupied, and Stella didn't wish to stand awkwardly in the corner, so she began to seek a place to sit while she felt the intense gazes of the other nobles burn into her back.

Eventually, she settled for a red sofa with a golden trim that was only half occupied by a small boy in the middle. Oddly, he had snow-white hair with streaks of crimson-like blood. Stella found it interesting as she had never seen mixed hair like that before.

Other than the boy, there was a large man that looked weirdly similar to Douglas perched on the end of the sofa. He gave her a disapproving look as he stood up, walked away as if repulsed by her presence, and stood near Kassandra Skyrend.

Makes sense, Stella mused as she saw everyone's reactions. *I am some unknown cultivator, whereas Kassandra is from the well-established Skyrend family. They have likely all known each other since they were young or from previous social gatherings. How annoying.*

Stella really hated the awkwardness of the dead-silent room with everyone staring at her as if she was some caged animal. She didn't even know where to look but was thankfully saved by one of the Academy people drawing everyone's attention.

"With everyone here, we can now begin the assessments. Kassandra Skyrend, please come and verify your knowledge and capabilities."

With a wide grin, Kassandra strode over to the table.

"First, a simple question," the middle-aged man with gray hair said. "Name a tier-one pill."

That's it? Stella's eyes widened a little. That almost felt a little too simple. Even some random mortal on the street should know at least a single tier-one pill.

"A minor wound cleansing pill," Kassandra answered, and the man nodded.

"Very good. Now please purify this small bundle of Qi Flowing Grass." The man passed over a small bowl with a ball of grass in it. "You have ten minutes and will be marked based on the volume of impurities you remove."

Stella's eyes narrowed. The Qi Flowing Grass looked almost dead from decay. It was likely overflowing with impurities. Wasn't this test a little too simple? Were alchemists really this inadequate?

The room became filled with thunderclaps and flashing lights as Kassandra blasted the ball of Qi Flowing Grass with blue lightning arcing from her fingertips. Thankfully for everyone's ears, she was finished in a minute.

The Qi Flowing Grass had a healthier shade of green, but Stella doubted it was usable as an ingredient. The bowl was caked in a thin layer of burned impurities that smelled awful.

Honestly, Stella wasn't sure Kassandra would pass...

"Fantastic job, Kassandra Skyrend. You passed,' the gray-haired man declared with a smile and gestured for a man Stella knew all too well about to approach the table.

"Dante Voidmind, you will be next." His gaze searched the room and landed on Stella. A slight smirk appeared on his lips. "And Miss Roselyn will be the last."

Stella felt weirdly targeted as all three examiners seemed to look at her with hostility.

65
THE PRELIMINARY ROUND

Stella felt very uncomfortable in the test room.

Not only were the other nobles showing open hostility, but so were the examiners.

Why did they look at me like that? Aren't the judges supposed to be from the Academy to avoid being biased? Or is corruption unavoidable even in a situation like this?

Stella scanned the room and pouted behind her mask.

Maybe they are trying to appeal to one of the nobles here? Actually, now that I look a little closer...

Stella realized that even with the lack of space on the lounge chairs, the way the various people were seated or positioned gave hints to a power dynamic or perhaps different factions within the group of nobles. It made sense that they weren't all equally friendly toward one another.

"Dante Voidmind, first I will ask a simple question." The middle-aged man with gray hair drew Stella's wandering gaze.

"As Kassandra Skyrend rightly pointed out, the minor wound cleansing pill is a tier-one pill. What type of wound is this simple tier-one pill unable to deal with?"

Stella narrowed her eyes as Dante thought up the answer.

Isn't this question far more challenging than the one Kassandra had to answer? I mean, this seems to teeter on medical knowledge rather than alchemy.

"That's simple," Dante said after a second of thought. "The minor wound-cleansing pill can heal wounds inflicted with mortal weapons. However, it cannot deal with wounds infused with foreign Qi."

"...Very good." The examiner seemed slightly irritated that Dante knew the answer. With a nod to the person beside him, Dante was handed a small bowl with a tiny bundle of Qi Flowing Grass that looked healthy compared to the one Kassandra purified.

Dante took the bundle of grass and placed it in his palm. Stella had to strain her neck to see what was happening, as it was difficult to track void Qi through spiritual sight. Funnily enough, she didn't feel out of place as everyone else in the room was also trying to get a good look by peeking over each other.

"I will begin," Dante said calmly as a flash of void Qi expanded out like a bubble, encompassing his entire hand. Not even a second later, the bubble retracted and was gone.

"Done," he said as he handed the bowl and bundle of Qi Flowing Grass to the examiner.

The gray-haired man took the bowl and briefly inspected it. "Where are the impurities?"

"Gone—none should remain after the void's cleansing," Dante replied, which earned him a raised brow from the examiner.

Stella was also skeptical. The Qi Flowing Grass from where she sat looked mostly the same, and she knew how hard it was to remove impurities. It was a mentally taxing process that took at least a bit of time... but Dante had done it so effortlessly in a second?

If that was really possible, Stella was starting to feel a little doubtful that this tournament would be as easy to win as she had first thought.

"Well, this is a problem." The examiner stroked his stubble. "The rules we set up clearly state that we measure based on the volume of impurities removed, as not all the examiners can detect impurities within the ingredients. If there are none, then you technically failed."

"So you will fail me?" Dante replied with an eerie calmness as if challenging the examiner.

The man seemed to glance over Dante's shoulder at someone in the room. Whoever it was had somehow given him good news as the man's face lit up a little. "No, there is no problem. We will make an exception and pass you."

"Tsk." Dante turned and walked straight for the door, his sunken eyes never looking at anyone as he left. There was an unspeakable, tense atmosphere from everyone in the room, as if their lives hung in the balance of this one man's mood.

Stella understood their feeling well. Void Qi had that uncanny ability to simply break the rules. She thought void Qi couldn't get any more ridiculous, but the fact it could delete impurities so effortlessly caused her great concern.

And if Elaine wasn't lied to, he plans to invade and somehow take over the city tomorrow? Luckily, it seems none of the other noble families here are that friendly with Dante, so he should be fighting alone with his own family, but they also seem somewhat terrified of him, so maybe they would help out his conquest purely out of fear of being next.

The door quietly closing behind Dante broke Stella from her worried thoughts. Dante was a problem for tomorrow. For now, Stella planned to pass her first-ever exam and not embarrass herself and ruin her Roselyn persona.

With Dante gone, the ominous pressure subsided as the examiner sighed in relief and called on the next person. "Roderick Terraforge."

The large man that looked creepily similar to Douglas walked up to the table.

Stella was very curious to see how someone with earth affinity could even perform alchemy.

"This is your question," the examiner said as Roderick loomed over him. "Is there a limit to the number of pills a person can take in one day?"

"Depends on the pill," Roderick answered. Stella swore she heard Douglas for a second as they sounded so similar. "Most can be taken as many times as the cultivator wishes, but it will have diminishing returns."

"Good enough answer." The examiner noted down something on his parchment and then handed over the bowl with Qi Flowing Grass. "Just like the others before you, please remove as many impurities as possible within the next ten minutes."

"Can I use some mud?" Roderick asked, and after some contemplation, the examiner nodded.

"Fine, but I will need to check it over."

So he can't use the earth Qi stored within himself to conduct alchemy. Already off to a bad start, but I didn't expect the Terraforge family to be any good at alchemy in the first place.

Stella felt like she should start making a mental list of those that would be her greatest opponents. So far, Dante was way at the top, with Kassandra annoyingly in second place. Although her question had been simple, she had removed a good amount of impurities in a quick time frame with her lightning. The process was just a bit messy.

While Stella had been thinking, the examiner had finished verifying there was nothing odd about the clump of mud Roderick had presented him with.

"Okay, with that out of the way, you have ten minutes," the examiner declared. "Please begin."

Roderick wasted no time pushing the Qi Flowing Grass into the mud that greedily absorbed the bundle. He then closed his eyes and placed his fingertips into the mud. It began to ripple, and after a minute, Stella started seeing black specs floating to the mud's surface.

How strange... Is he manipulating mud through those ever-changing pathways to push out the impurities? That sounds very slow and messy.

As expected, a full ten minutes went by, and the examiner had to snap the large man out of his meditation by tapping his arm. "Test is over."

Roderick frowned. "Already?"

"Yes." The examiner nodded impatiently. "Now dispel all the impurities from the mud into the bowl so I may check your results."

Roderick grumbled as he withdrew the mud, leaving behind the Qi Flowing Grass in a worse state and a small pile of impurities.

"You damaged the ingredient but produced the required pile of impurities..." The examiner tapped the parchment in his hand with his ornate pen. "I would count this as a pass but of the lowest grade."

Roderick seemed pleased with the result as he strode across the room and returned to his seat near Kassandra. From how Kassandra smiled at him, Stella concluded they had a positive relationship.

Not quite to the point of best friends, more like friendly acquaintances...but what do I know? Do I even have an acquaintance? I guess Douglas would be one, but I never really smile at him. Should I smile more?

As Stella began to feel even more alone than she already was while isolated from the others in the room, the examiner called up the next person.

"Celeste Starweaver, please step forward." Stella watched as a beautiful woman walked by. Her midnight-black hair with streaks of blue and gold seemed to have a gravity of its own as it went all the way to her feet like a cape…which wasn't that far as she was relatively short, around Diana's height.

The examiner scratched the top of his head. "So, for a question… What is the difference between affinities when it comes to alchemy?"

"I don't understand," Celeste said calmly, like the tranquil moon. "That is too broad of a question."

"Ahem, let me rephrase it a bit then." The examiner smiled. "Why would one affinity be superior to another when it comes to alchemy?"

"Compatibility?" Celeste didn't seem very confident. "Every affinity has its strengths and weaknesses…err… The more powerful the affinity, usually the harder it is to cultivate or source Qi for. To answer your question, err, some affinities have more finesse, making them better suited?"

The three examiners talked among themselves as Celeste stood there awkwardly. Eventually, they shook their heads. "Although your answer is somewhat correct," the gray-haired man said, "it was too long-winded and went off-topic, so I will have to fail you."

Stella blinked as she heard their verdict. *A noble actually failed? Is that even possible?*

Celeste sighed as she turned to leave, but the man stopped her. "Wait, although you failed the question, if you can remove the impurities, then you can still pass."

"Whaaa, really?" Celeste spun around.

The man nodded and handed her the bowl with the grass just like everyone else. "You have ten minutes."

Celeste's hair rippled with power as silver specks began to collect around her hands. Even from afar, Stella could feel such immense power despite the girl being in the Soul Fire Realm.

The bundle of grass floated up from the bowl, suspended between her two hands, surrounded with cosmic specks.

So this is the power of cosmic affinity? Sure does seem powerful. Stella narrowed her eyes, eager not to miss a thing.

However, nothing was happening.

Celeste's eyes remained closed, and Stella could feel an immense amount of Qi being used, but she couldn't see anything physically happening.

"Phew," Celeste said as her eyes fluttered open and her hair relaxed.

The silver specks orbiting her hands seemingly vanished, and the bundle of Qi Flowing Grass dropped to the bowl below. "Done!"

The examiner frowned. "No impurities? Just like Dante…"

Celeste shrugged. "I used cosmic radiation to obliterate the impurities. There should only be a few left."

"I see." The examiner inspected the grass and sighed. "There are indeed few impurities left, so I guess you can pass this round."

"Woohoo!" Celeste threw her hands up in glee and then wandered off. None of the other nobles offered an ounce of excitement for her accomplishment, so Stella guessed the Starweaver family was either weak or had bad ties with the noble families present.

Much like Dante Voidmind, Celeste Starweaver paid little attention to the others and waltzed out of the room, closing the door behind her.

"She was quite the character," Ashlock said as quietly as possible in her mind to avoid causing her mental fatigue. *"And one to be feared. She used far too much Qi on a test, but if used offensively, that cosmic radiation could be as dangerous as void Qi."*

Stella shuddered. How had this seemingly simple test been such a humbling experience? Had she been getting overconfident? How did such monsters in human skin like this exist?

"Maybe she got flustered, but she must have used a week's worth of Qi on that one purification," Ashlock continued. *"Definitely powerful, but much like Dante Voidmind, the amount of Qi they have to use to purify an ingredient that fast and thoroughly is not sustainable."*

"I see, that makes sense." Stella mentally sighed. "But since it's a two-day tournament, they have a massive advantage then."

"Don't worry about them. Your primary focus is Kassandra Skyrend."

Stella pouted behind her mask. Although that was technically true… now that she was this deep in, she wanted to win it all.

"Kane Azurecrest, please come take the test."

Stella looked to the side and saw the person sitting beside her get up. Kane brushed his long white hair with streaks of crimson to the side, giving Stella a look at his face. He had decent features, but an unmistakable aura of exhaustion overshadowed him.

Only now did she realize Kane wasn't a child but a teenager as he walked over to the table.

Everyone still in the room seemed disinterested in Kane, but Stella was curious how an air-affinity cultivator planned to remove impurities.

"Okay, simple question. What is the highest tier of pill?"

Kane looked up at the examiner and answered in a tired tone, "The Heavenly Tier is the highest."

"And what tier number is that?"

"Two questions?" Kane asked, and the examiner smiled.

"You know why I'm asking two questions. Don't play dumb with me."

Kane gulped as if caught in the act and swiftly answered, "It's the eighth tier."

"Good. Now here's the Qi Flowing Grass."

Why did he have to answer twice? Stella wondered as Kane placed the grass in his palm and closed his eyes.

A small tornado of light-gray flames shot forth from Kane's right hand and picked up the grass. What then surprised Stella was crimson flames like the Redclaws pouring from his left hand and joining the tornado.

The swirling, flaming tornado enveloped the grass.

"Kane seems to be a dual affinity. Those are rare. How did that happen?"

Stella also wanted to know. She ran through some ideas as she watched the mesmerizing display of duality when an idea hit her. "Didn't Diana kill someone from the Azurecrest family because they were a nocturne?"

"Oh, good thinking! Diana mentioned that everyone in the Azurecrest family was forced to take on a nocturne. So maybe Kane has a nocturne inside him?"

Stella nodded slightly as the fire tornado ceased, and Kane stepped back. The grass landed in the bowl alongside a pile of soot that was likely the impurities.

"Good job, you passed." The examiner marked on his parchment, glanced up, and instantly met eyes with Stella. "Your turn now, Miss Roselyn."

Stella stood up and felt everyone's eyes on her except Kane, who walked past her and quietly sat on the lounge chair.

So Dante, Kane, and Celeste aren't part of this mini faction of nobles. Stella surveyed the room and noted that House Skyrend and Terraforge seemed to be working together.

Stella strode forward with as much fake confidence as possible and tried to ignore the examiner's sly smile.

"First, a simple question..."

The words Stella had heard so many times today sounded particularly sinister this time.

"Tell me about the Bodhi Heart Pill."

Stella tilted her head slightly and only just about managed to hold back from shouting in this man's face. Asking a vague question about an obscure pill nobody has heard about was supposed to be on the same level as "name any tier-one pill"? This was so obviously a setup that Stella almost didn't want to play their stupid game.

Luckily if they planned to cheat, so did she—just better.

"Tree, a little help?" Stella asked mentally.

"One moment, that pill isn't used in the Blood Lotus Sect, so Elder Margret is pouring through a book to find its description right now."

Stella felt the gazes of Kassandra and Roderick on her back, and as the seconds passed, she saw the edges of the examiner's smile widen. "Roselyn, if you can't answer, that is fine. We can continue to the next step—"

"Elder Margret found it," Ashlock quickly informed her. ***"The Bodhi Heart Pill is..."***

Stella's laughed in the examiner's face as Ashlock relayed the information. "Why would I shy away from such a simple question, examiner? Although I have to wonder how the details of a pill only found in the Celestial Empire could be relevant to us?"

"Well, erm," the examiner's smile faltered slightly, "it's important to know our enemy's pill repertoire. Don't you agree?"

"Such deep foresight, as expected at someone currently working at the Academy here in Darklight City." Stella sneered. "But since you asked, the Bodhi Heart Pill is said to increase one's wisdom and understanding of the universe, allowing the user to break through mental barriers and comprehend profound truths."

Stella then crossed her arms. "Now, I don't know about you, but that doesn't seem like a significant pill for someone like me to know about?"

The examiner nervously chuckled and looked down at his parchment.

"You make a good point. Perhaps I made a mistake and read out the wrong question."

"I think you picked the wrong person to mess with." Stella snorted. "But go ahead, keep up the act."

"There is no act, Miss Roselyn. It was a simple mistake on my part." The man glanced down at the parchment in his slightly shaking hand. "How about another question?"

"Didn't I answer your 'simple' question already?" Stella shook her head as if deeply sad. "To think the Academy would allow a delusional old man with a declining memory to serve as a teacher."

"Fine." The examiner brought up an empty bowl despite the fact there were other bowls with Qi Flowing Grass already on the table—his spatial ring flashed, and a bundle of grass with a quality that Stella recognized appeared in the bowl.

"You passed the first round. Now all you need to do to qualify for the tournament tomorrow is remove enough impurities from this bundle of grass." He smirked as he set the bowl down in front of Stella. "You have ten minutes, starting now."

66
DEATH SENTENCE

Stella ignored the examiner's words to start; her focus was entirely on the Qi Flowing Grass presented to her. She picked it up, and after spending a moment to check, she let out a small sigh of relief behind her mask.

"It's not one of yours, Tree," Stella said mentally. "Although I almost thought it was, thankfully, there are still some impurities in here, so there's no way it can be yours."

"That's a relief. I thought Elder Margret had let my plants enter circulation for a second, which would have been terrible news as it would mean she somehow stole from the cavern and betrayed me."

"You didn't want her to distribute the plants for the tournament?" Stella asked.

"No, at least not yet. Because the plants are too perfect, their use in a tournament like this is questionable," Ashlock mused. *"Also, now that I understand their value, the other families may get suspicious if the Redclaws start handing out perfect Qi Flowing Grass for use by novices in a tournament."*

"I see," Stella muttered as she inspected the Qi Flowing Grass in her hand. Seeing the grin on the examiner's face made Stella grind her teeth behind the mask. Deciding enough was enough, she held up the near-perfect Qi Flowing Grass and glared at Kassandra Skyrend behind her.

"I didn't know the lofty Skyrend family would need to stoop so low to protect their fragile egos to the point of bribing the examiners and tampering with the ingredients," Stella said with calm fury. "How much did you even pay for this near-perfect Qi Flowing Grass? Was it all the allowance Daddy gave you?"

Kassandra's eye twitched. "Those are bold accusations, Roselyn. What evidence do you have that I have done such things? And you should stop wasting time accusing me. Time is ticking, after all."

Stella reined in her anger and focused on the task as Kassandra wasn't wrong. Time was ticking, and if not for the Mind Fortress pill helping numb her mind, she would be unable to concentrate, knowing that Kassandra was staring at her back with amusement.

"Are there enough impurities in that grass to pass the test?" Ashlock's voice helped Stella drown out the rest of the room and find a solution.

She could throw her hands up and call them out on their bullshit, but that would feel less satisfying than beating them at their own game.

"No, even if I removed every last one, it doesn't have enough, assuming the number of impurities Roderick Terraforge removed is the passing mark."

"Have you got a plan?"

"I think so." Stella's eyes briefly flickered to the bowls of impurity-riddled Qi Flowing Grass right in front of her, just an arm's reach away and under the noses of the examiners.

The way I remove impurities may not be as fast as void Qi or flashy as lightning, but I have one massive advantage—I can remove impurities from afar with spatial Qi.

"Tree, I plan to steal a few impurities from each of the other Qi Flowing Grass bundles on the table," Stella said mentally. "Could you flood this area with spatial Qi for me?"

"Just around the table?" Ashlock asked. *"Or do you want the whole room suffocating in my Qi?"*

Stella glanced up and locked eyes with the examiner while mentally replying to Ash. "Encompass the table and the examiners. Filling the entire room would be overkill and unrealistic."

"Got it," Ashlock replied, and just as the examiner was returning a slightly confused expression due to her staring at him, the area around Stella exploded with spatial Qi so pure and dense that it was almost suffocating even for Stella.

All three examiners stumbled back to avoid being killed by the Star

Core Qi that was far too dense for any normal human. The gray-haired man furrowed his brows as he glared at Stella. "What is the meaning of this?"

"For you to present me with such a high-quality ingredient, it would be an insult to the art of alchemy for me not to go all out." Stella tilted her head, her grin obscured by the cloth mask. "Wouldn't you agree, examiner?"

The gray-haired man gulped and nodded slowly. It was clear to Stella that the man was unsure what to do in this situation, and she relished in it briefly before getting back to work as a few minutes had already been wasted.

A minute was spent trying to remove a few impurities from the already purified Qi Flowing Grass in her hand. This was done for the sole reason of deliberately leaving a slight trace of spatial Qi in the grass so if anyone checked, they could confirm she had retrieved the impurities from this plant.

Slowly, specks of impurities formed next to the grass in the bowl under the scrutiny of the examiners.

Stella kept her eyes closed to not show any signs of losing concentration as she switched her focus to an impurity-rich Qi Flowing Grass in another bowl nearby.

Her heart was pounding in her chest as she very carefully made use of the incredibly pure and dense spatial Qi all around her from Ash to obscure her retrieval of impurities.

A tiny rift popped into existence over the impurities pile and deposited some impurities that had come from another Qi Flowing Grass bundle—the examiners seemed none the wiser as this had been the exact same process as before. And they had no way to spiritually check for the anchor point of the portal as it was hidden under the shroud of Ash's Qi.

Stella held back a smirk as she moved on to the next Qi Flowing Grass, removing only a minimal amount from each and leaving no trace of spatial Qi behind to avoid suspicion.

As time passed and Stella felt the end of her ten minutes approaching, she felt the Mind Fortress pill begin to wear away. The mental strain of performing alchemy without even having physical touch on the ingredient was so draining that Stella only managed to remove a minuscule amount, even with cheating.

As the examiner spoke up, the pile was only about the size of Roderick Terraforge's.

"Time's up. Please pull in your Qi and gather all the impurities into the bowl so I may verify its amount."

Stella felt Ashlock release his hold on the Qi and let it disperse into the room. The examiner leaned forward to inspect the small pile of impurities, and Stella saw a flash of surprise on his face before he quickly put back on his act.

Kassandra also walked over and loomed behind Stella, clearly interested in the contents of the bowl. Kane Azurecrest and Roderick Terraforge remained seated on the lounge chairs, with only Roderick showing a hint of interest in her results.

Tsk, this Skyrend bitch doesn't even care about being so obvious. Is her family name giving her the arrogance to cheat in the tournament this blatantly? Actually...even if they killed a Redclaw, nothing much would be done about it, so compared to that, what is cheating in a random tournament run by a "lesser" family?

Stella smiled behind the mask. *Of course, that would have been true with the old Redclaws, but now that the Ashfallen Sect is in charge, none of these bastards will be repeating their mistakes.*

"Ahem." The gray-haired examiner grinned as he put down a bowl with traces of mud and a pile of impurities next to Stella's. "Even with a quick glance, it's clear that you have slightly less impurities than Roderick, who I gave a barely passing grade to."

"Well, we all know what that means." Kassandra smirked. "The infamous Roselyn that dared challenge the Skyrend family was the only noble unable to pass the preliminary round! Isn't that right examiner?"

Stella stayed silent as the examiner nodded to Kassandra. "That is correct. She is just slightly below the pass threshold. Therefore Roselyn failed."

Kassandra burst out laughing. "You're just a pretty face that deserves to be chained outside our doorstep. To think you, a nameless cultivator hired by the Redclaw dogs, dared to humiliate us and thought you could get away with it—"

"What's this, then?" Stella reached forward and calmly pushed the bundle of near-perfect Qi Flowing Grass to the side of the bowl, exposing another small pile of impurities underneath that had been obscured from sight by the grass.

"In your own words, examiner, I was to 'gather all the impurities into the bowl,' which I have done," Stella said and enjoyed seeing the examiner frown and Kassandra's eye twitch.

"It's not my fault you rushed to conclusions without verifying all of the impurities in the bowl," Stella said as she reached forward and, with her finger, pushed the two piles together to form one taller and wider than Roderick's. In fact, it would even be clear to a blind bat that Stella had gathered more impurities.

There was an awkward silence as the examiner and Kassandra seemed to communicate with one another via irritated facial expressions.

Stella chuckled. "It's a shame you set the bar so low so you could pass Roderick."

"You cheated," the examiner said hesitantly. "You had to have gotten the impurities from somewhere else. Did you bring them in with you? Hidden in your clothes or perhaps your spatial ring?"

Stella raised a brow. "Even if I did, how are you so sure? Are you suggesting there wasn't this amount of impurities in the Qi Flowing Grass you provided me with?"

"Yes!"

"No, you idiot—" Kassandra tried to interrupt the man, but Stella had already gotten him to admit what she wanted.

"So if what you say is true, then the Qi Flowing Grass you provided me didn't contain enough impurities to give me a chance to pass the test." Stella crossed her arms and enjoyed the despair on the man's face. "Therefore, it was rigged from the start."

To Stella's surprise, the examiner nervously doubled down. "Ahem, even if I admit that, you still cheated somehow and I can disqualify you."

"But then I will report you to the Academy, and you will be fired," Stella retorted and didn't like the crazed look in the man's eyes.

"Guess we are both going down, then." The man grinned and tapped his parchment. "I disqualify you for cheating—that will be all. The test is over."

Stella was speechless at this man's shamelessness. Was there no honor left in this world? No integrity?

"I deposited Elder Margret in a nearby corridor via a portal. She will arrive any second."

Stella perked up behind her mask as the door abruptly opened behind her. She didn't even turn to look at the new arrival and instead enjoyed the examiner and Kassandra's brief expressions of pure annoyance.

"Elder Margret, how may I assist you?" the examiner said with a pleasant smile that made Stella's skin crawl.

"I just came to check up on the test to ensure everything is running smoothly." Elder Margret stopped next to Stella. "How are the results thus far?"

"Everyone except Roselyn here has already passed," the examiner calmly explained. "We were just verifying her results and have suspicions that she cheated."

Stella smirked behind her mask as Elder Margret raised a brow. "Oh? How do you believe she has cheated? That's a very grave accusation to make against a noble."

"She's not a noble," Kassandra muttered, which earned her a harsh look from Elder Margret.

"You mean she isn't a noble that you know about," Elder Margret retorted. "I would keep your thoughts to yourself or risk earning the ire of someone you can't offend."

Kassandra snorted. "Yeah, right, as if that person exists."

Elder Margret ignored Kassandra and turned back to the examiner. "So? How did she cheat?"

"Well..." The gray-haired man scratched the back of his neck. "I believe she obtained impurities from somewhere else."

"Interesting. Is this hers?" Elder Margret pointed to the bowl with bits of mud caking the bowl.

"No, that is Roderick Terraforge's," the examiner stated. "This is her bowl."

"Perfect, so neither has an awe-inspiring amount of impurities, but Roselyn's clearly has more, so she should pass on the volume collect alone. However, you claim she sourced them from somewhere else?" Elder Margret mused as she picked up the Qi Flowing Grass from Stella's bowl and closed her eyes.

A moment later, after Kassandra and the examiner exchanged a glance, Elder Margret opened her eyes with a frown. "This Qi Flowing Grass has had almost all of the impurities removed, and I detect some spatial Qi left over within the grass. Therefore, Roselyn either lost impurities, or this Qi Flowing Grass was of far too high purity for this test to begin with. So which one is it?"

The examiner cycled through contemplation and despair before finally giving up.

"Elder Margret, your words of wisdom have opened my eyes to this confused situation. I was unaware of the Qi Flowing Grass's purity and therefore made an almost terrible mistake." The examiner bowed deeply to the point his nose touched the table. "I hope you can forgive my foolishness."

"So you agree she passes the test?" Elder Margret asked, and the examiner nodded, hitting his forehead against the table.

"I do."

"What about you two?" Elder Margret sternly asked the two assistant examiners. "Do you agree?"

They glanced at one another and nodded. "We were just following the chief examiner's guidance."

You're both rats working for the Skyrend family with no backbone is what you mean to say. Stella resisted rolling her eyes. These people were beyond infuriating to the point she felt her hands itching to shove a dagger in their faces.

"Well then, that solves this minor issue. Congratulations, Roselyn, you and all the other nobles have been cleared to participate in the main event tomorrow," Elder Margret said as she turned to leave. "And you three examiners, I will be putting a word in about your performance today with the Academy."

And with those parting words, she left the room under the gazes of Kassandra, Roderick, and the three examiners. Kane Azurecrest didn't seem bothered by anything happening and mostly sat silently, looking at the floor.

"Fine, you win this round, but let's see if you can also cheat in the finals," Kassandra sneered as she left the room alongside Roderick, who shot her a scowl.

Stella ignored them and turned to the examiners, who all backed up a step under her glare. She debated saying something but held back with all her might and silently left, passing Kane on the way out.

The guard gave her a nod, but she didn't return it as she was too preoccupied with manifesting a portal to escape the colosseum's grounds. Stepping out into a nearby alleyway with piles of trash, she let out a sigh.

"I'm surprised you didn't try to kill them." Ashlock chuckled. *"You from just a month ago would be calling for their slaughter."*

Stella leaned against a nearby wall and clutched her hair in her hands. "What can I say? I've grown up and learned to tolerate annoying people."

"Mhm, I guess you have. Are you all right? You seem exhausted."

Stella massaged her forehead. "The Mind Fortress pill's effects have worn off, and I'm in a terrible mood. Could you retract your telepathy, Ash?"

"Sure. Do you need a portal back to Red Vine Peak?"

"No thanks. Since I am already here, I will walk around the city to clear my thoughts."

"All right, see you later."

Stella felt Ash's presence withdraw and finally felt the pressure on her soul subside. Performing alchemy in such an advanced and stressful way had worn down her mind, and she needed to relax.

Exiting the alleyway, she began walking in a random direction.

The stroll was supposed to be a peaceful one, but with every step, her anger only grew. She knew it was childish to give in to her rage, and she didn't want to become one of those young mistresses that killed anyone that offended them, but in this instance, she felt justified.

"Psst, Maple," she whispered as she stepped into a nearby alleyway and distorted her voice with spatial Qi. A second later, she felt some weight on her head; she reached up, and a a fluffy paw grasped her hand.

After giving some head rubs, Stella requested in a low voice, hoping Ash wouldn't hear her, "Maple, if you can kill those three examiners, I will buy you some acorns. They were nasty people working for a lady who wanted me chained up like a dog."

Maple tapped her forehead with his paw and then vanished in a bubble of void Qi, leaving Stella alone in the alleyway.

A smile spread across her lips as she exited the alleyway and hummed a happy tune to herself. "Now, where do I find some lovely roasted acorns?"

67
(INTERLUDE) NEW LANDS

Kassandra Skyrend glanced around the main hall of the Skyrend family mansion in Darklight City. The room was sunlit by massive windows obscured from the outside by a tapestry of runic formations running along the walls. Ten-foot-tall marble sculptures of the Skyrend family's heads encircled the room, with their stone eyes pointing toward a single seat that Theron was currently occupying.

Meanwhile, Kassandra sat beside him and noticed that her brother seemed deeply troubled as he drummed his fingers on the ornate chair's armrest.

Other than Theron, there was one more person present who, despite his rough-looking demeanor, glanced between the two of them with a hint of fear.

"Roderick, you understand the plan for tomorrow?" Theron eyed the Terraforge cultivator from atop his throne.

"Yes, absolutely, and if all goes well..." Roderick replied with an awkward smile.

Theron waved the man off. "Yes, yes, your branch of the Terraforge family will win the contract for our palace in the new lands."

"Thank you." Roderick bowed slightly as he got up to leave. "Do you require anything else of this humble one?"

"Show Henry in," Theron demanded. "He should be waiting just outside with his goons."

Roderick nodded and swiftly left the room under their lingering gazes.

Kassandra felt the atmosphere in the room tense up as Theron turned to glare at her and hissed in a low voice, "You had one job, Kassandra. How did you mess it up this badly?"

"I still don't know how she did it," Kassandra insisted. "Everything was set up perfectly. The question should have been impossible, and the Qi Flowing Grass was the purist one on the market that I could find at such short notice."

"What was the question?" Theron asked.

"The question was regarding the Bodhi Heart Pill."

"The Bodhi Heart Pill?" Theron frowned. "I have never even heard of such a pill."

"Right? I deliberately went out of my way to find the most obscure pill possible, and while digging through the records, I found a single mention of this Bodhi Heart Pill and a vague description of it." Kassandra sighed. "Yet she somehow knew of the pill? From the Celestial Empire, no less."

Theron's drumming of the armrest paused. "Celestial Empire?"

"Yes, that's where the pill originates from," Kassandra answered absentmindedly.

"So she knows about a pill from the Celestial Empire and refuses to reveal her family name or origins…" Theron's glowing eyes widened. "Is this not evidence the Redclaws are working with the Celestial Empire?"

Kassandra mused for a moment before answering. "Potentially farfetched, but the Redclaw Grand Elder did say he was more terrified of Roselyn's background than ours, which, now that you mention it…that would only make sense if she was from the Celestial Empire or a secret daughter of the Patriarch."

Theron leaned forward in his chair, his grin widening as his eyes glowed brighter. "This is getting interesting! I wonder what our dear Patriarch would do if he found out one of the noble families under him was conspiring with the Celestial Empire."

Kassandra snorted. "Obliterate them without leaving a trace."

"Exactly." Theron nodded. "If all doesn't go well tomorrow, I may need to make a trip to visit the Nightrose family."

Kassandra laughed but settled down when the doors to the room opened, and an absolutely terrified man with gray hair nervously walked in.

"Lord Theron." The man came to a stop a good distance away and bowed deeply. "I apologize for failing my duties."

Alongside Henry, there were two other middle-aged academy professors that they had bribed to fail Roselyn. Kassandra didn't even know their names, nor did she care.

"Henry, come take a seat." Theron pointed to the chair opposite him directly below an opening in the ceiling shrouded in an array formation to ensure anyone outside couldn't look in or hear what they were saying.

The gray-haired examiner glanced up at the hole in the ceiling and gulped. "M-my Lord…please give me another chance."

Theron smiled. "We are just going to have a chat. Why the hesitation? Come. Take a seat."

Henry's shoulders sagged as he trudged across the room and perched himself awkwardly on the edge of the chair. "My Lord, please let me explain!"

"By all means." Theron rested his chin on his fist as he lazily looked at the examiner with his glowing eyes. "You have one minute of my precious time."

Henry's eyes widened, and he didn't waste a moment and began to talk so fast he stumbled over his own words. "I-I had no idea how she passed the q-question nor handled the impurities. I ensured to p-provide her with the Qi Flowing Grass that Mistress Kassandra gave me this morning. I did everything as instructed, so it's not my fault—"

"None of that matters." Theron shook his head. "What matters is you failed. You have shown yourself incompetent and earned the suspicions of Elder Margret."

"But the Academy is an independent entity of Darklight City. So what if she is an Elder of the ruling family here? She has no right to have me sacked from my position in the Academy," Henry quickly retorted as he occasionally glanced up at the hole in the ceiling.

"Henry, you don't seem to understand your position here." Theron nodded at two silent cultivators wearing armor standing near the doorway to the room. They nodded back to Theron and slammed the doors shut, causing all three examiners to almost jump out of their skin.

"You are now an eyesore, and the Skyrend family doesn't tolerate such loose ends." Theron raised his finger to the ceiling, and Kassandra felt lightning Qi surge up his arm toward the sky through the opening in the ceiling.

All three examiner's eyes widened, and Henry jumped from the chair. "Wait!"

"This is the end—"

However, before Theron could finish his sentence, the ceiling exploded in a shower of rubble. Kassandra and Theron's Qi surged, and lighting arced out from their fingers to obliterate the large chunks of stone falling on them.

The three examiners turned tail and tried to run toward the door under the chaos, but before they could even be intercepted by the two guards, a giant claw of void Qi swooped down from the massive hole in the ceiling and slammed down on top of them.

"What in the gods!" Theron roared as his eyes were ablaze with power—lightning arced down his chiseled arms and coiled around his fingers as if waiting for their master to show them where to strike.

Kassandra was equally confused as she saw the void claw withdraw, leaving nothing but large gashes on the stone floor. The three examiners were either dead or had been taken off somewhere, as their bodies were missing. But why? How?

Theron seemed not to care for the reason as he blasted the retreating void Qi claw with all the lightning he could, filling the room with thunderclaps and light. "Dante, is that you?!?" Theron roared again as the void claw vanished out of sight.

Other than the sound of stone shards falling from the ceiling and smashing onto the destroyed floor below, the place was silent. The guards eventually walked over and hovered nearby, clearly concerned about another attack, but they also weren't brave enough to speak up to the enraged Theron, who continued to glare at the now wholly exposed sky.

Eventually, he calmed down enough to look at Kassandra with his wrathful countenance. "First, the Redclaws dare defy us, and now the Voidmind family?"

"Calm down, Brother," Kassandra said cautiously. "We can spit on the Redclaws with one arm behind our backs, but the Voidmind family is beyond us. Regain your composure and approach this carefully."

Theron's eye twitched, and he looked like he was going to say something but then sighed. "Your right. I'll go talk to him. We used to be sworn brothers, so this may be a misunderstanding. Although I can't see how we offended him."

Elaine opened her eyes as the door to the Void Chamber opened, and in walked Dante, who seemed to be holding back some anger.

Oh no, did the test go bad? Elaine began to panic. There wasn't much time left before the supposed invasion tomorrow, and she had yet to find an opportune time to acquire more information from Dante.

The reason behind the invasion made no sense to her. Dante claimed he wanted to conquer the city but never gave a good reason. Darklight City had few resources worth conquering for a family of the Voidminds' caliber, so there had to be a deeper explanation.

Dante ignored her and summoned a chair of liquid void. Only once seated did he meet her gaze with a deep frown.

Elaine felt her skin crawl under his gaze, so she asked to break the weird silence, "How did the test go?"

"Simple—a complete waste of time," Dante replied.

"So what is bothering you?"

Dante narrowed his eyes at her. "Tell me, are you working for anyone?"

"No," Elaine replied effortlessly. Her oath of secrecy to the Ashfallen Sect would never allow her to suggest otherwise.

Dante leaned back in his liquid void chair and stared at her with a scrutinizing gaze for a moment.

Did I mess up somewhere? How did he find out? Elaine tried to remember every little thing she had done since Dante's arrival. However, other than the meeting with Douglas in the dining room and writing out a note in ancient runes, she had avoided all forms of communication with the Ashfallen Sect until she acquired more information to share.

Not enjoying Dante's gaze, Elaine hesitantly said, "Why do you ask? Is it because of the invasion tomorrow? Is that what's bothering you?"

"The invasion is of little concern." Dante waved it off as he continued brooding, shifting his gaze to the void surrounding them.

"Say, Brother, I don't understand the purpose of the invasion," Elaine said as nonchalantly as possible, though her heart was pounding. "Of course, I don't doubt Brother or Father's vision, but I just wondered what its purpose was. I have lived here for many years, and I know of nothing here that the Voidmind family doesn't already have access to."

"Sister, my time is precious. In fact, the mere seconds I spend gracing you with my words is a waste of time. Do you truly believe I would be here in this backwater city for such shallow purposes? To conquer weaklings for fun?" Dante snapped at her. "These Redclaw pigs will surrender to me within moments, and the mortals get no say in who rules over them. So tell me, are there really no other conclusions in that ever-so-intelligent brain of yours?"

He then leaned in closer, seemingly enjoying speaking down to her despite his claims of not wanting to waste his breath. "Why am I here, Elaine? Tell me."

Elaine held back her anger and replied as sweetly as possible, "Your and Father's intellect far surpasses mine. How could I possibly hope to understand the depths of your plans?"

Dante grinned. "A good answer, my dear sister. You see, I gave you a weak reason for the invasion a few days ago and had my spies check for any sign of the Redclaws or anyone else suddenly preparing to fight an imminent invasion. But there have been no such signs, so it appears my paranoia was unwarranted, and for that, I apologize. I should have never doubted the loyalty of one with the same blood as me."

Elaine smiled and wanted to stab herself in the throat as she flattered him. "I am honored to be trusted by you, Brother."

"Well, with a day left to go, there's not much they could do even if they knew now, so I suppose there's no harm in letting you know the plan." Dante leaned in a little, and Elaine held her breath in anticipation. "The reason for the invasion is actually very simple—we need more airships."

"Airships?" Elaine was puzzled. "What does Darklight City have to do with airships?"

"Tsk, Sister, you are so short-sighted." Dante shook his head. "Have you not heard? The Patriarch has demanded an increase in airships from the Azurecrest family in anticipation of the move to the new land when the beast tide arrives."

"Okay…" Elaine frowned. "I still don't see the correlation between airships and Darklight City."

"It's only known to the top families right now, but the new land that the Patriarch picked out is apparently already occupied by a smaller demonic sect."

Elaine's eyes widened. "Which sect?"

"Lord Nightrose won't tell anyone to avoid any family getting a head start." Dante clicked his tongue. "But what he did disclose before entering closed-door cultivation to a few families is that there will only be one trip to the new land."

"One trip?" Elaine couldn't believe it. "But there are millions of people to be moved! Even with a drastic increase in the number of airships, there would only be enough room for most of the noble families and a small group of mortals with a single trip."

Dante nodded with a serious expression. "Exactly. And those airships will be split between each of the nine cities. Therefore, if we control both Slymere and Darklight City, we will have twice the number of airships at our disposal."

"But our family is rather small compared to the others, and so is Slymere," Elaine protested. "So what do you need more airships for?"

"If we bring an entire airship of mortal slaves, we can set up our industries and rebuild Slymere at the new location faster." Dante sighed. "But getting more airships was only one of the reasons I am here."

Elaine had been about to ask what Dante planned for the Redclaws if he was to seize control of Darklight Cities airships, but she held back because, as a Voidmind, she shouldn't care for what happened to them.

"What was the other reason for you being here, Brother?" Elaine asked innocently but shrank back a little under Dante's intense gaze.

"Do you know about the curse on our family?" Dante asked. "The shackles that bind our blood to this lower plane?"

Elaine nodded. It was known that nobody from the Voidmind family had managed to create a nascent soul.

Dante summoned the perfect pebble that Ashlock had given Elaine to help sell her lie about being cursed. "There's no way something like this could exist except in a higher realm. It now makes sense why Uncle holed himself up in this place. He knew how to ascend all along and wanted to perfect the technique away from the prying eyes of our family."

"How do you know he ascended?" Elaine knew what had really happened to her uncle if the words of the Ashfallen Sect were to be believed. He had initially died but was then taken away to a higher realm. So in a way, her uncle had found a way to ascend.

"Father has an artifact that can detect the presence of a person's soul," Dante explained. "There was a period where it was barely showing a reading, but that was during the time you said Uncle had gone in a rift, so that made sense."

"What does the reading say now?" Elaine inquired.

Dante held up the perfectly round but dull pebble. "Nothing. The artifact suggests that either Uncle perished and his soul has moved on, or he managed to find a way to ascend. Both options are terrible news for us."

"So he really found a way…" Elaine pretended to be amazed.

"We believe so, and if Uncle returns after forming his nascent soul or whatever realm of cultivation he is in now, he can come back down here and remove Father from his seat as the head of the family and put his branch in charge."

Elaine attempted to mirror Dante's grave expression. In truth, she didn't care what happened to her father or brother, nor did she care if Uncle somehow returned. Her life was pledged to the Ashfallen Sect, which would remain here.

The doors to the Void Chamber suddenly opened, and Clive, the butler of this mansion, had a severe expression. "Excuse my interruption, but we have visitors."

"Visitors?" Dante frowned. "Who are they?"

"Theron Skyrend is here. He wishes to speak with you."

"Did he say what about?" Dante asked as he stood up from his liquid void chair and reabsorbed the void Qi into his Star Core.

Clive nodded. "He wanted to ask if you were the one who just attacked their mansion with a giant void Qi attack in the shape of a claw?"

Dante's eyes widened, and all the color drained from his ghoulish face. "That was not me, and Father should still be back in Slymere. Is Uncle back?"

Clive lowered his head. "It hasn't been confirmed, but if Theron Skyrend's description of the attack is to be believed, I fear even your father could not produce such an attack."

Without delay, Dante strode out of the void chamber and followed Clive down the corridor.

Elaine watched her brother's departing back and wondered how she could get the information she just learned back to the Ashfallen Sect.

68
AN INSANE PLAN

After watching Stella tour the city for a while, Ashlock switched his focus back to Red Vine Peak.

The day of reckoning was soon upon him, and he started panicking a little. The tournament's main event was set to begin tomorrow afternoon, and he had yet to devise a solid plan to counter Dante Voidmind's invasion.

Information about the invasion was lacking, and so were his options for counterattacking such an attack due to the destructive power of void Qi, which made anyone who cultivated it challenging to defeat as it didn't really have any counters.

"If it's just Dante Voidmind attacking, I could defeat him with {Consuming Abyss} or send Bob to defeat him," Ashlock mused. "I could even tell the Grand Elder to try and wear him out, as once Dante is out of void Qi, he will have no way to replenish the spent Qi."

Ashlock knew he could win in a battle of attrition with his immunity to void Qi and his ability to acquire Qi through devouring monsters and from his vast network of trees. The issue was the location of where the invasion would take place.

"I had some suspicions of why Dante would wait until the finale of the alchemy tournament to attack, and now it's so obvious. He doesn't want to waste his precious void Qi, so he needs a location where many of the Redclaws are grouped together so he can threaten them all at once. He also needs a stage where he can force the Redclaws to surrender the city to him in front of all the other noble families present to make it more official."

Ashlock was at a loss. Should he cancel the tournament to deny Dante the stage he desired for his invasion and risk the Redclaws losing face or angering the other families present?

"If it was just Dante Voidmind and nobody else, and there was no risk of angering his family by killing him, then crushing him wouldn't be too much of an issue. However, if he brings multiple Voidmind Elders, Stella's safety alongside everyone else at the colosseum will be at risk," Ashlock mused as he absentmindedly watched the mist swirl around the wall of demonic trees encircling him as he tried to think of a way out of this.

But he was broken from his wandering thoughts when he felt a wave of pain through the root network.

He had naturally tuned out most sensations as ever since he became fused with all of his offspring, he had been bombarded with a mixture of emotions and pain.

Sometimes some kid from Darklight City that didn't know any better would hang off a weak branch of one of his offspring, causing it to snap, which obviously made the demonic tree cry out to him in pain. Other times it was a monster or animal that would lean against a tree out in the wilderness, causing it distress. All these were such minor things that Ashlock didn't have the time or resources to try and solve all these problems, so he simply ignored them.

But this time, it was different. It was a hot, sharp pain like someone stabbing a knife into his foot, so his vision blurred as he went to investigate. To his surprise, he found Elaine in the garden of the Voidmind mansion, quickly carving runic words with her nail into the exposed root of a demonic tree that had snuck under their wall.

"If only my roots were considered part of my body and were immune to void Qi like my trunk." Ashlock hissed as he tried to ignore the searing pain. "Then this wouldn't hurt so much. What is she even doing?"

Curious, Ashlock tried to read the words carved into the fused root between him and his offspring.

Skyrend mansion was destroyed by Void Qi... Dante speaking to Theron. Brother thinks the Elder is back and learned a way to

ascend. **My family wants Darklight City, so they will be allocated more airships to evacuate the beast tide.**

"Wait, what?" Ashlock reread the words to make sure he wasn't misreading them. "The Skyrend mansion was destroyed by Void Qi? Unless it was someone from the Voidmind family, Maple is the only one I know who can use void Qi. And what's this about airships?"

Ashlock debated using {Progeny Dominion} to take over the tree right next to the wall so he could talk to Elaine directly with {Abyssal Whispers}. Alas, he wanted to save the S-grade skill for tomorrow, and Elaine was unlikely to withstand his telepathy without the help of Stella's Mind Fortress pills, so that wasn't a smart idea.

Before Elaine could write any more ancient runes, she stood up as a guard of the Voidmind family was approaching from behind.

"Mistress, is everything all right?" the guard asked calmly.

Elaine smiled at the robed cultivator while blocking the view of the root with her body. *"Of course, I was just wandering the garden and thought I saw something interesting, but it turned out to be nothing worth my curiosity."*

"Then forgive my questioning." The man bowed slightly. *"Your brother requested you return inside as his talk with Theron Skyrend concluded."*

Elaine nodded and followed the guard back inside the mansion that Ashlock had no way to peek inside. However, by casting {Eye of the Tree God} and looking from above, he could see Theron leaving the mansion's grounds with a deep frown.

The giant man didn't say anything on his walk back to the Skyrend mansion, which was a few roads away. Once he arrived, Ashlock was baffled when he saw a large hole directly in the center of the mansion, as if a god had come down and pulverized it.

Through the hole, he could see most of the main room within the mansion.

"Marble statues...really? They seemed like they had never stayed here, yet there are statues?" Ashlock was a little happy to see a few of them had been damaged alongside the massive gashes on the floor. He didn't like them after hearing and seeing how they had treated Stella.

"This definitely looks like the work of Maple." Ashlock sighed. "But what prompted that nightmare squirrel to attack the Skyrend family?"

Ashlock quickly glanced over the city but was unable to locate

Stella. Returning his view to Red Vine Peak, he was about to ask Larry to go find them when he noticed Stella was lounging on the bench under his shade and feeding Maple roasted acorns.

"Stella never buys Maple acorns." Ashlock became very suspicious.

"Tree?" Stella seemed to somehow notice his spiritual gaze. *"If your attention is back here, feel free to use telepathy. I have recovered enough to handle it."*

Ashlock cast {Abyssal Whispers} and saw Stella wince. She quickly swallowed one of her Mind Fortress pills and then let out a sigh of relief. "Okay, Tree, you can speak now."

"Did you send Maple to attack the Skyrend family?"

Stella's hand giving Maple a head rub, paused. *"No...I did offer acorns if Maple killed the examiners, though."*

"I see... Did you know Maple destroyed half the Skyrend family's mansion?"

"Oh, how unfortunate." Stella shook her head and grinned. *"Bah, who am I kidding? That is a great outcome. I hate that family with a passion."*

Having finished the last acorn and seeing Stella wasn't giving any head pats, Maple sprawled out on Stella's head and fell asleep.

Seeing Maple's exhaustion, Ashlock could only lament that one of his trump cards had been seemingly wasted. "There has to be some way I can use this situation…"

Ashlock thought back to the words Elaine had written on the root. "Dante apparently thinks the Elder has returned. Is that because of Maple's void Qi? Hmm…I'll ask the girls."

"Hey, Stella, I got some news from Elaine—"

"Wait." Stella turned to look toward the water Qi demonic trees. *"Diana, come over here! Tree has some news from Elaine for us!"*

Diana seemed unresponsive as she was deep in meditation, so Stella opened a portal beside the bench and put her arm through to poke Diana.

Ashlock watched in amusement as Diana's eyes opened, and she glanced around in confusion while rubbing the spot on her cheek where Stella had poked her.

"What…?" she murmured while still half confused but brightened up a little when she saw Stella waving to her. Getting up and walking over, Diana asked, "Since when did you get back? How did the test go?"

"I passed, but I went for a stroll after the test to clear my head, so I

only just got back." Stella sighed. *"Can you believe those Skyrend bastards had paid off the examiners to ask me about a pill from the Celestial Empire, and then they gave me an already purified ingredient and told me to purify it?"*

Diana snorted. *"Did you really expect those egotistical bastards to play fair? It's obvious that they would rather die than face humiliation, so I'm surprised they didn't just try to murder you or something."*

"They didn't go quite that far..." Stella awkwardly laughed. *"But I might have."*

"You did what?" Diana's eyes widened.

"I might have gotten a little angry and asked Maple to kill the examiners." Stella smiled. *"But it's fine now. I am no longer angry."*

Diana let out a sigh of relief. *"Phew, I thought you actually went through with it for a second—"*

"I did, though?" Stella tilted her head in confusion.

"Eh?" Diana was in disbelief. *"Maple actually killed them?"*

"Well, obviously." Stella rolled her eyes. *"Why would I be in such a good mood otherwise? Oh wait, Tree had something to tell us."*

"Don't try and change the subject!" Diana crossed her arms and glared at Stella and Maple. *"You can't kill people from the Academy like that. They are sent by the Blood Lotus Sect!"*

"Oh..." Stella seemed to realize the gravity of her actions. "That's not good."

"No, of course not," Diana grumbled and then turned to look at Ashlock. *"What did you need to tell us?"*

"Stella, relay this to Diana. Elaine told me that the Skyrend mansion was destroyed by Void Qi and that Dante spoke with Theron. Apparently, Dante Voidmind thinks the Head Librarian is back and has learned a way to ascend. This is a big deal because their bloodline is cursed and doesn't allow them past the Nascent Soul Realm. Also, the purpose behind the invasion is because the Voidmind family wants to be allocated more airships for the evacuation. Does Diana have any good plans that make use of this information?"

After repeating his words to Diana, the black-haired girl fell into deep contemplation and began pacing around the courtyard. She even began muttering to herself, which earned her a concerned look from Stella.

"Diana? Are you all right?" Stella asked after Diana completed her third circuit around the hole in the courtyard's center.

"Shush, I am so close to a solution." Diana waved her off and continued pacing. She started drawing in the air, and the muttering only worsened.

Eventually, as the sun began to set, Diana finally paused mid-stride. "I got it!" she shouted, but her monotone voice made her sound more exhausted than excited.

Stella was shocked out of her trance where she had been petting Maple and just watching Diana pacing about. "What's your idea?"

"Okay, it's a little farfetched, but if we do it perfectly, I might have a way out of this," Diana said, and that was all Ashlock needed to hear to feel some hope.

Diana paused to compile her chaotic thoughts and then tried to slowly explain. *"As we are right now, we have no chance at defeating House Voidmind or Skyrend. Both are top-tier families for their fighting capabilities and political power within the Blood Lotus Sect. So our best solution here is to fight neither."*

Well, obviously—Ashlock didn't wish to fight, either. Even with his immunity to the void and ability to give lightning Qi resistance fruit to his allies, he still didn't want to try and resist the full wrath of one of these families.

If it were up to him, everyone would leave him alone, let him power up to be stronger than the Blood Lotus Patriarch, and then he would either overtake the sect or use his newfound power to fend off the beast tide.

Stella frowned. *"Diana, did you forget that Maple kinda obliterated the Skyrend family's mansion and killed three examiners?"*

Diana raised a finger. *"Let me finish, as that event might be our best bet. We need to sow discord between the two families. Have them fight each other rather than us."*

"Is that even possible?" Stella sat back and tapped her chin. *"I really don't understand all of this sect politics stuff."*

Diana grinned. *"Well, it's a good thing I do. Now listen here. This is how we can get them to fight each other. And hopefully, if I am not being insane, I won't be causing the death of us all."*

Idletree Daily Sign-In System

Day: 3531
Daily Credit: 4
Sacrifice Credit: 52
[Sign in?]

Ashlock awoke the next day with a pit in his nonexistent stomach.

Everyone knew their roles to make this insane plan successful, as they had discussed at length until dusk. But so much relied on their acting skills that Ashlock wasn't exactly happy to bet their continued existence on it. Alas, despite how insane it was, he had to admit it was their best bet.

Once his mind had awoken, his vision blurred as he checked up on the cavern. As expected, he saw Stella standing beside a burning cauldron of fruit with a line of ingredients on the earthen bowl's rim, including Mind Fortress fruit.

Stella had been hard at work throughout the night to improve her alchemy skills for the main event today, as she needed all the practice she could get to humiliate Kassandra in front of a live crowd.

According to Stella, the Skyrend woman had been somewhat competent at alchemy, and since it was almost guaranteed that Kassandra would try and cheat somehow, Stella needed to be on top of her game.

Her alchemy practice also doubled as a chance to make more Mind Fortress pills, as everyone would need one for today's plan.

Since Stella was still busy and there were many hours until the afternoon when the main event began, Ashlock returned his sights to the peak. Diana had already left to meet with the Redclaws and the Silverspires on Red Vine Peak, as without their complete cooperation, today could be his last.

Larry arrived in the courtyard as the sun bathed it in golden morning light with a sack of corpses on his back, which relieved Ashlock. He had been searching for monsters to devour for points near his demonic tree wall but hadn't found many, so he only had fifty credits stockpiled.

"Did you have a good hunt?"

"Yes, Master. I had a glorious feast befitting of a king, and now I am here to bestow upon you the finest delicacies of my hunt," Larry said in his gruff, almost Scottish accent as he unraveled the silk bag and deposited a small group of monster corpses onto the ground.

Ashlock greedily devoured the corpses with thorn-covered vines.

[+107 Sc]

"Only a hundred credits. Is this really the best of what you found?" Ashlock asked Larry, and the spider made a poor attempt at a bow.

"Master, this useless servant must apologize. I was hunting from dusk till dawn and only encountered a few monsters. My speech about a feast earlier was a joke in poor taste. There was almost nothing to eat. These truly are the best of the bunch I found! I would never lie to Master…"

"Okay, okay, this is enough for the plan today." Ashlock couldn't imagine needing to use his {Consuming Abyss} skill for longer than two hours.

Larry hissed in excitement, *"When do we begin the plan, Master?"*

"Patience, my many-legged friend." Ashlock chuckled. "Only a few more hours to go."

Time passed quickly, and soon enough, the sun sat high in the sky, signifying the main event would begin soon.

Right on time, Stella teleported to the peak after changing into her Roselyn persona. "Is Diana here yet?"

Ashlock checked the White Stone Palace courtyard with {Eye of the Tree God} and saw an exhausted Sebastian reluctantly shaking Diana's hand beside a grinning Redclaw Grand Elder.

Deciding their talks were likely concluded, Ashlock created a portal and brought Diana over.

"Did they agree to the plan?" Stella asked with excitement, and by Diana's mood, the answer was obvious.

"You bet they did! Are you ready to start the greatest civil war in the Blood Lotus Sect's history?"

Diana spread her arms and grinned. *"Today, Theron and Kassandra Skyrend will die."*

69
THE CROWDS ROAR

To kill the Skyrend family and blame it on Dante Voidmind was the focal point of the grand plan. Everything being done today was to set the stage for that moment.

Yet after Diana's great news regarding the agreement of the Redclaws and Silverspires to the insane plan that might start a great civil war within the Blood Lotus Sect, she remained excited as if she still had something even more ridiculous to tell them.

"Spit it out, Diana," Stella said. *"I can tell you have more news by that look on your face."*

Diana chuckled as if the news was too funny to share. Eventually, she gathered herself and explained, *"When I went over this morning to tell the Redclaws the plan, I happened to bump into someone rather unexpected."*

"Who?" Stella asked.

"Kassandra Skyrend," Diana said thoughtfully. *"My heart froze as, for a moment, I thought she had figured something out, and my mind was racing with so many questions, but she just casually walked past me without any interest as if I was a bug. It took a good minute for me to regain my composure."*

Stella's eyes were wide with shock, and Ashlock was also baffled. What was Kassandra doing at the White Stone Palace before the sun had even risen?

"So? What was she doing there?" Stella insisted.

"*Calm down. I was getting to that,*" Diana spoke quickly. "*We don't have much time until today's tournament starts, so I will be brief. Kassandra felt like the tournament only focusing on making a single pill wasn't enough, so she had come to the Redclaws to request a restructure of the tournament.*"

Stella narrowed her eyes. "*She wouldn't suggest anything that wouldn't give her an advantage. To think she would go this far just to try and get an edge over me.*"

"*You see, that's where she messed up.*" Diana smirked. "*Her grand idea was that after everyone had made a Body Strengthening Pill, the best ten participants would have a chance to compete against one another by making another pill.*"

"*But that wouldn't work...*" Stella furrowed her brows. "*The whole reason this tournament was cut down to making one pill was that the Redclaws struggled to get their hands on enough ingredients for other recipes.*"

Diana nodded. "*Exactly, so when the Redclaw Grand Elder explained that to her, she suggested that part of alchemy was the ability to source ingredients, and therefore in the final round, the participants should create the best pill they can with their own ingredients.*"

Ashlock couldn't believe Kassandra's arrogance. It was likely their fault that the Redclaws could not source anything more than the bare minimum needed for a single round that involved creating pills.

"Actually...to be fair, that is sort of the Redclaws' fault for being considered a lesser family that's easy to bully," Ashlock mused. "So, in a twisted way, Kassandra isn't wrong, but to stroll into the White Stone Palace and say that to the Grand Elder's face is crazy."

Stella crossed her arms and frowned. "*Other than the new Mind Fortress pill, we don't have the ingredients for anything else. Why are you smiling like that?*"

Diana's spatial ring flashed, and she brought out a beautiful pink flower and two glass bottles. One filled with a green dew and the other with sparkling water.

"*These are the ingredients required to make the Heavenly Purification Pill,*" Diana explained. "*This pill detoxifies the body of spiritual toxins or foreign energies that may have infiltrated a cultivator's body, purifying their Qi and ensuring smoother cultivation. It's a tier-two pill, apparently.*"

Stella took the petal and two bottles from Diana. "And these ingredients are?"

"That is a Celestial Peony Petal," Diana said, pointing at the pink petal. *"And then the green liquid is Heavenly Bamboo Essence, while the water is a diluted Nine-Tailed Fox's Tear."*

Stella looked at the items in her hand and frowned. *"I don't get it. How did you get these ingredients, and what should I do with them?"*

"Well, the Grand Elder was going to deny Kassandra's request of adding another round where we use our own ingredients, but then Elder Margret stepped in and told him to accept it only if they provided the ingredients of the pill they planned to create in the new final round." Diana gestured to Ashlock. *"I later found out this was due to Elder Margret's belief that Ashlock would be able to grow perfect version of the ingredients letting you get an easy win over Kassandra."*

Stella turned to Ashlock and asked through telepathy, "Can you grow these?"

"The Celestial Peony Petal is from a flower, so yes, I can grow that, and I believe bamboo is considered a flower, so that should be fine. But the tears are out of my capabilities," Ashlock answered truthfully.

"Okay, Tree says he can make the flower and the bamboo, but not the fox tears," Stella said. *"Did they say how many pills this bottle of tears was good for?"*

Diana shrugged as she summoned a parchment from her spatial ring. *"Elder Margret gave this to me. Apparently, it's the recipe for the pill."*

Stella scanned the parchment and then whistled. *"Quite the complex pill. Say, Diana, will a break exist between the round where we create the body-strengthening pill and the final round where I must make this pill so I can practice?"*

Diana shook her head. "Not that I know of."

"Mhm, the recipe says this volume of tears should be good for ten pills." Stella looked up from the parchment at Diana. *"How long until the tournament starts?"*

"Around an hour? But we should be going there now to set up."

"That should be long enough." Stella didn't waste a moment as she created a portal and vanished into the cavern below.

Ashlock's brought up his {Blooming Root Flower Production} menu and was glad to see both the Celestial Peony Petal and Heavenly Bamboo added to his growing list of potential flowers to grow.

His vision blurred as he followed Stella down into the cavern. She was busy frantically trying to learn the new pill, so Ashlock left her be and got to work designating two farming plots just above her head on the higher level to grow the two new flowers.

With a wave of power and Qi flowing from his almost overflowing Star Core, the Qi Flowing Grass wilted away and was replaced with shoots of bone-white bamboo in one plot and peony flowers in the other.

As with everything he made, they were perfect. Devoid of any impurities and ready to be harvested as ingredients.

Stella's eyes widened as she reached down and picked up the pill she had just created. It was the tier-two Heavenly Purification Pill in all its golden glory. The thing looked like an almost translucent nugget of gold and had a soft hue despite the cavern's darkness.

"I did it!" Stella gasped. This was her ninth try and was the first successful attempt. Even with the pill recipe provided by Elder Margret, it had been Stella's first time trying to make a tier-two pill.

Other than the three ingredients provided by the Skyrends, the recipe also needed Qi Flowing Grass and Dragon Marrow, which Stella had plenty of due to Tree's past efforts.

With exhaustion, Stella placed the Heavenly Purification Pill next to the glass bottle containing a single droplet of the fox tears.

"This is going to be tough," Stella muttered. "Only a single droplet of nine-tailed fox tears left, and I have only managed to make one of the pills so far. I might actually mess up and lose to Kassandra at this rate."

The plan already had so many moving parts that Stella had struggled to keep track, and now she had the stress of needing to beat Kassandra Skyrend in the final round with a pill she had only produced a single time out of nine tries mere moments before the tournament began.

"Focus up, Stella. This is for Tree and the others." Stella tried to hype herself up but was startled by a hand tapping her shoulder.

"You didn't even notice me sneaking up on you," Diana said. "You're too distracted."

Stella sighed as she touched her beating heart. "Phew, you scared me."

Diana tutted. "You need to calm down and try to relax your mind. Maybe take another one of those Mind Fortress pills."

"I already took three, just give me a moment to rest, and I'll be fine." Stella waved Diana off.

"Stella, the tournament technically started a minute ago," Diana said impatiently. "We need to leave right now."

I just created nine pills in a row while learning a new recipe that was sprung upon me last moment, and now I don't even get a second to catch my breath! These people all think too highly of me! Curse you, Elder Margret, and your faith in me!

"Okay, okay." Stella fumbled as she tried to collect all the needed ingredients. Besides the fox tears, she had manically harvested from the farms over the last hour as she didn't have time to purify the ingredients while learning to combine five different things into the intended pill, so she had a nice pile of Celestial Peony Petals, Qi Flowing Grass, and full bottles of Dragon Marrow and Heavenly Bamboo Essence.

"Patriarch, can we get a portal to the venue? We won't make it in time if we walk," Diana yelled at the ceiling.

Stella felt a wave of spatial Qi as a portal manifested, followed by some reassuring words from Ash.

"You will do fine. All those ingredients besides the fox tears are near perfect, so relax and focus on passing the first round."

"Thank you, Tree," Stella said aloud before walking through the portal alongside Diana, who was reaching up to fasten a white wooden mask to her face.

There was a pop in Stella's ears as she stepped through.

"I'm going to meet up with the others," Diana said the moment the floral scent of the cavern vanished and was replaced with the stench of the city. "Good luck. I'll be rooting for you."

Stella nodded with a smile behind her cloth mask and watched Diana vanish into a cloud of mist.

"Oh shit, I'm running late, aren't I?" Stella glanced around at the grand square and saw the line of people trying to enter was far smaller than yesterday, and the crowds around the market stalls were small. Everyone was likely inside already.

Although using techniques within a city was considered against the rules, Stella snapped open a portal that took her right to the front of the queue. She ignored the hollers of the mortals behind her and strode in.

"Roselyn," the same short Redclaw woman from yesterday called out to her, "the first round of today's main event is about to start. Quickly follow me!"

Stella wasted no time, and the two speedily walked through a long, straight corridor lit by glowing stones built into the walls. The sound of their shoes echoing on the tiles was soon drowned out by a deafening roar of excitement from up ahead.

You can do this, Stella. No, you are Roselyn right now. An arrogant cultivator hired by the Redclaw and Silverspire family with the sole purpose of humiliating Kassandra and carrying out the plan.

The Redclaw woman paused at the end of the tunnel and turned to smile at her. The sunlight cascading down the tunnel and reaching Stella's feet illuminated the woman's face, and she could see the vast sandy pit with people standing beside tables beyond the corridor's end.

"This is as far as I can go." The woman gave a slight bow. "You can pick whichever table is still free."

Stella nodded in appreciation and strode past her. The moment she emerged from the tunnel and out into the open, the crowd's roar was far louder than she had expected, and the sheer energy of the place was bewildering.

"How am I supposed to perform alchemy in these conditions?" Stella grumbled as she glanced around, trying to find an empty table. To her surprise, it was harder to find one than she thought. The place was packed with alchemists.

She walked past dozens of tables, all occupied by people of various ages and cultivation levels.

Are there really none free? Stella wondered as she started feeling awkward, having to walk around trying to find a vacant workstation.

"Roselyn, over here!" a voice called out to her. It was hard to tell who it was over the crowd's excitement, but her eyes narrowed as she walked toward it and saw an empty table…right next to Roderick Terraforge and Kassandra Skyrend.

Roderick was the one who had called out to her, and he seemed eager to point out the empty table beside him.

Stella spread out her spiritual sight but still failed to locate a spare table, so she reluctantly strode up to the table with all the fake confidence she could muster and stood beside it with her back straight.

"Sleep in?" Roderick snorted. "Or were you too busy sucking up to the Silverspire family to remember to show up on time?"

Stella was about to retort but held her tongue. She didn't remember Roderick being this talkative before, and his comments were such nonsense that they made her think less of him.

What's his goal here? Is he hoping to throw me off my concentration with snide remarks?

Stella glared at him and then returned her sights to the workbench before her. It was a simple wooden desk with a small black metal cauldron perched on top; beside it was bundles of Qi Flowing Grass, Starlight Lotus, and a pot of Dragon Marrow. All the ingredients needed for the Body Strengthening Pill.

Wait, what are these markings?

Looking closer, Stella saw random words etched into the table's wood and other drawings. At first, she thought it might be a secret message, but she couldn't understand it.

"Tree, do you know what these scribbles and words are?" Stella asked mentally. "They aren't runes. Are they a secret message? I won't be accused of cheating because of them, right?"

"Stella, these tables were taken from the Academy's classrooms. They are just the result of bored students leaving their mark on the tables. There's no hidden meaning behind them."

"Huh? Really?" Stella tilted her head in confusion. "Why would they be bored? Can't they just leave and do something more interesting?"

"That's not how school works." Ashlock chuckled. **"They have to sit in a classroom and listen to a teacher talk about a subject for hours. They aren't allowed to leave no matter how boring it is."**

"That's just torture. Why would anyone do that?" Stella didn't even care that Roderick was trying to taunt her or the crowd's roar. This information was so unsettling it helped her regain her focus.

Just breathe. Everything will be fine.

Stella tilted her head and looked at Kassandra.

Seeing the living, breathing woman that was the embodiment of pride and arrogance look back at her with such sinister confidence made Stella wonder one thing:

Does she know this is her last day alive? Can she feel it in the winds of change that her death draws near? I almost can't wait to finally see that smug grin buried in the sand.

"Everyone! Welcome to the first alchemy tournament of Darklight City!"

Stella was broken from her dark thoughts as she glanced up at a hastily constructed wooden platform on one side of the colosseum.

Backdropped by many levels of cheering people that seemed to stretch all the way to the clear blue sky was Elder Brent. He stood with his hands clasped behind his back as he used his Qi to empower his speech to reach everyone in this massive venue.

The moment he spoke, the crowd began waving their arms and drumming their feet. If that wasn't distracting enough, the shouts were deafening. Stella couldn't even understand what they were all shouting, but she didn't care. Her focus was on Elder Brent's words.

Elder Brent took in the atmosphere as he sagely looked around. It was hard to remember since Stella was basically his superior. But Elder Brent was a powerful cultivator and Elder of one of the noble families, so he was like a living god to the rogue alchemists and mortals in the crowd.

"Ahem, I am honored by everyone's excitement." Elder Brent grinned, and Stella could see the waves of his Qi-empowered voice spreading out in all directions. "Now before I explain the tournament rules, I believe it's only right I introduce everyone to the people behind today's event."

Elder Brent gestured to a large section of the colosseum stands that had been sectioned off opposite him. Stella followed his gaze and couldn't help but smile as she saw a large, demonic tree proudly rooted into the stone seats of the colosseum, shrouding the sectioned-off area in the shade of its canopy.

A fog began to swirl around the demonic tree, and under the thunderous cheers of the crowd, silhouettes of people lurking in the fog appeared.

"It is with great pleasure that I can introduce you to the Grand Elder of our Redclaw family alongside the event's main sponsor, Ryker Silverspire!" Elder Brent announced with gusto, hyping the crowd into a standing applause.

Stella held back a laugh as she saw the Grand Elder emerge from the fog and stand proudly beside a very confused-looking child. After a moment of the Grand Elder waving to the people in the crowd, a few more people emerged from the fog and stood at his flanks.

They didn't get a formal introduction, but Stella recognized them as members of the Ashfallen Sect.

Douglas, Diana, and even Elaine stood there with masks obscuring their faces.

"Who are those people?" Kassandra muttered under her breath as she squinted at the masked people.

Stella grinned.

You will be finding out sooner than you might think.

70
PILL ASSESSMENT

Stella ignored Kassandra's questioning of the masked people and glanced around the hyped-up colosseum. The atmosphere was ecstatic to the point that she began to fear that the giant stone building would collapse.

Eventually, the crowd's cheers calmed down, and Elder Brent continued explaining the tournament's rules.

"Now that I have finished the introductions, I believe it's time to explain what will happen today." His Qi-empowered voice made it sound like he spoke straight into her ear. "Yesterday, there was a preliminary round whose goal was to weed out the fakes from the adept. Therefore standing before you today are certified alchemists with some capabilities."

Stella looked around and saw many of the rogue alchemists had grins on their faces as they waved to the crowd. Meanwhile, all the nobles she could spot had blank expressions as if this bored them.

She couldn't blame them as she felt much the same way. If not for Kassandra paying off the examiners to try and fail her, the preliminary round would have been easy, and this was just another step to the final that truly mattered.

Elder Brent continued, "Today will consist of two rounds. The first will last twenty minutes, during which the participants will be expected to create a Mortal-grade Body Strengthening pill. Examiners will then go around and give each pill a score from one to a hundred based on a strict set of criteria. The ten people with the highest scores will then participate in the final round where they can create any pill within their capabilities with their own ingredients."

The moment he finished the explanation, there was a sudden roar from the crowd that helped to drown out the outbreak of discussion between the alchemists. Stella listened in, and it seemed many rogue alchemists had come without any ingredients and were shouting out about how unfair it was.

Elder Brent raised his hand to calm the crowd.

"Fear not. Those without any ingredients can create a second Body Strengthening pill." Elder Brent smiled. "But as we all know, part of being an alchemist is your ability to source ingredients."

Stella smirked behind her mask at Elder Brent's words as she saw Kassandra's eye twitch slightly. Kassandra was clearly annoyed at having her words repeated by someone from a lesser family.

Elder Brent then spread his arms and put a lot of Qi into his voice as he shouted to the heavens, "You all have twenty minutes! Begin!"

Stella spun around and eyed her workbench.

Okay, twenty minutes should be plenty of time. I can produce a Body Strengthening Pill within ten minutes if I concentrate hard enough and everything goes right.

Stella reached forward and picked up the Qi Flowing Grass.

Full of impurities, this is definitely an ingredient that the Redclaws sourced rather than one grown by Tree. Wait, isn't this enough to make two pills? Maybe if I work fast enough, I can make two and give the best one to be scored by the examiner?

Stella shook her head. The drumming of feet and shouting from the thousands of mortals around her made it hard to concentrate on anything more than her inner thoughts.

Turning her attention to the small metal cauldron, Stella frowned behind her mask. She had never used a real cauldron, as she had always used Ash's weird fruit cauldron that made performing alchemy far easier.

Focus on that later. For now, I need to remove the impurities from these ingredients.

Stella closed her eyes and was about to begin the process when she felt a blast of lightning Qi right beside her, followed by thunderclaps that made her hair and clothes rustle.

Glancing to the side, Stella saw Kassandra lording over her workbench. The giant woman had a bundle of Qi Flowing Grass floating between her fingers as she blasted it with lightning, making burned impurities rain and be carried away by a gust of wind into Stella's face.

Oh, this bitch. Stella gritted her teeth as her Star Core pulsed. If Kassandra could do something like this, then why couldn't she? Both Roderick and Kassandra were briefly stunned by the sudden pressure.

Now surrounding Stella was a field of distorted spatial Qi that stopped the impurities from reaching her and helped reduce the terrible noise. Was it a massive waste of the Qi she had cultivated over the past few weeks? Absolutely. Did she care? Not in the slightest. It was the Redclaws' fault for squeezing so many workbenches so close together.

Kassandra was broken from her concentration and glared at her, but Stella just returned a shrug and got back to work. Time was ticking, and she had already wasted a minute on nonsense.

Holding the bundle of Qi Flowing Grass in her hand, Stella activated the spatial plane, and the world around her became outlined in grids. Focusing on the grass, she identified tiny gaps where she could thread her Qi into the bundle of grass just like she had many times before.

Once inside, she directed her spatial Qi through shifting pathways and was astonished at the sheer volume of impurities within the grass.

Unlike the Qi Flowing Grass produced by Tree, which had clear pathways except for the occasional speck of impurity floating around, this grass's pathways were clogged up with impurities to the point it was blocking her Qi from progressing any further.

How had this Qi Flowing Grass even absorbed any Qi at all with pathways this blocked up? I can only thank the heavens that I am in the Star Core Realm and have saved up a lot of Qi for today. Otherwise, I would be running low on Qi from removing these impurities.

I wonder how someone like Kassandra even plans to have enough Qi left over to create that tier-two pill later. Actually, I know how. I bet she already has purified ingredients, so all she has to do is spend Qi on combining the ingredients. How smart.

The bundle of Qi Flowing Grass became the stage for a great battle between Stella and the impurities. Thousands of tiny portals barely the width of a single hair snapped open and closed to bring the impurities outside. It was clear to Stella that spatial Qi wasn't the most efficient when removing impurities in both time and Qi, but she didn't care. She would win anyways.

"Phew." Stella wiped the sweat from her brow as she set the near-perfect Qi Flowing Grass on the table. Up next was the Dragon Marrow.

Quickly glancing to the side, she saw Kassandra had already started purifying the Dragon Marrow, while Roderick Terraforge didn't even seem to have started purifying anything. Instead, he was busy looking around for something.

Stella was curious, so she followed his gaze and saw Dante Voidmind, Celeste Starweaver, and Kane Azurecrest a few tables away. All three of them had finished purifying the Bone Marrow and had moved on to the final ingredient, the Starlight Lotus.

She had no idea why Roderick was looking at them and wasn't focusing on purifying the ingredients, but to be fair, she was also getting distracted.

Ugh, it's impossible to focus! I miss my nice and peaceful cavern surrounded by quiet darkness and a pleasant floral scent. How can anyone perform alchemy under the scorching sun while having thousands of people screaming at you and working with such crappy ingredients?

Stella's brain was a clouded mess—she had been highly stressed for days as she oscillated between brute force learning alchemy without a teacher, participating in high society social events, and planning out how to start a civil war that has the chance to backfire and lead to the annihilation of the Ashfallen Sect and the death of Tree.

She was exhausted, but she had to perform. Feeling frustrated, she grabbed the jar containing the Dragon Marrow. To her surprise, it was far better quality than the Qi Flowing Grass, so purifying it only took a few minutes.

"Fifteen minutes remain!" Elder Brent called out, and Stella felt her hands shaking slightly as she reached for the Starlight Lotus. The Qi Flowing Grass had been riddled with impurities, while the Dragon Marrow had been quite good quality. How would the Starlight Lotus fair in comparison?

It sat in a small bowl of water, and from a glance, Stella could tell it was relatively low-grade because the coloring was off. The lotus had a dull gray pigment rather than the majestic blue of the Starlight Lotus that grew on the side of the monolith back at Red Vine Peak.

Picking it up confirmed Stella's suspicions. It was even worse quality than the Qi Flowing Grass, to the point it was half dead.

Stella couldn't help but glare up at Elder Brent and silently curse his nine generations for being so useless at sourcing high-quality ingredients. She understood this was supposed to be a test, and the ability to purify impurities was part of that, but this was just torture.

Time passed quickly as Stella wrestled the half-dead thing back to life.

"Ten minutes remain!" Elder Brent's words made Stella grumble as she set the now-purified Starlight Lotus on the workbench. It had taken her half the provided time to get a set of ingredients she was happy with. Nearly all three were as close to perfect as she could justify...

If only they had given us a full day so I could thoroughly purify them. Alas, with these ingredients, I think the best I could make is a low-grade tier-two-level pill.

Stella bit her lip behind her mask as she turned to the metal cauldron that dominated the workbench. A part of her had been putting this off because it would verify if her alchemy skills were really her own or just a result of being able to use Tree's cauldron and perfect ingredients.

Without further delay, as time was running out, Stella carefully placed half of the ingredients she had purified into the cauldron. It was only as she looked at the ingredients still on the workbench beside the cauldron that she suddenly realized she was an idiot—there had been no need to waste time purifying all the provided ingredients!

"Tsk," Stella clicked her tongue as she placed her two hands over the cauldron and closed her eyes. Once again, the spatial plane appeared in her mind as she bathed the cauldron in her soul flame.

Calming her breathing and focusing, Stella manipulated her soul fire as if they were ghostly hands to bring the ingredients together in a way she had done many times.

First, Stella had to mold the Dragon Marrow into a flat disc. She then layered the Qi Flowing Grass in an intricate pattern that was decorated with Starlight Lotus petals. Over and over, she completed this pattern, all while keeping her soul fire under control and making sure not to accidentally push some impurities from her soul flame into the ingredients and degrade the pill.

Okay, looking good, just need to do the final layer, and then I should have a near-perfect pill to be graded...

"Five minutes remain!" Elder Brent's Qi-empowered voice bypassed her spatial Qi field, briefly distracting Stella long enough for her to notice something shrouded in foreign Qi was running toward her at high speed.

Her eyes snapped open, only to face a grinning Roderick Terraforge shrouded in earth Qi barreling at her. Stella dodged to the side to avoid him, but her eyes widened when she realized his true objective had never been to hit her.

"Stop!" Stella called out as she tried to redirect the brute with a portal, but he easily smashed through it by flaring his earth Qi. She then tried to reach forward and pull him back from smashing into her table, but a tiny lightning bolt smacked her hand from grabbing his robe in time.

There was a loud crash, and everyone was broken from their concentration as they turned to see the scene of Roderick Terraforge lying flat on top of the workbench and cauldron.

The table was snapped in half, the cauldron shattered into pieces, and her almost-formed pill was ruined.

Stella stood there, unsure what to even make of the situation. It was unbelievable that they would cheat this blatantly to the point of attacking her. Was this really how the higher families acted while attending an event of a lesser family? Did they simply have no respect or care for consequences?

Elder Brent leaped down from the raised platform and arrived beside her in a flash of crimson fire. "I saw what happened, so there's no need for excuses."

Roderick Terraforge slowly stood to his full height, brushed off the sand and bits of ingredients, and looked down at Elder Brent with that same shit-eating grin. "Whatever do you mean, Elder Brent? I got too lost in my pill-making and tripped on my own foot. It's not my fault Roselyn was in the path of my unfortunate tumble."

There was a wave of boos from the crowd, and it was only now that Stella realized that the colosseum had actually gone relatively quiet with everyone, including the rogue alchemist, that should be busy making their pills curiously looking her way.

Elder Brent raised a brow. "What pill-making? You didn't even bother to purify a single ingredient."

Roderick awkwardly scratched the back of his neck. "Well, you see, I'm a novice alchemist, so it was all rather overwhelming."

"Your lack of skills does not give you a reason to meddle with another participant." Elder Brent snorted. "You are hereby disqualified and banned from all future alchemy tournaments hosted by us."

There was a round of cheers from the mortal audience, and the rogue alchemists surrounding them exchanged nervous glances. From their murmurs, Stella picked up that they couldn't believe a Redclaw would speak to a Terraforge in such a way.

But she didn't care about that as she ground her teeth in silent rage behind her mask. Roderick's dismissive attitude to demolishing her efforts and Kassandra's casual involvement in the incident infuriated her. Did they have no shame?

Elder Brent and Stella exchanged a glance, and it was clear what they were both thinking. Kassandra would normally also be disqualified, but as per the plan, she needed to make it to the finals.

Roderick raised his hands, his grin never leaving. "Okay, I accept my disqualification. Carry on with your little tournament."

Elder Brent seemed content to let the troublemaker leave, but Stella wasn't.

"Hold on a minute."

Roderick, Kassandra, and Elder Brent shot her questioning gazes.

"Why should I?" Roderick sneered.

Because if you leave so soon, I can't slit your throat. Stella held back her true feelings and said the first thing that came to mind.

"I believe what he did to me was done with nefarious intentions on behalf of someone else," Stella said loud and clear so everyone could hear her. "Therefore, I suggest he is detained so the Redclaw family may question his affiliation after the tournament has concluded."

The reason for his imprisonment was unimportant. All Stella wanted was to stop Roderick from leaving before she was done with humiliating Kassandra.

"Stella, this isn't part of the plan," Ashlock spoke within her mind.

"Nor was Roderick ruining my progress. It's not my fault he's dug his own grave," Stella retorted mentally. "You wanted a civil war, and I just thought of a way to get another family involved."

"Mhm, okay, I trust you. Just calm down and think carefully about what you are doing. Are you sure about this?"

Stella let out a breath and settled down a little. However, the second she looked back up and saw Roderick's face, she couldn't hold back.

"Tree, I have carefully considered and analyzed the situation and concluded that, without a doubt, I want to stab his fucking face."

Ashlock chuckled. *"I see. Well, I will handle this for you..."*

"Is that a good idea?"

"Absolutely, just blame it on the Silverspires. That's what we sacrificed some of our profits for!"

Roderick seemed to find Stella's words deeply amusing as he strode toward her. "Oh? You want to detain me? A descendant of the Terraforge family? I would love to see if you have the audacity."

Stella smiled behind her mask as she felt a ripple of spatial Qi spread throughout the area under the sand. A moment later, a large portal manifested behind Roderick.

The man turned to look behind with wide eyes. "What the—"

Before he could finish his sentence, the giant black wooden arm of Titus emerged from the portal and grabbed Roderick. Roderick tried to struggle and fight back but was powerless against the Star Core Ent that effortlessly dragged him away.

The portal snapped closed, sending a gust of wind that picked up the sand from the arena floor, making everyone squint. Everything happened so fast that even Stella might have second-guessed herself without a prior warning. But as the dust cleared, it was obvious that Roderick Terraforge was gone.

"What was that?" Kassandra shouted at Elder Brent. The man seemed clueless, so he gave Stella an odd look.

Stella shrugged. "Hired security by the Silverspires. They knew some arrogant nobles would think they could mess around and cheat, so they took countermeasures."

"But that seemed rather excessive even for the Silverspires." Kassandra's brows furrowed as she looked up at Ryker Silverspire standing under the shade of the demonic tree.

Stella didn't care for Kassandra as she went to look at the state of her purified ingredients. To her relief, the spares left on the side of the workbench had survived the fall and were just nestled in the sand.

Picking them up, she walked over to Roderick's hardly used workbench and set herself up. "Elder Brent, there are still a few minutes until the end of the test, right?"

Elder Brent nodded. "Due to the disturbance, I will add a few minutes as the test should have technically finished. Are you fine with that?"

Stella nodded, so the Elder returned to the platform and announced, "Test resumes! You all have five minutes left."

Only five minutes? Stella cursed as she scrambled to the cauldron. She had five minutes to create a body strengthening pill that would put her in the top ten out of all the applicants left.

Throwing all the ingredients in, she repeated the steps from earlier, just faster this time. The pattern of the Qi Flowing Grass was a little wonky, and the Starlight Lotus petals were sometimes placed a little too high or low, but Stella pressed on—there was no time to humor her innate desire for perfection. This was a rushed job.

"Time's up!" Elder Brent shouted right as Stella folded the Dragon Marrow into a ball shape and blasted it with her soul fire.

It was done.

Resisting the urge to collapse on the ground and nap, Stella fished the pill from the cauldron and inspected it.

Shit, I don't know much about grading pills, but this is worse than my first attempt at alchemy with the twins and Elder Margret. So it should be a Mortal-grade pill at best.

Stella looked to the side and saw Kassandra eyeing her completed pill, and she was grinning.

That's not a good sign...

Stella didn't have much time to wonder about her fate as the sandy arena became flooded with examiners holding parchments. They meticulously made their way through the participants, inspecting pills and cross-checking with one another to make sure multiple examiners reached a common consensus on a person's performance.

"Mortal-grade pill, score thirty-two."

"Failed pill, score zero."

"Mortal-grade pill, score fifty-six."

"Failed..."

Stella's heart pounded as she watched the examiners draw closer while keeping her ears peeled. She hadn't heard anyone get a score above sixty by the time a young man from the Redclaw family arrived before Kassandra.

"Kassandra Skyrend, please show your freshly created pill," he said while holding out his empty palm.

Kassandra proudly handed over a pill that looked like a glass ball with twinkling stars and dashes of green within.

The Redclaw man's eyes widened as he looked between his parchment and the pill multiple times. While the man was perplexed, two more examiners showed up, and they also seemed marveled by the pill.

After a while of intense discussions, they landed on a number.

"Spirit-grade pill, score eighty-nine."

Kassandra took the pill back from the examiner and smirked at Stella.

"Roselyn, please show me your freshly created pill," the Redclaw man asked, and Stella reluctantly handed over her pill.

There was a tense moment as the three examiners eyed her pill. However, to her surprise, they seemed almost equally impressed by her performance, and after a few moments of discussion, they reached a verdict.

71
SEVEN INGREDIENTS

Ashlock snapped the portal closed and watched as Titus stood at his full height out in the wilderness. In his cupped hands far above the ground was Roderick Terraforge, trapped within twisting black wood coated in fifth-stage Star Core Qi.

"There's no way Roderick can escape Titus, and even if he could, he wouldn't make it back to the tournament in time to meddle with anything." Ashlock almost felt bad when he heard shouts from within the wooden prison.

After taking a while to make sure Roderick really did have no way to break free, Ashlock's vision blurred as he returned to the colosseum.

"It seems that I missed the end of the round," Ashlock mused while observing the flood of examiners dashing between the workbenches and noting down scores.

On their parchments were diagrams and a list of things to look for to determine the quality of a Body Strengthening Pill. Elder Margret had drafted the list and handed it out earlier so that all the examiners could give accurate grades, regardless of their alchemy knowledge.

Of course, one person's judgment wasn't enough, so multiple examiners had to agree upon the same score. While this did make the scores accurate, it made grading slow.

While the event had taken twenty minutes, it took just as long to grade everyone. But the crowd seemed to love hearing the examiners shouting out scores, and whenever someone got a very high or low score, the crowd would either cheer or boo.

Ashlock was actually rather impressed with the tournament the Redclaws had managed to throw together over the course of a month with little help from him and limited resources.

His gaze drifted to those standing under the shade of the demonic tree he had left there all those weeks ago. Ever since he got the {Progeny Dominion} skill, he had left at least one offspring near every landmark in Darklight City.

However, he was yet to use the {Progeny Dominion} as he didn't want his presence to be too obvious until it was time to carry out the grand plan. So, for now, he was using {Eye of the Tree God} to watch the tournament from above, and he had opened the portal via roots he had buried under the arena's sand.

Standing around the tree were his sect members, including Elaine. Due to Diana's mist that shrouded them and the Grand Elder exerting his presence on the area, there would be no way for anyone to detect her Void Qi, the only risk was if someone recognized her despite the mask and black, hooded cloak she was wearing to hide her features.

Seeing how proud the Grand Elder looked as he surveyed the ecstatic arena, Ashlock could only reminisce about how far they had come together.

"It's already been a few months since that fateful day that Stella forced the Redclaws to sign an oath to me," Ashlock mused. "I remember when I promised the person who contributed the most to setting up the tournament a reward, but I already gave them all my truffles and access to the Mystic Realm."

Ashlock wondered if he should sign in for some low-grade items and give them as rewards instead. Would they even want his shitty items over his amazing cultivation resources?

"Spirit-grade pill, score eighty-nine."

Ashlock had been lost in his thoughts, but such a high number being called out by an examiner drew his attention. To his surprise, the examiners gathered around Stella had engaged in an intense discussion.

"Did Kassandra get eighty-nine?" Ashlock asked Stella through the telepathic link, and he saw her shoulders sag a little.

"Yes, she did. If that Terraforge bastard hadn't gone and ruined my work, I would have created a better pill than her," Stella replied. It was rather funny hearing how angry she sounded in her mind while she stood there motionless before the examiners while they debated about her pill.

"I see... Did you hear anyone else get a score near eighty-nine? I think the highest I heard was fifty-eight from one of the rogue alchemists."

"That's very high. From what I've gathered, I think seventy is the cut-off point for spirit grade, so fifty-eight from a rogue alchemist is impressive," Stella said. "However, I don't think the examiners have asked to see the other nobles' pills yet. They are the ones I am worried about."

"Why would you be worried? Look how excited the examiners are for your pill. What score do you think you will get?"

"Anything above a ninety would be great..." Stella paused. "But I believe that's unrealistic given that I made the pill in a rush. So maybe eighty-something?"

Ashlock was about to reassure Stella that everything would be fine, but the examiners had reached a consensus, so he stayed quiet and waited for their verdict.

The young Redclaw man turned to face Stella with a smile alongside the two others. He cleared his throat. "Ahem, Roselyn, we have deemed this pill as per the guidelines to be a Spirit-grade pill..."

Ashlock cheered as that likely secured her a spot in the top ten. He then saw Stella clench her hands as the Redclaw man continued after rechecking his notes, "With a score...of seventy-eight."

"Elder Brent, you bastard!" Stella screamed in her mind. "Why did he only give me five more minutes? Is he blind? Stupid? Did he not see what Roderick did? This is so unfair! If only he gave me ten minutes, I could have gotten a hundred points and spat in Kassandra's smug face."

"Stella, calm down. Look at Kassandra's expression right now," Ashlock pointed out and saw the blank-faced yet mentally raging Stella turn to look at Kassandra, who was frowning rather than smirking despite getting a higher score.

"She may have gotten the higher score, but you still made a Spirit-grade pill within five minutes even after she got her accomplice supposedly detained by the Silverspires." Ashlock chuckled at Kassandra's worried look. *"I bet she decided it would have all been*

worth it if you ended up with a Mortal-grade pill and didn't make it into the top ten, therefore winning her the bet. But you did it! You beat the odds."

Stella unclenched her hand, turned away from Kassandra, and stared blankly at the demonic tree. "But I lost. How can you twist it and say I won?"

"You may have lost the battle, but the war is far from over," Ashlock explained. "There is still one battlefield left: the only one that truly matters. The finals will begin soon."

As Ashlock finished his words, he saw Elder Brent make his way onto the wooden platform and begin to read from a parchment in his hands.

"I will now present the scores of the top ten, starting from the bottom."

Ashlock realized he had missed hearing the other nobles' scores while talking to Stella. "I wonder where she will place? A score of seventy-eight should still be rather high."

Elder Brent paused for dramatic effect and then began to read up the list.

"Spot's ten to eight are tied at fifty-five points. Congratulations, Tabitha, Dylan, and Ezra."

Ashlock noted the lack of a noble name, so these three were likely rogue cultivators or people undercover like Stella with her Roselyn persona.

"Seventh spot goes to Alaina with fifty-six."

"Sixth spot with fifty-eight points goes to Marcus."

Elder Brent's gaze then drifted to the middle of the area where the nobles mostly were. "The fifth spot goes to Roselyn with a Spirit-grade pill at seventy-eight points."

The crowd roared with praises, but Stella looked far from happy.

"Stella, you got fifth place after learning alchemy for a single week, and I am sure you might have even won if you had been given more time. Put your chin up. You did fantastic."

"But Kassandra got higher. It's not fair," Stella grumbled.

Ashlock sighed. "Life's not fair, Stella. Let Kassandra experience this final moment of victory as I'm sure she will think the world is far more unfair than yours when there's a void tendril through her heart as she draws her final breath."

Stella's eyes widened a little from his words.

"Next up is Kane Azurecrest with a Spirit-grade pill at eighty-one points," Elder Brent called out, drawing Ashlock's focus back to the tournament.

It was hard to tell the Azurecrest teen's reaction to fourth place as he leaned against his workbench and hid his expression behind his long white-and-crimson hair. Despite his lacking presence, he stood out among the nobles even when beside Dante Voidmind and Celeste Starweaver.

Not only did he have a dual affinity for fire and wind, which was one of the first dual affinities Ashlock had ever seen. But Kane also likely had a nocturne living inside him. If all that wasn't enough, the teen seemed to also be a rather talented alchemist, able to make Spirit-grade pills out of ingredients intended for a Mortal-grade pill.

Elder Brent continued once the cheers died down slightly. "Now for the top three, which happens to be between three very notorious noble families."

Ashlock felt the energy from the crowd reach a new height as Elder Brent gestured to each of the nobles. "House Skyrend, Voidmind, and Starweaver sent talented representatives, but which will come out on top?"

If Ashlock had to guess, it would be between Dante and Celeste. "Their affinities were far too good at quickly purifying ingredients, so the winner will be decided by the one most capable of forming the pill. Hmm, I think Dante might take the lead. He seems like a man who is way too arrogant to tolerate losing."

Elder Brent was a rather good showman, as he even managed to get Ashlock a little excited about who got the highest score. However, it was clear the nobles were bored as they had likely already overheard each other's results, but they stood there silently and let Elder Brent continue his theatrics.

"In third place is the ever-proud Kassandra Skyrend with a Spirit-grade pill at eighty-nine points! Just one step below a Profound-grade pill! Better luck next time..."

Kassandra's eyes glowed briefly, and she tensed her arm but then relaxed. That little jab at her arrogance despite coming in third must have rubbed her the wrong way.

"Next up is a surprising one." Elder Brent grinned. "In second place with a Profound-grade pill and ninety-three points is Dante Voidmind! Which means our victor is Celeste Starweaver at ninety-five points!"

The colosseum erupted in a thunderous roar as everyone stood from their seats and clapped.

Unlike the other nobles who stayed sullen, Celeste Starweaver waved to the crowd with a beaming smile.

Ashlock was surprised Celeste had managed to pull out ahead of Dante Voidmind. She had seemed rather clueless in the preliminary round, where she failed the easy question and then blew a week's worth of Qi on purifying an ingredient, but it seemed she also had some skill when it came to forming the pill.

"It's a shame Roderick ruined Stella's chance of being in the spotlight..." Ashlock sighed. "I wonder how Stella would have compared to these three if she had a fair chance."

He still wanted to recruit one of these alchemists for the Ashfallen Sect, but someone like Celeste Starweaver was part of a noble family, so bringing her on board was unlikely.

Would he have to pick between the rogues that couldn't get a higher score than Stella when she had only five minutes to rush a pill? At that point, was there even a point to hiring them other than to be Stella's apprentice?

"If anything, this tournament gave Stella the motivation to learn alchemy. If I can't find anyone from the winners I want to hire, I can get the Redclaw twins to do everything with Elder Margret's help."

Ashlock felt that was a good compromise as the crowd settled down.

"Those not in the top ten, we appreciate your attendance but kindly ask you to vacate the arena," Elder Brent called out as the examiners began to politely nudge the rogues that had failed to make the cut out of the arena.

Hundreds of alchemists of various ages and backgrounds were all funneled out of the few exits, and soon there was a very empty arena with ten people standing a fair distance from one another.

"Without delay, we will begin the final round." Elder Brent gestured to the empty arena. "You may go and pick any workbench you wish. Just make sure to space yourselves out so we can avoid another incident."

Ashlock heard Stella click her tongue as she strode as far away from Kassandra as possible and began setting up her ingredients on a random workbench.

Stella let out a breath and tried to calm down.

Today had been too much for her.

Far too much hatred, bloodlust, and exhaustion swirled around her mind in a constant war that overwhelmed her to the point that even three Mind Fortress pills had no hope of relaxing her mind.

Stella's spatial ring dimmed as she finished retrieving her ingredients and placing them on the workbench. She had to admit there was some solace in not having to purify the ingredients.

"Thank you, Tree," she said quietly in her mind. In a way, they were like a gift from him.

"Mhm, what did you say?" Ashlock's presence entered her mind, and his harrowing voice echoed within her consciousness. *"I was distracted by trying to study everyone else's ingredients so I can try and grow them later."*

Stella shook her head. "It was nothing—"

"Is everyone ready for the final round?!" Elder Brent's Qi-empowered voice boomed through the colosseum. "Participants, you have thirty minutes to create any pill you please with your ingredients. There can only be one winner, so there's no room for mistakes!"

Stella rolled her eyes as she reached forward and tried to mentally remember the complicated recipe for the Heavenly Purification Pill that she had only managed to make one of after nine attempts earlier in the day.

You got this, Stella, just concentrate, and everything will be okay.

She carefully placed all the ingredients in the cauldron and was about to begin forming the pill within her soul fire when Ashlock spoke in her mind.

"I have bad news."

"What is it?" Stella sighed.

"To the surprise of nobody, Kassandra has found another way to cheat."

Stella furrowed her brows. "How? We can do practically anything we want in this final round, so how could she cheat?"

"Well, to be fair, she hasn't exactly cheated, but she lied through her teeth. Remember when Elder Margret approved this final round

because Kassandra agreed to provide them with a copy of the ingredients she planned to use to make her pill?"

"Yes…" Stella didn't like where this was going.

"How many ingredients do you have?"

Stella glanced between the Qi Flowing Grass, Dragon Marrow, Celestial Peony Petal, Heavenly Bamboo Essence, and a single droplet of a Nine-Tailed Fox's Tear.

"I have all five needed for the pill right here," Stella grumbled. "So what's the problem?"

"Well, if I am counting correctly, Kassandra has seven ingredients instead of only five, and she put them all in the cauldron."

Stella's eyes widened as she shouted in her mind, "Wait, that means she has the recipe and ingredients for a Profound-grade pill!"

"I will go and question Elder Margret, but it would seem Kassandra is going to try and make a superior version of the Heavenly Purification Pill as the ingredients are the same except the extra two."

"Does she even have the skills to create a Profound-grade pill?" Stella asked.

"It might be a desperation play after seeing you create a Spirit-grade pill in five minutes despite her best efforts to sabotage you," Ashlock mused. *"So it might be a last-ditch effort on her part, but if she succeeds and manages to create this pill…"*

Stella looked at her ingredients and bit her lip. She only had enough fox tears for a single attempt, but if she managed to make the pill absolutely perfect on the first try, there was still a chance she could win.

"Tree, you said this was my final battle?" Stella glanced at the sky with the fire of passion in her eyes. "The one to win the war?"

"That I did."

"Ever since I was a little girl, it's been you and me against the world, Tree." Stella grinned behind her mask as she glanced back down and lit the cauldron with her soul fire.

"And I can't remember a single darn time we ever lost! If the heavens can't strike me down, what does the Skyrend family have on me?!"

"I believe in you, Stella. Go make the best Heavenly Purification Pill the world has ever seen. If anyone can do it, you can."

With a smile, Stella set out to accomplish the impossible. She had one shot, one opportunity to get a final win against Kassandra Skyrend before she drew her last breath on the sand beneath her feet.

72
NEWFOUND CONFIDENCE

Ashlock looked around the colosseum from high above and found Elder Margret standing under the demonic tree's shade.

She was calmly watching the proceedings of the finals with her arms crossed and tapping her foot. It seemed she was a rather impatient and fidgety person.

"Sorry, Elder Margret, but this needs to be done," Ashlock murmured as he reactivated {Abyssal Whispers} and targeted her consciousness. So long as she remained within the range of his roots, he could reinstate the telepathic connection anytime.

His only other options for communication would have been using telekinesis to write on the ground or utilize his soul flames, but due to sharing the spatial affinity with Stella, he didn't want to give Kassandra any ammo to use to accuse Stella of cheating.

So that left him with one option.

Elder Margret abruptly winced and clutched her head, earning her a confused over-shoulder look from the Redclaw Grand Elder.

"Everything all right?" the Grand Elder murmured through half-closed lips.

He never fully looked back as he tried to avoid drawing attention to Elder Margret's strange behavior as he was entirely out of the fog and exposed to the thousands of mortals. Whereas Elder Margret was a few steps behind and partially obscured.

While Elder Margret summoned a Mind Fortress pill to her hand and gulped it down, Diana calmly answered the Grand Elder's question. "She is receiving a mental projection from the immortal."

The fog carried Diana's voice to ensure nobody outside the demonic tree's shade could listen to their conversation.

"The immortal?" the Grand Elder murmured as his eyes widened a little. *"What does the Patriarch need of Elder Margret?"*

Elder Margret straightened up and tried to act like nothing had happened. "I will find out shortly. Just give me a moment."

Ashlock found it a little funny how they seemed to forget he could see and hear everything that occurred within many miles so long as he focused on the area.

"Patriarch, how may I be of service?" Elder Margret asked through the telepathic link.

"I have been observing the tournament, and I couldn't help but notice that Kassandra is creating a pill with seven ingredients, whereas Stella was only provided with five," Ashlock replied.

Elder Marget's eyes snapped open, and she searched until her gaze landed on Kassandra. There was a long pause as Elder Margret examined the cauldron's contents with her spiritual sight.

"You're right. Kassandra seems to be creating the Spiritual Enhancement Pill from the ingredients she's using," Elder Margret mentally replied. "Although she isn't cheating, this goes against our agreement. Do you want me to disqualify her and explain the reason privately?"

"There's no need to waste time and breath on a dead woman. All I care for is further establishing the Redclaws as a powerhouse for alchemy, so I need Stella to beat Kassandra in her Roselyn persona," Ashlock explained. **"Not to mention, if Stella won because we disqualified Kassandra, she would be furious."**

"The immortal is infinitely wise. What action do you require me to take?" Elder Margret asked, and that was a good question. What did Ashlock want from Elder Margret?

"I want to know, does Stella have a chance of winning? How does her pill recipe compare to Kassandra's?"

Elder Margret tapped her chin as she glanced over to Stella, who was hard at work trying to make the best Heavenly Purification Pill she could.

"If a pill's ingredients are purified and created to perfection, it's possible to start with a Mortal-tier pill recipe like the Body Strengthening Pill and increase its potency by multiple tiers. However, it's easier to start with a simple Mortal-tier recipe and perfect it to Spirit tier than to follow a Spirit-tier pill recipe from the start due to the escalating complexity that comes from more ingredients."

"I know little regarding the art of alchemy as it has evolved a lot over my time," Ashlock lied. **"But why would you want such a complex recipe with so many ingredients when you can use a lower-tier recipe and increase its potency?"**

"Because it's the ingredients that provide the pill with its effect. Therefore the more ingredients carefully crafted into a single pill, the more powerful the pill's effect will be," Elder Margret patiently explained. "I believe Kassandra has a fifty-fifty chance of creating a low-quality Profound-tier pill because she managed to create a Body Strengthening Pill with Spirit-tier potency."

"I see, but what happens if Kassandra manages to create the Profound-tier pill? How can Stella compete with her Spirit-tier pill recipe?"

Elder Margret sighed. "Stella must create a near-perfect Heavenly Purification Pill to be graded the same as a Profound-tier pill. How many ingredients does she have left?"

"She only has a single Nine-Tailed Fox's Tear droplet left."

"That's bad news. Anything can go wrong during the pill-making process, and a single slip-up will cause her to lose." Elder Margret frowned. "I'm not liking her odds here."

"I see. I appreciate your input on the matter, and I might be back later if another matter arises," Ashlock said as he withdrew his {Abyssal Whispers} skill and tried to find solutions.

There was a chance Stella wouldn't even need his help.

Kassandra could fail to follow the more complex Profound-tier recipe. However, if she succeeded and the created pill was also of good quality, then Stella's lower-tier recipe wouldn't be able to stand a chance even if the pill were of perfect quality.

Ashlock left Elder Margret to discuss their situation with the Grand Elder as his vision focused on Kane Azurecrest. His reason? The teen was still busy inspecting and preparing his ingredients, and he intended to try and analyze them to grow any of the flowers himself.

In the corner of his vision, he had the {Blooming Root Flower

Production} menu open, and he was trying to see if he could add the plants just by looking at them.

"Mhm, still grayed out," Ashlock grumbled. "How annoying."

He could see a white flower on Kane's workbench, and an outline of it showed up in his menu, but when he tried to click it, his system told him that he hadn't thoroughly analyzed the flower.

Ashlock had found the best way to analyze a plant quickly was to have it brought to him and placed near his trunk. He had done this for the Blaze Serpent Rose and the Dreamweaver Orchids.

But he knew for a fact he could still have his system analyze plants he had never had near his trunk before because when he had first learned the skill, there were already flowers like the Serene Mist Camellia, which grew in the forest between him and Darklight City.

Kane picked up the white flower and began blasting it with fire Qi.

Ashlock saw impurities falling out of the flower as soot. A minute passed, and the moment Kane placed the now-purified white flower onto his workbench Ashlock saw a flash of color in his menu.

"Moonlight Calla Lily?" Ashlock compared the picture in his menu to the plant on the workbench and confirmed they matched.

"So I can add flowers by looking at them so long as they have been fully purified? Then how did I add the Serene Mist Camellia?" Ashlock grumbled but now wasn't the time for useless thoughts. He had many ingredients to steal.

Stella felt sweat trickle down her forehead as she leaned over the cauldron filled with her soul fire. Bathed in the purple light of her flames was a beautiful golden nugget, much like the one she had made earlier in the day on her ninth attempt.

She felt incredibly focused—as if the world around her had slowed to a crawl. In this zen-like state, all she could hear was the blood flowing past her ears and her steady breathing. The chaotic world around her was white noise, and her vision was entirely tunneled on the pill.

The recipe was at the forefront of her consciousness as she effortlessly followed its complex instructions. Every ingredient had to be added at certain times and in particular ways to the point that the pill was a work of art.

Her right hand moved away from the cauldron's edge and carefully reached for the glass bottle containing the final Nine-Tailed Fox's Tear droplet. Grasping it firmly to ensure she didn't drop it, she brought it over and popped off the cap with her thumb. Tilting the bottle, she saw the glowing blue liquid wobble on the bottle neck's rim.

Stella let out a long breath; a single movement and the last droplet would fall, sealing her fate. Tilting the bottle, Stella watched as the droplet plummeted into her soul fire and splashed onto the golden nugget, making it pulse with power.

"Please be perfect," she whispered.

All she could do now was wait with bated breaths as the pill greedily absorbed the essence of the tear and morphed into its final form.

A heart-racing moment passed, and everything settled. Stella withdrew her soul flame and peered into the depths of the now-dark metal cauldron. All that was left in the bottom was a single golden pill.

Reaching in, she retrieved it with a slightly shaking hand, and as she held the pill between her fingers, she snapped out of her focused trance, and the world hit her in full force.

The crowd's cheers were so loud it felt like the ground was shaking, and as her tunneled vision on the pill expanded to encompass her entire spiritual sight, she felt briefly disoriented.

"Stella...Stella...STELLA."

"Huh?" Stella replied absentmindedly as she shook her head. "Tree? What's the matter?"

"You seemed about to faint for a second there. I was worried for you."

Stella blinked as the lingering sensation of the trance wore off. "Can someone in the Star Core Realm even faint if they still have Qi in their body?"

"I have no idea. How do you feel?" Ashlock asked. ***"You were zoned out and swaying side to side."***

"I feel...fine? I don't know what came over me, but I was incredibly focused," Stella replied.

"Mhm, strange... What do you think caused it?"

"No idea. Maybe a lack of sleep." Stella sighed as she looked down and realized she was still holding her freshly made pill. It smelled amazing, and she couldn't see a single defect from a simple glance.

It was perfect.

There was a moment of pure relief. "Tree! I did it, the perfect pill!"

"Elder Margret tried to appraise it from range, and she agrees," Ashlock replied after a pause. *"It should be in the Profound tier."*

Stella set the pill down on her workbench in a little wooden bowl and frowned. The brief euphoria from completing the task had subsided, and now all she felt was worry.

"It's not good enough," Stella muttered as she stared at the pill.

"Why not?" Ashlock asked, but Stella didn't have a good answer.

She wasn't sure why, but she was confident the pill was inferior. It was as if a small voice at the back of her mind was trying to warn her of an impending challenge to her rule and that such a weak pill wasn't enough.

"Rule?" Stella furrowed her brows. What nonsense was she thinking? Since when did she have a throne or palace to protect?

However, the feeling of an imminent threat only grew as time passed. Something deep inside was screaming at her to act in any way possible to get ahead of the competition. It was an almost primal feeling that was bubbling deep within her being.

"What is wrong with me?" Stella slurred as her head felt heavy, and she looked down at her hands; they were covered in blood.

Stella stumbled back in shock as she tried to shake the blood off, but it clung tight to her tiny hands… They were so small as if belonging to a child.

She glanced around and realized she was back home at the Red Vine pavilion—white walls topped with black wood and covered in red vines that had lived only in her memory were back, and her point of view was lower than she remembered.

The roaring crowds and burning sun were gone. It was night, and the stars were out. A cold breeze carrying the scent of death blew by.

Stella shivered as she frantically looked around. All around her were bodies littering the lush purple grass she hadn't seen in years.

Some corpses were cleanly decapitated, their heads lying to the side. Others had holes through the heart with shocking accuracy.

Stella felt a sudden weight. Looking down, she noticed a familiar black dagger she had made from the sticks Ash had gifted her in her blood-soaked hands.

Twirling around on her heel, she was relieved to see Tree was still there, just far smaller than he was now.

"Ash, is that you?" Stella asked but then remembered that back in these days, Tree couldn't talk. She circled him for a while in confusion, but nothing happened.

"Is this a dream?" Stella questioned aloud as she set out to wander the deathly silent pavilion hoping to find a way out. "Hello, anyone here?"

The moment she stepped out of the familiar central courtyard where she had spent most of her childhood under the tree's shade, the rest of the pavilion was a fractured mess.

Pieces of wall floated by as she stared down into an abyss. "What the…"

All that seemed stable was the cobblestone pathway that led to the next courtyard. Stella apprehensively placed her foot on the path as she had nowhere else to go, and the moment her foot touched it, she reentered that trance-like state, and everything slowed down.

Everything sped up with every step she took as the fragmented world began to fill in the gaps, including the abyss below. The floating wall pieces set into place, and rock surged up from below to fill in the void.

Alongside the world returning to normal, so did the details concerning the night of slaughter. It was as if she was piecing together her mind by walking through the pavilion.

This memory, like many others, had always been fragmented. Stella could recall small snippets of the night, but considering how traumatic killing hundreds of people should have been at the tender age of thirteen, she hadn't suffered any issues as she simply couldn't remember what had transpired.

She had chalked up her fragmented memory to the fact it had happened a long time ago or that she had been so overcome with rage that she lost her sense of reasoning.

But now as the memory returned to her while she walked the corpse-flanked paths of her old home, she realized that upon discovering the murder plot against her, that had been the first time she had entered a trance, and her body had moved to protect her domain.

The fight between her and the hired cultivators posing as servants had always been a blur, but now that she recalled the whole battle, she realized there was no logical reason for her to win against such stacked odds unless somebody challenged her throne.

Stella snapped out of her trance when she realized she had circled back around and now stood in the central courtyard before Ash.

Below his rustling scarlet leaves, illuminated by the twinkling stars and soft moonlight, was her throne. The wooden bench she had laid on while telling Ash her woes and where he had gifted her the earrings she still wore to this day. It was also where a servant had almost murdered her.

Perhaps throne was the wrong word. To Stella, the bench under Ash's inviting canopy was a sanctuary. It was the one place she felt safe and wanted to protect at all costs.

Stella began walking toward the bench as if it was calling out to her, but with every step, memories flashed through her mind. The first was surprisingly Larry, the oversize spider saying in his gruff voice, "Mistress, your bloodline may still be dormant for a good reason. The blood of a ruler takes longer to bloom."

As if a gong went off in her mind, Stella reexperienced her life as an observer. It all went by so fast. She saw herself as a little girl being told by the family's head maid that her father had passed away. One day the maid vanished, and the peak became infested by these gray-robed servants from the Ravenborne family.

Feelings of loneliness and despair led Stella to take refuge under the demonic tree. She felt like the whole world was out to get her, but then the earrings appeared. They were gifted to her by Ash, and upon putting them on, they gave her true power for the first time.

Stella saw a tiny, ghostly version of herself appear on the bench, gazing up at the tree's canopy while swinging her legs. "Tree, I did it! I didn't lose a single round, and by the end, they were calling me Demoness Stella Crestfallen!"

The ghostly form of a servant then walked into view. "Miss, would you like some tea?"

"Sure. Bring some for my friend here as well," the ghost of Stella said while patting Ashlock's bark.

I was so sweet and innocent, Stella thought as she saw the pure happiness in her former self. Where did that version of me go?

The scene then shifted to her past self standing over the cold corpse of the servant with a vacant look in her eyes and a bloodied dagger.

Her first betrayal—Stella now remembered this moment well. From here on, she'd closed her heart to others and avoided society.

However, the scene shifted again, and Stella saw her ghost training with Diana—the first person that had entered her life since that day.

"Is that the best you can do?" Diana's ghost asked while casually lowering her sword.

Stella remembered this moment. It was the first time she had felt an emotion that still followed her to this day: jealousy.

And it was this jealousy that drove her to improve constantly.

She tried to become the best in every way. At first, she had thought this drive was to please Ash, but it went deeper than that. As memories passed, Stella saw her ghost going through a constant cycle of feeling inadequate and then striving to improve.

Stella watched as her past self comprehended the ancient runic language so she could speak to Tree while Diana slacked off. She then trained day and night after having her life threatened by Tristian Evergreen. She learned runic formations after the arrival of Douglas, and more recently, she learned alchemy because she felt inadequate within the sect.

Before she knew it, she was standing right before the bench. The ghostly form of her past self vanished, and she was left alone in this weird dream.

"Is this my bloodline?" Stella clenched her hands. "The uncanny ability to always improve? Or is this just the start?"

She didn't feel any different—no demonic transformation or sudden power-up. Was Larry truly right in saying it would take a long time for her bloodline to manifest?

Actually, looking back, it has been alongside me my entire life, and my rate of improvement has only grown.

Stella clenched her fist as she looked at the bench—her throne. She went to sit on it, but it vanished, leaving her to tumble forward headfirst into Ash.

She reached out to catch herself, but rather than the rough wooden surface of Ash, her hands landed on a flat wooden workbench. Stella blinked as the crowd's roar hit her ears, and she felt the scorching sun on her neck.

A small smile appeared on her lips.

I am not yet worthy to sit on my throne as I have not yet finished defending it.

"Stella, I have bad news—" Ashlock said.

"I already know." Stella grinned behind her mask. "Kassandra managed to make the Profound-tier pill?"

"Yes…how did you know? Wait, that doesn't matter. We only have a few minutes left," Ashlock quickly explained. *"What do you want to do?"*

Stella felt the zen-like trance slowly overtaking her mind, filling her with confidence.

"Just give me the recipe and ingredients for a Profound-tier pill, and I will make a better one," Stella said in her mind as she straightened her back and looked to the sky.

"Stella, you only learned how to make a Spirit-tier pill this morning after nine attempts. What makes you think you can make a Profound-tier pill in a single go?"

"Call it a newfound confidence." Stella smiled. "If there's a chance to learn, who's to say I cannot succeed?"

"That's fair," Ashlock said, and then there was a long pause. *"I am growing the necessary flowers right now. How many times do I need to repeat the recipe for you to memorize it?"*

"Just the once is fine," Stella said as she entered her trance-like state, and the world became white noise.

"As expected of my daughter!" Ashlock laughed in her mind. *"You never were one to back down from a challenge."*

73
SPIRITUAL NULLIFICATION

Ashlock watched the colosseum from high above. Tensions were high as the final round was nearing the end, and the majority of the participants had completed their pill and stood idly next to their workbenches while watching their competition.

Dante Voidmind and Celeste Starweaver had already completed Profound-tier pills, and Kane Azurecrest was on his way to joining them. But Ashlock didn't care for them. His focus was on Kassandra Skyrend, and it wasn't looking good—her pill seemed almost done with no signs of a significant setback that could cause it to fail at the last hurdle.

Stella was going to lose. There was still time to hatch a plan and make a comeback, but the girl appeared zoned out as if she was in a trance. He tried calling out to her many times, but something was blocking his {Abyssal Whispers} skill from reaching her.

Her eyes were vacant and unfocused on the colosseum wall before her, and her expression was blank.

He wasn't sure what had suddenly overcome Stella. Since the final round started, she had been acting weird and unresponsive. Had someone poisoned her? Was she possessed?

"Stella! Are you there?" Ashlock shouted through their telepathic link, but there was no response. He was about to ask the Grand Elder to pause the tournament and check up on Stella when there was a sudden roar from the crowd.

"Oh no." Ashlock panicked as he glanced to the other side of the colosseum and saw Kassandra Skyrend holding a beautiful pill in her hand that radiated majesty. Even if it wasn't perfect, it was most certainly a fully formed pill of the Profound tier.

"Kassandra Skyrend has successfully created a pill in the Profound tier!" Elder Brent announced, and the crowd went ballistic.

How the pill compared to Dante's and Celeste's wouldn't become apparent until the examiners carried out a closer inspection, but to the average spectator, the fact cultivators from three rival powerful families had created pills that could compete with one another made them excited to see who could come out on top.

Meanwhile, Ashlock was worried as all eyes turned to Stella, including Kassandra's, as she was one of the only ones still working.

"Stella!" Ashlock kept shouting into her mind, and then as if someone had smacked her on the back of the head, she tumbled forward and caught herself on the desk.

Ashlock felt the weird barrier that had sealed Stella's mind from his {Abyssal Whisper} skill vanish, and he could exert his presence into her consciousness.

He shouted her name a few more times, and eventually, she responded. While she looked around the colosseum a little dazed, he tried to explain that Kassandra had already created the Profound-tier pill, but she somehow already knew. Had she been conscious while in that trance?

After asking what she wanted to do about it, he was somewhat surprised that she calmly agreed to try and make a Profound-tier pill while thousands of eyes were glued to her every movement.

"Since when was my daughter this confident?" Ashlock wondered and was genuinely baffled as she calmly stood there, waiting for him to confirm if it was possible with Elder Margret.

He reinstated his connection to Elder Margret, and the woman winced as he asked, **"Stella wants to try and create a Profound-tier pill. Do you know any recipes?"**

"Well, what ingredients do you have access to?" Elder Margret replied, and Ashlock listed every ingredient Stella had on her table and all the ones he had managed to analyze with his system from the other nobles.

"Mhm, from that list, I think the best one would be the Profound-tier Spiritual Nullification pill. It's popular among cultivators as it allows them to conceal their aura and appear like an average mortal." Elder Margret massaged her temples. "If I remember, the recipe goes something like this…"

Ashlock didn't have some godlike memory, and focusing on two conversations at once with {Abyssal Whispers} was tough. Luckily, Elder Margret and Stella were both within his line of sight, so he relayed the recipe to Stella as Elder Margret recited it since Stella claimed she only needed to hear it once.

Within Stella's consciousness, Ashlock saw the recipe manifest—as golden words on a ghostly parchment—at the forefront of her consciousness like a royal decree. It was bizarre to see an invisible quill writing down his words in real-time, and he tried to ask Stella what was happening, but she was being unresponsive again.

However, the moment he finished reciting the recipe, the parchment within Stella's mind flashed a brilliant gold and then dissipated into the darkness of her consciousness like golden snow.

"Tree, I am missing the Celestial Peony Petal, Dreamweaver Orchids, Nine Star Soul Grass, and Moonlight Calla Lily."

"Straight to business, are we?" Ashlock grumbled to himself before replying to Stella, "I'll go and grow them right now. How do you want them delivered?"

As they were both spatial users, even with many people watching, there were various ways they could exchange items without anyone noticing, and even if they did, the final round allowed people to bring their own resources, so it wasn't as big of a deal.

"I will start making the pill now," Stella replied. "So just create a small portal within the cauldron and pass me the flowers that way. It will look like I was summoning the flowers from my spatial ring."

"Okay, give me a moment," Ashlock said as his vision blurred, and he found himself back in the cavern under Red Vine Peak. He quickly opened his {Blooming Root Flower Production} menu, selected a few farm plots with Qi Flowing Grass growing, and told the system to replace them with the new plants.

After depleting some of his Qi reserves, his system's godlike power flooded the area. The Qi Flowing Grass wilted away to make way for a new batch of flowers and even a new type of grass, the Nine Star Soul Grass, described to him as a rare herb that grew in the regions where nine stars shone brightly. It cleansed the soul and spirit, bringing clarity and enlightenment.

In fact, almost all of the ingredients used in the Spiritual Nullification Pill helped cleanse the body.

"The Heavenly Bamboo Essence has the property to cleanse and purify the body and spirit, while the Celestial Peony Petal is also believed to have a high concentration of pure celestial energy that's beneficial for purification," Ashlock mused as he watched the new flowers and grass bloom from the soil at a supernatural speed.

"Then Stella will need to add the Dreamweaver Orchids to give that illusion shroud that helps conceal the Qi aura of a cultivator. What a useful little pill." Ashlock hadn't been terribly impressed with the pill recipes he had been shown previously, as they did nothing he couldn't accomplish with his own fruit and mushrooms.

"But this Spiritual Nullification Pill has an actual effect that makes it worth creating, and other than the Dragon Marrow, it's made entirely from flowers and grass, which makes it an ideal pill for me as growing rare flowers is no issue."

Ashlock waited another moment, and once the flowers were fully grown, he used telekinesis to pluck a few petals from the Moonlight Calla Lily, Celestial Peony, and Dreamweaver Orchids. He also grabbed a bundle of freshly grown Nine Star Soul Grass that glowed in a myriad of colors.

In a moment like this, he could truly appreciate just how broken his production skills were.

Just from looking at flowers on a workbench long enough, he had stolen them from the other contestants for free, even though they likely paid many spirit stones for them.

Then he grew the flowers many miles away from the tournament within a minute in a cavern devoid of any sunlight, starlight, or even moonlight, which some of these flowers required.

"Not to mention they are completely devoid of any impurities, which is a lifesaver in this situation as Stella won't have time to remove the impurities from all these ingredients within the little time she has left." Ashlock sighed as he felt the weight of the situation.

Yes, Kassandra would die, but he wanted the Roselyn persona to help sell pills to the merchants, and if she came almost last in the tournament, the merchants would brush her off as a nobody.

That aside, Ashlock had to deliver these ingredients to Stella as soon as possible, so keeping the flowers and grass floating there with telekinesis, his vision blurred as he arrived back at the colosseum.

"Stella?" Ashlock said through their telepathic link, but he was locked out of her mind again.

"How does she do that? {Abyssal Whispers} is an A-rank mental attack skill, so how can she block me out?" Ashlock wasn't sure what else to do, so he snuck a sliver of his spatial Qi into the cauldron and opened a tiny portal.

Stella didn't even flinch as her focus was entirely on the pill she was creating, but her spatial ring did flash with power to pretend she had the required flowers in there, and then she reached into the portal and pulled through the flowers and grass from the cavern and into the flames of her soul fire.

"Ten minutes remain!" Elder Brent shouted, and the crowd began to drum their feet and cheer.

A moment passed, and then a small pulse of fire Qi spread throughout the colosseum, and everyone turned to see Kane reach down into his cauldron and retrieve a blood-red pill.

"Another Profound-tier pill from one of the nobles!" Elder Brent announced.

Meanwhile, Kane Azurecrest placed the pill in the wooden bowl on the workbench and closed his eyes as he leaned against the table.

Ashlock wanted to know what the blood red pill was, but he hadn't been able to analyze half of the ingredients used in making the pill as they weren't flowers but rather weird vials containing suspicious viscous liquids.

"Mhm, although many pills use flowers and other plants, there also seem to be pills that have hardly any in them," Ashlock grumbled. "If I want to create any of those, getting the necessary ingredients is going to be a pain without a good relationship with the merchants, so I can only pray that Stella pulls through and attracts their attention."

Diana had met with a group of merchants back at the Immortal Gourmet Pavilion, and they seemed somewhat interested in working together, but if word could spread that there was such a talented alchemist, they might take more of an interest when it came to buying her pills and then giving her good deals on ingredients.

Stella felt her body fighting against her as she entered the final stage of creating her first ever Profound-tier pill. All she could hear was the blood rushing faster and faster past her ears, her body felt sickly with sweat, and something was squeezing her mind.

But she didn't stop. Nothing short of collapsing on the spot would deprive her of this hard-earned victory. So much had led up to this very moment that to fail here would break her on a deeper level than was possible to recover from. Not to mention, her throne was at risk.

Stella hadn't had time to contemplate the deeper meaning behind this mysterious trance-like state, but she knew this wasn't the first time she had entered it, nor would it be the last, and she planned to use it to its limit today to surpass the odds presented before her.

It had taken her an hour and nine grueling attempts to form a half-decent Spirit-tier pill with only five ingredients just a few hours prior, and now, under the scrutiny of thousands of people, she would have to craft a Profound-tier pill first try with eight ingredients and within a tight time limit.

She had always been one to defeat the odds, but at what point did it become arrogance? Stella didn't know and didn't want to fail to find out. So long as she kept defeating the odds, who could call her arrogant for her confidence?

Before her, bathed in her exhausted soul fire, was a mostly translucent pill apart from a milky white consistency that had appeared once she had added the sixth ingredient, the Moonlight Calla Lily.

"And now for the eighth," Stella muttered as she reached forward. Her hands were shaking slightly from a mixture of stress and fatigue. She felt ready to collapse there and then, and only sheer willpower was keeping her standing.

Why does using my bloodline tire me out so fast? Is it due to the complexity of the task? The time I have spent on it? Or have I not yet bloomed into a true ruler like Larry suggested?

Useless thoughts aside, Stella carefully plucked a petal from the Dreamweaver Orchids and carefully wrapped it around the translucent milky pill. Inserting some Qi directly into the petal made it melt into the pill as if it were greedily absorbing the offering, and the milky substance sloshing around in the pill took on a purple luster, which immediately faded.

Stella frowned behind her mask at the now utterly translucent pill. It was so see-through that it felt like she was holding a pocket of air in her fingers. Had she messed it up somehow? Why did it look so strange?

Fear began to grip her heart. Had she really messed up at the final hurdle?

The moment she removed the pill from the cauldron, she felt the pressure on her mind vanish alongside a sudden burst of golden flakes at the edge of her consciousness. Like the last few times, the world hit her in full force as the trance shattered, and she emerged from her focused state.

"Just in time, our final contestant Roselyn appears to have completed her pill!" Elder Brent announced, and Stella stumbled back from the workbench as she saw everyone looking at her with excitement. They were all standing from their seats and cheering while waving their arms wildly.

Stella just wanted to crawl into a hole and hide. This level of attention, coupled with her absolute exhaustion, making even standing difficult, was the last thing she needed right now. Had she succeeded or failed?

Could nobody tell her?!

"And it's in the Profound tier! We officially have five people that managed to create Profound-tier pills!" Elder Brent's Qi-empowered words reverberating through the colosseum didn't feel real to Stella. Had she really done it? Such an impossible feat?

"You did it, Stella." Ashlock's presence entered her mind. *"I don't know how...but you really did it."*

Stella looked down at the pocket of air she was seemingly holding. It was so empty, yet it meant so much to her. Weeks of slaving away in the cavern to learn alchemy was finally paying off.

"Thank you, Tree, but without you, I wouldn't have done it, nor would I even be here." Stella smiled behind her mask. For the first time ever, she felt on par or above the other scions and members of noble houses. They had received so much more education and care while growing up that she felt like she was always playing catch up. But now she was here, standing beside them as an equal.

Stella looked up and glanced around at the faces of the nobles littering the colosseum. Dante seemed indifferent to her achievement, Kane had closed his eyes, and Celeste seemed lost in thought and was staring into space.

They might not care for her or even see her as a threat. But it was all worth it for Kassandra's stare of utter disbelief. The pure confusion on her face was revitalizing, and Stella felt her back straightening a little with pride and strength returning to her weary body.

An examiner clad in the gray robes of the Academy then came up with a wooden bowl. "Please place your pill in here so we may take it to be appraised."

Stella absentmindedly complied and placed her pocket of air that was most definitely a pill in the wooden bowl. The examiner, who was a rather pretty woman with sky-blue hair, gave Stella a reassuring smile as she wrote on a parchment in her hand, "A Spiritual Nullification Pill, one of the most sought-after Profound-tier pills, good choice."

"Thanks?" Stella wasn't sure what to say as the examiner left with her bowl and walked through a tunnel alongside other examiners carrying the other people's freshly made pills.

Elder Brent surveyed the colosseum from his podium with his arms behind his back and explained, "As all five nobles created Profound-tier pills, they will be scrutinized and graded by a hired expert. This expert will not be informed about who made each pill to avoid bias."

His gaze shifted to the rogue alchemists in the finals. "All five of you performed admirably, but as none of you managed to produce a Profound-tier pill this round, there is no need to stick around."

To Stella's surprise, none of the rogues seemed particularly annoyed or angry. They just exchanged glances with one another and light smiles.

"Did they expect to lose?" Stella asked Ash. "Why do they have such calm attitudes?"

"It was mentioned in the invite that the top rogues would be offered jobs under the Redclaws if they so wished to take them," Ashlock replied. ***"We need grunt-worker alchemists to mass produce the simpler pills that we can easily sell. They can handle that part of the business and maybe even help train up some of the Redclaw family."***

Stella hummed in understanding and patiently awaited beside her workbench for the results. Only the five nobles remained now, with all the rogues gone.

Time passed by excruciatingly slowly, and Stella had her eyes glued on the dark passageway that must lead deeper into the colosseum where the pills were currently being graded.

After a few minutes, she really started to feel the fatigue of using that weird trance setting in, and right as she was about to either sit down or lean against a wall to cultivate some Qi, she saw movement within the dark passage.

Is it finally here? Stella wondered as a bearded man emerged with a parchment. He easily jumped up a few feet, handed the parchment to Elder Brent mid-air, and landed gracefully back on the sand, earning him a roar from the crowd.

The bearded man chuckled and wandered off back down the passageway without a care in the world.

Elder Brent seemed slightly baffled by the display but regained his professional composure. "Ahem, it appears the list of pill grades has been delivered. In fifth place is…"

There was a pause, and then Elder Brent furrowed his brows as he seemed to reread the list a few times. Eventually, he glanced up over the parchment and did a sweeping gaze at all the nobles present.

He didn't seem to be looking for anyone in particular, but Stella disliked how his gaze lingered on her for longer than the others before he returned to the parchment with the same confused look.

Please, not me. Stella tensed as Elder Brent cleared his throat.

74
DESCENDANT OF A FAKE GOD

"Let's start that again. I was rather confused why they gave me a list of pills rather than names." Elder Brent chuckled. "Anyway, in fifth place, we have the Blood Essence Revitalization Pill."

Everyone glanced at Kane Azurecrest, and he returned a nod to everyone and went back to looking at the floor.

Phew, I wasn't last. Stella sighed in relief as she tried to ignore the roaring crowd for her own sanity.

"Next up in fourth place was the Cosmic Alignment Pill." Elder Brent peered over the parchment, and Stella followed his gaze to Celeste Starweaver. She seemed genuinely baffled to have come in fourth and shot both Stella and Kassandra a look of suspicion.

Okay, I made it into the top three. I'm unlikely to beat Dante Voidmind, but I have to defeat Kassandra. Stella felt her heart racing as she exchanged a glare with Kassandra. The giant woman seemed thoroughly annoyed that it had come down to this as her eyes pulsed a chaotic blue.

Elder Brent paused for a dramatic effect that was not appreciated by Stella's exhausted legs before he read the words that would seal Stella's fate in this tournament.

"In third place…"

Although Elder Brent obscured the parchment from spiritual sight with his Qi aura, Ashlock could see the list over his shoulder with {Eye of the Tree God}.

However, despite knowing the results, he stayed quiet and let Stella have her moment.

"In third place is the Spiritual Enhancement Pill," Elder Brent announced, and the crowd roared as Stella stood there in shock.

Her eyes were wide as she slowly turned to look at Kassandra, who had stumbled back and caught herself on the workbench with a look of pure disbelief.

Eventually, Kassandra gathered herself and shouted to Elder Brent, *"I demand the pills get a second opinion! Mine were flawless. What makes hers better than mine?"*

"Well, according to the notes here, your pill had some impurities," Elder Brent calmly explained. *"Likely due to inferior ingredients or an inability to remove all the impurities before creation."*

"Inferior? Inability?" Kassandra Skyrend gritted her teeth as her eyes furiously glowed. *"Top alchemists purchased those ingredients, and I purified them to perfection! So what if a few impurities were left? It's impossible to grow perfect ingredients devoid of any defects."*

Stella crossed her arms and tilted her head at Kassandra as if she were a fool. "Didn't you know sourcing ingredients is an alchemist's job?"

"There's a limit, Roselyn!" Kassandra shouted as she strode over to Stella. *"You can only cheat so blatantly up to a point! I watched how effortlessly and quickly you made that pill. Unless you are the reincarnation of an alchemy god and have access to ingredients from a higher realm, I do not see how your pill could be better."*

Kassandra paused just before Stella, but the blond girl was entirely unbothered.

"Just admit you cheated," Kassandra demanded, *"or tell the examiners to get a second opinion."*

Ashlock quickly reminded Stella, **"Stick to the plan. Now would be a good time to start planting the seeds of doubt in Dante's mind."**

Stella gave a slight nod before she sneered and pulsed her Star Core, which sent Kassandra stumbling back. *"Maybe I do have connections to someone in a higher realm? In fact, it may be one that Dante Voidmind is familiar with. Isn't that right, Dante?"*

Ashlock found it rather amusing that to the spectators, they could see the nobles' lips moving but had no idea what they were saying as they carried out their conversation through Qi.

Kassandra shot a questioning glare at Dante. "Who is this person?"

Dante seemed equally puzzled. *"Good question. No, Roselyn, I do not know of this person. My family is cursed—"*

"Would a perfectly smooth rock perhaps jolt your memory?" Stella asked.

Dante's eyes widened a little, the void rippled, and he reappeared an inch from Stella. "How much do you know?" he questioned while looming over her.

Stella shrugged. "Everything."

"Tell me—" Dante began, but a burst of fire appeared between them, and the Redclaw Grand Elder cut him off.

"Please wait for the end of the tournament to finish this discussion," the Grand Elder said while flexing his cultivation. *"It wouldn't do well to ruin the young Silverspire's opinion of you, Dante."*

"Tsk." Dante clicked his tongue and stepped back. He waved Kassandra's questions off and returned to his workbench, but his abyssal gaze never left Stella for a single moment.

"How was that, Tree?" Stella asked through the mental link.

"Better than expected," Ashlock answered honestly. **"You are really good at getting under these nobles' skin."**

"Hehe, thank you." Stella grinned behind her mask at Dante's irate gaze, which only annoyed him more.

"Be careful, though. I will try to keep my senses ready to make a portal for you at a moment's notice, but he can silence you at the snap of a finger," Ashlock warned.

"Good point," Stella replied and stopped taunting the Voidmind scion by looking elsewhere.

Ashlock didn't think Dante would murder Stella because he would want to know what she knew about the Head Librarian ascending to the next realm of creation, but it was best to be cautious.

Having broken up the situation, the Redclaw Grand Elder vanished again in a burst of crimson flames and reappeared under the shade of the demonic tree, partially obscured by Diana's haunted mist.

The Grand Elder then gave a nod to Elder Brent, and the showman coughed awkwardly and then continued. *"In second place is the Spiri-*

tual Nullification Pill, which means the champion of the tournament is Dante Voidmind with the Void Traversal pill."

While the crowd became crazy with excitement, none of the nobles seemed interested in who won as they were engaged in a three-way staring contest.

Kassandra seemed unsure of who to be more mad at. Dante had his eyes dead set on Stella, and Stella taunted both of them with a cheeky smile behind her mask.

"Dante Voidmind, as the victor, please come up on the stage and give the crowd a speech," Elder Brent effortlessly lied. Elder Brent would have called for the top three to give speeches if Dante somehow came second or third.

The goal was simple: give Dante a platform to declare his invasion.

Dante slowly tore his irate gaze from Stella, and with a snap of his fingers, he reappeared on the wooden stage. The black-haired, ghoulish man seemed to contemplate what to say for a while as the crowd died down to a respectful level to hear the words of a noble family scion.

"Tree, is it time for the plan?" Stella asked through their mental link.

Ashlock gazed into the dense fog swirling around the demonic tree and could see the very faint outline of Larry's silhouette. Seeing that everyone was in position, he believed it was indeed time.

"Yes, get ready," Ashlock replied.

Dante brought out a crystal of pure darkness that had shadowy wisps evaporating from its surface.

"In truth, I care not for this pointless title granted upon me. Rather, I hope with the tournament's conclusion, I may say what I really came here for," Dante Voidmind said calmly, but his Qi carried his voice to all who dared to listen. *"I speak today to the great citizens of this beautiful city and the other nobles in attendance."*

His gaze briefly lingered on Ryker Silverspire and the Grand Elder before he continued. *"By the power vested in me as the scion of House Voidmind, I declare from this moment that Darklight City will fall under Slymere and ultimately my house's rule. Does House Redclaw accept this decision and agree to work with us to better this city?"*

The Redclaw Grand Elder stepped forward from under the shade of the demonic tree, flanked by swirling mist, and with his hands behind his back, he replied, "House Redclaw does not accept your forced servitude."

"I see, how unfortunate," Dante coldly said as he raised the void crystal. *"Then consider this a formal declaration of war—"*

"Larry, now!" Ashlock shouted.

The fog surrounding the demonic tree was pushed out of the way by a sudden tidal wave of ash that tumbled down the stands and into the area straight toward Dante Voidmind.

It moved with immense speed, destroying everything in its wake, including the workbenches and the wooden podium Elder Brent had been standing on. Luckily, the man had escaped, and so had most of the rest of the nobles by using various techniques, but hitting Dante Voidmind had never been the goal.

Kassandra's glowing blue eyes widened as she saw the tidal wave of ash cascade down the side of the stands and on top of her. She tried to call down lightning Qi to move, but the veil of ash above her easily absorbed the lightning bolt that descended from the clear blue skies.

"Ha, it worked!" Ashlock cheered. He had suspected that ash would be the perfect counter to lightning and the best way to trap Kassandra. It also acted as a way to obscure the following activities from the crowd of mortals and the other nobles like Kane and Celeste.

While hiding within the canopy of the demonic tree, the circle of ash orbiting Larry's crown of horns began to speed up, and the dense ash cloud began blanketing the arena to swirl like a forming tornado.

The mortals in the stands began to scramble to leave, and Ashlock made no move to stop them. So long as Kassandra Skyrend remained trapped, their plan would work.

Ashlock then saw a large chunk of the ash cloud vanish as if deleted from existence by a sudden bubble of void. Dante Voidmind stood in the center of the now-exposed area with the crystal far above his head. The ground around his feet looked like shifting tar, and three people in black cloaks slowly emerged from the darkness.

All three of them were in the Star Core Realm, and they all gave the scion a short bow.

"Young Lord, what are your orders?" a woman with long black hair in a ponytail asked.

"Elder Lilian, there is a blond girl with blackthorn tattoos somewhere nearby called Roselyn that knows about Uncle's whereabouts," Dante explained. *"You must find her at all costs, and I need her alive."*

"As you wish, Young Lord." Lilian nodded and then frowned at the

ash encircling them. *"This will be a problem. My spiritual sense is blocked, and forcing my way through it with void step will rapidly drain my Qi reserves. Do you have any idea where this girl could be?"*

Dante pointed in the direction Stella had been. *"I last saw Roselyn over there, so start your search in that area. I will ask Father to grant you more time in the Void Chamber in compensation for your sacrificed void Qi."*

"I would appreciate that, Young Lord." Lilian gave one last bow. *"I will go and find this Roselyn person now."*

With those words, she vanished into the void.

Dante then turned to a middle-aged man with a bald head and well-kept black beard. *"Elder Elias, kill all Redclaws, including the Grand Elder. Meanwhile, Elder Lucian, please watch my back and kill anyone else who gets in our way while we observe from above and ensure nobody important escapes."*

"As you command," both replied, and Elder Elias vanished into the void.

Dante and Elder Lucian hopped on swords and took to the skies before the ash cloud could finish encircling them and observed from above.

Ashlock watched as the Starcore Voidmind Elders reappeared within the ash by deleting a small amount around them and chuckled evilly as Larry slowly crawled down from the canopy of the demonic tree. "Have a good feast, but bring back their corpses."

"Certainly, Master," Larry replied and faded into the ash.

Guess it's time I also joined the slaughter, Ashlock thought as he cast {Progeny Dominion} for the first time.

His vision blurred, and he found himself far up in the sky above Darklight City. He was confused but noticed that many of the demonic trees, including the one in the colosseum, were glowing as if asking to be selected.

Ashlock picked the one in the colosseum, and a system notification appeared in his vision.

[Progeny selected: Initiating soul transfer...]

In the distance, his main body on Red Vine Peak trembled, and despite his point of view being so far away, he felt an invisible force tearing him apart from within.

[Soul fragmented: Damage to soul mitigated]

Suddenly he felt like a part of him was missing, just like when Tristan Evergreen stole a small percentage of his soul, but this time it was far more.

Weirdly, he noticed his system menu in the corner of his vision flickering as if it was having connection issues. Was the system this tied to his soul?

Ashlock then watched as the fragment of his soul, appearing as a glowing ball of spatial Qi, was dragged through the fused root network down the mountain peak, under the forest and streets of Darklight City, and eventually shoved into the demonic tree in the colosseum.

[Connection complete: Time till sundown 5:37]

When the system message appeared, Ashlock felt something drag him down from the sky at immense speed, and he watched the world blur as he plummeted toward the tree in the colosseum.

There was a ripple of power as his presence smashed into the demonic tree, and he felt his soul overtake the vessel. A moment later, he sensed his mind split between his main body and his offspring that he was temporarily overtaking.

Looking within, he saw the offspring's infant soul now encompassed within his own much larger soul fragment, like a tiny egg. He felt waves of happiness coming from it.

"Does it think I am giving it a hug?" Ashlock mused, but that wasn't important right now as he had identified his first target to attack. It wasn't Kane or Celeste who had retreated to the stands that were now half empty due to the fleeing mortals but rather Theron Skyrend, who was floating above the enshrouded arena on a small wooden boat.

His eyes glowed with immense power as he raised his arm. A great shadow loomed as the clear blue skies rapidly morphed into a violent storm.

He lowered his hand like an executioner, and a pure white lightning bolt arced down and blasted the ash cloud. It superheated a few meters in and then failed to penetrate deeper.

"Kassandra!" Theron roared as he raised his hand again. "Where are you?"

Ashlock activated {Abyssal Whispers} and targeted Theron.

The giant man stumbled on his boat and managed to support himself against its mast as Ashlock forced his way into his consciousness and laughed. "Would you like to meet her down there?"

"Who are you?" Theron bellowed as he clutched his head.

Ashlock took a moment to activate {Consuming Abyss} and watched as a black lake of void Qi spread out from the demonic tree he was inhabiting and snuck under the ash cloud below Theron.

"Tell me!" Theron shouted to the skies. "Who are you?"

"The one the Redclaws fear." Ashlock laughed. **"Roselyn's father."**

Before Theron could respond, Ashlock commanded a hundred void tendrils to shoot up through the ash and impale the Skyrend scion.

Theron tried activating his lightning Qi to teleport away, but Ashlock distracted him by saying, "Return to dust. Descendant of a fake god."

The wooden ship exploded as the void tendrils effortlessly tore through its hull and impaled Theron Skyrend. "Heretic…" was all Thern could gasp out as his head rolled back and his eyes dimmed. He then fell like a rock into the ash cloud below alongside a shower of splinters.

Ashlock sneaky opened a portal on the floor to secure the corpse.

"Y-Young Master, w-what was that?" Elder Lucian asked the Voidmind scion, who stood beside him on a floating sword.

Dante's eyes narrowed as he watched the hundreds of void tendrils retreat into the depths of the swirling ash.

"He's returned," Dante murmured. *"Uncle is really back…"*

75
BITTERSWEET REVENGE

Stella's eyes widened as a wave of ash so dense it could be confused for a landslide surged down into the arena with such force it made the ground shake.

Luckily, Stella had been expecting the incoming ash, so she had time to react and set an anchor point to quickly open a portal. As space tore open to reveal a path to safety, she winced as she saw the imminent surge of ash crash on top of Kassandra.

Within a second, half of the arena was consumed by the ash, and before it could smash into her, Stella stepped through the conjured portal and felt the temperature drop as she exited into a dark tunnel.

A burst of ash impacted her back as the portal collapsed behind her, not from her free will but because the dense ash cloud severed her connection as it devoured the spatial Qi.

Whew, I made it out with a second to spare. Stella let out a sigh. If she hadn't been forewarned about this part of the plan, she wasn't totally sure if she would have been able to escape in time.

And without my spiritual sight, I wouldn't have had a way to enter the spatial plane and set up an anchor to teleport out, so I would have been forced to try and find my way out of the ash storm.

Screams of mortals echoed from one side of the tunnel as they scrambled to escape the ash rapidly rising after blanketing the entire arena. Stella knew they would be fine, as Larry had no plans to kill them.

Brushing herself off, Stella could see the ash storm rising and swirling around the demonic tree through the tunnel exit.

"Roselyn!"

Stella turned to the voice and saw a beaming Elder Margret emerge from the tunnel's darkness. "I'm so proud of you!"

"Why?" Stella tilted her head.

Elder Margret laughed. "For creating a Profound-tier pill, obviously! I have never heard of someone learning alchemy as fast as you, and you came second!"

"Oh, thanks?" Stella replied with a feeling of awkwardness. She rarely received praise and wasn't sure how to respond correctly.

Stella then noticed the other Ashfallen Sect members and the Redclaw family standing behind Elder Margret. She wasn't surprised to see them hiding here as they had all been part of the plan. Under the shroud of the fog and ash, they would retreat here.

Diana and Elaine walked over and removed their masks.

"I'm surprised you're here," Stella said while looking Elaine up and down. "Won't your family notice you're missing?"

Elaine gave a weary smile. "They likely already have, but if I stay behind at the mansion, I will be forced back to Slymere with my brother, and I want to remain here with you guys."

"We did suggest she allow herself to be taken away to gather intel for us after this is all over," Diana chimed in, "but she said that getting information to us would be near impossible due to the void arrays that coat their mansion in Slymere."

Elaine bobbed her head in agreement. "Yeah, and I really don't want to see my father ever again."

Stella hummed and looked between them. "I see, so what are your plans now?"

"My job here is done." Diana shrugged. "So I guess I will wait here for a portal back to Red Vine Peak, and I assume Elaine and some of the others will join me."

"I will be remaining here with Sebastian and Ryker," the Grand Elder said with his hands behind his back, "to help start the civil war."

Stella nodded. "Okay, glad to see the plan hasn't changed."

"What about you?" Elaine asked. "Are you coming back with us?"

"No, I still have some unfinished business." Stella waved her off. "I just have to wait for the signal from the Patriarch—"

Stella felt the breath knocked out of her as there was a sudden presence. Her head snapped to look toward the source, and at the end of the tunnel, she saw the demonic tree that had previously felt like any other tree now had that distinctive presence of Ashlock.

"He's here." Stella smiled. "The Patriarch has arrived."

Everyone except the Grand Elder had stumbled back several steps and were in various stages of recovering from the sudden burst of power as if some divine being had abruptly descended.

Stella calmly watched the swirling ash beyond the tunnel, patiently awaiting Ashlock to tell her when it was time for her to kill Kassandra and end this hatred burning in her heart.

There was a burst of void Qi from the demonic tree, and then shortly after, a portal manifested in the tunnel. Everyone turned to look at it. Stella saw the dim cavern below Red Vine Peak through the wobbling, lilac-tinted portal.

"See you later." Diana waved to Stella and stepped through alongside the other Elders and Elaine, who also bid her farewell with words and waves.

The portal snapped closed, and silence briefly returned. Stella took this moment to eat a Lightning Qi Barrier fruit in preparation for the upcoming part of the plan.

"Theron is dead," Ashlock announced in her mind while she was finishing off the fruit. She paused mid-bite and shuddered a little.

The way Ashlock announced the death of someone that seemed so arrogant and powerful in her mind, as if he were talking about the weather, showed how little of a challenge killing someone like Theron Skyrend was to him.

I remember him as a weak little sapling that needed my protection. Since when did Tree grow so powerful?

Stella summoned the black wood dagger crafted from the sticks Ashlock had gifted her all those years ago. She felt its weight and rubbed her finger along the wood grain.

This dagger had been used to save her life from the conspiring servants, and now she planned to use them to execute a noble cultivator. Gripping it tightly, Stella asked Ashlock, "And what of Kassandra? Is she still alive?"

"Incapacitated within the ash cloud as planned," Ashlock replied. **"She's all yours. Just be careful. Dante Voidmind has a Star**

Core Elder combing the ash cloud to find you, and there are others."

"Star Core Elders?" Stella murmured in slight awe. "If not for you, a power like that would be enough to force many noble families to surrender their land."

"Indeed," Ashlock mused. **"However, with Larry's ash, a high-costing Qi affinity like void becomes a major disadvantage."**

Stella nodded. "That's true, but how will I fight Kassandra in the ash? Spatial is also a high-cost affinity, and I cannot locate her without spiritual sense."

"I will flood the area surrounding Kassandra Skyrend with spatial Qi and then open a portal for you," Ashlock continued. **"I know you are much stronger than her, so feel free to toy with her, but please keep the body in one piece. I might make an Ent out of her corpse."**

Stella could sense the slight anger and seriousness in Ashlock's tone. Clearly, she hadn't been the only one infuriated by Kassandra over the last few days, so Stella sighed. "Fine. I won't tear her limb from limb."

The dark tunnel leading outside rippled as space was torn apart, and a portal manifested, and through it, all Stella could see was the ash cloud.

Stella hesitantly stepped through, her vision a blur due to the swirling ash all around. Her Star Core flared up, and purple flames illuminated a mere centimeter around her, keeping the ash from invading her mouth and nose.

"Kassandra should be nearby." Stella glanced around but was completely blind. Without her soul flames fending off the ash, she would be suffocated to death.

Closing her eyes, Stella found she could spread her spiritual sense and perceive an area of a few meters around her due to spatial Qi being pumped into the storm from the tips of black roots poking out of the sand.

"There you are," Stella muttered as she noticed lightning Qi super-heating the ash around it in an effort to fight back. Due to Kassandra's towering height, her burning silhouette in the ash made her look like a blazing demoness that had crawled straight out of hell.

Licking her lips behind the cloth mask in anticipation of her screams, Stella lowered her body and dashed forward, cleaving her way through the ash and arriving right behind Kassandra.

"Who—" Kassandra shouted through the roaring storm as she seemingly sensed Stella. She started to turn and look over her shoulder, but Stella didn't waste a second and ruthlessly slashed at her ankles with her aflame black wood dagger and easily cleaved through her skin.

Stella frowned a little at how easy it had been to slice through Kassandra's defenses as blood spurted from her legs and was carried away by the violent winds and coated the swirling ash crimson.

"AHHHH!" Kassandra's Qi-empowered howl overcame the roaring winds of the storm as she stumbled forward a few steps. Her lightning Qi crackling across the surface of her skin flared up as if out of control and began lashing out.

Unfazed by the lightning burning holes in her clothes, Stella strode through the ash while twirling her dagger and stopped before Kassandra.

Despite the pain and confusion evident on Kassandra's twisted face, she still raised her fists up in the air and tried to pummel Stella with vengeful fury and a half-pained war cry.

"Who DARES!" The ash parted as Kassandra tried to destroy the person who attacked her, but Stella effortlessly raised her palm and caught Kassandra's fist.

With the power of the Lightning Qi Barrier fruit and her own dao comprehension, Stella easily resisted Kassandra's attack. Perhaps if the woman was trained with the sword or was more capable at stealth, this would be a more challenging fight…but Kassandra was clearly far too arrogant to use manmade tools and would rather depend on the lightning from the heavens to smite down all who opposed her.

But what was she without lightning? Just a somewhat strong Soul Fire cultivator—an ant in comparison to Stella.

The two exchanged a glare, and Kassandra's glowing eyes widened at the realization of who she faced. "Roselyn? So you finally show yourself." Blue lightning crackled down her arm, but Stella just tilted her head, entirely unbothered, as the lightning blasted into her hand and singed the sleeves of her clothes.

Realizing her attacks were having no effect and gritting her teeth through the pain, Kassandra tried to pull her arm back, but Stella easily held it in place.

"You were so arrogant before," Stella sneered. "Some bad weather dampen your spark?"

"You bitch," Kassandra hissed as she stumbled and fell to one knee due to her severed ankles finally giving out. "How dare you sneak attack me." She spat to the side and shouted over the storm, "Do you have no honor?!"

Stella tightened her grip on Kassandra's fist and twisted it, snapping her bone with a satisfying crunch. A chilling scream left Kassandra as she reeled back her obliterated arm.

Stella shivered in pure ecstasy. She had been hungering for this moment for days—a time when she didn't have to tiptoe or bow before this woman due to external factors like politics.

Here in this prison of ash, away from prying eyes and assistance, only the strength of the individual mattered.

"You speak of honor and demand it from others." Stella reached forward, grabbed the side of Kassandra's head, and kneed her in the face, breaking her nose and making her collapse to the sand. "Yet you cheated at every turn and hid behind your family name to bully the Redclaws who you refer to as lessers."

Kassandra spat a mouthful of sand and blood as she propped herself up. Her spatial ring flashed, and a group of pills appeared in her unbroken hand.

"Go on." Stella stood there with her arms crossed as the ash swirled around her. "Eat all the pills you want. You will die here all the same."

"Foolish girl." Kassandra had a blood-filled grin. "You dare act arrogant before me—"

Blood spurted out her mouth as Stella withdrew the dagger she had just thrust through a quickly conjured portal.

"You said…you would let me eat…" Kassandra gasped out.

Stella shrugged. "I lied."

Kassandra trembled as she reached up with her only functioning arm and tried to block up the hole in her neck that was oozing blood. A strange wheeze left her mouth as she tried to force the blood-covered pills down her throat but violently coughed them up, and they were whisked away by the fierce winds.

As Kassandra saw her pills vanish, Stella saw the arrogance fade and pure despair overtake Kher. Her glowing eyes dimmed as she kept wheezing and trying to breathe through her blood-filled neck with little success.

Stella slowly walked over, kicking up sand as she stepped closer, one step at a time.

Kassandra tried to shuffle away in fear as she stared death in the eyes.

Stella reached down and grabbed a fistful of Kassandra's hair and began dragging her by it.

"You wanted me to be chained to your porch as a slave to your brother," Stella said coldly over Kassandra's spluttering screams. "So how does it feel being dragged around like a chained dog? Humiliating, perhaps?"

With some force, Stella hurled Kassandra back down to the ground and then crouched and held Kassandra's face a few inches from her own. Only her purple flames illuminated both of their faces as Kassandra's lightning had died down.

As Stella stared the dying woman in the eyes, the pure hatred she had cultivated in her heart mellowed out, and all that consumed her mind was how pathetic this person was.

"You know what I hate, Kassandra?" Stella said. "Wasted potential. You were born with money, status, education, resources, and a loving home. And what do you do with this high station in life? You prance around flaunting your family name and pathetic strength while spitting on those you deem lesser."

Stella tightened her grip, making Kassandra groan in pain. "And all for what? We could have been friends and pursued immortality by uplifting one another. But you would rather boost your ego to the point you were so blind and offended the wrong person. Now look at you. Beaten and broken, alone in the sand."

Kassandra wheezed and clawed at her neck as if trying to free her windpipe from the blood, and Stella felt her words of ridicule die in her throat.

Why had her anger faded? Why did this feel so immoral? Kassandra had done so much wrong to her and the Redclaws, yet as she had the half-dead Kassandra in her hands, the idea of killing her didn't sit right.

Have I become like her?

Stella released her grip, allowing Kassandra to collapse to the sand, and stepped back. The image of the arrogant woman that she had dreamed about brutally murdering in her mind was broken when she stared at the pathetic sight.

What if Kassandra was just misguided and would be willing to repent? Would I even be willing to spare her?

Stella felt the chaotic ashen storm matching her jumbled thoughts. She had never had second thoughts about murder before… In fact, she had been the one to suggest killing Elaine. She had always seen murder as the most efficient solution to dealing with her problems, but now she wasn't so sure.

The dagger in her hand felt heavy as the tip pointed to the floor. If she killed Kassandra right here, wouldn't she be just as bad as her? Kassandra used her political weight behind her to spit on the lessers. Meanwhile, Stella had abused her superior cultivation to beat Kassandra half to death.

Who was really in the right here?

Stella looked down at Kassandra. "Do you wish to be spared?"

Kassandra's eyes briefly widened but then dulled. With a grunt, the dying woman pushed herself onto one knee and spat a large glob of blood onto the sand. "May I know your true name?"

Stella paused for a moment to consider, but she was curious how Kassandra would react to knowing she had a noble family name, so she honored the woman's request. Reaching up, she removed her mask.

"My true name is Stella Crestfallen…"

Due to her height, the two were at eye level; Kassandra grinned with blood-stained teeth and crazed eyes and said slowly, "Stella Crestfallen…to spare me would be an insult. I desire no pity from someone destined to be nothing but a lowly pill furnace."

Stella closed her eyes and plunged the black wood dagger straight into Kassandra's heart, causing her to groan and fall into her embrace. She supported the dying woman's weight and whispered into her ear as she drew her final breath, "I spit on destiny, just like you do on those you deem lesser."

Stella then twisted the dagger and ruthlessly pulled it out—ending Kassandra Skyrend's life.

She stepped to the side, and the colossal body unceremoniously crumpled to the ground. A mixture of emotions and thoughts spiraled in Stella's mind as she saw the lifeless corpse bleeding out on the sand.

It was over…yet why was it so bittersweet? Why did she feel like, in a twisted way, Kassandra had won?

She was prideful to the bitter end. Not even death could break her arrogance.

A portal opened nearby, and Stella watched as a black vine coated in spikes coiled around the corpse and then dragged it away.

"Satisfied with your revenge?" Ashlock asked within her mind.

Unfortunately, Stella wasn't sure what to say as she saw the foot of Kassandra's corpse vanish through the portal.

"Maybe not every problem can be solved with murder," Stella eventually answered, smiling behind her mask, "but this one certainly was."

Stella then spat on the blood-soaked sand where Kassandra had died. "And that's for the Redclaws."

76
VOID CALLER

Ashlock was glad to see Stella deeply contemplating her actions. She had a bad habit of acting first and thinking later, which wasn't the type of mentality someone trying to run a sect should have.

It had worked out so far, but there would come a day when Stella murdered someone over a misunderstanding and deeply regretted it. Elaine was already an excellent living example of this, as she had become an accepted member of the Ashfallen Sect rather than a cold corpse due to Diana and others resisting Stella.

"Tree, I can't make a portal out of the ash, my spiritual sight only spreads so far, and I can't even tell which way is up or down right now. Can you make me a way out?" Stella said through their telepathic link.

Ashlock realized he had been so focused on securing Kassandra's corpse that he had forgotten to make a portal for Stella to leave the swirling ash. Mobilizing his spatial Qi by using his progeny as a proxy, Ashlock could materialize a stable portal within the dense ash.

Stella seemed to have a lot on her mind as she absentmindedly walked through the ash toward the portal leading her back to Red Vine Peak. She was about to enter when Ashlock noticed something emerge from the ash.

"Watch out!" Ashlock shouted in Stella's mind.

She was snapped awake from her stupor just in time to notice a spear of pure void Qi cleaving through the ash and rapidly losing size as it deleted the ash from existence.

Stella's eyes widened as she threw herself to the bloodied sand below and barely managed to avoid the deathly silent attack.

It narrowly passed over her head, tore straight through the portal, and eventually fizzled out as it cleaved a few more meters through the ash. The portal naturally collapsed on itself with a hole carved through the middle, leaving Stella facing Elder Lilian Voidmind, who had been searching the ashen storm for her.

Lilian's eyes narrowed as they traced Stella's black thorn tattoos.

Without even saying a word, like a grim reaper, Lilian coated herself in void Qi that made her look like she was covered in liquid shadows and stepped forward.

She vanished.

"Void step," Ashlock warned Stella. **"Cover your flanks."**

Ashlock debated creating another portal to help Stella escape. But if the Voidmind Elder followed her before he could snap the portal closed, then Stella's chances of survival would drop drastically. She had the best fighting chance in the ashen storm that was drenched in his spatial Qi and near his progeny.

"Shit, where is she?" Stella panicked through their link as her soul fire flared up, and she tightened her grip around the bloodied dagger.

"I don't know." Ashlock cursed. Even with their environmental advantage, this was a void affinity Star Core cultivator with the sole goal of capturing Stella. **"I overheard Dante's conversation with Elder Lilian, and her orders are nonfatal capture, so she is unlikely to use lethal attacks."**

"That doesn't fill me with much confidence," Stella snapped back as she desperately glanced around. "Can't you do anything? One wrong move, and she could kill me."

"Not while she is hiding in the void," Ashlock replied. When the Elder showed herself, he could attack her with {Consuming Abyss} or his spatial Qi. But for now, all they could do was wait.

"Larry get over here," Ashlock called through their tether. "We need your help."

A few tense moments passed, with Stella flinching at every little movement within the ash. Her eyes darted as she kept moving, ensuring she never exposed her back in one direction for too long.

Suddenly a pocket of ash right behind Stella vanished, and in its place was a void Qi–coated woman. Stella didn't even have time to react before the Elder tried to reach forward and grab the back of her neck.

Ashlock's mind kicked into gear as he did three things simultaneously. Multiple badly formed Qi-dense portals that led to nowhere formed between Stella and the Elder. Each shattered as the Elder punched through them, but each shaved off a layer of the void Qi coating the Elder's hand.

By the time the Elder managed to grip Stella's neck, Stella could flare her soul flame to make the Elder reel back. The ground cracked open, and a black vine coated in thorns and ending in a spike shot out toward the Voidmind Elder alongside a surge of void tendrils.

Ashlock also attempted to cast {Abyssal Whispers} on the Elder, but the void Qi surrounding her consciousness was impossible to penetrate. However, that didn't matter. His objective had been achieved.

Stella stumbled forward while gasping for air because her neck was briefly grabbed, and Lilian was left fighting against Ashlock's onslaught.

"Agh!" Ashlock winced as the Elder grabbed his aflame black vine with void-coated hands and ripped it apart, tossing the decapitated spike to the sand.

"Void Qi is so overpowered,. Ashlock cursed as he decided to fight fire with fire and sent in his own void Qi attack, only to be left bewildered as the Elder easily grabbed the tendrils sent out to kill her and began absorbing his void Qi.

In the corner of his eye, he saw his sacrificial credits begin to drain. "Shit, how can she do that?!" Ashlock canceled the skill to stop giving her more precious void Qi to work with, but that left him with a problem.

Within a few seconds, the Elder had ruthlessly ignored or overpowered his attacks, leaving Stella defenseless.

The Elder surged forward like a haunted shadow; Stella didn't have time to conjure up a portal to escape, so she brought up her hands, and when the Elder was but a hair's width away, she unleashed a barrage of purple lightning she had absorbed from Kassandra.

Superheated ash pushed forward by a bust of spatial flames and lightning gave Stella a second of space to stumble backward.

Ashlock didn't waste time and opened a portal above the dazed Elder. Before she could react and void step away, Ashlock commanded Bob, the slime Ent, to fall through the rift and land on top of the Elder.

Lilian seemed to sense the imminent threat a moment too late as she glanced up to see Bob's giant foot descend upon her. She punched it to the side with a void-coated fist, but rather than deleting or exploding the threat as she was likely expecting, the gray slime's leg was only smacked out of the way and began to take on a black hue.

Remembering how Lilian had absorbed his void Qi tendrils, Ashlock cast {Consuming Abyss} on Bob and watched his sacrificial credits rapidly drain as hundreds of tendrils emerged from the black lake and linked up to Bob, pumping him full of void Qi.

When Ashlock deemed enough void Qi had been exchanged with Bob, he withdrew the void lake to prevent the Elder from stealing any more void Qi from him, as one of the best ways to deal with void cultivators was to force them to waste their precious Qi reserves.

Bob uttered a strange cry as the gray slime with a slight lilac hue rapidly transitioned into a titan of looming darkness.

Lilian seemed baffled as she stepped back from the strange monster she had encountered in the ashen storm that still violently swirled around her.

"Bob, I'm about to create a portal to evacuate Stella. Don't let that void lady anywhere near it," Ashlock commanded as his spatial Qi rippled through the area and tore open a rift right beside Stella.

His only concern was getting Stella the hell out of there.

Bob honored the order by lowering his body and encircling the suddenly formed portal—Stella dashed through, and the second the tips of her aflame hair had gotten through, Ashlock closed the rift, only to see it become corrupted with void Qi and notice the Elder was missing.

"Shit." Ashlock cursed. His fears of the Elder following Stella through a portal came true despite his best efforts to hold her back for just a brief second.

Stella stumbled out of the portal with fear she hadn't felt in a long time. She felt capable of facing most cultivators within the Star Core Realm, but something about the void element and its indisputable lethality sent shivers down her spine.

Gathering herself, she noticed the portal had led her to the tunnel entrance just behind the demonic tree that Ashlock was currently inhabiting. The ashen storm was just as prevalent here as it violently rustled the tree's leaves. Stella gave the tree a brief nod before turning her sights to inside the dark tunnel where she could see the Redclaw Grand Elder, Sebastian, and Ryker staring at her.

They all went wide-eyed simultaneously, and Stella heard Ashlock shout into her mind, "Behind you!"

Stella didn't even need to turn to feel the immense gravity of the Elder bearing down on her. Without thought, she threw herself to the ground and, shifting her body, glanced up at the Voidmind Elder standing over her.

"The Young Lord wishes to ask you some questions," Elder Lilian said calmly as she reached down. "So I will need you to come with me."

Stella watched Lilian grab at her with inhuman speed, but a blast of crimson flames pushed her back and ate away at the void Qi rippling across her skin.

Lilian conjured a javelin of void and hurled it at the Redclaw Grand Elder assisting Stella, forcing him to cancel his flamethrower attack and dodge to the side.

"Stop getting in my way!" Lilian seemed genuinely frustrated as she reached down and grabbed Stella's arm. The void Qi burned through the purple flames protecting her, searing her skin. As the two met eyes, Stella held back her screams of pain and activated her earrings as a last-ditch effort—her eyes became swirling abysses, but Lilian just sneered in response.

"Little girl, I stare into the abyss every day in hopes it will stare back." Lilian's eyes dimmed, and Stella felt a terrifying chill spread throughout her body, distracting her from the burning pain. "You think anything you can do or know would scare me?"

Stella was about to give up hope as the Elder pulled on her arm to try and force her to stand when she saw the void-corrupted portal behind Lilian collapse and then reopen; through the unstable rift, Stella could see many red eyes.

"Mistress!" Larry roared in the ancient tongue as his giant body emerged from the portal, and immense pressure bore down on everyone. The ash orbiting his crown of horns spun so fast it generated its own gale.

Lilian collapsed to one knee under the pressure, and Stella found herself totally floored on her back and unable to lift her head. Since when had Larry been this strong?

The surrounding ashen storm seemed to obey the will of its master as tons of dense ash smashed into Lilian, sending her tumbling to the side with a groan.

Stella strained her neck and managed to catch the enormous back of Larry as he crawled through the storm toward Lilian, who was struggling to stand under the surge of ash and immense pressure.

"Stay back!" Lilian shouted as she failed to stand on two feet. "My master will know of my death! Spirit beast, you would do well not to anger him."

"I only fear one master," Larry said.

"Spirit beast, I don't understand—" Lilian screamed as Larry opened his maw and dragged her inside with the furry pincers on either side of his mouth. There was a brief struggle as Lilian attempted to escape death, but the thick ash coating Larry easily absorbed the void Qi.

Stella's eyes widened—there was a sickening crunch, and the chilling scream abruptly stopped. A moment of silence passed as the storm calmed and the pressure subsided.

Larry slowly rotated to face Stella and the Redclaw Grand Elder, dragging Lilian's limp feet across the stone steps of the colosseum as he moved.

Stella gulped as she saw the Voidmind Elder that had terrorized her with a giant fang impaling her skull. Dead.

Dante Voidmind frowned at the void crystal in his hand.

Cracks had suddenly formed on its surface, and he could feel its power dimming.

I can't imagine an artifact my father gave me would be so cheap to break on me like this.

"Elder Lucian, do you know what's wrong with the Void Caller?" Dante asked the man standing on the floating sword beside him. The two of them were observing the chaotic ash storm from overhead and keeping an eye out to make sure nobody important escaped the vicinity.

"Mhm?" Elder Lucian had been using his superior cultivation to blanket half the city in his spiritual sense in search of anything interesting. Reeling it back in, he turned to look at Dante and then at the crystal.

He blinked in disbelief. "Young Lord, what is the status of the other Elders?"

"How would I know? They are within that darn ashen storm that blocks out everything."

Elder Lucian shook his head. "Dante, do you know how the Void Caller works?"

Dante frowned. "Father explained it briefly. All I had to do was insert some void Qi to call forth any who would answer the call."

"As you well know, void Qi allows us to cross great distances in a mere moment by traversing the void that lies beyond the physical realm," Elder Lucian explained. "The Void Caller allows you to call upon us from anywhere over any distance, but it has a catch."

"Which is?" Dante began to grow irritated. It was clear these cracks were a bad sign.

"We have to return to our point of call." Elder Lucian raised his hand and brought attention to a faint tether of void Qi between his fingers and the crystal. "For the price of instant movement, we can only remain here for so long and must pay our debt back to the void."

"So, the cracks?" Dante insisted. "What do they mean?"

"One of the Elders has perished, and the artifact took on damage as the void forcefully took back its debt," Elder Lucian said coldly. "If another Elder dies, the artifact may shatter."

Dante clicked his tongue. "Incompetent fools. How can a carefully raised Elder of our great family perish in this backwater city?"

"Perhaps it was your uncle's doing?" Elder Lucian suggested. His tone was as cold as the Void Caller in Dante's palm.

Dante paused.

It's possible, but all of this is strange. The void tendrils that killed Theron Skyrend were beyond my father's capabilities, so it could only belong to a void cultivator in the Nascent Soul Realm. So if it is truly Uncle, why has he not come to greet me? And what hatred could he possibly bear against the Skyrend family to waste so much precious void Qi on eliminating their heir?

Dante narrowed his eyes at the swirling ash. Something on this level also didn't belong to this realm. Had Uncle teamed up with someone to hunt down the Skyrend family?

Let's think... The only things the Skyrend family are known and regarded for are their arrogance and capability to defy the heavens.

Dante's eyes widened as he murmured, "Defy the heavens…"

"Young Lord?" Elder Lucian asked. "Is something the matter?"

Dante waved the Elder off. "Nothing, just keep an eye out for any more Skyrend family members."

Elder Lucian gave him an odd look but returned to his spiritual sight.

For Uncle to triumph over the curse on our noble blood and break the shackles that bind him to this realm, there would be no better family to ask than the Skyrends. Is Uncle murdering them so the secret doesn't reach Father's ears?

Dante understood it might be a leap in logic, but he couldn't fathom another reason for this nonchalant display of power against a random family like the Skyrends.

Just what is his angle—

The Void Caller in Dante's hand exploded, devouring his hand and sucking in Elder Lucian.

Dante blinked at his stump and watched the sword Elder Lucian had been standing on fall down into the ashen storm below. His mind was totally frozen in shock.

What had just happened? Were all the Elders dead? And where the hell did his hand go?

77
A BREWING STORM

Elder Elias Voidmind opened his eyes with a sigh. He stood on the third floor of the colosseum and was gazing out at the chaotic marketplace in the grand square.

"Where are these Redclaw bastards?" Elias grumbled to himself as he reeled in his spiritual sight. He had probed the thousands of mortals desperately fleeing down the streets and couldn't find any traces of fire Qi. It was as if the Redclaws had all evacuated ahead of time.

Elias's fingers drummed on the stone windowsill as the calm, warm breeze went over his bald head. The Young Lord would not be happy with his performance if he returned without blood on his hands.

Sighing, he pushed himself away from the windowsill and strode down the now-empty hallway. There was nothing else to accompany his thoughts besides the whistling wind that rustled his black robes.

Do I really have to hunt for them within that ashen storm? It will deplete my entire reserves, and I may set back my cultivation by years. Why did I think answering the void's call would be a good idea? Benefits? From a tyrant like Dante? Not a chance.

Elias clicked his tongue in annoyance as he rounded a corner and was met with a face full of wind and the burned smell of ash. Through the glassless windows, he could see the violent storm swirling around. The idea of setting foot in that storm and burning hours of cultivation per minute to stay alive was aggravating, but what was he to do?

The will of the Young Lord was absolute, and he had no plans to return empty-handed. Deciding to take the stairs to a lower level rather than simply jumping into the ashen storm blindly, he continued his walk through the empty hallway until he felt a presence.

Cautiously prodding it with his spiritual sense, he could feel the faint waves of gravity that could only belong to someone in the Star Core Realm, and to make things even better, there was the presence of fire Qi.

Grinning, Elder Elias popped a Spiritual Nullification Pill to obscure his aura. They were expensive and didn't last for more than a few minutes, but it was a small price to guarantee he had the severed head of a powerful Redclaw to present to the Young Lord.

Feeling the pill rushing through his body, he observed as his natural aura reeled in. A slight pressure from his Star Core remained, but that was almost impossible to entirely hide.

Sticking close to the wall, Elder Elias snuck up to the dark tunnel. He was briefly surprised at how long it was, but that was no matter as he could see the backs of two men and a child at the end.

Two wore white robes and, from their metallic hair, were clearly members of House Silverspire. Besides these two was a man with crimson hair and dark red robes—the Redclaw Grand Elder.

Why is he standing beside the Silverspires? Is their relationship closer than we thought?

Elder Elias narrowed his eyes as he crept down the tunnel. The Redclaw Grand Elder's Star Core seemed active as his fists were still aflame with crimson soul fire. Had he just been fighting something?

It was getting more questionable and risky the more he looked into it, but Elder Elias had no plans to disobey his Young Lord. If Dante wanted the Redclaw Grand Elder's head on a silver platter, that's precisely what he would get.

A few tense moments passed as Elias got closer; his finger itched to summon a dagger and coat it in void Qi, but that would alert the two Star Core cultivators just a few meters away of his presence.

In honesty, he was surprised they hadn't noticed him already. What could they be so distracted by to have no interest in a mortal behind them? Curious, he became a little bold and spread out his spiritual sight and almost shouted out in surprise when he saw the corpse of Elder Lilian in the mouth of a spirit beast far stronger than him.

Does that spirit beast belong to the Silverspires? Is it what's causing this powerful ashen storm?

For a brief moment, Elder Elias wanted to turn back and report the findings to Dante, but he could already imagine his reaction. He would question why he was informing him of trivial things instead of eliminating them for him.

Prideful bastard, Elias cursed in his mind but then froze in his tracks. Glancing down, he saw a fluffy white squirrel looking up at him with eyes of liquid gold filled with adorable curiosity.

And then it smiled.

Elias blinked in confusion and became even more disorientated when he realized the walls, floor, and ceiling of the hallway he had been sneaking through were gone and replaced with the endless abyss.

There he was, floating in the endless expanse of the void with nothing but a grinning squirrel to keep him company. He didn't feel anything out of the ordinary about the squirrel, but its bizarre grin that seemed far too human was irking him.

"Hello?" Elder Elias questioned the squirrel. "Did you bring me here?"

No answer—had he really been expecting one? Squirrels couldn't speak, but there was something so odd about it that he wasn't even sure what to do.

"I was hungry." A voice spoke directly in his mind, and worse of all, the words carried with it the pain of endless hunger. It was so extreme that for a moment, Elias couldn't even blame the voice's owner for wanting to eat him.

"Was that you?" Elder Elias asked the squirrel with a shiver, but the furry creature was still eerily grinning at him and didn't reply. Feeling creeped out, Elias glanced away and tried to workshop a solution out of this place.

He was in the void, but not of his own free will. Something had pulled him from the physical realm and trapped him in here. He tried to mobilize his own void Qi to tear open a doorway to the physical realm, but the void refused to answer him.

There's something nearby with far more domain over the void than me. My only hope is if the Void Caller is still working, it should be able to pull me back to my original location in Slymere, so I just have to survive until then—

Elias felt a weird pressure, so he glanced back and saw the squirrel roll its head back and open its mouth impossibly wide.

Its body then ruptured and exploded. A squirming mass of black tentacles expanded in all directions, forming an enormous body that dominated the endless void.

Elias hadn't even had time to register what happened when a single eye a thousand times his size glared down at him, and he could see the insatiable hunger in its gaze.

"A Worldwalker." Elias gulped as he closed his eyes.

He knew his death would be swift.

Ashlock had been listening in on the conversation between Dante Voidmind and the Elder beside him when something unexpected happened: the crystal in Dante's hand cracked and then exploded.

It all happened instantly. The air twisted into a singularity as if a black hole had formed, and a moment later, the Star Core Elder was missing, and so was Dante's hand.

"What the hell?" Ashlock murmured in disbelief. One moment there had been a Star Core Elder that he had been wondering how to deal with, and the next, he was just…gone.

Recalling the Voidmind's conversation, the only plausible explanation for why the artifact had shattered like that was that the Elder sent to kill the Redclaws had died.

"If the other Voidmind Elder has really perished, it makes sense for the void crystal to shatter. The void's hunger must have become too much for it to contain, but that raises another question…" Ashlock glanced around. "Who the hell killed a Star Core Voidmind Elder?"

Everyone surrounding the demonic tree within the ashen storm seemed oblivious to the situation that had just occurred high in the sky. And Ashlock couldn't see any evidence of this Voidmind Elder's corpse.

"Did he really die?" Ashlock couldn't believe it. "All of my strongest sect members are here. The Grand Elder, Stella, Larry, and even Sebastian. Who could possibly…"

Ashlock paused as he saw a fluffy white squirrel emerge from the dark tunnel.

Maple jumped and skillfully landed on Stella's head.

"Oh, Maple!" Stella lovingly patted the mythical squirrel. *"Where*

have you been? I could have used your help with this Elder that was hellbent on capturing me!"

Maple accepted the head rubs with glee and then laid on his back, letting out a satisfied burp.

"No way..." Ashlock let out a long sigh. This little rascal was always off doing his own thing and causing problems.

"You ate him, didn't you? You were the only person missing that's strong enough to pull off such a feat," Ashlock asked through their mental link, but Maple ignored him and slept.

"Bastard, those were valuable sacrificial credits," Ashlock seethed to himself. "And because that Elder died, the other one was also taken away!"

After a while of grumbling, Ashlock sighed. In truth, Maple had done him a favor by dealing with the Elder, and he should be satisfied that nobody on his side came out hurt or dead. But that wouldn't stop him from lamenting over the lost sacrificial credits.

"It's fine. I still have the two Skyrend corpses and one Voidmind Elder corpse," Ashlock mused. "I wonder if I should turn one of them into an Ent? Theron would make the strongest Ent due to his high cultivation stage, but what about a void element one from the Voidmind Elder's corpse?"

Ashlock's trail of thought was interrupted when he detected a flash of Qi in the sky. He focused on the source and saw Dante Voidmind talking into a glowing communication jade while staring at his stump.

The conversation was happening within a Qi bubble, so he couldn't listen in, but judging by Dante's worsening expression, whatever he was being told wasn't good news for him.

While this was happening, Ashlock noticed the clear blue sky on the horizon darkening. A giant storm system began brewing out of nowhere and moving toward him.

"Oh shit," Ashlock cursed as he noticed a small humanoid-shaped dot at the forefront of the storm.

Ashlock quickly opened a portal leading to Red Vine Peak. "Larry, take Stella and go. Leave the Voidmind corpse here."

Larry acknowledged his orders and nudged Stella, who had Maple on her head, toward the portal. The moment the giant spider left with Stella, the ashen storm began to settle down, and heaps of ash floated into the arena and covered the stands.

While keeping his eye on the rapidly approaching tempest, Ashlock wrote on his trunk in lilac flames, 'Grand Elder. He's here.'

The Redclaw Grand Elder translated the message, and his expression turned grave as he looked at the sky. *"It seems my prediction of him showing up has come to fruition. Time to try and reason with an arrogant self-proclaimed demi-god."*

He then turned to Sebastian at his side. "Remember your promise, Silverspire."

Sebastian patted Ryker on the shoulder and nodded to the Grand Elder. *"Of course, we would smear the Silverspire name if we were to dishonor a contract. This tournament is under our house's protection."*

"Then prepare the Voidmind corpse and get ready," the Grand Elder answered.

Ashlock was relieved to hear that everyone was on board as this was risky, but this was the pivotal moment of the grand plan to start a war between the Skyrend and Voidmind families to buy his Ashfallen Sect time to scale up.

He would need to advance his own cultivation and give his sect members another few rounds in the Mystic Realm before he felt comfortable fully exposing the Ashfallen Sect's existence and going to war against the top families and the Patriarch.

And it all depended on convincing the gigantic floating man that resembled the reincarnation of Zeus at the forefront of the massive storm fast approaching that they hadn't been the ones to kill his son and daughter.

The distant rumbling of a thunderous storm became louder as the sky darkened and the day turned to dusk. For some reason, this reminded Ashlock of that time the Winterwrath Grand Elder came to attack the Ravenborne family atop a titan of ice and flanked by a cataclysmic blizzard.

"They sure do like dramatic entrances—" Ashlock was silenced by the world going white as if a nuclear bomb had gone off. The storm overhead lit up all at once at the command of the giant man floating in the sky, and a bolt of lightning the width of the arena descended.

The moment the bolt hit the ground, there was a thunderclap so loud everyone present was pushed back a few steps and had the soul flames flickering across their skin briefly snuffed out. The Grand Elder had been expecting this and resisted the wave of superheated sand and ash thrown up by the attack with a wall of crimson flames.

Even with the wall of flames, if not for the spatial Qi drenching the demonic tree he was inhabiting with a fraction of his soul, the tree would have snapped in half and perished.

With color returning to the world as the lightning blast ceased, Ashlock witnessed a five-meter-tall man coated in golden lightning with similar features to Theron slowly descend to the arena below. The lightning bolt had transformed the arena into a beautiful art piece of ashen glass.

The man's golden glowing eyes were focused on a section of the glass tinted red. He bent down, running his fingers over the still-hot glass, and whispered, "Who dares…"

There was a moment of pin-drop silence as the man closed his eyes, stood to his full height, and then bellowed to the heavens above with a thunderous roar, "Who dares slaughter my children? Where are their corpses?!?"

Dark clouds overhead crackled and flashed to mirror their summoner's rage. Yet the heavens did not have the answer he sought, so his furious gaze landed on the Redclaw Grand Elder.

Kicking against the ground, he shattered the glass underfoot as he rocketed toward the calm Grand Elder.

"Magnus Redclaw," the Skyrend Grand Elder snarled, *"did you extinguish the life of my beloved children?"*

Ashlock was surprised. Only now did he realize the man had only ever been referred to as the Grand Elder of the Redclaw family and nothing else.

"Demetrios Skyrend, you know I hate that name." Magnus Redclaw narrowed his eyes at the towering man. *"And no, I did not kill your children."*

The two glared at one another for a moment.

Ashlock would believe Demetrios had titan blood in his veins. The man was so towering that he was almost the same height as the demonic tree he was inhabiting and was over twice the height of the already tall Redclaw Grand Elder.

"Magnus, I see the blood of my children smeared in the sand." Demetrios leaned in closer, his marble-like muscles swelling while containing his fury. *"My children came to attend your tournament to*

show face, so tell me why the heavens speak of their demise?"

"We were attacked moments ago during the final event by the Voidmind family," Magnus Redclaw explained. *"They must have died during the fight."*

"The Voidmind family?" Demetrios narrowed his eyes.

"Everyone here can confirm my claim," Magnus said calmly as he gestured to Kane Azurecrest and Celeste Starweaver, who were still in the colosseum stands watching the events unfold.

"Nonsense!" Dante Voidmind shouted from atop his sword while hiding his stump behind his back.

Demetrios ignored Dante as if he was a bug and turned to glare at the two nobles. "Are Magnus Redclaw's words true?"

Celeste Starweaver exchanged a glance with Dante.

Eventually, she sighed and empowered her voice with Qi so it would carry across the colosseum without her putting in much effort. *"Dante Voidmind announced his family was invading this city at the end of the tournament. However, I do not know how that involves your children."*

"We would never target your children. Our family shares a long history—"

"Silence, scion," Demetrios bellowed at Dante. *"Your Voidmind family has become far too suffocating to be around, and I will not be talked down to by a mere child."*

Demetrios then flexed his cultivation, and as if the heavens had descended, an immense pressure crashed onto Dante, knocking him from his sword and forcing him down to the ground like a meteor.

The ashen glass shattered as Dante was floored by Demetrios's mere presence. The ghoulish-looking man groaned as he pushed himself out of a crater and tried to stand under pressure.

Demetrios ignored Dante and returned to Magnus. "Now, explain what happened."

Sebastian coughed from the side. *"I can answer that. Upon the finals concluding, Dante Voidmind was allowed to deliver a victory speech. He utilized this opportunity to announce his family's plan to take over Darklight City. He then brought out a void-powered crystal and summoned multiple Voidmind Elders to assist his cause."*

"And the ash?" Demetrios questioned.

"A defensive artifact provided to me by Ryker Silverspire's mother for his protection in case of an assassination attempt," Sebastian lied.

"My mistress purchased it from merchants, and it was kept on hand for a situation like this."

Sebastian then gestured to the corpse of the Voidmind Elder. *"I was able to fend off one of the Voidmind Elders due to the artifact and because she was already injured."*

Demetrios eyed the corpse and then leaned closer. He traced his finger over the hole through her skull that was coated in silver. "Metal Qi used to impale her head." His finger traced to her chest. "And residual lightning Qi that I recognize as my daughter's in her chest."

He then closed his eyes. *"And I can't detect my son's or daughter's bodies anywhere nearby, so they must have been consumed by the accursed void."*

"Impossible," Dante shouted through gritted teeth as he tried to stand. *"I commanded my Elders to kill the Redclaw family and a woman called Roselyn. I never told them to do anything with your children! I swear under the heavens!"*

Demetrios rose to his full height and slowly turned to glare down at Dante with his glowing eyes that were like floodgates to a god's fury. In a single step, he was down to the glass-coated arena below.

The glass cracked underfoot like ice as Demetrios walked toward the floored Dante, still struggling under his godlike pressure.

"Foolish child, you thought you were so sneaky," Demetrios bellowed. *"Nobody here is strong enough to even touch a hair on my children's heads—except someone that betrays the heavens and gives into the temptations of the void's whisper."*

Demetrios raised one of his enormous arms, and golden lightning struck down. He caught the bolt and held it like a javelin.

"I didn't do it," Dante replied coldly. *"This is all a setup to pitch our families against one another. Think logically, Demetrios, don't make a mistake you may regret."*

"Then who slaughtered my children?" Demetrios' voice boomed, cracking the glass for a hundred meters. *"You didn't move a finger while standing on your sword to save my children. Will you claim ignorance to their deaths?"*

"That...I can't answer." Dante's eyes darted around as he took in everyone's faces. *"I will remember all of you who did this to me."*

"You can curse them in hell, you heretic." Demetrios brought his hand down with enough force to produce a sonic boom as he hurled the lightning bolt at Dante.

The world went white once more, and for a moment, Ashlock thought Dante would be executed.

However, as the bright white faded, Ashlock saw Dante half alive in the crater. His stump was gone as he sacrificed his arm to defend against the lightning. His face also appeared covered in void corruption that looked like a plague eating away at his face.

"If you hadn't taught my uncle how to ascend, none of this would have happened," Dante shouted. *"I watched as a void attack beyond even my father impaled your son. He didn't have time to react as he perished!"*

From his point of view in the sky, Ashlock could see ripples of void Qi around Dante. It was obvious he was trying to activate some sort of escape artifact and was trying to buy time.

"I would never help a heretic escape this realm," Demetrios said as he called down another javelin of heaven's wrath to his hand. "You are spouting nonsense!"

Dante grinned as half his face melted. *"You can try and hide it for as long as you want, but we will find out the truth soon enough."*

Demetrios' glowing eyes widened as he noticed the void Qi surrounding Dante. So without hesitation, he hurled the golden bolt, but Dante just manically laughed as he coated his remaining arm with void Qi and tanked the bolt.

"Get back here, you bastard," Demetrios roared as he dashed over and tried to grab at Dante, but he had already sunken into the floor and vanished into the void while screaming in agony.

Demetrios' entire body exploded with rage as he shot up into the sky and began to soar toward Slymere.

78
ASHFALLEN'S RISE

Ashlock and the others waited awhile, but Demetrios Skyrend never returned. The violent storm system dominated the distant horizon, and Ashlock suspected that Demetrios was giving a piece of his mind to the Voidmind family.

He would go and look, but his roots didn't extend far enough west to reach Slymere yet, and his {Eye of the Tree God} also didn't reach the city.

The Redclaw Grand Elder, who had his hands behind his back as he looked at the horizon, sighed in relief. His fire Qi then swirled around them to obscure his voice from others. "I must thank House Silverspire for mediating that conversation. Without your presence, I fear Demetrios would have taken Dante's side and wiped us out instead."

Sebastian frowned. *"It is indeed troublesome. When I agreed to sponsor the tournament for an extra percentage, I didn't expect to be dragged into a plot that may cause a civil war between the Voidmind and Skyrend families."*

"It's okay!" Ryker, who had remained silent for most of the day, grinned. *"Big Sister promised me lots of money, which means I might beat my brother and sisters for the silver core!"*

Ashlock almost felt like chuckling as he was reminded about the inheritance battle between the heirs of the Silverspire family.

"The poor Patriarch. He took his eyes off his Blood Lotus Sect for a few years to cultivate, and when he emerges, he will find all three of the most prominent families at war, two against one another and the last having an internal fight between the heirs," Ashlock sneered. "That's what he deserves for saving Stella as a pill furnace. In fact, the more the Blood Lotus Sect is in flames, the better. It will help camouflage our activities."

"Rascal." Sebastian ruffled Ryker's hair. *"Imagine your mother's face when she finds out."*

"Actually, she would be very proud of me!" Ryker smacked Sebastian's hand away. *"She always told me that war is good for business. People need weapons and spatial rings, which we sell, and then when they all die, we can move in and buy the land for cheap and start mining for metals."*

Sebastian and the Grand Elder exchanged a surprised look.

"Ahem...that is technically true." Sebastian nodded thoughtfully. *"The mistress is wise."*

"Of course she is." Ryker nodded seriously. *"My mother is the smartest woman I know!"*

"And how many women do you know?" the Grand Elder asked in jest.

Ryker replied thoughtfully, *"Only my mother and sisters, and my sisters are stupid."*

Sebastian snorted in amusement. *"Oh? What makes them stupid? They are your sisters, you know."*

"You and my sister told me Darklight City was a backwater place with nothing worth mentioning," Ryker said. *"But I found beautiful big sisters and lots of cool things here. So, Sebastian, you are also stupid."*

Sebastian seemed to stumble back with a painful expression as if an arrow had been shot into his chest. "Ouch, the young master's words hurt my heart."

"Good, let's head back," Ryker demanded. *"I want to cultivate after seeing the adults fight. I need to become stronger."*

Sebastian ceased his pained act. *"Grand Elder, is our presence here no longer necessary?"*

The Grand Elder looked at the demonic tree trunk, and when Ashlock wrote nothing, he gave Sebastian a nod. "I believe so. I will send someone to fetch you if something comes up."

Sebastian bowed slightly to the Grand Elder and the demonic tree. "I look forward to our continued business relationship."

Ashlock didn't want them to walk all the way back, so he created a portal for them to the White Stone Palace's courtyard. The two Silverspires departed, and the Grand Elder was also about to leave when someone unexpectedly approached them.

Kane Azurecrest floated through the air with a violent gale surrounding him.

The Grand Elder withdrew his fire Qi and faced the approaching teen.

Ashlock searched the colosseum stands and couldn't see Celeste Starweaver anywhere. Only the Grand Elder and Kane were left in the half-destroyed colosseum covered in shattered glass, ash, and rubble.

Kane touched down a few meters from the Grand Elder and offered a respectful bow. "Greetings, Grand Elder of the honorable Redclaw family."

"To what do I owe the pleasure scion of House Azurecrest?" the Grand Elder replied with a slight smile.

"I know I didn't win your tournament," Kane replied. He sounded exhausted, as if he hadn't slept in days. *"But I wondered if there was a way I could still be hired alongside the rogues?"*

The Grand Elder raised his brow. *"How unexpected. A scion from one of the top families asking for employment alongside rogue cultivators? Dare I ask the reason why?"*

Kane raised his head and looked at the Grand Elder through the gaps in his long white and crimson hair. "Could we take this conversation elsewhere? The subject matter is sensitive."

The Grand Elder looked him up and down with scrutiny and nodded. "Come with me."

After the two left through the portal to the White Stone Palace, total silence overtook the colosseum. A place that had once been alive with the cheers of a thousand mortals was now dead silent.

Ashlock opened a portal and slowly dragged the Voidmind Elder's corpse back to Red Vine Peak via a black vine.

He also retracted his view from his progeny and returned to his mountain because he wanted one of the girls to act as his spokesperson in the upcoming meeting between the Grand Elder and Kane Azurecrest.

He hadn't spoken to the Grand Elder through {Abyssal Whispers} before, and the man didn't have a Mind Fortress pill, so Ashlock needed someone to speak for him.

Stella was lying on the bench, passed out. A troubled expression was on her sleeping face as her chest peacefully rose and fell. Maple was sprawled out on her stomach, enjoying the late afternoon sun.

"She must be exhausted. When did she last have a moment where she wasn't learning alchemy or causing drama?" Ashlock laughed as he left her to sleep, and his gaze drifted a few meters away where a few corpses were lined up.

He closed the portal as quietly as possible to not awaken Stella, dragged the Voidmind Elder's corpse, and dumped it alongside the others.

Theron's body was in bad condition, with around half missing due to the void tendrils devouring him. Meanwhile, Kassandra's corpse was in much better shape as she had died from a dagger through the heart.

Ashlock was tempted to turn them into Ents or devour them for credits, but that could wait until later as he needed everyone's opinions. These were incredibly valuable corpses and weren't to be wasted.

"Mhm, I feel like I am missing one... Oh yeah." Ashlock realized that Roderick Terraforge was still trapped in Titus's hand prison. "I'll wait until Stella is awake to deal with that one. He can wait."

Ashlock looked around the peaceful courtyard and felt a sense of relief wash over him as the reality of the situation set in.

So much had occurred in just a few hours. It was hard to believe it was finally over. After months of planning and plenty of schemes, the Ashfallen Sect had come out unscathed while simultaneously gaining so much.

The tournament had concluded, and it was time to set his sights on bigger and better things. The Ashfallen Sect was about to welcome many new alchemists, and war may break out between the Skyrend and Voidmind families. A war Ashlock planned to profit off as much as possible.

But that wasn't all. A partnership had been formed with the infamous Silverspire family, and the merchants would soon come knocking to speak with Roselyn. Also, the Redclaws were now seen in higher regard by the other families, and Darklight City saw a significant influx of tourists due to the tournament.

So long as the plan had worked and Demetrios Skyrend didn't turn around and blast them with heavenly lightning, things looked up for Ashlock and the sect.

"Just a few more rounds in the Mystic Realm, and I should have a group of mid- to late-stage Star Core cultivators," Ashlock mused. "And if I can also get in there with my {Progeny Dominion} skill, then I might even reach the Nascent Soul Realm before the Patriarch comes out of seclusion."

Realizing he was getting distracted, Ashlock glanced around the mountain peak and spotted Diana relaxing under the shade of a demonic tree and embraced by the mist. She appeared much less exhausted than Stella and more just enjoying the sun.

"Hey, Diana," Ashlock spoke into her mind, and the woman was shocked out of her daze.

"What? Where? Who?" Diana shouted aloud, glancing around while blinking in confusion.

"Shhh, it's me. Stop shouting. Stella's asleep," Ashlock answered. **"I need you to head over to the White Stone Palace and sit in on a conversation and act as my spokesperson."**

Diana massaged her temples while standing up and then sighed.

"Fine, let's go," she said while popping a Mind Fortress pill.

Ashlock watched Kane and the Grand Elder sit opposite one another in the reception room of the White Stone Palace. The walls had arrays built in to stop other cultivators from eavesdropping, but the Grand Elder also used his own Qi to secure the area.

They were solid measures but not enough to stop Ashlock from listening in through a root under the floorboards. Not that the Grand Elder was in any position to have a conversation he was unaware of, but if he had no need to ask, that was for the best.

Ashlock effortlessly tore through the Grand Elder's Qi and produced a portal through which a white wooden–masked Diana emerged. She said nothing as she strode over, perched herself on an armchair, and glanced between the two other people in the room.

Kane gave her an odd look, but the Grand Elder just waved it off. "She is a trusted person. Feel free to speak your mind."

Kane sighed with relief as he sank into the sofa and seemed about to pass out. "I appreciate you taking the time to listen to me."

"You look haggard," the Grand Elder observed. *"Do you need something? Perhaps some freshly brewed tea or revitalization pills?"*

"Nothing works." Kane stared at the ceiling. *"I haven't slept in weeks, and all I can do is replay the events of a single night in my mind over and over."*

"Nocturne keeping you awake?" Diana asked.

Kane seemed to jolt in his seat and stared at her. "You know?"

"I have encountered them before," Diana said flatly. *"It didn't end well."*

"I see." Kane seemed a bit taken aback. *"And do you know anything about them, Grand Elder Redclaw?"*

"Small details have been made aware to me," the Grand Elder said, "but I will allow you to explain from the start as I am missing a lot of context."

"As you wish." Kane sighed. *"An order from the Patriarch had been given to my father before he went into seclusion, which sent the family into turmoil. He demanded that more airship pilots be available before the beast tide. The problem was that every abled person in the family was already working in the airship industry."*

"I see, and raising new talent takes a long time," the Grand Elder mused.

"Exactly." Kane nodded. *"So my father began to look for shortcuts, and he stumbled upon a demonic technique that allows for a rapid rise in cultivation."*

"Nocturnes," the Grand Elder said.

Kane's expression became grim. *"I watched as all of my siblings had duels over who would be sacrificed to empower the other. It was a harrowing experience to watch my elder brother Venik slaughter our sister and consume her soul for a surge in cultivation. I hid away in the servant quarters and tried to stay out of my father's sight for the duration of the sacrifices."*

"Venik...isn't that the one you killed, Diana?" Ashlock asked through telepathy.

"That's right," Diana replied.

"So how did you get here?" the Grand Elder asked Kane. *"And how did you end up with a Nocturne?"*

"Well, you see, there was an odd number of us, so I had hoped all of my siblings would fight it out, and I would be left alone, but the head servant reported me to my father." Kane gulped. *"If you don't know, my father is a lecherous man, which is one of the reasons he is such good friends with the Patriarch."*

The Redclaw Grand Elder nodded. *"There are some rumors regarding that man…"*

"I don't care what they are. They are probably true." Kane shivered. *"One of my father's habits is having children with rogue cultivators outside the family line. So when I was brought to my father's study one night, I was made to stand before a cage containing a red-haired kid who I later found out was my half-brother from one of those rogues."*

Ashlock did not like where this story was going one bit. Why did he have to be constantly reminded that he was surrounded by savages wearing human skin?

"You consumed him, didn't you?" the Grand Elder said, and Kane hesitantly nodded.

"It was either him or me. Father justified it by saying the boy had fire affinity and was, therefore, the lesser of us." Kane clutched his head. *"The fact that man would use the affinity purity argument while standing beside one of his children in a cage made me seethe with rage."*

"Then what happened?" Diana asked.

"I don't know." Kane began to quietly weep. *"I have replayed that night so many times in my mind I don't even know what really happened anymore. But all I know is I woke up in bed with a terrible headache, a voice in my head, and the ability to cultivate fire Qi. Father found it fascinating that I had become dual affinity, so he had me try and learn alchemy as the wind element is terrible at it."*

Ashlock had never considered that there would be ways to become a dual affinity after birth. "I wonder if there's a way I could use my skills to help my sect members unlock new affinities?"

"So that's how you ended up here." The Grand Elder hummed as he tapped his chin. *"And I assume you came to us looking for a way to escape your father?"*

Kane shook his head. *"Not initially. I came here to prove to my father that I had some skills in alchemy so he wouldn't send me to work in the airship industry. But then I heard you guys were hiring and saw the Silverspire family was involved. They are one of the only families that could help shield me from my father."*

"Diana, I need time to decide if taking him on would be worth the risk," Ashlock told Diana. **"Tell him we will consider his request to be hired over the next few days and for him to either wait here in the White Stone Palace or stay in the city."**

Diana relayed his message, and Kane gave a grateful nod.

"Thank you, I would appreciate it if I could stay here," Kane requested, and at the command of the Grand Elder, he was led away by a group of maids.

Although many significant threats were on the horizon, this conversation helped Ashlock refocus on things he had been putting off that needed to be resolved now that the Ashfallen Sect was more out in the open and time wasn't on their side.

"With the Redclaws more established now, I need them to focus on mass recruitment of cultivators, alchemists, and even mortals," Ashlock explained to Diana. **"The White Stone Palace was able to hold two families and their servants in the past. There is plenty of room to be utilized here, and we can always dig down and create more space within the mountain."**

Diana relayed the information.

"I see," the Grand Elder said. *"Are those rogue alchemists also going to stay here rather than in the cavern under Red Vine Peak?"*

"Yes," Ashlock said, and Diana nodded. It was time to start separating the two peaks. One was for his core sect members, while the White Stone Palace would be home for everyone else.

During the next few months, he planned for the Ashfallen Sect to rapidly expand in both size and power. His time lurking in the shadows was coming to a close, and the Blood Lotus Sect would soon learn their folly for allowing him to take root on their soil.

THANK YOU FOR READING REBORN AS A DEMONIC TREE 2

We hope you enjoyed it as much as we enjoyed bringing it to you. We just wanted to take a moment to encourage you to review the book. Follow this link: Reborn as a Demonic Tree 2 to be directed to the book's Amazon product page to leave your review.

Every review helps further the author's reach and, ultimately, helps them continue writing fantastic books for us all to enjoy.

ALSO IN SERIES:
Reborn as a Demonic Tree
Reborn as a Demonic Tree 2
Reborn as a Demonic Tree 3

Check out the entire series here! (Tap or scan)

Want to discuss our books with other readers and even the authors? Join our Discord server today and be a part of the Aethon community.

Facebook | Instagram | Twitter | Website

You can also join our non-spam mailing list by visiting www.subscribepage.com/AethonReadersGroup and never miss out on future releases. You'll also receive three full books completely Free as our thanks to you.

Looking for more great LitRPG?

For Noah Vines, death isn't the end. It's a weapon. *After standing around in the afterlife for thousands of years, Noah is all out of patience. So, when the opportunity to steal a second chance at life arises, he doesn't hesitate. Reincarnated into the body of a dying magic school professor, Noah finds that he got more than just a second chance — he got infinite. Every time he dies, his body reforms. With countless variations of runic magic to discover and with death serving as only a painful soul-wound rather than a final end, Noah finally has a chance to wander the lands of the living once more. This time around, he plans to get strong enough to make sure that he never has to wait around in the afterlife again.* **Don't miss the next hit Progression Fantasy series from Actus, bestselling author of My Best Friend is an Eldritch Horror. Featuring a strong, determined protagonist, a detailed runic magic system, loads of power progression, and so much more.** With 10 million views as a webserial, you can experience the definitive version of this smash-hit series on Kindle, Kindle Unlimited, and Audible!

Get Return of the Runebound Professor Now!

The Young Gods Tournament awaits. Only the victors will break through to the worlds beyond the heavens. *In an unfair world where a single monster can wipe out an entire village, Thomas is not one of the chosen few. He wasn't gifted with immense power from the moment of his birth, nor does he have a powerful backer to defend him. By the laws of the world, it's near impossible for him to rise to the top. But where the god's themselves have failed him, Thomas will push on and gain the strength to protect his friends, and his home, from the ever rising dangers of the world. There is only one true opportunity to break through the shackles of his life — The Young God's Tournament. After surviving a deadly ambush, he'll use every ounce of his strength as he faces off against his rival Prospects, a continent-wide conspiracy, and the ever looming threat from the once-slumbering Empire.* ***Western Cultivation melds with LitRPG as a single man rises against an unfair world in this new series from bestseller Cale Plamann (****Blessed Time, Viceroy's Pride****),*** *together with Alex Beaumont.*

Get Young Gods Tournament Now!

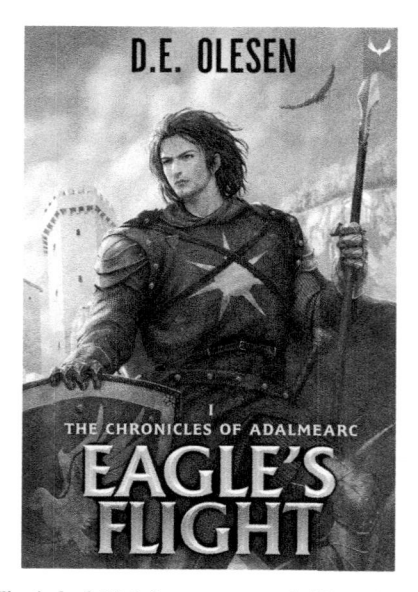

The King is dead. His heir too young to rule. Who will claim the crown? The noble houses gather to choose a new Lord Protector, sparking old rivalries. If they can't agree, civil war looms. That is if foreign kingdoms don't smell blood in the water and invade first. Lord Vale wants to take up the mantle, spurred by his ambitious brother Konstans. Lord Isarn likewise seeks this power. He is aided – or thwarted – by the return of his brother, the knight and war hero Athelstan, whose squire, Brand, hopes to restore his family's fortunes no matter the cost. Through all of this, an enigmatic traveler makes plans with jarls, scribes, and priests for his own mysterious purpose. Only one thing is for certain. War is inevitable. **Power-hungry lords scheme and warriors fight for glory in this epic fantasy tale from D.E. Olesen, which was one of the Top 10 highest rated Royal Road web-serials ever written. Equal parts Game of Thrones *and* Vikings, *the series digs deep into every level of a struggle of power, from lords to serfs. From political intrigue to the bonds between family. Join the fight for the soul of Adalmearc!*

Get Eagle's Flight Now!

The Connected System has come to Earth, bringing with it the apocalypse... *In an instant, life as it was known is gone, replaced by a System called The Connection. It doesn't come quietly as earthquakes rock the planet, the chosen survivors falling unconscious as the Connection takes their bodies and Adapts them. Lochlan Brady and his family were on their way home from a camping weekend when the Connection appears. He awakens with a new Adapted body, finding his wife missing. Now Loch must survive and thrive in this new world with his two teenage daughters, Harper and Piper. All Loch wants to do is protect his daughters and find his wife. A chance encounter with creatures straight out of myth will force the family to quickly confront the reality of their new lives, the changed world and give Loch a jump in power. But with that power will come responsibility and more danger. Along with the attention of some of the most powerful beings in The Connected System.*

Get Warbreaker's Rise Now!

For all our LitRPG books, visit our website.

Printed in Great Britain
by Amazon